D0854097

The FIVE

ROBERT McCAMMON

SUBTERRANEAN PRESS 2011

First Edition

ISBN
978-1-59606-341-9

Subterranean Press
PO Box 190106
Burton, MI 48519

www.subterraneanpress.com

. . . .

'Cause it's a bittersweet symphony, this life.
Try to make ends meet,
You're a slave to money then you die.
I'll take you down the only road I've ever been down.
You know the one that takes you to the places
where all the veins meet.

Bittersweet Symphony
The Verve

. . . .

ONE

DEATH OF A BAND

ONE.

Nomad decided he would have to kill the waitress.

< >

How he would do it, he didn't know. But it would have to be done soon, because in another minute he was going to go off like that dude in *The Thing* whose alien blood bubbled and shrieked under the touch of a hot wire. His neck was going to grow six feet long and spikes would shoot out of his arms before he tore the room apart. The waitress was cheerful and talky. Nomad hated cheerful and talky. He wasn't a particularly good guy, nor a very bad one. He was a musician.

Besides, he wasn't worth a damn before noon, and here he was at ten in the morning sitting in a booth at a Denny's restaurant just off I-35 at Round Rock, about twenty miles north of Austin. Everything was too bright for him in here. Everything was yellow and red and the sun was blasting between the blinds of the east-facing windows. His sunglasses helped a little, but underneath them his eyes were tired. And now here came the fucking waitress again, her third swoop past in as many minutes. She was an old hippie chick somewhere in the human wasteland of her late forties, he figured. She looked like she'd been somebody's groupie, back in the day. She was too thin and too old to be wearing her copper-colored hair in braids like some kind of Pippi Longstocking wannabe. She was bringing the coffee pot, she in her goldenrod yellow uniform, smiling, a big-toothed goddess of breakfast. Her nametag said *Hi I'm Laurie*.

"Oh, my God," Nomad said, to no one in particular.

"Fill 'em up?" Laurie asked, coffee pot poised.

There were various noises of assent. "Thanks," Mike said, when his cup was brimmed, and then Laurie answered, "No problem," and Nomad looked at the ketchup bottle as a weapon of murder because she'd just stepped on the nuts of one of his worst pet peeves. Where that damned *No Problem* had started he didn't know, but he wished he had two minutes in a locked room with the sonofabitch who'd first said it. Like a waitress or waiter was saying *Oh it's no problem that you're asking me to do something that I'm fucking paid to do, and that is part of my job description, and that if I didn't do I would be kicked in the ass out the door by whoever pays me to do it. Oh no, it's no problem at all.*

Then Laurie took a long look at all of them, at Nomad and Ariel and Terry in the first booth and Mike and Berke in the one just behind, and she gave a lopsided little grin and came up with the familiar question: "Are ya'll in a *band*?"

Nomad, whose given name was John Charles, did not rate breakfast at the top of his daily needs. Some of the others liked it. Mike and Terry did, especially, and had wanted to stop here before they headed up to Waco. Usually they stopped at a barbecue joint just outside Austin called Smitty's, where the one-eyed ex-Marine cook put eggs and beef hash in a blender with hellacious homemade hot sauce and called it a Texas Tornado, but Smitty had closed up shop at the first of the summer and so Denny's got the vote. They had never been in here before and had never met Laurie, but of course she knew. Probably because if there were thirteen hundred and fifty-two guitar players in Nashville there had to be fourteen hundred and sixty-three bands in and around Austin, so seeing musicians sitting in a Denny's was no biggie. But more clues were the bracelets of green vines and music notes—the opening bars of 'Amazing Grace'—tattooed around Ariel Collier's wrists, or maybe Terry Spitzenham's soul patch and shaved skull, or Mike Davis's heavily-tattooed arms, or Berke Bonnevey's silver nose ring and in general her do-not-fuck-with-me attitude, or Nomad's own shoulder-length black hair, sunglasses designed to shut out the world, and his dark demeanor.

Take all that together and you had either a band or a freak show, and some would say there was very little difference.

"We are," Ariel answered, and she offered the waitress the encouragement of a direct gaze and a smile, which Nomad had known was coming because Ariel—sweet, simple child—could never turn her face from a stranger.

"What's your name? Your band's name, I mean?"

"The Five," Ariel said.

There was just the briefest of pauses, and then Laurie wrinkled her brow and cocked her head to one side as if she'd missed part of that. "The five *what*?"

"Aces," Mike mumbled, into his coffee cup.

"Asses," Berke corrected.

But Laurie's attention was still on Ariel, as if she knew Ariel was probably the only person in this group who wouldn't steer her into a ditch.

"Just The Five," Ariel said. "We wanted to keep it easy to remember."

"Oh, yeah. Like the Fab Five, right?"

"Fab Four," Terry spoke up. The sunlight sparked off his round-lensed wire-rimmed glasses, which were suitably Lennonesque. "That was the Beatles."

"Right, right." Laurie nodded, and again she swept her eyes across the assembled Five, in all their glory of an early-morning saddle-up and an impending ride into the great unknown. "How come there are *six* of you?" She motioned with the coffee pot toward the place next to Berke where the sixth member had been sitting until about ninety seconds ago.

"He's the manager," Ariel replied.

"The slave driver," Mike said. "Keeper of the keys and the money bags."

"The *boss*, huh?" Laurie asked. "Well, I guess everybody's got to have one." She caught sight of another customer flagging her down for a refill, and she said, "'Scuse me," and moved away.

Terry started back in where he'd left off on his pancakes. Berke worked on buttered toast and a glass of water. Mike ate his scrambled eggs, Ariel sipped her apple juice and Nomad parted the window blinds a fraction so he could peer out against the glare into the parking lot.

The Little Genius was out there, talking on his cellphone. George Emerson by name, road manager, sound mixer, crisis mender, argument mediator, bean counter, and what have you. He was standing by their van, a battleship-gray 1995 Ford Econoline, three doors, with a U-Haul trailer hooked up behind. He was intent on his conversation, and he'd lit a cigarette. Nomad watched him, as he talked and smoked. George was five feet, six inches tall, had curly light brown hair—losing it on the crown a little bit, to be honest—and he wore horn-rimmed glasses and his usual button-down pale blue short-sleeved shirt and chinos. God only knew why George wore brown loafers with shiny pennies in them. Maybe it was for the shock effect. George was strolling back and forth now as he talked, trailing a plume of smoke. Not only was he a little genius, he was a little locomotive.

I think I can...I think I can...I think—

"Ya'll playin' here tonight?"

Laurie had returned, toothy and bright and braidy. She had posed this question to Ariel, who said, "We were at the Saxon Pub last night. Tonight we're at Common Grounds in Waco."

"Ya'll are from around here, then?"

"Yeah, we've been living here...how long, Terry?"

"Years and years," Terry answered.

"Our tour's just started up," Ariel said, in anticipation of Laurie's next question. "That was the first show."

"I'll be. What do *you* play?"

"Guitar. And I sing some."

"Oh, I would've known that," Laurie said. "You've got a nice speakin' voice."

Nomad had let the blinds go and was drinking his bitter black coffee, but he was thinking about George and the cellphone and the smoke signals in the air.

"My daughter plays the guitar," the waitress went on. "Just turned sixteen. She sings, too. Any advice I can pass along?"

"Stay sixteen," Berke said, without looking up.

"Move to an island," Mike offered, in his low raspy growl, "where agents and promoters are shot on sight."

Laurie nodded, as if this made perfect sense to her. "One thing I'd like to ask, if I could. Then I'll leave you guys alone. I've seen…like…musicians on stage do *this*." She transferred the coffee pot to her left hand, balled up her right fist and did the heart thump and then the peace sign. "What's that mean?"

Nomad studied her through his dark glasses. She was probably five or six years younger than she looked. It was the hard Texas sun that aged the skin so much. She was probably a little dense, too. Happy with her lot in life, and dense. Maybe you had to be a little dense to be truly happy. Or oblivious enough to think you were. He couldn't help himself; he said, "Bullshit."

"Pardon?" Laurie asked.

"It means," Ariel said evenly, "solidarity with the audience. You know. We love you, and we wish you peace."

"Like I said: Bullshit." Nomad ignored Ariel, who likewise ignored him, and then he swigged down the rest of his coffee. "I'm done." He slid out of the booth, put a buck down on the table, and walked out of the Denny's into the hot sunshine. In this mid-July of 2008, the fierce heat was unrelenting, day after day. Drought scorched the land. The air was hazy and carried the acrid tang of a brush fire, maybe from the next county. But where was George? The Little Genius was not standing beside the Scumbucket, which was the name Mike had given their van. Then Nomad saw a wisp of smoke rise up and waft away, and he walked over to the edge of the parking lot where George was sitting on a low brick wall, still involved with his cell conversation. Or, really, George was just listening, and taking a drag off his cigarette every few seconds as cars and trucks blew past on the long straight corridor of I-35.

Nomad quietly came up behind him. George must have felt the presence of a black aura because he suddenly turned his head, looked right at Nomad, and said, "Hey, listen. I've gotta go, I'll call you back, okay?" His phone buddy seemed hesitant to give it up, so George said, "I'll let you know tomorrow. Right. Early, before ten. Yeah. Okay, then." He put his phone away in its small clipcase on his belt, and then he drew the cigarette in as if it were oxygen to an air-starved man and spewed the smoke out through his nostrils.

Nomad said nothing. Finally George asked, "They ready yet?"

"No."

George continued to watch the passing traffic. Nomad sat on the wall a few feet away from him without being asked, because it was a free fucking country.

They were both wearing their uniforms, Nomad thought. George's was the uniform of the guy in control, the guy who met the accountants, if there were any accountants to be met. The guy who spoke to the banker about the loan for the new gear, if there was a banker and a loan and new gear to be had. Though George had three small silver rings in each earlobe, he still projected the conservative front, the voice of reason, the leash on these madmen and mad women who called themselves The Five. Nomad's uniform was his Army-green T-shirt, his well-worn black jeans, his black Chuck high tops and his black glasses that cut the glare and shunned the world until he was ready to let any of it in. His was the uniform of the fighter, the rager against the machine, the take-no-prisoners bard and bastard. The teller of truths, if there were any truths to be told. As if he *knew* any real truths, which he doubted. But you had to dress the part of whatever play you were in, that was for sure.

He had turned twenty-nine two weeks ago. They'd given him dairy-free birthday cake and soy milk ice cream, since he was allergic to dairy. They'd taken him paint-balling. Everybody got a birthday celebration, that was part of the deal. Not a written deal, but one that was understood. Just as on stage, everybody got their time. Their appreciation, for what they did. That was an important thing, Nomad thought; to feel appreciated, like you meant something in the world and your life and work wasn't just like a big busted-up truck spinning its tires in a mudhole. Like what you did mattered to somebody.

He was the good front man: six-one, lean and rangy, the hungry-as-the-wolf look. He could do the curled lip and the attitude as well as anybody on the knife and gun circuit. His nose had been broken in a bar fight in Memphis and he had a small scar on his chin courtesy of a thrown beer bottle in Jacksonville. He had been born in Detroit, and he had been down enough rough streets to know when to look over his shoulder and check what might be coming up on him from behind.

That was what he had decided to do now, with the Little Genius.

"Business call?" Nomad asked.

George didn't answer, which told Nomad all he needed to know.

But in time—ten seconds, fifteen, whatever—George did reply, because he was a stand-up guy and part of the family. He said, "John, I'm thirty-three years old."

"Okay." That was no news; Nomad remembered George's thirty-third back in April. "And?"

"Thirty-three," George went on. "Ten years ago, I was ready to climb mountains. I thought I was going to have it all. You know?"

"Yes," Nomad said, but it sounded more like a question.

"Ten years is a long time, man. In this business, it's like dog years. And I've been on the road with somebody since I was twenty. First gig, with the Survivors out of Chicago." George was a Windy City boy, born and bred. "They lasted about four months before they exploded. No survivors." He didn't pause to see if Nomad had cracked a smile, but that wasn't going to happen anyway. "Then with the Bobby Apple Band, out of Urbana. Have I told you this before?"

"No." There'd been many stories from George's complicated past, but not this one. Nomad wondered if he'd been saving it.

"The band was lame, just frat boys really. Bobby Apple—Bobby Koskavitch—was a skinny computer geek at Illinois, but he could belt it like a fifty-year-old black dude raised on misery. I saw him lift the gigs on his shoulders and just fly with them. Just take off, and leave the band behind. He was in some other space and time, you know?"

"Yeah." It was what every musician longed for: the rapture when nothing in the world mattered but the sound and it carried you away with a mindrush that was better than sex with sixteen women.

"They recorded two CDs in the drummer's basement," George said. "Solid songs, most of them original. Had some airplay on a local station. Swapped up musicians, people came and went. Tried a horn section for a bigger sound. But that force—the stage magic—in Bobby never translated." Not an uncommon thing, Nomad knew. If you didn't translate to CDs or mp3s or vinyl sooner or later the road would wear you out. "I mean, they had plenty of live gigs. We were making money, and Bobby was a trooper, and we had a few nibbles from A&R dudes but no bites. Then one day…he just woke up and asked me what town he was in, and he said he was going to do the gig that night at the Armory and to pay everybody up afterward, because he was going home. I tried to talk him out of it. We all did. I said, *Keep going, man. Don't give it up.* I said, *You've got a huge talent, man. Don't walk away from it.* But, you know, he was tired. He'd hit his wall. I guess I was tired too, because I didn't try harder. I guess I figured...really, there's always the next band." George took another draw from his cigarette and regarded the burning stub as if figuring it was time to kill it. "I've been thinking about him a lot lately. He went back to computer programming. Anti-virus shit. Probably mucho rich right now, laughing his ass off in Silicon Valley."

"Maybe." Nomad said, and shrugged. "Or maybe he lost his ass and wishes he was back in his old band."

"You ever wish you were back in *your* old band?"

"Which one?" Nomad asked, his face impassive.

"The one that made you the happiest," said George.

"That would be the current situation, so your question is null."

George pulled up a pinched smile. "I didn't realize how little it takes to make you happy."

"This isn't about me, or whether I'm happy or not, is it?" Nomad waited for George to speak again, but when the Little Genius did not, Nomad leaned toward him and said, "I *do* have eyes. I've got *some* sense. I've gone through enough bands to know when somebody's got the wanders. So be brother enough to tell me the truth. Who's making the offer?"

"Not what you think."

"Tell me."

A pained expression passed across George's face. He took in the last of his cigarette, blew out gray smoke that scrolled away like a banner of mysterious calligraphy, and crushed the butt into the bricks.

"My first cousin Jeff, in Chicago," George said, "owns a business called Audio Advances. They do the setups for auditoriums, town halls, churches...you name it. Mixing boards, effects racks, speakers, whatever they need. Plus training in how to run everything. He's doing real well." George stopped to watch a Harley speed past on the highway, its driver wearing a bright red helmet. "He needs a new Midwestern rep. He wants to know by ten tomorrow morning if I'm in or out."

Nomad said nothing. He was sitting in the frozen moment, thinking that he'd had it all wrong. He was thinking that George was being hustled—courted, if you wanted to put it that way—by some other band. That the GinGins or the Austin Tribe or the Sky Walkers or any of a hundred others they'd shared a stage with had fired a manager and come to steal George away with promises of bright lights, choice weed and semi-conscious nookie.

But no, this was worse. Because it was the real world calling, not this fiction of life, and Nomad could see in George's eyes that ten in the morning could not arrive too soon.

"*Jesus*." Nomad's tongue felt parched. "Are you giving it up?"

George kept his face averted. He stared down at the ground. Small beads of sweat had gathered at his temples in the rising heat. "What can I say?" was all he could find.

"You can say it, or not. You're giving it up."

"Yeah." George nodded, just a slight lift of the chin.

"We had a good night!" It was said with force, but not with volume. Nomad was leaning closer, his face strained. He took off his sunglasses, his eyes the fierce blue of the Texas sky and intense with both anger and dismay. "Listen to me, will you? We sold some *tickets* last night! We rocked the *house*, man! Come on!"

"Yeah, we did okay," George agreed, his face still downcast. "We sold some tickets, some CDs and some T-shirts. Made some new fans. Put on a tight show. Sure. And we're going to do the same in Waco, and the same in Dallas. And after that, in El Paso and Tucson, and San Diego and L.A, and Phoenix and Albuquerque and everywhere else...sure, we'll do fine. Usual fuckups and miscues, broken strings, sound problems, lights blowing out, drunks looking for a fight and jailbait looking to get laid. Sure." And now George turned his head and looked directly into Nomad's eyes, and Nomad wondered when it was that the Little Genius had hit his wall. On the last tour through the Southeast, when two clubs had cancelled at the last minute and they were left to scramble for gigs, to basically beg to play for gas money? Was it in that grunge-hole in Daytona Beach, under the fishnets and plastic swordfish, where drunk bikers throwing their cups of beer had brought a quick end to the show and the appearance of the cops was the opener to a collision between billyclubs and bald skulls? How about the Scumbucket's blown tire on a freeway south of Miami, with the sick sky turning purple and the winds picking up and off in the distance a hurricane siren starting to wail? Or had it been something simple, something quiet and sudden, like a gremlin in the fusebox or the death of a microphone? A floor slick with beer and vomit? A bed with no sheets and a stained mattress? Had George's wall been made of gray cinderblock, with sad brown waterstains on the tiles overhead and the grit of desolation on the tiles underfoot?

Maybe, just maybe, George's wall had been human, and had been one too many A&R no-shows at the comp ticket counter.

Just maybe.

"Like I said, I'm thirty-three years old." George's voice was quiet and tired and small. He squinted against the sun. "My clock is ticking, John. Yours is too, if you'll be truthful."

"I'm not too fucking old to do what I *love* to do," came the reply, like a whipstrike. "And we've got the *video*! Jesus Christ, man, we've got the *video*!"

"The video. Yeah, we've got that. Okay. We've had videos before. Tell me how this is such a magic bullet."

Nomad felt anger twist south of his heart. He felt the blood pounding in his face. He wanted to reach out and grab George's shirt collar and slap that blank businessman's stare away, because he wanted his friend back. But he stayed his hand, with the greatest effort, and he said in an acid voice, "You're the one who wanted the video the most. Have you forgotten?"

"I haven't. It's a good song. It's a *great* song. And the video is great, too. We needed the visual, and it's worth every cent. But I'm not sure it's going to change the game, John. Not in the way you're thinking."

"Well hell, how about telling me that before we spent the two thousand dollars?"

"I can't tell you anything you don't already know," George said. "Everything's a gamble, man. You know that. Everything's just throwing dice. So we've got the great song, and the great video. And I'm hoping for the best, man. You know I am. I'm hoping this tour is the one that lights the jets. But what I'm telling you *now* is that this is my last time out." He paused, letting that register. When Nomad didn't punch him or go for his throat in one of his infamous white-hot supernova explosions, which was what George had feared might happen when John heard it, George said, "I'm going to go for the rep job with my cousin. Until then, I promise—I *swear* to you, man, as a brother—that I will perform my duties exactly as always. I will jump when I need to jump, and I jump *upon* any sonofabitch who needs to be jumped. I will take care of you guys, just like always. Okay?"

There was a few seconds' pause, and then the person who'd come up behind them spoke: "Okay. Whatever."

George did jump a little bit, but Nomad kept his cool. They looked around—taking it easy, neither man showing surprise nor any hint of what they'd been discussing—and there was Berke, who offered them her own expression of absolute detachment. She wore faded jeans and a wine-red tanktop. She was twenty-six years old, born in San Diego, stood about five-nine, had short-cut curly black hair so thick it was a struggle to pull a brush through it, and eyes almost as dark under unplucked black brows. On the right side of her neck was a small vertical Sanskrit tattoo that, she'd told them, meant 'Open To The Moment', though her persona suggested more of a deadbolted door. She had sturdy hands with the strong fingers of the French farmers who swam in her blood. The veins carrying it were prominent in her forearms and wrists, blue channels beneath the white flesh. She was the drummer. Her arms were tight and sculpted, leaving no doubt her profession demanded physical exertion. She was a 'brickhouse', as Mike liked to say, due to good genes and the fact that she laced up her New Balances and ran a few miles every chance she got.

"Hey," Berke said, "Ariel wants to give our waitress a T-shirt."

George stood up, fished the keys out of his pocket and tossed them to her. "Tell her no free CDs. Got it?"

Berke retreated without comment. A couple of boxes of T-shirts and CDs were in the U-Haul trailer, along with the gear. In sizes of Small, Medium, Large and ExtraLarge, the T-shirt was red with a black handprint splayed across the front, fingers outstretched, and the legend *The Five* printed on the palm in a font that looked like embossed Dymo plastic label tape.

When Nomad put his sunglasses back on and got to his feet, George asked, "How much do you think she heard?"

"I don't know, but you should tell everybody before she does. Were you going to wait until the tour was done?"

"No." George frowned. "Jesus, no. I was just...you know...trying to figure things out."

"I hope they *are* figured out."

"Yeah," George agreed, and then he walked back to the van with Nomad following. Everybody else had already climbed in through the passenger door on the right side of the van except Ariel, who was coming across the parking lot from the restaurant.

"Those aren't freebies," Nomad told her, as George went around to get behind the wheel.

Ariel gave him a look that reminded Nomad of how the teachers in high school had regarded him just before banishing him to the office. "One giveaway won't break us. It's for her daughter. And you didn't have to be rude."

He climbed up into the shotgun seat beside George, who had retrieved the keys from Berke by way of Terry. Berke was sitting way in the back, with Mike; Terry was sitting behind George, and Ariel slid into the seat next to Terry. It was the usual arrangement, and only varied according to whose turn it was to drive. Jammed into every other available space were the suitcases, duffle bags and carry-alls of six individuals. George started the engine, switched on the air conditioning that stuttered and racketed and smelled of wet socks before it settled more or less into a hum, and then he pulled out of the parking lot and took the ramp back to I-35 North.

They were due at Common Grounds in Waco at three o'clock for load-in and sound check. It was Friday, the 18th of July. On a Friday night, the show would start about ten, give or take. First, though, they had the thing with Felix Gogo, up north of Waco. The instructions had been given by email to George: turn off I-35 onto East Lake Shore Drive and keep going west until he reached North 19th Street, turn right at the intersection and go past Bosqueville on China Spring Road about six miles, couldn't miss the place.

As they continued away from Round Rock, Nomad was waiting for George to come out with it. The Scumbucket rattled and wheezed across the flat landscape, passing apartment complexes, banks and stripmalls. Passing huge low-roofed warehouses with immense parking lots. Passing farmland now, cows grazing out in the distant pastures that seemed to go on forever.

Nomad was thinking that George might have changed his mind. Just in the last few minutes. That George had decided he wasn't going to give it up, no way. Give up the *dream*? After all the work they'd put into this? No *fucking* way. Nomad felt relief; George had decided to stick to the plan, no matter what lay ahead on what was—as always—a journey into the unknown.

And then, from the back of the van, Berke said casually, "Guys, George has something to tell us. Don't you, George?"

TWO.

To his credit, George didn't let the question hang. He had no choice, because only a few seconds after Berke asked it, Mike hesitated in plugging in the earbuds of his iPod and followed it up: "What's the word, chief?"

A good drummer and bass player were always in sync, George thought. They put down the floor the house was built on. So it ought to be even now, one playing off the other.

But before he said what had to be spoken, before he opened his mouth and let the future tumble out of it, for better or for worse, he had an instant of feeling lost. Of wondering if he was advancing toward a goal or retreating from one, because in this business—in any of the arts, really—success was always a lightning strike away. Yeah, he would do fine as the rep selling audio units on the road. He would get to know the products so well he would know what the client needed before he eyeballed the venue. But was that going to be enough? Was he going to wake up one night when he was forty years old, listening to a clock tick and thinking *If I had only stuck it out...*

Because that was the sharpest thorn in this tangled bush where the roses always seemed so close and yet so hard to reach, and everybody in the Scumbucket knew it. How long did you give your life to the dream, before it *took* your life?

"I have nothing," he said, which he had not meant to say and wished he could reel back in, but it was gone. He could feel John Charles watching him from behind the sunglasses with those eyes that could bore holes through a concrete block. Everyone else was silent, waiting. George shifted in his seat. "I mean…" He didn't know what he meant, and he was letting the Scumbucket wander over into the left lane so he corrected its path. "I've been doing this too long," he said, and again confused himself. But he had the wheels in control now, and his direction was set. "This is my last time out," he went on. "I told John, back at the Denny's. I'm giving it up." And there it was, the confession of…what? Shame, or resolve? "I've got a job," he said. "I mean, a *new* job. If I want it, which I do. In Chicago." He glanced quickly into the rearview mirror and saw that everyone was watching him but Berke, who gazed solemnly out the window. He was aware that he was looking at not just one band but a couple of dozen. Mike alone had played bass in six bands, most of them workmanlike, just solid craftsmen plying their trade, but one—Beelzefudd—that had shown flashes of brilliance and had opened for Alice Cooper on tour in the fall of 2002. It passed through George's mind that if anybody had paid their dues, these guys had, in bands like Simple Truth, Jake Money, The Black Roses, Garden Of Joe, Wrek, Dillon, The Venomaires, The Wang Danglers, Satellite Eight, Strobe, The Blessed Hours, and on and on. And because of that long list of experiences, they would know only too well—as he did—that people came and went all the time, due to burnout, exhaustion, frustration, drug addiction, death, or whatever. It was just life, cranked up to eleven.

He told them about his cousin Jeff, and Audio Advances, and his intentions. "But I'm telling you like I told John," he added, into their silence, "I'm not bailing on you." He didn't think that sounded exactly right, so he tried it again. "I'm not leaving until the tour's done. Okay? And even then, I'll stick until Ash finds a replacement." He hoped he could keep that last vow, because the Chicago job needed him by the middle of September. 'Ash' was their agent Ashwatthama Vallampati, with RCA—the Roger Chester Agency—in Austin.

"Well, *damn*," Mike said when George was done. It was stated flatly, more of an expression of surprise than of opinion.

"Listen, man, I was going to tell you—tell all of you—further down the road. I wasn't going to throw it at you, like, the last night or something."

"You're sure about that?" Berke asked, without turning her face from the window.

"Yes, I am. I want the tour to be a success. Got it? I wouldn't have pushed for the video if I hadn't." George glanced over to get John's reaction, but Nomad was staring straight ahead, watching the road unspool.

Nomad had decided to neither help George nor hurt him. This was George's choice. George had to live by it.

Another silence settled in. Then Mike broke it: "Sounds like a plan. I wish you well, bro."

"Same here," Terry said.

George was so relieved he almost swivelled around to thank them, but as there was a black-and-white Texas State Trooper Crown Victoria parked over on the right where it could clock the passing traffic he thought it would not be in the best interest of the band. "Thanks," he said. "Really."

"You're wrong, George," Ariel suddenly told him, and the cool clarity of her voice popped his bubble.

"Wrong? How?"

"About having nothing. You have the Scumbucket. And you have *us*, too."

"Oh. Yeah, right. That's true."

"Yeah, we'll come to Chicago and move in with you," Mike said, and George caught his lopsided grin in the rearview mirror. "Get a house with a big basement."

"Home theater with a candy counter," Terry suggested.

"Popcorn popper," said Ariel.

"Automatic joint roller," Mike continued. "We'll have to come *see* you, man, because in a couple of months you'll forget we ever existed."

"Besides," Ariel said, "it's not like you couldn't come back, if you wanted to. I mean...if things didn't work out, you could come back. Right, John?"

Nomad wanted to say *Leave me out of this*, but instead he thought about it for a few seconds and replied, "Probably not as *our* manager. By then, Ash would've found somebody else for us. I'm not saying it couldn't be worked out, but...who knows?" Ariel must not have liked that answer, because she didn't say anything else. "But George could get back in the game, sure," Nomad added. He figured he ought to lighten things up, before the cloud he felt he was under rained on everyone else. After all, he was the *leader* of this band, so he should act like a leader and buck it up. "Hey, we're putting the cart in front of the horse, aren't we?"

"*Before* the horse," Ariel corrected.

"That's what I meant. George isn't gone yet, we've got a tour ahead of us, we've got an awesome video and song to promote, and anything can happen. So we go from where we are. Right?"

"What he said," was Mike's affirmation.

"Yes," Ariel answered.

There was no response from Berke. Nomad looked back to see her curled up on her side of the seat, her head against the tan-colored cushion and her eyes closed. "Berke?" he prompted.

"What?" She didn't bother to open her eyes.

"Anything to say?"

"I'll wait for the written exam."

Nomad knew there was no use in pushing Berke for an opinion. When she wanted to disappear, she went deep. She closed her eyes and submerged into a realm no one else was able to follow. The word "loner" had been created with Berke in mind, but Nomad respected that, it was cool. Everybody needed their space. The only thing was, Berke's seemed to be so empty.

The highway stretched on between fenced-off fields in various shades of brown, with stands of bony trees here and there but nothing much to speak of except a few houses and barns in the distance. The route would take the Scumbucket past the small towns of Jarrell, Prairie Dell, Salado and Midway, then through the city of Temple and into Waco. The sky was bright and hot now, heat waves shimmered on the pavement, and dead armadillos drew the circling crows that dove in to tear off a swallow before the next tractor-trailer truck could scatter the feast.

"I've got something to say," Terry announced, when they were about three miles past the Prairie Dell exit.

Nomad turned around to look at him. There had been an unaccustomed note of urgency in Terry's voice. That wasn't like Terry; he could be excitable, sure, but he was usually calm and measured, as precise in his speech as in his playing.

Terry adjusted his round-lensed glasses, pushing them back up his nose with one finger. The air-conditioner was working all right, but Terry's face looked to be damp, and his full round cheeks—"chipmunk cheeks", Ariel called them—were blotched with red. His light brown eyes, slightly magnified by the lenses, appeared larger still, and his shaved skull was shiny with a faint sheen of perspiration.

Nomad's first thought was that Terry was having a heart attack, though Terry was in reasonably good shape except he was a little chunky and he had the beginnings of a potbelly, but he was only twenty-seven. Still, the sight of Terry in obvious distress unnerved him. He took off his shades, and there was a rasp of tension in his voice when he said, "Hey, man, are you *okay*?"

"Yeah. I'm okay. I just...I don't want you to blow up at me."

"Why would I do that?"

"Because," Terry answered, and he blinked rapidly a few times as if he feared being struck, "I'm leaving the band too. After this tour."

Beyond Terry, Berke had opened her eyes and sat up straight. She reached over to Mike, who had slid down in his seat and put his iPod on Shuffle, and pulled out the nearest earbud. He frowned at Berke and said, "What the *fuck*...?" but her attention was directed up front and he knew she wouldn't have disturbed him for no good reason.

"Oh my God," Ariel said, more of a breathless gasp. "*Why*?"

George glanced at Terry in the rearview mirror but did not speak; he figured his revelation had spurred Terry to make his own, and it was best he keep his mouth shut.

Terry looked agonized. He searched Nomad's eyes for the red candles of rage before he spoke again. "I was going to tell you last night. After the gig. But...we did so fine...and you were so up, man. I... thought I'd wait a while. But I swear I was going to tell you before—"

"What are you *talking* about? Have you gone fucking *crazy*?" Nomad's voice was angry and full of grit, but inside he just felt scared. If The Five had a retro/rock/folk vibe—as the promo materials from RCA said—then Terry Spitzenham supplied the retro component. Terry was the keyboard player who had his mind in 2008 and his heart somewhere in the mid-sixties, a time he lamented missing. He was particularly into the organ sounds of that era, the soul-stirring rumble of the B3, the high keening of the Farfisa, the gravelly snarl of the Vox and all their thousands of different voices. On tour he played a Hammond XB2 and a Roland JV80 with a tonewheel organ sound card, and he carried the Voce soundbox and enough effects boxes to generate whatever tone he could imagine. Terry could make his instruments scream, holler, growl or sob, as the song required. He could fill up a room with an immense throbbing pulse, or back it down to a nasty little chuckle. Nomad couldn't imagine The Five without Terry's keyboards, without his distinctive style and energy propelling everything forward. It was just goddamned unthinkable. Nomad had to draw a panicked breath, because he felt like all the oxygen had suddenly been sucked out of the Scumbucket. "No," he said, when he could find words again. "No way you're pulling out."

"Can I explain myself?"

"No way you're pulling out," Nomad repeated. "You go, the band goes."

"That's not true." Terry was speaking carefully. His tongue were testing every word for sharp edges. His armpits were damp under his blue-and-purple paisley shirt, one of many vintage shirts in his wardrobe. "I go, the band *changes*. Can I explain myself? Please?"

"Yeah, we'd like to hear it," Berke said. "Are you going into business with George's cousin, too? Well, shit, how about *me* being the California rep? Just show me where to sign."

"Cut it out, let him talk," Mike told her, and she made a noise of disgust and curled up again in her seat.

Terry glanced at Ariel, whose dark gray eyes were wide with shock. "Jesus," Terry said, with a quick nervous smile that hurt the tight corners of his mouth, "I didn't *kill* anybody. I made a decision, that's all."

"What, a decision to kill the band?" Berke countered.

"A decision," Terry said, focusing his attention on Nomad, "to go into business for myself." When no one spoke, he forged ahead. "Not my own band, if that's what you're thinking. I need a break from this. I've been at it a long time, John. You know I have."

Nomad did know. He and Terry had been together in the Venomaires—a tough ride—for over a year, and then in The Five for the last three. Terry had been through a half-dozen bands before the Venomaires, had gone through a divorce last summer that had weighed heavily on him during their Southeastern tour, and had had a brief flirtation with OxyContin before his band-mates helped him close the door on that dangerous romance.

Looking into Terry's face, Nomad thought he might be seeing his own. Or Mike's, or George's, or Berke's or—if you got past the blush of youth that was still fresh on her cheeks—Ariel's too. They were all tired. Not physically, no; they had strength enough to keep pulling the plow all right, and they would do their jobs and be professional, but it was a mental weariness. A soul weariness, born from the death of expectations. There were so many bands out there, so many. And so many really *good* ones, too, that were never going to get the break. Everybody could record CDs on the little portable eight and twelve-tracks these days; everybody could put up a half-assed video on YouTube, and make a MySpace page for their creations. There was just so much *noise*. How did anybody ever get listened to? Not just landing on a playlist as more noise, but *listened* to, in the way that people put down their cellphones and tuned out the fast chatter of the world for a minute and actually *heard* you? But there was so much noise, so much chatter, and faster and faster, and so much music—good and bad—going out into the air, but for all the purpose it served—all the worth it had—it might just as well be played on low-volume continual loops in elevators, or as background buzz for shoppers.

"Can I explain?" Terry asked.

Nomad nodded.

"I want to go into the vintage instrument business. I've got some money saved up, and my dad says he'll help me with a loan." The way Terry said it—a rush of words, an outpouring, a release—told Nomad that this decision had been working on him for a long time. Maybe it had begun as a passing thought, way back when they were with the Venomaires. Maybe it had just evolved over the years until it had grown wings and purpose, and now it was big enough to fly Terry away.

Terry went on, obviously relieved to rid himself of what he'd been keeping. His plan, he said, was to go back home, to Oklahoma City. To set himself up there in a business that would buy old keyboards in any condition—vintage Hammond organs in their many variations, aged Farfisas, Rhodes pianos, the Hohner keyboards, the Gems, Kustoms, Cordovoxes, the Elkas and the Ace Tones, the Doric and Ekosonic lines, and other proud ancient warriors—and bring them back to life. He already had most of the manuals, he said, and he'd always been good with fixing the vintage keyboards in his own collection. He thought he could repair just about anything that came along, and if he couldn't find the parts he could make them. These old keys were collector's items now, he said. They were a dying breed, and really most of the makes and models had died when disco boogied in. But there were those who wanted to either find instruments they'd played on as teenagers in garage bands or repair the ones moldering in the basement, he said. And he'd begun hearing some of them on new songs, too. He believed he could start an Internet search service for musicians or collectors looking for a particular electric keyboard, he told them. Some of the details had to be figured out yet, but he thought it would be a good start.

When Terry was done plotting his future course, Nomad didn't know what to say. He saw a billboard up ahead on the right, as they neared the outskirts of Temple. It showed from the waist up a trim Hispanic man with a silver mustache and thick silver mutton-chop sideburns; he was wearing a black cowboy hat, a black tuxedo jacket, a black ruffled shirt and black bolo tie with a turquoise clasp, and he was smiling and pointing to the legend *Sometimes Good Guys Don't Wear White*. Over his head were the big words, in red, *Felix Gogo Toyota* and next to that *Temple...Waco...Fort Worth...Dallas*. At the bottom of the overcrowded ad were the words "Walk In, Drive Out!"

"So," Terry prodded, "what do you think?"

Nomad didn't answer, because he was pondering the many ways a band could die.

He'd seen nearly all of them. The war of egos that ultimately exploded, the simmering resentments that built up over time, the quick flare of anger that hid exhaustion at its heart, the hard and final bang of a door slamming, the parking lot scuffle, the on-stage implosion, the rehearsal walk-out, the accusations of betrayal as cutting as the death throes of a marriage, the silence that screamed, the guitar flung across a motel room like a flying scythe, the fist into the wall and the broken fingers, Black Tar and Buzzard Dust, Twack and Shiznit, New Jack Swing and all the other combinations of heroin, crack, meth and whatever could be cooked, smoked, inhaled or injected.

Nothing was pretty about the death of a band.

He was staring into space, his eyes unfocused, but he thought he was looking into an abyss. Sure, they could go on without Terry. Have to find another keyboard player, if that's the way they wanted to go. But Terry provided a sound integral to The Five, ranging from raw and rowdy to the swirling of psychedelic colors to a dark bluesy wail that particularly complimented Nomad's own rough-edged, smoke-and-whiskey singing voice. Sure, they could go on without Terry. But it wouldn't be The Five anymore, not even with another keyboard player. It would be another band, but not this one.

And Nomad realized he would mourn this death, maybe more than any other. When it was running on all cylinders, The Five was tight and clean and everybody had their space. Everybody had their job to do, and they did it like professionals. They did it with pride. And though the life was tough and the money not much to speak of, the gigs could lift you up. There was nothing like being in the groove, like feeling the energy of the audience and the heat of the lights and the pure electric heart of the moment. It was so real. But more than that, Nomad had thought—had hoped—that The Five was going to find a way through the wall, that this band of any band he'd ever played in was going to get the record deal. Was going to get the moneymen behind it, with their engine of promotion and contacts and open doors.

Johnny, spoke the old familiar voice somewhere deep inside his head, *there's no roadmap*.

He could still see the little crooked smile surface on his father's mouth, and those blue eyes shining like Beale Street neon at midnight.

"Well," Terry said, "don't everybody speak at once."

Nomad knew what the silence was saying. Everyone was thinking the same thing: after this tour, when they trekked west through Arizona into California and came back through New Mexico to do a last show in Austin on the 16th of August, little less than a month away, The Five was finished.

"You can find somebody to fill my place." Terry proved he could read minds, if he had to. "It's not like I'm the one and only."

"I can't believe this." It was Ariel's voice, still hushed with shock.

"I can think of five or six keyboard players right now," Terry went on. He shifted uncomfortably in his seat. "It's not the end of the band."

George gave a faint noise, something between a sigh and a grunt, that only Nomad caught.

"You have anything to say?" Nomad asked him, more sharply than he'd intended, but George shook his head and concentrated on his driving.

"That's a great big load of hot mess for us to wade through," Berke said, and if anybody could sound more acerbic than Nomad, she took the prize. "Fucking *great*."

"Hold on, now." Terry turned around to face her. "I can be *replaced*. Look, there's nobody who's so all-that they can't be replaced."

"What are you going to do when you get tired of cleaning the cobwebs out of little plastic keyboards? Get a gig at the Holiday Inn bar? You going to put out your tipbowl with the five-dollar bill in it? Start playing Billy Joel requests?"

"Don't knock Billy Joel," Terry cautioned.

"I'm knocking *you*. Thinking you can walk away from music and be happy about it."

"I'm not walking away, I'm—"

"Repositionin'," said Mike, which caused Terry to shut up because it sounded good, or at least better than what he was fumbling to get out. "Yeah, I get it." Mike nodded and rubbed his chin. There were scrolled tattoos on the knuckles of each finger. "Repositionin'. Seems to me like everybody ought to reposition from time to time. Shake things up, see what falls out."

Berke scowled and was about to say something back to him, and maybe it would have been *What the fuck do you know about it* but in fact Mike Davis did know a whole hell of a lot about repositioning so she let it slide.

Nomad figured that for every bright star and flaming asshole in a band, there were a dozen Mike Davises. The solid guy, the workman. The man who steps back out of the spotlight to play, because he doesn't like the glare. Mike was thirty-three years old, stood about five-ten, but he was a small-framed guy—skinny, really—who looked like he was always in need of a good meal, though he ate like a grizzly bear just out of hibernation. He was tough and weathered and wiry in the way that said *do not mess with me for I will take your fucking head off and use it as a planter*. Nomad had seen

Mike stare down a murder clique of drunk football players from the University of Tennessee, in a dismal little club in Knoxville, and something had passed between Mike and those three mouthy, swaggering young men—something dangerous, some message between animals—that warned them off before they made a very bad mistake. Maybe it was the long beak of a nose, the cement slab chin always stained with stubble, or the dark brown eyes hollowed back in a chiselled face that generally betrayed no emotion. He nearly always won in their poker games on the road, because it was like trying to read the expressions of a crab. He had shoulder-length dark brown hair that was showing streaks of gray at the temples. He would say he'd earned it, and more, for all he'd been through. Eight bands that Nomad knew of, and probably more Mike didn't care to talk about. Two ex-wives, one in Nashville and one with their six-year-old daughter in Covington, Louisiana. Mike had been born just up the road from there, early Christmas morning, 1974, in Bogalusa. His life had been anything but holy.

It was the tattoos on his arms that people saw first, and those either scared the shit out of you and made you keep your distance or entranced you into approaching nearer, if you dared. He wore sleeveless T-shirts to show off his sleeves. Moby Dick rising from the sea was the first art on the knob of his right shoulder, and on the left was the grinning freckled face of a boy who Mike said was his older brother Wayne, killed eighteen years ago in a lumberyard accident. His first bandmate. Played a mean Fender Telecaster, Mike said. Blue fire, like a cut diamond. The Tele, not the brother. It was also there, underneath the boy's face, angled like a bowtie gone awry.

Nomad had always thought that people carried worlds within them. Whatever they had experienced, whatever they saw or felt, whatever joys or sorrows, those things could never be exactly duplicated by anyone else, so everybody carried their own world. In Mike's case, the tattoo artists—more than a half-dozen, in often jarringly-different styles—had depicted his world on his arms. From shoulders to wrists, it was all there in vibrant ink of many colors: faces of women and men copied from photographs, a variety of bad-ass or sorry-ass cars and—as Mike put it—pick-me-up trucks, numbers that had some meaning for him, a whiskey bottle here, a burning joint there, the bars of a cell, a long country road, a skull spitting fire, bass axes he had loved or lost or pawned, a white dog, a black dog, a devil, an angel, his little Sara's face, the names of the bands he wanted to remember which did include The Five, declarations such as *Trust Is Earned* and *Live Before You Die* and everything in a progression from the past to the present, shoulders to wrists. Everything, as well, underlaid by a phantasmagoric deep blue star-speckled background against which the trails of fiery red and yellow comets passed between the artwork. It had occurred to Nomad, as it surely must have to Mike, that he was running out of room.

Moby Dick? The first book Mike had read that he liked. Actually, he'd stolen it from the Bogalusa Public Library when the librarian said he was too young to check it out. He'd rooted for the white whale to make it out alive.

"Right," Terry said when it seemed safe to speak again. He was talking directly to Mike. "Repositioning is just what I'm doing."

"Why shouldn't we pull over and let you reposition your butt on the side of the road right now?" Berke asked, in her charming way.

"Because," he answered with great dignity, "I'm in it just like George is. For the tour. I'm going to do what I've always done. Nobody's going to say I'm slacking, don't worry about it."

"I can't believe it. I just can't believe it," Ariel was saying, and Nomad thought he'd never heard her sound so hurt before. "It's over when you go, Terry. Nobody can step in for you, no matter who it is."

"I don't know about that," George offered. "There are—"

"I think you ought to shut up," Nomad interrupted, and George's mouth closed.

"Fucking tell him," Berke said.

"Plug your lava-hole too," Nomad shot back.

"Happy happy joy joy!" said Mike, with a gravedigger's cackle. "Ain't nothin' like the *real* thing, bro!"

Nomad put his fingers against his temples and slid down in his seat. The air-conditioner was racketing, but was it *working*? He put his right hand against the nearest vent. A weak breath of cool air, but not cold. Hadn't George taken the Scumbucket in for a road check last week, like he was supposed to? That low, grating hum—sounded to him like an E minor chord strummed on a cheap Singapore guitar—seemed to have amped up in volume, and it was going to drive everybody batshitty by the time they reached Waco.

Bastard was already screwing up on his job, and they were hardly out of the gate.

"So," Terry said with a quaver in his voice, "Does everybody hate me now?"

God, it was going to be a long tour.

The last tour, with this lineup. Maybe the last tour with any of them together, because once a band started unravelling the emperor got naked real quick.

The thing is, he was the emperor. He'd never asked to be. Never wanted to be. But he was, and that was it.

He realized, as he listened to the hum from the dashboard and felt the oppressive silence at his back, that this shit could tear the band apart before they even finished up the weekend. At best, they were in for heavy weather. What could he do right now—right this fucking minute, while it counted—to show them he was still the emperor, and that The Five was still a band until he said it was not?

He found something amid the chaos, and he latched onto it.

< >

"Nobody hates you. I *ought* to, but I don't. I guess everybody has to do what they think is right," he said. "And I'm thinking we ought to write a new song."

No one else spoke.

"A new song," Nomad repeated, and he turned around to gauge the response. Berke's eyes were closed, Mike was staring vacantly out his window, and Terry was polishing his glasses on the front of his shirt.

Only Ariel was paying attention. "What about?"

"I don't know. Just something new."

"What's your idea?"

"I don't have any ideas. I'm just saying, we ought to write a new song."

"Hm," Ariel said, and she frowned. "You mean pull something out of the air?"

"No." Nomad understood Ariel's question, because this wasn't the way they worked. Most of the original songs The Five played—tunes like 'The Let Down', 'Pain Parade', 'I Don't Need Your Sympathy',

'Another Man', and 'Pale Echo'—had been written jointly by Nomad and Ariel. Terry had written a few more, both alone and with either of the two lead singers. But the way they worked was that Nomad or Ariel would come up with an idea and start kicking it around with each other, and it might go somewhere or stall and die, you never could tell about songwriting. The others would be asked their opinion, and for ideas on tempo or key, or Terry might come up with an organ motif or solo. Mike was quick to come up with an inventive bass line, and he might go through a few variations before he settled on what he wanted to offer. Berke supplied the core beat, the fills and embellishments, and sometimes she went for what was asked of her and other times she kicked it and went off in an unexpected direction. However it worked—and sometimes it was hard to say exactly *how* it worked—the result was another song for the set, though from beginning to end of the process might be anywhere from a couple of days to many weeks.

"Not just something out of the air," Nomad continued. "I'd like everybody to think about it. Put our heads together."

"*Our* heads?" That had brought Berke out of her sham sleep. "What do you mean, 'everybody'?"

"I mean what I said. I think we all ought to work on a new song, together. Not just Ariel and me, but the whole band. Start with the words, maybe. Everybody does a few lines."

Mike's thick eyebrows jumped. "Say *what*?"

"We all contribute to the lyrics. Is that so hard to follow?"

"Hell yes, it is," Mike answered. "I ain't no *poet*. Never written a line in my life."

"Me neither," Berke said. "That's not my job."

"Can I speak?" George asked, and in the space that followed he went on. "I think it's a good idea. I mean, why not at least *try*?"

"Yeah, I'm glad you think so," Nomad told him, "because you ought to contribute to the song, too."

"*Me*? Come *on*! I'm the last man in the world who could write a song!"

"Have you ever tried?"

"No, and that's because I *can't*. I know *sound*, but I am completely unmusical, man."

"But like you said, why not at least try?"

Before George could respond, Berke said, "Okay, we get it." Her voice carried a patronizing note that made Nomad think he ought to have punched her in the face a long time ago, and been done with it. "You're looking for some way to keep us *together*, right? Keep our minds straight for the tour? What is this...like...busy work for the *soul* or something?"

"Maybe it is." His throat felt constricted like it did when he had an allergic reaction, which was why he stayed away from all dairy. "Or maybe it's a productive thing for people to get their heads around."

"Good try, bro," said Mike, "but I know my limits."

"Yeah," Berke agreed, "me too. And it's not going to make me *forget*. Look, even if we all sat down in a circle around the campfire and wrote another 'Kumbaya', we're still going to know it's over. I mean, really. With George and Terry out, we're not who we were anymore. Yeah, we can find another road manager and audition for a keyboard player, but..." She paused, and in that instant of hesitation Nomad thought he saw pain disturb her features like a ripple across a pond that held its secrets deep. Then it was gonc, leaving Nomad with the impression that he was not the only one who'd already begun to mourn a death.

"It won't work," Berke said quietly, and she looked at him with what might have been sadness in those dark chocolate eyes. In contrast to that, a quick and nasty smile flashed across her mouth. Nomad thought she was torn up inside, just like himself, and she didn't know whether to cry or curse. But Berke was Berke, and so she said, "Fuck it" before she turned her gaze away.

THREE.

For a while they didn't seem to be anywhere, and then suddenly they were where they needed to be.

< >

"**Must** be the place," George said, as he pulled the Scumbucket and the U-Haul trailer off China Spring Road into a parking lot. They had passed through a nondescript area north of Lake Waco and the Waco regional airport surrounded by scrubby fields and scabby warehouses. He'd been directed by email from Felix Gogo to look for the red-and-yellow Delgado Cable van, and there it was, sitting next to a shiny black Toyota Land Cruiser from which the sun radiated like a blazing mirror.

"Watch out for glass," Terry warned. Jagged bits of it glittered on the heat-cracked pavement. Not only that, but broken beer bottles lay scattered about, and one of those under a tire would not only sound like a roadside bomb in Iraq going off but might lame their ride.

"Jeez." Berke was not impressed. "I thought we were going to a *studio*."

"Well, the guy evidently knows what he's doing." George eased the Scumbucket up next to the pristine Land Cruiser. He could imagine the Toyota saying to his van, in snobbish car-language, *Have you ever heard of something called a wash*? He cut the engine, put it in Park and pulled up the handbrake, and then he sat looking at what might have been a small stripmall before a meteor the size of a freight train must've crashed down onto it.

Nomad was thinking that a plane had arrowed in, short of the airport's runway. Blackened walls testified to fire. Windows were broken out and red metal roofs sagged. Here and there, on remaining sections of gray cinderblock, were the elaborate black and blue swirls of gang symbols. Looked to him as if two gangs had fought over the turf, and nobody won. But then he realized the place may never have been actually finished, because nearby stood two abandoned Port-A-Potties and beyond them, back where the thicket boiled up, were pieces of machinery that appeared to be part of a cement-mixing truck. A pile of old tires lay beside those, and a few beatup garbage cans full of burned lumber. Rags and other bits of trash hung in the brush like a hermit's laundry.

"This can't be it," Nomad said, but George was already getting out. Heat from Hell's oven rolled into the Scumbucket. And here came the hermit himself from one of the crooked doorways. He was a chunky Hispanic dude, a kid really, maybe nineteen or twenty, and he was wearing a baggy pair of brown shorts and a white T-shirt damp with sweat. His arms were crisscrossed with tats and his scalp was shaved except for a black stripe going back along the middle of his head. Nomad thought they were about to get jumped by a *cholo* until he saw the light meter hanging on a cord around the guy's neck.

"Hey, man," the dude said to George. "We're almost set up." He motioned with a thumb toward the doorway from which he'd just emerged, and he continued to the cable company van to fish something out of the back.

"Ohhhh*kay*," Mike said, mostly to himself. "Let's do this."

They climbed out of the Scumbucket. Sweat immediately popped from their pores. Their shadows were ebony on the bleached pavement, and as Terry, Mike and Berke followed George through the doorway Nomad stopped to wait for Ariel.

"Careful," he told her, because the broken glass had crunched ominously under his own sneakers. Where the others had gone was in relative darkness. He felt her hand grasp his arm, to steady her path over the glittering rubble. He thought this place looked like a fucking warzone, and why they'd come here to do the interview instead of a comfortable air-conditioned studio was beyond him.

"Listen," Ariel said, when she got up right beside him. "I like your idea about the song. I think it would be good for everybody."

"Yeah." He hadn't said anymore about it since they'd been south of Waco.

She still had hold of his arm, and she was stopping him from going any further since she wanted a moment with him. "I've got some ideas in my notebook. Fragments, really. But maybe we can find something to start it off?"

Ariel and her notebook, Nomad thought. It was decorated with glued-on gemstones of a dozen colors. Some of her song ideas began with a single word, or a descriptive line, or a question to herself. He'd never looked inside her notebook, but he knew how she worked. He was the fiery energy of a song, the hot red anger and the will to fight. She was the ocean depths, the cool blue mysticism of the currents, the surrender to the inevitable will of the tides. He presented a snarl and a fist; she offered a smile shaded with sadness and an open hand. She was twenty-four years old, of medium height and slender build, and she'd been born in Manchester, Massachusetts, just up the coast from Boston. She wore her strawberry-blonde hair in curly ringlets that fell across her forehead and down around her shoulders like, Nomad thought, a heroine in one of those Victorian novels who is doomed to fall in love with the callous cad. She dressed in that fashion, too: lace-trimmed blouses, lacy-puffed sleeves, fine etchings of lace on the necks of her T-shirts and sewn on the cuffs of her distressed jeans. Not that he knew a whole hell of a lot about Victorian novels, but he knew he hated them from high school English.

Ariel was pretty, in that old English way. Or maybe it was Irish; the scatter of freckles across her nose and the pale cream of her skin made him think of that country the green soap was named for. She did smell nice, he couldn't deny that. Sort of a faint honeysuckle aroma, caught sometimes when they were working close and she leaned past him. Everybody had a smell, of course. Take Berke, who smelled of friction.

But the thing that stood out particularly about Ariel Collier—leaving aside the fact that Nomad was grudgingly aware she left him in the dust on acoustic guitar, and her voice was a beautiful mezzo-soprano tessitura (which, she said, she'd learned when her parents had paid for operatic singing lessons)—was that the color of her eyes changed. Depending on the light, or her emotions, they could be gray from dove-to-dark, or show hints of sapphire blue, or sometimes display just faintly the sea-green of shallows where the reef almost touches the surface. He knew she was the baby of her family, with an older brother and sister, the former a corporate attorney in Boston and the latter a saleswoman with a yacht brokerage firm in Fort Lauderdale. Her father was an investment company executive. Her mother sold real estate. She was the baby of this family too, but she was no child to the hardships—challenges?—of the musician's life. Neal Tapley, the leader of the band she'd been in before she joined The Five, had driven his car off a county two-lane south of Austin and launched into a stand of trees at a speed, the police later said, of a hundred and thirteen miles an hour. Which surprised everyone who followed Neal and his band The Blessed Hours because Neal was a genuinely decent guy except for some bad choices involving crack cocaine and 3rd Street loan sharks, and nobody had ever figured his old Volvo clunker could get up much over sixty.

Hell of a guitar player, Neal had been. Another world, gone down in flames.

"Yeah," Nomad told her. "We ought to find something to start with." But he wasn't sure they could, and he heard his own uncertainty. He wasn't sure it was such a good idea, after all. What was the point? But directing everybody's mind to a new tune would give them a task to focus on, and pushing them to do what they'd never done before—a song with lyrics written by everyone, even the ones who thought they couldn't write—might ease the feeling of dissolution that could rip any band apart. And there was another reason: Nomad hoped, deep in his heart, that with such a song that was a testament to The Five in the band's darkest hour Terry would decide to stay, and George might find his own inner poet—however *bad* it turned out to be—and decide that he too was not ready to walk away.

Could, would, should...

Shit.

"Comin' through, man," said the tech dude. Nomad and Ariel stepped aside to let him pass carrying a coil of bright orange electrical cable, a can of Sherwin-Williams paint and a paintbrush.

"Little too late to be remodelling this dump," Nomad said, but the guy didn't respond on his way into the building. The darkness swallowed him up.

Nomad followed Ariel in. Once over the threshold he removed his sunglasses. The air was sweltering in here, in a rectangular room with a dirty concrete floor and gang graffiti spray-painted across every area of drywall that wasn't punched full of holes. Or *shot* full of holes, because it looked like guns had been at work in here. There was no furniture. A piece of metal tubing dangled from the ceiling and hung down to the floor like the cock of a giant robot. To emphasize that image, a few used condoms were stuck to the concrete. Over in the left corner, a garbage can overflowed and on top of the mess was a Shipley's Do-Nuts box. Good combination, Nomad thought: the tagbangers had sex first, got their blood sugar up with the doughnuts, and then finished off with a Glock orgy.

On the floor, off to the right, was a portable Honda generator mounted on a handcart. It was one of those super-quiet deals, rumbling like a cat getting scratched. Orange and yellow cables were hooked up to the generator, and snaked across the floor through another doorway about midway back and also on the right.

George appeared. "Back here, guys."

They went through the door, watching their step on the cables, and into a smaller room that was no less defiled. The others were in there already. Many impressions crowded in on Nomad: more graffiti and bullet holes, and places where it looked as if machetes had hacked the drywall; the sunlight streamed down through several bullet holes that had punctured the roof; the rear wall had been scorched shiny black by fire, and upon it was pinned a large clean American flag; cigarette butts, crushed beer cans and other trash littered the floor, but areas had been cleared to accomodate the tripod legs of two floodlight stands, their illumination powered by the generator. The tech dude was plugging in a plastic fan on a waist-high stand with the cable he'd brought, and a second young guy with a brown beard and a suffering expression had opened the paint can and was brushing bright blood-red over the gang symbols. Two pro camcorders outfitted with lights and microphones were situated on the floor, protected from the nastiness by virtue of sitting atop their individual Delgado Cable yellow canvas bags.

"We'd better do this quick," said the man who turned the fan's control knob up to Fast with a thick brown hand adorned with three diamond rings. He angled the breeze up into his face. "Fucking *warm* in here, huh?" When no one answered, he looked at them from under his black cowboy hat and scanned them all except for George, who stood beside him. "I'm Felix Gogo," he said. "But you already know that, huh? Seen my show before?" He answered his own question. "'Course you have. Who hasn't? I can tell you the numbers, week-by-week. Always going up. Amazing how many people tune in, late nights. Fuckers can't sleep, they're all worried and shit. They can watch me, I make them happy." He grinned, showing a blast of white teeth that had to be some dentist's dream house. "Hey, *amigos*! You get happy too, huh?"

Happiness, Berke thought, was different things to different people. She saw the glint of his eyes and some accusation came at her like a bullet, and then he'd swept his gaze past her and she stared at the American flag on the flame-licked wall and wondered whose god they had offended to wind up here, on such a happy day.

Felix Gogo, whose real name—according to Ashwatthama Vallampati—was Felix Goganazaiga, was obviously not only one of the biggest Toyota dealers in central Texas and the metroplex, and not only saw himself as the central Texas and metroplex late-night cable TV show Dick Clark—check that, make it Ryan Seacrest—but he had more than a passing familiarity with the term "photoshopping". He was about twice the width he appeared to be on his billboards. Black could not make slim he who would not lay off the enchiladas. He was maybe in his early fifties, with the same thick silver muttonchop sideburns and the silver mustache. Besides the black cowboy hat, he wore the black tuxedo jacket, the black ruffled shirt and black bolo tie with a triangular topaz clasp. On the jacket's right lapel was an American flag pin. Topside he was camera-ready, but bottomside was casual: he was wearing a pair of khaki shorts, gray anklet socks and a pair of expensive Nikes. He had spindly legs for such a hefty dude, Mike noted. Gogo's gut would've made a decent tractor tire.

"Can I ask a question?" George sounded timid in the presence of such celebrity. After all, the half-hour Felix Gogo Show had been an eleven o'clock Friday night—rerun, two-thirty Saturday afternoon—event for over ten years. It was on Delgado Cable in Austin, Temple, Waco and the metroplex. The guy had run music videos and interviewed hundreds of bands. He'd also interviewed stars such as William Shatner and Jenna Jameson, and there was still a video on YouTube of a shell-shocked Sandra Bullock watching a possibly inebriated Felix shimmy to Rod Stewart's 'Do Ya Think I'm Sexy?' back in 2002 on the studio set. There were the Gogo Dancers to keep things lively between segments. He was a showman and a character and a very rich man, and above all he seemed real happy.

"Go right ahead, George." Gogo spoke with the sincerity of a new best buddy. Nomad figured George had either talked to him by phone before the directions had been emailed, or George had shaken Gogo's hand and introduced himself just a minute or so ago.

"I'm wondering...how come we're not in the studio? I mean... isn't this—"

"A hellhole, yeah it is," Gogo agreed. "Well, the main studio's in *Dallas*. See, the thing is, I had my crew here scout a location. Find just the right place, suitable for your band. The interview, I'm saying. This was going to be the first stage of an office park, huh? New subdivision up the road. It went bust, and no more office park either. Then the bangers moved in. I wanted to find a place that went along with your video. Did I not succeed?" Before George could answer, Gogo said to the wall-painter, "Hey Benjy, just do from yay-high to yay-low. We're doing close shots, none of that area's going to light up. And we don't want to suffocate on the fumes, okay? Let it drip some, get that bloody look."

"Sir," said Benjy, obediently brushing.

"I tell you what, put that poster up there. Just stick it up right there next to the bullet holes and fling some paint on it. Kinda put it at an angle."

Benjy dutifully crossed the room and retrieved from one of the canvas bags a crumpled and wrinkled The Five poster, which showed their faces—all as serious as sin, couldn't have a musician smiling, that would be instant death—with the signature black handprint in the middle. Nomad knew Ash had sent Gogo a press kit, with their pictures and bios and shit, when he sent the video. "Angle it like so," Gogo directed. Benjy pushed the poster up against the wet paint as he was told. "Okay, fuck it up some," said Gogo, and Benjy flung droplets of red paint across it. "One more time. Yeah, there you go. Art for the artists," Gogo said.

"We're ready," the tech guy with the skunk-shave hairdo announced. He'd been shifting the floodlights around and checking his meter, and now everything was as he wanted.

"Let me tell you how we're going to do this." Gogo took a black handkerchief from an inner jacket pocket and wiped the sparkles of sweat from his cheeks, even though the fan's air was fluttering his bolo. "We're going to get you placed, and then I'm going to gab with you for about a minute in front of this wall," and here he indicated the red-spattered poster and the bullet holes. "Then we'll move you back there," a nod toward Old Glory against the shiny burn, "and gab for about two more minutes. That's your spot, three minutes. You really get more than that, 'cause remember, we're showing the video in between the backdrop changes. George, how about introducing me around real quick, huh?"

"Hey...can *I* ask something?" Nomad spoke up, before any introductions could be started. He didn't wait to be invited. The heat, a solid prickly thing, was making sweat itch the back of his neck and trickle down his sides. Gogo stared at Nomad blankly, as he put his handkerchief away. "I'm not getting what this place has to do with our video."

"I'll tell you, then." Gogo didn't miss a beat. His tone was flat and his eyes were still blank, as if he were conserving all his energy for the interview. "I *watched* your video, okay? Very technically well done. Who shot it for you?"

"Some film students at UT," George answered.

"The actors were students?"

"Yeah, but we hired local actors too." It was amazing how quickly a video project could eat up two thousand dollars, if you really wanted it to look pro: the costumes, the props, the smoke pots and blank ammo, the special effects and the editing work. In the end, as they were running out of cash, George sold an old reel-to-reel tapedeck he had in a closet, Nomad tapped the account that held the money he earned as a house-painter, Mike ditched an axe on eBay, Berke gave an afternoon of drum lessons to teenage wannabees at the Oakclaire Drive YMCA for twenty bucks, Ariel played for change several days running on the UT campus, and Terry donated from his gig giving piano lessons at the Episcopal Student Center on 27th Street.

"And it was shot where?" Gogo asked, still staring at Nomad. "Looked like some kind of abandoned building, about as fucked up as this one."

"An apartment complex," Nomad said, getting the point. "Turned into a crackhouse. A few days away from the wrecking-ball."

"There you go, huh? I wanted the interviews to have the same kind of backdrop as the video. Wanted it to be edgy. See, I even found you some bullet holes, so you should be grateful. They'll look good in the shot, won't they, Hector?"

"Yeah, *muy bueno*," said Hector.

"Okay, then. Christ, I'm melting. Introductions, Georgie. Who does what?"

George did a quick job of the intros, because it was obvious Gogo wanted to get to business. That was fine for everyone else, because they were all sweating and miserable in this mean little room. Then Gogo said, "Ready," the two techs got their camcorders, switched on the cam lights and checked the volume settings on the microphones. The generator's low drone in the other room wasn't loud enough to kill anything in here, and Nomad figured it helped the vibe.

"Okay, everybody move against this wall. Watch the paint... what's your name again?"

"Ariel."

"Wet paint, Ariel. Scruffy, move to your left about a foot. We want the poster to show." Mike obeyed without comment. "How's it look?" This question was aimed at the techs, who were peering through their rubber-rimmed eyepieces.

"Tall dude needs to shift to the right," Hector said, and Nomad moved. "That's got it. I think we're set."

"Count it down," Gogo directed. He turned off his personal fan.

"In five...four...three...two...one."

"I'm *here*," said Gogo with a dazzling smile and forceful emphasis, speaking into Benjy's camcorder, "with the Austin-based band, The Five. These guys have just started their new tour, and they're bringing us a look at their fresh redhot video. The song's called 'When The Storm Breaks'. We'll get to that video in just a minute, but first...you know...heh heh...I've got to ask a question." He turned his attention to the band. Benjy's camcorder stayed on his face, while Hector's was pointed at The Five. Nomad was aware of being at the center of bright light and black shadows. "Take a look at that poster," Gogo said. "Give us a tight closeup on that, Hector." Obviously, the techs were not only the crew but also part of the cast. "Okay, this is my question: which one of you is the *thumb*?"

There followed a few seconds of deafening silence. Nomad thought it was probably the most asinine question he'd ever heard. Their first minute was ticking away. He said, "I don't know who the thumb is, but *I* can be the middle finger."

"Cut it," Gogo told the techs. The lights on their camcorders went dark. Gogo scratched his chin and smiled without warmth. "Listen," he said, "let's understand that *I'm* the host, huh? I'm going for some humor. I'm not challenging anybody to a big dick contest. Now, to be honest with you, I'm doing this for Roger because he's a decent guy and he's sent me a lot of business. So save your attitude for the stage, and we'll all go home happy. Count it down," he told Hector.

The camcorders lit up again. "In five…four…three…two…one."

"I'm *here*—right here, wherever we are—with the Austin-based band, The Five. These guys have just started their new tour and we're going to get a look at their video, 'When The Storm Breaks', in just a minute, but first I want to remind you to check out our Weekend Special Deals coming up, see what Felix Gogo can do for you, doesn't have to be just the weekend, we've got deals *every* day of the week, walk in, drive out, and remember, my friends, sometimes good guys don't wear white." He'd been speaking directly into Benjy's lens, and now he looked at the band and gave an expression of exaggerated astonishment as if the light-washed figures had suddenly materialized before him like floating spirits. "There are *five* of you!" he said, clownishly. "I don' know what I wass es-pectin'!" He gave a big grin into the lens, put an index finger against the side of his head, lolled his tongue out and staggered like the village idiot, and Nomad just clenched his teeth and looked down at the trashy floor.

Ariel laughed, but it was all nerves. Beside her, Terry wore a frozen smile. His eyes were hot and sweat glistened on his scalp.

"Take you a long time to come up with that name?" was the next question. "Ariel?"

"No," she answered. "Not really." She felt herself trying to recoil from the lights, but there was wet red paint on the wall at her back.

"We thought about The Four, or The Six," Berke suddenly said, her voice calm and controlled, "but for some reason it didn't seem right."

"Duh!" said Gogo, with another fanatical grin into the camcorder. "See folks, you think my job iss *heeesey*? We got some great minds in here tonight! Okay, somebody set up the video. You went to Iraq to shoot this, right?"

"It's about the war," Nomad managed to say.

"Song's called 'When The Storm Breaks', by The—" Gogo held up his own hand, palm out and fingers spread, for Hector's camcorder to focus on.

"And cut," Gogo said. He walked a couple of steps to turn the fan back on, and he took the black handkerchief from his inside jacket pocket and mopped his face and did not give a glance at George, who stood about three feet away.

Gogo lifted his double chins to catch the breeze. "Have you people ever done a fucking *television interview* before? Pardon the truth, but you are *slow*. Benjy, get me some water."

"I don't think we got our full minute," Nomad said.

"What?"

"I said," Nomad repeated, "that we didn't get our full minute." He came forward, brushing between Ariel and Terry. George was shaking his head, warning him: *no...no...no*. Nomad stopped, but he had no intention of backing down. "You used our time for a commercial. That's not right."

"Oh, Jesus," Gogo said, as he took the bottled water that Benjy had brought him from one of the bags. He uncapped it, drank but did not offer any liquid relief to anyone else. "This whole *show* is a commercial. What'd you say you called yourself? Nomad? Okay, when you get the Nomad Show on cable, you can do what you please. Until then, the Felix Gogo Show is the name of this one, and I do what I please. Somebody fucks up, or acts like a moron, or doesn't appreciate the humor..." He shrugged. "There's the door. We can shut this down right now." He turned to George. "You want to shut this down right now, George? I can go sell some cars, huh?"

The tech guys were waiting to see how this turned out before they moved the floodlights. George looked from Gogo to Nomad and then back again, and he lowered his head and said, "Nobody wants to shut it down."

Still the tech guys waited. Gogo drank about half the water. Then he recapped it with a flourish, victor of this particular battle. "Okay," he announced, and the tech guys started working again.

Nomad caught Berke's gaze. Her eyes were slightly narrowed. She was asking him, *Do you believe we have to put up with this shit?* He didn't want to, anymore than she did, but they needed this. Even though the show would run too late to put anybody in the audience at Common Grounds, it and the Saturday afternoon rerun would bring people into The Curtain Club for their Saturday night gig in Dallas.

"Do you want to talk about the video?" Gogo asked them. "Or do you want to talk about your tour?"

"The tour," Nomad said, after a quick questioning glance at the others.

"Fine with me. That video's going to be about as popular around here as a cactus sandwich covered with turd sauce. But that's just my opinion. Okay, I want you all standing in front of the flag."

The band was in place (like mannequins in a store window advertising a small and hollow version of patriotism, Nomad thought), the floodlights were on, the camcorders lit up, the countdown done, and Felix Gogo got on the right track by mentioning their gig at the Curtain Club in Dallas' Deep Ellum. Doors at eight-thirty, other gators on the bill the Naugahydes, the Critters, and Gina Fayne and the Mudstaynes. Gogo asked Mike about the tattoos, and Mike said they were a history of his life. Gogo asked Ariel how long she'd been a musician, and she said she couldn't remember not hearing some kind of music and wanting to write down what she heard. Gogo asked Terry what his favorite song was that The Five had done, and Terry said it was a tough question but he probably had two favorites that were very different from each other and displayed their range: the slithery 'This Song Is A Snake' and the hard-edged 'Desperate Ain't Pretty', which they sometimes did as an encore. Gogo was a fly, landing here and there, long enough to start an itch, quick enough to slip a swatter.

Then Gogo looked directly at Nomad and asked, "You guys have been together three years, right? So how come you don't have a record deal?"

It sounded so sincere and sincerely interested, but Nomad knew they were having a big dick contest, after all, and Gogo had just pulled Nomad's jeans down to show the shrivelled little member that hung there.

In his allotted time, Nomad could not explain that Don Kee Records in Nashville had gone belly-up a month before their first CD was supposed to be distributed. He could not explain that their slick A&R rep with Electric Fusion Records in Los Angeles had been caught screwing the money-man's wife in a hot tub, and thus not only was Slick kicked, but every band Slick had picked was kicked. Nomad could not explain, in this happy moment, that the music business was a devastated landscape and that the sale of CDs fell every year and bands were fighting to survive on gigs that at best put a hundred dollars in the pot to be divided, but then again Gogo already knew this, and what was truth to working gators in the industry could sound like sour grapes to the paying audience. Anyway, Nomad decided, desperate ain't pretty.

He pulled up an easy smile. It was probably one of the hardest things he'd ever had to do because it felt so hideously, rottenly false, and he said, "We're working on it," which he'd heard many others say when they were sliding down the tubes.

"Well, good luck with that," said Gogo. He looked at Terry again. "Where you going after Dallas?"

"We'll be at the Spinhouse in El Paso on Friday night, the 25th. After that, we're at—"

"So I guess your fans can find you on the web, right?" Gogo interrupted.

"Uh...yeah. And we've got a MySpace page."

"Good enough. I want to give you a great big Gogo thanks for being here tonight, and I *know* you guys are heading for great things." He grinned into Benjy's lens. "And *speaking* of great, my friends, let's take a look at these great Weekend Special Deals. Felix Gogo Toyota makes it *eeeeeasy* to walk in, drive out any day of the week. Comin' at you right *now*." He pointed his finger into the lens and made his eyes pop and he pursed his lips as if trying to kiss the customer—or, at least, the customer's wallet.

"And out," said Hector.

The camcorder lights were switched off. Gogo mopped his face with his handkerchief again. "We're done," he said to no one in particular. "We'll edit it this afternoon. Check it out tonight, see what you think."

"We're working tonight," Nomad reminded him.

"Catch the rerun, then. Whatever. Fuck it."

The tech guys were unplugging. Ariel, Berke and Mike had already gone out as soon as the cams had darkened. Gogo left the room, followed by George, Terry and Nomad. Outside, in the parking lot, the air was only a few degrees cooler than the stifling room but at least there was the stale breath of a breeze. Gogo got on his cellphone and stood next to the Land Cruiser; the interview was finished, the favor to Roger Chester done, and what more was there?

"Thanks," George said as he went around to get in the Scumbucket, but Gogo stuck a finger in his free ear and concentrated on his conversation.

"I haven't had so much fun," Berke told Ariel as they climbed into their seats, "since the last time I puked on my boots."

"You're makin' me hungry," Mike said. "Anybody want a hamburger? We passed a McD's up the road."

Nomad was about to get in when Gogo closed his cell and said, "Hey! You! Nomad, come here a minute!"

Nomad's first impulse was to show him he really could be a middle finger, and a double middle finger at that, but he walked the few paces to where Gogo stood next to the Land Cruiser. The black cowboy hat was cocked to one side. Gogo watched him warily, animal to animal.

"The promo stuff I got from Roger says you wrote that song," Gogo said. "You and the girl."

"The song for the video?"

"Yeah. The anti-American anti-war shit."

Here we go, Nomad thought. He steeled himself for an argument. "I don't think it's anti-American."

Gogo looked at the ground and pushed rubble around with the toe of a Nike. "You don't? You think it says something *worthwhile*? Something *noble*? You trying to make some kind of political statement?"

"It's a song," Nomad answered.

"Let me tell you." Gogo stared into Nomad's eyes, and there was something about his expression that was at the same time both angry and weirdly fatherly. "I've seen bands come and go. Seen the bigshots and the blowhards pass through by the dozens. And they were all talented in some way, yeah, but talent's no big thing. Shit, talent's a piss-poor third to *ambition*, and ambition is second to *personality*. So I'm going to give you some free advice, huh? Don't get into political shit. Don't stir up anybody's water. You're an entertainer, that's what you do. I interviewed The Rock a couple of years ago. Remember when he was a wrestler? His motto was 'Know Your Role'. That's what I'm saying to you. Know your role, and you might get somewhere."

"Where would that be?" Nomad asked.

"Not in the crapper, which is where ninety-nine percent of you people end up. Listen, you've got a good voice and a good presence. I like you. I'm just saying, the reason blacks rule music these days is because their songs are about fun and sex. The guys sing about getting bling and finding fresh pussy, and the girls sing about getting bling and cutting the nuts off the guys who screwed them over, huh?" Gogo waited for that point to sink in. "White musicians are singing about angst and the cruel world and how nothing's any damned good. What's the fun in that? Who's going to dance to that beat, huh? Now you want to be fucking *political*. I'm telling you, don't go that way."

"Maybe I don't have a choice."

"What, because you're such an *artist*? Because you're going to teach the world to sing? Yeah, right." His face got up closer to Nomad's, and Nomad could feel the heat coming off it. "*Everybody's* got a choice. And if you've got any brains, you'll know your role. *Comprende*?"

Nomad didn't answer for a few seconds. He was feeling his own heat. "I think I'd better go," he said.

"One more piece of free advice," Gogo offered. "Ditch the dyke."

Nomad turned his back on the man, and he walked to the Scumbucket where his family was waiting.

The McD's that Mike had mentioned was about two miles back toward Waco along East Lake Shore. It was connected to a gas station, but it did have a drive-up window. George gave the orders: two cheeseburgers, Coke and double fries for Mike; a burger and a Coke for Nomad, and the same for himself. The others didn't want anything. They hadn't done much talking since the interview. The Scumbucket's air-conditioning continued its off-key humming, the sun beat down mercilessly upon the hood and windshield, the sky was almost white with heat, and all was not right with this world.

They were waiting for their order to come up at the window. Berke took a drink from her bottle of tepid water. "I'll bet he screws us over. I'll bet when we see the segment we won't even recognize ourselves."

"I don't *want* to see it," said Ariel, picking the silver polish off her fingernails.

"It'll be okay," George told them. "He won't screw us over. It was a favor for Roger, remember?" As if he knew Roger Chester well enough to call him by his first name.

"I'm sick of rude mechanicals," Terry said, frowning toward a distant field where cattle searched for shade. "They run the world."

"Yeah, but it's the only world we've got." Mike was watching for the sack of burgers to appear. "Have to live in it, bro."

Nomad had his sunglasses back on. He offered no comment. He felt worn out, his energy sapped by the heat, and it was hardly noon. Before they headed over to Common Grounds they were due to check in at the Motel 6 in South Waco. Two rooms, three and three, at forty dollars each. If they didn't sell enough T-shirts and CDs tonight, they'd already be behind the curve.

The chow came. George handed the stuff out and started off, turning right on East Lake Shore. Distractedly, Nomad put the Coke on the seat between his legs and started unwrapping his burger.

"So what'd he talk to you about?" George asked.

"Nothing."

"Had to be *something*, man."

"I guess he was warning me. Us, I mean."

"Yeah? About what?" Terry asked.

Nomad took a bite of his sandwich. "About knowing our—" Roles, he was going to say, but just as he swallowed he caught the tang of the melted cheese tucked under the meat and *smelled* it and he looked at the sandwich and saw it in there, yellow and gooey. He realized the guy at the window had screwed up the order, because his burger was wrapped in white paper and not yellow. It was down his gullet now, too late to spit it up, and he knew one bite of cheese was not going to lay him low, it would just cause his throat to itch, but it was one more thing to deal with and he yelled, "*Shit!*"

Startled, George hit the brake. Nomad grabbed for his drink, the plastic lid popped off, and suddenly his seat was awash in Coca-Cola.

"What is it?" George asked, steering toward the shoulder. "What the *hell*...?"

"Fucking *shit!*" Nomad shouted, as he crushed the offending hamburger in one hand. "Let me out! Stop the van, let me out!"

"Cool it, bro!" Mike said, his mouth full. "Come on!"

"*Out!*" Nomad repeated, and this time it was almost a shriek. He felt Ariel's hand on his shoulder and he shook it off, and he realized as if looking down on himself in a dream that he was cracking up, he was about to fly to pieces, he had been blindsided by a fucking cheeseburger but that wasn't all of it, no, not by a long shot, he was about to flail out and hurt somebody and he had to get out of this van...RIGHT...FUCKING....NOW!

"Okay, okay, okay!" George steered the Scumbucket off onto a dirt road that led into a thicket of pines and scrub-brush. Before George could stop, Nomad was out the door, Coke dripping from his crotch and the seat of his jeans, and he threw the balled-up burger as far as he could with an effort that he knew his shoulder was going to feel tomorrow morning.

This is a comedy, he thought. A comedy of errors, large and small. A guy standing on a dirt road in wet jeans, his fists clenched at his sides, his feet stomping the dust, rage in his heart and nobody to fight. It should be funny, he thought, and worth a real laugh on down the line.

Only he did not laugh, and in the next instant the tears welled up hot and blinding in his eyes and his chest shuddered with a sob.

He had to get away. But to where, he didn't know.

Just away.

"Hey, John!" George called from the van. "We'll get it cleaned up, man! No biggie!"

But Nomad, who had always thought his given name of John Charles made him sound incomplete, began to walk away along the road as if he were really going somewhere. He briefly took his sunglasses off to wipe his eyes; what a way to blow an image, he told himself. Big tough bad-ass reduced to a snivelling pussy. He was aware that the Scumbucket was following right at his heels, like an ugly dog begging for attention. A banner of dust floated up into the air behind the U-Haul trailer, and above the dark pines the sky was milky-white.

"Come on, John," George said. "Shake it off."

Nomad kept his head down. He kept walking. Space was what he needed. He needed to find a place to curl up and think. His heart was hurting. He kicked at his shadow, to get it out of his way. With George and Terry leaving, the band was done. It would be only a matter of time before the center could not hold. *Know your role*, he thought.

My clock is ticking, John. Yours is too, if you'll be truthful.

Behind him, George tapped the horn, but Nomad did not look back.

He was following this road for which there was no roadmap. His father had been right. It was the musician's path. His father had been right, even on the night of August 10th, 1991, when John Charles had seen him shot to death outside the Shenanigans Club in Louisville, Kentucky. And so rest in peace, Dean Charles and the Roadmen.

Know your role.

Someone tell me what that is, he thought. Someone. Please. Someone please please tell me where I fit, and where I am going.

Because I am lost.

"John?"

The voice had startled him. He hadn't heard her get out of the van, but Ariel was walking at his side. He kept his face averted from her.

"It's okay," she told him. She tried to take his hand.

"I don't need you," he said, and he pulled away.

She blinked back her hurt. She knew from experience that sometimes pain must suffer alone, but she kept walking beside him.

A bell began to ring.

It was a crisp sound, the ringing of bright metal. Not the low, sad tolling of a funeral bell, but a calling.

Nomad and Ariel came out along the road through the pines, and there before them was a wide field that held some kind of shoulder-high plants. Not a pot field, as was Nomad's first thought. It was more of an arrangement of thickets. And from among them people were emerging, as if answering the call of the bell. Nomad saw that all of them wore hats, some wore netting around their faces to keep away the bugs, and all wore gloves and carried baskets. A berry field, Nomad decided. He could see the dark berries in the baskets. Blackberries, most likely. Patches of the field were brown, but most of it thrived even in this ungodly furnace.

It was a small farm community, tucked away back here behind the trees about a hundred yards off the main road. Not so much a town as a Joadville, Nomad thought. Something straight out of *The Grapes Of Wrath*. Maybe fifteen yards from where he and Ariel stood the dirt road curved toward a building that looked to be made out of tarpaper and green plastic siding, with a wooden cross painted gold up over the arched doorway. In front of this building a large-hipped Hispanic woman with gray hair bound by a red bandana was holding a bell and methodically swinging it back and forth. Around her, other women were setting out platters of tortillas, beans and enchiladas onto a table under the shade of a huge oak tree. Before the church, on the sparse grass, stood a well made of brown stones.

It was lunch time, Nomad realized. They were calling the workers in from the field.

He saw on the far side of the church a dozen more tarpaper shacks and structures protected by the shade of other oak trees. The buildings were made of what looked like things wealthier people had cast aside: patio tiles, water-stained awnings, sheets of corrugated metal and plasterboard, multicolored chunks of glass melted together to make windows. Little concrete statues that maybe had once been lawn ornaments in some other world decorated the plots of dirt: a rabbit with one ear cracked off, a greyhound looking around as if in search of its lost hind leg, a cherub with arms ready to fire the arrow but for the missing bow and hand that had gone with it. Nomad wondered if there wasn't a dump somewhere nearby, where the people here found what they needed. A few old pickup trucks and cars stood about, sharing the indignity of rusted fenders and sun-cracked skins like the rough hides of alligators.

Nomad watched the figures in sweat-soaked hats and clothes coming out of the blackberry brambles. Even in this heat, most of them wore long-sleeved work shirts to ward off the thorns. He didn't know how they could bear it. He would've been crawling out on his knees. A chocolate-colored dog came trotting closer to Nomad and Ariel, followed at a distance by two other mutts. It stopped short, splayed its legs and greeted them with a series of ear-splitting barks that went on until one of the women spoke to it chidingly and threw out a tortilla for the dogs to tussel over.

Other than that, no one seemed to pay the two intruders much attention except for a passing glance, followed by a comment or a shrug.

"We'd better go," Ariel told him.

"In a minute." He was waiting for his jeans to dry out a little more, which wouldn't take too much longer in this heavy heat.

"Everybody okay?" Mike walked up on the other side of Nomad. "John, you past your fit?"

"I'm past it." His fit had been eclipsed by this scene of hardship. Nomad knew that things were rough, with his personal disappointments and the band breaking up and all, but at least he didn't have to labor in a blackberry field and live in a shack. Maybe he was heading that way, but not yet. He glanced back and saw that George had stopped the Scumbucket and had come around to the passenger side. George was using a towel from somebody's bag to mop up the seat. Terry had gotten out too and was walking toward Nomad, shaking his head and showing a wry grin.

Someone came out of the field and crossed the road in front of Nomad. He felt himself being examined. When he returned the attention, he saw it was a slender young girl with long, glossy black hair. On her head was a raggedy old wide-brimmed straw hat. The small buds of her breasts were visible under the open workshirt and sweat-wet gray tee beneath that, and she wore sun-bleached khakis with patched-up knees. On her feet were dusty sandals. Before he could catch her face, she had looked away; all he was left with was an impression of penetrating eyes in a pool of shadow.

He watched her take her basket of blackberries to one of the pickup trucks and give it to a man who dumped its contents into one of several smaller flat plastic containers. She said something to the man, who smiled and showed a silver glint of teeth. Then she removed her stained leather gloves and shrugged off her workshirt and put them on the ground, and she passed by the table that held the platters of food and also a supply of paper cups that one of the other women had brought. She went to the well, where she cranked the handle that pulled up the pail. She took a ladle from a hook and dipped it full. Instead of drinking it, as Nomad had thought she would, she turned around and filled the offered paper cup of an older, sweat-drenched woman who had followed her out of the brambles and had likewise given her blackberries to the man at the pickup truck. The girl spoke and touched the woman's arm. The woman's heavily-lined face smiled, and she nodded at the comment and went to get her food.

Then the next person, a white-haired older man who displayed thick, tattooed forearms after he'd removed his own workshirt, came forward with his offered cup. The girl filled it, and she leaned forward and said something and patted his shoulder, just a quick light touch, and when the man turned around to go get his lunch Nomad thought he could see a boy looking out from the wrinkled face.

"We're good to go!" George called, wringing the towel out on the ground. Two children about seven or eight years old were standing beside him, monitoring his progress. Their arms were crossed over their chests and their expressions as serious as any lord of the domain.

But Nomad was watching the procession. Between thirty and forty people had come out of the field. They were all ages, from early teens to elderly. All of them were burned dark by the sun, and all of them walked with a weary step until they reached the girl at the well, whose smile and touch seemed to revive them in some way Nomad could not understand.

Their day was most likely only half over. When their lunch was done, they would go back into the brambles. Maybe they kept at it until all the containers were full. Maybe they'd been at it since sunrise. Nomad figured the berries would be driven to a farmer's market, or to a winery, or somewhere to be processed into jelly or jam. It was a hard day's work, in anybody's book. He thought, watching the girl and the people who filed past, that she was giving them more than just the water. A pat on the shoulder here, a touch on the elbow there, a leaning-in, a nod, a comment that urged a laugh. Maybe her real offering was human kindness, he thought, which also quenched thirst.

He knew that, in her own way, she was giving them the strength they needed to keep going.

And the thing was...the thing was...she didn't pause in her work to get her own drink, though she was surely parched and thirsty like all the others. She had decided she was going to give everyone else their water first, and she would be the last to take one for herself.

Maybe it was just a small sacrifice, on this brutally hot day. Maybe it didn't mean much, really, but a sacrifice of any kind wasn't something Nomad saw very often.

"Let's saddle up, people!" George said, about to climb behind the wheel.

"You guys ready?" Terry asked.

"No," Nomad answered. "I'm not ready yet."

He was fascinated by the scene before him. How the girl—maybe fifteen or sixteen?—picked everyone up as they came past her. It seemed so effortless for her, and so important. Everyone got a few seconds of undivided attention. They were not rushed along. Most of them carried their own canteens, or half-empty water bottles pushed into pockets of work-aprons, but it was clear that they wanted—*needed*, maybe—water from the girl at the well.

He was struck by the desire to see her face. He had the feeling that if he did not see her face, he might never again have the chance. And then he asked himself what the big deal was. It was just a young Hispanic girl in a floppy straw hat giving people water. So what?

But he wanted to see her face, because he had the feeling that he would see in it a beauty he had forgotten existed.

"Will you dumb-asses *move* it?" Berke had gotten out and was standing next to the Scumbucket, one hand on her hip and the other holding her own bottle of water, which had about two good swallows left in it. The children had retreated a few paces. "You want to get heat stroke?"

"We're coming," Ariel said, but she did not leave Nomad's side.

And then the last person got his cup filled and went to join the workers who sat on the ground under the oak tree talking with each other and eating their lunches, and the girl at the well dipped her ladle into the pail and looked directly at the band members.

She held the ladle toward them, offering a drink.

No one moved or spoke for a few seconds, and then Mike said, "Well, shit, I'll get me some if she's givin' it out." He walked forward.

"It might not be clean," Ariel warned.

Mike said, "Hey, I was *raised* on well water. Didn't stunt my growth too bad." He nodded a greeting to the women who'd brought the food and cups, and took one of the cups from the table. Then he walked to the well, said, "*Buenos dias*," to the girl and held out his cup. Nomad saw the girl say something to Mike as she filled it, but it was spoken so quietly Nomad could not hear. Mike swigged the water down and came back to the group.

"It's *cold*," he said. "She says to tell you everybody's welcome, and not to be afraid."

"Afraid of what?" Nomad asked. He watched the girl, who seemed to be waiting for them. She still had not taken a drink herself.

"I don't know. That it's not clean, I guess."

"I think we'd better stick to bottled," said Ariel.

"Hey, we're *cooking* over here!" Berke came closer. "What the fuck's wrong with you guys?"

"Let me wash my mouth out," Nomad said.

He took Mike's cup and approached the girl.

She dipped the ladle anew and held it out for him. He could not make out her face in the shadow of her straw hat, only the shape of a face. As he got nearer, he took off his sunglasses so he could see what she looked like, but even then he only caught the shine of her eyes.

And then within reach of her he abruptly stopped, because something that was not fear but was very close to fear had shot through him and he was stunned by the intensity of it. He could go no further.

She was staring at him, from the shadow pool beneath the ragged straw hat.

The ladle was still offered, and from it a few drops of water fell to the dirt.

It seemed to Nomad that, yes, he was thirsty, and he wanted to get the taste of that cheeseburger out of his mouth but—as crazy as he felt it to be—he thought there was a price to be paid for accepting, and he feared knowing what that price might be. He was focused entirely on her, still trying to distinguish the hidden details of her face, but he could not. He felt also that she was focused entirely upon him too, and it terrified him even more. Her attention seemed to be almost a physical thing; he imagined he could feel it probing around in the innermost parts of himself, mind and soul, as if he were a puzzle to be figured out, or a walking Rubik's Cube to be assembled. But it was more than that, too; it was like a stranger rummaging through your dirty laundry, or getting too close to the box of porn DVDs up on the closet's shelf behind the folded-up hoodies.

She didn't speak. She only waited, and it seemed she had plenty of time.

He felt the sweat oozing from his pores. Well, who wouldn't be sweating in hundred-degree heat? He said to himself *No, I am not going out into those thorns*. Because that's what he thought she was asking him to do. There's a trick to it, he thought. Always a fucking trick to everything, because nothing is free. If he took that water from her, he would have to go out into that field and labor like a zombie, and maybe he hadn't looked hard enough, maybe those people he'd imagined were needful of her strength and grateful of her kindness were only stupid fucking zombies, and at one time or another all of them had simply been passing by on the road of their own lives until she'd lured them here and given them drugged-up water that blasted their brains and put them to work in the brambles. Made them *want* to go back, even when they were out. Made them happy with their misery. It was crazy what he was thinking, because she was just a kid, she was nobody to him, he could swat her down with one hand if he had to. And her sacrifice was false too, because she probably was the type who always had to be the center of attention, like Madonna of the junkyard or something, and so all this deal of standing at the well and giving to the others was a self-serving sham. He hated falsehood, even more than he hated bad waitresses. Nothing is free in this world, he thought. Not even a cup of water. And now all sounds were becoming muffled, as if from a great distance, and everything around them—the church, the well itself, the other structures, the trucks and cars, the dogs and children, the people underneath the oak tree—shimmered in the heatwaves and began to blur and melt together like the chunks of multicolored glass that made up the windows of the tarpaper shacks.

Oh no, he thought. *Not me.*

He took a backward step.

Everything came into sharp focus again, and all the sounds—dogs barking, the kids yelling at each other as they played, the voices of the workers talking under the tree—returned in a jarring crash. The girl was still staring at him, and as he stepped back another pace he crumpled the paper cup in his fist and let it drop to the dirt.

"What's wrong with *you*?" Berke asked as she passed him. She went to the girl, offered her the nearly-empty bottle of water and asked in Spanish, "Would you fill that for me?" When it was done, Berke came back with the cool bottle pressed against her forehead and she went past Nomad as if he were invisible.

George was standing between Ariel and Mike, bright beads of perspiration on his face. "Hi, how are you?" he said to the girl. "Guys, we shouldn't be bothering these people. Let's go, man!" This last entreaty was directed at Nomad.

"Did you see that?" Nomad asked them. His voice, upon which he depended so much, sounded like a cat being strangled.

"See what?" George frowned. He looked over Nomad's shoulder at the girl, who had turned away to refill someone else's cup.

"What happened just then."

"Um...." George gave Mike a brief glance. "Listen, you ready to hit it?" Berke and Terry were already walking back to the van.

"I saw what happened," Ariel said, giving him her patented look of disapproval. "You left your trash on the ground." She walked to the crumpled cup, picked it up and took it to the girl at the well, who held her hand out and accepted it in her palm. "*¡Perdón*," Ariel said. Even if she hadn't taken Spanish in both high school and college, life in Texas had a way of teaching you the language. "*El tiene maneras muy malas*." An apology for Nomad's bad manners.

The girl angled her head to one side, and Ariel caught a glint of ebony eyes in a dark face with a flat, broad nose. It was a face that might have been carved on ancient stone in a Mayan jungle, except for the outbursts of teenaged acne on both cheeks.

"*Gracias, senorita*," said the girl, and then she added in English with a heavy accent, "You are very kind."

"I just try to clean up the mess," Ariel answered, which she realized she had been doing, one way or another, for most of her life. She saw the girl look past her. Ariel followed her line of sight to track the others who were returning to the Scumbucket. Nomad was backing up as if he feared being jumped from behind.

"You have a long journey," the girl said, a statement instead of a question.

"Yes." The U-Haul trailer spoke for itself. Ariel felt the need to add, "We're musicians, on tour."

Her eyes were on Ariel again, and she gave a broad, warm smile that made Ariel want to move in closer, to bask in it. Her teeth were white, but she needed braces. "Oh!" she said. "What is your..." She paused, seeking the correct word. "Place?"

"I play guitar and I sing."

"I also like music," the girl said. "Very happy."

"Yes, it can be."

Behind Ariel, George tapped the Scumbucket's horn twice. *Come on, come on*!

Ariel thought that this life she'd chosen—or that had chosen *her*—was like what they said about the military: hurry up and wait. But everyone else was in the van now, she was the one holding things up, and she ought to go.

A movement caught Ariel's attention, and when she looked toward the blackberry field she saw the dark shapes of crows circling, circling, and then darting in to steal the fruit. They were coming in faster and faster, from all directions of the compass. Some of the other workers were already standing up, putting their workshirts back on. The labor had to be finished, or the crows would take the rest.

< >

Ariel returned her gaze to the girl. She said, "*Adiós*."

"I wish you safe travel," said the girl, and she frowned in search of translation for her next remark but settled on "*y a valor cuando usted lo necesita*."

"*Gracias*." Ariel figured the expression of care probably went back in the girl's family for generations. She turned around and walked away from the girl and the well, away from the tarpaper-covered church and the hopeful houses, away from the shade of the oak tree and the sun-scorched field of blackberry brambles, away from the past into the future.

But first there was the Scumbucket and the rest of the crew. Ariel got into her seat, George backed up being careful not to plow the trailer into a tree, and in another couple of minutes they were pulling away from the road in a plume of dust and onto the pavement of East Lake Shore again.

"Some life they've got," Terry said. "Not much of a place, was it?"

"Maybe they came from a worse one," Berke said. "You never know."

Nomad hit the dashboard with the flat of his hand, to try to silence the troubling hum.

"You're going to break it," George warned.

"Thing needs to be killed," Mike said. "Put out of its misery. Didn't you get it checked last week?"

"It's putting out cool air, man, that's all I know."

"Barely cool," said Berke. "We can hardly feel it back here."

Nomad swivelled around to face Ariel. "What did she say to you?" When Ariel paused, taken aback, Nomad continued in an aggravated tone: "She was talking to you. What did she say?"

"Just...stuff. She said she liked music." Ariel shrugged. "I told her we were musicians."

"*Were* musicians." Berke's voice was hollow, an intonation of doom. "I like that."

"She was weird," Nomad said. "Anybody else feel it?"

Nobody spoke for a few seconds, and then George asked, "Weird *how*?"

"I don't know." Obviously, no one else had shared his jolt of vertigo or the first stage of heat stroke or whatever it had been. He wondered if he ought to have a physical when they got back to

Austin. Check his brain for a tumor, maybe. He'd read about shit like this.

"You're on the ball today, bro," Mike told him. "Anybody's actin' weird around here, it's *you*."

"Oh," Ariel remembered. "It's not *weird*, really, but she *did* say something kind of interesting. Right when I was leaving."

"What was it?" Nomad asked.

"She said, 'I wish you safe travel, and courage when you need it'."

"Nice," said George. "Could be a song in that."

"Hm." Ariel considered it. "Could be."

Nomad turned around, facing the road again. He slid down in his seat. Jesus, he thought, I hope I don't have a fucking brain tumor. That had been a way-freaky minute right there. Shake it off, he told himself. Get the focus back, and jack yourself up.

One thing about what he'd seen back there, he thought, was that he ought to cast aside his pissy self-pity and concentrate on where he was and what he had. Things might be bad, things were not as he wanted them to be, but at least he was moving, he was on the road, he was going *somewhere*. The apartment he shared in Austin with two other working musicians had cable TV and good air-conditioning, and though he slept on a futon on the floor it was his own space, which suited him just fine. He was doing something he loved, something he felt had worth. He wasn't trudging out under the burning sun and tearing himself up in a bramble patch. Hell, no. There were lots of things to be thankful for. And they had the tour going on and the video, and Felix Gogo might have been a shit but it was okay, it was the plug for the Dallas gig that counted.

Things could be worse, Nomad thought. And who knows? Either George or Terry could change their minds. Both of them could. Nothing was written in stone. So it was wait and see, but in the meantime just try to put everything else aside but what was really important: the music.

In about two hours, they'd be going through their sound check at Common Grounds. It was a long, somewhat tedious process that was absolutely vital to run a show, because it ironed out potential problems. During the actual gig, there would be *different* problems from those ironed out by the sound check. It was worse than Murphy's Law, it was Finagle's corollary to Murphy's Law: Anything that can go wrong will go wrong in the worst possible way at the worst possible time.

Hi, guys. Thanks for coming out tonight, and we hope you enjoy the BZZZZZZPPPP.

This life made *Spinal Tap* look like a Bergman film.

Behind Nomad, Ariel leaned her head back and closed her eyes. She had a mild headache, from the heat. In her mind she saw the crows circling over the blackberry field, and the workers standing up to go in again, and the sun beating down from the pale sky and the shadow of the girl at the well lying across the ground at Ariel's feet.

You have a long journey, she heard the girl say.

Yes, Ariel answered. And then she was aware of the shadows of the crows on the ground as well, circling above them, and more and more, gathering together into a darkness, more and more, from all directions of the compass, and thickening the sky in their whirling eager hunger.

Courage when you need it, Ariel thought, and she opened her eyes because she imagined she could hear the vibration of black wings around her, about to fall upon her like an ebony cloak.

But it was just the Scumbucket's rumble and hum.

Just that, and nothing else.

TWO

ARE YOU MY PET

FIVE.

The night has taken Jeremy Pett. If there really is a Beast, he is in its belly, and he is already half-digested.

He lies naked in warm water, stretched out as much as he can in the stark white bathtub. The soles of his feet are pressed against the tiles, which are the color of wet sand. The water holds him around the torso, across the stomach, and up under his chin. He has gone days without a shave, and his face feels heavy. How many days? He's not sure, because time has turned on itself. It has become spasmodic, at times sluggish and then frenzied. Sometimes it seems as if hours crawl, and sometimes they whirl away like ashes in a hot wind. He believes it to be Friday night, because the movie *Gladiator* with Russell Crowe was on cable like the schedule said. He watched it, for maybe the fourth or fifth time, because he could relate to it; he used to have the dvd, but he gave it away to somebody, he can't remember who. Somebody borrowed it and never brought it back. But he can relate to it, to the man in the arena, the bloodied man, the man forsaken and cast aside, betrayed, yet the warrior spirit never broken. Never broken, because of his sheer willpower. The TV is still on in the other room, and shadows dance in its cold blue light.

Jeremy Pett takes another two Tylenol tablets into his mouth, and washes them down with another drink from the bottle of Nyquil. Those would be tablets number five and six. The extra strength kind, 500 milligrams each. He has read on the Internet that 7000 milligrams might put him over, but he's a big guy, fleshy. Weighs about two-thirty, stands a little over six feet. He's not sure exactly how many tablets and swigs of Nyquil he would need to do the job, but he's not going that way. He just wants to feel sleepy, wants the warm blanket to start to cover him over, and when that happens he's going to pick up the box-cutter that lies on the edge of the tub, near his right hand. He will start with the left wrist. He wants to watch himself bleed out, wants to test that willpower of which he's so proud. It seems to him like a good way for a warrior to go out, quietly, under the blade.

He is making the choice to go. It's done. The fork has been stuck in it. Tonight he is travelling to the Elysian Fields. Through the walls he can hear noises in the other apartments around him: the gurgle of a toilet being flushed, the hollow bass beat of music. They seem to be sounds from a different world, one that he no longer is connected to. His apartment is on the second floor. Number Eight, the Vanguard Apartments, southeast Temple, Texas. It is an area of abandonment, both of houses and people, where angry young men cruise in thugged-out rides looking for a reason to defend their territory. There always seems to be a pall of gray smoke in the air, and gunfire at night brings the shrieks of police cars. The one-bedroom apartment with its small kitchen has been cheap, and it's been comfortable enough though the carpet has smelled funky, especially in winter when the damp mist curls up against the bricks outside. But even so, the time has come to leave. He takes two more Tylenol and another drink of the Nyquil, and he waits. He's getting sleepy now, starting to feel the warmth creeping in, numbing his brain. That's what he wants most of all: an end to the echoes of the haunted house inside his head.

His stomach growls. I'm hungry, he thinks. But when did he last eat? A few hours ago? I ought to get up and get me some potato chips, he thinks. He believes there is still most of half a bag in the pantry. What would a few potato chips hurt?

But no, no...just lie still. You've had your last meal, boy. Chicken pot pie from the freezer. Microwaved as pretty as you please, but not much taste. He sure would like a few potato chips, just for the salt. But the warmth is creeping in, everything is getting dull and hazy around the edges, and he decides he is fine just where he lies.

He wonders who will find him, and when. It will most likely be Mr. Salazar, the manager, and Jeremy regrets that because Mr. Salazar has always been nice to him. Cut him some slack, went to bat for him with the realty company the last two months. Brought him a sack of tamales on the fifth of January, the day Jeremy turned thirty. Mr. Salazar has a crown of white hair and a heavily-lined face and a cigarette cough, and he says it's one hell of a world, *amigo*, when a hero like you has to live here like a dog in a cage.

But Jeremy has smiled at Mr. Salazar's kindness and answered, *Well sir, I'm really no hero, and I'm just passing through.*

Jeremy knows where the heroes are. He knows where the dead ones are buried, and where the ones who still breathe sit watching the sun rise and the sun go down. He knows all about the heroes, yes sir, and he knows he is not one of them. *But thank you, sir, for thinking of me in that way.*

He went to the hospital to see Chris Montalvo this week. He has gone every week since he moved to Temple from Houston, early last year. He always goes on Wednesdays. He recalls the day he went this week, because it was the day he put the unpaid bills and the Cancellation Of Service notices in a stack and decided he had gone far enough, he was not going any farther, and he ought to start making his plans. So then after he visited Chris he went to the pharmacy and got his pills and his Nyquil, and he went to the Wal-Mart Supercenter on 31st Street and bought the box-cutter. Then it was just a matter of when.

As he lies in the tub getting sleepy, drifting away from the world, Jeremy thinks of Chris at the hospital. The building with all the flags out front, on Veterans Memorial Drive. He thinks of the attendant wheeling Chris in, into the room with the wide windows where the morning sun streams through the blinds, and as always Jeremy leans down to his buddy and he sings in a soft whisper to the side of Chris's head that is not crushed inward, "Nice day for a white wedding."

< >

That never fails to make Chris smile, as much as he can.

It was what Chris always said when they went out on a mission, the two of them out there in the dust and heat against a world of ragheads for who knew how long, until the bullet was sent. *Nice day for a white wedding.* And Chris was awesome, because he could really snarl it just like Billy Idol. So, sure, Chris recognizes it, and he recognizes Jeremy too, and Jeremy dares anybody to tell him his buddy doesn't.

In his life Jeremy has loved only a few people. He has loved his mother and father in Nevada; he has loved the young woman and the little boy who smile at him from the framed photograph he has propped up against the sink, to look at as he passes over; and he has loved Lance Corporal Chris Montalvo, his spotter. People outside the Glorious Green Machine couldn't understand the kind of love he has felt for Chris. And that's okay, because it's a private thing, something he wouldn't talk about with anyone except another Marine. Only someone who'd been there would understand it, the way you love your brother in the Corps, the way you depend on each other, you watch each others' backs, you eat the same dust and smell the same blood and hope it's always Johnny Jihad who's lying there emptying out like a broken bottle. Once you hear the roar of hell with your brother at your side, and feel the fire lick your face, you are one person, indivisible, because that is the only way you are going to survive it.

So after things went wrong in Houston, Jeremy came to Temple to be near Chris, to go visit him every Wednesday and lean down to say *Nice day for a white wedding* and get that faint flicker of recognition. Maybe nobody else can see it, but Jeremy can. Any maybe Chris can't talk, and won't ever talk again, and maybe he just sits in the chair staring at nothing, but Jeremy knows his buddy—his friend, his loved one—is aware of him, in that room up high over the boulevard of flags. And he knows there was a reaction—just a movement of a corner of Chris's mouth, as if forming a reply—when Jeremy told him what he was planning to do, that it was time he was going to find Karen and Nick, and that the doctors here were good people, they knew their jobs, and they would always take the best care of him. *I'll see you on the other side*, Jeremy had said. *I'm gonna go on ahead, and scout it out for you. Okay*?

Jeremy had hugged Chris before he left, and he thought of how frail Chris was, how the bones felt as thin as a child's beneath the papery flesh. Chris had been such a strong guy, with the neck of a bull. Had played linebacker in high school, and had liked to work alongside his Dad on his father's vintage 1973 Pontiac Firebird. It was an incredible and fearsome thing, how quickly a human being could be wrecked. Jeremy had to stop in the men's room to wipe his eyes with a paper towel, but then what he had dreaded was done and he was all right with leaving Chris, it was okay. He believed in God, and he believed that God was okay with it too.

He takes a long, deep breath, and releases it as a sigh. The pills and the Nyquil are working, sinking him deeper. He knows the box-cutter will hurt, at first, but he has been through pain and it has to be done. He *is* sorry, though, that Mr. Salazar will have to deal with the mess. With a heavy hand he picks up the blade. He places the cutting edge against his left wrist, where the life flows. He wishes he'd lit a candle or something for the moment, because the bathroom's white light is way too harsh. He pauses a few seconds, the blade's edge pressing into his flesh; *this is where the old life ends*, he thinks, *and whatever's next for me is about to start.*

Help me across, he says to the woman in the picture, and then he pushes the blade into his wrist—a sharp, hot pain, but not too bad—and the blood wells up and trickles down his forearm, and he watches in a kind of hypnotic wonder as it drips into the water. He is creating his own crimson tide. He bites his lower lip as he presses the blade deeper, and then he begins to drag it across his wrist toward the veins, and he keeps his eyes on the picture of his wife and son because soon he'll be meeting them on that road that reaches the Elysian Fields, just as Maximus was reunited with his family at the end of *Gladiator*.

But Jeremy's hand suddenly stops, before the veins are severed. He pauses in his path to suicide, as the blood trickles down along his forearm and drips and drops into the water.

Something at the end of the hallway, in the other room, has demanded his attention.

In the chair that Jeremy had pulled up before the TV to watch the movie, a figure is sitting. It seems to be a man whose head is turned toward him, but whose face is a shifting mass of shadow. A hand is upraised, a finger crooked: *Come here*, is the instruction.

My God, Jeremy thinks, and maybe he's said it out loud. For the angel of death has arrived at Number Eight, the Vanguard Apartments, southeast Temple, Texas.

Come here, the instruction repeats.

"Give me a minute," Jeremy says, his voice slurred and hollow against the tiles. He intends to finish what he's started, and he's not really afraid of the death angel because in one way or another the death angel has been with him, riding shotgun, for a long, long time. So he says, "One minute," just to make himself clear.

But in the space of time it has taken Jeremy to speak, the death angel has created for itself the face of Chris Montalvo, complete with crumpled skull and childlike eyes that gleam in the TV's light, and the finger beckons Jeremy to come with an urgency that cannot be delayed.

Now, Jeremy knows he's got a lot of Tylenol and Nyquil in his system, and he knows the blood is running freely down his arm, and he knows his head is not right and his time is running out, and he knows this visitation is not really Chris Montalvo but maybe a costume of Chris Montalvo worn over a figure fearsome for human eyes—even blurred and cloudy human eyes—to behold, but still…it wants him to get out of the tub and come in there. It wants him, right *now*.

"Shit," Jeremy says, because it seems like such an inconvenient moment. It seems that for him to stand up and walk along the hallway into that room would be like rolling out of a bunk on the darkest oh-dark-thirty of his life, or reaching up and pushing away from a grave the stones he has nearly finished covering himself with. It seems like the hardest thing he could ever imagine doing, on this final night, yet with a gasp of breath, a strain of muscles and a wobble of belly fat he sits up, puts the box-cutter on the soap dish, and in a slosh of bloody water he steps out of the tub onto something resembling solidity.

Halfway along the hall he stumbles and crashes into the wall, and leaves a red streak there under the framed fake-oil painting of a desert scene that must've been the previous tenant's eBay Special. His knees nearly buckle; he is staggering back and forth, on his uncertain journey from bathroom to chair where the figure with Chris's face is sitting. He thinks how out of breath he feels, how lost he seems to be in this sack of skin. Use it or lose it, he thinks; five years ago he could run three miles in a little over eighteen minutes, do one-hundred crunches under two minutes and swim five hundred meters like Aquaman. Only thing super about him now was his appetite for junk food and the size of the junk he left in the toilet.

Oorah, motherfucker, oorah!

He makes his tortured way into the room. There the creature who occupies the chair turns its constructed Chris-face away from him toward the TV screen, and Jeremy hears a man's voice speak.

"It's about the war."

He looks at the screen, and sees there a dimly-recognized figure dressed in black and wearing a black cowboy hat looking back at him. "Song's called 'When The Storm Breaks', by The—" A hand is held up in front of the camera, palm out and fingers spread, and what appears to be an electric-blue flame ripples around the fingertips.

A few seconds of darkness appears, with small type down on the bottom left: "When The Storm Breaks" and underneath that, The Five.

Then what might be a flash of lightning or a camera's flash pops, and as a drum beats and guitar chords start growling, the scene changes to a herky-jerky handheld camera and what could be five or six or seven soldiers in full battle-rattle are advancing down a street between broken concrete walls. The color is washed-out, grimy, the sick pale yellow of Iraq. But it's not Iraq, and these fools aren't soldiers, because Jeremy instantly sees that some of them are wearing imitation desert pattern MARPAT camo and others are wearing imitation desert pattern ARPAT camo. So they're stupid fucking actors with pretend gear, and they're not any good anyway because they don't move with the caution of knowing your head could be blown off at any second, they're all twisting around and looking every fucking whichaway, a picture of chaos instead of control. Meat for Mookie, Jeremy thinks. Come right on down the street like that, old ladies, and get your asses handed to you.

The scene jumps to a band set up in the street: long-haired punk playing lead guitar, bass player with tattooed arms, skinhead fucker with glasses playing a piano or something on metal legs, hippie chick with reddish-blonde ringlets working a white guitar and another chick with short-cut curly black hair pounding the shit out of a drum kit, the cymbals flashing in the sun. Then it goes up close to the punk's face, right up in his angry baby blues, and he sings like a half-drunk black man whose throat has been worked over with a razor:

"*I was walking on a street under a burning sun,*
Put my visor down, thumbed the safety off my gun.
Heard a rumble, might be thunder in the sky,
Might be cannons or an F-18 fly-by."

Visor, Jeremy thinks. His lip curls. Guy doesn't know what he's talking about.

Now intercut with the singer's face and glimpses of the band are scenes of a house and some young dude's father showing him an old picture of a soldier, and in the background an American flag is flying from the front porch.

Then the punk goes again:

"*I was raised to think my blood's red, white and blue.*
I was raised to do what I was told to do.
Somehow in all that time I never did ask why,
It's the young men like me who go to kill and die."

Yeah, well, shit, Jeremy thinks. *Get a clue.* He believes he needs to sit down, his knees are weak and his stomach feels like it's got fish swimming in it.

With an explosion of drums, bass and guitar that sounds like a freight train crashing through a building, the scene goes to the face of one of the soldiers on the street and Jeremy sees it's the kid from the house, and now the herky-jerky shit goes wild because ragheads are shooting from windows and smoke curls up and the supposed soldiers run into another building except for one who goes down on his belly and jerks his legs like he's hit, and the singer goes:

"*When the storm breaks and the rain falls down,*
And the mighty laugh with a hollow sound,
We got money for oil, you got battles to fight,
And the heroes come home in the dead of the night."

Jeremy realizes the chair is empty. As he sinks into it, he is aware that the disturbed air around him smells like the hospital.

He doesn't know a whole lot about music, but this isn't bad. It's got a strong beat. It sounds muscular and hard-assed. The guitars sound like bands of sharp steel flying through the air. There's a firefight going on between the buildings, and then there's a blast of flame and tendrils of black smoke whirl up and that, right there, looks pretty real. Then another of the good guys gets shot and claws at his throat and Jeremy leans forward because the shadows in this part are dark.

Everything stops but the drums, and over their thud and rumble the punk growls:

"*This was somebody's child, this was somebody's dream,*
I hope they bury it where the grass is green."

And a second time, while the drums speak:

"*This was somebody's child, this was somebody's dream,*
I hope they bury it where the grass is green."

The music swells again, the bass and the guitars come up and so does a trembly organ part that is half tough snarl and half sad murmur. The young guy who's the hero of the video has somehow lost his helmet, he's got blood on the side of his face, and around him lie the bodies of his brothers. And then the singer goes:

"*I'm not saying this world will ever get along,*
Not saying everything is right when it's so wrong,
But I do believe that war makes some men rich,
And too many of them love that wicked bitch,
When the storm breaks, and the rain falls down..."

And now the young dude has lost it and broken cover, and wild-eyed he crosses the street alone and kicks in a door and nobody's in there except a figure on the rubbled floor who looks up at him, and the camera shows that it's an Iraqi kid maybe twelve or thirteen years old, who lifts his arms and crouches against the wall as the soldier raises his rifle and takes aim.

"*We got money for oil,*
You got battles to fight,
And the heroes come home in the dead of the night."

The camera backs out of the room and the soldier staggers from the doorway with an expression of shock on his dust-white, blood-streaked face, and he throws his rifle down and begins to run along the street in the direction he came from.

> "*This was someone's child, this was someone's dream,*
> *When the storm breaks,*
> *This was someone's child, this was someone's dream,*
> *When the storm, when the storm, storm breaks,*
> *This was someone's child, this was someone's dream,*
> *When the storm, when the storm, storm breaks, yeah when*
> *it breaks,*
> *This was someone's child, this was someone's dream...*"

And then the music stops and the punk's face fills the screen and he sings, in his husky razor-burned voice: "*I hope they bury it where the grass is green.*"

Fade-in to what Jeremy realizes now is the Felix Gogo Show. He's seen this a few times, has seen Felix Gogo up on the billboards. Felix Gogo is standing with the band—The Five, is that what they call themselves?—in a room of bright light and black shadows, and behind them on the wall is an American flag. He says they're going to play at the Curtain Club in Dallas on Saturday night. As Gogo asks them questions, their names come up underneath their faces. *Mike Davis* talks about his tattoos, and then the camera briefly shows *Berke Bonnevey* but she doesn't say anything, and *Ariel Collier* starts answering a question about how long she's been a musician, and suddenly the screen breaks apart into multicolored squares like the cable's about to go out, but the audio's still going and through a hiss of digital distress he hears the hippie chick say, "I wanted to be a musician so I can tell the truth."

"What truth?" Gogo asks, a distorted shape on the tormented screen.

"Like this," she answers, and there's a weird echo: *this...this... this*. "The truth about murder," she says, her image washed-out in a mosaic of pallid green squares.

Then the screen comes back like it ought to be, everything's fine, and Jeremy sees that *Terry Spitzenham* is speaking but now the audio is down and nothing is coming from his mouth. The screen ripples and breaks apart again, goes completely to black. The audio lets loose a burst of static and then picks up and the guy is saying, "...what this war's about is training killers, just a training ground for murder. You know how many kids have been killed by our so-called heroes?"

"Don't go there," Jeremy says numbly, to the black screen. "Don't you go there."

"Ashamed," says another voice, crackling with static. "They should all be ashamed, and they all deserve to suffer."

The picture reappears but everything is gray and ghostly, and the ghostly image of Felix Gogo says in a voice that sounds high-pitched and indignant, "So you want to make people believe our soldiers are shooting kids over there? That for everything they've done for this country, every sacrifice they've made, you're making them out to be child-killers?"

Another spirit image flickers in the gloom. Suddenly the picture clears and the singing punk is standing there with a fake smile on his face, and underneath it is the name *Nomad*—what kind of fucking name is *that*, anyway?—and he says, very clearly, "We're working on it."

"Well, good luck with that," Felix Gogo replies, and the way he's said it makes Jeremy know that if Felix had a gun he might have shot that long-haired, smirking bastard on the spot.

Jeremy loses the rest of it, because he's seen all he wants to see yet he does not have the strength to turn the set off. Where's the remote, anyway? In the kitchen, or the bathroom? A wave of weary sickness washes over him; he smells his own blood, leaking from the blade-cut on his wrist, dripping into a dark circle on the tan carpet. Now *that*, he thinks, is going to be one bitch to explain to Mr. Salazar.

Wait a minute, he tells himself. Hold on. I'm leaving tonight. Going back in there and finishing what I started.

Yet he does not get up. Nor does he even try.

It occurs to him, somewhere far back in his brain like a distant voice shouting for him to put it in gear and *move*, that he ought to get this wound bound up while he can still walk.

This is a weird world, he thinks. When you try to climb up a ladder, it breaks underneath you; but when you decide to jump off a cliff, a hook comes out of nowhere and grabs your miserable ass.

He doesn't fully understand this song and video, or why the death angel wanted him to see it. Death angel? *Whose* death? His, or...

He thinks the song was about rich men who never go to war making money off war, or maybe even starting wars to make money. *Duh*. Who didn't already know that? And nobody cared, even if they did know it. It was how the world worked, and so what? Like, maybe, it was news back in the days of the Civil War or ancient history. Yeah, and like that *band* wasn't trying to make some money off the war, too? Make me laugh.

But that crap about the storm breaking, and somebody's child and burying it and everything. Maybe that was talking about what was going to happen when the soldiers came home, and started thinking about...what? Doing the jobs we were trained to do?

Jeremy can feel the sweat rising from him like a hot mist. He feels sick to his stomach, he knows he's going to have to puke here real soon, and it is going to be an effort to get to the bathroom before his own storm breaks.

You know how many kids have been killed by our so-called heroes?

"What do you know about it?" he asks the TV screen, which by now has gone into another segment in which Felix Gogo is behind his desk in the studio, chatting up some huge-boobed Hispanic actress who sits on a red sofa shaped like a pair of lips.

The thing is, the video didn't actually show the soldier shoot the boy. Maybe he did, maybe he didn't. All Jeremy knows is that every block was a battleground. Especially in Fallujah, after the Blackwater dudes got waxed. If Jeremy had been the soldier in that video, he would've shot the boy. Damn straight. You shoot at me, I take you down. Then again...where was the boy's weapon? Maybe he'd just been in the wrong place at the wrong time. It happened. A casualty of the mission, no big whoop. You just put your head down and kept going.

So you want to make people believe our soldiers are shooting kids over there? That for everything they've done for this country, every sacrifice they've made, you're making them out to be child-killers?

We're working on it, that punk had said.

Jeremy lowers his head and closes his eyes, very tightly. An old rage has begun to awaken, and he thinks that if he had those lying scummy pieces of shit right here, he would wax them all, one after the fucking other. Just to shut their lying mouths.

And someone standing behind his right shoulder leans forward and says, in a bitter whisper that conveys both sarcasm and challenge, *Are you my pet?*

Jeremy's head comes up and he looks around, but no one else is there. It was what his old Gunnery Sergeant used to say to him, when Jeremy's lungs heaved from miles of uphill running, or when he was crawling through the mud in full gear, or doing the endless pushups, or whatever else the Gunny threw at him. *Are you my pet?* Translation: guy with a pussy last name ain't gone be no pussy, not in *this* man's Corps.

He can't wait any longer. He hauls himself up, staggers, crabs sideways, collides with the TV, gets his knees turned the way he wants to go, and starts for the bathroom. The hallway becomes the twisting corridor of a carnival funhouse he thinks he remembers going to as a kid, but this is no fun. Another collision, this time with the wall, and then he gets into the bathroom and falls to his knees in time to throw up about eighty percent of his troubled freight into the toilet, the other twenty percent going onto the floor.

After it's over and done and his retching has settled down, Jeremy struggles to focus on his wound. He is too tired to do much about it, and maybe he needs a few stitches but it looks to him as if the blood is crusting over. He can hear the old man in the apartment below knocking on the ceiling with what is likely a broom handle. Probably freaking about all the noise, thought his bathroom was about to cave in. The knocking stops after a few seconds, and Jeremy slowly gets up off the floor, turns on the sink tap and splashes cold water into his face. He wraps a towel around his left wrist. He blinks heavily, looking at the blood-stained water in the tub, the rivulets of blood on the white porcelain, the mess on the floor.

A job well screwed, he thinks grimly.

There will not be a journey to the Elysian Fields tonight. There are some things he has to think about, to get straight in his head. He takes the picture of Karen and Nick with him as he totters unsteadily to the bedroom. He flips on the overhead light. He places the picture on the bedside table, and then he takes his Remington 700 rifle with its attached Tasco scope from the closet and he lies in bed, staring blankly at the ceiling, with the weapon cradled across his chest.

This is my rifle, he thinks. *There are many like it, but this one is mine. My rifle is my best friend. It is my life. I must master it as I must master my life. My rifle without me is useless. Without my rifle, I am useless. I must fire my rifle true. I must shoot straighter than my enemy who is trying to kill me. I must shoot him before he shoots me.*

Since his honorable discharge, Jeremy has been through the jobs of construction worker, roofing man, yard workman, building supply warehouse security guard, mall security guard, video store clerk, car wash attendant, 7-Eleven clerk, and for the last four months garbage man until he was laid off two weeks ago because of cutbacks in the city budget.

It has become clear to him, before this night, that the task he is best suited for involves the tool that lies against his chest. The question is: how does someone use that talent—his God-given talent as a Marine Corps sniper—in the world beyond the battlefield? But this night, and the appearance of the death angel wearing Chris Montalvo's face, has made him think his task is not finished. And that video he saw has made him think he might have an answer to the question.

A hit man.

He could be a hit man.

People needed them, to get rid of their problems. Governments and corporations needed them, to make sure secrets stayed secure and enemies were silenced. Battered wives needed them, to get rid of abusive husbands. There were plenty of movies with hit men in them, doing the necessary thing. Where did they come from? The military, most likely. They were men just like him, trained to set up the target and send the bullet. One shot, one kill. Why not?

Maximus in *Gladiator* was a hit man, really. Trained for war, betrayed by his superiors, bloodied but unbowed, the man in the arena sent out to kill or perish.

That's me, Jeremy thinks. I can do that.

He has his rifle and a .45 automatic he bought for personal protection. Plenty of ammo for both of them, right up there on the closet's shelf. The Remington is not very different from the rifle he used in Iraq. The sight isn't as powerful, but at the shooting range up north of Temple he could still hit a target at five hundred yards, on most days. He has some money, not a whole lot, but he has a valid credit card. He has his dark blue pickup truck, banged and dented and seven years old but it can still get him where he wants to go.

All he needs to start his resume is a target.

Or *targets*.

Five of them, maybe.

If he hit them all, he could write his own ticket. In Mexico, maybe. God knows they could use his talent down there, against the drug lords. Because if he *was* a hit man, he would only want to work for the right side. And this band...this bunch of punks going on television talking about how United States of America soldiers are killing children in Iraq, about how they should be ashamed and suffer for what they do in the line of duty, just following orders, and sacrificing their futures and the futures of their wives and sons...they are throwing shit on the memory of Chris Montalvo, and every good man who puts his life on the line over there.

That band is definitely on the wrong side.

He thinks he needs to sleep now, to let himself rest. He thinks he might go to the pharmacy in the morning, get some disinfectant, gauze and bandages to tend to his wound. He might go eat a good breakfast at the Cracker Barrel on General Bruce Drive. He might head over to the library, go to the Internet room and look up The Five's website. Check them out, check out their tour dates. Come up with a plan. He thinks he might take his guns and the rest of his money and his credit card to Dallas, to where that band is playing tomorrow night. Scope them out, so to speak.

A hit man could make a lot of money these days. But first he would have to show any potential employers how good he was at the job. It wasn't as if he didn't have enough experience already.

That band...with their lies...they shouldn't be allowed to spread their poison. Sure, it's a free country, God bless it, and everybody could have their own opinion, but this...this goes beyond free speech into hate.

We're working on it, that bastard had said.

It is enemy action, clear and simple. It is a cancer that destroys from within.

Lying still and quiet, Jeremy suddenly knows he has found a reason to live.

He closes his eyes, listening to the thrum of blood through his veins.

And when the quiet, sarcastic challenge in his head whispers *Are you my pet?* Jeremy does not hesitate in his answer.

"Yes," he says. "Yes, I am."

SIX.

Nomad saw that they had left a porch light on for him. He wasn't sure if that was a compliment or not. He got out of the cab on the dark suburban street and paid the driver. The cab pulled away from the curb. It was on the weeping side of three o'clock. In fact, that was the name of a song Ariel and Terry had written for the CD The Five had recorded last year.

On the weeping side of three o'clock,
I walk alone down the city block,
I don't know where I'm going and I don't care,
'Cause I know when I go home you won't be there.

Had kind of a Loretta Lynn feel to it, made a little jumpy and strange by a pulsing B-52s-type Farfisa sound. Or it might have been something Joe "King" Carrasco and the Crowns could have recorded back in the mid-'80s.

Anyway, it was that time on Sunday morning.

The thing about Sunday mornings, Nomad thought as he walked toward the porch steps of a small house in this southwest Dallas neighborhood, is that they followed Saturday nights. It was quiet except for a dog barking maybe a couple of blocks away. The breeze was soft and the moon, just past full, shone down through the trees. The Scumbucket and trailer were parked in front of the house, across from a playground where this afternoon he'd watched

Ariel on the swingset. He'd been standing at a window, just watching. He knew she'd tried to get Neal Tapley off the pipe. He knew also that she had cared for Neal in a dangerous way, had let herself be too drawn into his trials and tribulations. She had cared too much for him, is all. People broke your heart, if you let them. If you got too close, and cared too much, you were just asking for it. He had seen too many bands destroyed in the aftermath of what passed as attraction, or need, or love, or whatever you wanted to call it. So as long as he was the emperor, there would be none of that in this band. No matter if you were sleeping in the same room, or in the same bed, and you were together more often than you were not, and you liked the way somebody smelled and you liked their smile and their voice and something about them spoke to the things you were not but wanted to be.

There would be none of that in this band.

He went up the steps, opened the screened door and was careful not to let it slam behind him. He hoped the front door was not locked; if it was, he'd be sleeping on the floor out here instead of on the floor in there. He'd find out in another few seconds which it was to be.

Five hours ago, he'd been in a totally different scene.

The boom and echo of his electrified voice over the heads of the Curtain Club audience: *Hi, guys. Thanks for coming out tonight, and we hope you enjoy the show.*

A quick flurry of drums from Berke, then into the kick-drum tempo at one hundred and twelve beats per minute, a hiss of hi-hat and the first chord, a monstrous D, crashed from Nomad's tobacco-colored Stratocaster. Ariel met him on the F chord and slid with him to the G on her glossy white Schecter Tempest. Mike took the bottom with his fire-red vintage 1978 Fender. Terry hung back, waiting. Many in the audience knew what song they were hearing, they knew it from the beginning chords because it had been on The Five's first, self-titled CD, and so they put up a shout as Nomad got up next to the microphone and sang it in his roughest, darkest snarl with a crimson spotlight in his face:

"Drivin' south down Main Street, I was takin' it real slow,
But in my pimped-up candy-colored ride, how slow could I go?

Saw the lights flashin', heard the siren start to blow,
Didn't know it then, Lady Law was gonna lay me low.
Bad cop,
She was a bad cop,
She said I was top of my class at bustin' bad boy ass,
She was a bad cop!"

Everytime Nomad sang the words "Bad cop!" their fans in the crowd shouted it back and swigged their beers, a ritual of sorts for this particular song that had started during their first tour. How those things began was anybody's guess, but Nomad glanced at Ariel and nodded with satisfaction because the wave of energy was lifting him up. Multicolored lights played over him, the different heats of blue, yellow and bright orange. The surface of the microphone on its stand before him glinted and flared as if made of exploding stars. He looked out upon his world.

"*Now lemme tell you, officer, I think you're mighty fine.*
She said whoa there, boy, I'm smellin' seven different kinds of wine.
And if you think a silver tongue's gonna save your sad behind,
Step out here right now, and you walk this crooked line.
Bad cop,
She was a bad cop..."

They were the second band on stage tonight, coming up after the Critters. Following their forty-five-minute set would be local favorites Gina Fayne and the Mudstaynes, and headlining at midnight were the Naugahydes, from Los Angeles, had a record deal with Interscope, had a song in the new Adam Sandler flick, and who sprawled around in the Green Room as if they owned it. Nomad used to be able to wear tight leather pants too, when he was twenty. Let them have their moment.

"*You sure do look good, you sure do fill out your blues,*
Now baby, I'm swearin' it, I haven't had that much booze.
She said, stop talkin' while you can, you got a lot to lose.

Get down on your knees and count to ninety-nine by twos.
Bad cop,
She was a bad cop…"

The beams of yellow and blue lights crossed in the air above the audience. Everybody was standing, some holding up cameras. Nomad didn't care if so-called unauthorized videos got onto YouTube. There was a party going on; it was all good. Maybe most of the people here had come to see the headliners, but for right now The Five was front and center, it was their time to show their stuff. Berke's drums were pounding the room, and then Terry started playing an organ tone that began as high-pitched and beautiful as a cherub's voice and suddenly dropped as low and nasty as the fevered gibberings of a meth-charged demon.

"*Bad cop!*
She was a bad cop!"

On the heels of the opener, Terry started up the pulsing Vox-toned intro to one of the '60s songs he'd brought in, 'Your Body Not Your Soul' by the Dutch band Cuby and the Blizzards from 1968, and Nomad launched himself at it as Berke's Ludwigs thundered at his back and spinning red lights descended from the ceiling. It was another fan favorite, suited to Nomad's persona and voice, and he could rip the motherlovin' shit out of it. Ariel stepped out front just after the chorus to demonstrate that her white Schecter Tempest could shred up a storm. The band moved on into the next song on which Nomad and Ariel shared lead vocals, a slow tempo bluesy tune titled 'Called Your Number'.

"*Called your number,*
Nobody was there,
Loving you is leading nowhere.
Called your number,

Won't you answer please?
Or cut loose this pain that is holding me."

It ended with a primal scream of guitars, Nomad and Ariel playing in harmony and then at dissonance. Next up was 'When the Storm Breaks', which Nomad introduced as their new video from their third and latest CD, called *Catch As Kukulkan*, on sale at the back with the other merchandise. "I hope we can get everybody out of the warzones and bring 'em back home," he told the audience as he stood in the white spotlight. He was going to let it go at that, but he couldn't. "Bush and Cheney are fucking liars, man," he added, and braced for the impact. Most in the audience whooped and hollered what Nomad took to be agreement; some were silent, and maybe too drunk already to disagree. Then Berke started the beat, Mike came in with the bass and they powered into the tune. It got a pretty good response, which Nomad appreciated since the song was so different from what they usually did.

At the set's midpoint, Nomad and Ariel stepped aside for Berke to do her drum solo that became a duel with Mike's bassline, and Terry brought the organ growling in to battle with both of them. This display of musical chops always went over well, and Nomad noted that Berke's female fans—also fans of Gina Fayne, an outspoken citizen of their Nation—were exuberant in their dancing over on the left side of the stage.

Nomad had read an article on Yahoo once that said Finnish scientists had run a test on a rock band to see how strenuous the work was. They'd found out it was as tough as being a manual laborer for the comparable amount of time. The job of being a guitarist and lead vocalist was like digging a ditch or moving furniture; the drummer worked as hard as a bricklayer, and the bass player's exertions were similar to those of a butcher. The body temperature went up to a hundred degrees, beads of sweat popped, and the pulse varied between one-hundred-twenty-eight and one-hundred-forty-four beats per minute. As the show wound down, he was feeling every bit of that and they still had the last number and encore—if the crowd wanted one—to do. They finished their regular set with 'Desperate Ain't Pretty', which was a high-octane rocker that ended with a furious rolling blast of toms and cymbals from Berke, then they went offstage for a couple of minutes to let the stew boil. When they returned and took their places, Nomad thanked the crowd for their response, reminded them that The Five CDs and T-shirts were on sale at the back, and then he intoned into the mike: “The universe is permeated with the odor of kerosene”, which was the opening of the second retro song that Terry had brought in, ‘The Blackout of Gretely’ by the garage rock band Gonn from 1966. It was a dinosaur-stomping earthquaker that Nomad sometimes feared could send a club crowd out into the street in a riot, if they were drunk enough. The song finished up in a dirty fuzz of distorted guitars, Nomad shouted, “Thank you, Dallas, and party on!” into his microphone, Berke threw the drumsticks into her throng of admirers, and The Five abandoned the stage for the next band’s setup, leaving the club’s crew to move their equipment to a holding area.

They were backstage in a dressing-room for only a few minutes, chugging down bottled water and hitting the tray of raw vegetables and three pepperoni pizzas, one without cheese, before George came to the door. “Great show, great show!” he told them, which if he said he meant. “Hey, John! There’s somebody out front who wants to talk to you.”

“Later,” Nomad said, settled in a folding chair with cheeseless pizza between his teeth.

“Yeah, well…I told him you’d be tired, but he says he’s got to hit the road. Drove a couple of hundred miles just to see you, he says. He’s asking you to sign six CDs and four T-shirts.”

“*Later*,” Nomad repeated. He frowned when George didn’t leave. “Come on, man! Give me a *break*!”

“Six CDs and four T-shirts,” George said. “Won’t take long.”

“Send the guy back if he’s so eager. We’ll all sign for him.”

“I already asked him. He says you have to come out there, and he just wants *you*.”

“What’s the dude’s story?” Mike was sitting with his bootheels up on the pizza table. “Sounds weird.”

“I don’t *have* to do anything,” Nomad said to George, countering his last statement. “I’m eating right now, tell him to wait.”

“You should go ahead,” Ariel told him. She was sitting next to Terry, both of them on folding chairs, and Berke was slumped over on a wooden bench, kneading the tight muscles at the back of her neck. “Maybe he runs a fan page.”

“All I know is, it’s *money*,” George said. “And it wouldn’t hurt any of you to come out of the cave and meet your fans.”

"This isn't a meet-and-greet," Nomad reminded him. He realized George wasn't going to leave without some kind of compromise. "Okay," he said, raising his hands in surrender, "give me five minutes."

"I'll tell him." George started to leave but caught himself. The staff handled the merchandise sales in the larger clubs like this one, true, but it might help if the band just walked out to the counter for a couple of minutes. "Listen," he added, "you'd better pray the day never comes when nobody asks you for an autograph. I mean it." He left before any further comments could be thrown at him.

Nomad let seven minutes go past, and then he stood up and said, "Okay, let me go do this."

"Nice to be the chosen one," Berke told him. "He's probably a freak, got a doll in his bed with your face on it."

"Look who's talkin'," Mike said.

Nomad went out of the room, down a short flight of stairs and through a door past the burly black-clothed security guard into the main part of the club, where knots of people were standing around talking and drinking, waiting for the next band. Instantly he was seen, recognized and shouted at, toasted with uplifted beer cups, focused upon by a half-dozen cellphone cameras, slapped on the shoulder, high-fived, all of it. Some girls rushed toward him, grinning, while their dates stood back at a distance. Nomad kept moving, even as the path before him began to close up. This was why he didn't particularly like to come out into the audience area after a show in a large venue, and why really very few musicians did: you never knew if somebody's drunk girlfriend would try to grab your ass, and the equally drunk boyfriend would start swinging on you, or some high-flying cowboy type decided he didn't like all the attention you were getting and he wanted to see if you were really as tough as you thought you were, or some nutjob had decided you'd stolen a song he wrote in a dream and he wanted to let you and everybody else in the club know about it, or somebody clung to you like you were made of superglue and started telling you how great you were and how there'll never be another voice like yours and could you please listen to this homemade CD that's got some kickin' shit on it, or...well, you just never knew. All those things had already happened to him, and more.

He saw George standing back by the counter where the merchandise was being sold. Keeping tabs on the action, for sure. A hand grabbed Nomad's shoulder and he turned around to bump fists with a wild-haired dude in a Kings Of Leon T-shirt. Then he was through another group of people who smelled like they'd taken a bath in beer and George said, "The guy's over here," and led him past three girls who looked as if they wore their dresses spray-painted on, all in different shades of red.

Suddenly Nomad was right up in front of a big, bulky dude with close-cropped brown hair and a long, unshaven jaw. The guy wore baggy jeans and a long-sleeved dark blue shirt with white stripes. His eyes were sunken in, almost as if he'd just awakened from a heavy sleep. In his arms was a green plastic bag.

"Here he is," George said. Nomad didn't know which one of them he was speaking to.

"Hi," the guy said.

"How's it going?" Nomad asked, aware that the three girls were coming up on him from the right. Two blondes, neither of them natural in hair color or boob-size, but the girl in the middle with auburn hair was the real hottie.

"Good, real good," the guy said. He blinked furiously, as if he was really nervous or he really needed glasses. And then he abruptly stepped aside and the thin woman who was standing behind him said, "John Charles!" She smiled, but only one side of her mouth worked very well. "Go Shamrocks!"

Shamrocks? he thought. East Detroit High School? Those Shamrocks? He had no idea who this person might be. She was a small, emaciated woman maybe in her mid-thirties. She leaned on the support of one of those curved metal walking-sticks with a black rubber tip that old people hobble on in hospitals. A bright, cheerful purple scarf was wrapped turban-style around her head, and fixed at the front with a gold-colored pin in the shape of a butterfly. *Chemo*, Nomad thought, because she had no hair. Her cheekbones and chin were so sharp they looked about to break the skin. She wore shapeless jeans and a white peasant-blouse top. A pink sweater was draped around her shoulders.

"I know you don't remember me," she said. "I'm Cheryl Buoniconti. I mean, I *was*. I'm Cheryl Capriata now. This is my husband, Ray."

"Heard a lot about you." Ray shook Nomad's hand. "You put on a great show."

"Thanks." Nomad felt as if he'd been knocked to the floor and he was still trying to get up. He'd gone to school with Cheryl Buoniconti, grades six through eight at Oakwood Middle School and then freshman and sophomore years at East Detroit. They were the same age. Cheryl and her family had moved away, summer before the junior year. The Cheryl he'd known had been a flirt, in fact one of the group called the Flirty Four, had been a whiz at math, a reporter on the school paper, had been—in all honesty—really kind of a snooty bitch who'd looked down on the hoods, thugs and sad-ass cases John Charles had hung with.

"Thank *you*," Cheryl said, "for coming out here. I don't do so well getting around in crowds."

"No problem," Nomad answered, and nearly choked when he heard himself say it. "Uh... *Cheryl*. Jesus. Do you live in Dallas?"

"No. We live just east of Shreveport. In Minden. Ray teaches algebra at the high school. I...I mean *we*...follow you on your webpage. Your band, I mean. Well, we don't exactly *follow* you, this is the first show we've been to, but..."

"We keep up," Ray said, helpfully.

"We do keep up." Cheryl smiled again, and this time Nomad saw a trace of the flirty teenaged girl way down in her dark brown eyes. But only a trace, and too quickly it was gone. "And we're not the only ones. I'm on Facebook with a lot of people from East Detroit." She mentioned several names, most of whom Nomad recalled as being in a different, higher atmosphere than himself. "Everybody's rooting for you. I remember that talent show when we were freshmen. When you got up on stage with your band. What was their name?"

"The Unwanted," Nomad said.

"I remember thinking you were going places. I remember thinking I wished I could find something as important to me as music was to you. But I guess I found it. Can I show you a picture of our daughter?"

"Absolutely," Nomad said.

From his wallet Ray produced a picture of a girl eight or nine years old. She had her mother's dark brown eyes, she wore her hair in bangs across the front, and she had an open, confident smile.

"That's my angel," Cheryl said. "Her name's Courtney, she's just turned nine."

"Awesome," Nomad told her, and it seemed to him that everybody needed an angel, of some kind. He returned the picture to Ray.

"I had to leave that summer before we were juniors. My dad lost his job at the Firestone plant. I didn't really get a chance to say goodbye to my friends, we just came down to Louisiana to live with my Uncle Burt for a little while, I thought we were going back after the summer. You know?"

"I guess that was tough," Nomad said, because he could tell it was important to her not only to explain this to him, but to get a response.

"Well…it was, but…I know it wasn't like…what happened to you, in the sixth grade. To *your* dad. I remember my folks talking about it. Listen to me, I sound like my mom chattering away in line at the Publix. Would you sign those for us? Ray, have you got the pen?"

"I do," said Ray, who brought from his pocket a silver permanent marker.

Inside the green bag were the CDs and the T-shirts. As Ray handed the first CD over to be signed, Nomad looked at Cheryl and asked, "Do you want my real name or my stage name?"

"Whatever you want to put. I'm just so glad to see somebody from East Detroit way down here. We had a good time, didn't we?"

"We did," he said, and he signed *John 'Nomad' Charles*. He wondered how long Cheryl had been sick, or what her prognosis was. He didn't want to ask, but she looked bad. At one point, as Nomad did the signatures, he heard Ray quietly ask her, "You all right?" and she said, "Oh, yeah." Ray put his arm around her, to steady her, and Nomad kept on signing.

The last T-shirt he signed, he put *Go Shamrocks!* under his name.

"Can we get a picture?" Cheryl asked, and Nomad said that was fine, as many as she wanted. As Ray took the shots, Nomad put his arm around Cheryl's frail shoulders and his face against hers. He was aware of the three girls coming up right beside him to take their own pictures with the ever-present cellphone cameras. They began to laugh loud and drunkenly, to jostle him with their shoulders and their hips and he told them as politely as he could to step back, that they were crowding him, and one of the fake blondes called him a dumb fuck and the other fake blonde put up the middle finger right in his face and the first fake blonde took a picture of it. But they moved off and away into the crowd, and when Ray finished up the pictures Cheryl said, "I brought something for you," and she reached into a pocket of her jeans and put into Nomad's hand a small piece of clear quartz crystal. He instantly recognized it as a type of crystal people carried when they were into natural healing.

"Thanks," Nomad said. "I appreciate you coming to the show."

"We wouldn't have missed it for anything. We can't stay, though, we've got to get back home tonight. I'll put the pictures up on Facebook. I know lots of people would love to see them. And if you ever come through Minden, we're in the directory. Under Raymond Capriata." She spelled the last name. Then she squeezed his hand with her thin fingers, and she smiled up at him. "I'm so happy to know," she said, "that somebody from East Detroit High School is living out their dream. Most people aren't able to do that, John. And I am proud to say I knew you back in the day."

Nomad nodded. *Back in the day.* His bitter sense of sarcasm welled up, and he wanted to ask, *Which day was that? The Tuesday when Quince Massey and two of his dickwads jumped me from behind in the parking lot, and when they were done they threw me into a garbage dumpster and slammed the lid shut? Or the Friday the booger-smeared note was left in my locker telling me that if I even looked at Sofia Chandrette again I could kiss my nuts goodbye? How about the Saturday, when I saw the knife in Quince Massey's hand outside the Olive Garden and I hit him as hard as I could in the throat and put him in the hospital and the police came to my house to arrest me for battery? Yeah, back in the day.*

But he did not ask these things, because by the time they had happened Cheryl was down in Louisiana, and maybe even then the cancer was a small darkness in her body.

Instead, he leaned forward and kissed Cheryl on the cheek, and he said, "You take care, okay?"

"I will." She had turned a little bit pink. A flash of flirty came up, very suddenly, from the depths of the soulful eyes. "*Nomad*," she said, and then her husband took her free hand and helped her through the crowd. She walked with a slow, careful step and she depended on the metal stick, and Nomad was struck by how very young all the other people in the room seemed to be, how young they moved and talked and looked, though by years they were not so much younger than Cheryl, nor so much younger than himself. He felt like twenty-nine had become the new fifty. But Cheryl was going home with her husband at her side, and a daughter when she got there. That wasn't so bad, was it?

When he turned away, he was shoulder-grazed by a big dude in a dark gray hoodie who kept going, on his way out the front door. Nomad started to say, *Where's the fire*? but he had the mental image of somebody hearing him and shouting *Fire!* out of drunken mischief or plain stupidity and that would not do. So he kept his mouth shut, a guy came up to him, said, "Fuckin' *mighty* show, man!" and flashed a camera in his face, and Nomad sought out the Little Genius, who had returned again to monitor the merchandise sales.

George was not only keeping count of the sales, but was tracking other numbers on his cellphone. "Hits on the new video," he told Nomad. "Three hundred and thirty-eight on YouTube, three hundred and sixty-one on MySpace, four hundred and twenty-six on the webpage. Not bad, it's still early."

"How many times have *you* watched it?"

"A few. Not many. You work everything out with those people? She told me she'd gone to school with you, wanted it to be a surprise. Was it?" George looked at him over the rims of his glasses.

"It was."

"You want to sign some T-shirts while you're over here?"

"I'm on my way to over *there*," Nomad said, and entered the main room where in a few minutes, give or take, Gina Fayne's band was going to start playing. He caught sight of Berke at the center of a group of five or six women down front, laughing and chatting each other up, and he noted—as he always did when he saw Berke mingling with her sisters—that a couple of them had shoulders like Longhorn tackles, were grim-lipped and fearsome in appearance while the others never failed to be hot enough to melt a steel dildo. It had to be the *idea* that they didn't need men that was such a turn-on, Nomad thought. Maybe it was the fact that unless they were going for the butch style they never overplayed their sexuality like straight women sometimes did. Nomad had seen Berke in the company of some stunning women who made you want to, as Mike had put it, "try and cry". It was the way they looked at you, too; either lingering, their eyes cool and remote, as if to dare you to cross an invisible line, or they sliced you up with a few quick glances and cut your throat with a knife-edged half-smile.

"Hi," said the girl who stood next to his left elbow. She was holding a beer and she leaned in closer, because of the noise. "Sorry they acted like assholes."

It was the auburn-haired girl who'd been with the two fake blondes. She looked to be about twenty or so, had light green eyes and a cute pug nose and the tattoo of a blue star on her right shoulder. "You're in that band that just played," she said, as if she wanted to make sure. Her eyelids were a little heavy. Maybe she'd been hitting more than just the beer tonight.

"Yeah," Nomad said.

"You wanna go somewhere?" she asked, and she held up a set of car keys that had a silver Playboy rabbit head on the chain.

The thing about being in a touring band was, people didn't realize what a grind it could be. They didn't realize that the only glamor in it was manufactured. They didn't realize that most of being on a tour was the miles and miles and hours and hours of travelling, and if not that then the waiting. There were three things that made the grind bearable: the actual gig, which could be either Paradise or Pandemonium; the frequent use of somewhat illegal but naturally-growing substances to ease the flow of electric energy given off by the Paradise so that one could sleep that night or the following day, or to lighten the self-anger or rage at one's bandmates following the disaster of a Pandemonium.

The third thing?

Nomad was looking at it.

"Sure," he said, as it had been said so many times before. "What about your friends?"

"Fuck 'em, they're bitches," the girl slurred. "And it's *my* car, anyway."

"Okay, but I think I should drive."

"Yeah," she said, and she gave him the keys, and it was that easy.

During the three hours that followed, Nomad was in an apartment off Amesbury Drive in North Dallas. There was evidence of a female roommate and a second bedroom with a closed door, but nobody came out of it. He smoked some weed with the girl, whose name was Tiffany and who worked somewhere at the Galleria doing something, he never could figure it out, and they made some margaritas in her blender and she showed him her collection of Barbie Birthstone dolls lined up on a shelf, they were real expensive she said and the only one she didn't have yet was Miss Opal of October, and then she asked him if he wanted to take a shower. He recalled that Ninja Warrior was on TV when he said he thought that was an awesome idea.

When they were wet and soapy Tiffany asked him if it would be a big deal if she got her video camera and took some clips in the bedroom, that it got her hot all over again to watch the replay and anyway she liked to be directed. Nomad, who had already seen the dolphin tattoo leaping up from the pink cleft between her thighs and had thought *Another fucking Flipper*, just shrugged his shoulders. This was not a first. In fact, years ago he'd considered bringing along a black mask to situations like this. More than once, a girl had gotten her friend to hide in a closet with a videocam. The techno thing was becoming ridiculous, it was like people couldn't *survive* without having some gadget near at hand. But there was no time for a rumination over the future of a civilization addicted to either porn or the electronic capture of special moments, because Tiffany was on her knees.

They progressed to the bedroom, where Tiffany proved to be an experienced participant and also a loud one, as she announced to her neighbors, the city of Dallas and most of north-central Texas how rough she wanted it, and in what orifice. Either her neighbors were deaf or they just rolled over in bed and said, "Oh, that's Tiffany being Tiffany," because nobody banged on the wall. Tiffany wanted to do things that would've made her Barbies blush, but Nomad hung in there. But as Tiffany thrashed about on top of him, he had the disturbing image of Ariel on stage, bathed in blue light, playing her acoustic guitar and singing,

This song is a snake, winding through the woods,
It's full of bitter venom and it would bite you if it could.
This song is a snake, coiled beneath the bed,
And if you love another girl there it will rattle by your head.

"Harder, harder, *harder*!" Tiffany shouted, but he could still hear the rattle.

When all was screamed and done, they slept. Then Nomad awakened when the man was standing next to the bed.

"Who are *you*?" His voice cracked. He grabbed the sheet and pulled it up to his chin like a naughty fop in a British sex comedy. But it wasn't funny, because this kind of scene was why his father was dead. Nomad was ready to fight for his life if the guy pulled a gun.

The dude was skinny, had a mass of tangled blonde hair and wore glasses. He had good musical taste, though, because he was wearing a black T-shirt with the symbols on it, in white, from Led Zeppelin's *Zoso* album. He was also either drunk or high, from the frozen grin on his face and the way he couldn't keep from drifting side-to-side. "Tiffany?" he said, shaking her starry shoulder. "Come on, Tiff, talk to me. Okay?"

She was wiped, and she muttered something into her pink pillow and swatted at him as if he were a tsetse fly. He kept on pleading for her attention like a sad child.

Nomad decided it was time to pull on his drawyas and get out. He slid from the bed, got dressed in a hurry, but careful not to make too much noise in case the punk went ballistic. Before Nomad could get out of the room, Tiffany sat up, rubbed her eyes and started talking to the guy. It was one of those *do you really really want another chance and why should I give you one* conversations, made totally bizarre when Tiffany seemed to remember Nomad was there and she said, "You can use the phonebook in the kitchen...call a cab."

"What's the address here?"

She shook her head, unable to process the numbers, and the Zeppelin fan who obviously had apartment key privileges said without looking at Nomad, "Just tell 'em the Zone apartments on Amesbury Drive. They'll know the place."

Nomad just bet they would. He remembered passing a twenty-four-hour Arby's near the entrance to the apartment complex, and when he called the cab company he said he'd be there waiting. He went out the door to the sounds of Tiffany's voice whiplashing the guy and the poor sucker nearly sobbing.

Rock'n roll, baby!

So it was that Nomad approached the door of the suburban house on the weeping side of three o'clock. He tried the doorknob and found it was, sensibly, locked against people like him. He was about to turn his thoughts toward curling up on the porch when the door cracked open and a familiar face peered out.

"Hey, bro," Mike whispered. He opened the door wider. "Heard a car pull up, figured it was either you or Berke."

"*Berke*? She's not here?"

"Must be a good party they're havin'. She and her friends left not too long after you went off with your *chiquita*. George saw you go. Watch it!" Mike warned, because in the dim light coming from a hallway he saw that John had almost stepped on Terry, who was wrapped up in a sleeping-bag on the carpeted floor. A few feet away from Terry, Ariel was also in a sleeping-bag. George was on the sofa since he knew the guy who owned the house and had worked it out for them to spend the night here.

Nomad saw that a backyard light was on, and that the sliding glass door that led out was partway open. "You sleeping outside?"

"Nope. Woke up a while ago. I was just sittin' out there, thinkin'."

"Sounds heavy."

Mike shrugged. Ariel suddenly stirred and lifted her head, and she looked groggily at the two figures, squinting to make out who it was. "John?" she said.

"Yeah."

"Some of us are asleep," she told him, and then she returned to her slumber.

Nomad thought that all fucking decent citizens were asleep at this hour, and everybody else was just thrashing around in their cages.

< >

"Hey," Mike whispered, "you want a cigarette?"

Nomad nodded. He followed Mike out through the glass door and slid it shut. Out back, in the glare of a pair of security floodlights mounted on the underhang of the roof, a few concrete steps led down to a fenced-in area with a small lawn. There was a picnic table, a playhouse meant to look like a wilderness fort, and a kid-sized plastic pool decorated with decals of smiling seahorses. The family who owned the house had two children, both under ten. They were sleeping in a back room, safely away from the scummy musicians. In fact, their father had been a roadie a few years ago, had travelled with some bands who were successful enough to need roadies and actually pay them money, but that was then and now he was the manager of an AMC theater that he was proud to say had sixteen movie screens.

On the picnic table was a coffee cup that Mike had been using for an ashtray. Beside it was his pack of smokes, his Zippo lighter bearing the logo of the New Orleans Saints, a small notebook with a green cover, and a ballpoint pen. By the light of the floods, Nomad saw three or four butts in the cup. He knew that Mike was waiting for Berke to come home, or what for the moment served as home.

"She can take care of herself," Nomad said, and realized this was a remark he'd made several times in the past, on occasions just like this.

And Mike's answer was the same, too: "Oh yeah, I don't worry about *her*, bro."

They sat at the table, one on either side. Mike offered Nomad a cigarette, took one for himself, and he lit both of them up with the Zippo.

Nomad blew smoke into the night air. "You guys hang around much longer?"

"Not much. Caught about half of Gina Fayne's set. Tight band, and she's got some pipes, I swanee."

"Yeah." She was compared to Janis Joplin on the Mudstaynes' website. Maybe not so much roughness in her voice, but she was only twenty. Nomad heard she was catching up to Janis in the department of drinking and drugs, and he hoped somebody wasn't stupid enough to let her try heroin to complete the picture. He glanced at the pen and notebook. "You writing something?"

Mike frowned, as if this question was improper. "Just playin' around."

"With what?"

"My *dick*," Mike replied, which meant it was not to be talked about any further. He smoked his cigarette some and listened for the noise of a car pulling up out front. That dog started barking in the distance again and another answered, but otherwise the neighborhood was Sunday-morning silent. "Nice house they got here," he said. "I like that pool. Hot night, you could curl up right there."

"Yeah," Nomad said.

Mike drew on his cigarette, exhaled and regarded the little red glow, as people will. Then he reached out, trying not to be so obvious about it but being obvious all the same, and slid the notebook away from Nomad about four or five inches. "Did you know," he said, "that Berke's stepdad died last month?"

"Huh? No, I didn't." Nomad smiled thinly. "Hey, she only talks to *you*, man."

"Heart attack. Had one about ten years ago. He had a pacemaker, took high blood pressure pills and all that, but the ticker got him. You know they weren't too close."

"I know she doesn't talk about him very much." Floyd Fisk had been his name.

"Yeah, well, the only reason I know is that she told me her mother called her. From San Diego. Said Floyd left her something he wanted her to have. The dude must've felt his time runnin' out, or maybe he was just gettin' ready. But Berke says he left a letter...like...stipulatin' his wishes and shit."

"What'd he leave her?"

"She don't know. Her mother don't know, either. Whatever it is, it's in three big sealed-up boxes in their garage. Letter said only Berke's supposed to crack 'em open. Anyhow, her mom wants her to come pick 'em up."

The Five were scheduled to play at the Casbah in San Diego on August 1st, a Friday night, opening for The Mindfockers and the Mad Lads. Nomad said, "Whatever," because that just seemed like a suitable, neutral comment.

They didn't speak for a while. Their cigarettes burned down. The dogs quietened. Mike shifted on the bench seat and said, "I've been thinkin'. You know that place with the blackberries? Somethin' wasn't right."

"What?" Nomad had heard him well enough, but the statement took him by surprise.

"Wasn't right," Mike repeated.

Damn straight it wasn't, Nomad thought. He'd been rubbing his skull for two days, searching for the swelling of a tumor. Could you even find them that way? He didn't know.

Mike took another draw on his cigarette, almost burning it to his fingers. In the glare of the floods, the pictures on his arms moved with the shifting of his ropy muscles. "Ever picked blackberries?" he asked, and Nomad shook his head. "Second time I ran away from home, I found work on a farm. Fella grew blackberries, one of his crops. Well, I remember the season ended up...oh...last part of June, first week of July at the latest. I mean, they're like...kinda fragile. The berry, not the fuckin' thorns. But they need a lot of rain, and this heat should've shrivelled 'em up to nothin'. I've been thinkin'...wonderin', I guess is the right word...how there could've been any blackberries at all in those brambles, it bein' so dry and so hot. Get me?"

"No, not really," Nomad admitted. "Maybe they were...like... resistant or something."

"I think they were just wild blackberries," Mike said quietly. "Growin' when they shouldn't be."

"Yeah." *Whatever*, Nomad almost said, but that might sound like disrespect and you did *not*, no way, no how, want to throw a diss at Mike Davis.

"That girl at the well," Mike went on, after a short pause, "spoke to me."

Nomad nodded. He recalled what Mike had relayed from her: *She says to tell you everybody's welcome, and not to be afraid.* "You told us."

"Not that." Mike turned his head slightly, and through a haze of smoke Nomad caught the sharp glint of the deep-set dark brown eyes aimed at him, like the first quick display of a weapon that had best not be ignored. "To *me*," Mike said. "Just to me. In English."

Nomad was almost afraid to ask, but Mike was waiting. "What was it?"

"She said...*welcome*." Mike started to crush his dying cigarette in the cup, but he took from it one more pull. "And...I could tell...I could..." He made a small gasping noise, and suddenly Nomad saw wetness bloom around Mike's eyes, and he looked away and Mike looked away and it was a shocking moment, really, for both of them.

"I could tell," Mike continued, when he got his voice steadied, "that she *meant* it."

Nomad didn't know what to say, so he made the wise decision and remained silent. He stared at the pool, at the surface of the still water.

"Do you know," Mike said in a distant voice, as if asking himself the question, "how many times somebody has said that to me, and meant it? How about...that was probably number *one*? I'm used to being thrown out of places, bro. At least, they fuckin' *try* to throw me out. And someplaces I say, okay, I'll go easy, and other places I say, let's see you *make* me. Like that all my life, John. Ever was, ever will be. Except that girl...she was like...glad to see me. Does that make any sense to you?"

"I can't say," seemed like the reasonable response.

"One thing I do know is that I can tell when somebody's shittin' me or not, and right now you can't figure out what the hell I'm talkin' about, because she was just a little Mexican girl passin' out water, and what of it, and you kinda think I'm dumb to begin with, and that's where we're at. Right?"

"I don't think you're dumb," Nomad said. "Where'd you get that idea?"

Mike blinked slowly and crushed what was left of the cigarette into the cup. "Because," he answered, "I *am* dumb. Oh yeah, I'm good with the bass axe. I do my part. I'm a pro, whatever that means. But as far as smarts take me, I've pretty much been hitchin' rides for a long time."

"I don't think anybody who read *Moby Dick* when he was a little boy can be dumb, do you?"

"Oh. That." Mike nodded. "It was more about the stealin' than the readin'. I figured if I could make myself get through a book that size, and understand it, I could..." He stopped abruptly and took another smoke from the pack. "I could be as smart as Wayne was," he said, as he fired up the Zippo and lit his cigarette.

Mike's dead older brother, killed in a lumberyard accident. The boy's face was tattooed there on his left shoulder. Nomad said nothing; he just waited.

When it came, Mike's voice was hushed and sad. "Wayne was everybody's golden boy. Star football runnin' back, A-student, popular...he was the bomb, bro. Gonna go to *college*. Scholarship lined up to McNeese State. And then he got a summer job at the yard. Same kind of job kids have been doin' there for years, summer after summer. A chain came loose, a safety gear that was supposed to lock up didn't catch, a load of timber fell...all she wrote, as they say. Only he didn't die for a while, he was busted and broken and they tried to put him back together in the hospital but he just...kinda gave up, I guess.

He never came to all the way, but I mean...he wasn't gonna be able to fuckin' *walk*, his spine was so tore up. That was a bad day, that one was. I loved my brother. He was gonna be the kind of man who turns out to be a good dad. You know? The dependable one."

"Sure," Nomad said.

"You mind if I talk about this?" Mike asked, his eyes narrowed. "This is on me tonight. You mind if I talk?"

"Oh, yeah. I mean...yeah, go ahead."

"It ain't pretty," Mike said.

"Well, neither are *you*," Nomad told him, and he saw Mike give a grim smile that did not last very long but at least was there for a few seconds.

Mike smoked and thought for a little while. Then he said, "See, he covered me. I just coasted in his shadow, and nobody ever had any expectations or shit for me. He made it easy for me to slide on by. But without him bein' around, my folks...they grieved for him, let's put it that way. They grieved for him, and they grieved for him, and they grieved for him, and our house was a fuckin' pit of grief, just seemed like the lightbulbs went out of the lamps one after another, and nobody put any new ones in. It wasn't long before I was hatin' him, and what he'd been, and I felt like they hated me, too, because I was the dumbshit brother, I was the pothead, the troublemaker, the *musician*. When they looked at me—wasn't too often—I knew they were seein' what was left. Wasn't gonna be no football star in our house anymore, no smart honor roll student, and no McNeese State graduate either. No sir, that bird had flown. And I knew that I had to get away from that house and those people, so I could love Wayne like I used to. So I could think of him like a mountain holdin' up the sky, with the clouds in his teeth. My big brother." Mike took a drag and blew smoke from his nostrils like the exhalation of a dragon. "And he would have been the first one to tell me to go. So I went. Came back a couple of times, when I ran into trouble. But then I left one night, to get away from the hate and the hollerin', and I got a ride on the highway with a black dude about a hundred and twenty years old, in a righteous old gold Cadillac with tailfins. He told me his name was Grover McFarland, and he was on his way to New Orleans from Montgomery, Alabama, to play in a blues festival. But he said he went by the stage name of Catfish McFarland, because he could play bass so deep he could just lie right there at the muddy bottom and grin." Mike himself grinned at that memory. "He was a drunk, cheated at cards, had two wives at once and had shot a preacher in Pascagoula in 1959. But that sumbitch, rest his soul, was not a liar. At least not about playin' bass." He touched one of the guitars tattooed on his right arm. "This one was his, the best I remember it. The one he taught me on. He called her 'Elvira, Mistress of the Darkies'."

Mike looked up suddenly, toward the street. "You hear a car?"

Nomad listened. "No," he decided. "She's not back yet."

"That girl needs a good girl to look after her," Mike said. "Drives me crazy sometimes."

Nomad had finished his cigarette and put it out in the cup, and he wanted to stand and stagger off to get a few hours of sleep before they loaded up to go to El Paso. Their gig wasn't until Friday night, but they might as well get on the road and have a few days to lie around a pool somewhere. He hoped the T-shirt and CD sales had made them enough money for a friendly neighborhood Motel 6. But he didn't go, because he felt that Mike still needed him.

"I never thought about playin' music for a livin'," Mike went on after a short pause to strain an ear for the car that was not there. "When I was a kid, I wanted to be a *vet*. I liked animals, I always got along with 'em. But you have to know math, chemistry...all that. I wasn't smart enough. Even my teachers told me I wasn't...and then the woman at the library, behind that desk, said...you're a little boy, you're not smart enough to read that big ol' book. She said, go put it on the red shelf over there, and you get yourself a book you can actually *read*. And then she said... wait a minute, wait a minute...you're Wayne Davis's brother, aren't you? Oh, is that book for *him*?"

Mike leaned his head forward and closed his eyes for a few seconds, and Nomad again looked away, at some invisible thing in the distance.

"It's a good word, huh?" Mike asked. When Nomad didn't respond, Mike said, "*Welcome*. It's a good word."

"Yeah, it is."

"Good place to start, maybe." Mike didn't elaborate on what that meant, and Nomad didn't want to push him. There was too much pain out here to be pushed.

At last, Nomad said, "I'd better hit it." He waited for Mike to answer, "Okay," before he stood up, just as a matter of courtesy.

A few steps toward the house, and Nomad turned back and said, "You don't have to wait up. You ought to—"

"I'm fine," came the reply. "Right where I am."

"'Night, then," Nomad told him.

"Mornin'," Mike corrected.

Nomad went up the steps, opened the sliding glass door, entered the house on quiet cat feet and slid the door shut behind him, and in the backyard Mike put the cigarette between his teeth and reached for the notebook and pen.

SEVEN.

Westward went the Scumbucket and its U-Haul trailer, following I-20 across the sunburnt landscape toward El Paso.

Everybody was present and accounted for. A red pickup truck with an International Gay Rodeo Association sticker on the back window had delivered Berke to the house just after seven o'clock. She'd climbed into a sleeping bag and hadn't budged until ten-thirty, which was why the Scumbucket hadn't gotten on the highway until noon. But they had plenty of time, it was all good.

"Three hundred eighty-two on YouTube, four hundred and six on MySpace, four hundred and fifty-four on the webpage," George announced, checking the video hits numbers on his cell. "It's early, man, still early." He was glowing today, freshly-showered and wearing his khakis and a crisp lemon-colored short-sleeved shirt. He felt like a million euros. Part of it was that he was so glad and relieved to have told everybody what his future plans were, and that they were past that, no hating going on, no name-calling or spiteful shit. Jeff in Chicago was good with the timeframe, no problem there. The Curtain Club gig had brought in three hundred dollars and change, a pretty decent haul. He felt like he wasn't leaving them in the lurch; he felt like something solid was in the making, something that was going to take The Five to a new place. The video had been expensive, sure, but he'd heard a lot of comments about it last night, and anything that got people talking was good. Media was the key. Once you got the media interested, that was half the battle right there.

Which was why he was okay with them spending money on a few days in a motel in the Paso, because they had an interview set up with the *Times* on Tuesday afternoon, six minutes on the KTSM morning show on Wednesday, a drop-in visit on KTEP's local radio talkshow on Wednesday afternoon, and on Thursday afternoon an appearance at Freaky Frontier Comics, Books and CDs on Pebble Hills Boulevard. You had to get the media shine, had to get the people interested and the talk going. So, yeah, he thought he was going to be able to leave them in a better place than when he came aboard, and that was important for him to believe.

Terry was behind the wheel. The iPods and the Gameboys had come out, each to their own to make the time pass. Terry drew George and Nomad into a discussion of which Who rock-opera was better, *Tommy* or *Quadrophenia*, with George going for the pinball wizard and Terry and Nomad for Jimmy's four personalities. Then they curved into talking about famous one-hit wonders, of which Berke thought the most obvious was The Knack and 'My Sharona', a song she remembered hearing over and over again at a bowling-alley birthday party when she was ten, about thirteen years after the song was first recorded. They realized they were getting into dangerous country, because Terry had an encylopedic knowledge of old dead bands and at any moment he could set off on a journey across what Berke called the Moldy Territory.

With eyes aflame behind his Lennon specs and passion rising in his voice, Terry would say that for sure bands like Kings Of Leon and Badly Drawn Boy and Band Of Horses were awesome, no doubt, but until you heard the Montells doing 'You Can't Make Me' or the Humans' 'Warning' or 'Real Fine Lady' by the Warlords you didn't know the fire and fever of pure garage rock. You didn't know what raw power could sound like in music. If you didn't move to 'Dinah Wants Religion' by The Fabs, or 'L.S.D.' by the Pretty Things, the coffin lid might as well be closed because you were one dead motherfucker. And then Terry would get onto the subject of "the rock star", who in his estimation could only be Phil May of the Pretty Things, and to see him in his finest sneering form there was a video of 'L.S.D.' on YouTube, the vid faded and gray and old and amateurish, but when Phil May in his striped Mod jacket glances past the camera and swings his long black hair away from his face and seems to chew the words to tatters before he spits them out, you know you have seen The Star.

According to Terry.

As the Scumbucket rumbled on and the air-conditioning hacked and wheezed, the highway speared straight between land colored both yellow and brown, with occasional stands of trees holding onto their faded green like desperate misers onto money, surrounded by thorn-bushes and waist-high scrub and dirt as dry as gunpowder. They passed Abilene around two-thirty. Ahead of them heatwaves shimmered and the pavement glistened like gray liquid.

"Weird bands," the Little Genius said, introducing another round of debate.

They came up with several. Uncle Fucker, described as "psychobilly country music on crystal meth", was Nomad's pick. Ariel said she'd seen A Band Of Orcs play in San Francisco; they were a heavy-metal band who dressed as Lord Of The Rings-style orcs, complete with battle armor and fearsome makeup. George said he thought ArnoCorps was pretty weird; they mostly did songs based on Schwartzenegger action movies, and they dressed the part. Berke mentioned Empire Of The Sun, with their off-the-wall costumes and strange but compelling electropop warblings. Mike had his eyes closed listening to his iPod, so he had no opinion.

"The 13th Floors," Terry said.

"We're not talking about prehistoric," George reminded him. "Current bands only."

"Don't care. The 13th Floors. And I'll say that the 13th Floors could blow us and every band we ever heard of off any stage anywhere."

"Oh, Jesus," Berke said. "Moldy Territory-time."

"Maybe." Terry glanced back at her in the rearview mirror. "But show me another band who actually *created* their own instruments. Show me another band who came up with such awesome sounds. And then they wrote songs from them that no other band in the *world* could've written. Show me—"

"Show me any remaining remnant of the 13th Floors," George interrupted, "except some warped LP in a collector's storeroom. Maybe they're legends, but those guys are long gone. How about we keep the discussion to *working* bands?"

Terry didn't reply for a few seconds. Then he asked Nomad, who sat shotgun, "Would you hold the wheel a minute?" When Nomad did, Terry dug the wallet from the back pocket of his jeans. "You guys know the name Eric Gherosimini?"

"Sure," George answered. "He was the keyboard player and front man. Flying high on acid all the time, wasn't he? And he vanished after the band split in...I don't know the year."

"1968," Terry said. "November." He brought a many-times-folded piece of paper from his wallet, passed it back to George and then took the wheel again. "You want to read that out loud?"

As the others looked on, and even Mike opened his eyes because he sensed he was missing out on something, George quickly scanned the paper. "*Shit*," he said quietly. "You've got to be kidding."

"Read it."

"*Terry*," George read, "*I don't have a computer out here but I went to the library in town. I looked up your band and I watched your videos. I found a CD in a store. There's some groovy keyboard shit on it. If you went to all the hassle to find me, and you want to hear her so bad, come see me. Not the best host, I can't put you up, but I'm working on something real. Like you to hear some of it, get a young ear. If you're coming from Albuquerque, follow 66 west for thirty-two miles, you'll see a road on the right with a sign to—*" He blinked and looked up. "These are directions to Eric Gherosimini's *house*?"

"You got it. He signed at the bottom, didn't he?"

"I'm not following this," Ariel said. "Who are we talking about?"

"The 13th Floors were—" George began, but Terry stepped on him: "*I'll* tell it."

Terry reached a hand back and waited for George to return the letter. Then he said, "The 13th Floors were together from 1965 to 1968. They did three LPs on the Polydor label and had a couple of singles that sold okay but didn't set the world on fire. If you can find those LPs now, and they're in good shape, you could make a lot of money. The 13th Floors did experimental rock, acid rock I guess you'd call it. They used weird effects, wrote off-the-wall lyrics and they made instruments out of things like gourds and metal pipes. Eric Gherosimini played a Rhodes piano, a Vox organ and a Mellotron, and he was always tinkering with them, taking them apart, rebuilding them, putting them together with parts from other keyboards. But George is right...the band played stoned most of the time. They were heavy acid hitters. It got to where they were hard to work with. They dropped gigs left and right. Their drummer jumped out the window of a Holiday Inn in Bathesda, Maryland—"

"Go, drummer!" said Berke, with a fist pump.

"—and he landed on a woman in the swimming pool and broke her back, and that was about the end of their road. They split and just merged with the giant whirlpool, man. Just got sucked down the drain, and gone." Terry shrugged. "But their stuff started showing up as samples in the '80s. Record collectors shot their LP prices up. A few critics who'd never heard of them got interested, and all of a sudden they were ranked with Procul Harum, Cream, The Doors... bands like those. Only stranger. Somebody found a fragment of a home movie in color of them doing a gig in Oakland in '68, a couple of months before the breakup...and on it, Eric Gherosimini was playing a white keyboard that nobody could identify. Vox? No. Rhodes? Mellotron? No. Too bad the fragment had no sound. But I think it must have been a keyboard he'd built from pieces of other instruments. I'd heard about it, it was kind of a rumor that floated in and out among the LP collectors. The keyboard was never on any record, there's no evidence it was ever used in any gig other than Oakland. But he had a name for it. Or, a name for 'her', I mean. Lady Frankenstein."

"Wait a minute, hold on!" George said. "If this is really the guy, how'd *you* find him?"

"Last year I was talking with one of my piano students at the Episcopal Center. We were just shooting the bull, and we started talking about old bands. This guy's only twenty, but he knows his retro. So he asks if I've ever heard of this band and that band...and I say yeah, yeah, and then he hits me with the fact that his *grandfather* was a roadie out on the West Coast in the mid- to late-sixties, that's how he got his interest. Then he hits me with the fact that Grandpa was not only a roadie, but was selling magic mushrooms, hash, acid and whatever to the bands he was working with. This dude was like...their Doctor Feelgood, man. So Grandson says Grandpa got busted in '67 getting high with a guy named Nate Cleave, that they were good buddies and they still kept in touch." Terry saw by the gas gauge that they'd better start looking for a station, because the needle hovered just above the E.

"Nate Cleave was the bass player for the 13th Floors," Terry continued. "Now he's Dr. Nathan Cleave, a professor of Astronomy at the University of Florida. I didn't find that out until later, but I figured I could start with Grandpa. I pleaded my case with Cleave, told him why I was so interested, and he said he knew where Eric Gherosimini was but the dude was a hermit, he didn't want visitors. Didn't have the Internet, didn't have a cellphone. Finally he said he'd write him for me. Snail mail, to a post office box. It took a few months, but back in May I got that letter. Inviting me to come see him. *Me*." Some emotion got in his throat and tightened it up. "Man, this is like the Holy Grail to a keyboard player. One of the greatest acid rock keyboard players *ever* is inviting me to come see an instrument he created. It's like.. the legend of legends. That's why I've got to go. I've got to go see it for myself."

"Okay, I get that," Nomad said. "But what's so special about it?"

"It sings like a woman's voice," Terry answered. "And more than that. Dr. Cleave says it was built to be like…a mood ring of instruments. Says somehow Gherosimini engineered life into it, that the tones change depending on your mood, on the state of your mind. He says it spooked everybody out, but the few times he heard it played no two people could get the same sound from it. And we're talking early tech, guys. Like primitive, before the big synthesizers that came along. I want to hear it. Just hear it, that's all."

A silence fell. The Five was scheduled for a gig at Staind Glass in Albuquerque on Saturday, the ninth of August. George figured, as he knew Terry already had, that if this visit to Eric Gherosimini was going to happen, it would probably be the following day, Sunday the tenth. And then Ariel broke the silence by saying, "I don't think that's all, Terry. I think that more than anything, you want to play it."

Terry nodded. "Yeah," he replied quietly. "That would be the truth." He saw a Shell gas station over on the right, at the next exit. "Gas time," he said, and took the ramp. As he left the highway, he noted in the sideview mirror that the dark blue pickup that had been behind them for many miles also took the exit. Terry turned again to the right at the end of the offramp; the pickup turned to the left, and drove away across the overpass.

"Get me somethin' to eat," Mike said, stretching forward so his back cracked. He had removed his earbuds and had heard most of Terry's story. "Terry," he said as the Scumbucket pulled up to the pumps under a yellow plastic sunshade, "it's been a long time since '68. I hope Lady Frankenstein don't turn out to be a snaggle-toothed hag that couldn't hum for her supper, bro."

Terry didn't respond; he was thinking of something Dr. Cleave had told him over the telephone, in one of their early conversations: *I'll have to caution you that sometimes the past is best left alone. But...if you really want me to write him...if you really do...I will.*

It was time for bathroom breaks and for getting replenished with soft drinks or coffee, candy bars, popcorn or whatever was available in the station's store. The place was painted yellow with red trim around the windows. Out in front was an ice machine and next to it a gizmo with a hose and nozzle to dispense air for fifty cents. Written on the plate-glass window in white soap-chalk were prices for six-packs of various beer brands, liters of Coke and quarts of motor oil. There was a stack of tires for sale, though there was no garage facility. George had the credit card they used for gas, so he started pumping while the others stretched their legs, used the bathrooms around back or went in to buy something.

The station was being run by a heavy-set Hispanic woman and her teenaged son, who wore a black baseball cap bearing the purple Nine Inch Nails logo. Nomad bought a bottle of water from the cooler and drank half of it down as he walked back and forth alongside the Scumbucket and trailer, from shadow to searing sun and back again. The heat today was a beast, probably a hundred degrees in the shade. Ariel emerged from the station with a bottle of cold water and also an Almond Joy candy bar, which melted in its wrapper before she could eat both pieces. As she came over to join Nomad, she saw a Texas Highway Patrol cruiser slide up to the pumps opposite the Scumbucket, and a trooper got out.

Inside the station, where the air-conditioning rattled as much as the Scumbucket's but worked at least twice as well, Terry bought a Coke and Butterfinger, and behind him Mike was ready with a ginger ale, a half-dozen glazed doughnuts and a bag of beef jerky. At the back, Berke had decided she didn't want coffee and was making a choice among the brands of bottled tea in the cooler.

She had had an interesting night. After her drumkit was safely packed up in the trailer and the Mudstaynes' set had ended, she'd gone off with some friends from Dallas and some friends of friends, two girls who knew Victoria Madden from Victoria's Inkbox tattoo parlor in Austin. They were numero uno fans of the Mudstaynes, and they were going to a party at this other girl's condo up in Highland Park, and later on Gina Fayne was supposed to drop by. So, since Berke was always open to the moment, she had climbed into the back of a cream-colored Mercedes CLK-350 convertible and, jammed in with sisters who smelled of Miss Dior Cherie and Amber Romance, went racing with the moon.

The party was full-on by the time Berke got there, maybe sixty women strong. Little lights twinkled in the indoor trees, candles burned where they wouldn't get knocked over and burn holes in the Persian rugs, Gina Fayne snarled from Bose speakers, the scent of weed swirled around, Cosmos and Appletinis were poured into glasses with Glowstick stirrers, and caps popped from bottles repping a dozen microbreweries. Berke watched a fashion parade of beaters and plaid board shorts dance past. Somebody put a girly gangbang video on the TV, but it was hollered off. Second up was some gay male porn, again shouted off. The next time Berke glanced at the flatscreen, somebody had put on *13 Going on 30*, and it was the part where Jennifer Garner starts doing the "Thriller" dance. That seemed to strike the right chord.

Berke was hit on almost continuously, by one or two or three at a time. She knew it was her cut guns, mostly. And though she was always open to the moment and had no problem instigating things, sometimes she just liked to find a place to sit, drink a beer, and observe. So she got a seat on the brown leather sofa, fashionably distressed, and watched the drama unfold. With sixty—and more coming in every few minutes, it seemed—lesbians in one condo, the alcohol flowing and the grass freely available, lethal drama was inevitable. Berke figured there had to be at least two hundred and twenty-four personalities in the place, and half of those would be derranged or embittered in a way that just saying "*Chi Ku!*"—swallow the bitterness—could not soothe. It might start with a rupture between two dyke-a-likes, or over the noise and music you'd hear somebody shout "I am Switzerland!" which meant war had been declared or a peace treaty broken and the girl in the middle was trying for diplomacy. A liplock might be attempted, an avoidance or pushaway countering it, and then the anger would uncoil like somebody's black snake. Or, on the other hand, a successful public liplock and tongue massage might be for the benefit of an ex, show her she's not the only game, and Berke had seen an ice-bucket dumped over firehouse-red curls due to that particular twist of the stiletto-heel.

It was a very entertaining show, this show after the show.

Berke noted that there were lots of young chicks in here. Like nineteen, twenty, twenty-one years old. Some really beautiful girls. Carried themselves with style and attitude. But everybody was looking for something, and hardly anybody knew what it was. Sex? Sure, but that was just the flesh-deep layer. It was hot flesh, it was freckled and moon-white, it was tanned and smooth, it was ebony and lustrous, it was young and soft and pliable. It was why everyone was here, it called the sisters together, and many would say this was what life was all about, this was the whole picture, this was the reality and essence of sex and domination and at the end of the night a last tender kiss or a caustic comment thrown like a slap. But, Berke thought, hardly anybody here really knows what they're looking for...which puts us right where straights are.

Maybe it was to hang on to something as long as you could. Youth, beauty, coolness...whatever. Maybe it was about power over other people, making them dance to your tune. Striking back at people, for past indignities and pain. Whatever that thing was that you needed to find, sex was just the outer skin of it.

Sitting on this sofa, watching the bodies go past and the games be played out, Berke thought of a card her father had sent her. Not Floyd fucking Fisk, but her real father, Warren Bonnevey. It had been sent to her on the eve of her first gig, when she was seventeen. Its colors were faded, it was spotted with yellow and looked like it dated from the '50s. On the cover were feminine-looking bees with long eyelashes flying around a hive. Where it had said *Congratulations On Your First Job*, the word *Job* had been marked out and *Gig* written in.

And inside, the verse had been:

Congratulations on your new position,
I know it's just what you've been wishin'.
I'd like to say a whole lot more,
But that's what cards like this are for.
Try and try,
Grow and thrive,
You'll be the busiest bee in a honey of a hive.

Only the last line had also been marked out, and written in her father's hand was: *Remember no one here gets out alive. Love, Warren.*

Strange, yes. Unsettling, for sure. But then again, her father was insane.

"Hi, I'm Noble," said the darkly-tanned woman with blonde-streaked hair who held a bottle of Sierra Nevada Pale in one hand and offered the other out toward Berke. She was maybe twenty-eight, twenty-nine. Had very beautiful green eyes, a confident voice. Wore a black tank top, slim-leg jeans and brown, scuffed cowboy boots. Nothing sparkly about her. Good enough.

Berke shook her hand, and when Noble asked if anybody was sitting next to her, Berke said no, she was welcome to park it.

"Hey, lemme ask you somethin'."

Berke turned from the cooler and her perplexing choice of bottled teas. Mike had come up behind her, clutching his ginger ale, box of doughtnuts and bag of beef jerky, which he'd already broken into. "Go," Berke said when Mike hesitated.

Mike glanced toward the door. Berke saw that a state trooper had just entered, a young very clean-cut looking Hispanic guy, and he came straight back to the cooler and got himself a bottle of apple juice. He nodded at them, Mike said, "How's it goin'?" and then the trooper took his drink to the counter and started a conversation in Spanish with the woman, whom he seemed to know pretty well.

"What're you gettin'?" Mike asked her.

"I don't know. Is that what you wanted to ask?" She knew it wasn't; he always approached things sideways, like a crab.

"Ever try the V8 Fusion stuff? The tropical orange is good."

She looked him in the eyes, because he seemed awfully nervous. "What's up?"

Mike watched the trooper leave. Except for the woman and the boy, they were alone in here. "Hey…I was wonderin'…have you thought anymore about that song idea?"

"What song idea?"

"John's idea," Mike explained. "You know, what he said. About everybody writin' words to a new song."

"Oh, *that* bullshit." Berke gave him a thin smile. "The Kumbaya song, right?" She decided to give the tropical orange a try, and reached into the cooler for it.

"Well…yeah, okay…but…you know, maybe it ain't such a bad idea." Mike followed her to the counter. "I know what he's gettin' at, but—"

"Busy work, that's what he's getting at," Berke interrupted, as she put her money up.

"Yeah, but…" Mike glanced out the window, through all the backwards soap-chalk words and prices written there. The fuelling was done. George had paid at the pump and was probably in the bathroom. Terry was getting back into the Scumbucket; it was Nomad's turn to drive. Nomad and Ariel were standing in the shade, a distance apart. The trooper had raised the cruiser's hood and looked like he was pouring water from a red plastic pitcher into the reservoir for his windshield-wash fluid. "Maybe it's a good idea," Mike said. "You know, to keep everybody together."

"We *are* together," she reminded him, and pocketed her change. "How could we be on tour and *not* be together?"

"Together…like…not gettin' pissed at each other. Not blamin' each other for the breakup. Like on the same wavelength or somethin'."

Berke had been about to go out the door, and now she stopped and stared at him very carefully, as if searching his face for a third eye. "Maybe I *am* pissed," she said.

He shrugged. The shrug said maybe he was pissed too, deep down, but repositioning was a fact of the musician's life. Take it or leave it.

"And who says we're breaking up?" Berke went on. "So George and Terry are leaving. We'll replace them and we'll keep going." Before Mike could respond to this wishful thinking, she narrowed her eyes. "*Wavelength?*" she asked. "What are *you* now, a pop psychologist?"

She again started to push through the door, and a little heat rolled in but Mike stopped her by saying, "I've started writin' a song. I don't have a whole lot of it, but...I was kinda hopin' you'd take a look at it, before I showed it to anybody else."

Berke was silent. For a few seconds she couldn't think of anything to say. Her face revealed no emotion—her barrier against the world, and everything that was in it—but her heart was touched. She thought for a quick fleeting instant that she might tear up, but no way she was going to let that happen. The truth was, she loved Mike Davis as much as she could love anyone. They were a team, the backbone, the foundation, the rhythm twins. He gave her a rough elbow to hold onto, and she gave him a punch in the ribs to show she needed it. They had clicked from the very first, if clicking meant the sharing of fart jokes and beer from the same bottle. And now here he stood, asking her to do this for him. It was important to him, she could see that in his eyes. *Before I showed it to anybody else*, he'd said.

But she was who she was, and even this could not be made easy. "You're not falling for this song-writing crap, are you? Tell me you're not that stupid."

He smiled, but the corners of his mouth were tight. "Maybe what I've written is no good...likely it's not...but nobody ever *asked* me to write words before. Yeah, I know it ain't what I do. What I'm *supposed* to do, I mean. But who says I can't give it a try?" He saw the flicker of derision in her faintest of half-smiles and he picked up his tempo like a double thumb slap. "If it was to be okay, and maybe start off a new song everybody could be part of...then I'd be doin' a good thing for the band, right? And...hey...you could maybe add *your* part, too."

"We're not the writers." Berke's voice was low and patient, as if speaking to a small child or a dog. "John, Ariel and Terry are the writers. I have no idea—none, *nada*—about how to write song lyrics. Come on, let's hit it." She went out, with Mike following right after her.

The trooper had lowered his hood, and with a squeegee was washing a layer of dust from his windshield that the malfunctioning fluid reservoir had failed to clear.

"*Please*," Mike said.

Berke had only taken a couple of strides from the door. Once more she stopped, because she realized there was a time to play the game of cruelty and a time not to be afraid to be kind. And this definitely, undeniably, was that.

She faced him. "Okay," she said with a sigh, "show me what you've got."

"In my back pocket. The notebook." Cradling his ginger ale and snacks, Mike turned around so she could get to it. "Listen, really...I appreciate it. But keep it to yourself, okay? For right now, I'm sayin'."

"Right." She was having trouble getting the green notebook out. With jeans that tight, his balls must be either the size of raisins or swollen up like apples. "Jesus! How do you get these damned things *on*?"

"Just pull."

"Hard ass," she commented, and then the notebook came free. The effort of it caused her to stagger away from him a few feet.

Something hit the window between them.

There was a sharp high *crack*, and suddenly a hole appeared next to the soap-chalk dollar sign of the price on a Budweiser sixpack. Berke saw it, and Mike saw it, and they watched as silver creepers spread across the glass from the edges of the hole. Then Mike turned his face toward Berke, to ask her what the hell just happened, and Berke saw a second hole appear as if by magic—fucking wicked magic, she thought in an instant of slow-motion shock—in Mike's forehead about an inch above his left eyebrow. The left temple bulged outward, as if a fist had struck it from within, his mouth remained open in what he'd been meaning to ask Berke, and at his feet the bottle of ginger ale burst like a bomb against the concrete.

Mike was aware of a great pressure in his head, and suddenly he was falling away from Berke, falling away from the Texas heat, falling away from the Scumbucket at the pumps and his friends who waited there, falling backward in time.

It was the damnedest thing. He was falling backward as if on a reverse rollercoaster, a fast trip, a breathtaking trip, and there was nothing he could do but fall. And in this falling, this ultimate repositioning, he possessed a life in rewind. He passed through a whirlwind of bands and gigs and smoky clubs; he went back past a table full of whiskey bottles, back past a jail cell that smelled of swampy August; he passed his daughter Sara, and he thought to try to touch her cheek, or her hair, or her shoulder, but too late, too late, she was gone; he went back past bad-ass cars and sorry-ass cars and pick-me-up trucks, and bass axes of many colors; he passed a white dog and a black dog and the face of Grover McFarland watching him with stern disapproval under a yellow lamp; he fell backward past many faces, many shadows, through a place of darkness and despair, and then in what seemed the last light of summer, the sad light, the light of saying goodbye to all that was, a hand with freckles across the back of it reached out of nowhere and grasped his hand, and a familiar voice said, very clearly: *Gotcha*.

He was dead before he hit the ground.

There was a second or two of silence, while Berke stared at the fine mist of blood that reddened the air where Mike had been standing. She saw that he'd dropped the doughnuts, but he had clamped hard to the beef jerky. His left eye had turned a vicious shade of crimson, and blood had begun to trickle from the hole in his head.

Even as Berke made a noise—a scream, choked sob or anguished moan, whatever it was she couldn't hear it—the young trooper was running toward her, and when he saw the wound in the fallen man's head and the bullet hole in the window he drew his own Sig Saur .357 semi-automatic service pistol. His eyes were wild; he was well-trained, yes, but two bullets from the blue had a way of turning anyone's Sunday afternoon a little chaotic. He shouted, "Everybody on the ground!" as he made a rotating scan with the pistol held in a double-handed firing grip. Nomad took a step forward, and the trooper levelled the pistol at him and yelled, "I said on the ground *now*!" because he didn't know who had a gun or not, where the shots had come from, or really what the shit was happening. So Nomad dropped, Ariel dropped, Berke fell to her knees beside Mike's body and, numbly, grasped his arm to shake him conscious, and alerted by the noise George came out of the bathroom pulling his pants up. "Get down! *Down*!" the trooper commanded behind his weapon. George went down, holding his arms out in a posture of surrender.

"You! Out of the van!" the trooper shouted at Terry, who immediately slithered from it and lay spread-eagled on the pavement. When the woman who ran the station emerged, with the boy behind her, the trooper told her in Spanish to get back inside, and she was trying to tell him that a piece of flying glass had hit Carlos and he was bleeding from the chin. Then she saw the body on the concrete and she backed up and the boy with the gashed chin gawked and started taking pictures with a cellphone camera.

"Get down! Get down! Get down!" the trooper hollered, his voice ragged, as he advanced on Berke with his pistol aimed and ready.

She was shivering. There were tears in her eyes, and she couldn't seem to draw a whole breath. But it occurred to her, in a blank cold place beyond the horror, that she ought to tell him disco was dead.

And so too, she realized, was her buddy, her rhythm twin, her rough elbow to cling to.

She lay down beside him, on the hot pavement, and suddenly she was aware of a breakage within herself, a rupture, a failure of a weak seam that had never before known such pressure. She began to weep quietly at first, and then began to openly and brokenly sob as she had not cried since she was a girl too young to keep a cold lid on her cup of pain.

Her friend was dead, and dead too was The Five.

Dead, dead, deader than dead.

EIGHT.

George stared at the black telephone. Your basic landline, no nonsense here.

"Nine to get out?" he asked, and the chunky detective, the guy who was always wearing the cowboy hat, nodded. The second detective, a foxy Hispanic woman in her mid-thirties with manicured red fingernails and eyes like pools of bittersweet chocolate, was watching him from her chair across the table.

George punched the nine, got the outside line and then dialed the rest of the number. He made a note of the time from the clock on the white plaster wall. They didn't want him to use his cellphone. They were going to sit in here and listen, and George figured the call was going to be recorded. The detectives were smalltown, but there was nothing soft or lax about them; they were interested in all the details, even what George was about to say. They made him as nervous as hell, and he hadn't even *done* anything.

The number rang in Austin. On the third ring, Ash's machine answered and left the usual message: *I can't pick up right now, but after the tone leave a yadda yadda yadda*. George had realized before that Ash had a little bit of a lisp, but it was very pronounced on the machine.

"Ash, it's George," he said when the tone sounded. "If you're there, pick up." He waited a couple of seconds. "I mean it, man. Really. Pick up like right now."

There was a click and Ash was there. A problem? Ash wanted to know.

"Listen," George said. And something about his voice made Ash repeat the question, only now in his firmest big boy agent inflection. "Mike Davis..." How to say this? Just the truth and nothing but. "Mike Davis has been shot," George went on. "He's been killed. He's dead." Like it had to be repeated. There was utter silence from Austin. "It happened about a hour and a half ago, a few miles east of Sweetwater. We're at the police station right now. In Sweetwater. Wait, wait, wait," George said, when Ash started asking questions so fast the clipped Indian accent was getting in the way. "Let me tell you. We were at a gas station. Mike and Berke were talking out front and all of a sudden...a bullet got him in the head." God, that sounded weird! Like something from any number of action flicks, but when it was real it was stomach-churning. George had already taken his turn at puking in the bathroom. "They say he was probably dead...like... right then." Ash started throwing more questions at him, rapid-fire, and the truth was that George had always had difficulty understanding him and now everything sounded like a freaking mashup of English and Hindi.

"About an hour and a half ago," George said again, because he caught that question. "Yeah, yeah...everybody else is okay. I mean... we're mindfucked, but we're okay." He paused, trying to grasp what Ash was asking. "No, they didn't catch anybody. They think..." He looked across the table at the woman. "Can I tell him?"

She nodded.

"They think maybe it was an accident. They don't know exactly yet where the bullets came from, but they're thinking it was from some woods across the highway. Yeah, I said *bullets*. There were two shots. They think maybe somebody was in there shooting a rifle, just dicking around." The detectives had told George that the little cluster of thorny scrub-brush and trees, maybe sixty yards wide on the other side of a cinderblock building where truck engines were repaired, drew shooters after what they called 'varmints'. There were rats, gophers and snakes in that mess, and kids with rifles shot it up. The repair shop had been closed, so nobody had seen or heard anything, and likewise from a few ramshackle old houses over there. "No, right now they have no idea who it was," George said.

The deal was, though George felt no need to say this, the detectives thought it might be an accident just from the distance involved.

The repair shop was two hundred yards on the other side of I-20 and the varmint woods was another hundred and fifty yards, at least. So it looked like an errant, careless couple of shots—high-velocity, for sure, but that wasn't so unusual, they said—that had carried right across the highway.

"They'll know more later," George said. "They've got cops swarming all over the place." When the Scumbucket had pulled away from the pumps, following the car the two detectives were in, the gas station had been secured with the yellow crime scene tape and it looked like a parking lot for police cars and paramedic vehicles. A slim yellow metal tube had been pushed through the hole in the window to show the angle of entry. What looked like a surveyor's tripod with a monocular attached had been set up in line with the yellow tube, aimed at the varmint woods across I-20. Over there were more police cars. The cops were prying the first bullet out of the station's rear wall. George assumed they would also remove the second bullet from Mike's brain, but when the Scumbucket had pulled out The Five—ex-Five—had left their bass player under a sheet on the pavement. George had been glad to be leaving, because he'd seen a body bag being taken out of the back of a white truck and the way Berke was so torn up...it was for the best they were getting out.

"The thing is," George went on, "they want to notify the next-of-kin. No, they want to do it from here. Right. So...I don't have that information. I know his parents still live in Bogalusa, but...yeah, right. Would you do that?" He put his hand over the mouthpiece and said to the detectives, "He's looking it up on his laptop."

They waited.

"You guys were on the way to El Paso," the woman said, without expression. It had been explained to her, the whole story, and she'd already checked their website, but around the station she was called 'the Digger', with those long red spade-shaped nails. The title was on her coffee cup. She could not stop until she got to the bottom. They were a team: Lucky Luke and the Digger, known to the general public as detectives Luke Halprey and Ramona Rios.

"Yeah," George answered.

"Going straight through, then," Lucky Luke said, chewing on a toothpick.

"That's right."

"Mr. Emerson, I have to ask you...do any of you owe money to anyone here? And by 'anyone', I mean a person who might feel they're not going to be repaid and may be...um...a little vindictive about it?" asked the Digger.

"No. Well...I don't. Owe anybody money," he clarified. "What're you saying? That this was a '*hit*'? Over money? I thought you said it was an accident."

It was Luke's turn to clarify. "*Might* be an accident, that's what was said."

"How about drugs?" The Digger's arched black eyebrows went up. "Anybody gotten on the wrong side of a dealer?"

"No! Hell, no! We've never *played* this area before. How would a shooter even know we were *here*?"

"That would my next question," said the lucky one. "Did you stop at that station because maybe you had a meeting planned with somebody?"

"Think about that before you answer, Mr. Emerson," the Digger cautioned.

"*No*. I mean...we didn't have any meeting planned. Wait a minute...go ahead," George told Ash, who gave him the number in Bogalusa. He relayed the number to the detectives, and Luke wrote it down on a notepad that advertised Big Boys Barbecue. Then came the moment that George had known was coming and that had to be done. "I guess that's it," he said, and when Ash didn't respond George spoke with what felt like a stone sitting in his gut, "We'll work out how to get Mike back, and then we'll come on in."

"We'd like you to stay here tonight," the Digger told him. "Let us call around, just to check some things."

"Stay *here*?" George asked, stricken by the thought of sleeping in a police station.

"A motel," Luke supplied. "Get a good night's rest."

"Oh. Okay." George turned his attention back to the matter at hand. "They want us to stay here tonight. And listen...you might as well start making the calls." Ash said he would, and that he was so sorry for this senseless tragedy and there would never be another bass player like Mike Davis, and for George to tell everyone else how sorry he felt. "One more thing," George said. "A woman from the local paper was here and asked us some questions. She said she wouldn't file the story until the cops gave her the go-ahead. I just wanted you to know."

Ash thanked him for that, then said he would immediately call Roger Chester.

"Are we done here?" George asked, and Luke told him the band members could follow them over to the Lariat Motel on East Broadway, get them checked in, and that there was a Subway nearby where they could eat dinner. Not said, but what George certainly felt, was that the detectives wanted to keep a rope around them and that the questions were far from finished.

He had his own questions. Who on this God's earth would have wanted to kill Mike Davis? And in *Sweetwater*? No, it had to have been an accident. A kid in the varmint woods. Had to be.

< >

In another room, a TV was tuned to the Weather Channel. The four people who sat on the orange plastic chairs in this room pretended to be watching it. Nomad had always thought that the Weather Channel was a kind of Zen; it emptied your head with its colorful images and soothed your mind with the illusion of control. Right now they needed all the Zen they could get.

A policeman came through to ask something of Lucky Luke and the Digger. Berke, who sat apart from the others and was wearing Nomad's sunglasses on her pallid face, sat up straight and called out in a strident voice, "Did you find it yet?"

The policeman, unnerved, looked to the detectives for help. The Digger said calmly, "We'll let you know when we find it. I promise."

Berke settled back in her chair. Her lips tightened. A weather map sparkling with sun symbols reflected in her glasses.

Nomad glanced quickly at Ariel, who sat a few chairs away with Terry on her other side. She was hollow-eyed and wan, and she occasionally made a catching sound in her throat as if awakening with a start from a very bad dream. Terry stared alternately at the television and at the floor, his eyes heavy-lidded behind his specs.

"We're going to a motel," the Little Genius announced. "Stay there tonight."

"You take them over," the Digger said to her partner, in a quiet voice. She took the Big Boys Barbecue pad with the phone number on it. "I'll do this one."

Nomad didn't think he could stand up. To an outsider, he might have appeared the most composed of the shattered group. He might have seemed the least in shock, the most able to bear this tragedy and to rebound the fastest from it. But the outsider would have been criminally incorrect.

In the past ninety minutes, he had relived his own personal nightmare a hundred times over.

< >

Johnny, *there's no roadmap.*

But.

It had been different that night. That August 10th, 1991. A Saturday, outside the Shenanigans Club in Louisville. Nearing midnight, and in a parking lot bathed in blue and green neon Dean Charles and the Roadmen starting to pack up the van after opening for the Street Preachers. John was a boy, a son, a fan. Dad was the bomb, the Killer. Played a gold-colored Strat that could cut through an arrangement like a razor through a hamhock. And *sing*...that man could wail. He was a bottle full of lightning. Up there on stage, front-and-center in the godly glow, all that power coming off him, all that energy and life. He was one of a kind.

And then out in that parking lot, when they saw the two flat tires on the van, the old blue cat sitting crooked on her paws, and somebody said, "Oh, shit," and somebody else growled, "Motherfucker!" because John was one of them, he had heard it all, he was a veteran of the road even at twelve years old.

Dean had looked at his son and shrugged and grinned in that way he had of saying nothing in this world was such a big deal that it tugged you out of shape, you could always find your way back to the center of the cool world the musician lived in, and he said as he always did in such situations, "Johnny, there's no roadmap." Then he'd paused just a second or two, maybe thinking it over for the first time, and he'd said to his son with that slip-sided smile, "*But...*"

"I'm gonna end it now," said the man who had just stepped out from his crouch behind a parked car, and Dean had regarded him only with mild surprise, as if expecting a visitor who was late in coming.

< >

John had been standing next to his father when the pistol in the man's hand spoke. It had shouted into his father's left ear, and John remembered how his father had winced at the loud noise, because his father had always cautioned John to guard his hearing, he only had one set of ears.

The pistol had gone off twice more as Dean Charles was falling, a whiff of gunpowder and a smell of blood in John's nostrils, the boy falling back in shock, falling as his father fell, one to be called dead four hours later in the hospital and the other left behind to relive the moment over and over again.

"I have to find it," Berke said, but to whom she was speaking was unclear. She hadn't moved from her chair.

"It'll turn up." George stood over her. "Come on, it's time to go."

Nomad counted slowly to three, and then he got to his feet. As he followed the others out of the police station into the solid heat of late afternoon, he thought how ridiculous this situation was. How utterly fucking ridiculous. Two days ago he'd been burdened with the fact that The Five would end their last tour in Austin on the 16th of August—the Month of Death, as far as he was concerned—and then it would be back to putting another band together, another name, another vibe, another set of personalities—and here he was, here *they* were, on the real last day come way too soon. And Mike dead. *Dead.* He had experience with sudden death, yeah, but at least he'd found out later that his father, one of the wiliest tomcatters to ever sneak in a housewife's back door, was responsible for a Louisville beauty-shop operator divorcing an out-of-work husband who owned ten guns. It would have made a farce, a black comedy directed by the Coen brothers starring George Clooney, but with blue contacts, and to complete the tragedy the man who had shot Dean Charles had walked about five yards away and shot himself under the chin, leaving behind two more children who would always feel an empty hole at their birthday parties. So as terrible as that was, it had made sense.

But *this*...if he believed in God, which he did not, he would have heard the sound of cruel cosmic laughter, funny to no one else. Now he had to stop seeing Mike fall down over and over again in his mind, and he had to stop hearing Berke's strangled scream or he was going to lose it right here on the Sweetwater street.

George took the wheel and followed the detective's car. Berke sat way in back, by herself. The sunglasses stayed on. Nobody could look at anybody else. Nomad stared blankly ahead and silently chewed on his insides.

On the drive from the gas station into town, Berke had suddenly come out of her state of coma and cried out, "The notebook! I left the notebook!"

"Hold on!" George had said. He was already about to jump out of his skin, and this outburst had nearly started the rip along his spine. "*What* notebook?"

"Oh Jesus, oh Christ! I dropped it! I had it in my hand, I must've dropped it!" Berke sounded close to hysteria, which put everybody else nearer the edge. "Did you see it?" she asked Ariel, who shook her head. "We've got to go back!" she told George. "Turn around, we've got to *go back*!" The last two words had been almost a shriek.

"Take it easy!" Nomad had said. "We can't go back right now!" They were following the two detectives, who might not have understood or appreciated the Scumbucket pulling off and turning around.

"You shut up!" Berke spat at him, her eyes enraged. "You fucking shut up!"

"Hey, hey, hey!" Ariel had turned around and grasped one of Berke's hands, and Terry was trying to console her as best he could, but Berke wasn't finished. She tried to jerk her hand away from Ariel's, nearly spraining Ariel's wrist, and she snarled, "Fuck you! Fuck you!" but Ariel kept hold of her and kept calmly repeating, "Settle down, come on, settle down," until some of the fight-against-the-world went out of Berke. When it went it went hard. Berke's shoulders trembled, she lowered her head so no one could see her face, and she began to weep—almost silently, but not silently enough. Through it all, Ariel did not let her go.

Nomad and George had exchanged quick glances. Berke Bonnevey, who made an art of detachment, was caught in the open with nothing to hide behind. No flippant remarks, no casual scorn, no big bitchin' set of Ludwigs. Just her, torn open. Witnessing it was almost as much of a shock as the shooting had been.

In another moment Berke's crying seemed to stop, because she sniffled and ran her free hand across her eyes. Nomad had said, "Here," and that's how she got his sunglasses.

At the police station, the story had emerged about the green notebook, which Nomad had remembered was on the picnic table next to Mike. "Something he wanted me to read," Berke explained. "It was important to him."

A call had been made to the scene, but Luke—maybe explaining the origin of his luck—reported back, "No dice. It's not there." Then, sensing Berke's slow and painful retreat into the sanctity of herself, he'd offered, "It'll turn up, though. When everything gets catalogued."

Nomad had taken that to mean it might have been thrown in with Mike's box of doughnuts and bag of blood-spattered beef jerky on the meat wagon, but he kept his mouth shut.

The Lariat Motel on East Broadway was small but clean, with a swimming pool behind a white fence and a sign that said *Guests Only, Swim At Your Own Risk*. The place had maybe a dozen rooms, all on one level. It was built to resemble a ranch house, with different brands burned into every door. George checked them in, got two rooms adjoining with free cable and complimentary Cattleman's breakfast of biscuits and jelly with coffee or orange juice in the morning. Luke waited for them to take their bags in. Before he left he said he'd check back with them around ten o'clock that night.

They ate at the Subway, which was in a stripmall about half a mile away. Picked at their food, really, but they knew they had to get something down. Berke kept the sunglasses on, even past the point where the sun began to set. She ate half a small bag of chips. No one talked very much; it seemed somehow disrepectful to talk about any subject but Mike, and that subject could not be touched.

Finally, when everyone had eaten as much as they could and the time had come to go back to the Lariat for a night of quiet Hell and mindnumbing cable fare, Terry said, "John..."

...there's no roadmap...

But no, Terry did not say that, as Nomad might have heard a ghost speak from a corner of the Subway where the sun had already left town.

Terry said, "What're you going to do?"

"Going to do? *When*? Like in the next minute? Five minutes? A fucking *hour* from now?" He felt the heat rising in his face, and he saw Terry's eyes widen behind the glasses and Terry shrank back a little from the table because the dynamite's fuse had been lit. "Is that what you mean?"

"No, I just mean—"

"Then *what* do you fucking mean?"

"Sir!" said the middle-aged black man behind the counter. "Please watch the profanity." He motioned toward a young couple with a little girl and an infant at another booth. Three sets of eyes were on Nomad.

"Oh. I'm sorry," Nomad said, to both the counterman and the other customers. The heat of anger became a blush of shame. He took a deep breath to get himself under control, and then he levelled his gaze at Terry again. "I'll tell you what I'm going to do," he answered. "I'm going back to Austin tomorrow, and I'm going to go home and sleep for a couple of days. Then when I can think straight I'm going to call Ariel and Berke and see if they're still in. If they are...and they don't need to tell me yea or nay right now...I'm going to work with Ash to find replacements for you and for Mike. And for *you*," he said to George, who sat impassively. George had a little dab of mustard on his lower lip. "Then we'll go from there, with whoever works out. We'll come up with a new name, we'll start rehearsing, and coming up with some new material. If Ariel and Berke want to be in, fine. If not, *fine*. But I'm going to keep on doing what I *do*. So that's my plan. What's yours?"

Terry hesitated. He felt himself falter. He liked peace, liked for everybody to get along. He liked to be *liked*. He knew that if he came across as calm and measured, it was because nine times out of ten he was stealthily backing away from confrontation. It had been one of the hardest things ever to tell them he was leaving the band. How many weeks had it taken to get those words out of his mouth? And he might have gone many weeks more, if George hadn't opened up first. One thing he truly feared, and he'd feared it since being in the Venomaires, was stepping into John Charles's rage radar, of being the target of the anger he'd seen erupt way too many times. There had been some pretty hideous scenes between John and Kevin

Keeler, before Kevin had suffered his mental breakdown on stage in Atlanta. But now Terry, who had thought Mike was one of the best bass players he'd ever heard and not only that but a real friend whom he would mourn in his own way, alone with one of his keyboards, decided that John was not going to blow up here in the Subway. There was no point to it; what was done was done, and even John Charles knew he couldn't roll back time before some kid with a rifle had fired two stupid bullets.

"When we get back," Terry replied, "I'm going to pack up my car and drive to Albuquerque. I'm going to visit Eric Gherosimini. After that, I'm driving home and take the loan from my dad. To start my business."

Nomad took the last drink of his Coke. What could he say to that? It was a plan. He realized that Berke would probably be wanting to get to San Diego, to open those boxes her stepfather had left her. Another plan. The Little Genius had a plan too, the bastard. Nomad caught Ariel's gaze from where she sat with George at the next table.

She said, "I'm still with you."

Something about that, he didn't know what it was, almost made him cry.

When they got back to the motel, twilight had deepened enough so the yellow neon sign out front was in its full glory. It was the kind rapidly disappearing from the landscape, an honest-to-God 1950s-style animated display of a smiling cowboy twirling a lariat over his head and then, in the next frame or step or whatever it was called in the neon sign lingo, twirling it around his boots. Ariel said she thought it should be in a book of photographs about motel signs, and Terry said maybe it already was, they should ask the manager. Yellow bulbs glowed in glass squares above every door. The Five had stayed in a lot of ratholes, a lot of dirty little motels where dawn brought forth a scurrying of disheveled women and sleepy-looking men to their separate vehicles of escape, but this place was all right. Nomad couldn't help but wonder what Mike would've said about the lariat-twirling cowpoke. *Looks like he's aimin' to rope hisself a big ol' dick, bro.*

Ariel and Berke took a room together. In the next room, a coin was flipped for the first elimination, and then the second coin flip pitting Nomad and George for the remaining bed earned George the small rollaway. But within a few minutes the door that connected the rooms was open and Ariel and Berke came in to watch HBO. Berke had removed the sunglasses; she looked like a swollen-eyed wreck, but she made a comment about George having to sleep on a baby bed that said she was coming back.

They weren't in there more than half-an-hour, watching TV sprawled on chairs and beds like the members of any family on a road trip, when they heard a knock at the door. Not *their* door, it seemed, but the door to Berke and Ariel's room, which was closer to the office. Ariel got up from her chair, drew aside the tan-colored curtain and peered through the blinds out the window.

"It's a guy," she announced. "I think…it's the guy from today. The *trooper*."

George opened their door. "Hi, can I help you?"

The trooper no longer looked so official, or so threatening. He was wearing dark brown trousers with freshly-pressed creases. Tucked neatly into the pants was a white polo shirt bearing what George recognized as the flag-and-eagle logo of the Penney's American Living brand, since he owned a few of those himself. A brown leather belt and brown lace-up shoes completed the wardrobe. The young man's combed hair was as shiny as fresh tar. No razor, not even the ones with four freaking blades, had ever scraped a chin closer. He looked like a nervous highschool kid but he must have been in his mid-twenties, or so George supposed.

"Um," was the trooper's first utterance, which did not bode well. Then: "Is the girl here? The black-haired girl?"

George almost said *Who?* But then he looked over his shoulder at Berke, who was the only female presence in the room with black hair, but to call her a *girl* was so very, very wrong. Just not feelin' it. He said, "I think he wants to see *you*."

"Me?" Berke stood up. Nomad was not the only one to note that she took a quick glance at herself in the mirror over the dresser as she passed it, and winced a little at what she saw.

"Hello," said the young man, when she peered out. If her eyes were swollen, her face blotchy and she looked like a five-car pileup, which she knew she did, his boyish smile didn't show he noticed or cared. "Um…how're you doin'?"

"Better."

"Good, good," he said. "I wanted to tell you...tell *all* of you," he prompted, and she moved away from the door and opened it wider so everyone could see him all neat and scrubbed in the yellow bulb's light, "that I apologize for losin' my cool out there. Wavin' my gun around and hollerin' at you. Not my best day."

"Hey, not ours either," George answered. "But you just did what you had to, we know that."

"Yeah." He looked down at the ground and moved some invisible grit with the toe of a shined shoe. "I'm supposed to keep things under *control*. Supposed to make sure nobody's got any guns I can't see. You know, you train for the worst...but when it happens, it's so fast."

"Did they find out yet who did it?" Terry asked.

"No sir, but they're still workin'. They're out in the woods right now, goin' through it with searchlights." His eyes examined Berke's face again and then he said into the room, speaking to all of them, "One thing I'll say...and maybe I shouldn't say it, but maybe I owe you...is that they haven't found the brass yet."

"The *brass*? You mean the shells?" George asked. His interest in *Cops* had just paid off.

"Yes sir, the ejected casings. There should be two. They've found some old ones, but not what they're lookin' for."

"So," Nomad spoke up, "what does that mean? They haven't found the right place?"

"They're where they calculated the shots came from, but..." The young man shrugged, indicating that was as far as he could go. He once more turned his attention to Berke. "Um...I know this is kind of a bad time...but...I was wonderin'...just maybe...if you'd want to go down the street and get a beer. The place isn't too far, I'd get you back in an hour, or...whenever you say. Just thought you might like to talk. But I'm sayin'...I know it's a bad time, I was just wonderin'."

The others in the room were riveted by this display of bravery. The trooper had come to ask Berke out on a *date*. At least a semi kind of date, of the beer-and-talk-in-the-dark-bar variety.

There seemed to be a common stillness of breath.

Oh, what tricks time could play. What a slow river the seconds could become, flowing down to the sandy sea.

At last Berke said, very firmly, "Thank you, but no."

"Okay, then." The trooper nodded, and maybe there was a shadow of disappointment on his close-shaved face but no harm was done. "I found this on the pavement," he said, and lifted his right hand from his side in what might have otherwise been a gesture to offer a bouquet of flowers or a box of candy. "I think it's yours?"

She looked at the green notebook, there in his hand.

"I got a radio call before I could give it to you," he explained. "I probably was supposed to hand it over to the detectives, but I looked through it and it's just your recipes."

"My recipes?"

"Yeah. It *is* yours, right?"

"Yes," she said, and accepted it. She realized that if he hadn't wanted a date with her, the notebook might have ended up in a trashcan. "Thanks, I thought I'd lost it." She opened it, and on the first page was a handwritten recipe for Sunshine Lemon Cookies. A woman's hand, certainly not Mike's. The next page had the instructions and ingredients for White Chicken Chili.

What a dumb-ass, Berke thought. Mike had taken the notebook from the kitchen of the house they'd stayed in last night.

"Some of these...have been handed down in my family," Berke said, figuring the trooper needed a stroke or two. "I guess I took it out to write something, I can't remember." She turned the pages. *Chickpea and Red Lentil Stew...Cornflake-Crusted Baked Chicken... Amy's Favorite Coconut Cake*. "Lot of love in here," Berke told him. "Thanks again."

"I'll head on," he said. "Sorry about your friend, and I hope I've helped a little bit."

"You have." She offered him a faint smile; she was thinking what must have sparked in his mind: *I've got to try for any female who can cook this stuff up*.

He said goodnight, Berke closed the door and locked it, and as she turned toward the others she thought to say to Mike, *News to the Street! I'm a lesbian!*

But Mike wasn't there.

"What's in the book?" Ariel asked.

"Recipes, just like he said." Berke began to flip through the pages. Chicken dishes, stews, soups and cakes flashed past. It was only a few pages from the back that she found where Mike had been writing.

"Here," she said, and she read it to herself. *I've started writin' a song*, Mike had told her. "The Kumbaya song," Berke announced. "Looks like he started it." She held it out for them to see.

The page was a mess. Things written and scratched out. Written and scratched out again. *Girl at the well* written there, crookedly. *Welcome* written there. *Welcome* written once more. The third time it became a doodle, with tiny eyes in the 'o' and a devil's tail on the last 'e'. The demon of creativity, hard at work in Mike's mind; Nomad, Ariel and Terry knew that devil, very well. Another line written down and scratched out, the word *Shyte!!* scrawled beside it.

Then there was a line complete and unmarred: *Welcome to the world, and everything that's in it.*

On the next page, there were two more attempts, two more scratch-outs and then: *Write a song about it, just keep it under four minutes.*

"That's it?" George asked, peering over Terry's shoulder.

"*Girl at the well*," Terry read, and frowned. "Is that supposed to be a title?" He looked up at Berke. "What was he doing, writing a song about that *girl*?"

"I don't know what he was doing. All I know is, before he..." Go on, she told herself. It's done. "Before he got shot, he said he was writing...this, whatever it is. You know. The..." *Kumbaya song* didn't sound right anymore. It was not respectful to Mike. "The communal song that John wanted everybody to write. The one I said was busy-work shit." Berke started to close the notebook, but Nomad held out his hand for it and she gave it to him.

Nomad read it again, first and second pages. Ariel slid over, sitting on the end of the bed next to him. They read it together. He was aware of the warmth of her cheek, nearly touching his own. He smelled her, the soft honeysuckle aroma. Maybe he had walked across a field sometime in his life where honeysuckles grew in wild and tangled profusion, and maybe he had paused there to take stock of where he was going. Her cheek was very close to his own. They were about to share a cheek-kiss. And then Nomad pulled away a few inches, looked at her and asked, "Do anything for you?" The words, he meant.

She also pulled away an equal distance, and kept her eyes on the tortured paper. One corner of her mouth pressed tight, as it did when she was thinking. "I don't know where he was going with it. But maybe…we could do *something*."

"Guys." George's was the somber voice of reality. "We're going home in the morning. Tour cancelled. All done."

Berke flared up. "Maybe they want to write a song for his *service*. Maybe we should have a last show, for *him*. A benefit. For his daughter, at least."

"We could do that," Ariel said. Then, to George, "Couldn't we?"

"Absolutely," he answered. "I'll run that by Ash first thing."

Nomad returned the notebook to Berke. *Welcome*, Mike had said last night in the Dallas backyard. *Good place to start*. Nomad didn't see any destination in those words, but Ariel and Terry might take them somewhere. Right now, all he wanted to do was go home to his own futon on the floor, curl up and leave the world until he either had to eat or had to…

It was going to be a bad night, in this motel with the lariat-twirling cowboy outside. They would probably all wind up in one room, piled around like ferrets in a cage, breathing and jumping and gasping in their ferret-like slumber. If anyone could sleep.

He did, well after midnight. Among his last thoughts before he went under was that somehow—for some reason—that girl at the well had gotten into Mike's mind. Had planted a seed in it. Just as she'd been trying to get into his own. Making him believe he had a fucking brain tumor, when he didn't let her in.

Oh no, he vowed. *Not me.*

Only he wasn't quite sure what he was vowing against. And, really, he didn't want to know. Whatever it was, he was too small for it.

About two o'clock, Ariel got up from her hour or so of sleep, put on her shoes, quietly unlocked the door, went outside and closed the door behind her. The neon sign had been turned off. East Broadway was silent, and stars covered the sky in a breathtaking panorama. By the yellow bulbs she saw that several more guests had checked in: along with the Scumbucket and trailer there was a white SUV, a silver or light gray Subaru and a black or dark blue pickup truck. The SUV had a New Mexico tag, the other two were from Texas. She noted on the pickup's rear bumper a metallic sticker that said *Semper Fi*. She wanted to walk, to breathe the night air, to feel the soft breeze on her cheek like a lover's touch. She started toward the swimming pool, and as she neared it she heard the quiet sound of movement in water.

Someone was in there, alone in the dark. Swimming back and forth, it sounded like. Not kicking, just pulling the water past them in a slow crawl. It seemed to her like a lonely thing, to be swimming back and forth in dark water under the canopy of night. She hesitated for a moment, listening, and then she decided to wander over that way, maybe to speak or maybe not, because she knew very, terribly well what it was like to be lonely.

THREE

BALLAD OF THE GREEK POTATOES

NINE.

When the sun was an hour old Berke was lacing up her running shoes, the black New Balances that had already taken her more than two hundred miles. Her oufit was spartan, meant to get sweaty. She tugged a black sweatband over the obstacle of her hair and got it positioned on her forehead. The streamers of sun coming between the blinds already carried a bite. This was going to be the hottest day yet, in a long summer of hot days.

The last time someone had died in her life, someone she'd cared about deeply, she'd gotten up from her bed the following morning, laced her shoes and gritted her teeth and gone out for a six-mile run. She didn't know if she could do that today, but she was going to try. Everyone else was still asleep. She couldn't believe that Mike wasn't here this morning, stretched out on his back with his hands behind his head because he hated the feel of a pillow. She'd never asked him why, thinking it must've had something to do with the number of hicktown jails he'd been hosted in, and lice or ticks or bedbugs or something like that. She couldn't believe she would never hear the rusty rumble of his voice again, and maybe that was the worst thing. He was really gone. He really, really was.

It looked to her as if she hadn't been the only one whose night was tortured. The guys had wound themselves up in their sheets, and George had nearly worked himself off the baby bed. And Ariel? Ariel wasn't in either room, or in either bathroom. She must've gone out walking, before the sun had even started to come up. Wherever she was, she wasn't here.

Okay, Berke said to herself. *Let's get to it.*

Out in the parking lot, she saw the three new arrivals: white SUV, silver Subaru, dark blue pickup. The air was still, and smelled of hot metal. There were a few cars on East Broadway, but only a few. Monday morning here wasn't quite like Austin. She stopped next to the U-Haul trailer for about five minutes to do a few stretches—Hang Tens, Lunges and Flamingoes, holding each one for thirty seconds—and noted the movement of a windowblind, in the room the pickup truck was parked in front of. Somebody else was an early riser, or else they wanted to be first up for the Cattleman's breakfast. She decided to go to her left and follow East Broadway toward the northeast. She would walk a little while first, work her pace up to running speed, and so she passed by the swimming pool beyond the white fence, and there was Ariel.

Ariel was lying beside the pool on a blue lounge chair. She was on her right side, facing away from Berke. Her knees were bent, her legs curled up beneath her. One shoe was on, the other lay on the cement beside the chair. Berke thought that Ariel's neck was going to be stiff today, the way her head was turned and her shoulders hunched up. That couldn't be comfortable. She thought briefly of going over and waking Ariel up, but she decided no, she wouldn't; Ariel might have had a tough time getting to sleep, and maybe had found some peace out here alone in the dark. So Berke walked on, picking up her pace, faster and faster. About two hundred yards along the street she started her run, heading away from the Lariat at a steady clip.

The detective with the cowboy hat had called last night at ten o'clock sharp. George had spoken to him. Any word on who did it? *They can't say much right now*, George had reported back. *But they're going to come talk to us in the morning*. And that had been the extent of it.

Berke ran on, her breathing measured, everything easy. The red fireball was sitting two hands above the horizon, aimed between her jawline and her right shoulder. She passed the usual sights of any small town, in any American state: small businesses, parking lots, churches and strip malls. She passed the Subway they'd eaten at last night, and a half mile further on there was a Dairy Queen which she wished she'd known about because she did like ice cream. Then she came upon an area of small houses, and past that some car lots and places where cars and trucks were serviced, a litter of car hulks and tires and the like. In this area was where a man in a passing white pickup truck shouted, "*Hey, muchacha caliente*!" but she kept her head down and her pace unchanged. She *was* hot, that was true enough; she was sweating pretty good now, the sun searing her right side. A few cars and trucks passed by in both directions, and somebody else honked at her but she looked neither right nor left. She stared only at the cracked brown concrete one stride ahead, and that was how you got through any demanding run.

She was thinking of Mike, and how senseless it had been, and how much she was going to miss him. It was still unbelieveable to her, something from someone else's bad dream. But so too had been the death of her running and rock-climbing bud, Melissa Cavanaugh, six years ago when Berke was living in Seattle and playing with the short-lived band Time Keeps Secrets. She had met Melissa at a coffee shop, a friend of a friend, and they'd immediately hit it off. Melissa had been a basketball player in college way down in Georgia, had been all-everything, an A-student, track star, student newspaper reporter, environmental activist, volunteer at a homeless shelter, lover of stray dogs and Kona coffee and The Clash's *Sandinista*. So why was it that Melissa Cavanaugh, twenty-two years old and with a great future ahead of her in graphic design in the Emerald City, had tied a cord around a support in her closet of stylish but tasteful clothes and with the other end of the cord around her neck strangled herself to death on a Sunday evening?

There had been no sex between them, no kissing, no hand-holding. They didn't talk about being gay, because in fact Berke was never sure Melissa *was* gay. She dated guys, and talked about how awful some of them were, and how some were really hot and fun but somehow...somehow...they weren't what she was searching for. Berke figured that if Melissa was gay, she would find her own way to it, eventually. But they were good friends, and they enjoyed being together. *My folks are so conservative*, Melissa had said. *And I've never disappointed them. I'd die before I'd disappoint them, they're looking for me to be perfect at whatever I do, only perfection for our family, you can go back generations and see our accomplishments, our lists of awards and honors. You can't disappoint a family of people who throw themselves at challenges and always win. You know?*

Yes, Berke had said. *I do.*

I know you're not very religious, but I thank God we met, Melissa had confided. *We can talk about anything.*

Except for that thing. The thing that was slowly killing her, and making her take notes in her mind of the strengths of different cords, and the perfect length she would need. Then when the time was perfect, and her mind perfectly fixed on this particular challenge, she had left this world because something in her could not abide the truth of her own heart, and she was too much the good girl to ever disappoint her family.

Berke had had no clue. Their last phone conversation, on that Saturday, had been about where they were going to eat pizza after they saw *Rabbit-Proof Fence* on Tuesday, their movie night. Melissa had said she was thinking about going down to Macon and spending a few days with her family. But everything had been bright, light, upbeat. Everything had been about the future, that blue-skyed place where all dreams come true and anybody can be who they want to be because This Is America. Melissa's roommate had found the body, on Monday afternoon. There had been no note, no blame, no incrimination: just a silence, to endure the generations.

The sun was hotter. Berke quickly looked around to get her bearings. She was in an area of dry brown fields, rusted barbed wire fences, and distant farmhouses that appeared abandoned. A few scraggly trees reached up from the miserable earth. It was time to turn around and head back. She was coming to a dirt road ahead that snaked off to the left across a plain of weeds. The air smelled bitter, with the drifting scent of roadkill. She decided she would turn around at the road.

Berke had never doubted her journey. Given the choice between a dress and a flannel shirt, she was glad in plaid. Not that she hadn't tried sex with guys, just to see what it was like. There had been three different guys, in three different states, in three different seasons. Three times, and three times only. Fuelled probably by alcohol or drugs, or maybe they were all mercy fucks. She couldn't really remember many details except the rough hands that didn't know what they were doing, the neanderthalic grunts that made her crush a laugh behind her teeth and at last—oh suffering Jesus, at long last!—the most godawful mess ever to scrawl across a bedsheet. *You want to put that thing* where? Uh uh, Bluto, my mercy's used up.

She wanted nothing to do with those kings of artless sex, those preening princes who thought they were a gift to all women of every size, shape and color and who fell apart in whines, tears and rages at the sound of "No". She did recall her three prizes as being ridiculously heavy, lying atop her like concrete suits. Their hairy backs and pimply asses...*urk*, she was going to have to stop thinking about this, or she would go over to the roadside and throw up.

She missed Melissa. She missed Mike, and she was going to miss him more as time went on. Maybe that was how the world worked, taking people you loved away from you with no warning, but if that was the best God could come up with She needed to rethink Her game.

Berke was almost to the dirt road. She looked along it and saw what appeared to be a haze of dust floating in the air, as if a vehicle had only recently driven that way. A sun-faded sign that used to be red, white and blue proclaimed *Land For Sale*. In the distance, a couple of hundred yards or so away and framed by skeleton trees, was a farmhouse the same color as the brown dry brush that surrounded it. The windows looked to be broken out, the chimney reduced to an iron pipe. But, oddly enough, a battered mailbox remained at the turnoff onto the dirt road, and on the mailbox was the name *Sam Dodge*.

She caught a quick flare of light from a front window. Sun on metal, she thought.

She heard a firecracker go off, not very loud of a *pop*.

Something zipped past her, a hornet or wasp, about level with her collarbone. She smelled the scorched air under her nose. She looked to her right and saw a plume of dust rising from the barren earth beyond a barbed-wire fence. And then it came to her very clearly that someone had just taken a shot at her, from the window of that house in the field.

Dodge, she thought.

She did better than that: she flung herself to the road and crawled into the weeds on the right. In a matter of seconds, her well-trained heart was pounding, her lungs gasped for air and a new bloom of sweat had burst from her pores.

Berke tensed for a second bullet. Her legs were still in the road. She pulled herself deeper into the weeds. When she looked toward the house again, she could no longer see it. But that didn't mean *she* couldn't be seen. A rush of emotions wheeled through her mind, culminating in anger: who the *fuck* was *shooting*? Her New Balances, her knees and her elbows pushed against the ground; she crawled through the brush along the barbed-wire fence. Then there was something right in front of her face that she thought at first was a piece of discarded rope, but since when did rope have scales and alternating light and dark brown bands? She couldn't see a head and she didn't hear a rattle but suddenly the thing shot away from her as if it had been touched with a hot iron, and just that fast it slithered through the brush and was gone. She thought she had peed a cup's worth in her lycra shorts.

She heard a car coming. She lifted her head as much as she dared. A pickup truck that might have been welded together from four or five other wrecked trucks of various colors was approaching over in the left lane, on its way into town. Two men were in the truck, their windows down, and in the back was a piece of machinery that maybe was an air-conditioning unit. On the driver's dented door was *Baumgartner Heating & Cooling* with a phone number. In another few seconds the truck was going to pass by. She thought that if she got up and ran for the truck, whoever was in that house was going to have another chance to kill her. But staying here was not an option, and even a snake had that much sense.

When the pickup was almost between her and the house, she jumped up and ran toward it with her arms waving. "Hey!" she shouted. "Stop! Stop!"

The driver hit his brake and the truck skidded to a halt. He had a mop of gray hair and a gray mustache, and the red letters in a white circle on his sweat-stained brown shirt said his name was *Roy*.

"Can you give me a ride?" Berke asked. Her voice was shaking. "To the motel?" Roy and his partner, a thin Hispanic man burned nearly black by the sun, just stared at her. "The *Lariat* motel," Berke explained. "I need a ride." She glanced through the cab toward the farmhouse, but it looked only empty and forlorn.

"You need a ride?" Roy obviously was the type to deliberate at his own speed. "What're you doin' out here?" He took stock of her outfit. "You runnin' in this heat?"

"Can I get in?"

Roy made a sucking noise with his lips against his teeth. His slow deliberation obviously also included sound effects. "Yeah," he decided, "get on in."

She edged around the truck. The Hispanic dude opened the door and scooted over. As Berke climbed in, the flesh on the back of her neck tingled in expectation of the bullet, but nothing hit it except a few gnats interested in her salt. She slammed the door shut, glanced again at the farmhouse and saw nothing move, no glint of metal, nothing. "Who lives there?" she asked.

"Land's for sale," Roy said. "Suppose it's vacant. You a buyer?"

By the time Berke shook her head, Roy had put a boot on the accelerator and with a tired groan the patched-up truck rolled on toward town.

"You ain't from around here, are you?" Roy asked, and Berke told him no, she was not. "Where you from, then?" Austin, Berke said, and added that she was going back to Austin today. "Big city," Roy remarked, after which he began to tell her about the time he went to his sister's wedding in Fort Worth, which was another big city but he didn't care for big cities, he had been here in this town for all his life and made a good living, had a wife and three sons, one worked on an oil rig in the Gulf and boy howdy did that little rooster make a wad of dough.

Berke had stopped listening about the time she'd said she was going back to Austin today. She knew someone had fired a shot at her. She *knew* it. Had felt the bullet go past, had *smelled* it. But... Jesus Christ...*why*? A bullet fired from an empty farmhouse? Yeah, well, it must not have been so fucking empty. What had she done, gotten some trigger-happy hermit mad at her? But this was too weird... Mike getting shot yesterday, and now this...

It was too weird.

Roy and the silent Hispanic stick-man were looking at her. She'd missed something. "What?" she asked.

"Did you fall down?" Roy repeated. "You're dusty, I figured you fell down."

"Yeah, I fell down."

They were getting close to the Lariat. Berke's fingers were on the door handle.

"Better be careful," Roy advised as he pulled the truck into the parking lot. Berke saw that the guest list had thinned; the silver Subaru and the dark blue pickup were gone. "Fella got shot dead out on I-20 yesterday afternoon," Roy said. "In the paper this mornin'. This is crazy times."

"Okay. Thanks for the ride." She got out while the truck was still rolling. The Hispanic guy raised a hand in farewell as Roy drove away. Berke was close enough to the swimming pool to see that Ariel was still lying on the blue lounge chair in exactly the same position she'd occupied about forty minutes ago. Berke opened the gate. She walked with long strides around the pool to Ariel's chair and touched her shoulder.

"Hey, wake up," Berke said. "Ariel! Wake up!"

Ariel's eyes opened. She turned her head toward Berke and immediately made a noise of pain. She pressed a hand to the side of her neck. "Ow," she said, massaging the cramped muscle. Her shoulder was stiff too; these loungers definitely were not meant to take the place of a bed, but it had been so nice out here, with the sound of the water and the panorama of the stars overhead. It was hot and bright out here now, though. Who was standing over her? She squinted to see. "Berke? What is it?"

"Somebody shot at me."

"Somebody...*what*?"

"Listen to me. Wake *up*. Somebody shot at me, when I went out running."

Ariel sat up, still working the offending muscle in her neck. She realized one of her shoes had fallen off during the night. "Went out running?"

Berke abruptly turned away and headed toward the room. Ariel was cute, smart, talented with lyrics and melody, a real trooper when it came to the grind, but before she got her bowl of granola and cup of silver needle tea in the mornings she could be as thick as a brick. Berke opened the door and went into the room, where George was sitting on one of the chairs staring at his cellphone's screen. Nomad and Terry were still laid out on their beds, asleep. Berke felt the heat of fresh tears at her eyes, because Mike wasn't there, and she wasn't sure she was ever going to get past this tragedy.

"I got—" *shot at*, she was going to say.

But before Berke could finish her sentence, George said, "Amazing. This is just...*awesome*."

"Listen to me. Okay? I got—"

"We sold one hundred and sixty-three CDs last night," George went on. "That's just figures for *Catch*. One sixty three," he repeated, for emphasis. He didn't have to tell her the CDs were ten dollars a pop, payable through PayPal. He consulted some more awesome numbers. "The video's up to five hundred and nineteen hits on YouTube, six hundred and thirty-eight on MySpace and...get this... seven hundred and twelve on the webpage." Behind his glasses, his eyes were shining. "Jesus!" he said. "What *happened*?"

"Yeah, great, I'm glad, but—"

"Guys!" George started shaking the others awake. "Get up! Come on, you've got to hear this!" They responded with snorts and snarls, like animals being dragged from their dens of refuge. "I *mean* it!" George almost shouted. "We made some fucking numbers last night!"

Nomad was the first to reply, his voice husky with sleep. "What the *shit...?*"

George's cell buzzed. He checked the caller. It was Ash. "Yeah!" George said, and listened as Nomad and Terry fought out of the bands of bedsheets that had wrapped around them during the night. Nomad staggered off to the bathroom. "I saw the numbers, yeah," George said. "What's the deal?" He was silent, letting Ash speak.

"Somebody took a shot at me," Berke told Terry. She didn't know if he'd heard her or not, because he was fumbling for his specs on the bedside table. The door opened again, letting in a blinding burst of sunlight from which Ariel emerged, still working her neck.

"Oh. Okay, right." George had eased down into the chair again. Something had changed in his voice; some of the happiness had evaporated.

"What's going on?" Ariel asked.

"Somebody took a—" Berke stopped herself. She could still hear the sound of that bullet zipping past, but now the whole event seemed dreamlike, surreal, mixed up with the *crack* of the slug hitting the gas station's window yesterday. She thought that the heat had gotten to her out in front of that empty farmhouse, or that she must be going crazy. Why would anybody be shooting at her? Did that make any *sense*? But had it made any sense that a bullet had hit Mike in the head and now he was lying stretched out on a slab somewhere?

"Really," George said. It was a reaction to something Ash had just told him. "No, we haven't seen it. Wow. That's all I can say, man… just…*wow*."

Berke put a hand to her forehead to see if she'd overheated. If anything, she felt clammy. Maybe she *had* overheated. Maybe she was going to throw up in another minute, because her stomach was roiling. This is like that syndrome soldiers have, she thought. That delayed stress syndrome deal. She felt cold sweat crawling on her cheeks.

"You okay?" Ariel asked. She'd heard Berke clearly enough outside—*Somebody shot at me*—and now Berke's face had gone gray. She thought Berke was having a nervous reaction from yesterday, and who could fault her for going to pieces?

Berke rushed away to the other bathroom beyond the connecting door, where she turned on the tap, splashed water into her face and then, trembling violently, leaned over the toilet and wracked herself with a series of dry heaves audible at least two rooms away. Ariel followed to stand outside the door if Berke called for help.

"Hold it, wait a minute," George told Ash. "Is she sick?" he called to Ariel.

"I'm fucking *fine*!" Berke shouted back through the cardboard door. "I'm fucking peachy-keen *fabulous*!"

"Who's puking?" asked Nomad as he came out of the other bathroom, his eyes sleep-stung and squinty.

"We're having an episode here," George said to Ash. "Go on, I'm listening."

"What the hell's happening?" Terry asked of no one in particular, then he hauled himself up and went to the bathroom Nomad had just vacated. Nomad returned to bed and lay there on his back, staring up at the ceiling tiles and wondering if Mike's daughter had been told the news yet. It was going to be a bad ride back to Austin, and not much to look forward to when they got there, regardless of his big plans from last night.

"Why are they calling it that?" The Little Genius's question into the phone snagged Nomad's attention. George was silent again as Ash spoke. Nomad propped himself up on a pillow, watching George's facial expressions to get some clue of the conversation. "We're supposed to hear from them this morning," George said. "I guess they'll tell us we can leave."

Talking about the detectives, Nomad thought.

"So...what's the deal?" At this question, Nomad's ears again went up. "Better than what? Fifty percent?"

Berke and Ariel returned to the room, one with a hand pressed to her stomach and the other rubbing the side of her neck. In the bathroom, Berke had gotten down a couple of glasses of water and felt a little better. She was deciding whether or not to pursue this tale of the farmhouse shooter.

"Jesus," George said. "Is he really *serious*?"

The toilet's flush announced Terry's exit from the bathroom. He looked quizzically at Nomad, who replied with a shrug.

George scratched his chin. "Can he go to seventy-five percent on the merchandise?"

"What's he talking about?" Berke asked, but no one could respond.

Nomad didn't want to say, but it sounded to him as if George and Ash were talking about a gig. He remembered, not without some bitterness, George's voice of reason in the Subway last night: *We're going home in the morning. Tour cancelled. All done.*

Well, it was morning, the tour was cancelled and The Five were all done. So what was this shit about?

"I hear you. I understand," said the voice of reason. "I'll run it by everybody. Yeah." He nodded, as more instructions came through the digital air from Austin. "Okay, thanks," he said, and put his cellphone away. Then he sat exactly where he was without moving, staring at the floor, as second after second ticked past.

"Are you going to make us *guess*?" Berke asked sharply, which was a very good sign.

"You would never," George answered in a quiet, measured voice, "guess this in the proverbial million years." He looked first at Nomad, then at the others. "Trey Yeager left a message for Ash last night. He wants us to keep the date at the Spinhouse." Yeager was the Spinhouse's booking manager, had been in the business for about thirty years at various clubs across the Southwest. "That's not all. They want to bump us up to headliner. It's a little more money, but Ash thinks we can get a way better percentage on merchandise."

Nobody spoke, because they just didn't know what to say. Then Nomad struck at the heart of the problem: "If you remember...we lost our bass player yesterday."

"Yeah, there's that. Ash says he can get Butch Munger to meet us in El Paso, or Trey can supply a local talent."

"Whoa, whoa, whoa!" Berke said. "I'm not playing with a gator off the street!"

"Not Butch Munger!" Nomad's tone was just as vehement. He was up off the bed and crouched like a fighter about to throw a right hook. "That bastard wrecked Hemp For Shemp last year!" Not only that, but Munger had a reputation for temper and had been arrested for breaking his girlfriend's nose, charges dropped because she just loved him so fucking much.

"Guys?" said Terry.

"Look, it's just the one show," George said. "I know Munger's rep, but he *is* good. And he kind of plays in Mike's style—"

"Don't you say that!" Berke came forward, crowding him, and George feared he was about to be torn apart by a ferocious lesbian. "*Nobody* plays like Mike! You hear it? *Nobody*!"

"Guys?" said Terry.

"Not Butch Munger!" Nomad almost shouted. "I won't step on a stage with him!"

The telephone on the bedside table rang, a shrill A above high C. George reached carefully between Nomad and Berke and picked it up. "Yes? Oh, sure. We *would* like the Cattleman's complimentary breakfast this morning, absolutely. Uh...that would be six. I'm sorry...that would be five. Just a minute." He put his hand over the mouthpiece. "Who wants coffee and who wants orange juice?"

"Orange juice," said Terry, and then he added, "Guys, *I* can pick up the bassline."

"Two orange juices so far," George reported into the telephone.

"Coffee. Black," Nomad said.

George paused with his ear to the receiver. "Yeah, that'd be great. Thank you." He hung up. "She says they're not real busy, so she'll bring a pot of coffee, five cups and five glasses of juice."

"Did you hear what I said?" Terry asked. "I can play the bass parts."

George didn't answer, waiting for Berke's reaction. She looked down at the floor for a long time, as if pondering whether Terry was strong enough to carry Mike's weight. Conflicting emotions fought on her face.

Then she lifted her gaze to George and said firmly, "That works with me."

Nomad nodded. "Me too."

"I can't believe this! We're going to go on without *Mike*?" Ariel's was not the voice of reason, but a cry of bewilderment. "I don't care if it's just one show!" she said before George could respond. "Shouldn't we...like...go home and...*mourn* him or something? It doesn't seem right to keep on playing!"

"I think," George answered, "you're wrong about that. Let me tell you what's happened, according to Ash. The story about Mike is in this morning's newspaper here. It's also in the Abilene paper. But last night it got picked up by the Associated Press and wound up on Yahoo in the news items. You know what the headline was? *Sniper Kills Member of Touring Band*."

"Sniper?" Terry frowned. "Who said anything about a sniper?"

"I'm just saying what Ash told me. The newspapers reported it as a 'rifle shot'. When it got on Yahoo, it became a 'sniper'. Let me just tell you...a *lot* of people have seen that item on the web. So even though they called us 'The Fives' on Yahoo, we sold a hundred and sixty-three CDs of *Catch* last night. In one *night*." The Little Genius waited for that to sink in. "We got some awesome numbers of hits, and I'll bet if I looked at the numbers again right now they would've gone up...who knows how many. Ash had a call in to cancel at the Spinhouse, but they want us because suddenly we are *newsworthy*." He caught Ariel's pained expression and he didn't dare even look at Berke. "Okay, I know it's a shitty way to get some media shine, but why do you think all of a sudden they want us to headline? Huh?"

No one answered, so George plowed on. "*Any* media shine sells tickets. We can think of ourselves as great and sensitive musicians, or rebels without a cause, or raging flames of angry righteousness, or whatever...but all the business cares about is, do you sell tickets? Okay, what I'm saying is—and we don't have to like it, but that's life—we need to buckle up and act like professionals. If we can headline and get a good merchandise split from the Spinhouse, we go play there. Any disagreements with that?" There were no replies, but George had one more point to make. "You think Mike would disagree? After working his ass off so long, and now we're invited to *headline*?" He directed the next question to Berke. "You think he'd say pack it in and go back to Austin?"

Berke was staring across the room, at the green notebook sitting atop the vanity. As far as she knew, Mike had never written a verse in his life, nor had he ever wanted to. Why suddenly now, just before he'd been shot dead by a...

...sniper?

"Mike would say go to El Paso and play the Spinhouse," Berke answered, speaking more to herself than to the others. "He'd say..."

No one here gets out alive?

"...buckle up," she went on, "but maybe not in those exact words."

"It doesn't seem right," Ariel said, but her conviction was wavering.

"We play the gig, and we tear the roof off the place, and I say Mike's family gets his cut just the same as if he were here." George's eyebrows lifted. "Everybody cool with that?"

They were, and Nomad spoke for them all: "Sure."

"Then it *is* right," George told Ariel. "Anything else would be wrong."

To that, Ariel had no reply.

Their complimentary breakfasts came, the biscuits, the jelly, the coffee and the orange juice. The woman who brought the tray looked quickly around the room to make sure it hadn't been trashed by this bunch, whom the police had told her were musicians, and she went back to her office relieved. There was no further mention of Mike as they ate, but Berke put the green notebook in her own bag for safe-keeping. She had decided not to say anymore about her experience on the road; it was just too weird to kick around, and George might want her to tell the cops, and now she wasn't sure of her own mind and she just wanted to get out of here. So she stayed quiet, and she went to the bathroom to take a shower and wash the dust out of her hair.

Around ten-thirty, with the sun up high and heat pressing against the window, the two detectives knocked at their door and came in to talk. Lucky Luke and the Digger both looked tired; it had been a long night and a hot morning in those scraggly woods, and neither luck nor digging had revealed more than they'd known before sundown. "I'll tell you," said Detective Rios as she and her partner stood next to the air-conditioner to catch a breeze, "that we haven't found fresh casings on the ground where we think the shooter was positioned. So either we're wrong about the location, or the brass was cleaned up. And that's kind of puzzling, because it's not something a kid in need of a course on rifle safety would do."

"Where does that put us?" George asked.

"In between theories, until we find the brass or somebody tells us something." Luke had his toothpick in his mouth and his cowboy hat sat on his head cocked a little to one side. "We may find the casings today, or they may be rattling around in the floorboard of junior's ATV. Hard to say."

That statement brought a flush of anger up in Nomad's cheeks. "Hard to *say*? Our friend's dead, and that's all you've got?"

"Easy, man, take it easy," George cautioned.

"See, this is our situation," Luke went on, his voice unhurried. "Was it an accident, or was it intentional? Was it a kid out dicking around or a random shooting, with intent to kill? If that's so, we've got a real problem."

Berke knew now was the time to speak up, if she was going to; but the moment passed and she kept her mouth shut because she wanted out of this town right *now* and they would get all tangled up with something she wasn't even positive had happened. The open road had never before seemed so inviting. Or so *safe*, for that matter.

"There are other possibilities," Detective Rios said, focusing on Nomad. "Somebody with a grudge against the gas station's owner. Or the oil company. We're bringing in for questioning some people you might call 'sketchy'. Got their guns and their anger issues. So we'll see if that leads us anywhere."

"Get the wrong person upset over any little thing, and that's why we've got jobs," Luke added.

"Sorry we can't offer you more," the woman said. Her voice carried a tone of finality. "You're going back to Austin?"

"No, on to El Paso," George told her. When she looked blankly at him, he decided to say, "We've got a gig there on Friday night, it's a pretty good deal."

"I guess you have to be dedicated to your music," she said, but no one replied.

What the detectives had really come to say, the Digger went on, was that the family had worked out transfer of the body back to Bogalusa from the mortuary, and that if anything further developed the Sweetwater police department would be in touch with Mr. Vallampati at the Austin number George had given them. She said Mr. Davis's belongings could be shipped from Sweetwater to Bogalusa at the UPS office, or that could be done in El Paso or wherever was most convenient. George said they'd do it in El Paso. He was thinking that he wanted to get on the road as soon as possible and that the bag of Blue Mystic weed in Mike's duffel ought not to be in there when the family got his stuff.

"We're very sorry about this," Detective Rios said, speaking for both of them. "I hope we'll have some news for you soon." With that, their visit had come to its conclusion. The two detectives left, closed the door behind them, and George scratched the back of his neck and said as he had said so many times before in so many different motel rooms, "Let's saddle up, people."

They paid their bill, Nomad took the Scumbucket's wheel because it was his turn to drive, Ariel rode shotgun with George and Terry in the seats behind, and in the back Berke sat next to an empty place.

They pulled out of the Lariat Motel's parking lot, and beneath the scorching sun they took the entrance to I-20 West on toward El Paso. They were silent for a while, and then Terry began to talk about a particularly memorable gig they'd done last June in Myrtle Beach, it was a club right on the beach, and it was early evening with the breeze blowing salty off the sea and the light was soft and blue and the place was crowded, everybody appreciative and cheering for the songs and only rowdy enough to be fun, and in the brief quiet between numbers Mike had come over to him, leaned close and said, *Bro, drink it up 'cause this is as good as it gets.*

Yes, the others said. They did remember the gig. They remembered it very well. And everyone agreed that now that Terry mentioned it, it seemed like it was only yesterday.

TEN.

When 'White Wedding' blasts from the speakers, Jeremy Pett allows himself a passing smile because he knows that he is in the right place.

"Are you a captain?" he asks the black-haired girl with the two silver bars piercing her nipples as she leans her head down to him (she smells like bubblegum and coconut suntan lotion, he thinks) and she returns the smile that she believes is for her and tells him he can call her anything if he'll buy another beer. He says yeah, sure, and she goes away into the purple light that is edged with crimson. He returns his attention not to the other black-haired girl who is coiled around the pole ten feet from him but to a table over on the right side where he saw Gunny sitting a minute ago but Gunny is not there anymore. Gunny is a prowler, and can't stay still very long. But Jeremy knows by now that Gunny is never far away, and this knowledge gives him comfort.

Damn straight, does he know! Gunny was all over his ass when he missed that first shot at the gas station. Jeremy could say it was a cold bore shot, he had no spotter to verify the range and the wind drift and maybe he *had* been unnerved when the trooper pulled in. He could say that he'd first taken aim at the lead singer, but the guy was walking back and forth from deep shadow into eye-zapping sunlight and that had thrown him off, and his second target—the guy pumping gas—had been obscured by the trooper's raised hood, and then also there was the traffic on I-20 to consider and it wasn't so easy to shoot between cars and trucks flashing past on a highway, but Gunny accepts no excuses. Then…oh Jesus, *then*…when Jeremy had heard someone walking past his door and looked out through the blinds thinking it was the old woman bringing his complimentary breakfast, but it was *her*, the drummer girl, all decked out in her jogging duds, and Jeremy had given some thought to the situation and decided he might could finish her off if the place and time were right, so he'd checked out, gotten into the pickup truck and actually passed her on the road looking for a shelter to set up his rifle and bipod. Maybe she would come this far, maybe not, but if she did he was locked and loaded.

It was another cold bore shot. The sun was in his eyes this time, too. That bullet couldn't have missed her by half-an-inch. It must've burned the tip of her nose on the way past.

But oh, Jesus, did Gunny give it to him when he drove out of there and swung east on I-20. *I thought you were supposed to be an expert,* Gunny had said, quietly at first but with a nasty bite of rising rage. *Supposed to be such hot shit at this. Killed how many ragheads over there?*

"Thirty-eight confirmed," Jeremy had answered, because he knew the count.

Great for you, Pett, but tell me this then…how many of 'em weren't kids?

Jeremy's foot had stomped down on the brake pedal and the pickup travelling at nearly sixty-five miles per hour had shivered and shrieked as if all the bolts were coming loose at once, and suddenly the truck was turning sideways and sliding, leaving smoking black streaks on the asphalt. He was aware of Gunny, the sarcastic shotgun rider, fading out to a gray presence. Jeremy thought for a second that he should go ahead and die, he should have died in the bathtub and this was just marking time, but then the survivor's will—the Marine spirit, the gladiator's fight, call it any of these—kicked in. He took hold of the wheel and fought to keep the truck from going over, a struggle that seemed epic but only lasted for a husky inhalation of burnt-rubber air. Then with a shudder and moan the truck gave its life back to him to control and it was slowing down, slowing down, its tires going into the weeds on the right-side shoulder…and WHAM came the burst of air and the indignant wail of a semi's horn as the beast whipped past, followed by a white BMW whose driver shook his head in disbelief at Jeremy's skill of four-wheel Mexican hat dancing.

Jeremy looked into the sideview mirror. No troopers yet, but they might be coming if they saw the dark pall of smoke rising off the treadmarks.

Drive, said Gunny, who was himself again. When Jeremy hesitated, Gunny said, *Get your mind back where it needs to be. Drive.*

He started off. The engine gave a rattle like a bagful of broken plates, but then everything must have fitted itself together again, God bless the American auto industry, and the pickup truck rolled on more lamb than lion.

The girl with the silver captain's bars through her nipples emerges from the gaudy glare, bringing his beer. She has the tattoos of thorny vines and roses on both arms and a small sad teddybear on her belly beneath the navel ring. He pays her from his wallet of dwindling money and then she leans her head toward him again, the better to be heard over the thundering music—a rap song, somebody Jeremy doesn't recognize singing about getting pussy twenty-fo' seven—and as she asks if he wants a lap dance she reaches down to place a hand on his right thigh. But instantly Jeremy has intercepted the hand and turned it away, earning from her a puzzled look in the sparkling dark. "Maybe later, okay?" she prompts. Her accent is strange; she appears to be a mixture of Hispanic, black, and Asian. They all do, except for the one with the flame-red hair and the thin blonde with the ponytail.

He says *maybe later* without meaning it, and she goes away again. He drinks his beer-flavored water and checks his wristwatch to see that Wednesday night has turned into Thursday morning. He does not want the girl touching him because she might feel the lump in his pants, hidden by the folds of his extra-large black T-shirt. The crowd—was there ever a crowd in here?—is thinning out, but the pole dancer is still energetic and the music is loud enough to churn a brain into oatmeal. He is watching Miss Ponytail give a lap dance to a Hispanic man in a dark suit who was in here when Jeremy arrived about an hour ago. The man is maybe forty, forty-five or so, with a bald brown pate and gray hair on the sides. There is a little gray tuft up top that Miss Ponytail plays with as she gyrates her ass on his crotch. The man is sleepy-eyed and grins too much. His teeth are very white, and Jeremy wonders if he's a dentist out on the town or visiting El Paso for a convention or something. Whatever he is, he likes to show Miss Ponytail his heavy wad of cash and she likes to lighten it for him, and Jeremy has been entertained by watching her set her lower jaw like a bulldog and scare off the other *chiquitas* who wander over behind their implants and try to score some of what he's throwing down.

Pull off where you can see the highway, Gunny had said. It was not a request, it was a command.

Jeremy had bristled up. Had clenched his fists on the wheel and given the engine more gas. Yesterday he had killed one of the members of that band, he had shot at another one today and he wasn't too happy with his record of one hit out of three bullets. The fact was, he wasn't nearly as good as he used to be. Couldn't even hit a slow-moving target at about two-hundred yards. Pitiful. But more than that...he couldn't remember exactly why he had followed that van and U-Haul trailer from the club in Dallas, had parked overnight in some suburban neighborhood to keep watch, and when they'd left Dallas he'd gotten on the highway behind them, knowing they were playing next in El Paso from the schedule on their website. He couldn't remember exactly why he needed to kill them, except for the fact that on that cable show they'd made some pretty vile comments and accusations about the soldiers in Iraq—which they hadn't repeated during their show at the Curtain Club—and that maybe he was going to embark on a new career as a hitman for the *federales* in Mexico. Call it training, then. But still...what had they ever done to *him*, really? It wasn't like lying in wait, hour after hour, for the enemy in Iraq. You knew then what your purpose was. You knew then that every bullet you sent would save the life of a brother, or maybe many lives. But this...he felt lost in his own mind.

You're not lost, Gunny had said, but Jeremy hadn't recalled speaking aloud. *You've been found. Don't you get that*?

Maybe Jeremy shook his head; he didn't know.

Pull off where you can see the highway, Gunny repeated. The voice was soft, caring, almost fatherly. *Then we'll straighten some things out.*

Jeremy sped past another exit.

Gunny said, *Oh, my. Don't you know yet that without me you're nothing? So...if you want to be nothing again, you can stop at the next gas station and let me out.*

Jeremy stared straight ahead. In another moment he realized he was alone, because he could no longer see Gunny from the corner of his eye. Yet he knew he'd always been alone; what he saw and heard as the image of his gunnery sergeant from training school wasn't there and had never been. It was something from within, just like when a lonely person starts talking to the mirror. He remembered some line from a movie, maybe he'd seen it on the base in Iraq, where the guy says you're not crazy if you talk to yourself in the mirror, but if you answer back you've gotta be fucking nuts.

He thought his image of Gunny, just as regulation spit-polished, side-walled and crisply buttoned-up as the man had been in real life, had to do with perfection. Maybe it was how he himself had wanted to be...had *planned* on being, until things messed up. He could've been an instructor at the school, no doubt about it. He could've served a long and useful life in the Corps. *Semper Fi*, that's what it was all about. So he knew that Gunny wasn't there, could never really be there, but he would accept any part of Gunny he could get because it took him back to when he was somebody, doing something important in this world.

It occurred to him as he was driving eastward, about midway between Sweetwater and Abilene, that his fingers on the steering-wheel seemed longer than he recalled. The knuckles were thicker, too. He wasn't excusing himself for those poor shots—no way, he was a professional—but his long fingers might have fouled up his trigger pull. It was something he hadn't noticed until now, and it hit him like a small shock that he did not recognize his own hands. When he moved the fingers, they rippled on the steering-wheel like the legs of a spider touched by a hot needle. He looked into the rearview mirror and saw with a strike of terror that one eye was the wrong color, and then he started talking himself down, muttering and gasping things that had meaning for him, like *grape popsicle* and *their daughter Judy* and *my name is Gladiator, my name is Gladiator, my name is Gladiator*. Until finally his spider-fingered hands pulled the pickup off at the next exit and Jeremy stopped at a gas station to get a cup of coffee.

He left the truck parked at the far corner of the lot, its bug-smeared grill aimed toward I-20.

It is nearly one o'clock by Jeremy's watch. In this pretend playhouse, with the Rolling Stones' 'Brown Sugar' now cranking from the speakers and the flamehaired girl taking her turn on the pole, the Hispanic dentist has had enough beers, even of the watered variety, to be swaying in his chair. Miss Ponytail is always a tit's touch away from him, guarding her gold mine. Jeremy has been to three other joints like this tonight. The first and second had a security guard out front, patrolling the parking lot, the third had floodlights and video cameras up on the corners of the building, but this one out in an industrial area is a windowless cinderblock slab designated by a portable sign on wheels to be Club Salvaje, Where The Wild Angels Play. There are lights in the parking lot, but they're angled so they throw huge pools of black shadow amid the cars, SUVs and trucks. Up on the building itself are two video cameras aimed down at the front door, which might have been a problem except for the fact that Jeremy thinks they're fakes because no red Record lights are showing. He thinks this joint is too cheap, too temporary, to afford a real video security system. The batteries for the false lights have probably burned out.

He needs money. He's used his credit card too much as it is, for gas, food and motel rooms; it was on the critical list when he left Temple, and pretty soon it's going to be shut down. If he doesn't have enough cash, the police will be called and that won't help him any. He was out last night, hitting some other strip clubs, spending his money on the crappy beer because they won't let him sit in these places if he doesn't buy something. But no opportunities had come up. He hasn't eaten today, saving his last few dollars for tonight. He watches the Hispanic dentist, and he wonders where in the lot is the man's car parked.

If you have any doubt about what you're doing, Gunny had said when Jeremy was back in the pickup with a styrofoam cup of coffee and a Milky Way bar, *know that you're making a new life for yourself. You're coming out of retirement. How does that feel?*

Jeremy hadn't answered, because if he did he would be talking to himself. His fingers were okay now, his hands back to what they were. He checked his eye in the rearview mirror and found that it too had returned to normal.

You've missed being useful, said Gunny. *Being needed for a task. A mission. Being the go-to guy. That was everything to you, wasn't it?*

Jeremy slid down a little in his seat and watched the passage of traffic going east and west on I-20.

Everything, Gunny repeated. *Well, you've got a mission again. Maybe you're not as good as you used to be, but hey…who is?* This time Gunny didn't pause for a response. *You're still very talented. Very able. And you still enjoy the hunt, don't you?*

"Yes," Jeremy said, before he could think not to.

They trained you and fed you and built you and set you loose. They created you to be what you are. What did they expect you to do, after they didn't need you anymore?

"I don't know," said Jeremy.

But they do still need you. They need men like you to step up and defend the honor of every veteran who put their boots in that dust over there. Who left their families, and who came back changed from when they went. Who died over there, or who came back as good as dead, like Chris. You think anybody in that band ever fought for their country? You think they ever would? *So they get up on their stage, on their platform, and make their accusations and their pronouncements, and play their music—which is shitty music, really—and people like them screw everything up until the flag looks dirty and fighting for your country looks like the act of a criminal. Are you a criminal because you carried out your missons? Does following orders make you a criminal?*

Jeremy shook his head. *No, it does not. Definitely not.*

He wasn't sure if he'd spoken aloud or if he hadn't, but Gunny could hear him.

This is not just about that shitty band, Gunny said after a stretch of silence. *Not just about smearing garbage on the memory of men like Chris. This is about* you. *Are you listening?*

From Jeremy: *I am.*

Gunny said, *This is your new beginning. You do this right—you be smart and careful—and you can live the dream. Every once in a while they bring you out of that white stone villa on the beach in Mexico somewhere, give you a target and you go hunting. You spend three or four days in the field, you send the bullet, and they heap praise and money on your head. And you perform a service for them, something they can't do on their own. Something they have to keep off the books. Dangerous? Sure. Could you get yourself killed, or strung up by the heels and cut up so bad you'd want to die? Absolutely. But where were you on Friday night, Jeremy? Cutting yourself up, weren't you? Living in misery and dying in sadness. So what do you have to lose from this point onward? And weigh that very carefully against what there is to be gained, won't you?*

That Gunny had a silver tongue, Jeremy thought as he stared at the highway through the waves of shimmering heat. That Gunny made everything sound so possible. No...*inevitable* would be the right word.

To get where you want to go, Gunny continued, *you have to earn your passage. It's not enough that one of them is dead. Not nearly enough. Think of them as being target practice. But don't fuck up again, Jeremy. Do you hear?*

"I hear," Jeremy answered. He had a question to ask, and now was the time: "How many do I need to kill?"

I'll tell you when to stop. Did you know that your candy is melting?

Jeremy looked down. The Milky Way, which he'd unpeeled from its wrapper, was oozing in dark sticky strands along his hand. When he looked to the right, he knew that Gunny would no longer be there; Gunny, after all, was a prowler and couldn't stay still very long.

Gunny had come to him on Saturday morning, after the failed suicide of Friday night. It had been a slow insertion, much as a sniper might creep in yard after yard under a ghillie suit that resembled nothing more than a bed of dry grass and dead leaves. At first Gunny had been a faint image in the bathroom mirror, next a pallid shape against a sand-colored wall, then a quickly-glimpsed human figure standing in a corner, and finally a revelation of the death angel's art, sitting in the chair where it had masqueraded as Chris the night before.

Jeremy had stared at Gunny, at the handsome sharp features and slightly-twisted mouth ready to snap out a command, at the straight-backed posture and slim wiry musculature in the ever-pressed uniform. Jeremy was more fascinated than fearful, more awed than afraid. He stood his ground in the dim room, and he said calmly, "You're not real."

Gunny's eyes had just fixed on him, the direct gaze of a man who is supremely confident of his own physical power. Seconds passed, yet the mouth did not speak.

"Not real," Jeremy repeated.

And then Gunny had smiled in that way Jeremy remembered; it was almost startling, like seeing a block of ice suddenly crack. It didn't hold very long, and Gunny's face settled back into its blank rigidity. *Pett*, said Gunny in the exact same voice Jeremy knew, *I'm as real as you need me to be. Now don't you have some work to get done?*

Gunny had lingered there for a short while, but in the space of a ragged breath or a slow eyeblink the figure was gone and Jeremy was left staring dumbly at an empty chair.

He knew what he wanted, and he knew what he needed to do. He wanted to live, and he needed to prove he was still worth something to someone...even if just to the shade of Gunny. The work to get done: packing some clothes in a bag, putting his rifle in its carrying case, taking the ammo and his automatic pistol and everything he needed out to the metal storage box in the back of his truck. Then going to the library, checking the Internet for The Five's website and writing down their schedule. The Curtain Club in Dallas tonight. El Paso next Friday night.

What was life, without a purpose?

Sitting in the truck facing I-20 with the melted candy bar all over his hand, Jeremy thought of something Gunny had just said: *And you still enjoy the hunt, don't you?*

For a sniper, the hunt was everything. It was what you had trained so hard for. What you lived, ate, and breathed for. What you dreamed about, when you slept. And when you had known what it was like to hunt a man, and had lived through it and been victorious as many times as Jeremy had, there was nothing better. Not even peace.

So, for sure...he still enjoyed the hunt.

He knew exactly why he was sitting with his truck facing I-20. He was watching for their van and their trailer. Wouldn't be hard to spot. He expected they would be leaving Sweetwater today before eleven o'clock, which was the Lariat's checkout time. They would be travelling east, back toward Austin, where their website said they were based. He would wait for them, and follow when they passed.

He did enjoy the hunt.

When he was in the swimming pool, there in the dark, the girl had crept up on him.

"Hi," she'd said, and he'd known who it was from her voice. Instantly he'd stopped his slow stroke through the water and glided over to the far side, where he'd hooked his elbows up on the concrete and hung there, his face hidden from her.

But she came nearer still, and after a few more seconds she'd said, "Lots of stars up there."

He hadn't answered. Wouldn't answer. He had nothing to speak to her that his rifle could not say better. But it was so close on his lips, so close, for him to say bitterly, *You think you know the truth about Iraq, bitch? You have no fucking idea.*

After a while, when he'd realized the girl had walked away, Jeremy had gotten out of the pool in his wet Fruit-Of-The-Looms and gone back to his room, where he'd expected—or hoped—to find Gunny waiting for him, but the room had been empty. So he'd channel-surfed across a TV-scape of movies and infomercials and reality shows until he'd gotten weary of looking, but he'd slept with the Made In China remote control in his hand and the TV soundlessly displaying a world in constant motion.

At the center of the pulse of purple light and throbbing noise that passes as music, Jeremy watches Miss Ponytail and the Hispanic dentist. A guy in a wife-beater T-shirt and chinos, a dark-colored ball cap on his head and chains around his neck, comes over to say something to Miss Ponytail, maybe wave a bill at her for a lapdance, but she gives him a tight catty look and says something back and he shrugs and moves away in apparent rejection, heading into the further darkness. The Hispanic dentist grins wider, glad to be her one-and-only. He peels off some more money for her, and again she grinds his front yard with an expert ass.

On that Sunday Jeremy sat in his pickup truck watching I-20, the van and the U-Haul never went past. He'd waited until almost sunset, and then he'd decided he should drive back to the Lariat. Their ride was gone. Where were they? *I think I left my cellphone by the pool*, Jeremy had told the woman at the front desk. *I was talking to a girl out there last night, she said she was a musician with a band. Did she check out?*

This mornin', came the reply. *No, nobody found a cellphone anywhere.*

Jeremy had thanked her and walked back to the truck.

He didn't have to ask for Gunny's opinion. He already figured they'd gone on to El Paso. Forward, instead of backward. Their website had said they were playing on Friday night at a place called the Spinhouse. He was surprised, because he'd expected them to pack up and go home.

It's not enough that one of them is dead, he'd thought as he'd started off westward again. *Not nearly enough.*

He'd found a cheap little motel on the eastern edge of El Paso, had spent most of Monday sleeping and watching TV and had called the Spinhouse that afternoon. His question had been: *Is The Five still playing there on Friday?*

Yeah, the guy had told him. *The Soul Cages start up about eight-thirty, The Five ought to be up around ten. It's ten bucks before Friday, twelve at the door. Gonna be a good time, come on by.*

Jeremy had said he would look forward to it.

Now, something has changed in the little play he is observing. The Hispanic dentist is leaning in, watching Miss Ponytail write with a pen on the inside of what appears to be a book of matches. Giving him her phone number? Setting up something more than a lapdance? Then she gives him a quick kiss on the cheek, a see-you-later kind of thing, and he stands up and staggers his way between the tables to the door. As soon as he's out, Miss Ponytail slides herself down beside a heavy-set gray-haired man in a UTEP T-shirt and puts her flirt on at full beam, but by then Jeremy is on his feet and heading across the room. He tries to make himself invisible, a slow-moving nobody in no hurry to go anywhere, but the truth is that he's tense inside, his stomach is roiling, and he's not just a little bit scared of what he has to do.

He steps outside, lets the door close but stands tight against it for a moment. If someone else comes out in the next couple of minutes, he'll need to scrub this particular mission. In the parking lot are eleven cars, pickups and SUVs including his own truck. Jeremy's target is walking among the vehicles, heading toward the right. Jeremy has no more time to think about it. He takes two quick strides forward, crouches down alongside a red Chevy Tahoe and spends a few seconds listening to the hammer of his heartbeat. Then he creeps after the man, and as he moves he takes from his pocket what he didn't want the stripclub girl to feel: a cake of heavy soap knotted up in a gym sock.

He peers up across a windshield and sees the Hispanic dentist standing beside a red Lexus, fumbling with his keys. Sweat is on Jeremy's face; after all the times he's set up shots with his sniper rifle, after all his association with violence and sudden death, he's never assaulted and robbed anyone before and never dreamed in his life that he ever would. But the time has come, and he has to move right now.

The man presses a button on his keychain and the lights blink as the doors unlock. Jeremy starts to stand up and rush forward, swinging his makeshift cudgel at the back of the man's skull, but before he can do that another figure suddenly comes out alongside Jeremy's own truck, which is parked just across from the Lexus, and a voice says, "Hey, man, got a light?"

The Hispanic dentist turns toward the sound and weaves a little on his feet.

Jeremy waits, the sock gripped in his fist.

"A light, man," says the guy with the wife-beater T-shirt, the dark-colored ball cap and the chains around his neck. He is holding out a cigarette.

The Hispanic dentist of course does have a light. He brings forth the book of matches Miss Ponytail just gave him, and as he offers it to the guy in the ball cap the third man in this drama, who wears a dark green knit cap and has shoulder-length brown hair, comes up behind the Hispanic dentist from where he's circled around and delivers a vicious blow to the back of his quarry's head with what Jeremy figures must be a blackjack of some kind. Before the man can fall, the two jackals are on him, and Jeremy watches them drag the body through a broken section of chainlink fence and down into a culvert on this side of a darkened warehouse with big trucks parked at the loading docks.

It has taken only a few seconds. Jeremy crouches down again and ponders the situation. A signal was passed from Miss Ponytail to the guy in the ball cap, for sure. The matchbook was given not to arrange a meeting, but to set up a robbery. Jeremy wonders if it's the girl's last night at this particular club, and if a police check might find other men were knocked out and robbed just before she pulled up her g-string and hit the road with her two buddies. Whatever, the problem is that Jeremy's money is being stolen while Jeremy crouches here against the side of a Ford Explorer trying to figure out what to do.

Fuck this, Jeremy thinks, as anger sets in. *I'm not letting them take what's mine.*

They're going to be fast about it. Get his wallet and maybe his watch too, if it's got any resale value. Hope the dumb fuck doesn't have any gold teeth.

Jeremy knows he has three weapons: the soap in the sock, his Corps training, and the element of surprise. If he wants the money, he has to get the job done. So he moves forward, his teeth gritted, and when he reaches the broken section of fence he can see them down there in the culvert, one going through the man's pants pockets and the other taking the watch off the right wrist.

One says something to the other, and the guy spoken to gives a short, wheezy laugh.

Before the laugh can end, Jeremy has slid down the side of the culvert and swung the soap-cake weapon against the side of the guy's green-knit capped head. There is a very satisfying *thunk* like woodblocks hitting together. The laughing thief is not laughing any more. He makes a strangled sound and as the man falls Jeremy sees blood drooling from his mouth and figures part of a bitten-off tongue has gone down his throat. The thief in the ball cap looks up and freezes, but he proves to be faster than Jeremy would've thought because in the next instant he scuttles away from the body before Jeremy can swing at him; then he turns and runs like flaming hell along the culvert in the opposite direction.

At once Jeremy is after him, because if that bastard's got the wallet then all this would be for shit.

The guy is fast, no doubt about it. Fear tends to speed the feet. But Jeremy is determined, and though he starts gasping for breath within the next ten seconds he can't let the thief steal his money. He tries his hardest to overtake the man, yet he can't quite get the boost of power his legs need. He is a very long way from his memory—fond, now—of running six miles in the rain at Camp Pendleton as fast as he could haul it.

If the Corps taught him any one thing, it was tenacity. It was stick to something until the something gives. The culvert keeps going on and on, but suddenly Jeremy's tenacity pays off, because the thief breaks his rhythm and tries to scramble up the sloping side on the left to get out. He reaches up and grabs a handful of weeds, one basketball sneaker slides on the dusty concrete seeking a grip, and then Jeremy is upon him. A swing of the soap cracks against the thief's left knee and buckles the leg. The guy says, "Oh man, oh man, come on," in a boyishly pleading voice, and Jeremy figures he must be just a kid, really, but that doesn't matter; this will be a night for the kid's education.

Jeremy hauls the thief down by his neckchains, and when the kid turns and kicks at him with his good leg and hits Jeremy a glancing blow on the left ribcage it does not go well for him.

Jeremy avoids a fist, twists his body to deflect a knee to the groin, and then he hits the guy across the face with his cake of soap and there is a popping noise as a nose explodes. He swings again, hits him below the black streaming mass on his face and from the sound of it probably has claimed all of his front teeth. A third strike bangs into the guy's shoulder, but by then the body is sinking down without resistance and the thief starts crying and puking at the same time there at the bottom of the endless culvert.

"Oh man...oh man," the kid is saying. If Jeremy didn't know what it was he wouldn't recognize it as English.

Jeremy tries to speak. First he has to get his wind back. His ribs are going to be bruised tomorrow. He almost swings the weapon again, out of pure rage, but he decides the thief has had enough education for one night. "You got his wallet?" Jeremy asks.

"OhmanI'mfucked," comes the garbled answer.

"His *wallet*, douchebag. Where is it?"

A trembling, bloody hand that has been clasped over a face unfit for public viewing digs into a pocket and comes up with a thin little piece of leather. Jeremy takes it. When he removes the money he realizes that this is not the Hispanic dentist's wallet, but the thief's own because he's holding a measly trio of bills that he can't make out in the dark.

"Where's *his* wallet?" Jeremy demands. "The guy in the suit."

But he's lost his audience, because the kid has leaned back against the culvert's side with both hands pressed to his face. Jeremy pats him down, finds some change in one pocket, a set of car keys in another. He keeps the change. The empty wallet goes into the weeds. Jeremy turns away and walks back to where the Hispanic man is still lying unconscious and the other thief is curled up on his side.

Beside the man's right leg is the dropped wallet. It has a satisfying weight of cash, which Jeremy promptly removes. Somebody could make some money off all the credit cards in there, but Jeremy's not that kind of player. He tosses the emptied wallet aside and then he kneels down and checks the man's heartbeat. It's strong enough; better a headache than a heart attack. The man begins to groan and stir, and Jeremy decides it's time to make an exit.

First, though, he takes the other thief's wallet and comes up with four bills. There are another two bills and change in the right pocket, along with a very nasty little length of black leather with a lead cylinder sewn up inside. He'll count his money when he gets back to the motel.

He throws the bloodied gym sock with its weight of soap as far as he can into the night, and then he climbs out of the culvert, goes through the broken section of fence, walks to his truck as if strolling through an English garden, and drives away. He expects Gunny to be there, to say *Good work* or *Nice job* or something, but Gunny does not show. It's okay, Jeremy thinks. Another thing they taught him in the Corps was the value of self-reliance.

On the drive back, through streets nearly empty, Jeremy has to pull over into a restaurant's parking lot because a fit of shaking has come upon him and cold sweat has exploded from his flesh. He can't get his breath, he thinks maybe he's got a cracked rib and what is he going to do now? But he sits holding onto the steering wheel, his knuckles turning white, and when at last he takes a deep breath and sees he's pulled up in front of a Popeye's Fried Chicken joint he has to give out a broken laugh because God has such a twisted sense of humor. A mean streak, really.

He decides he's all right. No cracked rib. Just the thrumming of violence through his nerves and the smell of blood up his nose.

In his motel room, under the light bar in the bathroom, Jeremy finds himself richer by three hundred twenty-eight dollars and seventeen cents. Not a bad night's work.

He congratulates himself by buying a Dr Pepper and two bags of barbecue-flavored potato chips from the vending machines down by the office, and when at last he passes into a twilight sleep he feels well-fed.

ELEVEN.

At six o'clock on Saturday morning the Scumbucket pulled away from the La Quinta Inn on Remcon Circle in El Paso. George was at the wheel, Ariel sat in the front passenger seat, Nomad and Terry were behind them and Berke had her usual place. There was no joking around, no cutting comments flying back and forth; in fact, it was way too early to do anything but mutter. It had been a hard gig at the Spinhouse last night, a series of frustrations. Today they had about two hundred and eighty miles to travel before three o'clock. They were heading in a northwesterly direction up I-10 into New Mexico, and would follow it when it turned off almost due west for Tucson.

The call from Ash had come on Wednesday afternoon, about an hour after their interview on KTEP's local radio talkshow. The Saturday night gig at Fortunato's in Tucson was still open if they wanted it, he'd told George. And if they went that far, they might as well go on to San Diego and the rest of the venues, finish up the tour, but it was the band's decision so if they needed some time to think about it they could let him know in the morning.

"How about the situation in Sweetwater?" George had asked as he lay on the bed in the room he shared with Nomad and Terry. This time, John Charles got the rollaway. "Did they find the shooter?"

There'd been no progress, Ash had told him. He said he had another call in to Detective Rios but was waiting to hear back.

George had thanked him, and when Ash had ended the call George said to his roomies, "We need to get Ariel and Berke in here and figure out what we're going to do after the Spinhouse. We're still on the schedule in Tucson and Ash is talking about us finishing the tour. What do you think?"

"Okay with me," Nomad had said. "If everybody else says yes." He'd lived in Tucson for two years in his early twenties, working at Budget Rent-A-Car at the airport and playing with a couple of bands that never got off the ground. It pleased him to go back to his old stomping grounds with some success under his wings.

"Me too," Terry agreed, but what was foremost on his mind was getting to Eric Gherosimini's house outside Albuquerque and seeing Lady Frankenstein.

"Let's find out what *they* say." George had reached back and knocked twice on the wall, and in a few seconds Ariel had opened the connecting door.

It had not been such a tough decision. They were professionals, and the show must go on.

That didn't mean the show was going to go perfectly, or even *well*. As George drove the Scumbucket under the glare of a cloudless sky and between craggy brown mountain ranges, the band lay back in a silent reflection of the night before.

The Spinhouse had been packed, the merchandise and CDs had sold at a brisk pace, but the troubles had started when the lead singer of the Soul Cages—angry at being displaced as headliners for the night and not a little bit drunk—made a remark to Nomad backstage that a lot of Mike Davis's fans were out there, they would've been smart to sell Beelzefudd CDs and T-shirts instead of The Five's shit. Nomad had given him a glare that could melt glass, though he'd held his tongue and temper. He'd been in bands that had been knocked down from headliner status before, he knew what that felt like, but for two nickels and a cup of warm piss from a leper he would've punched the oh-so-groovy young fucker's RayBans right off his face.

Then there was the show itself. Nomad had decided not to do the party song 'Bad Cop' and start it off with 'Something From Nothing', which rocked pretty hard but slowed down for a quieter chorus:

When things fall apart and the story comes to its end,
You have to make something out of nothing again.

Which was about the way they all felt.

Within a few minutes, Nomad had nearly put a foot through his malfunctioning monitor speaker before Ariel could calm him down. Her own monitor started going out during the third song, she couldn't hear herself and she was drifting off-key and screwing up the rhythm too. George had huddled with the tech guy, a well-meaning aged hippie who had tripped over the fantastic light way too many times and as a result moved in slow-motion suitable for an alternate plane of existence, trying to make sense out of the tangle of cables and connections in the beatup mixing console. Everything had looked and sounded good in the light of day at sound check, but in the dark with six mirrorballs spinning at the ceiling, the noise of contained thunder from Berke's drums, the hollering of beer-stewed fans and the speaker system throwing out shrieks and growls as it neared imminent overload and fuse blowout, the console revealed itself to be as addled and time-warped as its kaftan-clad master.

While George rode the sick console, Terry was trying to cover Mike's line on the songs they'd agreed really needed the bass bottom, and he'd missed a couple of cues for his own keyboard parts. That was shocking in itself, because Terry never screwed up his parts; the realization came pretty quickly that he was trying too hard, and Nomad told him to concentrate on his usual job and forget the bass, which pissed Berke off because she thought it was disrespectful to Mike's memory, like his part could just be thrown away and nobody would care.

But when the time came for Berke's drum solo, at the midpoint of 'I Don't Need Your Sympathy', she turned her anger into energy. With the opening blasts from her double crash cymbals the others knew to step back out of range. The stage was hers, and for almost three minutes she owned not only that platform but every ounce of turbulent air between the Spinhouse's black-painted walls. She put her head down and became a machine, starting up a funk groove with kick and snare, complicating it with hi-hats, buzz rolling, double stroke hits, then breaking into a free-form conversation between the ride cymbal, the kick and the high *crack* of snare rimshots, speeding up and slowing down, speeding up and slowing down, slower, slower, now into a brassy *click-clack* clockwork of hi-hats with the kick drum thudding below them, adding a display of triplets and single stroke sevens and returning to a strutting funk groove in the tradition of her father's soulful style before he lost his mind. With a brief shake of her head she waved Terry off at the two-minute mark when he came back onstage to add his keyboard part, and he drew away from the blue and red spotlights. Whatever she needed to say, she was determined to make it heard by her effort alone.

In the forty seconds or so that followed, Berke took her playing to the edge. She sat astride her throne at the center of a storm, and as her hands and her drumsticks blurred she went into a complex pattern between her floor toms, her snare, the kick and the sheet-brass Zildjian crashes. Nomad saw from his position the little lights of cellphone cameras sparkling out there in the dark. She was going so hard he thought she was going to destroy her kit, and as one drumstick snapped on the edge of the snare she reached into her holster of spares, drew another one out and kept going without missing a half-beat. Sweat gleamed on her face, her eyes were closed, she was a red-lit torch high somewhere in the drummer's nirvana. The pitching hard-struck cymbals shimmered with blue and purple light, the black walls spoke back to her the thunder she was speaking, and the other members of The Five understood that furious wild language: *I am somebody, I am here, I am somebody, I am here and I have earned this moment.*

Dig it.

Berke pounded a military tattoo on the snare like a machine-gun burst, and then she suddenly raised her arms with the sticks clenched in her hands and there was only silence. In the next second it was filled by the applause and shouts of approval from the audience—which was a good thing, because many audiences didn't give a shit about drum solos—but as the alcohol-fuelled admiration went on Berke did not lower her arms. The others knew: she was waiting for the low thump of Mike's bass guitar to bring her back to the steady 4/4 beat of 'I Don't Need Your Sympathy'. But it didn't come, the seconds passed, and just as Nomad, Ariel and Terry walked back onstage Berke lowered her arms and picked up the song as if she'd been listening to her bandmate lay down the bottom like he'd done in nearly three hundred gigs across thirty-six states and five Canadian provinces.

From then on, Berke had returned to her role in The Five: the engine of rhythm driving the music forward, supplying the fills and an occasional quick display of flash just for the hell of it. But whatever the tempo, she was always where she needed to be.

When the show was over there came the people asking to get backstage, who were the same everywhere except for wearing different faces. First were the honest-to-God true fans, the ones who bought the CDs and merchandise and knew the songs, and they wanted to take pictures and say how sorry they were about Mike and to ask how *Catch As Kukulkan* was selling because that was great, man, really great, the best ever. Thank you for being here, they said, and they meant it. Then came the people who knew the Spinhouse manager or had connections with this or that local entertainment rag and just wanted to be seen going backstage, and from this group there might be comments about how absolutely fucking amazing the new Death Cab For Cutie CD was, or how they'd really come to see The Soul Cages but you guys were right up there, almost as good. In this group there would always be several hot girls looking for action with whomever they could snatch, and a couple of snaky guys wanting to see if the band "needed anything", and usually one fugly bitch with bad breath and charcoal black around her eyes asking up in Nomad's face why they weren't as popular as some band like Ra Ra Riot.

Unlike the night in Dallas, The Five had packed up their equipment and driven back to the La Quinta Inn without any further distractions. They had gone to sleep like tired old geezers, because tomorrow—today, by now—was going to be tough.

They went through a McDonald's drive-in at an exit about sixteen miles out of El Paso to get breakfast. Nomad insisted on opening the wrapper to check that his Egg McMuffin was cheeseless, as ordered, before they went on. Then George got the Scumbucket back on I-10, hauling the trailer, and on both sides of the highway the sun shone hot and glaring off the hard yellow earth stubbled with spiny brown vegetation and the sparse thin triumph of an ironwood tree.

Ariel unwrapped and ate one of the granola bars she'd brought along. She washed it down with a drink from her bottle of silver needle tea, and then she looked back and said, "Berke, can I see Mike's song?"

Berke roused herself to activity, unzipped her travel bag and brought out the green notebook. She leaned forward to pass it to

Ariel, but Nomad—his eyes obscured by his sunglasses— intercepted it before it changed hands.

Ariel waited while Nomad opened the notebook to the last few pages and re-read what Mike had written:

Welcome to the world, and everything that's in it.
Write a song about it, just keep it under four minutes.

Nomad looked at all the scratched-out lines that had given birth to the surviving two. His eyes went to the *Girl at the well* written there, like a phrase of...

"Inspiration," he said.

"What?" Ariel asked.

"Here. Where he wrote *Girl at the well.*" Nomad showed her, and Terry tilted forward to get a look at it too. "I don't think that's a title. I mean...it doesn't have to be. I think it's something he wrote down for inspiration." He decided to tell them the rest of it. "Early Sunday morning, after the Curtain Club, Mike told me that girl spoke to him. Said 'welcome' to him, and it got to him because..." Nomad shrugged. "Because he said he felt like she was glad to see him. I guess he didn't get that from his family very much. Maybe it's why he started with that one word, out of anything else he could've chosen."

"He wrote that because of the *girl*?" George asked, glancing at them in the rearview mirror.

"I'm just saying, I think he chose that word because she spoke to him. Because that's what she said, and he got something out of it."

"Or *made* something out of it, you mean," Berke countered.

"Whatever. I know as much about this as you do." He continued the notebook's journey to Ariel.

There followed a few seconds of silence, during which Ariel studied the lines. George thought there was a lot of traffic on I-10 this morning, and most of it was passing him. The Scumbucket was pulling as hard as it could. He looked into the sideview mirror and saw behind him an array of tractor-trailer trucks, SUVs, pickups and cars all heading to points west.

"Kinda strange," Terry said quietly. Today he was wearing one of his favorite vintage shirts, a psychedelic eyeshock of blue paisleys against an orange background. "You travel with a guy so long, but you realize there's so much you didn't know about him. I never knew Mike wanted to write a song."

Berke took a drink of her bottled water before she spoke. "At the gas station..." Her voice sounded strained, so she stopped and tried again. "At the gas station, he said nobody had ever asked him to try writing. He said...if he started a new song everybody could be part of, it would be good for the band. I guess he liked your idea, John."

Nomad didn't return a comment. He was thinking about that girl. That damned girl with her ladle of well-water and her face hidden in the shadow of her raggedy straw hat. She was creepy, even now, even at this distance. He wished he'd never thrown his fit and gotten out anywhere near that place.

"Hey, Berke," Terry said, and twisted around to look at her. "Have you ever wanted to write a song?"

"Never. It's not what I do."

"You could write a few lines. Add something to what Mike set down. We all could, and we could come up with..." He stopped, because he realized where he was going.

"The last song," Nomad finished for him. His original idea had been for them to work on a song together to keep from falling into the squabbling that he'd seen poison the final weeks of many band's careers. As the emperor of this band, to give them a common purpose over and above the grind of the gigs. And—a wild desperate hope—to change both Terry's mind and that of the Little Genius by creating what Berke called, and maybe rightly, a 'Kumbaya song'.

Now, though, the idea seemed more like creating a legacy for Mike, something that would go on without him. But something that he had been courageous enough to start, and for sure it had taken courage for Mike to step out of his comfort zone and put those words on paper.

Nobody wanted to be rejected, or laughed at, or thought a fool. Nomad knew that was what you risked when you threw yourself into the wilds of creation, where often you didn't know where you were going but hoped you'd find the right path somewhere to lead you out. Nomad had been there many times, and so had Ariel and Terry. It was some scary shit, to feel lost in yourself.

But—bottom line—that was the life he'd chosen. Or had chosen him, he wasn't sure which. Had chosen all of them, the same. Deal with it or not, make or break, do or die, the world still went on. Just as the world would go on without Mike.

"We should finish it," Nomad said. "All of us, adding something."

"*All* of us?" George frowned. "I already told you, I can't write anything!"

"You can try. Mike did."

"And the point of this is…?"

"The point is, you might think of yourself as a manager only, but I think of you as a pretty valuable member of this band. Until you pack up and leave, I mean. So because I'm the boss of the band, I say you contribute to this song. I don't care what it is. Two or three lines, or two or three words. But this is going to be a group effort." Nomad took off his sunglasses, the better to match stares with Berke. "If it's our last song as the current lineup—and I guess it will be—then I want a part of everybody in the lyrics." He had a sudden energizing idea: "We can play it at our last concert back in Austin. Last show, last song. How about that?"

"It won't make any sense," Berke said. "It'll end up in fucking chaos."

"Mike didn't seem to think so," he reminded her. "You said he told you it would be *good* for us."

"Yeah, well, Mike isn't here to tell us where he was going with it."

"I have some ideas," Ariel said, and everybody else shut up. Nomad knew he might be The Five's leader and frontman, but Ariel was no doubt the band's creative soul. "I was thinking…maybe…" After writing or co-writing nearly seventy songs with Blue Fly, The Shamans, Strobe, The Blessed Hours and The Five, she still always felt a little uncomfortable being in the spotlight of attention, as if she feared embracing it would open her to the hurt of it being taken away. "I was thinking," she went on, because they were all expecting something, "that Mike might've been writing about the music business. The limitations, maybe. This part about keeping the song under four minutes." They all knew every music producer wanted singles, which rarely tracked over three-fifty-nine. "See, he's wanting to write a song about the world and everything in it, but he's limited by the four minutes," Ariel said. "Or…it might be a song about change, or choices."

Everybody was still listening. Some loose flap inside the air-conditioner went *thwack… thwack…thwack*.

"Change," Ariel continued, "in that he's saying it's impossible to write about everything in the world inside four minutes, so to make it fit...either the world itself has to be changed...or perceived in a different way...and that choices have to be made as to what to...wait, let me try something." She opened her fringed-leather bag and brought out her pen, which wrote with purple ink, and her own gemstone-decorated notebook. She found an empty page, paused in thought for only a few seconds, wrote a line, scratched it out, wrote again, then another short scratch-out, after which the purple ink flowed without interruption. "Okay," she said. "How does this sound as a next line?" She read: "*Got to figure what to keep, and what to leave behind, and like life it's never easy*." When she looked up, she found Nomad's face. "Rough draft," she said, and he noted that today her eyes seemed to be the blue where a continent ends at the mysterious deep.

Thwrip...thwrip...thwrip, spoke the air-conditioner.

"See?" Nomad said to George, and included Berke in his appraisal. "How hard is that?"

They declined to respond. Nomad slid his sunglasses on, Berke leaned back in her seat, folded her arms across her chest and closed her eyes, Terry listened to his iPod and George whacked the air-conditioner with the palm of his hand to clear its congestion.

Ariel gave her attention once more to the song.

She thought it needed something here, after the *like life, it's never easy*. Before you went into the second verse, it needed another line or two. Some other statement of choice, or change. Something short and decisive.

Whatever it ought to be, she couldn't find it yet. But she had time. They all had plenty of time to work on it. Tomorrow...the next day... next week...it would come together, in time.

She closed both the green notebook and her own, and she put her pen away. She gazed out at the brilliant azure sky, the yellow earth blotched with browns and grays, the march of mountains across the horizon. *I have come a long way*, she thought. *We all have...but me, especially me*. She caught Nomad's reflection in a trick of sun and glass. *I love my family*, she thought. *I love them, just the way they are. What am I going to do without them?*

Because choice and change were in the air. The choices of Terry and George to go their own ways, and change that could not be stopped. Already it had begun, with Mike's death. John and Berke would try to put together a new band, with a new name, and she would stand with them but it would never be the same as it was now. Could never be. The same river can never be crossed twice, she knew. The flowing water has no memory of footprints.

When she closed her eyes against the glare, Ariel saw what she had left behind: a large two-story brick house with a wide green lawn and a curving driveway made of paving stones, and at the end of that driveway a white Jaguar and a dark blue BMW convertible. A house that was not a home, for inside it she had drifted from room to room like a passing shadow. In that house, among those people who had birthed her and raised her and sought to have influence over her, she had been insubstantial. They all fit together—father, mother, older brother and sister—because they spoke the same language, they measured wealth by the thickness of folding green and happiness by the size of the television screen (which happened to be a line from one of the first songs she'd written). They were always so busy. It had been a house of furious ambition, nothing could be still and calm, surely no time for the weakness of introspection. Life was a combat against competitors, a battle of shiny possessions and numbers in bank accounts, and that was the only life they knew.

But Ariel had been the strange one. The one who didn't 'get it', as her father often said. The lazy girl with no ambition. The time-wasting daydreamer. Oh sure, she liked to write her stories and her poems, and pick on that guitar, but really...she's so quiet, so passive, she can melt into a wall, you don't know she's there until you trip over her. Professional young men want vivacious girls, girls with charm and sociability. Well, there was always the hope that the girl would wake up from her lethargy, or her somnambulism, or whatever, and if she's at all seriously interested in training her voice she'll apply herself to the operatic disciplines. After all, Madame Giordano did say she has a malleable tone.

Her sister had been the closest to her in age, but six years can become a vast distance. Her brother, the Boston lawyer, rarely visited because their mother hated his wife, a situation that caused rancorous arguments between her parents since the girl was the daughter of one of Edward Collier's partners. Ariel—christened 'Susan', but who'd taken that name from a British nanny who used to play guitar for her when she was a little girl—watched her parents descend into a pattern of chaos, a script of drinking and fighting that made her believe things had gone wrong between them years before she was born. It seemed to center around Ariel's brother, Andrew. But nothing was ever solved in the uneasy calm after the turbulence, and Ariel came to realize at an early age that her mother and father both needed the other to flail them with recriminations, to atone for some secret guilt or acts of disloyalty.

Except for the presence of a number of nannies, she was alone for as long as she could recall. Alone in the deepest sense, alone as if she had been left in a basket at the front gate of this house within salt-scent of Manchester harbor and taken in by strangers who thought they could put their thumbprints upon a spirit. She had nothing against possessions, against the shiny and the beautiful and the faddish, but she did have something against becoming a slave to them.

Wasn't there more to life than an existence, fevered by this year's model and passion for a cellphone?

Wasn't there?

She thought there was. Why she sought peace when her family revelled in chaos, why she valued books that told quiet, meaningful stories and were not written to encourage the application of Genghis Khan's methods to modern business, why she heard music in the night breeze and saw poems on paper before they were written, she didn't know. But she did, and what she'd told Felix Gogo was true; she couldn't remember not hearing some kind of music and wanting to write down what she heard. Or, rather, *capture* what she heard, which was very often a difficult task because some tunes—like wild animals, or like John Charles for instance—resisted being put into neat small boxes for the pleasure of the public.

Ariel believed that a song was a living thing. It could burst into the world prematurely, ragged and half-formed, yes, but she thought the best of them—the most fully-realized, the most able to go the distance—grew slowly from a seed, gradually developing its heart and mind, over time becoming male or female in its attitude, its swagger or its contemplation. It grew skin lusty or lustrous, it preferred night or day for its rambles, it dressed itself in the leather or suede or gossamer of a million colors. And the ones she remembered being touched by when she was alone and lonely among strangers had some message to give to her. To *her*, even though it might have been written for a different generation, like 'Wait For An Answer' by Heart or 'The Lady' by Sandy Denny. They offered her some secret solace, some friendship like a hand on the shoulder, a whisper of *I have been where you are, and now where are you going?*

Or they gave her a rap to the side of the head, to say *Wake up, girl, and get your ass in gear, because the thing that kills is a thing called fear.*

Which was also a line from one of her early tunes.

She had been gone from that house and the people who lived there long before she left. It had taken a handsome young man she'd met when she was playing her twelve-string Gibson in the Starbucks on Church Street in Cambridge to actually cut the last ties that held her to her old life. He was starting up a band, had a couple of players together who'd paid their dues in other bands, they were calling this band Blue Fly, and did she maybe want to audition. And he wasn't promising anything, he'd said, but they had some interest from guys who actually managed hot bands like Big Top and Adam Raised A Cain, so there was that.

Awesome, she remembered saying.

She thought it had been a relief to her mother and father, the day she'd told them she was quitting her job at Barnes & Noble in Brookline, that she was leaving the apartment she shared with two other young women, and that she was driving to Nashville with three ex-members of Blue Fly to start another band. She hoped she might get some session work there, too. She thought it had been a relief for her parents because they never once asked her to reconsider, or said that she was travelling too far from home, or that she wasn't wise yet to the ways of the world.

Maybe her father was glad that at last she'd discovered her ambition, even if it was unfathomable to him as to how she would make any money; maybe her mother wanted to mourn in solitude the loss of years that no plastic surgeon could replace. Maybe they both too were alone, each in themselves; maybe it was a state of being for the Colliers of Manchester.

Whatever it was, Ariel could not help them, and so she put aside the thing called fear and went out to help herself.

That had been the spring of 2003. Her stay in Nashville had been little more than a year, working with the bands The Shamen and Strobe, before she'd headed to Austin with a new band who called themselves The Blessed Hours, and the rest was herstory.

The morning moved on. In front of the Scumbucket, the long gray stretch of I-10 baked and shimmered. They passed across the desert where it lapped up against truckstops and small towns built around cemeteries. Always mountains stood hazy against the horizon, the sky was cloudless and more white than blue as if the very color of heaven was burning away.

Since Mike's death, a stop at the gas pumps to fill the Scumbucket's tank brought everything back in terrifying detail. Berke would no longer leave the van, somebody else had to go get her bottled water for her and whatever else she wanted. Whoever was pumping the gas couldn't help but look uneasily over their shoulder and scan the far distance, but what they were looking for they didn't know. Everybody breathed better when the transaction was done and they were back in the Scumbucket pulling away, because the Scumbucket—ugly as it was, worn down and beaten up by the thousands of miles it had carried them—was their protection. But from what, no one could say.

Except for a twenty-minute creepy-crawl when traffic on I-10 was backed up by one of those situations where a car or a truck has broken down and everybody and their dashboard Jesus has to gawk at the wrecker, they made the Tucson city limits in plenty of time. Nomad had always liked Tucson when he'd lived there; it was a beautiful city, artsy-craftsy, bright Mexican colors, the San Xavier del Bac mission, the dry mesquite smell of the Sonoran desert, lots of golf courses drinking that precious water and lots of old people, sure, because it was a retirement haven, but there were lots of goths and metalheads in Tucson too. The University of Arizona kept the funk going. There was a pretty hot music scene, a healthy variety of clubs showcasing different styles, some very good and cheap restaurants and some way cool bars like the Surly Wench Pub and Snuffy's. So in a way he felt he was back at his second home, though he didn't care to revisit the grimy "musician's special" apartment he'd lived in out on South Herbert Avenue.

Nomad had found them a way to save some money this time into Tucson, and he reminded George of the address and how to get there.

They were staying for the night with the cousin of one of his old bandmates from Uppercut, which had lived and died within the space of six months, but the cousin was cool, he'd let them rehearse in his garage. The house was in a development northwest of the city. They got there without a problem, said their hellos to the cousin and his wife, unpacked their bags and had time to eat the ham sandwiches and taco chips that were graciously provided for their lunch. Then they turned around again and headed downtown, to the brown brick Fortunato's on North Fourth Avenue, for their three-o'clock load-in and sound check.

The gear was unloaded, the check went well, management said the ticket sales were off the heezy, and everybody was in their groove. Their boxes of merchandise went into the same room where merchandise boxes of the other bands on the gig, The Yogi Barons and The Bella Kersey Band, were stored. The Five wasn't on until around nine, so they climbed back into the Scumbucket and returned to the cousin's house to grab a few hours of sleep, drink a beer or two, meditate over a candle, watch cage fight matches on cable and do whatever they needed to do to get up for the gig, each to their own.

Following a high-energy show by the Yogi Barons, The Five took the stage a little after nine and the pumped-up crowd gave a full-throated response to 'Something From Nothing'. Without interruption the band went into 'The Let Down', another hard rocker opened by Ariel on her white Tempest. The gig was going like clockwork, everybody was loose and easy, the crowd was hollering when you wanted them to let loose and quieter when you wanted them to listen. Berke did her drum solo, cutting back on the time and the frenetics, and she allowed Terry to enter with his keyboard part when he was supposed to. Nomad broke an A string during 'Your Body Not Your Soul' but it was okay, he was playing for the angels tonight. Forty minutes later they did 'When The Storm Breaks', which earned a big positive, then they left the stage, waited for the audience buildup and returned to finish with a thunderous, wall-shaking version of 'Blackout of Gretely'.

They met some fans backstage, had pictures taken, and did a quick question-and-answer with entertainment reporter Brad Lowell from *The Daily Star*, whom they knew from past trips through town. He praised their new CD, said he thought they were on their way to a breakthrough, and he would be the first to say *I told you so*. He touched only briefly on Mike's death, but they couldn't add anything he didn't already know.

They settled in backstage to watch some of Bella Kersey's band. They'd played several gigs with her before, and Ariel in particular was a big fan. Bella was in her mid-thirties, had long prematurely gray hair and the face of a serene earth mother, but she could kick out the jams and lay down some howling firepower with her cherry-red 1975 Gretsch Streamliner. The band was a family thing and they lived in Tucson; her husband played bass and her brother played drums. It was awesome to watch Bella work the crowd, her sultry voice soaring over the flaming chords. She punched the air with a fist and kicked it with a bright red cowboy boot. Then after a riotous rocker she went to her pedal steel and, bathed in blue light, did a slow, achingly-beautiful version of Shane McGowan's 'If I Should Fall From Grace With God'.

While Bella was playing, the Little Genius quietly said to Nomad, "I'll go bring the trailer around." He went out the stage door and back through the alley where the gear would be loaded.

The Scumbucket was parked in a lot on the next street over. Despite the tragic loss, George was feeling good about things. Anybody who might have been watching would have said he was walking like a man with places to go. The band had been hot tonight, very tight, the merchandise was moving, a check on the website said the CDs were selling now in the hundreds of copies, and the YouTube and MySpace hits were through the roof. Yeah, maybe it did have something to do with the kind of media shine that no band wanted, but there it was. Now there was the Casbah in San Diego to get ready for, and after that on Saturday the 2nd came the Big Show, the make or break, at the Cobra Club in Hollywood. The Sunset Strip, baby! What he had not told them—not yet, but he would—was that two A&R guys, one from Sonic Boom and the other from Manticore, were going to be in the audience. *Supposed* to be. Let's hope.

He was going to leave them in good shape, with a future ahead of them. He owed them that much.

He showed his parking pass to the attendant on duty and walked across the lot, under the bright yellow security lights. He fished his keys from his pocket, unlocked the driver's door and opened it, and he was thinking of finding a supermarket and buying a bottle of wine for their hosts when a hammerblow crashed into his right shoulder.

He thought that somebody had actually come up from behind and struck him, but when he spun around, gasping, no one was there.

George put his left hand to his shoulder. His shirt was wet. There was a hot throbbing pain, rapidly escalating. His shoulder felt knocked out of joint. He looked around, stunned. His glasses hung by one ear. It was getting harder to breathe; the breath had been knocked out of him, too. His heart…Jesus, it was really pumping…

He looked toward the attendant's hut. Saw the blurred shape of the man sitting on a stool, watching the screen of a small TV.

It came to George's mind to call out *Sir, I need some help please.*

But the words never left him, because another hammerblow hit him in the chest and he fell back against the Scumbucket. He tried to draw a breath but all he found was a gurgle of liquid. Something in his chest burned like a white-hot coal. He had to get it out, had to get rid of it, and he put both hands against his chest but he couldn't reach what he needed to find, his fingers were wet, he couldn't get his fingers deep enough. He clawed at his chest and he opened his mouth to shout for help but nothing came out, he no longer had a voice.

George staggered. His knees were giving way. He reached out to grab hold of the Scumbucket to keep him on his feet but it was no good, he was falling toward the pavement, and as he twisted and went down he saw in the last of his light his own splayed handprint dark against the battleship gray.

It was just like the logo on their T-shirt, except this one was melting in the warm Tucson night.

TWELVE.

"No, I don't," said Nomad.

He was weary and red-eyed. The video camera lights were not kind. Neither were the questions that came from behind them, and the one that had just been thrown at Nomad was *John, do you have any idea who might have wanted to kill him?*

"Dumb question, Dave," the Hispanic police captain sitting at the table between Nomad and Ariel said. "Don't you think we've been over this?"

"All for the public, sir," Dave the reporter from Fox-KMSB answered. He flashed a thin and humorless smile. "Doing my job."

"Miss...Bonneway, is it?"

Berke blinked heavily and directed her attention to the young woman who'd spoken. "Bonne*vay*. With a 'v'."

"Okay, got it. Am I hearing you've reported to Captain Garza that you were shot at by this sniper when you were in Sweetwater? After your bass player was killed?" The woman, blonde and sharp-featured and maybe twenty-two at the oldest, wore a nametag on the jacket of her beige suit that identified her as being a reporter from the *Tucson Citizen.*

"That's right." Berke had a blinding headache. She'd been sick to her stomach for the past two hours. "Yeah."

"So can I ask if you reported this to the police in Sweetwater or not?"

"I didn't, no. I thought...I wasn't sure it happened."

"Pardon me? You weren't sure you were *shot* at?"

"Jamie, this isn't an interrogation," said the public information officer, a dark-haired woman in her mid-forties named Ann Hamilton. She was sitting at the end of the conference room table, beside Terry. Her demeanor was quiet but obviously she could pull up some steel when it was needed. "Miss Bonnevay has explained that to Captain Garza. Next question, please."

The reporter from KVOA raised his hand, but the *Citizen* reporter wouldn't yield. "I'm just thinking out loud, maybe, that we have a sniper on the loose here because the police weren't properly notified in Texas. Am I wrong about that?"

"Let me answer," said Garza, whose deep-set ebony eyes fixed upon Jamie Layne and had the effect of nailing her to her chair. He had a jaw like a brick and a pock-marked face and his voice sounded like gravel being churned into cement. "First off, we're only starting our investigation. Where it'll take us, we can't say. Secondly, you're assuming that Mr. Emerson was shot by the same individual who killed Mr. Davis, which is far from being proven. And, Jamie, tossing around terms like 'sniper' is not going to endear you to the police department, I can tell you."

"It's a little premature," the PIO lady added, as a softener.

"Sir?" said the KVOA reporter. "Are you saying this was a *coincidence*?" It sounded ridiculous, the way he said it.

"I'm saying we have a young man who is fighting for his life." Garza would not rise to the bait. His expression was Buddha-calm, if Buddha had been born the son of a Juarez cop. The hospital public relations rep had only a few minutes ago left this room on the first floor of University Medical Center, after telling the assembled group of reporters, camera crews and various techs that George Emerson had been delivered by ambulance at eleven forty-eight in critical condition, a little more than two hours ago, and was currently in surgery with two gunshot wounds, one to the right shoulder and one to the upper chest. "Until we have more to go on, we can't draw any conclusions about *anything*," Garza said.

"But they were long range shots, is that correct?" asked the black female reporter from, ironically enough, KGUN.

"I can't comment on that."

"Mr. Castillo says he didn't hear any shots. He was right there when Mr. Emerson was hit. If they weren't fired at long range, then—"

"Under investigation. No comment." Garza pointed to the *Daily Star* reporter whose hand was up. "Go ahead, Paul."

"Thanks. How about some background on Mr. Emerson? What's his age, and where's he from?"

The others looked to Nomad to answer, but Nomad just stared at his own hands clenched together on the table before him. He wasn't feeling much like an emperor at the moment. He was feeling small and impoverished and lost again on the unmapped road. He was feeling caught between tears and rage and if he was to move his head one inch to the left he might start to weep and one inch to the right he might stand up and throw this fucking table over.

So he sat very, very still.

Terry cleared his throat. "George is thirty-three. He's from Chicago."

"Can I get a rundown of all your ages and where you're from?"

"Old," Nomad said when it was his turn. He wished he'd kept his sunglasses on, but Garza had told him to take them off when speaking to the press. *Just grit your teeth and get through it*, Ms. Hamilton had said. He could still feel the stiffnesss of dried stage-sweat in his red T-shirt. "Detroit city," he added, without looking up or moving his head.

"I think we ought to wind this up," Ms. Hamilton told the reporters after everyone else had answered the question. "You can imagine what these people are going through."

"Captain, are you planning on asking the FBI to help the investigation?" It was the woman from the *Citizen* again.

"That's not been discussed yet."

"Sir? Let me rephrase a question," said the Fox guy. "Does *anybody* at that table have *any* idea about why a sniper might be—*might* be—stalking your band?" He ignored both the abrupt birth of Garza's fearsome scowl and the outstretched palm of Ms. Hamilton's hand. "Or are we talking about music critics taking up arms?"

Nomad had had enough of this. His face impassive, he stood up and walked out the door behind Ms. Hamilton. Before he reached the elevators at the end of the hall, he was aware that three other people were walking with him. The police captain caught up with them and eased into the elevator just as the doors were closing. They began rising to the second floor, where they'd been given a private waiting area and a cop was on-duty to keep any reporters from intruding.

"As much as I don't want to hear that word or see it in print," Garza said before they reached their floor, "I know the media. They're going to be talking about a sniper all over this town by sunup, so get used to it. When it goes on the Internet and the networks, it's everywhere."

"This is crazy." Berke had dark purple hollows under her eyes. "Why would somebody be trying to kill *us*?"

"That's the question, isn't it?"

The doors opened. The cop was on a sofa in a small seating area, facing the bank of elevators. He put aside his *Sports Illustrated* magazine and sat up straight as a display of vigilance. On the table beside him was a stack of magazines and a dark blue coffee cup bearing a red 'A' outlined in white. Garza nodded at him and walked with Nomad, Terry, Ariel and Berke down the long hallway past a nurses' station to another door. He opened it for them and followed them in.

It was nothing special, just a room with a few gray upholstered chairs, a sofa, a couple of low tables and lamps, and a TV. On the cream-colored walls were framed paintings of sunwashed adobe houses and orange-tinted desert scenes.

"Okay," Garza said as the bandmembers got themselves settled. "Now I guess all you can do is wait. Unless you want to pray," he added. "If not here, there's a chapel at the far end of the hall and take a right."

"Thank you," Terry said. He pushed his specs back up the bridge of his nose. "Um...we can leave and walk around, can't we? If we want to take the elevator down to the vending machines? Like... we're not under arrest, are we?"

"You can go wherever you please. Just remember that if the reporters are hanging around, they can get to you downstairs. But probably most of them are going back to the crime scene." Garza checked his watch. "Which is where I need to be." He moved toward the door. "Anything else I can do for you?"

Nobody answered, but then Ariel spoke up: "I'd like to know," she said. "Where the shots came from. They *were* from long range, weren't they?"

"Miss, I just can't say. It's true Mr. Castillo didn't hear them. He didn't see anybody else in the lot but Mr. Emerson. So...the only thing we're sure of is that it wasn't a drive-by. Other than that..." He let the sentence die. "We have a lot of work to do," he finished.

"Thank you for doing what you can," Ariel told him. Her eyes were swollen and had the shine of shell-shock.

"Yeah. Well, the trauma team here is the best in the country. That's not just *my* opinion." He glanced quickly at Nomad, who was sitting in a chair slumped over with his hands to his face. "Hang in," he said, and then he left the room and shut the door behind him.

For a while no one said anything. At last Terry quietly breathed, "*Wow*," which served to sum up their collective inability to grasp the fact that the Little Genius lay on an operating table with surgeons trying to keep him alive. Also, they were so tired they could hardly move. It was a bad dream, and at its center a worse one. How long George had been bleeding out on the ground before the attendant had seen him was still unknown, though the police thought it had only been ten or fifteen seconds. Still...ten or fifteen fucking *seconds*? While George had been down with two bullets in him, and one right in his chest near the heart? It was more than they could bear to think about.

The attendant—Castillo—had recognized the blue parking pass as being from Fortunato's. Musicians parked their vans and trailers over there all the time, in a special area in the back. He'd called nine-one-one, reported a man down and unconscious and his chest covered with blood. About the time the ambulance and the first police cruiser had come screaming up, Nomad had walked out Fortunato's stage door into the alley to see where George was, and when he heard the sirens he later told Ariel that he'd felt like a knife had ripped open his guts because he knew something very bad had happened to their friend.

At the hospital, Nomad had called Ash on his cell and had gotten the *I can't pick up right now, but—*

"Pick up, you dumb shit!" Nomad had shouted into the cell. "It's John Charles! Pick up!"

"Hey, hold on with that language!" There had been some hot spice in Ash's heavily-accented voice. Little did he know how close he was walking to a burning crater in Hell. "Who do you think you're talking—"

"Shut up and listen!" the emperor had commanded, and Ash had shut.

Ash was coming to Tucson, would try to get a flight out by afternoon or at the latest by Monday morning. In the meantime, he would make the call to George's mother and father in Chicago. Ash had sounded stunned, and when he asked Nomad, "What is going on?" Nomad knew he was asking why two members of The Five had been cut down by bullets and to that there was no good or easy answer.

Nomad lowered his hands from his face. Terry was standing in front of him.

"Maybe we ought to pray for George," Terry said, and he looked at Ariel and Berke to gauge their reactions. "Don't you think?"

"I think we should," Ariel agreed.

Nomad closed his eyes and shook his head and masked his pain with his hands again. Berke said, "I'm not what you'd call religious."

"Can't you be? For just a minute?" Terry asked, but Berke turned her face away. Terry went over and sat beside Ariel, and they grasped hands and put their heads together, and when Terry began with "Dear God," Berke got up and left the room.

When their prayer was finished, Nomad sat back in his chair and rubbed his temples. If he'd only gone to get the van with George, he thought. Maybe it wouldn't have happened. If only, if only...

"John?"

"What is it?" Nomad watched as Terry pulled a chair up in front of him and sat down.

"Don't you believe in God?"

"No," came the reply. "I believe in myself." He saw his lamplit face reflected in Terry's Lennon-specs. "God is a myth made up to keep people from freaking out about death." Terry was silent, as if waiting for something else. "Listen," Nomad said irritably, because Ariel was watching him too, in that expectant way she had when they were writing a song together and she was waiting for him to supply a line. "I want to rest. How about leaving me alone."

"I'm just asking."

"Don't ask."

Terry started to slide his chair back, and then he seemed to think better of it. He drew a long breath, as if preparing himself.

"What do you *want* from me?" Nomad asked, again on the verge of either anger or tears. "You want me to get down on my knees and pray for George's life? You want me to promise I'll be a good boy or some shit like that, so George will come out of that operating room *alive*?" He felt his mouth start to twist into a snarl. "It doesn't happen that way. Praying to a myth doesn't get it. Either he lives or he doesn't. Okay? And anyway...if God wasn't a myth, why should He care about George? Why should He care about anybody in this room, or this city, or on this fucking *earth*? Huh?"

"I don't know," Terry said, but the way he said it told Nomad that maybe Terry had already asked himself these questions, many times over.

"Damn straight you don't know." Nomad looked to Ariel for support, but she was staring down at the floor. "Nobody knows, and for damn sure those fucking preachers don't know. So what are we sitting here talking about?"

Terry's face was impassive. Whatever he had been preparing himself for, he was ready. He said, "Can I tell you a story?"

"What kind of story?"

"A true story. Something that really happened to me, in a church about—"

"Oh, shit!" Nomad interrupted, scowling. "Come *off* it, man!"

"Terry?" Ariel's voice was quiet but firm. "You can tell *me*."

Terry nodded, but when he spoke again he was still staring at Nomad. "In a church about forty miles northwest of Oklahoma City," he went on. "A small town called Kingfisher. Did I ever tell you about my dad?"

Nomad didn't speak. Ariel said, "You told us he has a furniture store."

"Not just a furniture store. He's the White Knight there. That's his chain of stores. White Knight Discount Furniture. Two locations in Oklahoma City, and four other stores across the state. One in Little Rock and one in St. Louis. My dad's loaded. I mean, *his* dad started the business, but he really made it go. He's a hard worker. He puts his nose to that grindstone, man. But it takes its due from him, I can tell you. With that many people working for you, and jumping when you say jump...it makes you into a bully, always pushing for what you want. Which he was, when I was growing up. It was his way or the highway, know what I'm saying?"

"Everybody has it tough," Nomad commented.

"Yeah, that's right. Ever hear this: Be kind to everybody you meet, because everybody's fighting some kind of battle?" Terry paused for a response, but Nomad made none. "My dad was fighting one. His dad was, and back and back. But the deal was...you never said 'no' to Clayton Spitzenham. The White Knight just wouldn't hear it. So I was seventeen years old and I'd been taking piano lessons since I was ten, and I told my dad I wanted to be a musician because music just...spoke to me...it was like food to me. I said I wanted to make music. Maybe join a band, or start one. I said I didn't want to go into the family business. But you think he listened to me? You think he *heard* me?" A bemused and slightly bitter smile moved across Terry's face. "Don't think so. He said I'd outgrow all that. He said, Terry, you don't know your own mind. You don't know what's good for you. You look around yourself, he said, and you'll see that everything you have comes from that business you seem to want to turn your back on. This is a *family* business, he said. You have to realize what your place is in this family."

Know your role, Nomad thought, remembering Felix Gogo's advice.

"We really went at it," Terry continued. "I was sticking to my guns and my dad was making the plans for me to get a business education." He shrugged. "Hey, maybe it would've been good for me. Maybe I would've come to it myself, in time, but it wasn't what I wanted. But he was pressuring me day and night, cutting down my music, cutting me down...everything he could do to get me in the box."

The dreaded box, Nomad thought. For an artist, it was the worst thing. The safe, predictable thing that can lead a creative person to boredom, drugs, insanity and early death. Wasn't that the point of the box? To kill risk, which was the life and soul of creation?

"He said everybody needs furniture," Terry said. "But the world can go on just fine without music."

"*Oh*," Ariel said, as if she'd been punched in the stomach.

"I told him that wasn't a world I wanted to live in. Without *music*? Without...my *food*? I mean, it's like bread and wine to me, and you know what I'm saying. But there was nothing I could tell him, because when Clayton Spitzenham makes up his mind, it's a done deal. And I guess I could've left home, just hit the road and gone, but I didn't want it to be that way." Terry hesitated, and now he was staring past Nomad at a distant place, his eyes lit up with lamplight behind the round lenses. "I guess I wanted him to give me his blessing, because for whatever he is, I did love him. I *do* love him. But like that was ever going to happen. Then…something *did* happen. On a Sunday morning, in a church in Kingfisher. And nobody knows about this but my folks, I've never told anybody because it just sounds so…" He trailed off, searching for a word.

"*Holy-rolly*?" Nomad prompted.

Terry gave a faint smile. "No, not that." He found his word. "So *awesome*," he said. "Maybe scary-awesome. But it did happen to me, just as I'm telling it. See, this church was building a camp for kids. They were going to be buying furniture for the cabins and the main building, and my dad wanted to get the contract. So he loaded me up, I guess to show how great of a family-man he was that he would bring his son with him to church even though he never set foot in one in Oklahoma City and neither did my mom, and we drove there and went in. He wanted to be seen, and to glad-hand people, but neither one of us knew anybody there. I mean, it was forty-something miles from our house. So we're sitting there in the pew, about midway in, and it's a nice big church, modern, still smelled new, and the pastor gets up front and says there's a special speaker that day."

Terry was silent for a moment, working his fingers together. "When it came time for the speaker," Terry said quietly, "the guy stood up at the lectern and looked out at the congregation. I don't remember his name, but I remember that he was just real ordinary-looking. Kind of flabby and going bald, and he was wearing a tan suit. It was late June, warm outside. So he said hello to the people, and cracked a joke or something, and said he was going to talk about some mission work somewhere. And all of a sudden…just like that… he leaned over the podium and I remember…he trembled. His eyes closed, and he trembled, as if he was about to pass out. I remember that people gasped. Then the pastor jumped up to help him, and some other men at the front stood up…but then…that man lifted his face. He opened his eyes, and he'd gone pale and he was sweating, and he said, 'I'm speaking to Terry'."

"Oh, *right*!" Nomad said, with a crooked grin. "Did he like... have one of those booming voices that made the walls shake, and sawdust fell from the rafters?"

"No," Terry answered, his own voice still quiet and controlled. "It was the same as it had been before. Just the voice of an ordinary man. I'm telling you what happened, John. It's no joke, and it's no lie."

They stared at each other, until Nomad's mocking smile faded away.

"Go on," Ariel urged.

"The man spoke my name." Terry turned his attention to Ariel and then back to Nomad once more. "And, sure, maybe there were other Terrys in the church. I think there were maybe eighty or a hundred people in there, so there could've been other Terrys. And he never looked at me, he just seemed to be staring at the back wall. But then he said, 'Don't be turned aside. Music will be your life'. And let me tell you guys...when you hear that from a stranger in a church you've never been in before...far from your home...what you feel is *fear*. The awesomeness came later. Right then, I just wanted to put my head down and hide, because I was afraid."

Terry waited for that to sink in. From Nomad there was no sign of interest or emotion. "He didn't speak to me only. He spoke to two or three other people, but I can't tell you what he said. Told them stuff he never should've known, is my guess. Then he just seemed to get tired, and he lowered his face again and he kind of staggered back, and the pastor got up and told the people to stay where they were, that everything was all right. He helped the man to his seat, and the man put a hand to his face and I could tell he was crying. Then my dad said to me, 'We're getting out of here', and his face was the color of spit on a sidewalk. I mean, he was *gray*. So he got up and I got up and we went, and that was the end of him wanting that contract. I don't think he ever went back there. I know *I* didn't."

Terry's specs had slid down his nose a little bit, so he pushed them back into place with a forefinger. "We never talked about it. I guess he told my mom. Maybe he didn't. But the thing is...after that happened, he was done trying to force his will on me. Whatever I wanted to do with music—whatever I wanted to *try*—he stepped aside and let me go my own way. I don't think he was ever happy about it, but he accepted it. He still does. That's why he's helping me start the vintage keyboard business. He likes that word, *business*. But it took a stranger in a church for him to respect *me*, and what I wanted to do with my life. We didn't *know* anybody there, John. There was no *way* it could have been anything but..." Again, he searched for his destination.

"The voice of God?" Nomad's voice had a cutting edge. "Is that what you're saying you heard?"

"I heard a man speaking," Terry answered. "I'm not going to pretend to know where the words were coming from. But he said something that was meant for me and me alone. I'm sure of that. And the deal is...all I've ever wanted is to build a life with music in it, John. That was always my dream. Not to play on a stage in front of thousands of people or make tons of cash, or be anybody's superstar." He included Ariel with another glance. "I've gotten what I wanted... and more, really."

"Okay, so you're saying everything is like...preordained, right?" Nomad challenged. "It's all written in the fucking stars?"

"He said 'Don't be turned aside'," Terry answered. "So no, I don't think it was preordained. I think I had a choice. He was just telling me how to get where I wanted to be."

Nomad shook his head. "That's bullshit."

Terry grinned at Ariel, but his eyes were sad. "Now you see why I've never told anybody. Not even Julia." His flighty, ethereal ex-wife, to whom he was married for less than a year before she took off from Austin to Florida with an old boyfriend. Nobody had known what he saw in her, except she was very pretty, she played classical piano and made great crepe St. Jacques when she wasn't popping little blue Xanax tabs.

"Bullshit," Nomad repeated, for emphasis.

"Do you think you know every-fucking-thing?" Terry asked, and now the sadness was gone; now he had some heat in his face and his eyes were bright with the beginning of anger and he had decided that right this minute—this minute—he was through backing down from John Charles because he knew what he'd seen and heard and—"Nobody on earth is going to say I'm a liar," he said, his voice tight. He blinked rapidly; maybe he *was* still a little afraid of John, but this was important enough to fight for. "You don't know everything. Not nearly. And I'm telling you I don't either, because I don't understand it and I never will, and I'm not trying to holy-roll anybody, but there's a lot more to all this than we can see and hold. I mean, there's like a world beyond this one. A dimension or something that we can't get our minds around."

"Oh, you're talking about Heaven now? With the angels and the harps?"

"You make it sound stupid."

"It *is* stupid, Terry. It's stupid for stupid people." When Terry paused, Nomad said, "Go on, let's hear some more. Set it up so I can knock it down."

But Terry stared at the floor and worked his hands together, and he didn't answer as outside in the hallway there was the *bing-bing* of an intercom followed by a woman's voice paging what sounded like 'Dr. Pajiwong'.

At last Terry said, "It's not as simple as you make it out to be. Or as simple-minded. See, you laugh and say it's 'bullshit' because you've never heard a stranger speak your name in a church before. Nothing's ever happened to you that shook your foundations, or made you think that you don't know everything. I'm a human being, I can't see through the dark glass. My personal belief is that there's a Heaven and Hell of some kind, but—"

"Pitchforks and golden halos," Nomad interrupted. "When I die I want to go south where the action is. I want a slut from Hell giving me an eternal—" *Blow-job*, he almost said, but he felt Ariel's presence and he amended it to, "Lap dance."

"Are you afraid," Terry asked, as he lifted his gaze to Nomad's, "to even let yourself *wonder*? Does that scare you so much?"

"No, it doesn't scare me." Nomad's eyes narrowed. "I just don't want to spend any time wondering about being nothing. Because that's what you are after you die. Everything you were and thought, gone to nothing. Just like the dark blank before you were born. How come your stranger in the church didn't help you out a little more with these kinds of questions, Terry? How come he like...hit and ran, without saying what everybody in that church really wanted to know. Huh? How come he just didn't say, 'I'm speaking with the voice of God, and I'm telling all of you there's an eternity where everybody finds happiness...whatever that is'. How come he just picked out three or four people and left the others feeling like they were skinny kids in a schoolyard too nerdy to join the cool team?" He let that hang, and then he asked, "How come your stranger didn't tell you why innocent children and good people like Mike get killed every day of every week, every month and every year? Now *that* would've been worth hearing. So if you're saying it was the voice of God...he's going to have to speak a whole hell of a lot louder before I'll listen."

Terry stared at him for a few seconds longer, with the reflection of Nomad's face suspended on the lenses of his specs. Nomad stretched his legs out, leaned his head back and closed his eyes as an instruction for Terry to go find another place to sit. After a while Terry got up and pulled his chair over nearer Ariel, who gave him a faint smile and a nod but who saw that he'd been defeated in his purpose of making John Charles grasp the possibility of the Unknown Hand. That was how she'd always pictured God. An Unknown Hand, moving for the greater benefit of human beings. It seemed to her that when it could move it did, but there were times it could not, or for some unrevealed reason it *did* not.

John had asked some good questions, she thought as she watched him either feigning sleep or searching for it. Some questions that were asked by believers and non-believers alike. Believing didn't mean the questions should be silenced, she thought.

She didn't have the answers. No one on this side did, and if they pretended to they were probably lying to make money from frightened people, which made them deceivers that the Unknown Hand should have crushed...but it did not. Just as the Unknown Hand did not move to bring justice against the wicked, or stop evil, or eliminate suffering in an outpouring of miracles.

Because, she thought, that work depended upon known hands, the hands of men. Maybe the Unknown Hand moved things beyond the understanding of men, or set things into motion that asked men to make choices, and whatever choices men made they had to live with for better or worse. Maybe the Unknown Hand directed men, or prodded them, or presented them with problems to be solved and men were unaware of its presence in the chaotic life of day-to-day. But maybe the world belonged to men, it had been given to them as a gift, and whatever they did with that trust was their burden and responsibility, and the Unknown Hand—like the voice of a stranger in a church—could guide but not compel.

She didn't have the answers. Like everyone else, all she could do was wonder.

Berke came back in with a can of Coke she'd gotten from the first-floor vending machines. "All done with the prayer meeting?" she asked, but no one bothered to reply. She sat down on the sofa and propped her feet up on the table that held a stack of months-old magazines. What she didn't intend to tell them was that, though she was far from being religious, she'd been curious about the chapel and had walked down that way to take a look. She'd stood on the threshold of a small, dimly-lit room with two pews, a lectern and a picture of Jesus kneeling in a garden. Maybe she'd said something in her mind about George. Maybe. It had been quick, just a passing thing. For good luck, if anything else. She'd always figured Jesus was kind of like a four-leaf-clover. A tip wouldn't hurt either, she'd thought, so she'd put a buck in the slot of a little white lockbox screwed to the top of a table. Next to it was a white book where people wrote down the names of who they were praying for.

Better make it two bucks, she'd decided, but in the end it had been five.

About forty minutes after Berke's return, an Asian doctor wearing blue scrubs and a surgeon's cap came into the room. He told them in perfect English, his calm quiet doctor's voice tinged with a trace of Southern accent, that George was out of surgery and in the ICU, and that the next twelve hours would be, as he put it, 'the crucial period'. More than that, he couldn't say. Nomad took that to mean the doctors had done all they were able to and now it was George's fight.

They thanked him, and after he left they settled back into their places to wait some more. They were good at waiting; they did far more waiting than playing, so they'd made their peace with that necessary aspect of the musician's life. But never before had they waited out the life or death of a bandmate, and it was going to be a trial for all of them.

And maybe most of all for Nomad. The walls were closing in on him. He hadn't particularly liked hospitals before his father was shot, but afterwards...when he'd sat in a room similar to this, smelling the hospital's odors and sensing the impending news, in front of him some dog-eared Batman, Green Lantern and Captain America comics a nurse had found for him, until one of the other Roadmen had come in and told him his dad was gone...

The Month of Death had arrived early this year.

As Ariel and Terry dozed and Berke watched through heavy-lidded eyes an old black-and-white TCM movie with Bette Davis on TV, Nomad stood up. He told Berke he was going downstairs to the machines, and did she want anything. She said no, she was okay.

He left.

At first he'd only intended to walk outside and breathe some non-hospital air, some air without bad memories in it. Then he decided to walk a little ways, not very far, just to get the blood moving. That waiting-room was killing him. To go back to it...no, not right now. He would walk a while down the city block, on this weeping side of three-o'clock.

Exactly when he'd decided to step out and hail the cab he saw coming, he didn't know. But there it was, he waved an arm and it veered over to pick him up.

"Where to?" the driver asked.

Nomad sat thinking. *Where to?* was the question. What was open twenty-four hours downtown, say within two or three miles? Where had he used to hang out, at all hours, over a cup of black coffee, a steak sandwich and a platter of...

Greek potatoes, he remembered.

"The Argonaut," Nomad said. He gave the driver the address, on East Congress Street, and the cab took him away.

THIRTEEN.

Walking into the Argonaut was like returning home to a house your family had sold and moved out of without letting you know. Sure, it had been years since he'd set foot in here, and it looked pretty much the same and had that same aroma of charred lamb kabobs and peppery fish soup he remembered so distinctly. But there were differences. The exterior that used to be painted soft 'Aegean blue' was now a hard yellow, making Nomad think of the color he saw in his mind when he closed his eyes and belted out the sustained A note at the end of 'I Don't Need Your Sympathy', because it was true he did see mental colors when he sang. Another difference was that when you used to step into the place, a series of small bells chimed over the door; now there was only the whirring of the ceiling fans, but at least those were still there.

The cash register sat atop an unchanged and probably immovable scarred and battered wooden desk that looked as if it had been deck planking from one of those fighting Greek ships, but where was Jimmy? Short, barrel-chested Jimmy with his black crewcut and his mile-wide grin, and from his mouth a rusty barbed-wire voice that always launched the same words when you came in—*Hey, ya hungry?* and when you left, *Howja like ya food?*

Fine, Jimmy, just fine.

But Jimmy was not there, his place taken by a somber-looking girl with long dark hair who was texting somebody on her cell.

"Hi," Nomad said.

"Sit anywhere," she told him, her eyes never leaving the blue screen.

There were lots of wheres to sit. The seven or eight tables were empty, but a few people sat in the red vinyl booths. Lamps with gold-colored shades shed light upon the early-morning patrons. Nomad counted three guys—college students, they looked to be—in one booth, a young couple cuddling close in another and in a third a solitary middle-aged man reading a book and drinking iced tea. Nomad took a booth away from everyone else, near the windows that gave a view onto East Congress, and he waited for a waitress to show up. From his seat he had the full impact of the mural of a Greek galley painted on the opposite wall, next to the kitchen door. It was a thing of beauty, and it had sailed through the years with only minor modifications to the original, which according to Jimmy had been painted in 1978, the year the Argonaut had opened.

It was of course the *Argo*, the ship built to carry Jason and the Argonauts to find the Golden Fleece. Under a sunlit sky decorated with lacy streamers of clouds, the Argo's sharp prow cut through the dark blue waves. Seagulls flew before it, and a dolphin's gray dorsal fin emerged from the white-capped water. The sturdy Argonauts pulled at their oars, in this rendition twenty on either side. Standing before the mast with its billowing russet-colored sail was the dark-bearded Jason, his right arm outthrust and index finger pointed to indicate the destination ahead. Nomad had always thought it was a really cool mural, its style similar to the beautifully luminous works of Maxfield Parrish he'd seen in one of Ariel's art books. At the bottom, where the sea waves began, was signed the name 'Myalodeon', though whether that was the original artist or a later restorer Nomad didn't know.

He was still waiting. Somebody had to be working in here, because the other customers had food and drink. He wished he'd thought to bring a magazine from the hospital, but then again, no: hospital magazines smelled like hospitals. He needed something to look at but his own hands, so he shifted a little in his seat, reached into the pocket of his jeans and brought out an object of interest he'd been carrying since that night at the Curtain Club.

It was the piece of clear quartz crystal Cheryl Buoniconti—now Cheryl Capriata—had given to him. He set it on the table before him and just stared at it. He was trying to understand the depths of belief.

Somehow, Cheryl believed healing crystals might intercede for her in her fight against cancer; somehow, Terry and Ariel believed God or Jesus Christ or whoever might help George in his fight for life. What was the difference? To him, he'd go for the crystal, because you could hold the fucking thing in your hand, and whether it did any good or not it was real, it had weight and it was solid. At the very least, it was a pretty cool paperweight.

He rubbed his eyes with the heels of his hands. Who had shot George? The same person who'd killed Mike? Different snipers, at different times in different places? Was there any possible sense to be made of that? And Berke saying she thought she'd been shot at, too? Was it open season on The Five, and if it was—and here he realized he might be sitting too close to the window—who was going to be next in the sniperscope?

He was tired, he needed some coffee. He saw a waitress come out of the kitchen door, and she saw him and then she retreated back into the kitchen. So much for that. Come on, damn it! He looked again at the crystal and wondered what his father would have thought about it. Dean Charles, in his never-ending—some might say fanatical—quest for women, would have spun a romantic story about it, a tale of it holding the image of a future lover, and when a man peered into it just right, and held it just so, he could see the face of a beautiful—not to say sexy—angel in it, and baby oh baby...there you are.

From what he knew of his father now, and what in time the other Roadmen told him, Nomad thought that everything Dean Charles had done was for the purpose of dipping the wick in as many honey-pots as he could find. Except the music. Or maybe that's what Nomad wanted to believe, so he had his own depths of belief too. He wanted to believe that the music had mattered, and that when his father threw flaming guitar chords at the audience and got the microphone up close to his sweating face to holler the lyrics to 'Memphis' it was for pure love of the music. But those women had been everywhere. Up front and backstage and in the restaurant after the gig and hanging out by the van and just 'happening by' the motel. There were bar girls and secretaries and housewives and waitresses and shy girls who wanted to show him their songs and brassy girls who wanted to crash into show business. There were quiet girls and loud girls and blondes and brunettes, redheads and streaked heads and the occasional soul queen. Nomad had been taken for a lot of ice cream cones, pizzas and to see a lot of movies by the other Roadmen in a lot of towns both big and small, and the number of Do Not Disturb Signs hanging on the doorknobs of Dean Charles's motel rooms had been legion.

They'd never really talked about it, but gradually the kid who adored his dad grew up enough to notice how women dragged their gaze across him, how they talked to each other while looking at him from the corners of their eyes, how they grinned at him and touched him and got up close to breathe his hot musician's sweat and his soured English Leather.

Johnny? his father had said one Friday night in a Best Western in Mansfield, Ohio, while they were watching *The Dirty Dozen* on cable TV. *Would you mind goin' over to finish this flick with the guys?*

A few minutes before he'd spoken, there'd been a quick check of the wristwatch.

No, Dad, Johnny had said, as he'd sat on the edge of the bed and put on his shoes. *I don't mind.*

But when the son had turned to look at his father, on his way out the door to a room down the hall, both of them knew what they were looking at.

Dad? John had asked. *Don't you love Mom anymore?*

Are you kiddin'? came the answer, with a quick harsh laugh. *'Course I love your mother! Know why I love her so much? 'Cause she gave you to me, that's why. Us two men, on the road. Freedom and music, what could be better? Hey, you go tell Danny I said you guys call out for pizzas. 'Kay?*

Okay, Dad, the son had said, because Dean Charles was the light of his world and for years now in that little house in East Detroit, between Center Line and Roseville, Michelle Charles had been sitting on the living-room floor surrounded by her many Bibles and religious pamphlets, her brow furrowed in concentrated study, her eyes moving desperately from line to line to find something she could believe in, for she had discovered the letters in her husband's shoebox.

But like Butch Munger's girlfriend after he'd beaten her half-dead, Nomad thought as he waited for service, Michelle Charles was loyal and faithful and true and what was a woman like that doing with Dean-a-rino? Giving him space, Nomad mused. Letting him wander, knowing he would always come back home, if just to restring his guitar.

His mother was okay now. She lived in an apartment near her sister's family in Sanford, Florida, and she worked in hospice care and had taken up tennis with a group of friends. She didn't mind telling them her son was a "rock'n rolla". Life, like the show, must go on.

Suddenly there was a waitress standing next to his booth, watching him think. He realized she wasn't the same waitress he'd seen at the kitchen door, because that one was pouring iced tea for the middle-aged man.

"Um...I'd like a cup of coffee, please," he told her. "Just black."

"Is that all you want?" She was about forty or so, on the short side, had dark hair and dark eyes and she looked either very tired or supremely bored, as if she wanted to be anywhere on earth but the Argonaut at about three-thirty in the morning.

"No, I'd like the steak sandwich special."

She didn't write it down. "Steamed vegetables, Greek potatoes, or au gratin potatoes?"

"The Greek." He felt he had to say the next thing, because the first time he'd ever come in here and ordered those they'd been way too oily, and because the waitress turnover was high, almost everytime he came in he had to say the same thing. "Can you ask the cook to hold back on the oil?"

"He just makes 'em one way," she said.

"Yeah, but...you know...I've had them before and there was too much oil, so—"

"He just makes 'em one way," she said, and this time there was a grim belligerence in her voice that made Nomad set his mouth in a hard line and stare up at her.

"Hey," he told her, "trust your cook, okay?" He tried to smile but it wouldn't happen. "He'll get it right, if you ask him. Just trust your cook."

She was silent for a few seconds, her mouth partly open. Her face was an expressionless mask, her eyes two small bits of unshining coal. "I'll ask him," she said tightly. "I know what I'm doing. I'm telling you he only makes 'em one way."

"Alright, thanks," Nomad said.

She said, "No *problem*," as she was turning away from him, and he felt the hair on the back of his neck stir as if from a hot breeze.

OhmyGawd, Nomad thought when she had gone. Shimatta! What a bitch! Whatever was going on with her, he hoped she didn't spit in his coffee before she brought it to him. His heart was beating a little hard. He thought he could write a song about this. A ballad, maybe. Right. Call it 'The Ballad of the Greek Potatoes'.

First verse: *He stumbled in for want of food,*
And found a waitress fucked-up and rude.
A steak sandwich, he asked for, and potatoes Greek.
She glared at him like he was a two-headed freak.

Or something like that.

Here she came again, bringing him a cup of coffee. He noted she didn't make eye-contact with him. The cup was banged down, and some sloshed over onto the table. But then she'd turned around again and headed into the kitchen, and Nomad thought,

This is going to be war.
He asked the waitress to trust her cook,
And got for his trouble a dirty look.
This used to be a place he liked to go,
But now the service in this fucking joint doth blow.

Well, the meter was screwed up, but it got the point across.

He would eat his food, call a cab and get out. Simple enough. He stared again at the lump of crystal. Something to believe in, he thought.

He used to believe he was going somewhere in this business. He used to believe that one day all his dues would be paid. That he would come up with the Right Song, at the Right Time. With the Right Band, of course. He'd thought—believed, wished, whatever—that The Five was the Right Band. That in The Five the talents and the personalities and the desires meshed, as much as they could in any band. Were they perfect? No. Was The Five perfect, as a band? Absolutely not. But they had tried, so so hard...

He remembered what Felix Gogo had said, and it was the bitter truth: *Talent's a piss-poor third to ambition, and ambition is second to personality.*

And add these necessary ingredients: connections and luck. But even with all those things combined, something could still go horribly wrong.

He imagined a splitting of himself, a division between the Nomad and the John Charles. In his imagination the John Charles stood up from the Nomad and sat down on the other side of the booth.

"A shitty, shitty deal," John Charles said. "You know what I'm talking about."

"Yeah," Nomad said in his mind, to his mental boothmate. He was talking about the new music the Austin band Ezra's Jawbone had finished back in February. Nomad was friends with both the lead singer and the keyboard player, who also wrote all their songs. They had wrapped up a project they called *Dustin Daye*, had given him a copy of the test CD to hear and then sent the package off to their label, MTBF Records. *Dustin Daye* had been a rock opera, about a young man who suddenly awakens in a hotel room in an unknown city and has no idea who he is or where he's come from. As the music progresses, the idea is raised that Dustin Daye, who gets his name from the faint impression of a signature on a notepad in his room, might be the Second Coming or he might be the Devil in human flesh, and even he doesn't know which one, but someone out there—or more than one person—is trying to kill him before he can accomplish what he feels he has to do, which he doesn't know will ultimately be for Good or for Evil. Or is he just an escaped lunatic? Nomad wasn't religious, but he understood the light versus dark concept. It was in all the best horror movies.

"That's some awesome music," John Charles said, and Nomad had to agree. The fifteen songs, two nearing the seven-minute mark and one up there over ten minutes, were absolutely mindblowing. They flowed from and into each other, they went in unexpected and amazing directions, the arrangements and vocals were off the hook and there were mid-song key and tempo changes that should never have worked but to Nomad sounded like some of the freshest, most vibrant music he'd ever heard. Plus it had a last song, 'The Last Song', that made Nomad lie awake at night hearing it over and over in his head and thinking this was going to be a huge breakthrough biggie for Ezra's Jawbone.

"You know how that went," John Charles reminded him.

"The fucking suits," Nomad answered. He remembered hearing from his shell-shocked friend the lead singer that the first impression of *Dustin Daye* from MTBF was that there were no singles. That some of the tunes—fucking 'tunes', they called them—were way too long, that kids wouldn't listen to tunes that long. That this really was, and sorry but we have to be truthful, one of the worst, most confusing collection of tunes we've ever heard. That Ezra's Jawbone had already set up its hard rock/country funk vibe on its first two releases, so this attempt at a product does not play to the market. That there's no sense to be made of people sitting talking to themselves, or having ghosts—or whatever the fuck they are—roaming around. And then there's the religion angle, and we'll be the first to say we respect all views and opinions but this is really where the shit starts to slide. MTBF is not a contemporary Christian label; have you seen our iTunes hit list lately? No religious tunes on there, *nada*. So when you get into this area, you are walking on sinking sand. Your audience wants to be *entertained*, not preached to. This is an *entertainment* business. So we have to say, and we're all in full agreement on this, that *Dustin Daye* is not releaseable as it is. Now, having made that clear...we can hook you up with a proven production team we have in mind who can help rework this record, but you're going to have to give them more control to do what needs to be done, because Bogdan Anastasio and Ji Chao require complete authority.

"Those sick fucks," sneered John Charles.

"Can you *imagine* that scene?" Nomad asked. "The suits sitting in a conference room listening to *Dustin Daye* and saying it's shit because there aren't any *singles*? And these are the same guys who've driven the whole fucking business over the cliff, you know."

"Right," said John Charles.

"Didn't lower the cost of CDs when they could have," Nomad said. "Should've dropped them to half-price. So there go the independent CD and vinyl stores down the tubes, and those indie stores were the lifeblood, man." He stopped to sip his black coffee. "It won't ever come back to what it was," he told himself, in his mental voice.

"You have to keep on keeping on," John Charles said.

"Do I?" Nomad asked, and then he saw the waitress coming with his food and John Charles slipped back into him because they both were hungry.

She again offered him no eye-contact. She thumped the steak sandwich plate down and then the platter of...

"What's this?" Nomad asked.

Her eyes became slits when she looked at him. "It's the au gratin potatoes, just like you asked for."

He had smelled the yellow cheese striped across the top of the potatoes before he saw it. "I can't eat that," he said.

"You *ordered* it," she answered.

"No, I ordered the *Greek* potatoes."

"You ordered the au gratin."

"Listen, ma'am," Nomad said, feeling his guts start to clench. George would've said *Easy, take it easy*. "I know what I ordered." She just stood there staring at him, her coal-black eyes fierce and her head cocked to one side as if it were getting ready to fly from her neck and bite his dick off. "Okay," he said, and he put up both hands palm-outward to keep the peace. The other customers were watching. "Just forget it, okay?" He pushed the offending potatoes aside. "I'll sit here and eat my sandwich, that's really all I—"

"No, if you want Greek potatoes, I'll get you Greek potatoes!" said the waitress, as she snatched up the au gratin. Her face was all screwed up and getting red, the anger about to burst forth like snot from her nose and spittle from her mouth. "I'll get you Greek potatoes, but you *didn't* order 'em!" It had almost been a shout.

You dumb shit, you didn't write it down, Nomad nearly said. But he did not. He took a long deep breath and he grasped the edge of the table with both hands and he tried to force a smile that did not take. "Listen," he began.

"Quit telling me to listen! I can hear you, you think I'm *deaf*?"

"No, I'm just saying—"

"You want Greek potatoes, I'm gonna get 'em for you!" She began backing away from him, as the other waitress rubbernecked out from the kitchen and the cashier girl poked her head around the corner.

It came from Nomad with surprising force: his rough whiskey voice, demanding "*Stop*!"

She took two more steps in retreat before she obeyed, and then she seemed to hunch her shoulders forward like a pit bull bitch about to attack.

"Please." Nomad heard his voice tremble, as rough as it was. "*Please*." He was starting to shake, he was starting to come apart at the seams. Mike was dead. George might be dead within the next twelve hours. The crucial period, the doctor had said. But right now, right this minute, this felt pretty crucial too. The Five was staggering toward its grave. Nomad thought his heart was beating too hard, he needed to calm down, *easy take it easy* George would say but the Little Genius was not at his side and might never be there again.

"Please," Nomad breathed, "just let me eat my sandwich. Leave me alone and let me eat my sandwich. Alright?"

A burly sandy-haired man in a cook's apron had come to the kitchen door and was looking over the top of the other waitress's head.

Nomad's waitress gave a tight little grin, a nasty little smirk of victory, and she said in a voice like a hammer driving a nail into Nomad's skull, three beats: "No. Prob. Lem."

Then she turned around with a dramatic sweep like Bette Davis in that movie Berke had been watching and carried the platter of cheesy potatoes away. The cook and the other waitress retreated before her. The kitchen door closed.

Nomad started eating, but he couldn't taste anything. Whatever war he'd walked into the middle of, whatever was eating at this dominatrix waitress and made her flail out at him, he wanted none of it.

"Stay cool, man," said one of the students, who must've thought Nomad was the cause of the trouble. When Nomad glanced at their table, all three of them were staring at him so he couldn't tell which dork had spoken. He returned to chewing his way through the sandwich, and then one of the guys made the mistake of letting out a chortle, a slobbery laugh hidden behind a fratboy's greasy hand.

Nomad felt the flashfire burn across his face. He turned his head toward them, picked out the heftiest one to aim his full beams at and said, loudly enough to be perfectly understood, "Hey, are you Moe, Larry, or that fat fuck who gets his ass whipped?"

They all glared back at him without speaking. Suddenly the couple got up from their booth and, hand-in-hand, headed for the cashier.

He wanted to tell them not to worry, that nobody was going to get hurt, that he had his spike of anger under control and they didn't have to rush out the—

Something was slammed down upon his table so hard it made him jump.

He looked up into the face of his waitress, who had come up on him so fast he hadn't realized she was out of the kitchen.

"There," she said, with a twisted smile. Her eyes were small black circles of rage, but at the center of their darkness was a red glint of triumph. "That suit you?" Medusa couldn't have hissed it better.

Nomad saw that she'd brought him a platter of Greek potatoes.

Oil kept to a minimum.

Just as he'd asked.

They were perfect.

She grinned at him.

He could not let this stand.

George was not here to talk him down. Ariel was not here, to be at his side whether he wanted her there or not. The memory of Mike's body being put into a white coroner's van and George's body being lifted into the back of an ambulance and Dean Charles's body lying sprawled on the pavement mixed together, bled into each other like the songs on *Dustin Daye*, and from that neon-lit, heat-stroked Hell Felix Gogo told him to know his role and a sniper in a suit reloaded his rifle and three fratboys laughed behind his back and the waitress gave him perfect Greek potatoes and said it was no problem.

He was a mass of clanging alarms and trapped terrors, and just like that he broke.

It was a quiet breakage.

He said, with sweat sparkling on his cheeks and forehead, "Ma'am?" Whose voice was that? He didn't know it. He was aware of the other waitress, standing again at the kitchen door to watch.

Well…it was showtime.

"Ma'am?" Nomad said again. "There's something in my food."

"*What?*"

He picked up the platter of Greek potatoes and slid out of the booth with a slow, smooth motion, and he said, "Your fucking face," in a mild matter-of-fact tone before he grasped the back of her head and pushed the platter into her stunned mug.

She shouldn't have screamed as she did, like a wild animal. She shouldn't have reached out and clawed at his face and kicked at his shins. Because he would've thrown down a tenner and walked out, but with lines of blood rising from the scratches on his left cheek and one of his shins nearly cracked he also gave an animalish roar and shoved her away from him, and she fell back over a table and chair and went down on the floor still screaming.

The three stooges should not have jumped him from behind, either. They should not have tried to catch his arms and pin them at his sides and drop him to the floor by kicking his legs out from under him. All that just made Nomad punch loose from them, pick up a chair and start swinging. "Come on, man! Come on!" shouted one of the guys, but whether he was wanting Nomad to stop fighting or to advance on him was unknown, because the chair crunched him across the left shoulder, he grabbed at his injury and scuttled away and he didn't say much after that.

The middle-aged man fled with his book. The other waitress was screaming *Call the cops! Call the cops!* The waitress with lightly-oiled Greek potatoes on her face came rushing at Nomad with a dinner knife raised in a stabbing position, and Nomad in his red rictus of rage got the chair between them and drove her back across another table. "Jesus Christ! Stop it!" someone shouted, and Nomad saw the cook standing in the kitchen door. Then the bravest or most stupid of the young men caught him around the neck from behind and tried to wrestle him to the floor. Nomad dropped the chair and thrashed like a maniac to get loose. The blood was pounding in his head and dark spots swirled before his eyes. He gave the guy an elbow shot in the ribs, followed up with another one that drew a grunt of pain, and then he broke free, turned around and swung a right fist that popped a jaw crooked. A second punch to the face ended the discussion because the guy ran for the door holding a bloody mouth.

It might have finished there, if the waitress had not thrown the ketchup bottle at Nomad's head.

"Fuck you, you motherfucker!" she shrieked just before she threw it, giving Nomad enough time to dodge it and save his skull, but the bottle crashed through the front window. Then Nomad, who heard George's voice in his head begging him to stop but who was now locked into what seemed almost a catharsis of hallucinatory violence, picked up another chair and threw it at her, and she ducked down as it passed overhead. The chair crashed into the *Argo*, the painted ship upon the painted sea, and knocked a plate-sized hole in the mural's wall just above the waterline.

Two seconds after that, the cook came out of the kitchen holding the pistol.

He was red-faced and shaking and he held the gun out toward Nomad with his finger on the trigger and he bellowed, "I'll *shoot* you, you sonofabitch! I'll—"

The gun went off.

Nomad only had an instant in which to flinch, because then the bullet had sizzled through the air past his left ear and followed the ketchup bottle through the glass onto East Congress. The cook was looking at the pistol with horror, as if he were grasping a spitting cobra. Nomad staggered to the side, against the booth he'd been occupying, as he saw the cook bringing the gun back to bear on him.

"Don't move!" the cook shouted, but by then the coffee cup that Nomad had thrown was on its way, and as the man lifted an arm to deflect it he—by accident or by intention—fired again.

The bullet punched a neat round hole in the booth's red vinyl seat. Nomad saw the pistol's barrel searching for him. In either desperation or madness he picked something else up from the table and flung it and the lump of healing crystal hit the cook smack on the collarbone, causing him to stagger back against the wounded *Argo*.

Nomad attacked. He propelled himself at the cook with his head down and his shoulders ready for collision. He was his own bullet.

Before Nomad got to his target, the waitress on the floor grabbed at his legs and tripped him up. Still, his momentum was enough to hurl him forward, and before the cook could get the pistol between them Nomad hit him so hard they almost crashed straight through the *Argo* into ancient Greece, or at least the kitchen. They fought face-to-face, the cook trying to get the gun in position and Nomad trying to pin the gunhand. Then Nomad head-butted him and suddenly all the fight jumped out of the other man, his fingers opened and Nomad was holding the pistol.

"Run! Run!" the cook shouted, as he—a truly brave soul—tried to push Nomad back so the waitress could get out. She ran for her life, trailing a shriek, and then the cook let go of Nomad's shirt and he ran too.

And then Nomad was alone in the Argonaut with three lines of blood on his face and a gun in his hand.

He heard the sirens coming.

His fire had diminished, but it was not yet embers. He put the pistol down on a table and listened to the sirens. Music, of a sort. Ariel could do something with this situation. She could write it out so you could feel the pain and frustration and sadness as if you were living it yourself. Because, really and truthfully, she was so much better a songcrafter than he.

Now there were red and blue lights spinning out on East Congress, beyond the broken window. He didn't know how many police cars were out there, but it looked like a cop convention. He could hear people shouting. Heard what might have been the voice of that damned bitch of a waitress, raised to ear-breaking decibels.

He had been a bad, bad boy.

"Oh my God," he said, and though he did not believe in God, who were you gonna call on when the shit hit the fan?

A bullhorn spoke from the street: "Attention in there! Throw your firearm out the window and come to the door with your hands locked behind your head! Nobody's going to get hurt!"

Nomad just stared at the busted wall and the broken mural, as his shadow danced in a world of red and blue spinning lights. Poor fucked-up Jason, he thought. Standing at that mast, directing a ship that never moved. Believing he was actually going somewhere, getting closer to a golden fleece.

He thought he would put Jason and the other Argonauts out of their misery.

The bullhorn repeated its message, but this time it left out the last line.

Nomad picked up a chair and began to demolish the mural and destroy the wall. When that chair broke to pieces he picked up another one and kept on knocking holes in Jason's stupid dream. With the breaking of the second chair he picked up a third, and this was hard work now, very hard, but he was determined to finish what he'd begun, he wasn't a quitter, no way Dean and Michelle Charles had raised a quitter, and so he was still working hard when the two small torpedo-shaped canisters came through the window and he didn't even turn around, he didn't even care because he was involved in his emancipation of Jason, and when the gas swirled up around him like purple snakes and his skin began to burn and his eyes involuntarily shut tight because they were full of wet fire he kept swinging in the dark because it was all he knew how to do.

He was on his knees, surrounded by broken chairs, when they came in. They entered as if from another world. They looked like mad combinations of frogmen and masked wrestlers from parts unknown.

They drew his arms back behind him, snapped white plastic restraints on his wrists and ankles, and they hauled him out like yesterday's garbage.

FOUR

STONE CHURCH

FOURTEEN.

It wasn't so bad. He'd paid money to stay in motels that were worse than this. But the bright orange jumpsuit...now, *that* was ridiculous. The thing had its own inner glow, and you still saw it pulsing when you closed your eyes. The huge black-lettered word JAIL across the back wasn't too cool, either.

The situation being what it was, though, Nomad was impressed by the Pima County jail. It was clean, well-managed and seemed more like a strictly-run—*very* strictly-run—dorm for wayward men. The roach-overrun lockup was dead in the modern era of physical confinement. Now the "cells" were cubicles fronted with impact-resistant glass. Each cell held eight inmates, and eight cells made up what was called a "pod", each pod with its own dayroom. The place was cheerfully lit and the air conditioning was kept on the chilly side. Books, magazines and a TV were provided. He'd already seen himself on the television screen, several times in fact, and he was a real celebrity around here.

It was nearing ten o'clock on Tuesday morning. He'd been in jail for about fifty-four hours, but who was counting? He didn't care that he'd come to the end of this particular road; at his arraignment he'd been so tight-lipped and uncaring about the whole thing that the judge had wanted to run him through a battery of psychiatric tests. Nomad had just shrugged. "Whatever you want to do, man," he'd told Your Honor. "Fuck it."

Which had not gone over so well. He wasn't going anywhere soon, because Your Honor had decided to postpone a decision on setting bail until the nutbag questions were done and some mental health geek had filed three hundred and thirty-three reports on the state of Nomad's mind. But Nomad didn't have anyplace he really needed to be, The Five was over, everything was done, so why not just stick here for a while?

His call had been to the University Medical Center. He'd asked to have Ariel Collier paged.

"John?" she'd answered. "Where are you?"

"Around. Any word on George?"

"They think he's going to make it. They're not sure yet, but they're saying his vital signs are looking good. John, tell me where you are."

"I went out to get something to eat. Maybe I went a little too far." He heard a drunk guy shouting and raging over in the booking area. The cops would take care of that outburst in a hurry, but he figured Ariel had probably heard it too. "I might not be able to get back for a while."

"What's that noise?"

"Loud party goin' on."

"On a Sunday *morning*? What's the number there? And what's wrong with your voice?"

"Listen to me." His voice was tired and scratchy. Tear gas was not gentle on the vocal chords. He'd been scrubbed clean, all the purple dye washed out of his hair, and he'd been allowed to curl up in a holding cell and rest until he had enough strength to talk, but it had taken some time. "I'm glad George is going to make it. I'm just going to hang out where I am, so don't worry. Okay?"

"*John.*" The way she spoke his name told him she knew. "Are you in trouble?"

"A little."

"Tell me where you are," she said tersely. "I *mean* it."

Nomad allowed himself a slight smile. It tugged at the scratches on his left cheek, which wore a pink shine of disinfectant. He'd never seen Ariel angry, never heard her lose her temper. She sounded close to it, right now. That would be a sight, he thought; Ariel Collier, in sympathy with the vibrations of the cosmos, going batshit. "You need to get back to Austin," he said. "You, Terry and Berke. When Ash gets there, tell him...I don't know, just tell him to get you guys home." The drunk dude was really hollering now, about his rights and all that, as three cops were dragging him into a holding cell. "Go back and start over," he said.

"*Start over*? What do you mean, *start over*? We're still The Five, John. We don't have to start over."

"Oh yes, you do. Believe me."

"What've you *done*?"

"I don't want to talk about that. Get home," he told her. And then he was silent and she was silent and he didn't know what she was thinking but he was thinking he had really let them down this time, he had screwed up when they needed him the most and he couldn't stand to look into her face again and see her disappointment. He couldn't stand to look into the faces of any of them again, but especially not hers, because...because he thought she really didn't need The Five, she was talented enough to go out on her own, and in these last three years he had known that and had never said anything. Never encouraged her to at least think about it, because he was the emperor and emperors could hide their jealousy under their crowns of tarnished tin.

He remembered her saying *I'm still with you* back in Sweetwater. Her loyalty was like a knife to his heart. She was wasting time in this party band, and that's what The Five was. A band pumping out pablum to be washed down by a flood of cheap beer. A broken-down, sad merchandise machine. One song like 'When The Storm Breaks' didn't make any difference. He knew she was a better guitarist and a better singer and a better songwriter than he, and he believed his leaden earthbound influence was keeping her from finding her own path, because—Christ love her—she meant it when she said *I'm still with you.*

So now was the time for him to find his guts and say it.

He did.

"You ought to go out on your own." He had to pause for a few seconds, to clear his throat. "Put your own band together. You front it. Audition the players, make the sound you want. You can do it. You could've done it straight out of The Blessed Hours, if you'd wanted to."

"Oh, no," she answered, in a quietly stunned voice like a child being told to leave the house. "Oh, no."

"You *can*," he said. "It would be all yours. What would be wrong with that?" He recalled all the times they'd been working together on songs and he'd steamrolled her, just plowed her under when she'd made a suggestion to transpose it to a different key or add this or take away that or whatever. Even though down in his deep dark grudge he'd known she was right—*usually* right—he couldn't have let her take control. Once she figured out she didn't really need him, then where would he be?

But now it was different. Day was night and up was down. Mike was dead and George was shot, the *Argo* had sunken in a sea of broken drywall, The Five had played its final gig and Johnny, there is no roadmap.

"I couldn't do that," Ariel replied. "I couldn't leave my family."

"Your *family*?" It was said with incredulous sarcasm. "Oh, a few people travelling together in a busted-up van? *That* family?" He hesitated, but when she didn't respond he went on, because his blood was up and he was ready to hurt her to make her let go. "Musicians are a fucking dime a dozen," he said. "Bands fall apart every day, so what's the big deal? When it happens, you just go latch onto some other group of nobodies. So we were together a while, we went through some good shit and some bad shit, but that doesn't make us a family. Far from it."

"What, then? What does it make us?"

"It makes us *nothing*. Because we're over. Don't you get that? Now, if you want to live in your land of rainbows and moonbeams, that's up to you. But I'm not living there. I'm telling you, The Five is finished. Okay? And I'm not coming back, so you and Berke and Terry get yourselves to Austin and do whatever the fuck you need to do. I'm out of it."

"You don't mean that."

"Listen, stop holding onto me!" he said, with maybe more vitriol than he'd intended. "Either put your own band together or go home to Massachusetts, but quit fucking around with losers like Neal Tapley. If you want to try to save sick animals, go be a vet." He knew that was a hard punch, because Ariel had tried her best to get Neal off the crack, the speedballs and everything else he was loading himself up with to fight his depression, but she couldn't hold him strongly enough to keep him from flying off that two-lane in his Volvo clunker. Nomad didn't know if there was more to that story, if there'd been a "romance"—that's how they would've put it in those godawful old

English novels, "romance"—but he'd figured long ago that Ariel was searching for someone to believe in, to trust and to follow.

It ain't me, babe.

"Go back to Austin," he said, wearily now. "Just go."

Still she didn't leave him.

She spoke softly, but with grit in her voice: "Don't you know that we're all over the news? Front page of the morning *Star*, with pictures. We're on NBC, CBS, ABC, Fox and CNN. The sniper story has gone nationwide. Haven't you seen a TV?"

"No."

"We need you back here with us. I'm speaking for Berke and Terry, too. Wherever you are, come back."

"No," he repeated, very firmly, and with that he had hung up the phone.

Hey, amigo! You that guy on the TV? Right there! You that guy?

Early Sunday afternoon, an officer had come to get him from his cell. Police Captain Garza was here, he was told. Wants to talk to you.

"No," Nomad had said again, and had stretched out on his bunk. The officer had gone away, and there had been no further word from Captain Garza or, for that matter, anyone else.

So, it wasn't bad. A clean bunk, good food, plenty of people to talk to when he decided he was ready to talk. Didn't a lot of cool musicians pay their dues in jail? Not so bad. Except for the Day-Glo orange jumpsuit with the JAIL stenciled across the back. But he would bear that indignity, too.

He was out in the dayroom sweeping the floor when two of the badasses came up behind him. Not prisoners, but guards. Moates, the one with the bald skull and a mole on his forehead, the one Nomad had been warned by some of the other dudes not to look at because he really really *really* did not like to be looked at by pond scum such as themselves; and Kingston, the thin black guy with the goatee, the constant unsettling half-smile on his face and the snakes tattooed on his ropy forearms.

"Charles," said Kingston, "somebody wants to see you."

"Right now," said Moates.

"Who is it?" Nomad asked.

"Move," said baldie-with-a-mole, and he hooked a thumb toward a red-painted steel door across the dayroom.

"I don't want to see anybody," Nomad said.

"Ain't askin' you," said Kingston. "Put the broom aside. Let's *go*!"

Nomad weighed his options. The two men planted themselves before him, relaxed but ready. They were the real deal, citizens of the world of hurt. Nomad put his broom aside, and he followed Kingston with the bald dude right at his heels.

A plastic pass card was used on a slot in the door, followed by a key. Nomad was led into a stark hallway painted off-white, with several doors on either side. The door was closed and locked behind him. Moates gave him a shove just because he could.

Kingston opened another door without having to use a key. "Get in there," he directed. "Sit down and wait."

Overhead fluorescents spread even light on a table and three chairs, one across from two. The walls were the same stark blankness as the hallway. A cork bulletin board held no bulletins or pushpins. There was a smell in here as if it were a place the guards sneaked in to smoke cigarettes.

"Who am I—?" *Waiting for*, he was going to say, but Moates and Kingston were already going out and the door closed. Nomad didn't hear a lock turn.

He sat down on the side of the table that faced the door. Damned if he knew what this was about. Whatever it was, he didn't like it. He had the feeling that if he walked to that door and opened it, he might return to his cell in the shape of a pretzel.

In about thirty seconds, the door did open. A man entered. He was carrying a brown folder. He shut the door behind him and he did not look into Nomad's eyes until he was sitting down on the other side of the table.

They stared at each other.

"You're in some trouble, John," the man said.

Nomad's first urge was to shrug off the comment, to present a stone face like he'd seen the other inmates do when they were trying to act all-that in the presence of pressure or despair, but he didn't because he knew the man was right, and the way the man had spoken was no-nonsense and required respect. But Nomad didn't answer, and he spent a few seconds putting together impressions of his visitor.

The man was about fifty or so years old, in very good physical shape. He had a ruddy, outdoors coloring. His gray, close-cropped hair was retreating at the temples and sat on his head like a tight cap. He was so clean-shaven a razor might have been his religion. A military man? Nomad wondered. The man's thick eyebrows were still black, his eyes a pale sky-blue. He had the square chin of a comic-book hero but the crooked nose of a boxer who has gone a few bad rounds in his life. He was wearing khaki trousers and a dark gray polo shirt. Nomad had seen that he was wearing a black belt and black wingtip shoes. The man stood maybe six-one, had wide shoulders and forearms that looked as if he could chop wood for a living. His hands were veiny, one of the few signs of the toll of years. He had a few deep lines in his face, bracketing his mouth and at the corners of his eyes, but he didn't have the saggy look that old people get. He didn't have their sad look, of lost chances and yesterdays receding into the rearview mirror. In fact, this dude didn't look like he'd lost any chance that came his way. The pale blue eyes were keen and careful. He wore a thin gold wedding ring and a nice but not flashy wristwatch. He kept both hands pressed flat against the brown folder on the table in front of him.

"Who are you?" Nomad asked.

"My name is Truitt Allen. I'm an agent with the Federal Bureau of Investigation, based here in Tucson. Want to see my ID?" He made a move for his wallet.

FBI, Nomad thought. Almost military. This dude was a tough old hoss. But he said, "Yeah, I do," and he waited as the wallet was opened to display a gold-colored shield and the official identification card that bore a picture of Allen's unsmiling, all-business visage.

"Okay. Now...do you want to see who killed Mike Davis and shot George Emerson?"

That question hit Nomad like a double blow to both heart and stomach. "*What*?" he managed to croak.

"Here he is." Allen slid from the folder a sheet of paper and pushed it toward Nomad. On it was the color photograph of a man's face, his eyes hooded in shadow. "This is his most recent driver's license photo. His name is Jeremy Parker Pett, born January 5th, 1978 in Reno, Nevada. Ever seen him?"

Nomad was in a daze. He thought he shook his head. "No."

Allen let him stare at the face in the picture for a few more seconds, and then he returned it to the folder. "The doctors are giving Mr. Emerson an eighty percent chance to pull through."

"That's good. Thank...um...why..." Nomad couldn't make sense of what he was trying to ask, so he waited for it to come together. "Why...is this...Pett guy after us?"

"You've figured that out, have you? That Jeremy Pett is following you? Stalking your band, I guess would be the better way to describe it."

Nomad swallowed thickly. "What's he got against us?"

"We'll talk about that," Allen said, his gaze steady. "First we have to talk about some other things. You're pale. Want some water?"

"I'm all right."

"Sure about that?"

"Yeah," Nomad said, and he meant it. He drew a long breath and let it out. "This isn't...what I expected to be happening today. So how did you find out this was the guy?"

"Later. Right now we have to talk about your future. I understand you refused to see Captain Garza when he came here. I've talked to Miss Collier about the phone conversation you had. One would think you wanted to curl up in here and try to make the world stop turning. Is that what you want, John?"

"I want to be left alone."

"Hm," Allen said. "Sorry, I can't do that. You're much too important to me to be left alone."

"Important? How?"

Allen leaned forward slightly, his hands still on the brown folder that held the picture of Jeremy Pett. "I want you to walk out of here with me," he said. "Today. In fact..." He checked his wristwatch. "Within the next half-hour."

"Oh, right!" Nomad couldn't supress a crazed grin. "Just walk out of jail! After the shit I stirred up? Right!"

"Yes," Allen said. "Right."

Nomad searched the man's eyes, which had taken on a flinty color. "Are you *serious*? How the fuck can I just walk out of here? I'm a *prisoner*!"

"I can take you out. Simple as that."

"You can...*take* me out? Uh uh!" Nomad leaned back in his chair; he wanted to laugh, but he didn't think Truitt Allen would like the sound of it and he decided he'd better not piss off Truitt Allen. "It's not simple, man. I don't know what this is about, but I know it's not simple."

"You did cause some damage, yeah. You did kind of fly off the handle. But, some things have come to light since you were brought in here."

"What things?"

Now it was Allen's turn to lean back, and cross one leg at the ankle. Nomad saw he was wearing socks the same color as his shirt. "Number one: the wall you tore down. With the mural on it."

"Okay, so what?"

"The building inspector found an electrical wiring hazard behind it. If you hadn't broken the wall up and exposed it, the place might have caught fire sooner or later. So maybe you saved the restaurant, and maybe the owner is grateful to you."

"I'm sure he is," Nomad said sarcastically.

"The nightshift cook had no permit for his pistol," Allen went on, his expression nearly the same as in his picture ID. "So he's in a little trouble himself. The waitress you attacked turned out to have a few skeletons in her own cupboard. One big one, like being wanted under her real name for the sale of crystal meth in Amarillo two years ago. Seems her current boyfriend has been cooking the stuff in a rented house on North Edith Boulevard."

"What've you been doing?" Nomad asked. "Beating the bushes?"

"Beating them 'til they bleed," Allen said.

"I hit a guy in the mouth. I think I might have broken his jaw." Nomad cocked his head to one side. "Are you going to tell me he needed oral surgery anyway and I saved his folks some money?"

"No. He's an honor student at UA with a father in the banking business. Big Wildcats supporter. The other kid whose shoulder you dislocated is a trombone player in the marching band. So...you're still up for assault and battery, aren't you?"

"I don't know. Am I?"

A slow smile crept across Allen's mouth, but his eyes remained cool. "A real tough guy, huh? Mad at the world? Think it owes you something?"

"Wrong. Nobody owes me a fucking thing."

"I wish you wouldn't use that word."

"What word?"

"The four-letter word, and don't play stupid. How come you people use that word all the time? You use it so much it doesn't mean anything. Noun, verb, adjective...using it says your mind is lazy because you can't come up with another descriptive."

"What *people* are you talking about?" Nomad asked, doing his best Clint Eastwood squint.

"Young people," said Allen. "If this is the voice of the future, I'm glad I won't be around a whole lot longer to hear it."

"That's *your* problem," Nomad said, and he wished he had a cigarette because in the time-honored tradition of prison movies he would've spewed smoke in the old fucker's face.

Or maybe not, because he didn't particularly care to wind up in the infirmary today, and anybody with the first name of *Truitt* probably had a lot of practice putting people in plaster casts and bandages. And to tangle with an FBI agent, even a geezer like this? No way.

After a long pause during which Nomad thought he could hear the geezer's wristwatch ticking, Allen said, "Let's talk about *your* problem, John. Which I think is not going to go away anytime soon."

"What would that be?"

"Jeremy Pett," came the answer. "You know, we think the bullets that hit Mr. Emerson were fired from the top level of a parking deck. We didn't find any brass, he cleaned up after himself, but we believe we've calculated the firing angle pretty well. It definitely was a downward shot. A difficult shot. You know how far away that parking deck is from where Mr. Emerson was hit?" He didn't wait for a guess, which wasn't coming anyway. "Across the street and three blocks away. He had a sliver of a view to work with, but he found a position to watch the van, and he might've been sitting there for hours. Just waiting for somebody to come get it after the show. Probably didn't matter who it was, as long as it was a member of your band."

"George is our manager," Nomad said. "He's not on stage. How could this fu...how could this guy recognize George?"

"He may have seen him at one of your shows, or—"

"Gigs," Nomad corrected, for the sake of it.

"Okay, thank you for that. Or, as I was about to say, he probably got a good look at Mr. Emerson when he was scoping you at that gas station outside Sweetwater. Bear in mind, Pett has likely—I'd say without a doubt—gone to your Internet site and made note of your stops during this tour. Am I getting anywhere with you? Impressing you on how serious this young man is?"

He was. Nomad frowned and looked down at the green-tiled floor, but no answers lay there. "Why does he want to kill us? We haven't done anything to him."

"That you know of," Allen said.

Nomad lifted his gaze back to meet the other man's. "What's that mean?"

"It means," Allen said, in a slow and deliberate voice, "that Jeremy Pett is probably not going to stop what he's doing—for whatever reason he has, whatever grudge he's holding—until he's satisfied. I'm telling you that Mr. Emerson—"

"George. That's his name." Nomad felt both clammy and feverish. Wasn't the air-conditioning working in this part of the jail?

"George, then. I'm telling you that George is very, very lucky. It helped him that UMC has one of the best trauma teams in the country, and they got him within what they call 'the golden hour'. But in time he'll be wheeled out of here, and—"

"Whoa! 'Wheeled out'? You mean he's going to be crippled?"

"No, he'll walk again, but that bullet to his upper chest did tremendous damage. It'll be a slow process for him to come back."

"Oh, shit," Nomad breathed, and came close to slamming his fist on the table. But he didn't, because there'd been enough of that just lately.

"He *will* come back," Allen said. "But at the very best, he'll be in the ICU for several weeks, and they'll be watching him for infection or other complications."

"You sound like you've been there."

"Not me personally, but I know some who have." He checked his wristwatch again. "In a minute or two there's going to be a knock at the door. It'll be someone bringing your clothes and shoes wrapped up in brown paper and the contents of your pockets in a plastic bag. There'll be some forms for you to fill out and sign. I'll step into the hallway and give you some privacy. Just leave the jumpsuit and the jailhouse clogs on the table. Then we're going to walk down the hallway to another door, we're going to go through that, past a guard at a security station—who you will not speak to or look at—and out into the parking lot to my car. You understand that I've pulled a lot of strings and called in a lot of debts to get you out of here?"

"Yeah, I do. But *why*?"

Allen stood up from his chair, gripping the folder between his hands. “You come with me, and I’ll tell you. Not only that, but I’ll tell you Jeremy Pett’s story.” He walked to the door and then stopped. Nomad thought he moved with the crisp economy of a man who could without a doubt take care of himself in a fight. Again... military? Maybe more than the FBI?

“I’m not sure I want to go,” Nomad said. “Seems like it’s safer in here than out there with a sniper trying to kill me.”

“One big problem with your attitude, son.”

Son? Nomad had almost winced at that particular cheese sandwich.

“Your three bandmates aren’t in here with you,” Allen continued. “So to save them... you’re going to help me catch Jeremy Pett.”

Came the knock at the door. Allen opened it and went out, Kingston entered and dumped the package of clothes and shoes and the plastic bag of pocket stuff onto the table in front of Nomad. Kingston put down a ballpoint pen and a clipboard with some forms in it. Then he also left the room, without speaking a word.

Nomad sat looking at his belongings.

For better or for worse, the emperor had his clothes back.

He tore open the package. Then he got himself out of the jailhouse suit.

FIFTEEN.

Nomad realized he might be out of jail, but he was still definitely in custody. This message was sent to him by the sound of the doorlocks engaging on Truitt Allen's black Acura TL sedan as soon as the engine started. The interior of the car was to Nomad disturbingly spotless, not an errant Kleenex nor crushed paper cup nor old hamburger wrapper in sight. Even the dashboard had been polished, and everything metal gleamed with psychotic perfection.

"Where're we going?" Nomad asked as they pulled out of the lot.

"The medical center." Allen had his sunglasses on against the glare. In profile he looked like a hawk with a lopsided beak. "Everybody's waiting for you."

"For *me*? Who's waiting?"

"Sit back and relax," Allen said, a command both benign and emphatic.

Nomad obeyed, figuring he couldn't do much of anything else. As they approached the medical center, he saw a crowd of maybe forty or so people across Ring Road from UMC. They were gathered around two camera trucks, one from KVOA and the other from KMSB. Some of the people were dressed in long white robes and held handlettered signs. Nomad caught sight of what a few of the signs said as Allen drove past them, things like 'God Hates The Devil's Music' and 'Secular Music Praises Satan'.

"Are they protesting *us*?" Nomad asked.

"Protesting your music in general, I guess," Allen replied, steering for the parking deck. "Any chance to be on camera, and people get themselves worked up."

Nomad nodded. He had a secret. It would have amazed the other members of The Five, at least as much as it had astounded them that Mike Davis was a fan of *Moby Dick*, to learn that from age twelve, just after the death of his father, to about age fourteen John Charles had been an interested listener to WQRS-FM classical radio in Detroit. He'd discovered it after listening to the Cramps' *Stay Sick* late one night on his record player and his mother had come into his room and asked him—begged him, really—to cut out the loud noise. So he'd gone radio surfing, hitting the FM rock stations, until suddenly he'd found a man talking about a piece of music called the Resurrection Symphony, which he'd learned later was Gustav Mahler's Symphony Number Two. The man—a music professor—was talking about the vocal parts of the Fifth Movement, translating them from German to English, and what stopped Nomad's travels across the dial was the man's calm, measured voice saying, *O believe, You were not born for nothing.*

Sometimes in the dark and the quiet, especially after his father was gone, he'd wondered what he'd been born for. Where was he going? What was he supposed to do with his life? They were heavy questions for someone his age, and there were no answers, and in the dark and quiet he could hear his mother reading Bible verses to herself in her own room, and sometimes crying a little bit as if what the Bible had to give her was not nearly enough of what she needed, and that was why he grew to despise the dark and the quiet.

But that weird music with the strings and the piano and the horns and the harps on WQRS pulled him in. Some of it could put you to sleep for a hundred years. But some of it sounded like war. Some of it sounded like the questions he asked himself about his life, if he were to put them to music. Here and there would jump up a piece that made him think of his dad swaggering across a stage, and then there would be music that sounded like a procession of ghosts carrying their lamps through a cemetery at midnight.

Kind of like the Cramps, only not as loud.

From the public library he'd checked out a book called *The Lives of the Composers*. He'd kept it way overdue until he'd finished it.

Now, some of those fuckers had waded through swamps of deep shit. Writing by candlelight and thrown out into the street when they couldn't pay their rent, and people hating them and acting like they had no place on earth because they heard things in their heads the mundanes didn't.

Those protesters back there. Nothing new about them, Nomad thought. People hated that Resurrection symphony, the first time they'd heard it in Berlin. That Russian guy Stravinsky, the first time his *Rite of Spring* was played, in 1913, there was a huge riot. And there was that story about Mozart, the Michael Jackson and the Prince of his era, writing an opera for an emperor and the emperor saying, when it was over, "Too many notes, my dear Mozart!"

To which Mozart had replied, "Just as many as are necessary, Your Majesty."

Even Mozart had had to deal with the suits, Nomad thought. The dudes who timed the songs and checked the notes in search of a single. The *Dustin Daye*-killers.

Same as it ever was.

Nomad couldn't fail to note a police presence around the hospital. A cruiser was prowling slowly along Ring Road and a second was sitting at the front of the hospital where its occupants could see and be seen. Allen found a slot about mid-level up in the parking deck and pulled in. The door locks clicked open. Nomad got out and followed his new warden into the hospital. Allen carried the brown folder with him. They went past the elevators and took the stairs. Allen paused in the hallway to show a police officer his ID, and then they entered the waiting room that Nomad had walked out of early Sunday morning.

It was reunion-time. Ariel, Terry and Berke were there, all of them looking as tired and haggard as if they'd been the ones spending two nights in the lockup. Also present were three other people: a brown-haired young man in a dark blue suit and a red-striped tie whom Nomad didn't recognize, and two others he did—Ashwatthama Vallampati and, unexpectedly, Roger Chester, the 'RC' of RCA. Everybody but the unknown young man, who wore a Bluetooth headset, had been sitting down when Allen and Nomad walked in, and now they stood up to show their good Texan, Oklahoman, Massachusetts, Californian and New Delhi manners.

"Dude!" said Terry, smiling as he came forward to bump shoulders and knuckles. "You enjoy your state-paid vacation?"

"No swimming pool," Nomad said. "Not a lot of chance to sunbathe, either." It was obvious they knew where he'd been; Captain Garza had probably told them on Sunday. Nomad saw sleeping bags folded up in a corner. He guessed the floor and sofa were not very comfortable. Maybe his bandmates had changed clothes and cleaned up in the public bathroom, but a scatter of soft drink cans, water bottles, candy and granola bar wrappers completed the story. They had been right here at UMC since Sunday morning.

Berke came over to slap him a high-five and comment on the bitch kiss he'd taken to the cheek. Suddenly Ariel was standing right in front of him. He looked into her eyes. Today—this moment—they were dark gray, the color of rain from a troubled sky. He recalled the things he'd said to her from the Pima County Jail. *Your land of rainbows and moonbeams. Do whatever the fuck you need to do. If you want to try to save sick animals, go be a vet.*

And maybe the worst: *Stop holding onto me.*

Because he knew it was the other way around, and without Ariel's presence he feared his anger—at the world, at his father for betraying his mother and being so damned *good* at it, and at himself for being not nearly as talented as he pretended to be—might rise up and eat him alive.

She hugged him.

She put her arms around him and leaned her head against his shoulder, and he realized that the most awesome thing…the most totally amazing thing…

…was that he did not pull away.

Then after a few seconds she looked at him and nodded, to welcome him back to his family, and he said a little nervously, "I missed you guys."

"John?" Roger Chester thrust a brown hand at him, and Nomad shook it. "Glad we could get you out of that situation." He had the kind of voice that takes over a room. He was trim, in his early sixties, and was tanned year-round from either playing golf or spending time at his second home in Cozumel. He wore tortoise-shell glasses that slightly magnified his dark brown eyes. He had curly white hair and a neatly-trimmed beard. His blue jeans were the trendy dirty denims, and he wore a red cowboy-style shirt with pearl-snap buttons under a dark blue blazer. Nomad had met him only once before, on the day he and the others had signed the contract for representation, and even then it had been brief because Roger Chester had just stopped by Creedy's office to ask a question about the new CD from Creedy's hot zombie-goth band I Died Yesterday. Creedy was Ethan Creed, who'd been The Five's agent for about three months before he took off for another talent group in Miami. Then The Five's career was handed over to the new man at the agency, Ashwatthama Vallampati.

"Hello, Ash," Nomad said, and Ash said in his clipped accent, "Hello, John."

He didn't really care much for Ash, and he didn't think Ash cared much for The Five. Ash was twenty-six years old, tall and fashionably slender, was handsome in an exotic way that could slay the Texas chicks—or the Texas dicks, because it was unclear which way he swung—and he always wore black suits and white shirts with neon-colored ties. His blue-black hair was always combed straight back and fixed with glistening pomade. He always smelled of bitter lemons. He always looked to Nomad as if he wore a faint half-smile of smug arrogance. The Roger Chester Agency handled maybe thirty bands and another dozen or so single acts. They had a couple of country-western heavy hitters, the Austin All-Nighters and the Trailblazers, both of whom had won Grammys. Roger Chester handled those personally, as well as the monster heavy-metal thrash band Shatter The Sky, who'd just recently returned from a European tour. Of the rest of the bands fighting for attention and a place in the public sun, The Five was probably down in the basement with the mutts. Or at least that's how Nomad felt Ash viewed them. To Nomad, Ash was all talk, big plans and no energy, and when something fizzled Ash just shrugged and let it go like he wasn't responsible.

Nomad figured Ash was on his way to Los Angeles, and thought of his job as more of a babysitter for spoiled wailing brats than a professional working to break a band out. Yeah, he did *some* things, like getting the spot with Felix Gogo, and obviously he was doing something for the other five or six bands he handled, but Nomad always remembered that one time in Ash's office Ash had said to him, "Your band doesn't really make any money for us, but we keep you around because we personally like you."

Nomad and Ash didn't shake hands.

"I am grieved about this tragedy." Roger Chester was standing so close to Nomad that Nomad could smell the orange Tic-Tac on his breath. "Mike Davis was a great bass player, a great musician. As for George Emerson...thank God he's going to live."

Nomad doubted that Roger Chester even knew who George was. "Are his parents here?" He'd directed the question to Allen.

"They flew in Sunday night. I've spoken to them, they're good people."

"Like I say, thank God he's going to live," Roger Chester repeated, as a way of gaining control of the room again. "All right then, Mr. Allen—or should I say *Agent* Allen?—where do we go from here?"

Nomad had already assumed that Allen had previously paid a visit to this room, speaking to Berke, Terry and Ariel as well as to George's parents, but he had no idea what Chester was talking about. Nomad frowned. "Go from *here*? Back to Austin, that's where. The tour's over." He got no response from anyone. "Listen, if we've got a fu..." He decided he didn't care what Allen thought about his language. "If we've got a fucking *sniper* after us, I think we'd better go home! Don't *you*?" He looked back and forth between Chester and Allen.

"It's not that simple," Allen told him, and those four words had the sound of doom. "Why don't you sit down?" He motioned toward one of the folding chairs that had been brought in for the extra people. "Everyone take a seat. I want to tell you what you're facing."

Nomad sat down in a chair beside Ariel. He was thinking of what Allen had said at the jail: *You're going to help me catch Jeremy Pett.* When all the others had settled, except the young man in the dark blue suit who remained unintroduced and who stood silently by the door, Allen took the central position in the room and opened the brown folder.

"I've already told you who he is, but I haven't told you *what* he is," Allen said to the group. "He's a veteran Marine. He served two tours of duty in Iraq as a sniper, so he knows his business. Training to be a sniper is the toughest discipline in the Corps. They teach the doctrine of one bullet, one kill." He paused for emphasis. "That's the ideal. It doesn't always go that way on the battlefield. But Pett's record says he had thirty-eight confirmed kills and another forty-two probables. His last kill was in 2004, though, and now is now. He's been through some hardships. They've worked on him. He's probably let himself slide physically. Mentally, too. So he's not nearly as sharp as he used to be...*but*...he's given himself a cause of some kind. He's invented a mission. Which obviously involves killing the members of your band. He followed you to Sweetwater and got himself in position across from that gas station. He must have been right behind you all the way from Dallas."

"Hold it!" Berke said, lifting a hand. "How do you *know* all this? How do you even know this guy is the one?" She'd seen Jeremy Pett's driver's license photo when Allen had introduced himself to them this morning, and he'd told them he would explain everything later but he had to go get John Charles out of jail first.

"The police passed along to us some information from a Detective Rios in Sweetwater. She did some digging after you'd left town. Nothing was making sense to her, but the fact remained that the shooting looked professional. So she went to your website and saw your latest video. She started thinking that maybe the video had triggered somebody with a military history, somebody who had experience with long-range shooting. If that was true, then this person might have decided to follow you to your gigs." Allen glanced quickly at Nomad, to show he had a good memory for a guy his age. "To stalk you, and to set up his shots. That sounded to her like a military sniper. The question was: where did he start from? So...she took it upon herself to make calls first to the Austin PD and then she spread out to the PDs of the towns between Austin and Dallas."

"Looking for what?" Nomad asked.

"A recent missing person report, filed around the 20th. The problem was that, if this sniper fits a psychological profile, he'll probably live alone in a rented house or apartment, he'll have trouble making social contacts and trouble keeping a job. So if he's taken off on the road to follow you, there might not be anybody left behind to notice he's gone. But...in this case, Jeremy Pett *had* made a contact, and there *was* a missing person report that caught her interest, filed on Monday the 21st, in Temple, Texas."

Allen pulled up another sheet of paper from the folder to be sure he got the name right. "Pett's apartment manager, Teyo Salazar, told the Temple police he went into the apartment with his key to leave a sack of tamales because, as he said, Jeremy was very depressed about his finances. Inside, he found blood on the carpet, on the wall and in the bathroom. The tub had been drained, but there was blood evidence in there as well. Also a box cutter, and some drugs in the apartment. So Mr. Salazar calls the police, and they start looking for Jeremy Pett but he's nowhere to be found. They relayed this information to Detective Rios, who started a search of Pett's personal history. She discovered that Pett was a decorated Marine sniper, discharged in January of 2005 after the second battle of Fallujah. Then she turned to his credit card history. She learned he'd used his credit card to buy gas at a station about ten miles west of the one where Mike Davis was killed. The time on that transaction was twenty-some minutes after Mr. Davis's death."

"Oh, shit," Terry said, a stunned exhalation of breath.

"That's not the kicker." Allen's cool blue eyes scanned his audience. "He used his credit card again on the night of the 20th, to pay for a room at the Lariat Motel."

Berke made a noise, kind of a soft gasp, but no one looked at her.

Nomad said with a mixture of shock and anger, "The fucker was right in the motel *with* us? Christ, man! What the *fuck* have we done to him?"

Roger Chester stood up. "Take it easy, John." The real reason he'd stood up was that his hemorrhoids had flared on the flight from Austin and his folding chair wasn't making him feel any better. He looked at Truitt Allen. "It's got to be more than a *video*. Who kills somebody because they don't like a video?"

"I can't say. But I do know from experience that people can create extraordinary circumstances in their own minds. Especially disturbed individuals, which I think is fair to say is the case here. They can create scenarios that would boggle the imagination of anyone we consider 'normal'. Do you remember the Beltway sniper shootings in 2002? In Washington DC, Virginia and Maryland?"

"I do."

"Ten people were killed and three critically injured," Allen went on. "Four people were killed in a single morning, during a two-hour time span. As you may recall, it turned out to be the work of one man and a boy. The man was an Army sergeant in the Gulf War, qualified as an expert with the M16 rifle. After he was caught, he explained his motives. He'd planned to kill six people a day for thirty days. He was going to extort millions of dollars from the government to stop the killings, and then he was planning on travelling to Canada, stopping at YMCAs and orphanages to recruit children who could also be trained as snipers." He raised his black eyebrows. "He was going to be a father figure to an army of young snipers. They would then be sent to major cities across the United States to carry out mass shootings. Insane? To us, yes, but to him it made perfect sense. It was an achievable goal. It gave him something to—shall I say—shoot for."

That's not fucking funny, Nomad wanted to say, but he kept his mouth shut.

"I'll point out that a check of Jeremy Pett's firearms licenses shows that he owns a Remington Model 700 SPS rifle, which fires the same .308 Winchester caliber long-range bullet that killed Mike Davis and hit George Emerson. The rifle is similar to what he would've used in Iraq, and with a decent scope and an open field he can make shots at over five-hundred yards. Maybe not every shot, because he's lost some of his ability and he doesn't have a spotter. He also owns a .45 automatic, so he can be deadly at close range too, but I think he trusts his sniper skills more than his pistol ability." Allen managed a sad smile. "It's what he's good at."

"So find him, then!" Nomad realized his voice was a little too strident. "Trace his credit card or something! Do you know what kind of car he's driving?"

"Just before I came to get you, his license tag number and a description of both him and his pickup truck were released to the media. It should start showing up on the local channels this afternoon and on the national broadcasts as soon as they're ready to put it in rotation. As for the credit card, he's stopped using it. The last credit purchase was again for gasoline in El Paso, on the afternoon of the 23rd. He's gotten himself some money. Maybe pawned the pistol…who knows?"

"Okay, great," said Terry. "But can't you…like…call around to the front desk of every motel in town and try to find him? I mean, could it be that hard?"

"We're working on that. Nothing's turned up yet," Allen answered. "I love my town, but I'll be the first to tell you that there are some pay-by-the-hour holes here he can disappear into, and if he's paying up front with cash nobody's going to ask for an ID or write down his plate number. He might have decided not to use his real name.

Understand that this man may not be who he once was, but he still has his Marine training and he knows how to improvise."

"Maybe he's gone," Ariel ventured. "Maybe shooting Mike and George was enough."

"Maybe. It depends on what's happening in his head."

"But he *could* be gone?" Roger Chester's gaze had sharpened. "It's a possibility?"

"A possibility," Allen agreed, but cautiously. "He could be in Mexico by now."

"That would be a good thing for The Five." Chester looked at the bandmembers in turn and then directed his attention to Nomad, because Ashwatthama had briefed him on who the leader and decision-maker was. "John, are you aware that in the last forty-eight hours, your band has sold almost twenty thousand CDs?"

Nomad couldn't speak. He thought he'd heard a voice talking to him from another world.

"Twenty *thousand*?" It was Berke, sounding choked. Her throat was not used to such a number.

"Eighteen thousand, three hundred and forty-six at last count about an hour ago, and that's just the new CD," Chester said. His voice was growing muscles, taking over the room once more. "We're getting orders from all over the country, Canada and Mexico. We're starting now to see orders from England, France, the Netherlands and Germany. Your backlist has picked up and is also selling in the thousands, and your single downloads on iTunes at nine o'clock this morning was more than forty thousand. Your YouTube and MySpace hits are off the chart and your website crashed with the traffic on Sunday night. You're a lead story—most viewed and most emailed—on Yahoo. It's in newspapers everywhere. *People* magazine called the office this morning. Yesterday the sniper story was running every hour on CNN and Fox News. It's on the World News Network." He paused to catch his breath; his face had become flushed. "I don't have to tell you what national—correction: *international*—media exposure can do for product and for artists," he said. "We're all lucky you guys look so good on television."

Nomad felt light-headed and woozy. He felt a little bit sick, really. How could he be happy, at a time like this? He realized that The Five was suddenly a success, though the only thing that had changed in two days was the fact that a sniper was after them, the media had jumped on it and the public was intrigued. He figured a lot of those CDs were being sold as morbid collector's items, or to be resold on eBay after...what? After all of them were dead?

That damned Little Genius, Nomad thought. Got that media shine going bigtime, but I don't want it this way.

"Can't you people say anything?" Ash prompted, and Nomad nearly got up and smashed him in his bag of curried nuts.

"What do you want us to say?" Ariel stood up. For a few seconds the glint of volcanic flame beneath the sea in her eyes made Nomad think she was going to do the job of smashing Ash herself, which amazed him so much all he could do was sit there and gape. "*Thank you*? For what? We did all the work. And the thing is, we're no different a band than we were on Saturday night, but suddenly we're *famous*? Because Mike is dead and George is in the ICU? What are we supposed to say?"

Roger Chester cleared his throat to get her attention. "You can say," he answered calmly, "that you'll keep going to the end of your tour. You have...what?...eight more dates? What's the schedule, Ash? San Diego on Friday and Los Angeles on Saturday, I think you said."

"Yes sir...but there's the other thing, if they want it."

"*What* other thing?" Berke asked.

"Stone Church." Ash chose to look at Nomad instead of the woman. "An invitation to play Stone Church came into the office yesterday afternoon. They're offering—"

"No," Ariel interrupted. "Not Stone Church."

"May I finish?"

"Not Stone Church," Ariel said again, defiantly. "I won't play there."

Nomad realized something of what he'd said to her over the phone had taken hold. *You ought to go out on your own. Put your own band together. You could've done it straight out of The Blessed Hours, if you'd wanted to.*

He saw in her face—the set of her jaw, the new fire in her eyes—that she believed him.

But the new Ariel Collier wasn't yet ready to take the stage on her own after all, because the old one peered out like a little child and said, "I'm sorry, Mr. Chester."

"I've heard of Stone Church," Allen said. "Used to be a mining town, wasn't it? Up near Gila Bend?"

"Yeah, now it's an outdoors music festival." Nomad gave him a sardonic glance. "If your idea of a music festival includes badass biker gangs, death cultists and Satan worshippers, that's your nirvana."

"What are we talking about?" Berke demanded. "Somebody's trying to kill us and we're just going to go out and play more gigs? Not me. I'm heading—" She abruptly stopped. *To San Diego*, she realized she was about to say. To open Floyd fucking Fisk's boxes in her mother's garage. Her mother was going mental; she'd been calling Berke every few hours to make sure she was okay.

When it was apparent Berke was not about to finish her declaration, Roger Chester said, "Let me spread this out for you. They're offering six hundred dollars for one show. The festival opens up on noon Thursday. You'll be the headliner on Thursday night. We can negotiate with them on the merchandise split." He aimed his attention at Nomad. "One show, six hundred dollars. Local and national media will be there. You play an hour and a half and you're done. They need to know by two o'clock today, to put you on the promos. We'll find you a new road manager. You say the word, and Ash goes out to buy a new van; you just tell me what you need."

The Scumbucket belonged to George. There would be no more Scumbucket in the lives of The Five. Nomad didn't know what to say. He could feel Ariel urging him to reject it. "The only reason they want us there," he said, meeting Chester's gaze, "is because of the death thing. You know that."

"They won't like our kind of music," Ariel added. "We don't play what they want to hear."

"Garth Brickenfield wants you there." Chester was unyielding. "He's asked for you personally."

"Who's Garth Brickenfield?" Allen asked.

Chester told him. Nomad knew that Garth Brickenfield was the Big Dipper in the Southwest promoter's sky; he ran his business out of Tucson and had created the Stone Church festival. He was in his sixties, a hermit in his sunset years, and legend had it he'd twice attempted to climb Mt. Everest, he had a private airstrip and a collection of vintage planes, and he owned an alligator farm in Louisiana. When he was a top gun in the record business, he'd had long-standing bad blood with Bob Dylan and once had challenged Mick Jagger to a swordfight.

"Let me ask you a question." Allen was speaking not only to Nomad but to Terry and Berke. "If I can get you eight hundred dollars and I can provide security, would you play? And we're talking about an afternoon spot, not night time."

"Sir?" The tone of Roger Chester's voice was a little frosty. "We're in control of this, thank you. I've dealt with Garth Brickenfield many times, and when he makes a money offer, that's it. Also, no way in Hell is he going to pay that much for an afternoon...*spot*, as you call it. Those are for the hasbeens and wannabees. The Five is star material."

"How about letting the *stars* talk?" Nomad asked, dripping acid. He got to his feet, standing shoulder-to-shoulder with Ariel. "What's this about, man?" He was addressing Roger Chester. He'd been gentleman enough to leave out the *old*. "A crazy guy's killed one of us and almost killed another, and he may be in Mexico or he may still be after our asses, and you're wanting us to finish our *tour*? Why? Because we're worth more to you dead than we are alive?"

Berke and Terry remained seated; one was thinking about the contents of three boxes in San Diego, the other about a rock legend with a strange keyboard in a house outside Albuquerque.

"Continuing your tour is *my* idea." Truitt Allen was speaking to the floor. "I ran all this past Mr. Chester this morning." He looked up into Nomad's eyes. "Why do you think I got you out of jail? I told you already, I need your help to catch Jeremy Pett."

"Oh, I get it! We're supposed to be fucking *bait*, right?"

"Cheese for a mousetrap," Allen said.

"I'm allergic to cheese," said Nomad. "Especially the kind that can get me—us—killed."

Allen shrugged. "Okay, so you go back to Austin. Go back to your routines. If Pett's still hunting you, how does that make you any safer? He can pick you off one by one, when you're alone. Until he's found, believe me...you're safer together, on the road. Especially if you do what I say."

Nomad scowled. "Yeah, right! What are you gonna do, be our new road manager?"

The man scratched his perfectly-shaved chin. "Well," he said, "that *would* solve one of your problems."

This was too much for Berke. "You're a whackjob, man! We don't need an FBI agent as a road manager!" It had taken all her willpower not to drop the f-bomb on him.

"Yes," Allen answered, "you do. Because you need the security I can put together for you. You need a team of my men trailing you on the highway, watching your backs. You need a team travelling in front of you, to check out where you're going. And this Stone Church thing…you need to play there on Thursday afternoon, and there need to be promos flooding local TV and radio and items on the newscasts building it up, so Jeremy Pett will see them and bring his rifle to Gila Bend, where I'll have tac teams up in the hills waiting for him. *That's* why you need to play in daylight. And that's why I jumped through hoops to get you released into my custody…Mr. Charles," he finished.

"Un…fucking…real," said Berke, but she sounded resigned to whatever lay ahead.

Ariel tried her protest again. It, too, had weakened. "That's not our kind of crowd. We shouldn't play there. Not Stone Church."

"Your being their road manager aside," said Roger Chester to Allen. "The elephant in this room is that Garth Brickenfield wants them at *night*. Once he makes up his mind, it's done."

Allen nodded thoughtfully. "How about if I give him a call and ask him? And while I'm at it, I also ask for eight hundred dollars instead of six? Just to show I can do my new job."

Ash gave a mocking laugh. "Nobody calls Garth Brickenfield! You call his office and talk to his people!"

"Really?" Allen looked at the young man standing next to the door. "Ken?"

"Yes sir?"

"Get the home phone number of Garth Brickenfield. Then get him on the phone for me, please," Allen told the young man, who started talking to someone on his Bluetooth.

"That's ridiculous!" Ash said. "You're not going to find a number for him. It's unlisted and his people make sure that no one gets through without—"

"They're bringing it up now, sir," Ken announced. "Garth Orwell Brickenfield, on North Summer Moon Place. Call's going through."

"He owns *several* houses," Roger Chester said; his face had gotten flushed again. "I doubt if—"

"Hello ma'am, I'm Agent Kenneth McGuire with the Federal Bureau of Investigation here in Tucson. I'm trying to reach Mr. Garth Orwell Brickenfield. Is he in?" There was just a short pause. "Would you tell him that Special Agent Truitt Allen would like to speak with him, please? It's very important." Ken gave a nod to his boss. "Yes ma'am, I'll hold." He said to Allen, "She's calling him out at the hangar; he's been working on his planes today. She says it should just be a few minutes."

The door opened.

A young auburn-haired woman wearing blue scrubs looked in. "Excuse me," she said. "Mr. Emerson is awake. He's asking to speak to his friends."

They knew who they were.

On the way to the ICU, they were briefed that they were not to touch anything in George's room and that they could stay only a few minutes. They came to a middle-aged man and woman standing in the hallway just outside the unit's cream-colored doors. Nomad stopped to speak to them in his most decent and caring tone of voice. They thanked him for what he said about their son. Nomad would've recognized George's father anywhere: not by his short stature, but by the shiny pennies in his loafers.

Nomad, Ariel, Terry and Berke followed the young woman through the doors. It was cooler and quieter in this area of the hospital. There was the low hiss of respirators in action and the electronic beep of crucial machines, but otherwise everything was hushed. Doctors and nurses in scrubs moved about, either talking calmly to each other or checking their clipboards. Along the corridor between rooms separated by closed curtains there was a blue-cast underwater light.

"This way," said their escort. She took them to one of the rooms on the left and drew aside the curtain.

They moved into the room, Nomad first and Ariel right behind him. Terry was last in, and his thought when he saw George lying in the bed at the center of all the monitor screens and gray wires and IV drips and black rubber cables was that George was now more machine than man.

Nomad had the feeling that he was not looking at George, but at a wax replica of the Little Genius. Surely this moon-colored face wasn't the real thing. George was wearing an oxygen mask, he was packed into the bed with the sheet up to his neck and there was something over his chest, bandages or medical dressings or whatever, that made it bulge like a muscle man's. Tubes snaked out of the bed to and from various receptacles. Clear fluid was dripping in and yellow fluid was dripping out. A vertical bank of monitors about six feet tall stood next to the bed. Things chirped and beeped and suddenly George's legs rustled the sheet—a heavy, painful sound—and he looked at them with his bleary, swollen red eyes and said in a voice like the scrape of a dead leaf blown by the wind along a sidewalk, "Hi, team."

Ariel turned away from the bed. Berke put a hand on her shoulder and left it there like a steel clamp until Ariel could get control of herself again.

"You're all wired up," Terry said, and he gave a weak little laugh.

"Oh yeah," George answered, more of a breath with words than a regular voice. The sound was made hollow by the mask. "Getting tuned," he said. "Weird thing. I can see better now."

Nomad walked to the side of the bed, wary of all the life-sustaining machinery. He didn't know what to say, so he said what welled up when he looked into the pale, waxen face. "They're going to get the bastard, George."

"Same guy," George said; it was not a question, because he knew.

"Yeah. We're going to finish the tour." Just that fast, smelling the lingering burned scent of a critical wound that he recalled had hazed the air around his father's body there in the Louisville parking lot, Nomad had made his decision. "We're going to help get him."

"Finish...?" George blinked, maybe thinking he was more out of his mind than he'd realized. "The *tour*?"

"Thanks for asking *us*," Berke said, but when both Nomad and George looked at her, she frowned as if she'd stepped on the crack that broke her mother's back. "Shit." The lines on her forehead only deepened. "Okay, screw it. I'm in."

Terry said, with a shifting of his shoulders that was not quite a shrug, "I guess I'm in too."

Ariel didn't speak.

"Crazy." It was a distant voice from a faded man. "All of you."

A silence stretched. Nomad was not good with hospitals; this was torture, wanting to be gone but needing to be here.

"I almost let go," George said.

Ariel had composed herself. Her eyes were red, but she came forward to stand where she thought she should be, beside John Charles.

"It was up there." George lifted his chin toward the ceiling. Toward the corner of the ceiling, up on the right where the curtain guide was.

"What was there?" Nomad glanced up to where George had indicated. Ceiling, curtain guide, nothing else.

"Folded up," said George. "Sharp edges." He took a few slow breaths before he spoke again. "I couldn't see a head. No face. But I knew. It was watching me. It was like...the wings of a crow. Or like black origami. It was waiting. Right up there."

"Waiting for what?" Ariel asked.

And George answered, "For me to die."

Terry gave that nervous laugh again. "You're not going to die, man! Get real!"

"You're not going to die," Berke said. "You're past the worst part." She hoped. "Listen, we probably need to go so you can rest. Okay?"

"That's not all," George said. "I was fighting. Really fighting. Hard. And I don't know...when it was...but I heard somebody speak my name. It was like...a voice I knew. Maybe... a teacher I used to have. Somebody who cared about me. I knew that voice." He made a noise that sounded as if he were struggling to breathe, and Nomad almost went for the nurse's call button but then George said, "I opened my eyes and that girl was here."

"Who?" Ariel asked.

"That girl," he repeated. "Where they were picking the blackberries. You know."

Nomad and Ariel exchanged glances. Terry looked quickly at Berke, but Berke was just staring down at the floor.

"Standing in the corner. *There.*" George lifted his chin toward the left-hand corner. "She said, 'I believe in you, George,' and then...she smiled at me...and she nodded. That voice...somebody else's voice... I don't know whose. I was afraid. Closed my eyes. Tight. I thought... if I burst a blood vessel...least I'm in the hospital already." He had to stop and take a breather. "She was gone when I looked," he said. His eyes found Nomad's. "John...I thought...she was the angel of death. But now...I think she was the angel of life."

"You had a dream," Berke said quietly. "That's all."

"Right. A dream. But listen...if you guys...drove back there. To that place. She'd still be there...right? That whole place...it would still be there. Right?"

"Yeah," Nomad told him. "It would."

"Go back...and find out," George said.

Nomad had no idea what he was talking about. It was time to leave; past time, really.

"Take the Scumbucket," George said. "Old warhorse. Good for nothing...but following the music."

"We can't do that," Ariel said. "It's your van."

"Done with me. 'Member, John?" His voice was getting weaker. His eyes were wanting to close and stay shut. "I said...I was with you guys. Said I'd take care of you. Like always." He moved his legs again under the sheet, seeking some kind of comfort. "Dad's got the keys. I'll tell him."

The young woman with the auburn hair came in. "George," she said in a light, friendly tone, "I'm afraid your visitors are going to need to leave." She made a quick visual check of the monitors and systems.

"Hey." George roused himself from his impending slumber. "The song. Don't you want my part?"

"The *song*?" Nomad shook his head.

Ariel knew. The song Mike started, probably the last song they would ever write. "Yes, George," she said. "We do want your part."

"I'm adding...what the girl said. To you, Ariel. *I wish you...safe travel...courage when you need it.*" The Little Genius offered them a wistful smile. His eyes glistened. "You need it now," he said.

"I'll see you on the other side of this," Nomad vowed.

They said their goodbyes. Terry, who had been last going into the room, was the last out. Berke walked on ahead, moving quickly, her head lowered.

Ariel kept pace with Nomad. Heavy-burdened, they went back to the room where the suits were waiting, and where their new road manager had just gotten them eight hundred dollars for ninety minutes in the afternoon sun at Stone Church.

SIXTEEN.

"**Tell me** what I don't already know about Stone Church," said Truitt Allen.

"What do you already know?" Nomad fired back, from his seat behind Ariel.

"Damn, look at that fool!" Allen tapped the Scumbucket's brake. The purple-and-blue spray-painted camper just ahead had swerved into the right lane without a turn signal. "Nothing pisses me off worse than a careless driver." There were maybe a dozen stickers on the camper's rear bumper, things like *Eat Me, Not Meat* and *What Would Jesus Shoot*?

Nomad thought Mr. Driver's Education had better get used to it, because the train of huge recreational vehicles, campers, Volkswagen vans, pickup trucks and motley rusted-out mutts on four tires heading up I-10 was only going to get longer and more piss-worthy the closer they got to the junction of I-8 and the straight shot to Gila Bend.

The U-Haul trailer was an orange thumb that indicated they were on their way to Garth Brickenfield's little bitty ole festival, as he'd described it to Allen over the phone. It was indeed thirteen years old, but it was no longer little bitty. The highway, at ten o'clock on Thursday morning, was already a demolition derby in the making. The troopers were out in force but so were the wreckmakers. A few minutes earlier, they'd passed the blinking lights at a fresh mess and seen crashed in a ditch one of those gargantuan black pickup trucks meant to carry Paul Bunyan's lumber. Around it on the ground sat seven or eight people who looked to be made out of tattoos. One of the shirtless baldheaded young men was raging at the troopers as the plastic cuffs were being locked on his wrists, and none of The Five could fail to note on the man's sunburned back a tattoo of a downward-facing pentagram with a red goat's head at its center.

Have fun in the Pima County Jail, Nomad had thought. But what concerned him was that there were many more music-lovers just like that guy who weren't going to crash their rides today.

It was going to be crazy on the two-lane road that left I-8 a few miles west of Gila Bend and twisted up into the mountains on its way to Apache Leap. The weathergirl on KVOA had said it was going to be cloudless skies and a hundred degrees at noon, so maybe at three o'clock, when The Five took the stage, it would be in the upper nineties. But it was dry heat, so they would bake instead of steam.

"I have a question for *you*." It was the first time Berke had spoken since she'd climbed into the back seat about thirty minutes ago. She was dressed, appropriately for the weather of this 31st day of July and her current state of mind, in black jeans and a black wifebeater T-shirt. One thing new she was wearing was a small silver pin in the shape of a bass guitar that she'd bought yesterday in a crafts shop on North Campbell Avenue. "What handle are we supposed to give you?"

"What *handle*?" A pair of intense blue eyes glanced back in the rearview mirror.

"Your name," Berke clarified. "Like...what? Allen? Mr. Allen? Truitt? I mean, if you're pretending to be our road manager, then—"

"No," he interrupted, and she stopped dead because she could tell when he spoke that word he meant it. "I'm not *pretending*. If I'm asking you to do...what I'm asking you to do...then you need to make some money off it. And if Pett doesn't show up here, we'll be ready for him in San Diego. Or Los Angeles, or wherever. But believe me...are you listening?" He'd seen her look away with a pained expression.

"I am," Berke said, but she still stared out her window at the white sea of sand and clumps of spiny vegetation, darkened green by the newly-tinted glass.

"Believe me," he repeated, "I'm going to do a real job." He didn't have to tell her he'd gone over his new role very thoroughly with

Roger Chester. Organization was his mantra; how difficult could this be? "By the way, are you feeling the air-conditioning back there?"

"It feels great," Terry said.

Nomad grunted. He had to give credit where credit was due. Mr. Pep Boy had taken the Scumbucket somewhere—maybe the agency garage—and had the van scrubbed and detailed, though scrubbing and detailing didn't do much for beat-up battleship gray. Still, it was amazing that there wasn't a single crumb of last year's marijuana brownies anywhere on the floorboards, not a forgotten straw nor a plastic cup lid. In fact, there were new rubber mats, still with the new rubbery smell. The multitudinous variety of soft drink, tea, beer, mustard, hot sauce and other stains that had blotched the seats for years like a collection of Rorschach inkblots was gone as if absorbed by a magic ShamWow. The air-conditioning worked like an oil sheik's dream. And it was nearly *silent*.

But what really blew the top off the Awesome Meter was the fact that Mr. Dark Glasses At Night had gotten that tint job done within a single day. For the ordinary man, it would've been a week on the wait. Windshield, side windows and back glass: all were pimped with the cool green, which made sunglasses unnecessary and also helped the air-conditioning.

Nomad knew the reason for that, as they all did: somebody—Jeremy Pett by name—wanting to fire a shot into the van wouldn't have as clear a target as before.

On first seeing it, Nomad had asked their Scumbucket benefactor if the pop-up machine-guns, the oilslick shooters and the automated armor shields were in working order, and which seat was the ejector?

"I'm not sure of that other stuff," came the reply, "but how about riding shotgun today?"

Which was how Ariel had wound up in that front passenger seat, though of course Nomad had known Mr. Fit-At-Fifty was just pulling his chain.

He hadn't slept very soundly the last couple of nights, and today he was feeling it. When he closed his eyes, he saw George's face with the oxygen mask strapped to it, in that bed in the hospital whose smell took him back to a death in Louisville. He saw George looking into one corner of the room—*It was waiting. Right up there*—and then into the other.

I opened my eyes and that girl was here.

Why would George have dreamed about that girl? Of all people...*her*?

I believe in you, George.

It was creepy, Nomad thought. Way creepy. And then adding that line about *safe travel* and *courage* to the song. Ariel had written it down in her notebook, with the other lines begun by the word *Welcome*.

That single word had been powerful enough to bring tears to Mike's eyes. And powerful enough for him to dare to start writing a song.

Creepy, he thought. But it could be explained. Dreams were just dreams and Mike had been a lot more sentimental than he'd let on. So there was really no big deal. It was a song. And what else would it be?

"So how about it?" Berke persisted, speaking to their driver. "What do we call you?"

He thought it over. There *had* been a name for him, back in the day. Before he'd gotten so serious...well, no, he'd always been serious...but, still...

It had been given to him...no, he'd earned it, as he'd earned everything in his life, the hard way...by his fraternity brothers at the University of Oregon. He decided it was good enough for now, as well.

"True," he said. "With an 'e'. Opposite of 'false'."

Berke tried it out, to see how it sounded and felt: "True. Okay, I guess that works."

"I can't see calling you that," Ariel said.

True frowned. A big fat-assed red SUV was right in front of him, he couldn't spare even a quick glance at her. "Why not?"

"I don't know, I just can't."

"Oh." He got it. "Right. Because I'm *old*. Because you're thinking you need to be saying 'sir' to me, and calling me 'mister'?"

"I didn't say you were old." She paused, trying to figure out exactly what she *was* trying to say. After a moment more of uncomfortable silence, she asked, "How old *are* you?"

"Fifty-three. Coming up to fifty-four in November. My story: met my wife in college, at Oregon, married her after graduation, been married—very happily—for thirty years. We have two daughters, one in enviromental science for the city of Tucson, and another an FBI agent in Dallas. We have one grandchild, a boy named Wesley Truitt Adams. My wife and I like to go on cruises when we can, and we enjoy river rafting and mountain biking. I like reading military history. I have a stereo room, and I listen to a lot of Bruce Springsteen and the Eagles but I also like Tony Bennett and bluegrass. What am I leaving out that you might like to know?"

"Big jump from Oregon to Arizona," Nomad said. "How'd that happen?"

"I was actually born in Yuma. Went to high school there. Played football with the Criminals. Senior quarterback until a Kofa High King got through the defense and knocked me into orbit, three games from the end of the season. But I guess I wanted to see something green. I wanted to see a forest and hear rain and...you know...do something that you feel you need to do. So you go do it. Anything else?"

"You were a policeman before you joined the FBI?" Ariel asked.

"Oh, yeah. Did all that grunt work." True was trying to read the white-on-black sticker on the bumper of that red SUV. He sped up a little bit, getting closer. The SUV had a Texas tag. The part of the sticker he could read said *Have Some Fun*. Underneath that were small words he couldn't make out. *Nun*? He gave it some more gas.

Nomad asked, "You were a cop in Tucson?"

"Hold it, hold it, I'm trying to—" And then he *was* close enough to read the smaller words. The second line read *Fuck A Nun*. About two seconds after seeing that, he saw a black decal with an upside-down cross on it at a corner of the rear glass, and then he realized something was staring at him from the back of the SUV.

He could see the whites of two eyes and below them a gleam of bared teeth. It was a black dog, he thought. A big dog. Its eyes were fixed upon him as if it could see him clearly and distinctly through the green tint. Maybe it could. The way the thing stared at him, immobile though both the van and the SUV were doing about sixty miles an hour and the highway was flashing past underneath, made True think that if that dog could get at him it would rip his throat open from ear-to-ear.

A Melville quote came to him: *I saw the opening maw of hell.*

True felt the small hairs on the back of his neck tingle. Suddenly a white arm braided with a barbed-wire tattoo emerged from the dark within, hooked around the animal's neck and pulled the dog away from the glass...

...and then the SUV's brakelights flared red, True saw a rear-end collision about to destroy his perfect driving record and perhaps the way his head sat upon his spine, and he swerved the van and trailer into the left-hand lane directly in front of a Winnebago painted a sand-colored camo scheme. He came within inches of scraping that hideous sticker off the metal and he felt the whipsaw of the trailer shudder through the van's frame. The trailer swayed back and forth a few times, as True cut his speed to keep the rig from dragging them off the interstate. The shriek of tires and blare of horns followed.

"Jesus Christ!" Nomad hollered.

"Hey, man!" Terry said, righting himself after his seatbelt had nearly cut him in half. It was a pain, wearing these seatbelts, but with an FBI agent at the wheel, what were you gonna do? "I thought you could *drive*!"

"Sorry." True checked the sideview mirrors. Thank God, he was leaving no accidents in his wake. The driver of the red SUV dropped back, turned on the blinker and merged smoothly into the left-hand lane a few vehicles behind the Scumbucket.

"*That* was different," Berke said. "I used to have a drum kit back in that fucking trailer instead of shit and splinters."

"It'll be all right," he told her. He felt such animosity from her, he couldn't resist saying, "It would've been busted up if it hadn't been repacked."

"Repacked?" Terry asked; it had also gone through his mind that his keyboards, even in their hard cases, weren't up to that kind of rock-and-rolling.

"I had everything repacked by experts," True said, feeling a little superior. "They filled in the empty spaces with styrofoam cubes and put color-key labels on everything."

"Color-key *labels*?" Berke leaned forward as far as her sealtbelt would let her. "What for?"

"There's a diagram taped to the inside of the trailer. It shows how everything should be packed, according to the colors." When no one spoke for a time, True said, "More efficient this way."

"Yeah, well, *George* had a system." Berke wasn't ready to let it go. This guy with his pressed khaki trousers and his dark burgundy-colored polo shirt and his white sidewalls and fucking control-freak attitude was starting to crawl up her butt. "He just *knew* where everything went. He didn't need...like...an agency full of government flunkies figuring out what color label ought to be stuck on my snare."

"I'm sure he did a great job." True's voice was cool; he was somewhere else now, though, concentrating on the task ahead.

"He was one of *us*," Berke said, and let the obvious rest of it hang out there. No further comment came from the government man. She leaned back and closed her eyes to escape the moment and recharge her batteries. There would be a huge sunshade awning up over the stage, she'd been told, but hot was hot and drumming made its own heat. Fuck it, she'd be ready; she always was.

"If your boys had seen that move," Nomad said to True, "they might take your Good Driver's badge away. That wasn't them crashed in that ditch back there, was it?"

"No." His 'boys', dressed the part of Stone Church music fans, were in two vehicles ahead of them and two vehicles behind. Another team of 'boys' had gone to the site early this morning to get everything organized, and more 'boys' were at this moment setting up on their stations. True had had an interesting meeting with his site coordinator yesterday, when True had said he needed metal detectors in operation between what they called the 'Midway' and the entrance to the 'Amphitheater'.

Metal detectors, sir? The site coordinator was thirty-two years old, an ex-SWAT guy and a big fan of a band called Green Day, which True had never heard of. *Sir...do you realize how many times those detectors are going to go off with this crowd? It'll be a constant buzz. And...begging your pardon, sir, but some of these people are going to be carrying metal in places you'd rather not know about. Male and female both.*

True had taken it upon himself to find on the Internet some examples of what was being talked about, and when he was looking at a picture of a split cock with metal rings dangling from both halves his wife had happened to come up behind him in the study and spilled his nightly Ovaltine all over the carpet.

So much for the metal detectors. The undercover guys were going to have to eyeball the crowd, but it was unlikely Pett would try to get in close for a shot. The rifle was his instrument, and long range his protection. The biggest responsiblity would be with the tac teams surrounding the venue. But to this point, everything had been going as planned. Pett's picture, his tag number and a description of his dark blue pickup truck had been on the local news and on CNN and Fox. Last night Nancy Grace had put up the information before every commercial break; she was a bulldog about such things and could be counted on to help. On the other hand, the media was always hungry for hot stories and the sniper story had lost some of its heat, being knocked off centerstage by new developments about the missing little girl in Florida and the fourth rape by the so-called Duct Tape Rapist in Los Angeles.

The local TV stations had been helpful in promoting Stone Church. They'd been running the frenzied, quick-cut video ads that Garth Brickenfield had paid for, and also getting in on the newcasts mention that The Five—*you'll remember they're the rock band that's been struck twice in sniper attacks both in Arizona and Texas*—would be playing there for one show at three o'clock on Thursday afternoon. *Promoter Garth Brickenfield assures us that of course security will be tight and every precaution will be taken.* Brickenfield had insisted on that last bit, and he said he didn't give a shit if the FBI or the IRS or GWB himself had some questions about his last three years' tax returns, he couldn't scare off his paying customers.

Didn't really matter, True thought. For sure Pett knew security would be tight. Would he see it as a challenge? A way to show what he could do, now that he was back in the arena?

Time would tell.

By the looks of the crowd on this highway, nobody was being scared off. They'd be pouring in from the eastbound side too, coming from California. Brickenfield's promotional efforts—on TV, radio, and newspapers—covered the entire southwest and half of the left coast, and the website was slick and professional but the band pictures were nearly as disturbing as the image of the cock with two half-heads. In True's day, bands had wanted their faces to be seen; they didn't want to wear over their heads executioner's masks, wire cages and coiled things that looked like French sex toys.

The first band started up at noon. Stone Church went until midnight Sunday with bands playing around the clock. He'd gone over the roster, but he didn't know any of the names: Triumph Of The Dark, Skullsplitter, FTW, The Black Dahlias, Rat Scab, Monster

Ripper, Anus And Candy, The Descenders, Mjöllnir, The Bleeding Brains, The Luciferians, Dear Mother's Blood, Fist Deep, Dreams Of Sharp Teeth, The Sick Crabs, The Slain, and on and on.

He recalled thinking how weird Adam and the Ants seemed back at the beginning of New Wave. Now they were as quaint as the sound of the Mitch Miller records his own father used to listen to after dinner.

The question was...what was coming *next*, to give these current bands the scent of moldy age? His tac leader had called them 'death-thrash bands'. True remembered what John Charles had said to Roger Chester: *The only reason they want us there is because of the death thing.*

Garth Brickenfield had not gotten where he was by being dumb. Or being caught napping in an easy chair. He knew what his paying audience would pay to see. Those other bands might thrash all they wanted to about death...but The Five had seen it up close, in its bloody truth.

They were going to be real celebrities at this shindig.

"Jeremy Pett," Terry began, and then he let that sit for a few seconds. "He might have headed to Mexico. Right?"

"Maybe," True answered, watching the road and all the vehicles in front of him. He was dreading that traffic on the two-lane. "Like I told you, it depends on what's in his head."

"You mean if he decides killing one of us and putting another one in the ICU is enough?" Nomad prodded. "To satisfy him, I mean?"

"That's right."

"Well, what is so fucking *bad* about that video? Okay, it criticizes the war. Other bands do videos criticizing the war, but they don't get popped because of it! Why *us*?"

"You'd have to ask him."

"I'm asking *you*!" Some fire jumped into Nomad's face. "You've seen it! What's so bad about it that we should get killed?"

"John," said Ariel, in a soothing voice, "he can't answer that. He doesn't know. Nobody knows but Jeremy Pett, and he must be out of his mind. Maybe he saw something in the video that reminded him of what he went through. Maybe something he *doesn't* want to be reminded of. That's what *I* think."

"Yes," True agreed. "I'm thinking that, too."

"Should I go on TV and apologize?" Nomad asked, speaking to both of them. "Should I get up on the stage and say I'm sorry we did this video and got Mike killed for it? Or maybe it's the song? Should I say I'm sorry we wrote this song, and never again will there ever be another song written in the world that has the power to piss anybody off? You know what you get when that happens?"

"Yeah," Berke said. "Lame Van Halen tunes. Which I'm sad to say we've done a lot of. Like 'Bad Cop'."

"What's wrong with Van Halen?" True asked.

"What's wrong with 'Bad Cop'?" Nomad twisted around in his seat to the limit of his restraining belt. "It's a party song, people like it."

"Drunks like it," said Berke, with a wicked little smirk. "The bartenders like it."

"And the club owners like it."

"It's not going to fly with this audience," she pointed out. "We go out doing shit like that and they'll bum rush the stage. You want to join George in that ICU? Not me, bro."

"*What*?"

She realized what she'd said; a message delivered from another world. "I mean…not me. Period."

"I *like* Van Halen," True said to Ariel.

"I'm just saying," Berke went on, now that she was geared to go, "is that we need to play for this crowd. If we don't connect with them in a hurry, they're going to take out their fucking power drills and give us new assholes right in our foreheads. So I'm thinking…maybe we ought to kick it off with 'Bedlam A-Go-Go'. Distort the shit out of it. Go fucking monster loud. In fact, distort and go freak wild on *everything*. And when you sing, John, get your mouth right up on the mike and scream it out so nobody can hear what you're saying. Just eat the fucking mike. How about it?"

There was a silence.

After a while, Nomad nodded. "Sounds like a plan."

"Distortion is my name," Terry said.

"And we ought to pick the tempo up on everything," Berke told them. "What was slow gets fast and what was fast gets ridiculous. Okay? You guys follow my lead and I'll carry you through."

< >

"My kind of gig," said Ariel. "If my hands fall off in the middle of 'Sympathy', will somebody please put them in a refrigerated box?"

"We've got this knocked," Nomad said, with a smile that might have been described as jittery. "Yeah. Ninety minutes of noise, distortion, and speed. We may have to play some songs *twice*, but we've got this knocked."

I-10 curved into I-8. About six miles past Gila Ridge, True and nearly everybody else heading westbound turned off on the two-lane that stretched out flat for a distance and then began its climb into the heat-hazed, brick-red mountains toward Stone Church. The road was jammed and traffic slowed to a crawl. In front of them the passenger of a gray van lowered their window and threw yellow liquid from a bucket onto the pavement, where it bubbled and steamed. Young men wearing umbrella caps that bore the red legend *Stone Church 9-2008* began appearing, walking among the vehicles to sell bottled water, T-shirts and umbrella caps that bore the red legend *Stone Church 9-2008*.

"A decorated Marine," Ariel suddenly said. It had come to her as she was thinking about George lying in his hospital bed. "You said Detective Rios told you Pett was a decorated Marine." She waited for True to acknowledge her with a glance. "What decoration?"

"The Bronze star for valor." True stared straight ahead, guiding the Scumbucket ever onward. The mountains had grown rugged and huge. "It happened in Fallujah, in November of 2004. He was in position in an abandoned building with his spotter, looking for targets. Evidently they'd been seen and tracked by an insurgent scout. The report I read says that a rocket-propelled grenade was fired into their hide. The blast wounded Pett's spotter. It was a cranial wound, ended up being severe brain damage that put him in the Veteran's Hospital in Temple for life. Right after the RPG came in, an estimated thirty to forty insurgents with assault rifles stormed the building."

True's jaw was set. In it, a muscle twitched. Ariel thought his blue eyes had turned the color of steel.

"According to the report, Pett was in shock and bleeding from his own wounds, but he started making shots," the man continued, in a slow and even voice. "He hit a few of them. Knocked them back on their heels. Then they brought in a truck loaded with more

RPGs, and they started blowing the building apart room by room. According to the report, Pett dragged his spotter with him as he kept on the move. Gave him whatever first aid he could. Pett was calling for help on his radio, but by that time the building was surrounded and there was no way out." The steely gaze wandered toward Ariel. "Can you imagine what that must've been like? What that young man must've been thinking? He was trained, sure...but that kind of warfare...trapped like a dog in a cage...the RPGs tearing in and blowing holes in the walls all around you and your buddy with his brains falling out of his head...what does a man do, in a situation like that?"

After a short pause, True said, "What he did, was to get himself and his spotter down to the basement, in the dark, and find a protected area where he could get his back to the wall. Then he waited. There were battles going on all over the city. Help was coming, but it wasn't going to get there quick and it was going to have to fight to get to him. So, according to the report, Pett stayed in that basement with his spotter for nearly three hours, with his buddy's head cradled in his lap and his rifle aimed at the square of a doorway at the top of the stairs. They kept firing the RPGs in, but they wouldn't come in after him. It was almost night when a squad got him out. He had killed six insurgents, likely wounded twice that many. The squad had trouble separating him from his buddy, so they let Pett carry him with them up the steps. That was Pett's last combat mission. For staying with his friend and showing heroism under fire, he was awarded the Bronze Star. The Temple police found it in his apartment, up on a closet shelf in a box with letters from his wife."

"His *wife*?" Nomad was amazed to hear this fact. "Where is she?"

True didn't answer for a time. He was watching the mountains come nearer, and now they looked to him like a massive line of broken teeth.

"One night in February of 2004," he said, "Pett's wife and his seven-year-old son—Nick was the boy's name—drove out of a mall's parking lot. They were hit at the next intersection by an SUV travelling at what the Houston police say had to be nearly seventy miles an hour. The two teenaged girls were high on pot and the driver was arguing with her boyfriend on her cellphone. Witnesses said she never braked for the red light. I read the police reports and the newspaper article." The picture in the *Chronicle* had been horrendous, showing what used to be a minivan reduced to a shapeless mass of metal, the impact having spun the wreckage through the front window of a Popeye's Fried Chicken restaurant. "Pett's wife died at the scene. The little boy lingered until the next day. As for the teenaged girls, the driver died a few days later and the passenger was crippled. Pett went home to the funerals of his family, but he turned around and went back to active duty a few weeks later."

"*Why?*" Terry asked, sounding stunned.

"I'm sure," True said, "he knew they needed him in Iraq. They were his second family. I'm supposing from everything I've read that Pett intended to make the Marines his life career. He was very good at his fieldwork, but I doubt you can sustain that too long. I'm thinking he wanted to be a gunny. A gunnery sergeant. Teaching the discipline to the new boots. Maybe training new snipers. But after what happened in Fallujah...the sad thing is that you can be tested and pass the test, but something fundamental is changed about you. Something is pulled out of shape. I've seen the same thing happen to agents in violent situations. They do everything right, they go by the book, maybe they even win citations for bravery, but you look in their eyes—you look deep—and you see...something has gotten down in the dark, in that basement, and it presses its back against the wall for protection and it knows...it knows...that next time, the fear might win. And it's the fear that causes you to make an error and get yourself killed. I'm thinking that after Fallujah, the next time Jeremy Pett fired a rifle he couldn't hit a red barn at two hundred yards, because when he held that weapon everything came flooding back. So the Marines discharged him with his Bronze Star and sent him home to Houston where the bodies of his wife and son were lying in the cemetery. It wasn't too much longer before he moved to Temple. Obviously he wanted to be close to the VA hospital. The visitors' records say he went to see his buddy every Wednesday."

"Wow," was Berke's quiet response. If anything, she could relate to loyalty.

Nomad was having none of it. "Are we supposed to feel *sorry* for him?"

A grim smile moved across True's mouth, and then it went away.

He said in an empty voice, "Feel the way you need to feel. No skin off *my* back."

They were climbing into the jagged brown teeth. The traffic would move for a few minutes and then it would clog again with an exclamation of brakelights all down the long line. A helicopter swooped low over the road.

"Hey, a chopper!" Terry said. "I'm impressed!"

"Not mine," True told him. "Might be media or Brickenfield's security men making a display. My guys aren't meant to be noticed."

Nomad thought that was an understatement, considering how smoothly Truitt Allen had stashed a small soft leather bag down beside the driver's seat when he'd gotten behind the wheel. Cellphone? Walkie-Talkie? Compact handgun? Probably all three.

"Question?" True asked, as if he were reading Nomad's mind.

"I don't have a question, man."

"I'm saying I *do* have a question. I was about to ask…what's the story behind Stone Church? It didn't start out with that name." True knew that much; it had been the Apache Leap Festival when it began in 1995. In the year 2000, it became Stone Church. "The highest peak up here is called Apache Leap, correct?"

"I guess."

"Well, who *knows*? I'm interested in why the name changed." He'd never thought to ask Garth Brickenfield or Roger Chester or even his own tac leader, with all the other million details that had to be worked out for this operation, and anyway it was hardly an essential point. But still, he was curious. "Anybody help me out?"

"I've read about it," Ariel said, though she was underestimating her knowledge. She'd talked to other musicians who'd played Stone Church, and from their experiences she'd dug into the subject like Detective Ramona Rios on the track of a missing persons report. "The legend about Apache Leap is that—"

"A brave climbed up there to fight an evil spirit," True interrupted. "He jumped off the peak when he realized the evil couldn't be beaten, because it was part of himself. Yeah, that's schoolboy stuff. I want to know about Stone Church."

"The legend and Stone Church tie together," she explained. "It's been a place of evil spirits for a very long time."

"You're quoting someone?" He gave the Scumbucket some gas;

they were moving again, but once more the line of brakelights flared ahead. The helicopter passed, throwing its shadow like a huge dark bird. "Or is that your opinion?"

"I'll tell you what I've read and what I've heard, if you want to listen."

"Shoot," he said, and instantly thought that was a very poor choice of words.

Ariel began.

SEVENTEEN.

She was good at painting pictures with words, and so now Ariel painted them for Truitt Allen: yellow dust blowing through the mountain air, the stillness of the red-rimmed stone, the sun burning hot upon the cracks and fissures of a dry, old earth, and deep down below that baked brown crust the men sweating in the light of their lanterns as they swung pickaxes in the sweltering rooms of Silver Mine Number Three.

The Spanish had worked the mine before, using Indians as slaves, but not until 1887 did the industrious white men find the hole in the ground and haul up a taste of what was in it. They brought their pack mules, their tent canvas, their lumber boards and their picks and shovels by the hundreds, and then with the arrival of the barrels of nails and a proper team of construction surveyors paid for by the San Francisco investment company, wooden buildings took shape. The two whorehouses were given painted signs. The four bars earned their solidity, their batwing doors and their brass spittoons. Wagons began bringing in the wives and children. At night the wind picked up, and under the stars it sang through the telegraph wires that stretched down along the poles to Gila Ridge. A school was built, well away from the saloons and houses of ill repute. It was the third silver mine owned by the Company, and by now the managers knew how to build a town around a dream of wealth.

A lot of silver was coming out of that mine. Some other things too: a little lead, a flash of zinc, enough gold to quicken the pulse and cause women to crave the gleam and men to go buy a pocket pistol, just for protection. But a lot of silver was coming up, and Silver Mine Number Three was going to make a lot of people very rich.

A man of God arrived, in the summer of 1890. He introduced himself at a town meeting as the Reverend Daniel Kiley. He brought with him his own wife, his two young sons, his baby daughter and a wagon full of Bibles and hymn books. He was a good man. He was an intelligent man. He was a man who had his own dreams, of making a difference in a world that needed salvation.

He was a man.

Daniel Kiley had had some difficulty in Denver, their last place of residence. It might have had to do with the power of whiskey, or the power of a woman who whispered things in a man's ear that a wife would not dare to speak, and who did those things laughingly and then laughingly watched a man's face crumble along with the plans for a new church on Blake Street. He had been cast out of that Eden, and had wandered long in search of a purpose to redeem himself in the eyes of God, in the eyes of his wife and in the hearts of his children. He had to win his way back, and the only way he knew to do that was to build something holy, something that would last, something like a beacon to lead sinners home from the dark path. Because he knew what lay at the end of that; he had seen his destruction in a pair of green eyes and a pair of green-gloved hands. He had seen it in the distorted reflection of his own face in a mirror down along the hallway where a red curtain hid his secrets.

It was to laugh at.

The Company was all for what Daniel Kiley proposed: a church to settle the community, to give the beginnings to the law and order that towns needed, to give the people a place to wed, a place to bring their babies for baptism, a place to prepare for the journey that every man and woman must make. The church kept workers satisfied. It would go up at the center of the fledgling business district of Silver Mine Number Three, and at Daniel Kiley's urging the Company would build this church not of ordinary timber and tar, nor of bricks fired from the town's new kiln, but from the stone of the mountain itself. It would be built to last a hundred years, and in mid-1891 a great hurrah rose into the red-dusted air as the shovels bit first earth, after which there was a pause while the photographer loaded his glass plates into the camera, repositioned the scene and memorialized the moment with a bright flare of magnesium powder.

When the church was finished, it was a thing of beauty. A thing of pride and of promise. The stones were tight and precise, the mortar as white as God's beard. In front of the door, stone steps stood chiseled and firm underfoot, to guide the needy to their places. Who knew what the future of the town might be? The silver was still coming up, and much more to be found. This town of over four hundred people might be a city one day. A city on a mountaintop, to rival even Denver.

Oh yes, said the Reverend Daniel Kiley, from his new pinewood pulpit to his congregation in their pews. That's a nice thought.

Within a month of the church going up, the mayor called a meeting. With the Company's permission, he was suggesting a new name for their town. He was suggesting Stone Church, and may it stand for a hundred years as the beacon of this community.

"No one knows exactly how it started," Ariel said, as the Scumbucket crept up the mountain road. "But it did start."

"What started?" True asked.

"The end," she said.

Maybe it started with the mine itself. But it wasn't that the silver ran out. It didn't stop gleaming in the walls when the lantern light touched it. But the streams of silver ran deeper down, and to get to them the miners went deeper too, and day after day—week after week and month after month—the miners went deeper. And deeper still.

Who was it who first had a nervous drink at a saloon and said he'd seen something, down in the passageways and gloomy rooms where heaving pumps brought in the gritty air? What had he seen? What did others see, that made them come up from that hole, pack into their wagons their picks, their shovels, their wives and their children, and leave their houses with bedspreads still on the bed and dishes in the cupboard?

Some talked, before they left. Not going back down in that hole, they said. No sir, not for any coin on this earth. Because there are *things* down there. There are things that watch me from the dark, and when I hold my lantern up I only see their shadows as they pull back into the rock. Did you hear me, sir? I said...*into the rock*.

The town's doctor was an old man named Leon Lewis who had seen his own share of visions among the lotus eaters of San Francisco. He told the mayor and the council that he thought these hallucinations were a result of bad air down in the chambers. The bellows pumps were outdated and inefficient at the depth the mine had reached, he said, and it was time to present the Company with a plan for a steam boiler that would run a new air circulation system.

The Company's response was to study the plan. In the meantime, more men were emerging from the rooms and vowing never to go back. Most would not talk, not for money or whiskey. When one of them spilled his story to a prostitute, it was likely the town would be less both one miner and one prostitute in the next day or two.

More than the shadows, more than the glimpses of figures standing where they should not be, more than the quick shine of eyes in the dark, it was the music that began to shred their nerves.

It was always faint. Always just at the edge of hearing. But all who did hear it were sure it was a brass band playing a march. Down in the deep dark of the mine, down in a place where picks and shovels had just begun to pierce the earth, a brass band was playing a John Philip Sousa march. There was some difference of opinion over whether it was 'The Washington Post' or 'The Gladiator' or some combination of the two, because there were only seconds of it to be heard, drifting amid the wheeze of the pumps and the scrape of the shovels.

Doc Lewis said working at that depth could affect a man's inner ear, in such a way that phantom music might indeed be heard. He volunteered to go down himself, with Sheriff McKee and the head foreman.

"Ariel, you're creeping me out," Berke said. "You're making half this shit up, anyway."

"I *wish*. There are three books I know of on the subject, and last April there was a documentary on the History Channel."

"What've you been doing? *Studying* this?" Nomad asked. Christ, he wished he had a cigarette! The higher they climbed up this freaking mountain, the more nervous he was getting, and he did *not* as a rule get nervous.

True followed the car ahead through an open orange metal gate. A small adobe-style building stood next to it and out front were a couple of guys in white shirts and sand-colored shorts. They wore caps that had *GB Promotions* on them. The security men looked like fleshy ex-football players, and one was making the devil horns hand to four girls in a Jeep while the other was hollering at somebody over a cell phone. True saw a sign ahead: *Campgrounds*. An arrow pointed to the left. He was supposed to keep going straight on, to the artists' area.

"I think maybe you've been reading too much Stephen King," he told Ariel. "But go ahead."

She did.

When the doctor, the sheriff and the foreman came back up from the mine, they spoke to none of the other men waiting at the entrance. They walked straight to the stone church, and it was seen that Sheriff McKee had to help Doc Lewis because the doctor's knees buckled at the foot of the steps. Then they went inside and didn't come out for a while. Nobody followed them in, but one of the miners ran to get Daniel Kiley, and when the reverend arrived and went into his church he didn't come out for a while, either. Finally everybody went home, and that was the first night the telegraph in the Company office started tapping out the message *News! News! News! Stone Church has been destroyed* over and over again from somewhere down the mountain, but nobody in Gila Ridge was sending it.

What got out, over the next few days, and what was whispered in the saloons over the half-guzzled bottles and the forgotten whores, was that the three men who'd gone down into the mine had followed the faint snippets of music, the 'Washington Post' or the 'Gladiator', whatever it was, the kind of music that ordinarily would have made a man doff his hat and salute his flag in a fine frenzy of patriotism. They had followed the music from chamber to chamber, armed with lanterns and in Sheriff McKee's big ruddy paw of a hand a Colt Navy revolver. And, the whispers went, the music drew them deeper and deeper, until suddenly it stopped and the woman stepped out into the lantern light.

She was a striking-looking woman. A beautiful woman, in an elegant dress. She wore green gloves, and—so the whispers went—she told the three men she wanted to speak to the Reverend Daniel Kiley. She said it would go hard for the town, if he wouldn't see her. She said it would go hard for the town even if he *would* see her, because that was how things were. But, she said, at least from such a righteous gentleman as him she expected a courtesy call.

The wagons began to roll out. The head foreman and his wife were gone the next morning after it had happened, left everything behind that couldn't be thrown into a single trunk. Sheriff McKee had to be awakened from a drunken stupor by the thin Chinese girl who slept on his porch like a lovesick mongrel. Even Doc Lewis thought about running for it, but he was on his last legs anyway, he had no family, he was a horse waiting to be shot. He decided to stick it out, with a little lotus leaf to steady his nerves.

Daniel Kiley called a gathering in front of the stone church. It had to be in broad daylight, because no one walked the streets after sundown. He addressed the remaining seventy or so frightened people in what many considered a voice carved from the Rock Of Ages. He stood firm before them, with his family at his side, and commanded the crowd to also stand firm. He lifted up his Bible and told them he had found his purpose here, his calling, his truth. He had found what he'd been looking for, in one way or another, all his weak and miserable life.

He had found a fight with Satan. And by God he was not going to let Satan take his town.

At that point, about thirty more people headed to their wagons at a pretty quick clip, but the forty who stood their ground spat their tobacco and scratched their balls and hollered back at the reverend in the Greek language, in Chinese, in the Nordic tongue, in the brogues of old Ireland and the burrs of Scotland and in the toughened timbres of men who have learned to sleep standing up with one eye open.

They would send their wives and children down the mountain to safety—if they could, because some of the wives spat their tobacco and the children scratched their balls just like Papa did. But what was life if it was lived like a scared sheep?

"Now that's where it runs off the tracks," Nomad said. "Nobody would've stayed in that town. *Nobody*. My ass would be going down that road." He realized, quite suddenly, that his ass was currently going *up* that road.

"Maybe." Ariel saw, as True did, a double sign pointing to a turnoff on the right. The top sign said *Vendors* and the bottom one *Artists*. "But, according to what I read, the people who elected to stay were told the Company was sending a bonus for every man who would go back into the mine. The Company didn't know what was happening—they thought it was a work stoppage over the air pumps—but they were sending a strongbox of gold dust from San Francisco. And no one had been hurt yet. There was the music, the woman, and the threat of harm from the telegraph, but the telegraph had stopped its chattering."

"What do you mean, no one had been hurt 'yet'?" Berke frowned. "That sounds fucking ominous."

"For a few weeks, nothing else happened. The miners went back to work. The music had stopped. There were no more half-seen figures in the dark. Even some of those people who'd left came back. Then whatever it was...evil, Satan, whatever you want to call that force...left the mine and entered the town."

Did Daniel Kiley want to go into the mine, to meet the woman—the creature—who called him? Did the reverend's wife throw herself in his way, and beg him not to go? He didn't go. Then...one morning they found their little girl dead in her bed. There were bruises on her face. The reverend's sons woke up to the noise of horror...and one of them said he'd had a dream, a bad bad dream, in which he'd walked quietly into their room while they were sleeping and looked into his sister's bed and had seen a snake coiled next to her head. And in this dream he'd had a pillow already in his hands, and he'd smashed it down upon the reptile, had pressed down hard with all his strength, and when he'd tried to call for help...the strangest thing...his voice was gone. His voice had been stolen from him, there in the night. But he kept pressing down, and pressing down, and at last he'd lifted up the pillow and seen that the snake was dead. He'd told his father that he thought he was a real hero, in that dream, and maybe he ought to earn a medal.

A Company wagon bearing the strongbox of gold dust from San Francisco arrived the next day. It was accompanied by four men with the names of Barton Taggett, Miles Branco, Jerrod Spade and Duke Chanderley. They wore dirty Stetsons on their heads and notched Colts in their holsters. They were ready to declare war, in the name of the Company, on sluggards and malingerers and weak-willed sonsofbitches who didn't want to dig for silver just because of an old air pump. When they found fifty or so people where four hundred used to be, and the new head foreman a red-bearded Scotsman with one leg, they changed their attitude. When they heard the stories and talked to Sheriff McKee and Doc Lewis and Daniel Kiley, and when they saw the body of the little girl in its casket and the haunted eyes of the boy who'd suffocated her in a bad dream, they sat down for a while in the last remaining saloon with the last of the soiled doves looking on, and they drank some whiskey and smoked some cigars and figured they were getting too old for this shit.

But the thing was, they were moral men who had had immoralities thrust upon them. So as the night went on and the lamps burned across Stone Church, and the church itself stood silent and solid in the center of the town, the Company enforcers decided they didn't know if demons could bleed, red blood or black, but maybe it was up to four Civil War hellraisers to find out.

"They went down into the mine with Daniel Kiley and Sheriff McKee," Ariel said, as the Scumbucket passed a huge gated parking lot full of trucks, vans and trailers. *Vendors Park Here*, a sign directed. "They went down to find the woman. The thing. Whatever she was. *It* was. And that's the end of the story."

"The *fuck* it is!" Berke had nearly yelled it.

"Come on!" Terry said. "That can't be the end!"

"There's no *good* end," Ariel clarified.

True scanned the vehicles in the vendors' lot. *Rings Of Saturn Tattoos, Inc. Body Art by Sarafina. ShockIt Tattoos. Tribal Attitudes. The Living Needle.*

"Finish it," he said, as he drove on.

"I've heard and read about a daily journal in a library somewhere. Kept under lock-and-key, available for study only to parapsychologists and the clergy." Ariel said quietly. "It was written by one of the Stone Church prostitutes. The story is that she and all but two others of her profession left on a wagon as the enforcers, the sheriff and the reverend were walking into the mine. The women didn't look back. But all the details come from that journal. They talked about it in that documentary on the History Channel. The women heard nothing. They just kept going. But when the Company didn't hear anything more, they sent a Pinkerton's detective from Tucson to find out what was happening with their investment. The detective found...nothing and no one. Fifty-something people, and the four enforcers, were gone. There was no evidence of a fight. The horses, mules, cows and pigs...all gone. There was not a living thing left in Stone Church. But clothes still hung on lines, dishes were stacked up in washbasins, and mops and brooms leaned in corners as if their owners had just stepped out for a minute. A pan of browned biscuits sat on a table. Some of the doors to the houses were open, some closed. The strongbox was locked in a cell in the sheriff's office. All the sacks of gold dust were still there. An empty casket was found in the parlor of the reverend's house. Child-sized. Two other things...the Pinkerton detective found that all the gravestones in the cemetery had been knocked flat, and the windows had been blown out of the church from the inside." She'd been looking to her right, through the green tint, and now she narrowed her eyes slightly. "There it is," she said.

They saw what she was seeing.

It was maybe two or three miles away, commanding a slightly higher elevation. The roof had collapsed; if there ever had been a steeple, there was not one now. The stone walls formed a shell around a hollow center. Even at this distance, in the midday sun, some of the lines of mortar could be made out. Below the walls the earth was an ashen color. Here and there piles of timbers lay jumbled about. The open frame of a building that the wind had gnawed to pieces was still standing, but its days were numbered. But the stone church itself...it had lasted for a hundred years, and might last a hundred more though its congregation now was likely only the lizards and the scorpions. Nomad could see a massive iron gate across the road that wound up to Stone Church. It was secured by what might have been a dark fester of chains and coils of barbed-wire. The wire was strung all around the mountaintop, like spiky hair circling a scabby pate. Day-Glo orange signs were set at intervals in the ground. He couldn't read them, but he imagined what they probably said: Danger. No Trespassing. Proceed At Your Own Risk. Trespassers Will Be—

What? he wondered.

Swallowed up by Hell?

"That whole story's some jimcrack bullshit," he said, but he didn't say it very loudly.

A wall of brown rock stubbled with brush came up between the Scumbucket and the stone church, and it was gone from view.

EIGHTEEN.

True was thinking. The answer to his original question was that Garth Brickenfield had decided to retire the name 'Apache Leap' for a darker image for his annual music festival. It was the kind of story you could email ten people about and a hundred—several hundred?—would know it by the end of the day. Publicity, publicity, publicity. That and a note of weirdness, a smell of Satanic brimstone, and bringing in the vendors that Brickenfield cultivated for this thing and there you had it: an old guy pretending to putter around with antique airplanes while he was building a flying zoopalooza.

Around the next bend, they could feel the music.

It was always the bass, first. It vibrated through the Scumbucket before they could hear it. Somebody's big huge speakers were cranked up to big huge numbers. The amphitheater's gates had opened at noon, and by the schedule True had gotten the first band to take the stage was The Bleeding Brains.

They were very, very loud.

True slowed the van down. It rolled toward the orange gate where the GB Promotions security boys were checking the entry passes with hand scanners. True lowered his window and caught the full thunder of bass guitar and bass drum echoing off rock walls and maybe a couple of hundred shaved skulls. He felt like one of the Company's enforcers; he was way too old for this kind of mess, but to call himself a man he was going to have to go down into that mine.

"Thank you, sir," the security guy with blue sunscreen on his face said to True when the passes were scanned, and then he looked past True into the van and shouted, "Kick some *ass*!" as he pumped his fist into the air.

They drove onto the dirt lot behind the huge stage, which like any lot behind a festival stage was a phantasmorama of many elements: the military encampment, the neighborhood block party, the mad scientist's cluttered lab of crates and boxes and strange electronic gizmos, the power station in a constant state of emergency, the lineup of battered trucks, trailers and vans from that seedy auto dealership in the bad part of town, the grimy place behind the colorful banners at the state fair where all the half-eaten candied apples seem to end up.

True found a place to stop, in between a line of green Port-A-Potties and a purple van painted with grinning silver death's heads. They had arrived.

The first thing for The Five to do was to go to the large black hospitality trailer with GB Promotions in red on the sides, get their stage passes and some bottled water, eat whatever sandwich and chips they were offering, and figure out exactly what the set was going to be. They had about two hours to settle in. The equipment would have to be unloaded, everything plugged in and checked as best as possible in this environment. They wouldn't have to worry about unloading any merchandise, because that had already been shipped from RCA to Brickenfield's company and would be for sale up on the 'Midway' where the sea of vendors was located. But it would be barely-controlled chaos, no matter how it was sliced.

True's first task was to take his leather bag out of the van, walk to the other side of the Port-A-Potties to get some relative quiet from the Bleeding Brains, unzip the bag and reach in next to the lightweight aluminum Charter Arms .38 Special. He removed his small black Motorola Walkie-Talkie with its eighteen-mile range and secure codes. He turned on the voice activation capability.

"This is Prime setting up shop," True said. "Scout, you guys out there?"

"Affirmative." The reception was so clear Tony Escobar could've been standing right next to him.

"Knave, you copy?"

"Affirmative."

He went through Lance, Logic, Shelter and Signet. He'd chosen the names from the Admirable Class of minesweeping ships in World War II; the guys rolled their eyes at him, but he was the big dog. "All I can tell you is to stay sharp," he said when the teams had reported. They knew their business, they had their high-powered binoculars and wore camouflage suits that blended them in with the mountain terrain. Their rifles, all Remingtons with scopes similar to what Jeremy Pett would be carrying, were also camouflaged with earth colors. The tac teams were spread out around the clockface of the amphitheater, and were experts at staying invisible. A thought struck True. "Hey, Clark!"

"Yes, sir?"

Clark Griffin was the leader of the Shelter team. He and his men would be hunkered down in a position nearest to that place up on the higher elevation. That place.

Watch your backs, he almost said.

But that would've sounded stupid. It would not be wise for the operation leader to sound stupid. So he said, "This is your kind of music down here."

"Nobody in that lineup can hold a candle to Buckethead," Clark answered back. "I'll make you a fan yet, sir."

"I'm still in my Crosby, Stills and Nash period," True said. "Okay, let's put on our bigboy faces. One reminder: we are *not* shooting to kill. Check you." He switched off the voice control. Then, satisfied at least that everyone was where they ought to be, he walked back around the line of portable toilets and went into the nearest one to relieve his aching bladder.

On their way to the hospitality trailer, Nomad's pace slowed. Ariel noticed and also slowed down. He was staring at something off to the right. "John?" she said, and followed his gaze to an Airstream trailer where a nearly-naked man with tattoos on his arms and chest and long hair the color of butter was sitting on a lawn chair in the sun, his face offered to the rays. Nomad told her to go on ahead, that he'd be there in a few minutes. She hesitated only briefly, as Nomad began to walk toward the Airstream, and then she followed Terry and Berke across a landscape strewn with cables.

Nomad had known this man was going to be at Stone Church. His band Mjöllnir—pronounced "Mole Near"—was scheduled to take the stage at eight o'clock tonight. He had gotten here early, to kick back, mix and mingle, to check out the flashy young tail, to score some good dope, to listen to the new bands. Maybe also because his tour calendar was a lot lighter than it had been ten, twenty years ago. Mjöllnir was the name of Thor's mythical hammer. The man in that lawn chair, catching sun with his eyes closed against the glare, was a fallen god.

Nomad came up on him silently, as the Bleeding Brains thrashed and screamed onstage about a hundred yards away, but fallen gods still retain their sixth sense, and the man opened eyes as green as new emeralds and with The Look speared Nomad in his tracks.

"You just passing through, or what?" Nomad asked, unable to keep a grin off his face.

"There's the *kid*!" said the blonde-haired man, in a raspy growl that used to be known by the millions and imitated by dozens of lesser vocalists. He stood up, matched Nomad's grin and opened his arms wide, permitting entrance. "Come on over here, you little motherfucker!"

The man was wearing only a black Speedo and brown sandals. The lump at his crotch was huge. Nomad said, "I'm not getting any nearer to *that* thing."

"It's been tamed," the man said. "Hey, I'm not wasting it on *you*. Come on, gimme a hug."

Nomad walked forward. Suddenly the long-haired man with the black Speedo and the huge crotch-log crouched over and rushed him. In the next instant a shoulder as hard as reinforced concrete hit Nomad before he could brace himself. He staggered back. He would have gone down had not the buttery-haired bastard grabbed him around the waist to keep him from falling. Then he swung Nomad around like a ragdoll and neatly set him down in the lawn chair.

Thor Bronson gave an explosive cat squall of a laugh into Nomad's face. "That's for fucking my mind, Johnny! I thought I was opening for you tonight! How come I'm not?"

"Ow! Jesus! You trying to break my ribs?"

"I ought to break your ass! Come 'ere, I love ya!" Thor grabbed the back of Nomad's neck and gave him a big wet kiss right on the forehead. "You little *shit*, you never heard of email?" A shadow passed over his face; the half-crazed grin slid away and the emerald eyes darkened. "About Mike and George. Oh man oh man, is that a bad scene. Who the fuck is Jeremy Pett and what did you do to him?"

"You saw that on TV?"

"*Every* fucking station. For a while. Then the world spun on. Did you know the fucking Duct Tape Rapist nailed somebody I used to *date*? A secretary at Rhino Records. Man, I do not like the way things are headed. Beer. You want a beer? Sure you do."

"No beer," Nomad said. He saw a pack of Winstons and a lighter on a little table next to the chair. "I'll take a cigarette and some bottled water, if you've got it."

"Light it up. Let me go get another chair." Thor went into the trailer, leaving Nomad sitting alone in the harsh sun. Nomad got his cigarette going. In another minute Thor came back out, gripping two bottles of beer by the necks and carrying a second lawn chair under his arm. He handed Nomad one of the cold brews and set up his own chair. "Hey, we can't have a pale pussy like you getting a little sunburned!" he said. "Here you go." He reached over into a plastic bin and brought out a large red-striped umbrella, which had a rubber vise-grip on the handle. He opened the umbrella and screwed the grip to one of Nomad's armrests so his guest would be sitting in the shade.

"Comforts of home," Thor said. He sat down and clinked his bottle against Nomad's. They both drank, and then Thor stretched his wiry legs out and uptilted his sun-lined, rough-weathered face to the celestial Sol.

Nomad's gaze slipped toward the man on his right and then away again. He took another drink. He hadn't seen Thor in a couple of years; the last time had been at an outdoor festival in Santa Cruz in June of 2006. Thor was about forty-five years old, give or take. His website said he'd been born in 1963, but that was up for debate. His website also said his own musical influences growing up as a rebellious kid in Bayonne, New Jersey included Judas Priest, Blue Oyster Cult, Mountain, Black Sabbath and of course Led Zeppelin, with special props to Mark Farner of Grand Funk Railroad, Peter Wolf of the J.Geils Band, and Jim Dandy of Black Oak Arkansas. That part was true, but Thor Bronson was a fiction.

He'd been born Saul Brightman to a father named Maury, also known as 'The Lighthouse'. Many beers, tequila shots and spliffs of whackyweed had gone into these revelations, drawn out over the course of several months when John Charles had been a hanger-on and band wannabe in Hollywood in 1997. At age 18, Nomad had taken the bus from Detroit with great expectations of quickly finding a band and making his mark; within a couple of weeks he was walking the streets looking for any place to play, living on chili dogs and crashing in a dumpy apartment on North Mariposa Avenue with four other big shots like himself. He had finally found semi-steady work as a house painter. And lucky to get that, too. But he had wound up painting an apartment for a young woman in Hermosa Beach who, when she'd found out he wanted to be a musician, had told him her sister was dating an "old guy" who used to be somebody famous in music. Like he was named after that dude in the comic book, that guy with the helmet and the horns.

That guy was playing on Saturday night at the Addiction in Downey, and maybe if a girl could get a discount from her handsome painter there might be an introduction?

That guy was on the cover of many of the old records John Charles had left behind in his teenaged bedroom, in there along with the Aerosmith, AC/DC, Guns N' Roses and Motley Crue vinyl. That guy used to take the stage with his heavy-metal band, him with his long flowing Nordic-blonde hair, his bared chest thrust out to the world, his body lean and ripped and his voice "a dark broth of pure grimy rock mixed with black-lacquered soul mixed with red mud field hollers mixed with the primal scream of urban desperation".

That had been straight from the back copy of Mjöllnir's first album, *Hit It*, which had done some monster sales, especially in Germany, Norway and Sweden.

"They'll find the sonofabitch," Thor said after another swig of beer. "Nobody gets away clean these days. They'll find him on a satellite picture or something."

"Yeah, they probably will," Nomad agreed.

"I like it hot," Thor said, and then he grinned at Nomad because the Bleeding Brains had come to the end of a song and up rose the ragged voices of the multitude, the throng, the infernal engine that kept the wheels of rock 'n roll on the burning rails to Hell. The voices, hundreds strong, merged together into a mass of knotted noise and came rolling across the lot behind the stage like the thunder of a medieval siege machine. "Listen...*listen*," said Thor. Nomad saw him close his eyes for a few seconds as if he were hearing a choir of angels, be they however deranged. The sound rolled over them and past, and before it was gone The Bleeding Brains' drummer started pounding his bass and two guitars shredded the air as they fought for supremacy.

"New band," Thor told him. "Young dudes, scared shitless. I told the lead singer that if he ever felt things getting out of control, he ought to drop his jeans and moon the crowd. Nothing like an asshole on display to show 'em who's in charge of the party."

"I think you gave me the same advice."

"I guess I did, huh?" Thor turned his chair slightly so he could face the kid, which was what he'd always called John Charles. *Where's the kid with my fucking water? Where's the kid with the fucking Phillips screwdriver? Where's the kid with the fucking electrical tape?*

That's what John Charles was, at first: the gofer, unfit as yet to move speakers and carry equipment alongside the guys who'd been with Mjöllnir for years. He had started at the bottom of the crazy birdcage, where all the shit dropped down on a young punk's feathers.

"How're you doing?" Thor asked him. "Really."

Nomad could've asked Thor the same question. His old friend—the first person who'd given him a chance to show what he could do, after that long hard summer of grunt work—was looking much older than his years. But then, rock years were like dog years. Thor had been an iron-pumping brute in his prime; now he was more shrivelled than ripped. Coiled around the remains of his biceps were bands of jagged black tattoos. Over his heart and much of his left shoulder was the black-and-red tattoo of the Viking symbol for Mjöllnir, topped with a skull. He hadn't had those adornments until he'd needed them to stay current. True, he could still knock Nomad sprawling, yet he seemed thin and diminished. Knots and veins stood out under the burnished, sunfreckled skin. The hair plugs were showing in the front, the dreaded "doll's-hair" effect. His expensive set of teeth had worn down, like those of an old lion that has chewed up too many calcified bones. But he still had the gleaming green eyes, and he still had The Look, and with those two things alone you could go a long, long way.

"This has been tough," Nomad answered. "About Mike and George. I don't know if you heard, but George is going to be okay."

"That's good. You've got guts, kid. Keeping on keeping on. *I* wouldn't be out here, if I was you. I'll get my little tight ass home."

"Would you?" Nomad asked, and blew out a long stream of cigarette smoke.

Thor didn't respond. He just gave a small laugh and shrugged his shoulders and drank some more, and then he said in a lighter tone of voice, "I see you're still riding with the lesbo, the geek and the hippie."

"Still am."

"You fix me up thirty—*fuck*, no—fifteen minutes with that butch babe and I'd leave her blinkin' and thinkin'."

"I don't think that'll ever happen." Nomad listened to the Brains bleeding on the stage. He drank his beer and heard all sorts of clams coming out of those widowmakers. "Who's with you tonight?"

"Guys you don't know. More fucking kids. But they *can't—*" and here he balled up his fist and gave Nomad a painful shot to the right arm "—keep up with the sugardaddy. It's like fucking music kindergarten with those guys behind you. But they've got great hair, I'll say that for 'em."

"Here's to great hair," Nomad said, and lifted his bottle.

"Used to have it, now I buy it," Thor said. He clinked Nomad's bottle and drank his beer almost empty. "You want another?"

"No, I've still got plenty."

"Okay." Again Thor lifted his face toward the sun. After a moment of silence he said, "My dad passed away last December. If you ever emailed or called people who give a shit about you, I would've let you know."

"I'm sorry." Nomad had heard the stories about Maury 'The Lighthouse' Brightman, drawn from the memories of the son who'd tramped along with his father and mother to the hotels and clubs in the fading sunset of the Borscht Belt, the Jewish Alps, otherwise known as the Catskill Mountains in upstate New York. The Lighthouse had played such resorts as Grossinger's, The Concord, the Friar Tuck Inn, and Kutsher's Hotel and Country Club. His show had been called "The Boardroom", in which he sang and did skits in the voices of Tom Jones, Ray Charles, Vic Damone, Al Martino, Jerry Vale, Sammy Davis, Jr., Billy Eckstine and Steve Lawrence, among others, ending of course with Mr. Sinatra the Chairman.

"I bought a black suit, a black tie and a white shirt at Penney's," Thor said. "I stood up front and sang 'My Way' for my father. Blasted that mother out, made the fucking walls shake. I think he would've liked it."

Nomad nodded. Maury's gift of vocal prowess to his son was Saul's ability to speak with no accent at all, or to pull up a dirty drawl in the South or conjure a New England drone or a Midwestern nosehorn or for that matter a British street cockney or a German staccato. His voice was a citizen of the world. All you had to do to hear it was listen to his stage patter, connecting with his audiences like a hometown boy wherever he was, on the *Mjöllnir Circles The Globe* double album released in 1986.

John Charles recalled something this man had said to him once, after sound check in an empty Long Beach club ten years ago: *You want to be like me, kid? Four ex-wives, a taste for the white lady, about sixteen ulcers in my fucking gut and debt up to my ass? You want to be like a fucking nomad wandering the desert? Okay, then, if it means so much to you...and you can take it, which is real doubtful...then you pick up that fucking guitar, you stand up there and sing me something. And you better make it good, because I am not about to let you enter my world if you're just a fucking slacker.*

"Funny," Thor said after a while, as he looked at the world through his bottle's amber glass. "A dream I'm having lately."

Nomad smoked his cigarette down and tapped ashes on the red dirt.

"I can see a woman dancing in a club. All alone. And everything's dark in there, I can't make out her face...the color of her hair... nothing. Just occasionally a light passes behind her, so she's like... outlined. You know."

"Silhouetted," Nomad offered.

"Yeah. That. So she's dancing...slow...like she's waiting for somebody. The music...it's not *my* music. Maybe she keeps looking toward the door...expecting somebody to come in, and when they don't she just keeps dancing, but there's something about the way her shoulders slump, or the way she brushes her hair back from her face with one hand...that says she's getting tired of waiting." Thor angled his face toward the stage, where a particularly bloody B-minor chord had just been launched from the quivering strings. "I don't know," he said. "I think I lost my time."

"Lost your *time*? Get real, man!" Nomad tried to bring up a caustic laugh, but nothing would emerge.

"I'm not talking about the so-called fucking golden days. Can't remember half of 'em, anyway. I mean that I lost my time to find my soulmate."

Nomad didn't know what to say, so he stared silently across the lot at the vans and trailers that continued to pull in. A Fox News truck was among them.

"I'm incomplete, man," said Thor. "That's my fucking problem, right there."

"*Incomplete*? What've you been smoking today?"

"Not anything nearly strong enough." Thor's eyes had again taken on a deep green shine. "Listen, Johnny. I'm serious. I think this woman in my dream is my soulmate, but I don't know where she is. I don't know where to go to find her. And she's waiting for me, but she doesn't know she's waiting, and pretty soon...real soon now... she's going to give up waiting because it's been years and years...and I never came to her. Maybe I met her somewhere, but she didn't have any flash about her, and back then it was all about the flash, and I didn't see her for what she was so I just brushed her off. Or maybe I never met her. Maybe it's not my music she's dancing to in the dream, because she doesn't even know me. Never even fucking *heard* of me. But my dream is telling me she's out there, but the time I spent...the time I lost...it may be too late for me to find her before she just...goes away."

"Soulmate," Nomad said, and he took the last draw from his cigarette before it burned his fingers. "I never understood if you're supposed to...like...instantly know your soulmate, or if this person—saying there *is* a person who fits you like that—grows on you over time, or what. I don't even know if I believe in that or not."

"Oh, I do," Thor said, his face getting animated. "Absolutely. It's your Bashert, man. The Zohar talks about it. You know, the Kabbalah. It's like...when God makes a soul, He creates the male and female together as one, but as it enters this world it like...gets fucking ripped apart. A whole soul is the combination of male and female, those two that got torn away from each other. God Himself is supposed to bring the two halves together again. See?"

"I don't mean any disrespect for what you believe," Nomad said, "but I'm not sure that idea's been working out so well in the last few thousand years."

"Yeah, yeah, yeah, but this is how it's *supposed* to be. I mean... you're supposed to find your missing half, and when you find it... *if* you find it...you're not incomplete anymore."

"So how come God doesn't put a big neon sign over your soulmate's head? How come He doesn't tell you in that dream exactly where she is? Huh?" Nomad didn't wait for an answer. "That's kind of cruel, not to let you know something so important. Right?"

Thor heard an element of the music that he liked, and he listened to that for a moment with his head tilted to one side. The sun was radiant in his hair. Then he said, "God is not a nice guy. He's a hard teacher, Johnny. He's tough, nothing soft about Him. Oh yeah, He can show mercy. He's all about mercy. But He's all about *teaching*, too. He's the hardest fucking teacher you could ever have. Sometimes you don't want to hear it, so you turn your back. Sometimes the lessons are pushed right in your face, you can't turn away. What we call cruel, maybe He calls...necessary, in some way we can't wrap our minds around because we only know the right here, right now. How come He won't put a sign over her head in that dream and say, 'There she is, Saul, there's your missing half, and go to this exact address and find her and then marry her like you did those four other women and go crazy in the middle of the night and fuck your soulmate up with drugs and bad shit because that's who you are, Saul, and you would even screw up this thing if I was to let it happen.'"

Thor seemed to catch himself, to hear what he was saying as if some voice other than his had spoken it.

He blinked and looked at his own right hand, and curled the fingers up before his face as if trying to envision it holding something that was not there.

"So," he said. "'Here is your lesson, Saul. And it is that I will let you know that there *was* a person meant for you, you alone out of every other person in this world, but you're so fucked up with yourself that you would destroy even your soulmate. She's better off walking alone than with you, and I'm not going to help you find her, Saul. I'm going to let you know she's there somewhere, and she's getting tired of waiting, and maybe...maybe...if you *do* ever find her by that time maybe...maybe...you will have learned how to be a *man*, you brainless wasteful piece of flesh'." Thor gave Nomad a startling, ferocious and terrifying grin. "Class *dismissed*."

Nomad may have made a noise. A quiet murmur, a hiss of breath, whatever. At last, when Thor looked away from him, Nomad dropped his cigarette butt into the beer bottle.

"I guess I'd better go check in," he said, and he got out from beneath the umbrella and stood up. "Jesus, it *is* hot out here."

"The deal is," Thor told him in a quieter voice, "I should've found somebody who wanted to help me drive the car."

Nomad had no idea what that meant, so he waited patiently for the rest of it. God might not be a nice guy and He might not be so patient, but God hadn't been given his first chance on stage by Thor Bronson, nor had Thor Bronson given God the names of some dudes he knew in Tucson who were looking for a solid lead vocalist/guitar player.

"Every woman I ever found," Thor said, "wanted to *ride* in the car. Wanted to kick back and let the sugar daddy do it all. And driving that car...it gets mighty fucking hard. Mighty fucking lonely. Yeah, they wanted the money, the clothes, the parties, the drugs, the *glamor*." That last word had come out like a drool of disgust. "But not one of 'em wanted to help me drive the car. Hey, maybe that's why I had so many fucking wrecks." When he looked up at Nomad he was now not so much a lion as a puppy begging for affection.

Nomad smiled. "Maybe." He was thinking of one wreck in particular, the one with the blue Porsche Targa on the Pacific Coast Highway that had happened years before John Charles had met him, the one that broke both of Saul Brightman's legs, shattered his jaw and injured his spine, ending his onstage gymnastics and his amazing and fabled leaps from the thundering speakers through walls of pyrotechnic flame. The doctors thought he'd be lucky if he ever again managed to hobble on crutches, but that long-haired Jew from Bayonne, New Jersey...he was one tough *shtarker*.

"The one who wants to help you drive the car," Thor said. "Maybe she's the soulmate, maybe not...but she's definitely the keeper." He reached out to rub his scarred kneecaps, which felt so much better in the heat of the sun. "Having a party after our gig. Fun to be had by all. Bring your condoms and your fucking youth."

"We're pulling out after we play," Nomad replied. "Hitting the Casbah in San Diego tomorrow night."

"Okay, yeah, I saw that on your website. Hey, how about checking out *my* site? And before you pull out, let's exchange email addresses. Of course, I'm not up in your range anymore, fuckers like you getting eight hundred smacks for ninety minutes on an *afternoon* gig. Yeah, everybody knows about that, man, so don't try to look dumb, and don't shrug like a gutless motherfucker either. You're either worth it or you're not, and you've got to *believe* you're worth it to *be* worth it. Anyway, you guys have been chosen by somebody up in the penthouse, some Jew *momzer* smoking a big Cuban and looking for his next meal ticket. So go and enjoy it and work like a sonofabitch and don't fuck it up, and what is there left to say?"

"I guess that says it all." But Nomad knew it didn't. He knew he should say *this is our last ride* or *we're ending it after Austin* or *I'm going to hunker down for a while and figure out what to do next,* but then Thor would've gotten up on his wiry legs and scarred knees and blasted him with Norse fire and the statement *Don't give me that, Johnny, because you know just like I do that the show must go on.*

To which Nomad would've answered with a question: *But does it have to go on and on and on and on?*

Thor stood up. He and Nomad exchanged high-fives, bumped fists and shoulders and then, running out of affectations, they hugged each other.

"Think about me out there, kid," Thor said.

How could it be otherwise? How could Nomad go onstage and *not* think about Thor Bronson and the long shadows of the road warriors who had gone before?

"Catch you later," Nomad told him, and he walked toward the hospitality trailer. Before he got there, he looked back over his shoulder and saw Saul Brightman, the dutiful son of a great and loving father, sitting in his lawn chair again with his legs outstretched, like any middle-aged fan at an outdoor concert. Nomad saw him give a fist pump, at some part of the music that he thought particularly deserving.

Then Nomad turned his face away, and he went on.

NINETEEN.

"You guys ready for your intro?" asked the skull-faced clown in the red Stone Church 9 T-shirt, the sparkly green shorts, cowboy boots and black tophat. The curls of his orange fright-wig boiled out from under the hat. He wore a red nose with a blinking light powered by the battery pack at his waist.

"Ready," Nomad said, speaking for them all.

The clown, whose handle at this gig was Eezy Duzit, headed out onto the stage through a corridor lined with black curtains. A chorus of whistles and a roar of anticipation went up from the audience, which Nomad hadn't seen yet. The clown had said he estimated about eight or nine hundred people were out there, and more would be coming in from the 'Midway' as their show went on. There were no seats; the audience brought their own or stood up, and the front half of the place was a mosh pit where people danced or thrashed or fought as they pleased. However many there were, they sounded hungry.

As Eezy Duzit went to one of the mike stands, a ragged chant started up and gained both strength and volume: *The Five...The Five...The Five...The Five...*

"Are they saying 'You Die'?" Berke asked.

In the space between Duzit picking up his mike and the chant quieting down, somebody out in the midst of the crowd shouted, very clearly, "The Five fuckin' sucks!" which brought a storm of laughter and more wicked shouts and catcalls concerning The Five's abilities to suck donkeymeat, eat shit and take cocks up their collective ass.

Nomad turned around and looked into the faces of his friends. On Terry's scalp and chipmunk cheeks shone an oily sheen of sweat, his eyes huge and frightened behind his Lennon specs. Ariel's mouth was a grim line, her face pale but her eyes the dark gray of a stormy sea. Though Berke wore a faintly bemused expression, her eyes were dead black and her hands were on her hips in an attitude of somebody ready to kick dogturds off the sidewalk.

Nomad was the emperor. He had to say something in this moment of heat and pressure. He had time for only three words, spoken in a whiskied rasp that even Thor Bronson would have admired: "Tear them up."

"You've heard about 'em!" Eezy Duzit's amplified voice came out of the huge speaker stacks capable of sixty thousand watts of mind-blowing power. The voice hit rock and came echoing back. "You've seen 'em on TV! Welcome to the Stone Church stage, from Austin, Texas, the band that will not die....The Five!"

As a raucous and not altogether sober cheer went up, Berke pulled in a deep breath, squared her shoulders and walked out through the corridor. Nomad stared into Ariel's face, and she into his. They were following a short set by the Cannibal Cult, whose Asian female lead singer Kitty Kones had, at a breakthroat tempo, screamed songs into the Electrovoice that seemed to be the Korean language mixed with a shrill outpouring of English profanity, as far as Nomad could tell. Whatever she was saying, the crowd had responded with basso woofs and the kind of noise that could bend metal. Her response to their response was to throw her microphone on the stage in the middle of Cannibal Cult's fifth song and storm off, teeth bared in her white-powdered face.

The stage crew had come on to clear away Cannibal Cult's mess and set up for The Five. While the band got themselves ready in whatever way they needed to, the crew swarmed the stage to move the Cult's drumkit off and bring in The Five's, set up the keyboards, plug everything in, check the sound levels and the stage monitors, and generally get the transition from band to band done as smoothly and quickly as possible.

As Nomad had been waiting for the crew to finish, he'd thought of an incident that had happened in the hospitality trailer just after he'd left Thor. He'd gone into the trailer's air-conditioned chill and walked between the chow tables set up with pre-packaged sandwiches, chips, fruit, candy bars, soft drinks and the like. His available choices of sandwich had been chicken covered with melted American cheese, turkey with melted provolone cheese, ham and melted Swiss, and some kind of pimento cheese nightmare. Pizzas were on display, all layered with his throat-closing favorite. But when he'd gone to the check-in table to get his stage pass, the very nice older lady on duty had looked at the green mark next to his name and said, "I see you get a special lunch. Are you allergic to dairy?"

"I am, yeah."

"I've got a couple of sandwiches without cheese set aside for you."

"Oh...okay. Well, that's great. Um...how did you know?"

"Your manager told us," she'd said.

Nomad remembered saying to Truitt Allen at the hospital: *I'm allergic to cheese.*

Where was he, anyway? There'd been no sign of him since he'd unlocked the trailer and they'd taken the gear out, over an hour ago. He hadn't even walked them to the stage.

Some manager *he* was.

Over the surly noise of the crowd, Berke started her drum intro to 'Bedlam A-Go-Go'. It was a snap of snare, a flurry of toms and a bright hiss of cymbals. Then on the bass she pounded a beat that was nearly double what they'd done on the original song, from their first CD.

It was time to get it done. Nomad nodded at Ariel, who walked out along the corridor; he clapped Terry on the shoulder and Terry walked out, and then Nomad got in step right behind him.

The light was a harsh white glare. A dry wind blew into their faces. Above them, a huge canopy of black cloth flapped and twisted. The crowd hollered again, and surged forward against the waist-high chainlink fence that stood about twenty feet from the stage. Uniformed GB Promotions security guards were waving them back, while between the chainlink and the stage, photographers were snapping pictures and news teams were aiming their video cameras.

The band that will not die, Nomad thought as he crossed the stage to his position and picked up his Strat from its stand.

He kinda liked that.

Terry slid behind his Hammond, with the Roland on his left and a rack of effects boxes on his right. He turned up the Fuzz and

Distortion settings to their max. On the other side of the stage, Ariel stood in front of her mike and picked up her Tempest. She adjusted for tone. Without looking at the audience she hit the song's first howling chords—B-flat, D-minor, G—which brought Nomad in to repeat them and add an F chord to the structure. Terry came in with an ear-piercing little stab of notes, and then Nomad got his mouth up to the microphone and half-sang, half-shouted the words as Berke drove the drums into a frenetic, warped disco beat.

"In my dream I had a third eye.
My dog and I we liked to fly
High above the wasted earth,
High above the dirty surf.
We saw a city burning red.
We heard some voices
And what they said,
Come join us it's party time,
Come join us the party's fine.
Come on down we never close,
Come on down enjoy the show.
We live it, we love it
But we never can rise above it.
Bedlam A-Go-Go.
We live here, we love it.
The kings and queens of nowhere scenes,
In Bedlam, Bedlam A-Go-Go."

Nomad looked out across the audience as Terry launched into a short instrumental strut—a demonic boogaloo—between the choruses. He saw the oval shape of the natural amphitheater, which was about the size of two football fields. A control tower stood at its center, topped with a glassed-in booth and bristling with multicolored parcans, follow spots, strobes and other special effects lights. Back and to the left were the turnstiles of the entrance area, and beyond it the 'Midway', where vendors from all over the southwest and California had come to display their artistry.

Business was booming among this demographic. He saw blue, red and purple flames tattooed on bald heads. He saw faces transformed into Escher artwork. He saw the calligraphy of a hundred hues written across shoulders and chests and breasts and stomachs, each man and woman their own Book of Life. Here, dancing and capering, was a bearded figure whose original color of birthflesh had disappeared beneath the new skin of blue ink and black proclamations; there whirling 'round and 'round was a topless female with red pigtails and an intricate painting of a multicolored dragon clinging to her back, its arms extending down across her shoulders and the black nails of its claws circling her nipples. Technicolor serpents coiled around throats, arms, thighs and calves. Flowers grew from navels and foreheads were crowned by shooting stars and pentagrams. Marilyn Monroe, Charlie Chaplin, Alice Cooper and Hitler pushed their faces forth from sweat-glistening meat. And there in the crowd...and there...and over there...stood in this blur of constant motion the few motionless figures who stood staring at the performers on the stage with eyes in a visage no longer recognizable as being earthly; they were creations from another realm, a strange and frightening beauty of human matter carved upon and recolored by needles both insane and awesome. There was the face made of layered scales like the gray hide of a desert lizard; there was the face created from a dozen interlocking other faces like a grotesque human jigsaw puzzle; and there was the face that was none at all, but rather a pair of eyes, nostrils and a mouth suspended against a bruise-colored, crackled parchment of indecipherable markings. It seemed to Nomad to be a document of rage.

He almost missed his cue. The disco beat became nearly a slippery-slidey rap, echoed back to him as if the mountain itself had a voice:

"Bedlam A-Go-Go!
Two wrongs, they make a right.
Peacekeepers, they want to fight."

The song had been their first video. The Five had danced down a Soul Train of demons and angels. A UT computer graphics major had digitized James Brown dancing down the line, followed by, among other public figures, George W. Bush, Bill Gates, Saddam Hussein, Mother Teresa, Oprah Winfrey, a black-and-white leering

Satan from an old movie called 'Dante's Inferno', Godzilla and John Barrymore's hunchbacked Mr. Hyde from the silent film. The video had been up for two days on YouTube before the plug was pulled, in a big way.

"*Vampires, they sleep at night.*
My straitjacket, it's way too tight!
Bedlam A-Go-Go!
Mad mister murder he came to play,
Brought a butcher knife and he carved away.
The homeless sit on barren fields
While the bankers sit on their golden steals.
President says to embrace that fear,
But he's on the first plane out of here.
Bedlam A-Go-Go-Go!"

At the end of the song, sweaty and energized, Nomad stood at the edge of the stage as he took in the response, so far so good, and he shouted into his mike a statement for that other Gogo, the Felix, over in Dallas or Fort Worth or Temple or Waco or wherever he was today, selling his cars and grinning his grins: "*Fuck* your role!"

Which got, really, a stronger response than the song had.

By the end of the third song, the Terry-penned 'Don't Bleed On My Paisley Shirt', Ariel was dropping chords and lagging behind the beat. Her concentration was out of the groove and it wasn't just because of the speed and intensity. Those she could handle; it was the feeling here that was eating at her. It was the atmosphere of Stone Church itself, a hard steely dark sense of...what was it? Hatred? Contempt? She was out of her element here, she felt vulnerable and threatened. She felt, quite simply, like an easy target. She'd realized, as well, that the stage's backdrop and wings were painted to look like mortar lines and red stones.

Everybody else was going full-throttle. Occasionally she would get a questioning glance from John or Terry, a lift of the eyebrows to urge her to tighten up, but her nerves were betraying her talent. As the show went on and the hot wind blew around the folds of the black canopy above their heads and more and more bodies came through those turnstiles and ran to join the slam-dancing, bone-smashing tribe, Ariel felt herself falling away from her friends.

It had bothered her so much, since that visit to George in the ICU. Day or night, bright or dark, she couldn't shake it.

It was up there, George had said. *Folded up. Sharp edges. The wings of a crow.*

< >

Waiting for him to die, he'd told them.

And then...the apperarance of that girl.

I believe in you, George.

I thought she was the angel of death, he'd said.

But now I think she was the angel of life.

Ariel dropped another chord and stumbled over a trill in the first chorus of 'Your Body Not Your Soul', which really earned her a puzzled look from John Charles. She had a solo coming up at the bridge of this song, she had to focus, but...why had George seen that girl from the well in his hospital room? Of all people he might have dreamed of seeing? Of all the people he had ever met?

Why her?

And that thing about driving back and finding out if the place would still be there...why *wouldn't* it be there? It was there, they saw it, why wouldn't it be there?

Don't you want my part? George had asked.

The song.

She thought about Mike, writing the first word: *Welcome.*

Again, drawn from that girl at the well.

And George's part: *I wish you safe travel...courage when you need it.*

The song.

Her solo was upon her.

She was a half-step late, but she swung her Tempest up and stepped toward the edge of the stage, and she was shredding metal and flailing it out in thick dripping incandescent blue-white coils above the heads of the Stone Church crowd when some of the people on the left side started sliding over the chainlink fence.

She faltered in her playing, mangled a hot handful of notes and stepped back, but then she picked it up again because she was a professional. Nomad, Terry and Berke had also seen the tattooed bodies coming over the fence. Garth Brickenfield's security men were trying to push them back but now on the right hand side they started coming across, and over there the security men were shoving back and shouting but Ariel could only hear the voice of her guitar through her stage monitor. There was a human crush against the fence, a straining of flesh against chainlink, and suddenly the fence collapsed. It just went down and disappeared under the boiling wall. The bodies rushed forward, swarming around the security guards who were caught up in small battles of their own. The camera crews struggled to get out of the way, but there was no way to get out of the way; they were caught in a floodtide and shoved hard against the stage, and when there was no more empty space before the stage the real party, the hard-core crash of tattooed, sunburned and red-eyed music fiends, could begin.

< >

"**Prime,** this is Shelter."

"Go ahead, Clark."

"We've got a vehicle coming up the road behind us. Black Range Rover. We'll get a visual on the tag in just a few seconds. Yeah... okay, it's an Arizona tag. Driver's stopping at the gate. Doors opening. Looks like...three males and a female. Two males, two females. Not quite sure there."

Join the club, True thought. He'd been walking around the lot, checking things out with his Walkie-Talkie ready, strolling in between the trucks, vans and trailers, and so far he'd seen plenty of unidentifiables. True stopped alongside a small U-Haul truck and faced in a southeasterly direction, where the Shelter team was located. The gate Clark mentioned was the one festooned with chains and barbed wire. "What're they doing?"

"Um...well...it looks like they're wanting to climb the gate. One's trying it. No go, he's backing off."

"Kids who ought to know better," said True, though he could remember climbing over plenty of barbed wire and locked gates when he was one of those who ought to know better. He started walking again, his black wingtips stirring up puffs of red dust. "They moving on?"

"Still in place, sir. Looks like...checking with the glasses...looks like they're smoking some pot now."

"Prime, this is Signet," another voice came in. "Fly on the wall. Do you copy?"

True felt his face tighten. All joviality at pot-smoking unidentifiables vanished in the fraction of an instant. "Copy that," True said. "Got a distance?" He was already turning toward the northwest. The music was thundering from that direction. The fly was coming up from the opposite side of the mountain, and would seek a clear shot at the stage.

"Three hundred and twenty-seven yards."

That distance, calculated by a range-finder, would put the fly more than five hundred yards off the stage. Still climbing up, unable to get a shot yet until he reached Signet team's height. True said, "Give me some details."

"Definitely carrying a rifle," said the Signet leader.

True wasted only the time to swallow. "Go get him. You know what I want. Logic, you're on standby. Copy?"

"Copy that," said the Logic leader.

True kept walking. After a few minutes he realized he was going in circles. He checked his wristwatch. He checked the sun. He walked past a nearly-naked guy with long brown hair and a topless, scrawny girl sprawled together in the water of a small blue inflatable baby pool. He brought the Walkie-Talkie to his mouth.

"Signet, you copy?"

No answer. They might be a little busy right now.

"Signet, this is Prime. Copy, please."

He heard a sound from the amphitheater. The sound of wailing guitars, the driving drums, the fiery keyboard and the raw voice of John Charles, yes, but something else too. It was a sound like the wings of a thousand birds. When True looked up he saw only a sky of white fire.

John Charles abruptly stopped singing. There was an explosive *boom* and feedback shrieked. Something made a horrendous crash and twang.

True heard the next two noises and knew exactly what they were.

Crack. Crack.

Gunshots.

He ran for the stage.

< >

Ariel had seen the goose-steppers. There were six of them, bald-headed and pale, wearing white T-shirts, black jeans and shiny black boots. They were going back and forth through the crowd at full-speed, doing their Nazi salutes as they jammed into other people and fought through the crowd like battering-rams. No one was listening anymore; no one in her range of sight was actually paying them any attention, but they were hearing the music like escaping prisoners hear the sirens at their backs, and all they wanted to do was smash through every obstacle in front of them.

She was playing rhythm guitar to 'Desperate Ain't Pretty' and trying to keep up with Berke's frenetic beat. Terry sounded like he was playing the Hammond with his fists, and even John had started to miss notes. He had his mouth right up on the microphone, he was bellowing it out like a hundred-year old field hand scarred by a Georgia bullwhip.

"*Some fine woman you made yourself out to be,*
If you had your evil way they could hang me from a tree.
You take my money and then you spit in my face,
Somebody ought to take you from this human race.
Won't be me, not today, not me,
'Cause I want you to live to see me go free,
Want you to live to see your pretty face fall,
Want you to cry before that mirror in the hall.
'Cause desperate ain't pretty, baby, you're gonna know that's true,
Desperate ain't pretty, baby, ugly's gonna show on you."

Nomad stepped back from the microphone while Terry went into his organ solo. The hard, heavy vibrato was full of glittering golden pain. Nomad looked out at the audience, at the figures who slammed into each other and, snarling, twisted away again. He saw at the very edge of the stage a few people who had ceased their warfare for the moment and were staring at him with glazed eyes. When they saw him looking, they reached out to him their tattooed hands and arms, and the inked figures and shapes moved on their necks and shoulders and shifted on their naked chests as if a multitude of souls were confined in each body and trying to climb out by using him as their ladder. He saw a big burly dude with close-cropped black hair staggering around, clipping people left and right with dangerous elbows. His red T-shirt read *Nug Nug Nug*. Another formidable guy with a goatee and Celtic tattoos blackening his throat ran head-on into one of the Nazi freaks and knocked the goose-stepper on his ass. Nomad thought of something his mother used to say: *It's all fun until somebody starts to cry*. In this case, *starts swinging fists*.

As Terry ended his solo and Ariel picked up her rhythm part again, Nomad stepped up to his mike. He caught sight of a slim kid with neatly-trimmed blonde hair pushing through the crowd to the front of the stage, moving slowly but avoiding elbows, knees and skulls with the grace of a dancer. The guy was wearing jeans and a loose-fitting gray T-shirt with a color travel picture screened on the front and the green legend *Vietnam Golf Vacations.com*. He had his eyes fixed on Nomad, who got his mouth right on the mike once more.

"*This part you've been playin', you know it has to end,*
Nothing worse in the world than the murder of a friend.
Could've been so much to you, been the steady one,
But what I have to say to you won't be spoken from a—"

Gun.

The sun sparked off metal.

The wind rustled through the black canopy overhead. Nomad stopped singing.

He saw it in the blonde kid's hand. It was a small pistol. It had come up from underneath the T-shirt. The barrel's eye looked at him.

Then the kid blinked, his eyelids maybe freighted with drugs, and he turned the pistol toward Ariel.

Nomad had no time to think; he just jumped.

He knocked the mike stand over and carried with him the guitar on its strap around his shoulder. There was a hollow reverberating *boom* as the mike slammed down, followed by a squeal of feedback. An effects box or something crashed to the stage and made a noise through the speakers like a Strat in its death agony.

His guitar hit the kid first, and then Nomad. From the pistol in the outstretched hand came two shots, but the shooter was already going down to the dirt. Nomad was on top of him and fighting for control of the dude's arm, which snaked this way and that and then suddenly the kid's head came up and slammed against Nomad's right eye. Sizzling lights and pain zigzagged through his head; he thought his skull had been fractured, but he had to get that fucking gun. He just started beating the kid, started whamming at him with both fists, every damned thing he had.

Somebody grabbed him under the arms and pulled him up and somebody fell on the shooter like a blanket. The blanket was wearing a red T-shirt, and as he pinned the kid's gunhand to the ground with one knee, he looked up at Nomad and the guy holding him and said tersely, "Get him on the stage! Now!" His T-shirt read *Nug Nug Nug*. Another figure knelt down and started twisting the kid's white fingers off the pistol's grip. He had a spiderweb tattooed—painted?—on one side of his face and hexagonal steel gauges—definitely real—in his ears.

"Back! Everybody get back!" shouted the dude who was helping Nomad climb up over the edge of the stage. Ariel was there, her face drained of blood; she reached down and grasped his hand, and Terry leaned forward to grab hold of his shirt.

Nomad scrambled up onto the stage and then fell to his knees. The socket of his right eye was throbbing. Maybe it was already swelling shut. God, that was going to get black! Fucking took a shot! He felt like he was going to puke, the smell of gunpowder was still in his nose. He saw that the guy who'd helped him had a headful of spiky brown hair, a brown beard and on his bare chest a—fake?—tattoo of a horned red devil sitting astride a Harley. The bearded devilish Harley fan was holding out an open wallet and showing a badge to the crowd.

Berke knelt down beside Nomad and said something. It was all gibberish, he couldn't make it out. "I think I'm going to puke," he told her, or thought he did because he could hardly hear himself either. He began to try to fight free from his guitar, but it wouldn't let him go.

Ariel was trembling. She backed away from the crowd. She could feel what was coming just about to break; she saw it in their faces, in their clenched fists, in their rage at having been born between the wasted earth and dirty surf. As the young man who'd tried to shoot her was being pulled to his feet, his gun now in the possession of Agent Nug, one of the Nazi Six stormed in and kicked the kid in the ribs with a black boot.

Maybe their anger was spilling over because he'd screwed up the show. Maybe they just wanted to beat somebody to death. Whichever it was, they started coming in at him and in another moment the FBI agents were fighting for the life of their prisoner.

Nomad sat on the stage. Ariel turned away, and thinking she too was going to be sick she headed through the corridor lined with black curtains. She ran into Truitt Allen, who looked questioningly at her and then ran past her to the stage. His .38 Special was in one hand, his Walkie-Talkie in the other.

Berke sat down behind her drumkit, where she felt the most comfortable in the world. She stared into the distance, at nothing. Terry stood watching fights break out across the amphitheater. He saw a young man in a blue shirt being knocked back and forth between two tattooed and grinning bruisers; the young man fell to his knees, blood streaming from his nose. Another dude, thin and bearded, was being stomped on by a guy in a Wildcats T-shirt.

Terry went to Ariel's mike. Through it he shouted, "Stop it! Please, stop it!" but no one listened, and no one stopped.

True came to the edge of the stage, and looking out upon the madness he raised his gun into the air and began to fire bullet after bullet toward the silent red mountain.

TWENTY.

When Jeremy Pett finishes the job of shaving his hair off with the new electric clippers he's just bought, he emerges from the men's room at the Triple-T Truck Stop just off I-10 about nine miles southeast of Tucson.

He has taken a shower and used the facilities, and now—clean and refreshed and shaven to the pink—he goes out to the grocery section to buy some food. He needs items that don't have to be cooked or even heated up, because there's no electricity in his hidey-hole. The truck stop is only a few miles from where he's been living since seeing his face, the description of his pickup and his tag number on television. He saw it yesterday when he was lying on the bed in Room 15 at the Rest-A-While Motel on South Nogales Highway, and after he saw it he stood up, quickly got his gear together, paid the old Hispanic man who'd asked him when he'd checked in on Saturday if he wanted a nice young college girl for company that night, and then he had hit the road. But not too fast, because he wanted to stay invisible.

He roams the aisles, picking up a few cans of pork 'n' beans, a can of chili, three bottles of water, a pack of doughnuts and a bag of potato chips. He needs the sugar and salt, because it's very hot where he's living. He sees a rack of ball caps, and chooses a tan-colored one that has the red Triple-T logo. A candy bar or two would be good. He has parked around back, in among the protection of the semis at rest. His eye is always on the front entrance. In the waistband of his jeans beneath his light blue cotton shirt is his automatic pistol, loaded with a clip of eight.

At the Rest-A-While, which came equipped with many nice young college girls who knocked on his door after dark and smiled at him with meth-rotted teeth, he kept up on the news. The cable reception was fuzzy, hard to look at, but it had shown him what he'd needed to see.

One dead in Sweetwater, one in the ICU in Tucson. Sniper Stalks Rock Band. Tucson police and the FBI need community help in finding this man, a Marine veteran who served in Iraq and may still be in the area. GB Promotions Presents Stone Church Nine at Gila Bend Thursday July 31st through Sunday August 3rd. The Five Appearing Thursday July 31st at 3:00, one show only. Tickets on sale at the site or available online through Ticketmaster. GB Promotions assures the fans that security will be tight and every precaution taken.

Don't go there, Gunny had told him in Room 15, as Jeremy had been packing his stuff. Gunny had been standing in the bathroom door, his boots in the puddles of the toilet overflow from last night, the soggy towels lying like dead white dogs. *I want you to rest today and tomorrow*, Gunny had said.

"I've got to get out. They're on me." Jeremy was thinking one word and one destination: Mexico…Mexico…Mexico.

Gunny had told him they were not on him until they had him. Now, it was true they knew his name and face and the make and color of his pickup truck and his tag number, but…they're not here, are they?

"Matter of time," Jeremy had said.

Then you know what you need to do, Gunny had answered as he moved across the room. *Dig yourself in.*

"Mexico, Mexico, Mexico," Jeremy had said. He'd zipped up his rifle case.

You're not ready. Jeremy? Dig. Yourself. In.

And the way Gunny had said that, with all the iron-hand-in-the-velvet-glove persuasion that made a man admire another man, caused Jeremy to look toward the corner where Gunny was standing, just at the edge of the blazing light that slipped around the crooked curtains.

"Dig yourself in," Jeremy had repeated, as if he'd come up with the idea. "How? Where?"

You're supposed to be the Marine, Gunny had reminded him, with a dark stare.

Translation: guy with a pussy last name ain't gone be no pussy, not in *this* man's Corps.

Jeremy stands at the Triple-T Truck Stop's cash register, waiting as the lady bags his groceries. She is also talking on a cellphone, so she's working one-handed. And slowwwww. Up on a shelf behind the counter is a small TV for her entertainment, and it is from a KGUN-9 News Minute that he sees a young female reporter holding a microphone. At the bottom of the scene is the legend *Violent Afternoon At Stone Church*. That sounds like one of the many paperback Westerns Jeremy had read at Camp Fallujah.

"It happened about an hour ago, Guy," the reporter is saying to, presumably, the anchorman. Her mane of brown hair whips in the wind and she makes a move to control it but no luck. Behind her, people with tattoos are milling around, mugging at the camera over her shoulders, showing the devil horns and sticking their tongues out. "During a performance by The Five band, a man drew a handgun and fired two shots. There were some minor injuries in a scuffle, but no one was seriously hurt and the shooter was taken into custody. We have some pretty startling video to show you."

There is just a brief clip of bodies flailing around, the camera getting knocked back and forth, a glint of what may be a gun in someone's hand, and then a figure with shoulder-length black hair jumps off the stage into the crowd.

Jeremy knows who that is.

"Guy, we'll have more of this video, more details on this story and interviews with the actual Five band members at six o'clock. For now, a GB Promotions spokesman says Stone Church will continue as planned through Sunday night."

"Amazing video, just amazing," says Guy.

"Cap?" asks the woman behind the counter.

Jeremy focuses on her and realizes what she's asking. "I'll wear it," he answers, and then he breaks eye contact because that's one way to stay invisible. But she's back on her cellphone as soon as he has the bag in hand, and he walks out into the hot yellow sunlight of late afternoon and goes around to his truck. He drives away, slowly and unhurriedly, but he keeps watching all his mirrors for a flashing light.

Jeremy drives to the southeast, toward what he found yesterday afternoon when he left the Rest-A-While in search of a place to dig in. He found it when he followed a series of signs that said *Houses For Sale* and repeated underneath it was *Casas para la venta*. It is not quite four miles from the truck stop. It is on a main road past a residential area of middle-class homes with cactus gardens and red tile roofs, three different types to choose from. Many of the houses here are For Sale. Some appear to have been For Sale for a long time. It is past a stripmall with a drugstore and a Mexican takeout joint and a consignment shop and a nail parlor, but the grocery store and the video rental store are For Rent though their signs still hang in place over empty windows. It is the next turnoff on the right, within sight of the dying mall. It is built upon God's own country, hard desert earth under a stark blue sky with cactus-stubbled foothills and gray mountains to the east. At the turnoff, there is a stand of mesquite trees and among them a rock wall with the words *LaPaz Estates* hammered into it with tarnished brass letters.

And beyond the turnoff and the trees and the wall are dusty streets with no names that lead to the empty driveways and bare garages of nine small houses built in the adobe style, three different types to choose from, all with red tile roofs. Beyond the nine houses, there are two more half-built and one hardly started. The streets wander a distance past wooden stakes that define the borders of their estates. Here and there are sacks of concrete and forgotten wheelbarrows and black garbage bags melting in the sun. Past the last estate where any work has been attempted, marked by piles of stones and brown cactus, the streets surrender to the desert, and that is the end of someone's dead dream.

Dead it is. Jeremy steers toward his very own adobe-style piece of heaven, which stands back off the main road far enough to be careful. The For Sale signs are everywhere, though some have collapsed due to wind and fatigue. Open House, some of them proclaim. New Low Price, some of them plead. He has seen a coyote here this morning, trotting down the middle of his street.

No one is home in any of these houses. Jeremy figures it was a construction deal gone bad, or somebody ran out of money, or the bank stopped throwing away good cash until some of the existing LaPaz estates started selling. Whatever. Somebody's loss, his place to dig in.

He has to go there now, and think. Figure things out. He is so close to Mexico he can smell the freedom in the breeze. He can smell the new beginnings, like the odor of onions frying in a pan. He pulls into the driveway, the ninth of nine, and he lets the truck idle as he gets out and pulls up the garage door, which normally would be opened by someone's electronic garage door opener but that person is not coming here today and Jeremy has previously disengaged the latch.

Then he drives in and pulls the garage door shut again, and when he takes his bag of groceries into the kitchen he almost feels like calling out *Honey, I'm home.*

There is no kitchen yet, really. There is a white counter and some cupboards, you can tell this is supposed to be a kitchen, but there are no appliances. The new linoleum floor is protected from workmen's dusty boots and spatters of paint by a bright blue tarp. The same sheet of blue in every room, protecting the carpets. The money must have run out suddenly, because the painting was never finished and several empty paint cans lie around.

There is something about this color that bothers him. There is something about it that makes him want to run away, and in the room where he sleeps he has taken up the blue tarp and gotten it out of there, so he can curl up on the thin sand-colored carpet with a pillow of clothes under his head and find some rest.

He thinks maybe he remembers it as the color of a body bag. He remembers seeing it on the roofs of New Orleans houses on TV. Or... maybe...something else...something...

He wants and needs and badly desires a nice powdered doughnut.

You need a car, says Gunny, whose face slides in across Jeremy's shoulder.

It is hot in this house. The air is still, the sound of humanity absent.

A car, Gunny repeats, as if to a mentally-deficient child. *Do you understand why?*

Jeremy does. He's been lucky so far, going back and forth to the truck stop. He hasn't seen a police cruiser, and neither has one seen him. But the thing about digging in is, digging in can be a trap of your own making. He can't get out on the highway to Mexico in his pickup truck. He can't make it to freedom and lose himself in his future. So, yeah, he needs a car.

Gunny asks him, in that quiet and penetrating way that Gunny has, where Jeremy thinks he might find a car.

"A car dealership?" Jeremy asks, but he knows the correct answer.

Some place where cars are parked.

He takes his powdered doughnut and his bag of chips and a bottle of water into the room where he sleeps. Before he sits down in his corner he removes the .45 from his waistband and puts it on the floor at his side. Then he eats a little and drinks a little and thinks as he stares at the gun.

He is proficient with his rifle, but a pistol is a different animal. You have to be close. You can so easily miss with a pistol, unless you're really close. He has always thought of a pistol as a defensive weapon, a rifle as offensive. That's why he didn't try to use his pistol on the drummer girl back in Sweetwater. Sure, he could've just driven up beside her and shot her, but what if she'd been quick enough to dodge a killing bullet? Then she's got his face behind her eyes, and if she's able to talk the police have his face too. And if somebody drives up before he can finish her off…wow, that's messy. Well, they've got his face *now*—and how that happened he couldn't figure out—but still, at the time he didn't think he should risk a close encounter. Look what happened to that amateur at Stone Church. Two pistol shots, wasted.

Kind of an interesting thing, though, why somebody *else* would've wanted to take those fuckers out. Maybe he wasn't the only one their lies had stirred up?

He can feel that Gunny has entered the room, and is standing right over there.

Jeremy eats and drinks and stares at the gun.

The rifle is a creature of dignity. To die by a long-range rifle shot is, really, a dignified death. It is the coming together of engineering, geometry, and God-given talent. But death by pistol is nasty and brutish, and way below his standards.

What he does is art.

But he knows what Gunny wants him to do.

"Do I have to kill an innocent person?" Jeremy asks, with powdered sugar on his chin.

Gunny tells him again that he needs a car.

Jeremy remembers a day when he had some downtime and he was connected through the Internet with Karen and Nick on her laptop. It was morning in Iraq and near midnight in Houston. He remembers that she had put on makeup for him, and how pretty her hair looked. He remembers that Nick had stared at him through the screen seven thousand six hundred and a few miles away and asked him one question: *Daddy, when can you come home?*

And Jeremy had answered, *I can come home when the good guys win.*

"Don't make me kill an innocent person," says Jeremy, but there is no begging in it. A Marine does not beg. A Marine gets the job done, and then he can go home.

Gunny tells him that he doesn't have to kill anyone today. What he has to do is get a car, and if that means taking a person out in the desert two or three miles from a road, giving them a bottle of water and directions in which to go and making them walk in the cool of the evening, then what is the problem with that?

"You make it sound so easy," Jeremy remarks.

Gunny says that the sooner he gets this task done, the safer he will be and he will not be trapped in this place with those blue shoes on the floor.

Jeremy doesn't move; he's not sure he heard what he thought he heard.

Gunny asks to be forgiven. He says he meant to say *blue sheets*.

Neither of them say anything more for a while after that.

Jeremy knows that Gunny is right. There's not much use in arguing with Gunny. If he wants to get out of here, he needs a car and he needs to go to a place where cars are parked.

Like that stripmall up the road.

He picks up the gun. He stands up and puts the gun in between his flesh and the waist of his jeans, under the shirt's flagging tail. He needs to get this done in a hurry, but it occurs to him that he should leave his pickup hidden right where it is. He will need time to transfer his gear from the truck to whatever car he can jack. So with the Triple-T cap on his head and the .45 automatic under his shirt he leaves the house through the back door and sets out, walking around the house to the street and then along the street toward the stripmall.

A few cars pass him, but not many. This could go very, very bad. Or very good. Or it might not happen at all. Maybe when he gets to that stripmall, he'll decide to buy a burrito and go back to his hide. He walks not briskly, but he doesn't amble either. He is a man with a purpose, but to anyone passing by it wouldn't look very important.

When he reaches the parking lot there are ten cars in it, most in front of the drugstore. They look to be grandpa cars. Sedans with lots of room and old American gas guzzlers, except for one white Honda Accord. As Jeremy stops and pretends to examine the sole of his right shoe, a man and woman in their fifties come out of the drug store. The woman is carrying a bag and the man has his arm around her shoulders; he looks toward Jeremy and nods, his eyes cautious. Jeremy nods back and moves on as if he's heading for Mexican food, and the couple get into a silver Buick and lock their doors before the engine starts. Jeremy pauses at the door of the Mexican joint as the car pulls away.

Maybe he *will* get a burrito after all, he decides, because his heart is beating hard and he thinks he needs to sit down in some air-conditioning.

As he starts to go in, a woman with shoulder-length gray hair emerges carrying a brown paper bag. He waits for her to pass. The interior of the Mexican place is dark, nothing much to see in there but an old dude walking back through a swinging door into a kitchen. Then Jeremy sees that the woman is heading toward the Honda. She is well-dressed, crisp like someone who works in a bank or a real estate office. She is wearing sunglasses, and has the strap of a dark blue leather handbag around one shoulder. A red-white-and-blue scarf is tied around her throat. A real Grandmother America.

She is not very much overweight and has a young walk. She probably has young legs under her turquoise-colored pants suit. Jeremy decides she's the kind of woman who could walk herself out of the desert.

She is unlocking the driver's door when Jeremy comes up beside her and says in an easy, nonthreatening voice, "Excuse me, ma'am. Ask you something?"

She is startled just a little bit, and when she turns her face to him Jeremy sees a slight quiver of her pale pink lips that means she doesn't know whether to be afraid or not. He quickly says, "I'm lost, can you help me?"

"Lost?" she asks. She has the throaty voice of a lifetime cigarette smoker. Maybe she's in her middle sixties, with a sharp chin and deep lines bracketing her mouth. Lots of worry lines across her forehead. "What're you looking for?"

"LaPaz Estates," he answers, and instantly—*instantly*—he knows this is something he should not have said.

"Well...it's—" She glances in that direction, and then Jeremy takes the gun out and holds it just south of her takeout food, and he says, "I'll shoot you if you scream. Get in the car." And he's had to say this as if he really means it, because she must obey him before somebody else comes out to the lot.

She trembles all over. Her mouth is slightly open. Her teeth are also gray. "Put that bag in the car, down on the floor," he tells her. "Get behind the wheel. Do it *now*." She doesn't move; maybe she *can't* move. "Ma'am," Jeremy says, the sweat crawling on his neck, "I'm not going to hurt you. I want your car." She starts to give him the keys. "No, you're going to drive and I'll let you out up the road."

"Please don't hurt me," she says in a smoky gasp.

"I'm going to let you out up the road," Jeremy repeats, and he says, "Go on, now, be a good girl. Unlock the other side. If you touch that horn, I'll get very upset. Okay?"

"Please don't hurt me," she says again. "I'm going to my sister's." She unlocks the passenger door and puts the paper bag on the floorboard as Jeremy quickly walks around to the other side, keeping his eyes on her. She gets in and he gets in, and neither of her trembling hands touches the horn. She is being a very good girl.

Jeremy closes the door, and when he feels her suddenly tense up as if she's decided she needs to make a break for it, he says calmly, "Just do what I tell you." He keeps the gun down low, so she can see it from the corner of her eye. "Start the engine and drive."

"Alright," she says, and something catches in her throat. "I will."

Just then a heavy-set woman comes out of the consignment shop carrying a red table lamp with a shade that appears to be decorated with Indian symbols. Jeremy's captive turns her head toward this other woman, who has paused to pick up a shopper's newspaper from a wire rack.

"Start the engine and drive," Jeremy repeats, and now he aims the gun at her side.

Grandmother America does as she's told. The other woman with her red lamp and her shopper's paper walks past the Accord, and continues on to her Ford Taurus a few spaces away.

"Which way do you want me to go?" Grandmother America asks, and now it sounds as if she can barely get the words squeezed out.

Jeremy realizes he's made a big mistake. A big omission. He has forgotten something very important. He could grind his teeth down over this one.

He has forgotten to bring a bottle of water for her to drink in the desert.

He can't just put her out somewhere nearby. Can't put her out on one of these streets. So he decides he has to go get a bottle of water for her, so nobody can ever say he was a bad guy.

"Turn left," he tells her.

Then, about a mile further on, at the stand of mesquite trees and the rock wall with the tarnished brass letters: "Turn right."

He directs her to his street and his house. He directs her to pull the Accord up alongside the house where its blinding sunlit whiteness can be hidden. And then he tells her they need to go inside because he's going to get her a bottle of water before he sets her free out in the desert.

"Alright," she says, in that weak old smoky voice. "I'm going to my sister's, she's waiting for me."

"This will just take a minute," he tells her.

In the house, in the kitchen with its floor covering of disturbingly bright blue, Jeremy picks up a bottle of water as Grandmother America stands with her back in a corner. He has a thought, and he gives it a voice: "Do you need to go to the bathroom?"

"Please," she whispers. "Don't hurt me."

"It's okay, it's okay." The way she's standing, as if she's trying to press herself into the wall, to also become invisible just as he wishes to be, touches Jeremy. "My name is...Chris," he decides to say. He takes his cap off, to show her his shaven head. When the police find her, she will say a shaven-headed man named Chris took her car. "What's your name?"

She doesn't reply. Her head is down, her hair stringy over her shoulders, her crispness all burnt up and gone.

Gunny comes to stand in the doorway on the other side of the kitchen, just looking in, just marking the progress. Then he goes away again.

Jeremy can't see her eyes behind the sunglasses, and this bothers him. "Would you take your sunglasses off, please?" He motions with the gun.

Those thin, veiny, trembling hands come up and remove them. She has brown eyes, sunken down in nests of wrinkles. She will not or can not look at him.

"I'm from Texas," Jeremy says, but why he tells her this he doesn't know. "Do you live around here?"

She makes a noise that sounds like *muh*, like her lips are stuck together, and a slow tear courses down through the wrinkles on her left cheek.

"I'm in a little trouble." Jeremy realizes this is the first person he's spoken to, for any length at least, for...how long? Really *speaking*, that is. Human to human. Gunny is his angel, but Grandmother America looks to him like she would be a very good listener. "There are some *bad* people in this world," he contiunues. "Some liars, about what happened in Iraq. They're carrying lies around with them, and they're poisoning the air. And you can bet...you can fucking *bet*...they wouldn't have lasted one *day* over there. Because, you know, sometimes you don't get a choice about the things you have to do. No, ma'am, you don't. You go right along following the road, doing what you're supposed to do... what you've been *trained* to do...and all of a sudden, *wham*!"

Grandmother America flinches at this, and tries to push herself further into that corner, and another tear slides down her face but on the other cheek.

"All of a sudden, something crashes into you from the side and you never saw it coming," Jeremy says. "That's what."

He stops speaking, because he feels there is a movement in his face that he can't control. He feels like insects are in the muscles and bones of his face, winnowing down in there, breaking up all the structures that make him appear to be a human being, and when they are through eating at him, when they are finished eating and laying their eggs and destroying his face in their eagerness to consume him so that *they* might live, whatever will be born inside him will be a monster that used to be a really good guy.

He stares down at the blue tarp on the floor, at the sickeningly bright blue, and he remembers. In remembering, there is a hot passing flash and a shockwave that tells him exactly why he is here.

The young lieutenant that everybody knew as a Fobbit came in the middle of the night to get Jeremy and Chris out of their bunks. They were taken to an Ops tent at the center of the base, and at a table with directional lights around it sat a captain neither of them knew, and a civilian in his mid-thirties, wearing a khaki jacket, a white shirt and jeans. He looked like cowboy material, or maybe a Christian In Action.

Color photographs and the map of a section of Baghdad were arranged on the table. *This is the task*, said the civilian, who was not introduced. *You will be accompanied by a squad to this position at oh-five-hundred. You'll make your way here, to this building, and set up by oh-five-thirty. The target will walk along this alley between oh-seven and oh-eight hundred. Our source tells us he will in all probability be wearing either black or gray cargo shorts, a red, black or camo T-shirt that might bear a Nike swoosh and either a red Houston Rockets cap or an orange cap with a Fanta logo. I understand Houston is your home, Sergeant Pett, so this might be called 'fate', if you believe in that. The target will be moving toward this opening here, in this building on the northeast corner. He should be removed before he reaches it. I can't answer or acknowledge any questions, but I can say that the removal of this target will help us put a stop to some of these goddamned IEDs. One more thing: we need positive verification of the kill. That can be done by bringing back an article of clothing. His cap will do. One more thing, gentlemen: however this mission turns out, our meeting never happened. Good luck and good hunting.*

At the site, hunkered down in the yellow building under the dust-hazed sun at oh-seven-forty-one, Chris had been watching the alley through his spotter scope when he said quietly, "Target. Orange cap."

Jeremy had peered through his own scope. Yeah, there he was. A gangly little bastard wearing black cargo shorts, a camo T-shirt—plain, no swoosh—and the orange Fanta cap. That little dickwhacker *wanted* to be seen, because in addition to the orange topper he was wearing bright blue plastic sandals, a common type of cheap footwear for these ragheads. That little dillweed was lit up like fucking neon, and he was burdened under a black backpack that was not built for speed.

It was barely a two-hundred yard shot, easy squeezy, but Chris started feeding in the ballistics numbers to his small PDA. Chris took another scope-look, and then another, and the target was walking along getting ever closer to the opening in that building he was not supposed to enter before he was hit, and then Chris looked over at Jeremy and said, "That's a little kid."

"A kid? No, he's—" *One of those really small Johnnies*, he was about to say, and then Jeremy had adjusted his scope to get a sharper view of the face, and he saw that their target was maybe ten years old. He pulled his eye back as if a hot ember had spun into it.

The kid in the orange cap was walking right along. Maybe thirty feet now from that opening, a square dark hole in the rubbled building on the northeast corner.

"That's our target," Chris had said, in the grim voice of finality. "The motherfuckers have sent us out here to kill a kid."

"No way." Jeremy had exhaled it. "No way, no way. *No*."

"He's moving, man. What are you gonna do?"

"That's not the target."

"The *fuck* it's not. Man, he's almost to his hole. You want the wind call?"

"Don't push me," Jeremy had said, with only a hint of the panic that was rushing upon him. Kill a *kid*? Somebody had to be fucking *insane*. Who was this kid, Saddam's baby brother? Was he a messenger, about to go down into a lamplit pit where the IEDs were being loaded with nails, broken glass and ball bearings? Did he have a couple of dozen cheap cellphones in that backpack, to be used as triggering devices?

The kid was there, and now he started to bend over to get into the hole because it was a narrow opening not much bigger than himself

"Jeremy, do you want the wind call?" Chris asked, also feeling the panic.

The kid was going in.

"Shit," Jeremy whispered. His finger rested on the trigger. He put his eye to the scope and readjusted, bringing his target in for the kill. "Shit shit shit *shit*," was all he could think to say.

The kid was almost all the way in, almost gone.

Jeremy's finger did not move. God help me, he thought, and he wanted to weep.

Those IEDs. Those IEDs were cruel bastards, and the people who put them together and the kids who brought them backpacks full of American tragedy should not be allowed to live.

The kid stopped. He was backing out. A strap on his backpack had been caught by a piece of exposed pipe. He reached up to free himself, and that was when Jeremy sent the bullet.

"They don't know, they don't know," Jeremy says to Grandmother America. "What that's like. They don't know. They don't want to know."

"What...*what* is like?" she asks, because he has voiced none of this.

He draws a long, sad breath, and he tells his captive that he would like for her to go into the bathroom. He would like for her to get on her knees in the bathtub, because the plan has changed. The new plan, he tells her, is that he will have to hit her on the back of the head with his gun, and then he will leave her and go away. He says all this with the gleam of sweat on his brow, and he has begun to fidget with the safety.

She goes, stumbling along in front of him, her hair in her face. On the way, Jeremy gently takes her handbag from her and lets it drop to the blue-covered floor in the unfinished hall. She is sobbing, but not very loud. "I'll try not to hurt you," he tells her. "I'm a good guy, really I am. I'm just...you know...in a little trouble."

In the bathtub, when she is on her knees in the cream-colored tub with her back to him, she gasps, "I'm going to be sick," and then she shivers and heaves and throws up. "Please," she says, as she struggles for whatever dignity and hope she can hold onto. "Please, please, please."

A shadow moves across the mirror. Gunny is standing behind Jeremy; Jeremy sees the reflection, beside his own.

Jeremy aims the gun at the back of Grandmother America's head. When Jeremy retracts and releases the slide to cock the pistol, feeding the first round into the chamber, Grandmother America suddenly turns toward him with hot rage in her eyes, as if she is condemning him for telling such a lie. The bullet he fires digs a smoking groove across the side of her jaw. She does not scream so much as make a catlike mewling, but she is no meek pussy; in the next instant she comes up out of the tub with a bitter snarl and tries to claw her way past him and out of her death chamber. He shoots her again, somewhere in the midsection, but she keeps going, a desperate woman leaking out her life and trying to get to her sister's.

Jeremy shoots her a third time, in the back in the hallway on the blue-tarp floor lah de dah de dah la *boom*. She is made of strong stuff, because though she nearly collapses against the wall she still keeps going, and he thinks of himself back at his apartment in Temple, staggering along a hallway between life and death.

Oh, how far we have come.

In the front room, she goes for the door. She is making a high whining sound now, not unlike air escaping a tire at several punctured places. She falls upon the bright blue before she gets there, and yet amazingly—and there are some hardcore members of the Green Machine who could *learn* from this lady—she continues to crawl and reach and wheeze.

At last, so very close to the door yet so very far from who she was an hour ago, Grandmother America flops over on her back and looks up with hateful reproach at Jeremy, who puts a bullet between her eyes.

This is one big mess, Gunny tells him from the gory hallway.

Jeremy realizes he did not finish his story. He did not tell her that when the bullet was sent, it hit the kid in the side of the neck and the kid had slithered into the hole in the building and out of sight. And that he and Chris had to go through those streets, turkey-peeking over every wall and around every corner, and raghead men and raghead women were gawking at them and screaming like they were from another world. Then right in front of that hole was one of the kid's blue sandals, a bright blue, a happy blue, unforgettable. Lots of blood, too. And going in after that kid, they'd found his other blue shoe on the broken concrete. And him too, lying curled up. His orange Fanta cap was still on his head and he hadn't yet left this life, and over in the corner was—would you believe this, lady?—a fucking goat tethered to an iron bar, and a water bowl next to it. And—get this, now—the kid is crying, and bleeding from the mouth and the neck, and somebody—a woman—at the entrance really starts wailing, and Chris says Man, we've got to get our asses *out*. So, an order being an order and because I am the *prince* of my profession, I shoot the kid in the head and take his cap, and then we haul ass out but you know the woman, his mother it must be, is silent now, just staring at us as we go past, and she is holding that fucking blue sandal against her cheek like it was the perfect rose of Araby. See what you missed, lady?

And then...and *then*...at the base we get flash-blasted by that captain we don't know. Done in the middle of the night, in a secure place where nobody else can hear. He roars at us, Did anybody *tell* you to take out any secondary targets?

Secondary targets? Oh...I know what he means. The goat. He's pissed because after I killed a kid who had gone to feed and water his pet goat, I shot the goat in the head since there was no civilian Christian In Action standing around for me to kill. See, I figure...and I've thought about this a long time, I've had a *lot* of time to think... that the whole shitbag was about the goat. A feud between families, maybe, or between tribes. Was information about IEDs passed along because I killed a kid who stole another kid's goat? Or did I kill the kid who stole *back* the goat that some kid stole from *him*? Did I do somebody's dirty work for them to exchange for info on the IEDs, and I brought back the cap to prove it?

"I don't know, lady," Jeremy says to the body on the floor. "They don't tell you everything over there. They just say some things are fate."

He sighs deeply. He's going to miss having someone to talk to. But there's always Gunny.

In the bathroom, Jeremy looks at himself in the mirror and sees the bones and muscles of his face moving beneath the flesh. A lump comes up on his right cheek and subsides; another rises, squirming, on his forehead. A third bulges up alongside his left eye, and it appears his jaw is trying to break loose from its hinges.

Gunny was right, he thinks. I'm not ready yet for Mexico. Before I get there, I have to—

Shut their mouths, Gunny says from behind him. *Somehow, they know. That video speaks volumes, Jeremy, and all it can do is hurt you and the good soldiers who carry out their jobs. Now here is the thing...they have to be silenced, because they're doing something that is going to hurt so many, many other people. They don't even know what they're doing. That amateur today had his chance. But you...*

you are the professional, Jeremy. You have a car now. It's time to get packed, and get serious.

Jeremy agrees. He will leave the pickup in the garage, right where it is. How long will it be before anybody finds it? How about...a month of Sundays?

Time to get serious. If they played at Stone Church, they might be going on to their next date. The list he wrote down from their website said The Casbah in San Diego, tomorrow night. If not there, then the Cobra Club in Hollywood on Saturday night. He figures he ought to go through Grandmother America's handbag, check it out for cash. It would be for a very patriotic cause.

Yeah.

Time to get real serious.

Jeremy's face has stopped moving, for now. He is himself again. He almost sobs, almost lets out a wail that would've echoed in this little bathroom and scared him enough to keep him sweating and sleepless every night for the rest of his life, but the feeling of dark despair soon passes. He forces it to pass, because a person can't live with that kind of feeling inside him. She was collateral damage. She'd been in the wrong place at the wrong time. It happened. A casualty of the mission, no big whoop. You just put your head down and keep going. And one thing he knows is that after he's completed this mission he'll be doing the good guy work against the druglords of Mexico and saving thousands of lives, so it all evens out. It is called fate.

Gunny gets up close, cheek-to-cheek in the mirror, and he says that there is one more thing Jeremy should know. That the new police advancements in computer and forensic science make it possible for them to cut open a victim's eyeballs and see the face of a killer burned on the retina by the inflamed optic nerves, and maybe it would be wise if Jeremy did something about that.

Jeremy thinks about it, and then he agrees with that too.

Time to get way fucking serious.

FIVE

THIS SEAT IS SAVED

TWENTY-ONE.

Ariel had lost her way.

She was wandering in a place unfamiliar. It was a hot thicket of leafy green vines that nearly blotted out the sun. What she could see of the sky was a white glare. She knew only that she had to get from where she was to some other place, that she couldn't stay where she stood, and so she pushed onward through the wall of vegetation ahead as another closed at her back.

There were thorns in here. They were stabbing her and cutting across her skin whenever and wherever she moved. It was treacherous, this going forward. It was painful and almost unbearable, but she had no choice; she must bear it, to reach the other side.

She smelled earth, and heat, and the raw green growth that surrounded her. She was aware also of another smell, a sweet aroma, a rich scent nearly like wine, perfuming the air. She saw small dark berries hanging from the thorned vines by the hundreds, some wholly black and others touched with red, and she realized she stood in a dense thicket of blackberry brambles that went on in all directions.

The question was: which way led out? Or, another question, and more troubling: was there *any* way out?

She continued onward, in the direction she had chosen though she couldn't remember making such a decision. It had been made for her, it seemed. She could always stop, turn and go another way, but it seemed to her that sometimes in this world you just have to trust *something*.

She had not gone very far when the man came through the brambles, and stood before her as if to block her path.

Ariel knew him. She knew his face, from a driver's license picture. She knew what he'd done to two friends of hers, and she knew now what he wanted to do to her.

As she backed away, he followed. He wore no expression. Fear tightened around her heart and hobbled her legs. He came on unhurriedly, with a supreme and terrifying confidence, and as he closed the distance between them his face began to change.

Ariel saw the flesh ripple and move, like clay being reshaped by a phantom hand. The bones began to shift beneath it. With a series of cracking noises the features distorted and destroyed themselves as one cheek swelled outward and the other caved in, as the nose collapsed into a widening fissure and the forehead lengthened like a slab of veined stone. One eye retreated into the dark while the other burst out like the eye of a fish popped by a hook.

All this, while his lower jaw slid forward. Then with a sound like sticks being broken it began to unhinge itself from the upper jaw, and as Ariel backed away through the slashing thorns she put her hand up before her own face to push aside the image of a reptilian mouth yawning open, stretching itself to impossible size, dwarfing even the misshapen head upon which it had grown. The grotesque body lurched toward her, staggering through the brambles, its arms at its side and hands gripped into fists, its single eye wet and gleaming on the edge of the voracious mouth.

Something dark flew out of that gaping hole. It was followed by another, and another still, and then three at a time and five at a time, ten and then twenty, a vomiting forth of dark sleek projectiles that in an instant grew wings and black feathers and spun around Ariel like a living whirlwind.

The crows flew in black swarms from Jeremy Pett's straining mouth. Some of them came at Ariel, jabbing and clawing, their small red eyes ticking this way and that, but most of them fell upon the fruit, and this they tore from the vines and swallowed in dripping beaks as they fought each other for the next swallow. They tumbled through the black-stained air in vicious struggling knots, their shrill cries nearly human in their expressions of greed, triumph and frustrated anguish.

Thousands of crows blighted the air. They battered themselves into Ariel's face, they battered into each other and, still fighting and tearing at each other over the sweet pulp, flapped on broken wings in their death spirals. Through chinks in the black walls that circled her, Ariel saw Jeremy Pett spinning around and around, his arms outstretched wide like the cylinders of a bizarre machine, the engine of a carnival ride that has popped its rivets and burned out its regulators and now must spin and spin until it spins itself to pieces or shatters itself in a blast and roar. As the crows streamed out of him, he had shriveled. His clothes had fallen away, revealing a body that had become an emaciated horror of gray flesh. The hideous head with its gaping mouth had darkened like an old wart and was flagging back and forth, boneless, on the spindly neck. It began to implode, and as the last few black feathered things struggled out blinking their red eyes and already tearing at each other, the head collapsed like an airless balloon.

In all this shrieking noise, in all this flurry of feathers and chaos of claws, Ariel watched the skeletal body fall, still locked in its spinning circle, and she thought, *He is a vessel.*

The crows came at her. They tangled in her hair and jammed against her nostrils. They squirmed against her eyes and thrashed across her mouth. But as she staggered back, seeking some place to protect herself in this field of life that had become the province of hell, she realized that they were only coming at her because she was between them and the few vines of fruit that remained unseized, and they would not stop until they had it all, every last bit of it.

Look at me, someone said.

Ariel turned her head. Standing beside her was the girl.

She looked exactly as Ariel remembered her. She wore the same clothes and the same raggedy straw hat, and she stared at Ariel through ebony eyes that were both serene and impassioned. Her cheeks were marred by scatters of teenaged acne, the same as before.

Walk with me, the girl said. Her voice had no accent yet it reminded Ariel of a voice she had once heard and trusted, somewhere in the long-ago.

When the girl held out her hand Ariel took it.

The crows continued to swirl around them, but none penetrated the space between.

Whether the girl moved first or she herself did, Ariel didn't know. But they were walking together side-by-side through the brambles, hand holding hand, as the black curtains of crows flapped in their faces and hissed at their backs. Still, not one entered the space they occupied, and as Ariel and the girl walked forward the crows retreated before them. Speaking in shrill tongues of indignation, the solid walls of feathers and glinting crimson eyes began to break apart like so many crumbling leaves shaken off a dead tree.

Ariel awakened and lay staring at the ceiling. A fan was lazily turning up there, creaking very softly. The sunlight was bright through the pale yellow window curtains. A dog barked somewhere along Benton Place, and a motorcycle went past. She turned her head on the pillow in search of a clock. The one on the bedside table said it was about ten minutes after ten, the hands in a pleasing symmetry. She stretched and heard her backbone pop, and she started to push aside the sheet but she decided she would lie there until ten-fifteen and try to absorb her dream.

She was in bed in the guest bedroom at Berke's mother's house, in an area of small but neatly-kept homes in the northeast section of San Diego, perched on a hill above Interstate 15. They'd gotten here last night, after a two-hundred-and-eighty mile drive from Stone Church. When they'd reached the house, they were so wrung out by their experience that all they could do was mumble some pleasantries to Mrs. Fisk and find a place to stow their bags before they crashed. Truitt Allen, though he'd driven the whole distance, had gone into the den with his laptop, cellphone and a cup of coffee and shut the door. Ariel assumed the white GMC Yukon with dark-tinted windows that had trailed them up through the winding streets and parked in front of the house was still there; she would check, just out of curiosity, when she got out of bed.

It was interesting, she thought, how they handled the gas situation. Last night when they needed to fill up, True had given some kind of code over his cellphone. When the Scumbucket had pulled up to the pumps at a Texaco station, the white Yukon and another Yukon, this one a metallic gray, had stopped on either side of The Five's van and trailer. From each SUV two men dressed like True, in casual slacks and shirts, had gotten out to stand facing the darkness on the far side of I-8. They would have looked like ordinary business travellers stretching their legs except for the weirdly-shaped pairs of binoculars they were using as they scanned back and forth. "Night vision," Nomad had told her. "Either that, or thermal."

True had pumped their gas. A third man from both the SUVs had filled those tanks as well. There'd been a brief discussion among the agents and a pair of them went into the gas station and came out each carrying two bags of popcorn and four cups of coffee in a styrofoam tray. True had asked if anybody needed to use the restrooms, and when all the band members said they did, they got an FBI escort who waited outside the doors. Never was there a time when two of the agents did not keep watch with their night vision or thermal or whatever it was. Ariel had the impression that there was a fourth man in each Yukon, riding in the back, just from some movement she thought she detected and from the fourth coffee. Nine men on duty, including True. Ariel figured that had to be a lot of taxpayer money being spent, to safeguard the lives of four musicians whose deodorant had worn off a *long* time ago. *Plus* True had put their gasoline on his own—or his agency's—credit card. No wonder this country was so deep in debt.

Ariel lifted her head and looked at the other single bed in the room. John Charles was still asleep, tangled up in his sheet as if he too had dreamed of blackberry brambles and the striding specter of Jeremy Pett. His face was turned away from her, toward the window. She hated to see what his right eye looked like today, because last night it had been swollen shut as tight as an oyster and colored a curious mingled palette of black with purple edges and olive-green highlights. The icepack they'd given him at the medical trailer had helped some, she guessed, and so had the supply of Excedrin Extra Strength.

He had saved her life.

She still couldn't get her mind around yesterday afternoon. It had been just like the cliché: everything happened so fast. When John had stopped singing and the music had faltered, and then John had stage-dived like a lunatic...it was too much to handle. And later learning that the young man—nineteen years old on his California driver's license, True had told them—had been aiming that gun at her...too much to handle.

The shooter had been taken away very quickly and efficiently. After The Five had gotten offstage and the techs had cleared their gear, Monster Ripper had started setting up about an hour later, but soon after that—past a visit to the medical trailer and brief interviews with reporters from the Tucson TV stations and Brad Lowell from *The Daily Star*—the Scumbucket had pulled out of that particular circus with True behind the wheel. On I-8 West, the two Yukons had gotten into position, the metallic gray in front and the white behind them, and that was how they rolled.

He had saved her life.

It was going to take her a long time to put this gift on a shelf, if ever.

He snorted a little bit, as if reading her thoughts. His hand came up to touch his eye, but even in sleep his brain figured he probably shouldn't do that and his hand sank back down again across his chest.

True hadn't told them the young man's name yet, though he'd certainly seen it on the license. He'd said he would let them know what developed, and that was last night before he'd secluded himself in the den.

Ariel allowed herself to return to the dream, and play it back again. It was so bright and sunny and cheerful in the bedroom. There was the spicy odor of air fragrance, which maybe Mrs. Fisk had sprayed around this morning to counter their need for showers. It was difficult to think of dark things, in here, but now she must.

He is a vessel.

She remembered thinking that. What did it mean, exactly? She retained the vivid image of the crows, swarming at the fruit and tearing it from the vines. And she retained the vivid image of the girl.

The girl.

Walk with me.

Ariel was struck with a desire—a need—to see the song. The Kumbaya song, Berke had called it. She leaned over to the floor, where her fringed-leather bag was parked next to her blue suitcase. She opened the bag, removed from it her notebook with its glued-on gemstones of a dozen colors, and then turned to the page upon which she'd written what they had of the communal song. The last song, it was supposed to be. Performed at the last show in Austin, on Saturday the 16th of August. The song that was a testament to The Five, that was written by all of them together, that held a little of their souls in its words and music.

Welcome to the world, and everything that's in it.

Write a song about it, just keep it under four minutes.

Got to figure what to keep, and what to leave behind, and like life it's never easy.

I wish you safe travel and courage when you need it.

And that was it, so far.

Unremarkable.

A song in progress.

Something in progress.

Ariel scanned the lines again. What she'd written down, she realized, began and ended—to this point, at least—with words spoken by the girl at the well.

Sitting up on the bed with a pillow at her back, with a dog barking down the street and the sunlight streaming through the yellow curtains, Ariel felt a transcendent truth come upon her, a sense of wonder that had some fear mixed in with it too, yes, but it was like being locked in a tight and exhilarating groove of rhythm and tempo, the knowledge that everything was *right*, was flowing as it should, and that to break this rhythm, this strange and somewhat frightening connection, this forward motion that led to an unknown counterpoint, would not only be unprofessional, it would be tragic.

Ariel thought that the girl—whoever and whatever she might be—was helping them write this song.

"John?" she said. And again: "John?"

"No," he mumbled, "I don't want any."

She was relieved, in a way. What was she going to tell him? How was she going to explain what she *felt*? And it was just a feeling, that's all it was.

Walk with me, the girl had said.

Ariel decided she needed to get up. Like right now. She needed to take a shower and wash the red dust of Stone Church out of her hair, and then she needed to get dressed and find a quiet place to work on this song.

It was time to get serious.

Terry was still asleep on the floor, in his sleeping bag. Berke had taken the sofa in the basement's little junkroom. *It's good enough for me*, Ariel had heard Berke tell her mother before she'd carried her suitcase down the steps. Ariel figured Berke had wanted to sleep as far as possible from the room where her mother and stepfather had lain together for nearly ten years. As Ariel understood the story, Berke had been fourteen when her mother and father had divorced, and later her mother had sold the house where Berke had been born and she and her daughter had moved in with Floyd Fisk, the divorced father of a twenty-year-old nursing student, after the wedding.

Ariel took her shower, washed her hair and got dressed in jeans and a purple long-sleeved peasant blouse with a floral print and ruffles of white lace at the cuffs and neck. One of her many finds from vintage clothes shops, though now these were nearly as expensive as the newer items. When she emerged from the bathroom she ran into a bleary-eyed Terry, who just grunted a greeting and shambled past in his tatty gray bathrobe.

Ariel saw that John was still conked out. Maybe that was for the best. She took her notebook and her purple-inked pen and walked through the hallway into the kitchen, where she found Berke's mother monitoring a crockpot while she was watching a soap opera on a small TV.

"Good morning!" Berke's mother had been born Kim Chapman, but somewhere in her days as a thespian and cheerleader at Patrick Henry High School she'd been called 'Chappie', and it had stuck. Her face lit up with the presence of someone else in the room. She was an attractive woman, tall and lean with her daughter's strong bone structure. But her brown eyes, many shades lighter than Berke's, were sad. Ariel had met Chappie on several occasions when they'd played San Diego but had never been to this house. She knew that Chappie was forty-nine, that she was the middle child between two brothers, that her own father was a retired technical worker for Northrup Grumman who had once shaken the hand of Howard Hughes, and that she used Clairol Medium Brown to cover up the creeping gray in her long, still-silky hair. She was wearing a pair of beige slacks and a black sleeveless blouse.

"Morning," Ariel replied. "Smells good."

"Veggie stew for lunch. Do you want breakfast? I can make just about anything."

"Really, all I'd like is a glass of orange juice." She reconsidered. "Maybe some toast would be nice. And some jam?"

"Juice, two slices of whole-wheat toast and some strawberry jam. Does that sound all right?"

"Great. I'll get the juice." Ariel made a move toward the refrigerator, which was covered with bright little flowery magnets in different hues holding a variety of color photos, some faded with age. She saw glimpses of a different world: a smiling, balding heavy-set man wearing horn-rimmed glasses and sitting amid piles of books; a slim girl about sixteen years old with thick, curly black hair pounding away at a drum set with her eyes closed; a terrier of some kind, head cocked and looking quizzically at the camera; a scene in a bar with maybe a dozen people, most of them long-haired and gray-haired, lifting their beer bottles; the balding heavy-set man, now in sunglasses, standing with his arm around a happier Chappie Fisk and behind them the natural wonder of the Grand Canyon.

"Oh, I'll get it," Chappie said, and she swooped in as mothers will and got the container of orange juice out before Ariel could even register exactly where it was.

"I guess Berke's still asleep?" Ariel asked as Chappie poured juice into a glass.

"Haven't heard from her. Here you go. Now, for your toast."

"Thank you." Ariel drank some of the juice and gazed around the kitchen. Like the rest of the house, it was a sunny place. A homey place, with homey knickknacks collected from different tourist destinations. Everything neat and clean, everything orderly. It was difficult to grasp, in this sunny kitchen with the soap on TV and Chappie busy loading up the toaster, that Chappie's husband—her second husband—and Berke's stepdad had died last month, yet there *was* a feeling in this house, however bright and neat it was, that someone was missing and would not be coming home.

Ariel, and none of the other band members as far as she knew, had ever met Floyd Fisk. Berke had told her mother well in advance of their gigs in San Diego that she didn't want him anywhere near her, and so he'd never shown his face.

Floyd fucking Fisk, Berke had said to Ariel one day at rehearsal when they were talking about—or talking *around*, really—their parents. *Don't you think that sounds like the fucking dumb-ass barber in Mayberry? You know, the Opie show?*

What's so bad about him? Ariel had asked. *I mean…is he like… cruel to your mother?*

Cruel to my mother, Berke had repeated, as if trying that on as a reason. *No, he's not cruel to her. She loves him. But he's not my dad. You know?*

Ariel wasn't sure she did know, but Berke's mood had gotten black-cloud stormy and that was a good sign not to travel any further without a lightning rod.

"Can I ask you a question?" Chappie asked as she spread strawberry jam on the two pieces of toast. "This…is kind of weird to ask, but…are you…Berke's *friend*?"

"I'm her friend, yes."

"Well…I mean…" Chappie gave her a quick sidelong glance. "Are you her *good* friend?"

"Oh!" Ariel realized what the subject of this was. "Oh, no. Not that kind of friend."

A blush of color rose into the woman's cheeks. She shrugged. "I didn't know. I don't ask Berke very much." She offered Ariel the toast on a yellow plate with brown ceramic flowers around the rim. "She can snap your head off when she's in a bad mood. But I don't have to tell you, do I?"

"We all get edgy sometimes."

"Oh…I'm supposed to let you know…Mr. Allen went downtown this morning. He said he'd be back by early afternoon."

"Did he take the van?"

"No, he got into one of those huge SUVs. Do you know he ate *four* eggs and just about finished off all my bacon? He said he'd reimburse me, but still…that man can eat." Chappie pretended to watch her soap opera for a moment, but Ariel could tell she was formulating either another statement or question because the corners of her mouth moved. "Let me ask you something else," she finally said. "Do you trust that man to protect you? I mean to protect all of you. The whole band. I watched that video over and over. I saw how close you came to getting shot. Aren't your parents worried about you? Haven't you heard from them?"

"I've called them," Ariel answered. "When it first happened, in Sweetwater. I called them again from Tucson."

"And…what? They don't want you to come home?"

"They didn't mention that. I didn't expect them to." Ariel took a bite of toast and chewed it. "Anyway, I wouldn't go, because that's not my home anymore. I live in Austin. But...next year...it may be somewhere else."

"Berke *did* tell me that the band is breaking up," Chappie said matter-of-factly. "I'm sorry to hear that, because she always..." Here she paused, as if deciding whether she was betraying a confidence or not. She went on. "Always believed in you guys," she said. "More I think than she's believed in any of her other bands. She particularly believed in John and in *you*. That you would find success. Make a hit record. Get the recording deal. Whatever. Jesus, I am *old*, but I swear I didn't date Elvis Presley."

Ariel smiled.

"But I *did* date Todd Rundgren," Chappie said. "I had a little thing going on with Joe Strummer. I used to give backrubs to Iggy Pop. *And* Robert Plant kissed my hand one night in Hollywood, standing right on the Sunset Strip, and something like that you never forget."

"I guess not," Ariel said.

"Wow, the music scene back then...it was in—" There was just the briefest of pauses and Ariel thought she was about to hear the f-bomb dropped, but Chappie caught herself. "—credible," she finished. "So much going on, so many bands. It was just electric. And we were right in there. People wouldn't believe how many songs were written about the sisters."

Ariel nodded. Chappie wasn't hesitant to admit her membership in the sisterhood of groupies. To hear her tell it, as she'd told it before, Chappie and the 'sisters of comfort' were all about maintaining the sanity of their rocker men and keeping them well-supplied so the great works could keep on coming. Flowing. Being created. Ariel finished her orange juice and again said thank you.

"I've got coffee. Do you want some?" Chappie motioned toward the pot. Her own cup, a piece of merchandise—maybe an original—that bore a picture of The Eagles, sat on the counter. "Oh...you're a tea drinker, aren't you?"

"Right."

Chappie refilled her cup. "So you think Mr. Allen and those men out there can protect you?" She reached up to a cupboard, opened it and with a smooth, unhurried and completely unselfconscious motion she brought out a half-bottle of Jack Daniels. It was the most natural thing in the world to pour a small bite of Jack into your coffee before noon, which she did. "You trust the FBI?"

"I guess I do, so far."

"So far, you're not dead." Chappie capped the Jack bottle and put it away. She sipped at her high-octane fuel. "Neither is my daughter. But you know that was a close call yesterday, don't you? Nancy Grace said last night on TV that this guy at Stone Church was probably copycatting Jeremy Pett, and she thinks there'll be others. Listen, if you were *my* blood, I'd get on a plane and come collect you. I'd say no tour or music or ticket sales are worth getting killed for. I'd say put it all away until that nut is in jail."

"Have you said any of this to Berke?" Ariel asked, knowing what the answer would be.

Chappie took another drink before she replied. "This is the biggest cliché in the world, what I'm about to say. But Berke has always walked to her own beat. She's her own different drummer. She might be scared, but she's not going to show it and she won't back down from anybody...not even that..." Again, the f-bomb was poised to drop. But no. "*Nut*," Chappie finished.

"Berke is a strong person," Ariel agreed. "I envy her strength. Her knowing how to get what she wants."

"Yeah, it'd be a great world if everybody was like *her*." Chappie attempted a smile that didn't quite work due to the bitterness at its core. Then she walked a few steps away to check on the crockpot.

Ariel decided it was time to move on. "I think I'll go outside for a while." Last night she'd seen, in the front yard, the wooden park bench under the eucalyptus tree. "Thanks for the—"

"I'm surprised she even agreed to come here," Chappie interrupted, and Ariel braced for an onslaught. "Even with Floyd gone. I'm surprised, that's all."

"Well..." Ariel felt as if she were walking on treacherous ground. "I guess she wanted to make sure you were okay."

"I had to almost beg her to come. To get what he left her. He said to me very plainly, early last year, that if anything happened to him he wanted her to have what he'd saved for her. It was very important to him." She nodded. "Very important. And the letter too. I told him, nothing was going to happen, he was fine and he was going to have another checkup to make sure. Mandy came over twice a week to watch him take his medicine and check his blood pressure. But...he said he was tired sometimes. Just tired. Everybody gets tired." She started to take another drink, but lowered the cup before it reached her mouth. "They did what they could for him. The emergency team. I watched them work, so I know they did what they could. But oh my God, how I miss him." Her hand came up and the fingers pressed against her lips. Her eyes glistened. "And the thing was...he tried so hard...so hard...to be a father to Berke, but she wouldn't let him in. She turned her back on everything he tried to do for her. Okay, so he wasn't...like...the world's greatest drummer, like Warren thought *he* was. Floyd didn't know music, and he didn't keep up with bands, and he liked most of all just reading, or sitting on the couch watching football or old movies, and he wasn't flash...but he was *substance*. Do you understand what I mean?" She looked hopefully at Ariel, and Ariel said she absolutely understood.

When Chappie spoke again it was in a tone of reverence. "Floyd was no Todd Rundgren. He was no Joe Strummer or Iggy Pop. He was no Warren Bonnevey, either. He didn't say he was going out for cigarettes and three days later he was calling you from Los Angeles asking you to send money because he was on the edge—right on the *edge*, he said—of getting a gig with the latest hitmaker, whoever was high on the chart that week. He didn't knock holes in the walls because he didn't get a callback. Jesus, if that house Berke grew up in could talk, it would fucking scream. Excuse my mouth, but it would. Floyd didn't holler and yell and go on a rampage at three o'clock in the morning because he thought I was stealing his sticks and burying them in the back yard. And then he didn't go sit in the bathtub and start shouting that if he had a gun he'd kill everybody in the house and then himself. Oh, those were some choice days and nights, Ariel. And the terrible thing was...Warren really *was* good. He had a great talent. He had the fire inside, you know? But it was a horrible thing, to watch someone you loved burn alive from the inside out."

Ariel had no idea what to say, so she said what she felt: "I'm so sorry."

Chappie blew air between her lips and waved Ariel's comment away and took another drink of Jack and java. "Life," she said. "It's not bubblegum. See, the deal is...Berke asked me one time—oh, she asked many times, in that very nice way she has of asking—why I would give up on her father and marry—her description—a total loser. The Mayberry barber, she called him. The bookworm, that was another one. She said, Mom, he's just so *nothing*. And I looked her right in the face, I stared her down, and I said I love Floyd Fisk because he loves me, and because he loved *her*, whether she wanted to accept that or not, and because they call it 'flash' for the reason that it goes up in smoke so fast, but you can hold onto 'substance', and it holds onto you. 'Substance' honors responsibility, and you can say... oh, man, that's so *old*...but the truth is, I wanted to be happy and I wanted to be loved. I wanted things to be settled. If that's old, you can wrap it up for me because I'll take as much of that as I can carry."

Chappie's eyes suddenly filled with tears. "*Oh*," she said softly, and brokenly.

Ariel saw a box of Kleenex on the counter. She pulled a couple of tissues out and gave them to Berke's mother.

"Thanks," Chappie said as she dabbed her eyes. "You're sweet."

Ariel stood with her a while longer until it was clear Chappie had unburdened herself as much as she was able, and now Chappie was focusing back on the soap opera again, and she had finished her Jacked-up coffee and put the cup aside. Ariel said she was going to go sit outside and think about some things. Chappie told her to enjoy the bench out there, it had been where Floyd liked to sit and read when he got home from the bookstore in the afternoons.

The house was a light tan with darker brown trim around the windows. A picket fence guarded the property. There was a rock garden in front, and the eucalyptus tree threw shade over the park bench. The Scumbucket and the trailer stood in the short driveway, behind Chappie's vanilla-colored VW Beetle. When Ariel emerged from the house and started down the front steps, two agents got out of the white Yukon parked on the street and began talking to each other as if discussing baseball scores or some other interest between men. Ariel saw that they were wearing sunglasses and they didn't really look at each other as they spoke; they were scanning the street and the houses and hills. She approached them, and when one of the men recognized her presence she asked if she could bring them something to drink but the man said, "No, miss, we're good, but thank you."

Ariel wondered if there was a toilet in the rear of that giant SUV. It was likely there was some sanitary setup for their convenience. She sat down on the bench, under the tree, and opened her notebook to the lines of the song again as the men, no longer talking, stood with their backs to her.

It was a puzzle to her. What this could possibly mean. She had no idea where it was supposed to go or what it was supposed to say. She considered the idea that if she closed her eyes very, very tightly and thought very, very hard, maybe the girl would come to her again from the green mist of the blackberry brambles and tell her exactly what it was supposed to mean, or if the girl was feeling particularly salvatious today she would offer up the next line or two.

But deep down Ariel knew it was not going to work that way. The Unknown Hand was not going to write this for them. The song, like any other act of creativity, was no good if it wasn't strained through the joys and woes of human experience. It was no good if it was not in some way personal. It would not come fully-formed from a girl in a dream. It would have to be worked on, trial and error, writing and scratching out, searching for rhyme and struggling for reason.

Just as it always was, no different.

"Inspiration?"

Ariel looked up at Terry, who had taken his own shower and was dressed in gray shorts and a seagreen shirt covered with small blue and gray paisleys, circa 1969. "Going over our song," she told.

"You mean *the* song, right?" He nodded toward the empty half of the bench. "Can I sit?"

"This seat is saved," she said, "just for you."

Terry sat down. He angled his head to read the lines and Ariel cocked the notebook toward him so he had a better view.

"Say anything to you?" she asked.

"No, not really. To you?"

"I guess it's about change. A summing up of things. Where you *stand*," she decided. "Like...where are you in your life. What do you need to keep and what do you need to let go of, in order to move on. Does that make sense?"

"Yeah," Terry said. "I can see that. So you're wanting another couple of verses and a chorus?"

She thought about it. "I don't know what I want," she said. What she meant was: I don't know the *why* of this song, much less the *what*. It sounded so crazy, so spooky-oooky, to say that the girl at the well was directing them. That maybe John had come up with the idea of the communal song on his own, it was something he felt was necessary to keep the band on the same page, but the girl had... what?...read his mind, or planted a seed in Mike's head, and made a passing statement of care that had struck George strongly enough to remember it in his ICU bed, and maybe...planted the desire to finish this song in Ariel's own psyche?

But if that were true, in a Twilight Zoney way, then what was the *why* of it?

"I have to ask you something," she told him. "This is going to sound strange, but have you had any weird dreams lately?"

His eyes blinked behind the specs. "The night before Stone Church. I was pretty tense about that gig. I had a weird dream that I was playing the Hammond and it bit my hands off at the wrists."

"That's not what I mean. I know you believe in God and a Heaven of some kind—whatever that is—and you believe in the *other* side of that, too. Right?" She waited for him to nod. "I want to tell you about a dream I had last night...or this morning, or whenever it was. I just want you to sit and listen, and then I want to talk to you about some things that are on my mind, and if you think I'm losing it... okay, fair enough. Maybe I *am* losing it. Maybe I'm the one who ought to be hanging it up for a while and taking a break." She stared directly into his eyes. "But I don't think so." She hesitated, to underscore her resolve at this statement. Then: "Can I tell you?"

"Yeah, sure. Go ahead," Terry said.

How trustingly he said that, Ariel thought. How bravely he said it. In the next few minutes, she would find out how trusting Terry was of his system of belief, and how bravely he could handle her interpretation of the Unknown Hand at work.

Because she was already thinking that the other side also had its unknown hand.

And it too might be at work.

TWENTY-TWO.

When Ariel had finished and they'd talked it back and forth for about ten minutes, Terry felt either that the incident at Stone Church had snapped her strings or something was happening to The Five that he could not explain or understand. He didn't know which he believed. It was one thing to hear your voice spoken in a church by a man you could not possibly know, and that was strange and frightening enough, but *this*...

This was like looking at your reflection in a mirror and putting your hand up against it, and suddenly your hand pushes through the mirror like it's a thin pane of ice and beyond it is a world that was right there all the time, and maybe you suspected it was right there all the time, and you talked about it and made theories about it, but to actually look into it, to actually see the fearsome wonder that lies hidden beyond the mirror...

Or it was like swimming in the sea at night, under a million stars, and swimming further and further out from the lights of shore until a current takes you and you can't get back, and you swim and swim against the current until you're tired, but you have to rest for a while, have to tread water and get your strength back, and then in that night-black water something massive and covered with the scars of time slides along under your feet, and it just keeps sliding on and on, an entity too awesome to look at, and you know the leviathan has either come to eat you or give you a place to stand with your head just above the waves.

What Ariel had told him, and her thoughts about that girl and the song, about George seeing her in his hospital room and calling her an *angel of life*, about crows flying from the mouth of Jeremy Pett in the blackberry bramble battleground...it was too much for even a believer. It was too much for even someone who had heard his name spoken by a stranger in a church far from home.

"I don't know," he told her, sitting on the park bench in the fragrant shade of the eucalyptus tree. She had just asked him if he thought they should talk this over with John and Berke. He could tell that she wanted to, but she needed him to agree. "I'm not sure they're ready for this."

"You mean, *you're* not ready."

"Ariel...listen...I'm trying to make sense of this, okay?" Terry felt himself floundering, like that swimmer in the night far from shore. "You saying this song is...like...divinely inspired, right? By that girl, and she was something *other* than an ordinary girl? But John had the idea for all of us to write the song before we got to that place."

"No, he had the idea for all of us to write *a* song before we got there. He came up with the idea, but she..." Ariel hesitated, as lost as she'd been in her dream. What exactly was she trying to get at? "...is refining it," she said, for want of a better term.

"*Is* refining it? *Is*? Ariel, here are the lines of the song, right here on this page. In this notebook. Your notebook. And you came up with this line about figuring what to keep and what to leave behind, didn't you? *You* did, not...her. So how can *she* be refining the song? How can she have anything to do with it? Okay, maybe George had a dream about her in the hospital, just like you did last night, but I don't see—"

"Why would George have had a dream about her? He hardly spoke to her that day."

"That's the way dreams work. Things pop in and out. Look, *I* haven't had any dreams about her. As far as I know, neither have John or Berke. If she was like...some kind of supernatural *force* or something, then why wouldn't she speak to all of us at the same time?"

Ariel almost said it, but she didn't: *Maybe she spoke to the one who would listen, and maybe she trusted that listener to carry the message forward.*

"What would be the reason for it?" Terry had his hand on her shoulder, like someone might do to calm a deranged person. "Honestly, now. Are we supposed to write a song that brings about whirled peas? Come on! Are we supposed to write a song that makes us... like...a huge success and suddenly we're the great big music stars? If you've noticed, we're all over the news right now, and you know who made that possible? It wasn't that girl." He leaned in closer, as if confiding a secret, but Ariel already knew what he was going to say. "It was *Jeremy Pett*. It was Mike's murder, and George getting shot. It was some nut with a .25 at Stone Church. Yeah, I believe there's a God, and I believe there's a Satan too. I believe in a Heaven and a Hell, and all the stuff that a lot of people laugh at. But *this* is just a few lines of a song."

"A .25?" Ariel asked. That was the first she'd heard of it. "True didn't say what kind of gun it was."

"It sounded like a .25 to me. A small gun. My dad's a collector. Handguns, not rifles. He took me out to a pistol range a few times." Terry shrugged. "It's one of the man things he was pushing on me." He reached out for the notebook and the pen. "Can I show you something?"

She gave the two items up.

Terry sat for a while looking at the lines, and then beneath the last line he wrote in the purple ink *Won't you move my hand, please tell me what to write.*

Then he waited, pen poised.

"Okay already," Ariel said. "I get it."

Terry's hand moved, and he began to write.

I'm sitting here like a candle on the darkest night.

I've got my hot flame, got my flicker on, but where am I when my light is gone?

I wish you safe travel, courage, you're gonna need it.

Terry looked up and handed her back the pen. "Second verse. Did that girl write it, or did I?"

Ariel took the pen and also the notebook. She closed it.

He was right. Of course he was right. But she couldn't help thinking that if she hadn't been sitting out here on this bench, saving a seat just for Terry, and if she hadn't told him what was on her mind, this second verse would not have been born today.

"What a way to earn a living." Terry was looking at the two FBI agents who were still scanning the street, the houses and the hills. When he spoke again, his tone was a little wistful. "I'm so sorry about Mike and George. But the awful thing—the thing that makes you really sick—is that the media attention has already made us a *success*, if you want to use that word for it. It's already sold thousands of CDs that we wouldn't have sold just going on like we were. No telling what doors are about to open. And we're just doing exactly what we were doing *before*." He gave a small bitter smile. "Because before all this press and shit, where were we going? Around in a circle." He didn't have to remind her of what they'd shared for the last three years: the grinding road trips, the gigs where you hoped to sell enough T-shirts to pay for a motel room, the indignity of opening for bands—some younger and much less experienced—who got the lucky break of a record deal early on, and you never saw your own break coming, no matter how hard you worked or what you did. "That just wears you down," Terry said. "You know? It wore *me* down. Way down. And before that I was there with the Venomaires, watching that death battle between John and Kevin Keeler over who was going to run the band, and then Kevin having his nervous breakdown on stage in Atlanta. With all that, and then Julia and the pain pills."

When he sighed, it was the sound of a man whose joy has become a burden. "I don't know what you guys are planning to do, whether or not you'll keep the name and soldier on with some new faces. I'm leaving because I want to do the vintage keyboards thing, sure, but the other part is...where am I when my light is gone? What have I *done*? What am I *going* to do? Have I mattered to *anybody*?" He paused for a moment, and he straightened his glasses on his face as if to be able to see a little more clearly. "I need some time and space, all my own. I need to get off the bus and find out where I am."

Ariel said, "The man in the church. The voice. About music being your life."

"I'll always play, if just for myself. I'll always write songs. Maybe I'll kick in with another band someday. Maybe I'll record at home. I'm not doubting what he told me. I just want to know why he took the time to speak to me, if that's all there is." Terry sat staring at the ground, where the edge of the eucalyptus shade met the promise of the California sun. "Well," he said at last, and he stood up a bit creakily, like an old codger artfully disguised in a young skin. "That stew smelled pretty good in there. I'm starving."

Ariel also got to her feet, holding the notebook close to her side. "Let's get at it," she suggested. She took his hand and they walked into the house together, and behind them the FBI agents returned to their Yukon.

In the kitchen, the two lovely birds of morning had emerged from their slumber nests and had already been served with bowls of veggie stew. One bird had touselled, curly black hair and dark hollows under her equally dark eyes, she wore a loose-fitting T-shirt and a pair of camo-print men's boxer shorts and she was sullenly nursing a cup of coffee that may or may not have been spiked like momma's own. The other, wearing the Five tee and the gray PJ bottoms in which he'd slept, had an even more wildly cockscrewed bedhead of long black hair and—

"Christ, what an eye!" Terry said, not without admiration.

"Thanks, and go eff yourself," Nomad replied, being a gentleman in front of the older lady.

The first thing that had jumped into Terry's mind upon seeing that eye was the title of King Crimson's 1974 album *Starless and Bible Black*. Except the swollen-shut lump of head-butted flesh wasn't completely black, it contained splotches and streaks of green in maybe four different sick shades. It had been bad last night but today...whoa! It was time for the phantom to put his mask back on.

"Are you going to be able to do the gig?" Ariel asked.

"Yes, I am." Nomad's voice was huskier than usual. His good eye looked bloodshot. "Don't worry about me." He kept eating his stew, though his spoon seemed to have trouble finding his mouth.

Ariel nodded, but the fact remained that she did worry about him. She remembered apologizing for John's behavior to the girl at the well, and telling her *I just try to clean up the mess*. It was her path, it seemed. She had tried to clean up the mess for many people, most of them guys she'd been involved with. Most all of them musicians, the messiest of the bunch. Like Neal Tapley, and before him Jess Vandergriff, who was one of the best acoustic guitarists on the East Coast but one of the worst in believing everything was either perfection or crap, nothing in between. And before him, others. After

Neal had driven himself off a county road to his death, in the aftermath of one of the messiest drug scenes/breakups/breakdowns Ariel had ever tearfully and agonizingly witnessed, she had sworn off men of the music. There was not going to be any involvement with any guy in any band she was in ever again, no romance, not any little funky and innocent—mostly—fun fuelled by a few vodka shooters when she knew she ought to be drinking silver needle tea and getting the broom ready. Nothing.

And yet.

She had looked at the shape lying in the other bed last night, his shoulder and the wounded side of his face touched by the faintest iridescence of moonlight, and it had crossed her mind that if Terry was not lying on the floor in the sleeping bag she might have drawn aside her sheet, gotten up and gone to John, as silent as a spirit.

She might have slipped in beside him, and gently touched his forehead as if to draw from it the fever of his pain. She would bear that for him, if he would let her. She would ease the trouble in his bones and smooth the worry from his mind. She would take the fire of his anger in her hands, and make of it a candle.

He had so much potential. He was so very good, in so many ways, without knowing he was. She thought maybe that was a great part of why she admired him so much; he didn't strut or brag, he just *did*. She wished she had a few embers of his flame, to heat up the sometimes too-cool hallways of her own house. She knew he could be abrasive, he could be childish, he could throw his tantrums and say things his mouth wished seconds later had never tumbled out. He could be terribly human, is what he could be. Human, cranked up to eleven. But she wished she had his ability to go full-throttle, to open up his engines and let the roar of life thunder out. If he made a mistake, the same kind of mistake that would have paralyzed her with the fear she might commit it again, he kicked it aside like an old sack full of ashes. He just kept going forward, even if he didn't know exactly where he was going. To be honest, sometimes he played his guitar like that, too. But his passion and energy always made up for his lack of direction. At least, in her opinion.

She had asked herself if she was falling in love with him. *Love*. That was not a word used by members of a gigging band for each other, unless it was in the concept of *I love my brother* or *I love my sister* or *I love my whole dysfunctional road-crazed family*. She wasn't sure, but she did feel for him—what would be the word used in those old Victorian novels by the Brontë sisters that she liked to read in school?—oh, yes....'stirrings'.

But only stirrings, because she had tried—and failed, mostly—to clean up so many messes, and her own heartbreak was not a mess she was eager to tackle, her own weeping side of three o'clock had come and gone so many mornings when John had left a club with one or two girls laughing and rubbing themselves all over him, but that was the Nomad part of John, the persona, and she had tried very hard and so far successfully to sing and play 'This Song Is A Snake' with no hint of a hiss.

Anyway, there was not going to be any involvement with any guy in any band she was ever in again. No romance. No little funky fun.

But something Terry had said out under the eucalyptus tree had made her heart sink: *I don't know what you guys are planning to do, whether or not you'll keep the name and soldier on with some new faces.*

Three could not be Five. Changes were coming. If two new players came in, the chemistry would be altered. If it didn't work, John might even decide to join another band. After all, this was a business. Wasn't it? Berke might split and go her own way. A business, that's what it was. Not really a family, after all.

She thought she should be considering what to keep and what to leave behind, because this life was never easy.

After his statement to Ariel, Nomad put down his spoon and very gingerly touched the piece of puff pastry that seemed stuck to his face with searing hot Super-Glue. "Maybe you should stretch your acoustic set out tonight. Do two or three extra songs. Since this is such an acoustic crowd."

The Casbah, on the corner of Laurel Street and Kettner Boulevard in Little Italy, was one of their favorite venues. The music room was small and the club sat under the noisy flight path of aircraft in and out of San Diego International, but it was a fun and friendly place and in the three times they'd played there the reception had always been stellar. One thing Ariel particularly liked is that her acoustic set, usually a couple of quiet songs delivered soon after Berke's drum solo, went over well at the Casbah. The audience really paid attention unlike at a lot of other clubs where the cry was for louder and louder.

"Sure," Ariel said, pleased at this suggestion. "I'd be glad to."

A cellphone's ring tone burbled a couple of bars of The Clash's 'London Calling'. Chappie checked the incoming number, which she didn't recognize, and then she answered, "Hello?" She listened for a few seconds, as Terry walked over to stick his nose into the crock-pot's aroma. "Any of you guys know a DJ Talk It Up?" Chappie asked with the phone at her ear. "From Rock The Net? *Pardon*?" She was speaking to the caller. Then, to her houseguests again: "Rock *Da* Net."

"No," Terry said.

"*Fuck*, no," said Nomad, his gentlemanly demeanor over and done.

"He wants to talk to *you*." Chappie held the phone toward Ariel.

"Me? No, I don't want to talk to anyone."

"She doesn't want to talk to anyone," Chappie told DJ Talk It Up. "That's right. Okay, I'll let them know. Uh huh. Listen, how did you get this number?" Evidently that question was not to be answered, because Chappie put the cell down and said, "I guess they've found you. Mr. Allen told me they might. Anyway, DJ says to tell you he does a podcast from Los Angeles. He says to check out his website. Rock Da Net." She couldn't hold back a grin. "Have you ever heard anything so fucking lame?"

"Got that right," Nomad said, aiming his spoon in what he hoped was the vicinity of his mouth.

"Says he'll be at sound check today and would like to do an interview. Get ready for it. That place is going to be crawling with media. But that's what you want, right?"

No one replied. Because Nomad was the emperor, sometimes his thoughts exactly mirrored those of his subjects, and that was now the case. He was thinking, as they all were, that success—if it meant acceptance, or fame, or money, or revenge on those who looked down on you as if you'd just crawled out of a gutter—was not worth the death and injury of two bandmates. All those things would be great, the dream of every working band, but this price tag was way too steep.

"What I want," said Berke, and she let that hang for a few seconds before she finished it, "is to get this over with." She turned her haggard face toward her mother. "The boxes."

Chappie left the kitchen and came back with an envelope. She put it down on the table next to Berke's coffee cup. Written in block letters on the front was *Berke—Open The Boxes First*. The word *First* was underlined.

"They're waiting for you," Chappie said, her voice betraying no emotion.

Berke took the envelope. She stood up and headed for the back door. She was wearing her running shoes without socks. When she realized nobody was following, she said with forced and farcical cheer, "Come on! Let's make it a party!"

It was a small free-standing garage whose contents, Berke knew, had gradually choked off enough room for a car. When Chappie unlatched the door and pulled it open, the odor that rolled out was not of old oil and grease but instead of old library stacks. Sunlight had already revealed the dozens of boxes, the precariously-leaning metal shelves jammed full of books and the layers of newspapers and magazines that stood everywhere, but Chappie switched on an overhead light to complete the illumination.

Berke looked around, with her mother at her side and her bandmates behind her. Floyd fucking Fisk had really laid his crap heavy in this hole, she thought. It was a paradise for cockroaches and silverfish, probably for mice too. That smell...she remembered that sickeningly-sweet smell of decaying bindings and newsprint from Floyd fucking Fisk's downtown store, Second Chance Books. It had been there since before she was born; he'd bought it from the retiring owner who'd had it like since Abraham Lincoln stopped shaving.

This shit was so fucked-up. She looked high and low, at all the murder of trees. An open box to her left invited a glance. It was full of moldering magazines in plastic bags. The covers of the ones she could see were adorned with spaceships and weird alien-looking faces and had the titles *Galaxy, Worlds Of If, Analog* and *Astounding Science Fiction*. That figured, she thought. Floyd fucking Fisk probably didn't even know what really good sci-fi was, like Star Trek and Star Wars. In other boxes and on other shelves she saw titles like *Argosy*, *Esquire*, *Ellery Queen* and *Alfred Hitchcock*. And who the *fuck* ever needed so many sets of encyclopedias? They were bound up with cords and looked like weapons of mass destruction. And then there was the *ancient* stuff in here, the books that appeared to be bound from slabs of wood or crinkly cowhide. There had to be a book of dirty jokes written by Nero around somewhere: *The One-Handed Fiddler and 101 More, Or: Pluck It Baby*!

But this was no fucking joke in here, this was a serious place. It was where the family car had alternated with Berke's early—"junior", the ad had called it—drumkit. It was where she busted some sticks and hammered some heads. It was where she'd been, many times, when the police car pulled up and the cop who got to know the Fisk family said if the girl just didn't play so late at *night*, they could work this out with the neighbors. It was the bass beat that was coming through the closed garage door, so maybe they could muffle it with a few pillows?

Sweet sound of rolling thunder, crashing above the mediocre sea of the whitebread world. Dad would have understood. Dad would have said, *Pump up the volume, kid, and don't ever let it get so quiet that you have to hear yourself think*.

"There they are." Chappie motioned toward three large cardboard boxes lying side-by-side-by-side on the floor toward the back of the garage. Berke saw that the one on the left bore the black marker numeral 1, the middle 2 and the one on the right 3. They were sealed with regular white masking tape, but it wouldn't be any kind of job ripping them open.

"Man, this is a lot of books," Terry said, as he turned in a circle between Ariel and Nomad. "Wonder if there are any old keyboard manuals in here. Would you know?" he asked Chappie.

"I wouldn't. This is special stuff that Floyd wanted to keep. You should see the backroom at the bookstore."

"Did he make a good living?" Nomad asked. "Just selling old books?"

"He got orders from everywhere once he started selling on eBay. We weren't getting rich, but he was able to pay off the house."

There was an abrupt tearing noise as Berke stripped the tape off the top seam of Box Number 1.

"You got it?" Nomad asked.

She didn't answer. She stripped the tape off the edges and pulled the box open.

Chappie stepped forward to see, because she had no idea what Floyd had left their girl.

Berke didn't know what she was looking at. That pungence of old newsprint drifted up into her face, and she thought if she blew her nose the snot would be yellow. Whatever they were—papers of some kind—they were protected in the plastic bags and backed with cardboard. She brought the first of them out into the light.

It had a strange fold. She removed it from its plastic, and a few tiny pieces of paper spun out around her. Almost dust, but not quite.

There was a gray field of newsprint and a headline *The High Cost Of Music and Love: Where's The Money From Monterey?*

There was a black-and-white photograph of John Lennon, unmistakably John Lennon in specs just like Terry's, dressed as a British soldier with a webbing on his helmet, his eyes narrowed against the glare of the sun, his lips pursed in either surprise or the beginning of a whistle.

Above the photograph there was a logo that read *Rolling Stone*. And beside it was the date: November 9, 1967.

She handed it to Terry, who had also come forward to see. She took the next paper from its plastic. This *Rolling Stone* bore a cover photograph of Tina Turner—it said this young woman was Tina Turner, right there in the caption—caught in a blurred moment of dramatic intensity on stage, and there was a story with the headline *Bob Dylan Alive In Nashville: Work Starts On New LP*. The date was November 23, 1967.

"My God," said Terry in a stunned voice, as he peered into the box of treasures. "It's a mint set. The golden age of *Rolling Stone*."

The third issue that Berke brought up had a photograph of a group of about thirty or so people in all manner of clothes sitting on a series of steps in front of a building. She spotted the Fab Four—Paul McCartney was so *young*—among them. The headline was *New Thing For Beatles: Magical Mystery Tour*. The date was December 14, 1967.

"Mint," Terry said again. He shook his head in awe. But for the aging of the paper itself, each *Rolling Stone* looked to be right off the press.

Berke continued to bring them up from the darkness of the box, into the light. She looked at the papers, at the covers and at some of the pages within, and then she passed them back for her friends to see. A lost age revealed itself to her. It was captured in gritty and startling black-and-white pictures with colored borders. It was held in headlines like *The Los Angeles Scene* and *American Revolution* 1969 and *Forty Pages Full Of Dope, Sex and Cheap Thrills*. It was offered up from the past by the announcements that Cream had broken up, that the Rolling Stones were on the verge of the great comeback of their career, that Johnny Cash was playing a concert at San Quentin, that Janis Joplin might be the Judy Garland of Rock, that Fillmore West was closing, that Paul Is Not Dead, that the Underground Press of America was alive and well, that Chicago's Conspiracy Eight was the Trial Of The New Culture, that contained in these pages was All The News That Fits, and that this publication would steadfastly present its Continuing Coverage Of The Apocalypse in this turbulent summer of 1970.

The second box held more, all pristine, all protected in plastic. In the third box, the front covers became full color and the paper quality slicker. As Chappie returned to the house to get some more coffee, Terry encouraged Berke to keep going to the bottom. It took Berke a while to get to the last paper, which was dated April 29, 1982, and had on its cover the black-and-white photo of a very sad-looking dark-eyed, dark-haired man whom the caption identified as John Belushi.

"An interview with Sun Ra," Terry said, carefully holding one of the early papers open. The images and typeface bloomed large in his specs. He sounded like he might be about to faint from ecstacy. "Oh my *God*."

Nomad was regarding a cover picture of Elvis Presley decked out in black leather. Ariel had just turned a few pages in the *Stone* she was holding and abruptly stopped. On the page before her was the wild, ink-spattered drawing of a distorted, one-eyed, American-flag-draped figure whose mouth was stretched impossibly wide, and from that cavernous drooling hole spurted forth a vomit of spiky missiles and speeding jet airplanes. The artist had signed a name in crazed and crooked letters at the bottom of the art, and that name was *Steadman*.

She closed the paper. It was a little too disturbing.

"Three hundred and forty five issues, give or take," Terry said when he'd recovered himself. Most of them had been replaced in their plastic and returned to the boxes, though not in order this time.

A few of the older papers were still lying about. "You're gonna need another U-Haul."

"Yeah." Berke nodded. "I guess I am." Her mind was reeling from the faces and names these boxes had yielded up to her: Van Morrison, Jeff Beck, Frank Zappa, Marvin Gaye, the Jefferson Airplane, Joe Cocker, The Grateful Dead, David Bowie, Cat Stevens, Joan Baez, MC5, the Doors, Steely Dan, Brian Wilson, James Taylor, Steve Winwood, Elton John, Pete Townsend and Roger Daltry and Keith Moon and John Paul Jones and...it just went on and on.

Ariel picked up another issue, because on the cover she recognized the face of a very young Joni Mitchell, whom she'd liked to listen to as a teenager in the solace of her room and who actually had influenced her own playing and writing. The date was May 17, 1969. Joni Mitchell looked out at the viewer with a hint of anger in her eyes, as if adamant that her private space not be invaded. In purple hippie-type letters was the headline *The Swan Song of Folk Music.*

"The letter." Chappie had returned with her Eagles cup. "Aren't you going to read the letter?"

"Oh. Yeah, I am." Berke picked up the envelope from atop a set of encyclopedias where she'd put it aside. As she tore it open—carefully, so as not to damage the letter—she realized her fingerprints were being left upon it in forty-year-old ink. Chappie stepped back to give her privacy, and the others quietly continued their inspection of the long-dead counterculture, and from the two-page letter that was probably printed out on the computer in the den, Berke heard the voice of her stepfather.

Dear Berke, I hope you enjoy these. I found them years ago in a warehouse in San Francisco, and I've been saving them for you. I guess I'm dead now. Ha ha.

I didn't really have a premonition of when it would happen. I just had a feeling that my time was running out. Through the hourglass, like on that soap opera your Mom watches. My hourglass was getting empty.

I'm no musician or expert on music, and I can't say that I care much for the modern stuff. (When I say 'stuff', I don't mean to be disrespectful :) I was a pretty conservative young man, everything Rah Rah and Apple Pie. I voted for Nixon. You can imagine.

But I did know what the Rolling Stone is. I read some of these from cover to cover, and they made me realize how proud I am of you. I know you didn't want me around very much, or to come to your shows, and I understand that, but I hope that now you'll give me a chance to speak.

You can look at these and see what you're a part of. This world you have chosen to live in. I guess you chose it, but maybe it chose you???? I think you should know, if you don't already, that you're a citizen of a blessed and magic world, though I'm sure sometimes blessings can seem like curses, and there's not much magic to be found in a dingy old motel room. (Your mom has clued in me on The Road. At least as much as a stodge like me can handle :)

I remember when we went to the Battle of The Bands in August of 1996. It was at the auditorium.

Oh yeah, Berke thought. She remembered it was something she'd decided to forget. Her mom and Floyd Fisk had just met and he was trying to get to know her.

I remember you were watching one of those bands and the drummer was going strong, and I saw you start playing along with him on your knees, just using your thumbs, and your foot was tapping the bass. He really tore it up (at least I thought he did) and when I asked you what you thought of him you looked me right in the eyes and you said, "He was good, but I can do better."

You said it so positively, from that moment on I believed you.

I've seen you on those YouTube videos. You were right. But I never doubted you.

I wish you could have been my real daughter. Then again, I couldn't have given you the talent that your Dad gave you, but I'd like to think that I gave you something.

So...these papers in the boxes.

If you ever doubt what your place is in your profession, or if you ever doubt what changes for the better music can make in this world, open these and start reading. Oh yeah, there's the sex and drugs and rock and roll part of it, but I mean the soul of it.

I believe that at its best music exists to give a voice to people who sometimes can't speak on their own. I believe it helps weak people find their strength, and frightened people find their courage. I believe it helps people understand with their hearts what their minds can't comprehend. I think it may be the truest link to a higher power, if you believe in that. (And I know you don't, but I had to get that last one in ;)

Never, ever doubt that you have an important place in this world. Look at these papers and see who came before you, and then think about who came before them, and on back to the hornpipe players and the troubadours and the poor man who played a Jew's harp in a cold house for the pleasure of his family.

This may be hard to think about, but someday someone is going to watch you playing, either at one of your shows or on your videos, and they'll say 'She was good, but I can do better'. And that's how your blessed and magic world works.

Please take care of yourself and your Mom. She's the most fun woman in the world.

Love, Floyd.

Berke read again the final five paragraphs. Then she returned the pages to the envelope, and she sat down on a box full of dead men's ideas and turned her face toward the wall, and she sat there so long without moving that her mother asked her if she was okay.

"Yeah," Berke answered, her voice very soft and very distant. "Okay."

It had occurred to her, sitting in this garage she'd not visited for many years, that pain had a way of pushing everything else out of a person. It had a way of owning you, and you didn't even know you were being owned. She felt she had a long road ahead of her, to escape from that particular master, and maybe she never would—not completely—but it seemed to her that to recognize how it had enslaved you day-in and day-out for so many years was a first step in breaking the chain.

"Ariel," Berke said, because sitting here holding the letter in her hand and surrounded by all these old decaying books and magazines that were once so new she'd had a sudden clear and pressing thought.

"What is it?" Ariel asked.

"Our song." Berke turned around to face her bandmates and her mother. Berke's eyes were red, but she was a big girl, a tough girl, a strong girl, and she was not going to cry today. "My part for our song," she said, and she drew it up from memory: "*Try and try, grow and thrive*," she recited. She decided to alter one word. "*Because no one here gets out alive*."

"Weird," said Terry, and Berke thought that was exactly how Mike would've expressed it.

"Have I missed anything?"

They all turned to see Truitt Allen, wearing a white polo shirt and gray slacks, standing in the open doorway. Before anyone could answer, True took stock of Nomad's eye. "Ouch," he said. "That even hurts *me*."

"Where've *you* been?" Nomad asked.

"Why? Did you miss me?" True was carrying a leather satchel that held his laptop.

"Like salt misses pepper in vanilla ice cream," Nomad told him. He still felt dazed and his eye was throbbing. "If I even *liked* ice cream."

"I think you need to go back to bed for a few days," True said. "But not starting today." His voice had gotten serious, and he looked from one bandmember to another. "Come on, let's go inside and I'll tell you how you music stars are going to handle this..." He glanced again at Nomad. "*Gig*."

TWENTY-THREE.

"I can tell you more about him now." True was eating a bowl of vegetarian stew and having a glass of iced tea at the kitchen table. Joining him at lunch were Terry and Ariel, while Nomad, Berke and Chappie stood at various points in the kitchen. "His name and address on the driver's license checked out, and his parents were notified yesterday evening. The information was released to the press while I was there, so it'll probably be on the next news cycle." By *there*, he meant the FBI field office on the corner of Aero Drive and Ruffin Road. He'd spent the morning planning security for the 'gig' tonight and smoothing everything out with the San Diego police, at the same time keeping a call in for details from the FBI and the police in Tucson.

"I told you already he was nineteen and from California." True spent a few seconds to wipe his mouth with a red-checked napkin. "His name is Connor Addison. He's from a nice middle-class neighborhood in Oceanside. From what we've learned, Connor took his father's car on Wednesday afternoon, hit the San Diego Freeway using the dad's credit card for a fillup, and headed to Stone Church. Where he got the pistol from, no one knows."

"It was a .25, right?" Terry asked.

"Yeah, a .25 Beretta Jetfire. You've had experience?"

"I just figured, from the sound. My dad's a pistol collector. He took me to the range a few times."

"Small gun," True said, speaking to all of them again. "Easily concealed." He didn't say that when he'd heard the pistol fire at Stone

Church he thought it had been at least a .38, due to the sound being amplified by the microphone Nomad had knocked over. "Anyway, Connor lives at home with his parents. He doesn't have a car of his own. He's gotten into some trouble with meth and cocaine, flunked out of community college, lost a couple of jobs, wrecked his car last year...kind of a mess."

"He was copycatting Jeremy Pett, wasn't he?" Chappie asked. "That's what Nancy Grace said last night."

"Maybe." True took a sip of iced tea, which was very cold and very minty. It had been released to the press right after the incident that the shooter was *not* Jeremy Pett, but Addison's name hadn't been put out there for the media until the details were taken care of. "He's not talking. They can't get him to utter a word."

"He's a nut," Nomad said. "They ought to go ahead and throw him in the nuthouse." He was a nut with a hard fucking head, though.

"Addison has an interesting story." True continued to eat his stew, taking small spoonfuls and then some of the wheat bread that had been offered with his lunch. The agents outside, God bless 'em, would have to make do with trips to the nearest fast food window. "His family was in the news there in Oceanside in 2003. One evening his parents went out and left him at home to watch his eight-year-old sister. Addison evidently got pissed, called some friends over to do drugs, and he told the little sister to go out and ride her bike. She did, and that was the last anybody saw of her until her bones were found in a trashbag in the marsh just off Jefferson Street, five months later." He took another drink of tea, to wash down the bread. "Some material in the bag was traced to a laundry, and they got a Russian immigrant who lived maybe five miles from Addison's house. This individual's great pleasure in life was driving through neighborhoods searching for little girls to kidnap, rape and murder, which he had enjoyed doing in Portland and in Sacramento. And oh boy, did he enjoy *talking* about it to the Oceanside cops. Just painted a very beautiful picture of it, which wound up in some of the sleazier news rags." True decided he'd had enough lunch, because he'd seen the digitized articles the field office guys had pulled up for him.

"So what does this have to do with a scumbag druggie nut trying to kill Ariel?" Nomad asked. "And where's Jeremy Pett?"

Good questions, True thought. He'd been going over both of them at the field office, in a conference call connection with the Tucson office, the Tucson police, the San Diego badges, the city attorneys and, it seemed, everybody else with any splinter of a stake in this. He'd even gotten a call from Austin about an hour ago, and that brought him to his next statement.

"Hold onto your questions," he said. "Roger Chester called me. You're headlining at the Casbah tonight."

"Oh whoopie whoopie yay yay!" Nomad was nearly back to his bristling, snarly self. "Where's that fucking Jeremy Pett, is what I want to know!"

"Just listen for a minute." True couldn't begin to tell John Charles what he'd been going through with the Casbah management to meet the security standards. One big problem was that, being out by the airport, the area was full of parking decks. There were a couple of them right across the street, and he was going to have to put men on every level. "*After* the Casbah is what I'm talking about now. *Tomorrow* night. The tickets have sold out at the Cobra Club, and you're headlining there too, by the way. They're wanting you to headline again on Sunday night. Then, on Monday night, you're booked into...wait, let me get this." He reached for his wallet, a slimline, and brought out the piece of paper with the FBI seal at the top that he'd used to write down The Five's new schedule. "Okay. You're booked into the Sound Machine on Santa Monica Boulevard on Monday night. Headlining with—I cannot believe I'm saying this—Sack Of Buttholes." True looked at Ariel. "Is that for real or did I get set up?"

"It's for real," she told him. The SOBs were also out of Austin and were repped by the Roger Chester Agency.

"Jeez," True said. "Alright, then. Pardon this paper, I'll get all the info to my PDA. Now...on Tuesday night, you're playing at Magic Monty's in Anaheim. Chester thinks you'll sell out of merchandise tonight, so he's making direct shipments to Hollywood and Anaheim. You still with me?" He looked up at his charges.

"This is crazy," Chappie said, her eyes wide. "Are you *wanting* them to get killed?"

"Mom," Berke cautioned. "It's our job, okay?"

"You don't need to be killed for it! Christ Almighty! Get back to Austin and wait until they catch him!"

"Go ahead," Berke said to True. "What else?"

"Then you're back to the regular schedule: the Red Door in Phoenix on the 8th; the next night Staind Glass in Albuquerque; on the 15th the Lizard Lounge in Dallas; and on the 16th back in Austin at the Vista Futura." True had realized, after speaking with Roger Chester, that he was facing a massive endeavor in scouting out all these locations and setting up security, much less keeping the mobile teams rolling. City lawyers were not so keen on putting their citizens at risk, the police departments didn't want to feel they were being pushed around by the FBI, and for the first time today True had heard from the Tucson office the mention of all the money that was sinking into this operation. Though True was the big dog, he was not the only big dog and there were large hands on the leashes. Also today, the large hand on the leash in Tucson had pointed out that, while reports were coming in of Jeremy Pett being sighted in a dozen states including Alaska and Florida, if Pett had any sense of survival he would have headed straight to Mexico while he was so close to the border. Had he made it in soon after his description had gone public? Had he already gone *before*? The pickup truck's tag hadn't been seen on any of the cameras at the border crossings, but a man who wanted to get through could walk it.

Careful with this one, Truitt, the warning had been delivered. *This could really blow up in your face.*

This road managing job was hard work. He was a detail guy, sure, but planning the gas stops and the meal stops and where the band was going to stay in all those cities, and then putting together the security both outside and inside the clubs and clearing his operation with the local police and mobilizing agents from different field offices…it was tougher than he'd expected.

He wouldn't be doing this, if he wasn't—

"How about Pett's family?" Nomad asked, breaking into True's thoughts. "His mother and father. Have you checked his house?"

"The first day," True answered. "We're watching the house and we got their okay to set up a tap and an intercept. They haven't heard from their son since the accident in Houston. He briefly visited them before he went back to Iraq. I'll tell you that Mr. Pett is also a veteran Marine, of the hard-bitten old school, who I am told seems to think his son lacked the toughness to make it a career. Pett's mother, I also am told, is hardly a presence in the house. The agent who went there described her as 'trying to make herself invisible'."

"I think he's probably gone to Mexico." Terry finished his stew and put the spoon aside. "I think he's done what he wanted to do, and he's gone."

"You don't know that!" Chappie said. "I think it's *insane*, you putting yourself out there like—" The Clash played their little snippet of 'London Calling' again, and Chappie looked at another number she didn't know on her cellphone screen. "Sitting ducks," she finished, before she answered. "Hello? Oh, Jesus. Wait a minute." She asked the gathering if anyone wanted to talk to the *National Star*.

"Another thing," True said when Chappie had refused the call. "At your sound check this afternoon—in about ninety minutes from now—there are going to be all sorts of media folks present. Roger Chester clued me in that *People* magazine is sending a reporter and photographer. The local news will be there. Maybe some other magazines and who knows who else."

"DJ Talk It Up will be there," Nomad said. "Trying to get a little piece of Ariel."

"*Who*?"

"Don't mind John," Ariel advised. "It's a guy with a podcast. He called this morning."

"Nobody gets past *me*." True's blue eyes were burning bright. "That's what I want you to know. I see all credentials and talk to everybody who wants a piece of whomever. Right?"

"You're the road manager," Berke said.

"And I thought *I* used to be fucking crazy," Chappie muttered into her coffee cup.

True grunted but said nothing more. All this talk about *crazy* and *insane*.

He had decided not to tell them the rest of it, either about Connor Addison or the guy with the .22 rifle who'd been captured making his torturous climb up Hell Mountain. No, best not to tell them. He didn't want anybody to get—what was the term Berke had used?—'creeped out'.

"I'm going to take a nap for an hour," True said as he stood up. He took his bowl and glass to the sink, and he realized he was avoiding eye contact with everyone. Then he went directly to the couch in the den, where he had set up his 'command center' on the desk next to the computer and wireless cable modem that Floyd Fisk had used.

When the Scumbucket pulled up to the Casbah just before three o'clock with True at the wheel, it was clear the circus had come to town. Satellite trucks bearing TV news logos were nearly blocking Kettner Avenue, and the police were on hand to try to keep everybody moving. The Casbah's crew helped with unloading the gear. The music room was small—intimate, they would say—and only held about a hundred and thirty or so patrons, but there were at least forty news media people milling around waiting for The Five. The ceiling was low and the stage was backed with a wall of what appeared to True to be black leather seat cushions. He introduced himself to the owner and the manager and talked to them for a few minutes, and then as the equipment was set up on stage True put himself between the band and the media hounds and tried to maintain some order.

Ariel was amazed at this turnout, at the shouting for attention and the glare of the camera lights that followed her as she made her way across the room. Berke didn't look right or left. Terry ducked his head down, suddenly a lot shyer in a spotlight than he'd ever thought he would be. Nomad just laughed; here were all these cameras grabbing his image for national exposure, and instead of a young long-haired, street-tough Elvis he looked like the loser in a four-man cage fight.

The Casbah's owner, a bearded man named Tim Mays, got up on stage and told the assembly that they were welcome to do their interviews for one hour—starting *now*—but after that they had to clear out so the checks could be done and everything prepped for the show tonight.

True was true to his word and started asking to see credentials—business cards, personal identification, whatever—of people lining up for interviews, which seemed to piss some of them off but he couldn't care less about that; the way he blocked the path to the table where The Five had parked themselves said he was the big dog in this room, and if anybody didn't like it they might as well pack up their digital capture gear into their black bags—which had to be searched, for the sake of security—and move their asses on out da doah.

The *People* magazine team, a young Asian-American woman wearing pink eyeglasses and a lanky guy with curly brown hair who carried his expensive Nikon like it was a five-dollar basketball, came on in and set up to do their interview. *How does it feel to suddenly be so successful? Now, how long have you guys been together? John, what did you think about when you made that jump? Oh...yeah... you go by the name Nomad, right? Do you guys have any idea how you got on Jeremy Pett's radar? What about Connor Addison? Tell me a little bit about yourselves, just a brief bio. What's your plan after this tour is over?*

Everybody looked to Nomad for the answer to that one. He said, "We're working on it."

"Good luck," said the *People* reporter, after the pictures had been taken of The Five on stage against the black cushion background, their faces pressed together as if they were one single entity, their right hands extended, palms out, each five fingers strong. No smiling, exude confidence and toughness, and let your shiner and the fading scratches on your cheek speak to every poor man's son.

"Ariel? Hi, there."

The voice caught her as she was returning to her seat at the table and her bandmates were in their own conversations with other reporters. A hand touched her elbow. She looked to her left, at a smiling, heavy-set young man wearing a white ball cap with DJ on the front in gold glitter.

"How ya doin'? Okay if I set up and get a couple'a questions in? Your manager passed me through, I'm clean." His smile never quit. His wide shoulders strained against a white nylon jacket that was really a couple of sizes too small; he stood about five feet seven and had big front teeth. The cap was pushed down low and tight on his head, with a huge curved bill. His hair was a sandy color on the sides and his deepset eyes were light brown. He had a bulbous nose that could round a corner before his Pumas did. "Just be a minute," he told her. He was already setting up a tripod for a video camera next to the table. A black camera bag lay at his sneakered feet. "Go ahead, siddown." Somebody else behind him told him to hurry up, and he shot a dark glance at the guy and said, "We're all pros here, right? You shoulda got here *early*." Then he switched his smile back on for Ariel, and he reached in to help her with her chair.

"DJ Talk It Up," he said when Ariel was sitting. "A.K.A. Dominic Jankowski, but don't let that get out. Pleased to meet 'cha." He offered his hand and she shook it; he was wearing a ring on every finger. "Lemme get this thing ready, we'll be off and runnin'." He was attaching the camera to the tripod, which had seen heavy use and suffered some mishaps. One of the banged-up legs looked to be secured by a thick winding of duct tape. "I didn't mean to cause nobody no worry when I made that call," he explained as he worked. "I just believe in goin' for what you want. *Got* to, all this competition out here. You know what I mean."

"Yeah, I guess," she said.

"You are a *talented* person," he said, throwing another smile at her. "I saw your videos. Got a fan-fuckin'-*tastic* one of you on YouTube doin' the snake song. You wrote that?"

"I did."

"I like what that says. Very beautiful. Okay, we're ready." The camera was positioned on her face. "Just...lemme...get this little *fuck* turned on." The switch was fighting his finger.

Ariel shifted in her seat. The next two people behind him were trying to get her attention, waving cameras at her. "Can I ask what this is for?"

"My website, Rock Da Net Dot Com. Didn't you check it out?" He didn't wait for an answer. "It's where DJ Talk It Up *lives*, my lady. Where he fries the night wires, talkin' it up. There ya go." The red light came on. "In business."

"Talking up exactly what?"

"Ariel!" DJ Talk It Up spoke to her as if they were dear friends who hadn't seen each other in years. "Talkin' about *you*. And your band. And every other band I think is shootin' straight for the stars. We're recordin' now, this'll be for my Sunday night show." He came around to peer into the lens over her shoulder, his cheek next to hers. She thought he was wearing a cologne that smelled like Band-Aids. "DJ Talk It Up on da Sunday *night*, yo yo yo!" He slung the fozzie finger. "We're down here in San Diego at da Casbah, talkin' to Ariel Collier, she be da *dream* girl of Da Five, check 'em out on this clip right here." He straightened up and adjusted his cap. "I'll edit the clip in, you'll like it. You from up Boston way?"

"Manchester."

"Philly," he said, with a heart thump that went into a peace sign.

"Detroit," said Nomad, who suddenly came up beside the DJ. "Can whip Philly's ass."

"Hey, my *man*!" DJ Talk It Up gave a crooked grin and balled up his fist to bump knuckles, but he only punched air. "Mr. Nomad, lookin' mean!" He dropped his ghetto-by-way-of-bad-acting-lessons accent. "We're recording here, see the light?"

"Rock Da Net Dot Com," Ariel said, lifting her eyebrows.

"Excuse me, I'm with the Globe magazine." A bearded man in a dark blue coat and open-necked shirt leaned in, a camera ready. His voice was a little testy. "Do I have to make an appointment to ask a few simple questions, or should—"

"Don't push me!" DJ Talk It Up spun on him with a ferocity that even made Nomad step back. "I'm standin' here, don't push me!"

"I'm a *professional*, don't you raise your—"

"Get your motherfuckin' ass to the back of the line, dickweed! I've been waitin' here for hours!"

"What the *hell* is this about?" True shouldered the Globe reporter, or freelancer or whatever he was, to one side. "Anybody causes any trouble in here, they're going out. Are you causing trouble?" He directed this question to the Globe man.

"Sir, I am waiting my turn. That is all. This individual is wasting the hour that we professionals have been given to—"

"Bite my dick," said DJ Talk It Up.

The upshot of all this was that the Globe spun toward the door, True walked away rubbing his temples because he had a ferocious headache, and after the crimson heat receded from DJ Talk It Up's face he said this video would go over great on the website, his fans would go crazier than shithouse rats.

The interview went on for about seven more minutes, during which Nomad learned that DJ Talk It Up recorded the podcast in his aunt's basement in L.A., where he was staying until his new crib in Westwood was redecorated. DJ Talk It Up said he'd just put the finishing touch on track number finito for his new CD, his own style of music he called grindhop, and both Dizzy D at Walkaround Records and Jasper Jack at Mutha's Angry Boy were interested, and he'd used lots of samples from bands like Insane Clown Posse to make his statement. Maybe Ariel and Nomad would like copies? He could bring them to the Cobra Club tomorrow night.

"I don't really have a lot of time to—" Nomad began, but Ariel said, "Sure, I'll listen to your music."

DJ Talk It Up smiled. "Okay," he replied. "Yeah. Great. I'll get it, like, cleaned up." He stood silently for a few seconds, staring at her. Nomad thought the dude was zoning out. Or maybe he was *in love*. Then the DJ's smile widened and he said, "I guess that does it." He turned off the camera. "Hey," he said before either of them could turn to the next person waiting. "Ariel, can I ask a big favor? I might have some more questions for you. Could you—and you might say no, and I'd understand—work me a backstage pass? Since I'm coming anyway. I could shoot some more video." His grin showed the big front teeth. "Swear to God I won't bring my fucking Uzi."

"No can do," Nomad said. "And you know, that's not very funny."

DJ Talk It Up smiled broadly at Nomad, but his eyes were vacant. "Sorry, man," he amended. "Us Philly guys, we don't got no class."

"I can get you a pre-show pass," Ariel told him, as Nomad looked on in astonishment. "You can come back before our set. Will that do?"

"Like honey on money," he answered, which Nomad thought must've been something this guy had heard in a '70s black exploitation flick, something like *Super Fly Goes To Hell Up In Harlem*.

When DJ Talk It Up had packed his camera and taken his tripod and gone, Nomad asked Ariel if she had lost her mind today, if she didn't smell the whiff of bozo like he did, and if they wanted a loser like that anywhere *near* the Cobra Club, much less backstage.

"Pre-show won't hurt," she said, and her voice was firm. "Everybody deserves a chance."

Nomad didn't reply, but he knew the City of Angels. It made people want things before they'd earned them. And anyway, *deserve* was not a word in his dictionary.

TWENTY-FOUR.

The hour passed and the sound check went on. They returned to Chappie's, rested as True went into the den and hit his cellphone making sure all the last-minute security details were in place, they ate the dinner Chappie made for them, whoever wanted to change clothes and shower did so, and then they headed back to the Casbah. The place was overflowing. First up were the Mindfockers, six guys from the San Francisco area who delivered heavy-guitar distorto-and-vibrato-drenched head-banging rock, and after the Mindfockers' double encores the Mad Lads got up there in front of the black leather seat cushions and the big clunky air-conditioner that looked like it was about to fall out of the wall and those four dudes laid down some serious vibe with funky guitars and a bright red Elka X-705 combo organ that made Terry salivate. The Mad Lads' lead singer opened a music case, brought out an accordion and knocked the house down with a rollicking Cajun-peppered version of 'In The Midnight Hour'.

It was half past the midnight hour before The Five took the stage. They started the gig with 'Bedlam A-Go-Go', slowed to its original tempo. By the middle of the show, when Berke did her drum solo and Terry came in on the gutsy growling Hammond to trade back and forth with her, they were a smooth and powerful engine of sonic flight, up in the orbit of the spinning spheres, way up where the music looked to the mind of the player like geometric shapes constantly changing themselves against the pure black of space, collapsing inward and reforming like a multitude of kaleidoscopes or, the best that Nomad could describe this sensation of being one with the music, as existing for a short time within a Kenner Spirograph drawing set, where you put the tip of your colored pen in a series of interlocked wheels placed on a piece of paper, and when your talent and discipline took you where you were supposed to be—with guitar, or vocals, or drums, or keyboard—again and again and again, an intricate design began to appear that was a perfect and stunning combination of both mathematics and art. After going that far into the dream, the applause and appreciation of the audience was like a call to let go and return to earth, because no one could stay at that height very long, and wanting to get up there once more was part of the drug called creativity.

They were back at Chappie's house around three-thirty, drained of energy but satisfied—like good sex—after two encores and a version of 'Blackout of Gretely' that had nearly lifted the roof off the Casbah. Chappie had some cold cans of beers on hand, and passed them around as everyone sprawled, half-dead, in the living room. Terry was sitting on the sofa between Ariel and Berke, with Chappie in a wicker chair and Nomad lying on his back on the gold-colored carpet. True sat in a green chair and gratefully accepted a beer; the night had passed with no incidents, and all the agents who'd put their lives on the line for him and The Five were by now at home with their families. Except, of course, the ones in the Yukons on sentry duty out front.

He drank his beer and listened to them talk. They were tired, sure, but they were still 'up', as they would call it. Terry was fretting about an intro he thought he'd flubbed, and Nomad told him to forget about it. Then Nomad sat up, turned his lasers on Berke and said he thought some of the songs were still running fast, and she said he was wrong, the beat was right in the pocket. He faced her down for a few seconds, and then they both shrugged and returned to their beers and that was the end of it but the point was delivered for Berke to rethink her timing. The small talk came back up, they laughed at the recollection of the Mad Lads' lead singer going buck wild with his accordion, and suddenly Chappie got to her feet and asked, "Anybody want a nightcap? Something a little stronger than beer?"

"Mom," Berke said, "don't get started on that so late."

"What's *late*? Jesus, I hardly ever see you and you're here two nights and leaving again at...what?...ten in the morning?"

"We can stay until eleven," True said.

"Okay, eleven then! You! Mr. Secret Agent Man. You want a Jack and Coke?"

"Um...well..."

"Coca-*Cola*," she told him, in case he was that much of a stranger to the human race.

"I'll take one," Terry said.

"What the hell," Berke said. She shrugged and leaned back, throwing her sneakered feet up on the coffee table and in the process kicking some magazines off to the floor. "Sign me up."

"That's my girl. Anybody else?"

True looked at the others in the room. They were so young. He had the sudden feeling that he was very far from home, and after this was over all of him might not *want* to go home. It had been, to him, an amazing night. Maybe most of it had been senseless noise and barely-controlled chaos, but still...all that youth, and passion, and life under one roof...it was eye-opening, is what it was. In his day, it would have been 'consciousness-expanding'. If you believed in that.

"I'll take a little drink in a shotglass, if you have one," True decided.

"Do *I* have a shotglass?" Chappie grinned at him. "What color, and from which bar?"

"*Mom*," Berke said. "Stop fucking around."

"You ought to help your mother," True told her when Chappie had gone to the kitchen. "With the drinks, I mean." He glanced at her well-worn sneakers. "And you probably ought to take your feet off the table."

"Oh my God!" Berke spoke with breathless mock surprise. Her eyes had widened with pretend shock. "Guys, our road manager has become our barracks sergeant! Yeah, I knew that was coming. It doesn't bother my mom, why should it bother you?" She did recall, however, that it had bothered Floyd.

"It's not ladylike," True said.

Countdown to blastoff, Nomad thought. Five...four...three... two...

"Go help your mother," True said, and this time his voice carried the hard stamp of official business. "She needs you."

One, the loneliest number, never fell.

Berke's face seemed frozen, her mouth partly open and her black eyes as shiny as new glass. She slowly blinked, she said, "Okay," with a quiet that nearly blew her bandmates' minds, and then she got up and left the room.

"'Danger' is your middle name, huh?" Nomad asked True.

"My middle name is Elmer," he said, as he retrieved the magazines from the floor and put them in a neat stack back where they were, and Nomad, Ariel and Terry thought that name sounded just fine.

True finished his beer. The drinks were served from a wooden tray painted watermelon green. True's shotglass was full to the brim and had a logo that said it was from the Funky Pirate on Bourbon Street in New Orleans. He took half of it down and did not fail to note that Chappie had opened a fresh bottle of Jack Daniels and it was on the coffee table where her daughter's feet used to be. Berke returned to her place on the sofa with her drink, and nary a hiss was hissed nor a curse unfurled like a battleflag.

But those fucking drums would sure take a beating tomorrow night, Nomad thought as he settled in with his potion. Or...maybe not.

True came to the bottom of his glass. He was still thinking about the Casbah, and how the audience—a decent audience, an appreciative audience, not like that mob at Stone Church—had responded to The Five's music. This was a different world. He couldn't imagine how courageous a person would have to be, to get up for the first time on stage in front of strangers who could cut your dream to pieces. Chappie was offering him another pour, and he accepted it. They were talking about the gig tomorrow night, how they needed to tighten up here or stretch it out a little bit there—'let it breathe', Nomad said, as if the song were a living thing—and the talk was easy and relaxed, the conversation of people who respected each other and, it was clear, really did share a strong bond of family, of professionalism, of...*honor,* really.

He understood that kind of bond.

He'd almost gone through his second shotglass when he said, "I used to be in a band." It had come out of him so abruptly he hadn't heard it coming, even in his own head.

The easy and relaxed talk silenced.

"Look at all those eyes," True said, and when he smiled he thought his mouth felt heavy. "It's true. I mean, *I'm* True. But it *is* true. Really."

"What'd you play?" Nomad asked, with a semi-smirk. "Bone fiddle for the Cavemen?"

"No, honest to God." He was aware of Chappie refilling his shot-glass, and that was okay, they weren't leaving until eleven. He would sleep until eight, he never needed much sleep anyway, this was a nice night and it was okay. "I played acoustic guitar in a band called the Honest Johns. Three guys. And me. I mean, three guys in all. When I was a junior in high school." He took another drink, and boy was he going to sleep well tonight. This morning. Whenever. Time got weird when you were in a band. "Well, we never actually played anywhere. We just rehearsed in my friend's rumpus room."

"Say *what?*" Nomad asked.

"Downstairs room," True explained. Jeez, these kids acted like adults but they knew as little about the world as children did. "My friend had an eight-track reel-to-reel. Tape recorder."

"Cool," said Terry.

"We played…let's see…Buffalo Springfield's 'For What It's Worth'. We did 'One Toke Over The Line', by Brewer and Shipley—"

"My *man*," said Terry with admiration.

"We did 'Blackbird', by the Beatles. And I guess the nearest we came to perfection was 'Suite: Judy Blue Eyes' by—"

"Crosby, Stills and Nash!" Ariel was nursing a glass of orange juice. Her smile was sunny. "Oh, wow! I used to play that song all the time!"

"Really? I remember it had a strange tuning."

"Oh yeah, the E modal tuning."

Nomad just had to ask the next question: "Who sang the lyrics?"

"We all did," True said, not realizing what kind of trap he was stepping into. "We did the three-part harmony." He took another drink, and thought of himself as a young man in a rumpus room, two friends on either side, singing into a microphone while the reels of a huge tape recorder caught the moment, to be forever lost except for the imprint in his mind.

"Sing the first few lines for us," Nomad said.

"Huh? Oh, no. I haven't sung that song for years."

"Don't you remember the words? You're not *that* old."

"John!" Ariel caught his gaze and shook her head.

"You've got to remember the *tune*," Nomad went on. And why he was pushing like this, why he was showing a little streak of mean he didn't know, except for the fact that the gig tonight had been a big success, the media thought they were a big success, the *People* magazine article would say they were going to be a big success, the future for this dead band said Big Success in huge flashing neon with dollar signs twenty feet tall, and he felt like a creepy-crawly piece of shit because it wasn't about the music, it wasn't about their talent and dedication to their craft, it was about death and sniper's bullets, and how could a person with any ounce of self-respect call that a big success? He thought that the others, for all their smiles tonight and their afterglow of accomplishment, had to be feeling the same, or they just weren't letting themselves think about it.

"If you remember the tune," Nomad said, unyielding, "the words may come back."

True nodded. "I do remember the tune." His shotglass was empty once again, and Chappie moved to refill it because it was fun having a new drinking buddy, even if it was an FBI agent, but she stopped when she looked into her daughter's face and those steady black eyes said *No more.*

"I'd like to hear some singing." Nomad drew his knees up to his chin. "Man, you might be like…a lost talent or something."

"Come on, John," Terry said, and Nomad looked at him fiercely and asked, "Where are we going?"

Without warning, without an intake of breath or an explanation that his voice was rusty or that he couldn't do this in public and he was sorry he'd even brought any of this to light, True began to sing.

His pitch was perfect. His voice was softer and higher than they would've expected. It had an element of a junior high schooler in it, singing for his friends in a downstairs room.

"*It's getting to the point,*
Where I'm no fun anymore.
I am sorry.

Sometimes it hurts so badly
I must cry out loud.
I am lonely.
I am yours, you are mine, you are what you—"

True's voice faltered. He stopped and looked at his audience, who were all staring at him. He started to take a drink and realized the shotglass in his hand had nothing in it. Now I've gone and made a damn fool out of myself, he thought. Damn old man, he thought.

Damn old man.

Maybe someone should have clapped, to break the silence. Ariel thought about it, and came close to doing it, but she did not.

It was Berke who stepped into the breech. "I bet John hopes he can sing like that when he gets your age," she said to True.

"Well," True said, and shrugged, and looked at his polished black wingtips.

"Not bad," Nomad had to admit, after a few more seconds had drifted past. "You want to sign up for vocal lessons sometime, I'll only charge you a hundred dollars an hour."

True turned the shotglass between his palms. He had forgotten himself, he realized. He had forgotten why he was here, and what he was about. It was time, maybe, to let them know so he wouldn't be allowed to forget again.

"In the van," he said. "On the way to Stone Church." He was still staring at his shoes, but he was speaking to John Charles. "You asked if you were supposed to feel sorry for Jeremy Pett."

"Yeah, I remember."

True nodded. He felt a pulse beating at his temple. "Have you ever fought in a war?"

"No."

"Ever been in the military? Ever served your country?"

"Served my country?" Nomad's voice had taken on a defensive edge. "Like how? Getting killed so a contractor can make big bucks and the flag-maker's stock goes up on Wall Street?"

True lifted his gaze to Nomad's. The agent's eyes were sad. "Don't you believe in anything?" He directed the question again, to all of them. "Don't any of you believe in a higher calling than...what you're doing?"

"A higher calling?" Terry asked. "I believe in God, if that's what you're—"

"I'm talking about service to your *country*," True emphasized. "To the fight for *freedom*. Not just here, but around the world." His gaze fixed again on Nomad. Maybe he was still feeling a little light-headed and stupid from the Jack, but he had to get this out. "You can say whatever you want to about Jeremy Pett, and I'm not going to defend him for what's he done, but that young man…that young *Marine* has served his country to the best of his ability, and no matter what he's done or what he's planning to do, no man who refuses to be a Blue Falcon can be all bad."

"A Blue Falcon?" Ariel asked, frowning. "What's that?"

"A military term for a soldier who leaves a wounded buddy on the battlefield. It means Buddy—" He just couldn't say that word, it was undignified. "Effer."

It hit Nomad. Hit him hard and square, right in the brainpot. *Our barracks sergeant*, Berke had said.

"You never told us where you were a cop before you joined the FBI." Nomad's voice sounded thick. "You were in the military, weren't you?"

True's gaze did not waver. "Military Police. United States Marine Corps." He had joined right after college, knowing the MP experience would put him on the fast track for the job he really wanted.

Nomad saw the whole picture, even as it came clear for the others. "This isn't about saving us. It's about saving *him*."

"That's right," said True.

"*Shit*," was Berke's caustic response. She leaned toward him in full attack mode, her teeth clenched. "You're *hoping* he'll try to kill us?"

"Planning for it," True corrected.

True is False, Nomad thought. "Our road manager," he said, the old familiar rage growing in his heart, "wants to save his boy. His little wayward nutbag Marine. Doesn't matter if one or two or *all* of us get drilled. Is that it, Gomer?"

"Not exactly, but close." True again stared at his shoes. He liked to keep them well-polished. He liked everything neat and clean and polished, but unfortunately life had a habit of getting very messy. He could feel, of all them, the girl staring at him with hurt on her face. He liked the girl. Really, he liked everyone in this room. Life had a habit of getting so very messy. "No one wants any of you to be injured," he said, keeping his face lowered. "I knew there was a chance Pett might come after you at Stone Church. Every possible precaution was taken."

"Yeah, except for one fucker getting in with a pistol." Nomad's voice was a whipstrike.

"Every possible precaution, except metal detectors. And, yes, I was hoping he'd show. I was hoping he'd try something when we stopped on the highway."

"Christ!" said Berke. "Are we *that* worthless?"

"With the gear they've got—what you've seen and what you haven't seen—my men only need a single shot from the dark to pinpoint a location. I've already told you how good a sniper Pett used to be. He set up that shot on Mike Davis with some of his old precision, but he didn't hit with the first bullet. Did he?" True watched Chappie pour herself another drink. Her hand was slightly trembling. True waited until she was finished before he went on. The way the girl was looking at him—he could see her with his peripheral vision—made him wish this hour had never arrived.

"So Pett's skills have diminished," he told them. "It's unlikely he can make a kill with a first shot, unless he gets lucky or close, which he doesn't want to do. You knew you were bait when you agreed to do this. I believed then and I believe now that if Pett is still in this country, if he's still following us and he wants to kill any one of you, he'll try again. It doesn't matter where. You go back to Austin and call it a day...guess what? It's *his* call." True aimed his cool blue eyes at Nomad, whose mouth was twisted with disgust. "But you're absolutely right, John. My first priority in this situation is capturing Pett alive and getting him the help he needs." He paused long enough for Nomad—for all of them—to absorb that. "That's why *I'm* here, and not an agent from the office who wasn't a Marine. Let's just say, veterans look out for each other. For *life*. Or let me say...they *should*. What this young man has gone through, both in Iraq and here after he was discharged...that's a tragedy I'm not willing to let continue by having someone shoot him in the head and drag him off like a piece of filth. Which he is *not*." True felt the heat rising in his face, and maybe it was the Jack or maybe it was because he was just plain effing angry.

"I want to get this straight," said Berke. "You're saying you value his life over ours? And if he pops up somewhere, your people won't shoot to kill?"

"My men are well-trained in what I expect them to do," came the answer. "I want him in a mental hospital, getting the best possible care. Not in a cemetery."

"Our government in action," Chappie said, with a bitter smile. Her eyes had gotten small. "Fuck the people!" She lifted her glass in a toast.

Nomad had finished his own drink. He wondered how quick the old man's reflexes were, and if he could dodge a glass thrown at his skull. "If your men sighted Pett before he could get off a shot at any one of us, they wouldn't try to put him down for good? They've been *ordered* not to kill him if it comes to that?"

"Pretty much," True said. "Yeah."

Ariel got up from the sofa and carried her empty glass to the kitchen. True avoided looking at her, and she did not immediately return.

Silence filled the room. Or, rather, it hollowed out the room.

"You don't understand," True said, with a harsh note of steadily increasing anger, "what those young men have gone through. You don't understand what they've seen. You *can't* understand, because you take everything for granted. Everything you have. You've never fought for anything worth dying for, have you? Answer me!"

"Who gets to say what that is?" Nomad fired back. "*You*? The President? Some corporate chairman who's got plans to build a shopping mall and a megaplex in the middle of Baghdad? *Who*?"

"See?" True gave a crooked smile, but his cheeks were flushed. "You don't get it. Some things, like freedom, are worth dying for whether you think so or not. If everybody turned their backs on their responsibility, where would they be?"

"A lot of them," Terry said, "would be alive."

"Easy to sit here and not have to *do* anything. Nothing required of you. Just sit and take." True almost got up and put an end to this, because it was about to get very messy and it was not going anywhere, but he had something important to say. Something he wanted John Charles and everyone else to hear, whether they wanted to hear it or not. He was aware that Ariel was standing in the kitchen doorway. Good. She should hear this, too.

"What you don't understand and can never understand is that the young men and women over there are fighting for *you*," he said. "For your *future*."

"Oil for my car?" Nomad returned a ferocious grin. "Is that what you mean?"

"That's part of it. Our way of life, until we can get other energy sources going. But you don't get that Jeremy Pett and young men like him went over there with courage and purpose, to do a job they were obligated to do as soldiers in the service of this country. It didn't matter if they wanted to go or not; they weren't asked, and they didn't want to be asked, because this is what they were *trained* to do. And I can tell you, Pett's training as a sniper was far harder than most. It's incredibly difficult, and only the best of the best pass through. You couldn't qualify to carry his socks." A stabbing finger drove that point. "So he's the best of the best, doing what he's been trained to do, and then something terrible happens to him there and at home and the spirit drains out of him and leaves him basically a broken shell. But he has no serious and long-lasting physical injuries, and maybe he can cover up his psychological wounds because he's been trained to be tough and to deny pain, and his own father has taught him a lot of that, so nobody follows up on Sergeant Pett. No, the VA hospitals are understaffed and overworked, so solid, tough guys like Jeremy Pett are given a certificate that says how much the Marine Corps appreciates their service. Maybe they're awarded a medal too, like Pett was, so they can remember what sets them apart from men like *you*. Then this broken young veteran who's been trained to kill people at over eight hundred yards goes out into the world looking for *work*." True's blue eyes were no longer cool; they were aflame, and they dared Nomad to interrupt him.

The dare was not taken.

"Well, it's a tough world out here," True continued. "We all know that. We use whatever skills we have, don't we? And there's so much competition for jobs, and people having to take whatever they can get. And maybe, if you were Jeremy Pett, you'd had plans set out for your entire life, that you were going to work harder than anyone else—I mean bone-hurting, back-breaking hard—and earn yourself and your family a home in the Corps. But you know, plans sometimes just don't work out. Little things go wrong, here and there. Oops, sorry. Here's your certificate, and this fine medal for you to look at and remember the day you were *somebody*. But now, you need to go out in that world of civilians and find yourself a job, you with your training to be the best of the best and to kill people at over eight hundred yards."

True leaned forward in his chair. "And maybe in time…after you keep hitting a wall that will not move…and after you realize you live in a world that can't ever measure up to what you once knew…you start trying to find a new enemy, because only a battlefield makes you feel worth living." True nodded. "I think that's his story, and I won't be another bastard who's kicked him to the curb. If it's within my power, I'm going to save his life."

True stood up, with the shotglass in his hand. "Thank you for your hospitality, Mrs. Fisk. I'm going to bed now." The couch in the den, he meant. "I'll set my alarm." There was no need to set his alarm, he woke up at whatever time he decided to awaken the night before, but he wanted them to have confidence that he would not oversleep. He never overslept. He headed for the kitchen, to place the shotglass in the sink, and Ariel retreated to give him room.

Before True entered the den and closed the door, Nomad said, "One question, man. What if Jeremy Pett aims the rifle at *you* first? Still figuring to save his life if that happens?"

True didn't answer. The door closed at his back.

Near six in the morning, True's cellphone buzzed. He was on it at once, his eyes bleary and his mouth tasting like wood shavings from a barroom floor but his senses already sharpening.

"Good morning, Truitt," said the familiar voice. "I'm sending you an email attachment. It's something you need to see *post haste*."

"What is it?"

"Connor Addison started talking around midnight. It's all on the video."

"Okay." True rubbed his eyes with one hand. "Send it over."

"Something else."

"Go ahead."

"We've got a few dozen Pett sightings to go through, but there were two yesterday in Nogales. Made within hours of each other.

One by a local policeman. We've got some people asking questions down there, strictly unofficial and very low-key."

"Alright. Good."

"He could've made it over," said the man at the office in Tucson. "You know, we might need to talk here pretty soon about cutting back. This is taking a *lot* of resources."

"Yeah, I'm aware of that."

"A lot of manpower. I've got other things going on."

"Sure, I know," True said. He had slept in his clothes. Every part of him felt wrinkled.

The question came, as he'd known it was going to: "Can you make do with one team?"

True sighed. Heavily, so it could be heard.

"Just asking. Would you consider it and get back to me?"

"Yeah," True said. He worked a tight muscle in his left shoulder. "I'll get back."

When the caller had finished, True put his laptop on the desk and turned it on. He checked that all the lights were where they were supposed to be on the den's wireless cable modem, and then he yawned so wide his jaw muscles cracked and he went to work.

TWENTY-FIVE.

True didn't like their two rooms at the Days Inn Motel on West Sunset. He thought the windows were too open to a parking lot on the east side of the building, and though the teams in the Yukons would be sitting out there taking turns on shift with their day binoculars and night goggles he just didn't feel good about it. He had their rooms changed to the west side, where the windows were blocked by another structure. Then he went to his own room down the hall, unpacked his gear, splashed some cold water in his face from the bathroom tap, and lay on his back on the bed while he called his wife and asked her how her day was going.

Everything's good here, he told her. California sunshine. Traffic wasn't so bad. The band's doing a remote interview from the Cobra Club—yeah, that's the name of it—with Nancy Grace this afternoon, you might want to watch that show tonight. You remember the talent agency guy I was telling you about? Roger Chester? He set it up. Greta van Susteren's people are supposed to call me. We're doing a couple of radio interviews before the gig. Do you like that word? So, anyway, it's shaping up to be another mad minute like yesterday.

Her phrase: mad minute. A period of chaotic activity where you just put your head down and held on like a cat in the curtains.

He told her everything was under control. He had what he needed. Yes, he knew he'd forgotten his fish oil supplements, he'd left them on the vitamin shelf. His clothes steamer wasn't working like it should, he thought they'd gotten a bum one from that whole stack of them at Target. But he had what he needed. He told her there were palm trees lining the boulevard outside just like in the movies, and she would go crazy to see the huge Off Broadway shoe warehouse that was almost right across the street. He said for her not to worry, he was going to find a place with a good salad bar.

He didn't tell her about the IHOP across the way, because she knew how he liked to mix syrupy pancakes, crumbled-up bacon and yellow-drippy eggs into a scrumpdiliumptous feast that laughed a hearty big fat man's laugh at Omega-3 pills, but he didn't have that very often. Only when there was an IHOP within range.

Love you, she told him.

Love you, he answered. I'll call tomorrow.

Needless to say. He called her every day he was out of town.

Be careful, she said.

Always, he answered.

Their ritual, their touching of hands over distance.

He put the phone down and lay back on the bed, and he stared at the cottage-cheese ceiling and wondered if and when he should do it.

Before their sound check? After the gig?

Should he do it at all?

Would he want to know, if he were one of them?

This was one of the decisions they paid him to make. It was his call. Those young people up the hall were adults. It wasn't right, keeping this from them, but then again...what good did it do, to show them?

He asked himself another question: if he was the *father* to any one of them, would he want his son or daughter to know?

He lay there a while longer, turning his decision this way and that to give himself an out if he wanted it. Then he got up, took his laptop and left the room.

"Mr. True," said Nomad when he answered the knock. "How do you *do*?" The air had been a little tight today, a little frosty on that drive up from San Diego, but True had survived tighter and colder climates.

"I have something to show you," True said. "While I set up, would you go get the girls?"

"The *who*?"

"The *women*," True corrected.

When everybody was in the one room and True had the laptop powered up, sitting atop a writing desk that had never seen a pen put to a letter, he asked if all of them could see the screen clearly. It was displaying the white seal of the FBI against a black background.

"What is this, show and tell?" Berke asked, sitting cross-legged on a bed.

"Yes." True guided the trackball pointer over the shortcut to his image program and clicked. He hit the Browse All Images and a series of fifteen color thumbnails came up. He had gotten these pictures in a secured email attachment from Tucson yesterday morning, when he was at the field office in San Diego. "These are graphic," he warned, and found himself looking at Ariel.

"I think we can handle *graphic*," Nomad said with a hint of a sneer. His eye was mostly green today, and he could see out of it. He was still burning about that mess unloaded on them last night. To tell the honest truth he was deeply and bitterly disappointed in Mr. Half-True.

"Okay. First picture." He clicked on a thumbnail and an image filled the screen in high resolution.

They didn't know what they were looking at. From his chair, Terry asked, "What is that?" The image showed what looked like... pale, freckled flesh? And on it was...what? A shiny brown tattoo of some kind? The depiction of a wine glass with an 'X' at its center, and a 'V' at the bottom under two curling tails?

"It's a brand," True said. "It would be right about here." He touched an area just above his left shoulder blade. "Those who know this kind of stuff say it's a portion of the seal of Lucifer from a book called 'The Grimorium Verum', printed in the 18th century." He clicked on the next image. Again there was a shiny brown mark against pale flesh, but the flesh was puckered by long ragged scars.

"Somebody's been using a whip on him," True said before he could be asked. "Somebody who *really* likes to use a whip. This symbol is supposed to be an all-seeing eye, again as related to Satanism."

"*Hold* it!" Nomad had been sitting on the other bed, next to Ariel, and now he stood up. "What *is* this shit?"

"These are brands, the scars of several different kinds of whips, razor slashes, wounds made by fish hooks and broken glass—and other implements the experts haven't figured out yet—on the back and chest of Connor Addison. They found them when they took him to the medical trailer after that melee. The Tucson police took these pictures." True clicked on the third image, which showed in closeup more scars, these crisscrossed as if inflicted by the furious digging of a small metal object in the shape of a sharp-tipped, five-fingered claw.

"Je...*sus*," Berke breathed.

"On his lower back, right side," True said. The images were tagged with the locations of where they'd been found on the body.

The next image caused Ariel to shrink back, Nomad to narrow his eyes and Terry to whisper, "Oh, man."

It was the brand of a large downward-pointing pentagram, with the head of a half-animal, half-human goat at its center, the eyes completely blackened burn marks, the horns outlined and quite artfully decorated in burn, a '666' burned across the forehead, everything done with detail and obvious passion and creativity, if working with red-hot irons and electric pyrography chisels was the artist's joy.

"This one is at the center of his chest," True said. "You can see that his nipples have been burned off, as well."

"I can't look at any more." Ariel put her hand up and averted her face.

"Okay, we don't have to go through all these, but I wanted you to see a few." True closed the image program and navigated to another file. "Now...this is Connor Addison speaking to the police around midnight, last night. He suddenly wanted to talk, so they wanted to hear what he had to say. You ready?"

Nomad was still on his feet. He'd moved between Ariel and the laptop as if to shield her from these hideous images of tortured meat. "Why are you showing this to us?"

"Because you need to know what's out there," True replied calmly.

"We *already* know, man!" Terry said.

"No," said True. "No, you don't."

He double-clicked on the video file, and it began to play.

The scene was a view of one of those small interrogation rooms from every reality cop show on the planet, taken from a camera positioned in an upper corner. Two men, a gray-haired dude in a white shirt with a red-patterned tie, the other in a dark blue shirt with the sleeves rolled up, sat on one side of the table. The gray-haired cop was rubbing his eyes, as if it had been a long hard slog to midnight. The man in the blue shirt had short-cut brown hair and was husky, with the broad back and shoulders of a wrestler. A notepad, pens and what looked to be a voice recorder was placed between them. On the other side of the table sat a thin, pale young man wearing the eye-shocking orange jumpsuit that Nomad had known and loved so well. Addison's hands were folded on the table in an attitude of prayer. His neatly-combed blonde hair looked damp, as if he'd just taken a shower before coming clean.

Time and date stamps sat down on the lower left of the frame, and a frame counter on the right. The time was twelve-oh-nine.

"Let's get started, then," said the older cop. He had a radio rumble of a voice, like the bass presence was turned up a little too loud. "You can state your name."

"Apollyon," said the young man. He spoke with composed authority, in a soft voice that suited his looks but not the raging nightmare under his jumpsuit.

"Say 'gain?" asked the second cop, who sounded like a hardcore cowboy type: *careful there, feller, I got five beans in the wheel.*

"Apollyon," the soft voice repeated, and then he spelled it out.

Cowboy wrote it down on the notepad.

Radio's fingers tapped the tabletop. "And what's your home address?"

"You know all that," said the young man, Connor Addison or Apollyon or whatever he was calling himself.

"We'd like to hear it from you."

The young man looked up directly at the video camera. He had a black and swollen left eye. A bandage covered his chin and his lower lip was puffed up. Nomad suddenly felt awfully proud of himself, though he knew most of the damage had been done by the Nazi Six.

"Call me Apollyon," said the soft voice to the camera. "I am not from this place."

Cowboy tore the page off the notepad and started to leave his chair.

"I can tell you what it means, you don't have to go look it up on the Internet."

Cowboy paused, thought about it, almost went anyway because his horses were restless, and then he sat down again, smoothed the page out on the table and stared across at Apollyon.

"I am the destroyer," said the pale young man. "I am everything you fear, and I am everything you would like to be."

"That so?" Cowboy asked, and he looked down at his piece of paper.

"That is so," said Apollyon.

"Would I like to be in jail facing a very serious charge of attempted murder, Connor?" Radio rumbled.

Apollyon looked up again at the camera, and his battered face beamed. "They need their ears checked here."

"Okay, then. *Apollyon*." The way Radio said that, he could be announcing an '80s hair band. "You wanted to talk, so we're listening." His chair creaked as he leaned back. He spread his arms out, palms open. "Let's hear it."

"I'd like a candy bar. Something sweet."

"After you talk to us. Let me start you out a little bit, with a question. Why did you intend to commit murder on Thursday afternoon? That *was* your intention, correct? To shoot as many people on that stage as you could?"

"That's three questions," said Apollyon.

"Answer the first one, how 'bout it?" Cowboy directed.

"I'd like a Snickers. Really, anything chocolate."

"Okay, let's stop this foolishness." Radio stood up. "Come on, we're through here."

Apollyon didn't move. After a few seconds, he said, "The seventh mansion the Furies possess."

"What?" Cowboy asked, straining to understand.

"I was told to go to Stone Church," said the young man. He folded his arms around himself, around that thin body bearing the savage multitude of scars and burns. "I saw the ads on TV. I saw who was going to be there. That band the sniper's after. Playing on Thursday afternoon, at three o'clock. One show. I looked them up on their website. I looked up the website for Stone Church." Then he stopped speaking.

"Go ahead," said Radio. He sat down once more, but he perched on the edge of his chair ready to jump up and rattle the sword again if he needed to.

Apollyon remained silent.

Cowboy tried his hand: "Who was it *told* you to go to Stone Church?"

Apollyon began to very slightly rock himself back and forth. He had a fixed smile on his face. Looking at it, even from this distance of time and space, made Ariel's flesh crawl.

"Who was it *told* you to go to Stone Church, Apollyon?" Cowboy repeated.

The young man said something. It was so soft they couldn't make it out.

"What was that?" Radio asked. "*Who?*"

Apollyon spoke a little louder. A name, spoken quickly. Spoken like something that even a destroyer should be afraid of.

A girl's name.

"Bethy," he said.

True froze the video.

"Bethy was—" he began, but Ariel interrupted him because she already knew.

"His sister," she said. "His raped and murdered sister."

True stared at her as if seeing something in her face he'd never seen before, or hearing in her voice a firm certainty that he didn't quite understand, and Ariel was aware of the others staring at her too, and she didn't fully understand her own feeling either, but watching this video—seeing this young man's sick smile and hearing his eerily soft voice speaking the name of a dead little girl—made her aware of places in this very room where the light did not completely settle, and where a shadow seemed to shift and shudder at the edge of the corner of the eye.

"This kid's a lunatic," Nomad said. "A fucking nutbag." Even as he made that statement, he was wondering about the lunatics and fucking nutbags who'd decorated Apollyon's body with fire and blood.

"There's more," True told him.

"Show it," Ariel said.

True clicked on the small circle with the Play arrow in it.

"Who's Bethy?" Cowboy asked, proving he hadn't fully done his homework, but as Apollyon sat silent and motionless Radio wrote something on the pad. He slid it in front of his partner, and Cowboy read it and gave a brief nod.

"Bethy told you to go to Stone Church and kill people. Is that correct?" Radio asked.

Apollyon didn't reply and it looked like he wasn't going to, as the time counter displayed the passage of twelve seconds. Then he answered, "She told me to find a gun, to steal one if I needed to from Cal Holland's house, and go kill the girl."

"What girl?"

"The girl in the *band*." Apollyon's bruised mouth showed the faintest curl of annoyance. "The girl singer. Bethy told me to kill her, because if she dies they won't finish it."

"Finish what, Apollyon?" Cowboy asked.

"What they're doing." He continued to rock himself back and forth. "Bethy says they don't even know."

"Hm," Radio said. "So...did Bethy tell *you* what it is?"

"Oh, no." Apollyon shook his head. He gave a sad smile, the smile of an intelligent but nerdy high school kid who has been snubbed by the cool dudes at the cool table, and who finally and forever knows his role. "I'm not allowed."

"Stop it!" Nomad commanded. True's finger was slow. "Stop it *now*!"

The video froze.

True looked at Nomad, his dark eyebrows upraised.

"How do you figure this is helpful to us?" Nomad's face was fearsome with its angry mouth and swollen sick-green eye. "You think this is *helping* us go out to the sound check, meet-and-greet the news people, do interviews and keep ourselves together? This is supposed to pick us up for what we have to do?"

"John?" Ariel said softly. "We need to watch this."

"No, we don't." He pointed at the video frame. "This is a crazy, pain-addicted Satan *freak*. Nothing else. Okay?"

"What else *would* he be, John?" asked Terry, and in that question Ariel realized Terry was sitting next to her again, in that seat she'd saved for him on the bench under the eucalyptus tree, but now he was listening to her. He was listening to every single word.

Nomad was unable to answer. He looked from Ariel to Terry and back again, and then to Berke for her caustic acid that dripped upon every unmanagable thought or uncomfortable idea and melted them down to Silly Putty.

This time, it didn't drip. This time, Berke chewed on her lower lip, and she gave a small nervous laugh and shook her head as if to say she had nothing to say.

"Finish *what*?" True asked, directing the question to all of them. "Just for interest's sake. Do you think that's a reference to your tour, or—"

"The dead don't speak!" Nomad had nearly shouted it. "Ghosts don't come back and tell people to do things! The dead are *dead*! They're *nothing*!"

But as he said it, he heard his own ghost tell him that Johnny, there was no roadmap.

No, that was different, he thought. That was a memory. His father was not a ghost telling him to steal a gun and kill a girl because if she was dead, a song would not be finished.

Oh, yeah. Here we go, he thought. Here we go. The communal song. And that girl at the well. That girl in her raggedy straw hat with her ladle of water, trying to stuff him into her sack of buttholes. *The angel of life*, George had said. God's voice speaking to Terry in church, and Heaven and Hell and all that garbage for people who were afraid to think for themselves. Oh, yeah; here we go.

"Set it up," he told them, "so I can knock it down."

Ariel's eyes were dark gray with hints of sapphire blue, like gleams of something mysterious in motion just beneath the surface of a sea. "You know what this is about, John. You know best of all, because it was your idea."

"It's a *song*," he said, almost pleadingly. "Not even finished yet. No music to it. It's just some words strung out in lines. There are no hidden meanings. No big flash of light. It was just...a way to keep..."

"Us together," Ariel said, helping him. "I know that's how it began, but now I think it's more."

"A new song?" True asked. "You're writing a new song? Is there mention of it on your website?"

"No," Terry said. "We just started thinking about it when we left Austin."

"How would Connor Addison know about it, then? And according to him...according to his sister...you don't know what you're doing. So how can that be?"

"That freak's sister is dead! Stop talking about his sister!" Nomad feared he was about to blow his circuits; they were going to have to load him into an ambulance and take him to the Hollywood ICU, and maybe the girl would come to him in his room and say *I believe in you* and he could shout back, *Fuck you, I don't believe in* you!

True said, as calmly as he could, "There are just a few more minutes of the video. I'd like to show you the rest of it."

"Berke!" Nomad said. "Come on, let's go find us a fucking bar!"

"No," she told him, and she glanced quickly at him and then away. "I think I'll stick here. Anyway…it wouldn't be safe, just walking around."

True clicked the Play arrow. Nomad did not leave.

Cowboy tap-tap-tapped his pen on the edge of the table. Radio rubbed his mouth, readying it for another rumble.

"Who gave you those marks, Apollyon?" Radio asked. "They're Satanist symbols, aren't they?"

"Two questions, one answer: the seventh mansion the Furies possess."

"Yeah, we heard that already. Is there a meaning to it, or is it gibberish?"

"It has a meaning to *me*," said Apollyon.

"Enlighten us."

"Would I ever like to," came the reply, "but you wouldn't understand the game."

Cowboy jumped in with both boots. "Game? What game would that be?"

Silence from the destroyer.

Tap-tap-tap went Cowboy's pen. Radio cleared his throat like a burst of static. "Your father told me yesterday that you used to be a model student—"

"I'm still a model student, but I've changed schools."

"We'll get to that. He said you were active in the chess club. Is that the game you're talking about?"

"You wish," said Apollyon, with a crimped smile. "Am I ever going to get my candy? I would talk so much better with something sweet in my mouth."

"Uh-huh." For a few seconds Radio searched the young man's bandaged face, and then he said with the resigned air of a weary soul who really, really wants to go home. "Billy, would you go get him something? What do you want? A Snickers bar?"

"Anything chocolate," Apollyon said.

Billy the Cowboy got up, dug for change in his pocket and left the room.

"*Bad idea*," Nomad heard True say under his breath.

No one spoke on the video until Cowboy returned. "This suit you?" He put a small bag of M&Ms down in front of Apollyon.

"Fine, thanks." Apollyon delicately tore open the bag and dumped its contents into a pile. He began to separate the candies into areas of blue, green, yellow, red, brown and orange. He took a yellow and a green and chewed them.

"Would you tell us," said Radio, "how Bethy told you to go to Stone Church?"

Apollyon kept arranging the colors, eating a candy or two or three.

"Did you hear that question?" Cowboy asked, his patience growing thinner than a snake on a dust diet.

When Radio spoke again, his bass voice was dangerous. He was done playing. "Your sister is not among the living. So how can you sit there and tell us—and try to make us believe—that she told you to steal a gun and kill someone? That just kind of defies logic, don't you think?"

Apollyon ate a few more candies, and then he met the cop's gaze. "Logic," he said. "is a creation of men. It's a narrow door to a very large house. In that house are lots of rooms. Some you'd want to live in, others...not so much. Logic is a shirt that's been dried too hot, so when it comes out of the machine it's too tight around your neck, it chokes you and it binds your shoulders, and your mom tells you you're going to wear it no matter what, because you were wearing it that night and she's never going to let you throw it away. Then when you do outgrow it, and there's no way you can fit it on you, she makes a pillowcase out of it for your bed. Is that logical? To make a pillowcase from a shirt?"

Neither cop said anything for a few seconds. Cowboy shifted his weight in his chair. Radio rubbed his fingers together, his elbows supported by the table. He said, "We're talking about your sister. How did she come tell you to do this? Did she...like...materialize? Out of the air?"

"She just comes. She's there and then she's not." Apollyon continued to eat the M&Ms, as if he had all the time in the world.

"And you do whatever she's tellin' you to do, right?" Cowboy asked. "This is *her* fault, is that it?"

Apollyon stopped chewing.

He did not move nor speak, as the seconds ticked past.

The two cops looked at each other, as if they suspected a trigger had been pulled, or a rope twisted, or a shirt tightened enough to make a person scream.

"Her *fault*," said Apollyon, staring at nothing. And again: "Her *fault*."

They waited, and in the Days Inn Motel room the viewers could see that the young man's face had become shiny with sweat, and his smile flickered on and off with erratic speed, and he had placed his index fingers on two M&M candies like they were the opposite poles of the battery that was keeping him alive.

"I was about to hang myself," he said hollowly, "when she came the first time. I was about to step off the chair. And then Bethy was sitting on my bed looking up at me, and she said, 'Connor, don't do that.' She said, 'Someone likes you a whole lot, Connor, and they want you to know how much. But you have to show them how strong you are, Connor. They don't like weak.' So she told me to go to a place in front of a carwash and wait and somebody would pick me up, and it was a man who gave me a drink from a water bottle and then he drove, and I got sleepy. When I woke up…I was in a room in a house, and the people there asked me if they could do things to me. They were very polite. They were smart people, I could tell that. At first I had to drink a lot from the bottle, but…after a few times, it was all right. When my mom and dad saw, they were going to go to the police but I told them what Bethy said to me, that if they didn't test my strength here, they were going to test hers *there*. And she told me all of it. She told me how much that man had hurt her, and what he'd done, and she was afraid they would find out she wasn't strong enough and they would cast her out where the weak things walked, and she begged, 'Connor, would you please please pretty please take it for *me*?'"

"I said I would," the young man told them. "And she said, for that, she would try to forgive me." His eyes moved from Radio to

Cowboy and back. His smile flickered: on, off, on, off. "They gave me a new name, and they birthed me. They told me why I was born. They made *sense* out of everything. And when you finally, finally see the sense of things...you know a power that is beyond..." He paused, searching. "*Logic*," he said.

Apollyon continued eating his M&Ms, crunching them a few at the time.

When Radio spoke again, some of his bass presence had been muted. "Why'd you say Bethy told you to go kill that girl?"

"She was upset. Bethy was. Early Wednesday morning, when she came. She said it was something I had to do to show I was strong. She said Connor had died, and Apollyon had been born. Born in *pain*. I was the destroyer now, and that was my job. To destroy." He frowned, with a red M&M held to his lips. "I think I fucked up, though." He slowly eased the candy into his mouth. "I was going to shoot the lead singer first. I hated his voice. Then...I thought I'd better do what Bethy wanted, or they might get mad at her. They might hurt her, and I couldn't...I couldn't take that. Because...you know... she's such a *little* girl. So I think I fucked up."

"I think I fucked up," he repeated.

"I think I fucked up," he said again.

"I think I—"

With sudden terrible speed he grasped a handful of M&Ms, threw them into his mouth, crunched down and inhaled with a hideous rasping howl. He took hold of his own throat and squeezed with both hands. He went sideways off his chair and the two cops scrambled around and over the table to get at him before his airway was blocked. Cowboy started trying to get the hands loosened as the body kicked and writhed beneath him, and Radio ran out the door shouting a garbled unintelligible shout that sounded like he was hollering through a boom box.

True clicked the video off.

Nomad suddenly realized where he was.

He was nearly in the corner. He'd been backing up, a few inches at a time, until the corner was right behind him and there was nowhere else to go.

He felt an incredible pressure, as if he was in one of those centrifuge things the astronauts use, he was spinning around faster and faster and the flesh was being pushed back from his skull. He thought of a crazy thing. The thing that musicians shouted when everything went wrong, when the fuses blew, when the speakers made everything sound like muddy shit, when the lights malfunctioned, when half the CDs were broken in their cases, when the crowd lost their patience and hollered for blood or refunds, when every note you hit was a clam and every word you sang was lost in a looping shriek of feedback.

He thought: *More cowbell.*

But down below that, down deep in a horrible place, he was thinking that he had never dared to consider the possibility of an afterlife, the possibility of something human beings called in their limited knowledge Heaven and Hell, never *dared* to, because if he considered those things, if he let them in, then he would have to believe that his hero...his idol...that *man*...would be called upon to suffer for the pain he had inflicted on a woman who'd loved only him.

And John Charles would remember that when they told him in the Louisville hospital his father had died from a trinity of gunshot wounds, his first silent judgement and ever to remain silent had been: *He deserved it.*

Oh my God, John thought, behind the hand he'd put up to cover his mouth. Oh my God.

"They rushed him to the hospital," True explained. "He's all right. Physically, that is. If you can look beyond...all that damage. But he's gone inward. They've got him on suicide watch."

Terry breathed out with a whooshing noise. Berke couldn't look anywhere but at the floor. Ariel's gaze went to John.

"We caught another man," True told them. "Coming up the side of the mountain with a .22 rifle. Obviously he was intending to get in position for a shot, though I can tell you he probably would've shot himself first, by accident. He's a part-time handyman and full-time... what was your term, John?...nutbag. Lives in a trailer park about forty miles north of Stone Church. His neighbors say he's always talking about hearing voices. He's mounted all sorts of homemade antennas up on the roof of his trailer, says he was an electronics expert in the Navy. Not verified. Anyway, his neighbors say he thinks his trailer is sitting on what he calls a 'comm line'. Know how he described it to the police? An 'angel line'." True's smile didn't stick.

"He says there must be a really important reason for the girl in that Five band to be dead, because the angels are very disturbed with her. Disturbed with the whole band, really. He says the angels are putting it out on the line everywhere, every second of every minute of the night and the day, to everyone who can hear. He says they're getting a little...his word...frantic. Kind of like a telegraph line of the spirits, I suppose," True said, and he shrugged. "If you believe in that. So this guy, he decides if the angels want her dead, this is a good way to show what side he's on. If you believe in that."

He closed his laptop.

He arranged the notepaper on the writing desk that had never seen a pen put to a letter.

Then he turned to The Five, and very clearly and as forcefully as possible without sounding—as Berke would say—'creeped out', he said, "I want you to tell me—right now, nothing held back—what you people have gotten yourselves involved with. Whatever it is, and it may sound strange, or...illogical, or whatever. You may not even know what kind of boundary you've crossed. But listen...do not hold *anything* back. Anyone want to speak?"

"They're two crazy people," Nomad said, but for one time in his life his voice was weak because he knew he was lying. He was still standing with his back against the corner, his hands up at his sides and curled into fists, ready to knock something down.

"I'll speak," said Ariel.

TWENTY-SIX.

From the front on the sparkling, electric-bright Sunset Boulevard the Cobra Club was a dreary brown-painted building with no windows, no sign and no evidence that it was in use except for clear plastic displays on the walls showing band posters and an ornate black gate that was locked over the entrance until eight o'clock.

Inside, at a little past midnight, the club's stage crew had finished setting up for The Five. The place was packed and noisy. It was another black box club, the walls deepest ebony. The bar in the lounge was lit by yellow bulbs behind ceramic fixtures shaped like cobras. Behind the stage was a backdrop of a large red-eyed cobra rising from a basket, painted on black velvet. The big, silent black-and-silver JBL speakers, still cooling down from the hard harmonics of the previous band, Twenty Million Miles To Earth, promised the moving, chattering crowd a continuation of mind-blowing entertainment to go along with the three-dollar beer, the mixed drinks and the house specialty, the Cobra Cock.

Rock and roll, baby.

The particular difference on this night, of any other night of the club's checkered and sometimes violent existence, was that everybody who wanted to come in had to stand just beyond that open black gate while two men in Cobra Club T-shirts scanned their bodies with metal detecting wands. The women had to open their handbags. Everyone and everything coming in had to be scanned. If a nipple ring or a Nefertiti piercing or a labia bead made the wands squeal, or in the case of the male a dydoe, a dolphin, an ampallang or any of the other insertions into or through the summer sausage, then it was either go let the female or male police officers stationed inside pat you down in a curtained-off room or take your metalled pride somewhere else, like the Viper Room further along the boulevard. No likee, no have to stayee.

Some left. Most stayed, because they wanted to say that not only had they been felt up by the cops, they had seen the Band That Will Not Die.

It was a hectic scene backstage. The road manager and four members of Twenty Million Miles To Earth were still moving their gear out along the narrow green-painted corridor to the stage door while being trailed and delayed by a knot of various people who wanted something. There had been a problem with the Lekolites and the techs were going over the wiring. Two of the crew were arguing with the stage manager about who had last had possession of a missing gobo, and someone had left a handcart full of coiled elecrtrical cables out where its metal edge nicked the ankles of anybody going past, like a cobra bite.

Through this confusion, Ariel moved in a hurry because she had to pee.

The several bottles of silver needle tea she'd consumed during the long afternoon and at dinner had been going right through her. It was nerves, she thought. It was from the video of Connor Addison's attempted suicide by M&Ms and True's story of the man who heard voices in the trailer park. It was from her own revelation of what she believed the song to be, and her belief that the girl at the well was using them to write it for reasons unknown. It was from her retelling of the dream, and her revisiting the image of Jeremy Pett vomiting forth his dark air force. It was from the interviews with the news media here at sound check, and from the guy who'd shown up with a business card saying he was the head of A&R at Manticore, and he had some great ideas for their future but since there were no longer five of them they shouldn't be called The Five, they should be named Death Ride. It was from talking John down when he wanted to tear the guy's head off his neck, because John was in a fragile state, and she would never have said that about him but he wore the sick and uneasy look of a little boy caught walking through a cemetery at sundown. It was from warding off other A&R people with other business cards and other great ideas, and from the radio interviews and the throngs of people who were waiting outside the radio stations with CDs to be signed and more questions to be answered.

And it was from True's instruction, given in his very clear and forceful voice, that nothing seen or spoken about in that room at the Days Inn should be discussed with *anyone* outside it.

Silver needle tea in, silver needle tea out.

She got past the handcart without being bitten and she went into the bathroom.

It was small and the white-tiled floor was not the cleanest in the world, but neither were musicians. It was unisex with two stalls and a pair of urinals, one sink and a mirror. The ceiling light, a simple glass bowl, was stark and harshly unflattering, as a glance in the mirror told her. She entered the stall furthermost from the door, closed the stall door and latched it, unzipped her jeans, pulled down her lace-edged panties, sat down on the toilet and went "Ahhhhhh." She had a sudden fright and looked to make sure there was paper. About half a roll, so she was okay.

As she relieved herself of the silver needle pressure, she worked her hands, moving her fingers back and forth, getting them ready for the guitar.

There was always the guitar. And the wonderful thing was that it always waited for her.

She had to get all this off her mind and focus on the show. That's what it came down to, no matter what. Focus on one performance at a time. Actually, it was focus on one *song* at a time. No, down to even smaller increments than that. One bar at a time...one note. That was how you did it, when you were troubled or anxious or scared. One note after another, and then suddenly you were free.

What was really bothering her, apart from Jeremy Pett and Connor Addison and the idea that the spirit line was lit up and the angels were very disturbed with her and her bandmates, frantic even in their disturbance, was that she hoped she could hold her next pee until Berke's drum solo.

She heard the bathroom door open and close.

She heard the lock on that door turn.

She heard the *click* of a dirty switch, and the light went dark.

"Hi, I'm in here!" she called out.

No one answered.

"Hello! I'm in here!"

She heard someone walking across the tiles. The squeak of sneakers.

"Please turn the light back on!" Ariel said, and she fumbled to find paper. The roll moved on its cylinder with a metallic squeal.

Music began.

It was a thump...pathump...thump...pathump. Low bass beat, low-fi, scratchy. Maybe from a voice recorder?

Ariel blotted herself, grasped her panties and jeans and stood up. She wriggled her bottoms back on. She was about to ask whoever this was to stop playing around when the gasping, gutteral echo-enhanced male vocal kicked in, backed by a clattery rhythm of tambourine, cabasa, and drumsticks being cracked together.

"*When I come ta kill ya,*
I'll come right through ya door.
I'll bring my best man and my little midget whore.
We'll cut off ya face, won't it be groovy,
then we'll sit down and watch a shemale porn movie.
That's right...that's right...that's right...that's right."

"Hey, stop it!" Ariel said. She heard her voice quaver. "Turn the light back on!"

"*When I come ta kill ya,*
I think I'll eat ya brain,
then I'll stand with my bloody teeth out in da rain.
I'll curse da sky above and da fool who made me,
then I'll go kill another one, or two, or three.
That's right...that's right...that's right...that's—"

The music abruptly stopped.

He came right through the door.

It burst open in her face, propelled by a single savage kick. The door hit her and knocked her back over the toilet, she thought her nose had been smashed and her lips split open, and before she could do anything but make a soft bleat of terror he was upon her. She put her arms up for protection, as if from a whirling mass of crows coming at her through the dark. A hand flailed for her and caught her hair. A fist crashed into the side of her head. She saw stars and lightning bolts and tasted blood. Her knees gave way, and she felt something sticky being wrapped around her mouth. Around her head. Catching in her hair. Around and around and around.

She realized it smelled like Band-Aids.

He grabbed her by the neck and threw her, and she skidded out in the dark on the dirty tiles. She was on her stomach, she tried to get her knees under herself and stand up, but her arms were wrenched behind her to their breaking point. She screamed beneath the tape that sealed her mouth. He had her arms, and he was wrapping the tape around her wrists, binding them together.

He was very fast and he was very strong and he had done this before.

He grasped her jeans and yanked them down, scraping her flesh with his fingernails.

Then he started pulling off her panties.

Dazed, bleeding, her mind full of cold shock, she thought someone was going to come save her. Someone was going to put a stop to this. It was ridiculous, is what it was. She had a show to do. One note after another, and then suddenly you were free.

She felt his hard penis, pressing against her vagina from behind.

No, she said but her mouth would not repeat it. *No*.

His grasped her hair with both hands, and he began to push himself in.

No one was going to save her. She realized that, finally and fully. She could lie here and be raped waiting for the rescuer who would not arrive, or she could fight until this man killed her.

Ariel twisted her body away from him. He wrenched back on her hair and kept driving in. She twisted once more, and she heard him say, "You fuckin' bitch," and then he hit her again, an open-handed, disdainful slap swung against the right side of her head just above the ear. Hard harmonics buzzed in her brain. Tears were hot in her eyes, they were spilling over down her cheeks, but when he tried to push into her a third time she arched her body backward and flung her head up as hard as she could and the back of her skull hit something—collarbone, shoulder, chin, something—and his weight was suddenly off her.

She pushed forward, feet and knees, across the floor.

"You dirty little fuck," he said from the dark. "You little shit."

She heard the squeak of his sneakers, coming after her. She turned over, the weight on her trapped arms causing her to gasp with agony behind the tape, and she kicked out with both feet toward the sound.

Her right shoe hit something solid. A shin? A knee?

"Fuck," he said quietly, a painful sound. "You're fuckin' dead."

She recognized that voice, only now it was a gutteral growl dripping with snide menace. It was the voice of a thousand horrorcore and death rap songs. She kicked at him again but found nothing. He was coming at her from the side; she thought she could see the smear of his movement. She scrabbled backward and clunked her head against what felt like a metal pipe. She was up under the sink. A shoe grazed her ankle. She kicked at it and missed. She was pulling her leg back when his fingers caught her foot. He jerked her out from her little unsafe haven and dragged her across the floor, and she kicked out with her other foot, swung it wide and hard, missed on the first swing but tried again with the heel, and this time she hit bone and he made a hissing noise but held on tight. His shoe came down into her crotch and started pushing there as he wrenched at her leg, and she thought he was trying to tear away the part of her that interested him and take it home to his aunt's basement.

Someone was at the door. Ariel heard the knob being worked.

"Ariel!" It was Berke. "We're on! Let's go!"

He released her.

"Ariel?" The knob was turned back and forth. "You okay?"

Ariel got up on her knees, facing the door. She tried to scream, tried as hard as she could. The sound came out as a muffled moan, and then he was down on the floor with her, one arm snaking around her throat from behind and his face buried in her hair. He was breathing raggedly into her ear. As he breathed, the pressure of his arm steadily tightened.

"Open up!" said Berke.

Ariel felt pressure building in her head. Felt it begin to push her eyes out of their sockets. His arm was crushing her windpipe.

The doorknob rattled once more, back and forth.

And then Berke was gone.

Outside in the hall, Berke was about to go back and get John. She thought Ariel must be sick, and what were they going to do?

Then she saw a camera tripod leaning against the wall next to the door. It was a pitiful thing. One leg of it was wrapped with duct tape. On the floor beside it was a black camera bag. She unzipped it. The video camera was in there. It was a nice one, it said ten-point-six megapixels on the side. Who would leave something like this sitting around? With a light meter in there, and a battery pack, extra lenses, filters, the works. Ripe for the stealing.

She knew tech people swore by it and used it in all sorts of situations, but, she wondered, who really needed to carry around four fucking rolls of duct tape?

In the bathroom, behind the locked door, he was choking Ariel to death.

She tried to fight him. She tried to twist, to arch her back, to thrash him off, to strike with a backwards blow of her head. But he had her, and he breathed in her ear as he was killing her, and his free hand was working on himself, fast fast fast, and he started to make the noise that men make when they have mistaken possession for love and pornography for sex, a high keening whimper and to the world an announcement of, "Oh yeah, I'm gonna cum, oh yeah I'm gonna—"

The bathroom door blew off its hinges.

Berke hurtled through, shoulder-first.

The light that streamed in fell upon the swollen-eyed face of DJ Talk It Up, his lips wet with saliva and his hair sticking up in spikes stiffened with product. He was wearing a dark brown hoodie, the jacket twisted on his torso and the hood lying down across his shoulder. Tonight he had left his rings at home, because he'd wanted to dress down.

Berke saw the duct tape over Ariel's mouth, saw the terror in her eyes and the guy's arm squeezing her throat. She saw blood streaming from both of Ariel's nostrils, making a mess of her pretty lavender-colored blouse with the puffy sleeves that Berke herself would never have been caught dead in.

Berke thought she was going to have to kill him. She was ready.

He shuddered, came to himself and his current predicament with a jolt, and he let Ariel go. He pushed her aside and sprang up, like a stocky panther searching for escape. The zipper of his jeans was open. Before Berke could think to shout for help, DJ Talk It Up charged her and swung a fist at her face, but Berke saw it coming and warded it off with one arm while the other punched five into the fool's bulbous nose.

She gave it all she had, and she had one hell of a lot to give.

His nose exploded like a blood balloon. But that didn't stop him, he was enraged and desperate and so he kept flailing at her, grabbing at her hair, her breasts, trying to claw her eyes out.

Fucker fights like a girl, Berke thought just before she drove a knee right up into his balls.

Maybe that did hurt him, from the way he whined, but he was running on nerves and adrenaline and he was not going to be stopped by a bagful of smashed nuts. His face might have gone ghost-white, but he still wanted out. He clawed his way past Berke and through the door, tearing himself out of his jacket as Berke grabbed hold of the hood, and then in his flagging white T-shirt stained with tonight's Hungry Man dinner he started to limp to the left but there were still people who'd gotten backstage passes from Twenty Million Miles To Earth in the corridor, jamming things up, and now they were gaping at him and Berke was shouting, "Stop him! Stop him!"

So DJ Talk It Up turned to the right and tried to get past the handcart that nearly tripped him up and took a bite from one of his ankles as he passed. Two more ball-dragging staggers in search of a way out and suddenly from a door in front of him stepped the Detroit dude.

"Stop him, John!" Berke shouted, holding a dark brown hoodie with nobody in it.

Maybe Detroit couldn't always beat Philly's ass. It had been a general statement.

Tonight, though, it was pretty much true.

Nomad got three punches in before DJ Talk It Up realized he was being pounded. They weren't just ordinary back-behind-the-bar or parking lot disagreement shots; they had some meaning behind them, some muscle, and they were well-placed to make DJ Talk It Up understand he was on his way to the hospital. Another trio of punches, fast fast fast, and DJ was speechless and also toothless in front.

Nomad gave him one to the throat, not as hard as he'd given Quince Massey in front of the Olive Garden that day years ago, but one that would be remembered.

Then the DJ was on his knees. His face was not so much a face as a model for an abstract painting. Nomad stood over the Study In Scarlet With Nose On Forehead. Terry looked out from the door at his back, his eyes wide behind his specs, and he determined to stay right where he was, out of harm's way.

There was a frozen moment, as happens in the aftermath of sudden violence.

"John! Terry! Help me!" Berke called, and the way her voice trembled pierced Nomad's heart.

He looked along the corridor. Berke was supporting someone he could not possibly recognize. They were walking slowly, painfully, toward him, and the crew and techs and people with backstage passes and even members of Twenty Million Miles To Earth were around them trying to help.

Nomad saw the duct tape across her mouth, wound around her head and caught in her tangled hair. He saw the blood. He saw her rubbing her wrists, and how a long silver ribbon of tape hung down from one of them. He saw how the lavender-colored blouse with the puffy sleeves had been ruined. One of her favorites, he knew. She lowered her face when she saw him looking, as if in shame to let herself be seen like this.

"Oh, Jesus!" Terry cried out, and he rushed past Nomad to go to Ariel.

Somebody flashed a camera.

Nomad would have torn that person's eyeballs from their skull and made them examine their own asshole, but he didn't have to. One of the stage crew darted in and grabbed the camera. There was a protest and two Cobra Club guys suddenly were taking out the garbage.

Nomad looked again at Ariel, being supported by Berke as Terry worked to get the tape off her mouth and out of her hair. The people around them were stunned into silence. When the tape came off, Ariel took a step forward and then she bent over and vomited on the floor. "It's okay, it's okay," Berke said, rubbing her back. Ariel had to lean against the wall, and somebody offered a towel to hold against her bloody face.

Beyond the door that led to the stage, the audience began to chant for The Five.

Nomad stared down at DJ Talk It Up.

The rage came up in him. It sizzled through his veins like life's blood. Maybe for him, it was. He decided he would end it now.

He reared his right foot back to kick the DJ's brains out of his head.

The young man lifted his chin. The bleeding face was weeping. Tears mixed with blood coursed along the corners of the mangled mouth. His eyes were sightless, fixed on something far beyond the dude from Detroit.

Nomad was about to let swing.

But he hesitated.

He wondered what more he could add to this cup of suffering. He heard the DJ's chest rattle as the sobs rolled out. He saw the DJ put his hands up to his eyes as if to hide from the blinding light. Nomad wondered what kind of shrunken shirt this young man had had to wear, and what had been burned and scarred into his mind and soul. He could imagine this kid leaving Philly with a big-lid ball cap and big dreams. Gonna be a big star, Mom. Gonna set 'em on fire.

Instead, he came to the place where people want things before they've earned them, where you are nobody without power and money, where the heat of the dreams melt you down to size, and hey, Mom, lookit me now.

It was not for Nomad to add anything more.

He lowered his foot. When he turned back toward Ariel, he saw that True and two cops had come into the corridor, along with the club's manager, a spindly guy wearing all black with a trimmed black goatee. True was talking quietly to Ariel, his face close to hers, and Nomad saw her nod. The two cops came over and pulled DJ Talk It Up to his feet. His knees promptly gave way, so they half-dragged, half-guided him into the Green Room. True said tersely, "Call an ambulance!" but Ariel shook her head and grabbed at the manager's sleeve.

"No," she said. "No ambulance."

"Go ahead," True directed.

"No!" Ariel's voice was louder. "I'm not going to the hospital!"

Berke said, "Listen, baby, you've *got* to go. We'll be right there with you."

"No," Ariel repeated. "No, I'm going on."

"Going *on*?" Terry shot a quick glance at Berke and then at True, whose flesh seemed to have tightened over the facial bones just in the last half-minute. "Going on *where*?"

"On stage," Ariel answered, holding the towel against her bleeding nose. It was numb, she didn't know if it was broken or not. She'd already explored with her tongue to make sure her teeth were still there, and though she'd discovered a few unfamiliar edges she thought she was okay. "They're calling for us," she said. "He hurt me, but he didn't rape me." She repeated it to make sure they understood. "He didn't rape me."

"You're going to the hospital," True said, searching her eyes. "Whether you want to or not. Go call the ambulance," he told the manager.

Ariel took the towel away from her face and screamed.

It was a word.

The word was: *No*.

The manager stopped and no one else moved either, not even the dude who was mopping up the mess. Out front, the chanting went on, louder and louder and *time to get this party started*.

Nomad walked to her. He saw her eyes tick toward him, and they were her eyes, yes, but they were different now. They had seen things he wished she'd never had to see. They were bloodshot and they were frightened down in their gray depths, but most of all they were angry.

"Nobody's stopping me!" Ariel said, to all of them, and maybe to the world too. Her teeth clenched; she could taste her own blood and feel all her new sharp edges. "Nobody's going to stop me from doing this! *Nobody*!"

She pulled loose from Berke and from Terry. She stood on her own.

"*This is what I do*!" she cried. "*I was born to do this*!"

When Berke reached out to touch her shoulder, Ariel pushed the hand away.

"No, just let me...let me..." Ariel shook her head and put the towel to her nose again, and when more of the blood was captured she dropped the towel to her side and her eyes blazed into True's. "Nobody's stopping me," she told him, "from doing what I was *born* to do. This. Music. I didn't work this hard...I didn't come all this way...all the bands...the people...everything...to have someone tell me I can't go on when I say I *can*."

And there was more to it, but she was about to sob and she feared breaking apart and not being able to pick up her pieces, so she didn't say that she thought the darkness that had just tried to destroy her *wanted* her to tuck her tail between her legs and go speechless and spineless to the hospital. She didn't say that she thought the darkness revelled in the wounded silence of broken hearts and raped spirits, that it grew strong on the bitter memory of the crushed dream. She didn't say that she thought to *not* go on would be the biggest surrender of her life, because to fight that darkness, to push back its encroachment, meant you had to be determined to stand up. You had to play your guitar and sing, if that's what you were born to do. You had to go out there, bruised and bloody, and let them know you were where you were supposed to be in this world, and *nobody*—surely not that greedy, stupid-minded little *thing* that had tried to throw you out of it—was going to stop you.

She didn't say any of this. But she did say, "Now listen to *me*. My nose might be broken. There might be a doctor or a nurse or a med student out in the crowd. Somebody who can look at me. I know there's got to be a first-aid kit here. My head's hurting, maybe he can find out if I have a concussion. The *doctor*," she said, so they'd understand. "I need one hour. If I pass out or keep throwing up, then okay...call an ambulance. But I need one hour. And I...shit...I need a new top."

"You can't be serious," True said.

"I need to get cleaned up," she continued, as if he'd never spoken. "Wash my face. I can't go back in *there*, though." They knew what she meant. "Oh Jesus," she said wearily, "I've got to pee again."

"You're in shock," True said.

"No," she answered. "Too much tea."

True was about to say something, to deflect her crazy arrow, but he couldn't remember what it was going to be. He didn't smile, he kept his face as grim as a rock. But the determination on this girl's face got to him. He knew why he liked her. She was probably the toughest one of the bunch, but before this moment she'd never needed to be.

"Will you let me—*allow* me to—take you to the emergency room after we're done?"

"Yes."

"You need one hour? That's all?"

"That's all," she said, and he knew she meant it.

"Suit you?" True asked the manager.

"You got it."

"You guys okay with this?" True asked his band.

Terry and Berke looked to Nomad.

"Solid," he replied. If Ariel could go on with her busted nose, he could go on with his swollen knuckles. This was going to be a gig for the ages.

< >

The corridor was clearing out. In the Green Room, the cops had called for a cruiser to take into custody a suspect they thought was most likely the Duct Tape Rapist. The manager went out on stage, faced the happy beer-sodden and Cobra-Cocked crowd and got to speak into the microphone a question he never thought in a million years he would ever ask: "Is there a doctor in the house?"

Suddenly, when True and Terry and Berke moved away, Nomad was right there in front of Ariel. He stared at her, as a wry and admiring smile slowly crept over his face. He didn't understand about Jeremy Pett, about that girl at the well, about that song or what it meant, but he did understand that he could fall in love with Ariel, if he let himself.

And maybe he was halfway there.

He touched his bad eye and then he tapped his nose. He said, "I think we're two of a kind."

Who reached for whom first? It was too close to call.

He hugged her and she held tightly to him, and he found himself crying, just small tears squeezed out between his eyelids, because he was so very very sorry that this terrible thing, this soul-sickening thing, had happened to her, that though—thank God—the DJ had not violated her, some part of her had to have been touched by his ugliness, by the vileness that had been shaped by his suffering, whatever the cause. But those were things of the world, and he couldn't protect her from them any more than he could protect himself, or any of them. Besides, all that went into the stew they called 'writing'.

He put his head against her shoulder and breathed in her aroma. It was a faint smell of honeysuckle, like a sunlit summer meadow. It was the proper aroma for a heroine in one of those Victorian novels who is doomed to fall in love with the callous cad.

But that would not be him, because though he was his father's son he was not his father, and he would never be.

Ariel pressed her hands against his back, and when she heard him sniffle like a little boy she whispered in his ear, "It's all right."

And again, so he'd be certain of it.

TWENTY-SEVEN.

The wheels *on the bus go round and round…round and round…round and round.*

A children's song, Terry thought. He wondered if that was how it had begun, for all of them.

Music, heard when they were children. A tune from a local TV show, one of those disappearing breed where the host in a captain's cap shows cartoons to kids and does magic with balloons and napkins, somebody always named 'Cousin' or 'Cappy'. A snippet of a Christmas carol in a department store, with all the festive lights ablaze and Santa on his way. A tinkling outpouring of silver notes from a music box that holds a tiny dancer, slowly pirouetting. A guy playing a harmonica in one of those old black-and-white westerns or war movies. The distant keening of a train's whistle, lonely in the rainy night.

Something had been awakened in them early, of that Terry was sure. Something that other children might hear, but not keep. He was sure they all had heard something and kept it, and had it still, hidden away in a place of safety. He knew what his was. He knew very well.

True tapped the brake. The Scumbucket slowed at the top of a rise. Not much of a rise, on this straight and flat stretch of Interstate 40, also known as Route 66, but enough of one. He checked his sideview mirror, looking past the U-Haul trailer.

That white car was still there.

Maybe half a mile behind? Now this was kind of ridiculous, he thought, because there was all sorts of traffic heading west from

Albuquerque this Sunday afternoon. There were small cars and big SUVs and tractor-trailer trucks and vans and pickups, all makes and all colors. But that white car—a foreign make, maybe a Honda?—had for a while been close enough for True to catch a glimpse of a man behind the wheel. Wearing sunglasses—*duh*, heading west into the sun, right?—and a ball cap bearing some kind of logo. But then the white car had slowed down and dropped back, had let three or four cars get in between them, and now seemed to be maintaining a constant speed. Or, rather, matching the Scumbucket's speed.

Which was *slow*.

A white car. Foreign make. Young driver, he looked to be.

How come he didn't blow right on past?

"What're you slowing down for?" Nomad asked, from the seat behind Terry.

"Resting my foot, I guess," True answered, and he gave the old engine some more gas.

A white car. Foreign make. Not a dark blue pickup truck.

True looked straight ahead again. The first layer of this highway could have been laid down using a single gigantic rubber band stretched on stakes across the New Mexico desert. Just pull it tight and pour the asphalt in its shadow. He didn't know if they'd had rubber bands back then, but they could've done it that way if they'd had them.

He was getting loopy, he thought. Life on the road. No wonder these people started smoking dope, drinking too much and throwing television sets out of motel windows. He jumped a little bit—just a hair, nobody noticed—when a tractor-trailer truck roared by, sending an insulting wind slapping against the Scumbucket. True noted it was a Hormel meats truck. A meatwagon, he thought.

He'd never smoked dope before. He wondered if anybody in this van had some in their possession. He'd never asked; he didn't really want to know, but at least they hadn't lit up in his presence. This highway was so straight it was hypnotic. On both sides the desert was stubbled with small brown clumps of vegetation that he figured could stab thorns in your ankles at the slightest graze. He wondered how many rattlesnakes were out there, coiled under those ugly clumps, their forked tongues vibrating on the scent of prey.

He knew he was going loopy, because he was starting to think about asking his band what marijuana tasted like.

He shifted in his seat.

"You okay?" Terry asked from the passenger side, and True said he was fine.

True glanced quickly in his rearview mirror. Ariel was drowsing. The bandage was still across her nose, hiding the bruise, but the darkness under her eyes had gone away. Her sniffer hadn't been broken, though it had really swelled up and hurt her the next day and she'd blown out dried krispies of blood until after Anaheim. She had two cracked front teeth that were going to need some work. She was one hell of a trooper. John Charles was staring into space, thinking. His right eye was ringed with pale green. He had a lot to think about. In the back, Berke was listening to her iPod, eyes closed, head slightly nodding to the beat pumping through the earbuds. That girl could play drums like a machine, but True had made the mistake of asking her what she thought about drum machines and for that he'd gotten a year's supply of f-bombs packed into his ears. Terry was alert and excited, of course. This was his day.

There were lots of cars on this highway. Every sort of make and model, big and small. But that white car back there...well, he couldn't see it now, but he knew it was still there.

What was making True so jittery was the fact of the slow decay. The reality of the money pit, even for the FBI. The large hand on the leash, pulling the little dogs home.

After Anaheim, that next morning, the call had found him.

He would have to make do with one team. The money this was costing was out of all proportion to the situation, he was told. He just loved that bean-counting language. He was told, and to be truthful the voice that told him was not as warm and ole-buddy-buddy as usual, that this whole thing might well be a wash. *I know this was important to you, but—*

Ouch. It hurt when you realized you weren't as big a dog as you'd thought you were. And, really, *nobody* was that big of a dog.

The team in the metallic gray Yukon had peeled off the caravan. So long, guys. We're going on.

And then, this morning, after the gig at Staind Glass last night.

True had been shaving in his bathroom at the Comfort Inn when the call had found him this time. "Good morning," True had said, with lather on his upper lip. "Are you being a heathen and skipping church today?"

"Truitt, we need to talk."

"Obviously. You've called me."

"Are you sitting down?"

"No, but I have a razor in my hand." He'd known what it had to be. He'd hoped a phone call was going to lead a team of agents to a motel where Jeremy Pett was holed up, afraid to open his curtains or door to let in a sliver of sunlight, afraid to leave his crummy flea circus of a room for a takeout pizza because of the media noise, but hoping wasn't about to make it happen. Pett had plain and simply vanished. Gone to Mexico? That was the theory. But where was his truck? It hadn't shown up, so where was it? Abandoned somewhere on the border, was the theory. Driven into a gulley, or parked amid the mesquite trees and head-high sticker bushes just north of many of the paths grooved into the earth by the shoes of Mexican illegals. After all, those paths went both ways. Another theory: maybe Pett, trained in the art of going to ground, had actually gone *underground*. Maybe he'd found a tunnel across. Those things were out there.

Jeremy Pett would have to be totally insane to stay in this country with his face and his license number all over TV. That was the theorists talking. He would have to *want* to be caught. And why in this *world* should he follow that damned band to California when he could slide right into Mexico from Tucson?

"Truitt," said the Sunday morning heathen, "we're pulling the second team."

Ouch. True had nicked himself under his left nostril.

"There's no need for you to stay out. Call it off and bring them in."

"Slow down, take it easy." He'd realized he was talking to his heart. "The tour ends six days from now, and they've only got two more gigs, in Dallas on the 15th and in Austin on the 16th. Then it's done. We're checking out this afternoon and driving to see somebody Terry wants to visit. That's the keyboard player."

"I saw the story in *People*. Hell, I *know* their names."

"Okay. We're hitting the road right after that and driving to Amarillo. Then, tomorrow, on to Dallas. I figured they could hang out in Dallas for—"

"Excuse me, did you say 'hang out'?"

True had heard himself sigh. It was a sound of exasperation; those mundanes—Terry's word—just don't *get it*. "They're good people," he'd said. "Hard workers. You wouldn't believe how hard."

"I know they're a big hit now. Selling thousands of CDs, aren't they?"

"Yeah." Not only that, but every gig since that night at the Cobra Club had been jammed solid. Which actually put a strain on him, trying to get the security locked down. The news that The Five had aided in the capture of the Duct Tape Rapist had really made the engines rev. Roger Chester was calling him, giddy with glee, saying he had offers from three networks to do a The Five reality series and publishers were calling with quickie book deals and somebody wanted them to be spokespeople for a new energy drink. It was off the hook, as John said. Yet he didn't say it with a convincing display of joy. So what was up with that?

"Six days, two more gigs," True had said into his cell, as he'd dabbed the small red dot under his left nostril with a bit of tissue paper. "Can I finish it with them? And can I get some support from the field offices?" Boy, did that sound like begging.

"Truitt," said the voice attached to the large hand that held the leash. "You do understand you're not really their manager. Right? You do understand your role, don't you?"

"I do. But...you know...I told them I'd finish it out." He'd paused, trying to think of something else to say to pierce the silence on the other side. "They *really* are good people."

"I heard that the first time."

"I can't leave them," True had said.

"I hear the word *won't* in that, Truitt."

"Yes, sir," True had replied. "That's correct."

The silence had stretched a little longer this time, and had been a little more solid.

During it, True had wondered if he should tell his old friend and compatriot and superior that Ariel Collier thought the song they were writing was being directed—well, not really *directed* exactly, but guided in a way, but not exactly that either—by a girl who was not exactly human, but something more than human if you believe in that, and this song they were writing was just a regular song, nobody could see any big thumbprint on it, no hidden meanings or mystical codes as far as they could tell, and if it was supposed to break them through into being a success it was a little late, because the song wasn't finished yet there was The Five in *People* magazine and their CD catalog was going back for a hundred thousand more pressings, and they were selling big numbers now all over the world, so they were already a success, and by the way Terry Spitzenham—oh, I forgot you know their names—believes the same thing, that this song has a divine inspiration, and Berke Bonnevey and John Charles don't quite know what to make of it but they've come around to admitting nothing ever shook their foundations but this was putting some cracks in the mortar, and also—a *big* also—Ariel thinks there's a link between Jeremy Pett, Connor Addison and our trailer park communications wizard, maybe even the Duct Tape Rapist too, because this *thing*—this greedy *king crow*, she calls it, only she says that's not exactly what she means—wants to stop the song from being finished so it has reached out to human hands to do the dirty work.

And that's my story and I'm stickin' to it.

"Truitt?"

"Yes, sir?"

"One of your best qualities is that you're determined to see a situation through to the end. I appreciate that. I'm going to tell you that you can see this one through, but you'll have to go it alone." The voice had paused for True's reaction. None was forthcoming. "I've told the second team to stand down. As of thirty minutes ago, they were relieved of duty and instructed to come home as soon as they can pack up. I imagine Casey's going to be knocking at your door any minute now. You say you have an errand to run this afternoon?"

"Right."

"I can't justify the cost, Truitt. Now, I can work with you on providing security at the venues in Dallas and Austin. But as far as having that caravan burn money and time on the highway...I just don't see the point."

True had known there was no use in arguing. When the large hand on the leash didn't see the point, there *was* no point. It wasn't as if he could single out anything that had happened in the past week as a reason to keep one team on the road. Everything had gone like oiled clockwork except for that incident at Magic Monty's in Anaheim last Tuesday night, where a young man stoned on pot had set off a string of firecrackers in the crowd. The Five had stopped playing just long enough for the cops to haul the kid off to jail, and then they'd picked it right up again.

When Agent Casey had come to the door to announce what he knew True already knew, True had told him he appreciated the good work and attention to detail, and he would make sure everybody involved got gold stars on the reports. True had been so tempted to ask Casey to wait two hours, until the band had roused themselves from their late night gig at the converted church, and follow them out along Route 66 before taking off for Tucson, but he couldn't do it. The orders had been given. The men were anxious to get home to their families.

So long, guys. We're going on.

But after Casey had gone, True had had trouble steaming the wrinkles out of the gray slacks he intended to wear, the steam just wouldn't come out of the nozzles, and suddenly he'd felt a hot surge of anger and when he banged the steamer against the bathroom counter he was holding a piece of broken plastic dripping water all over the floor. He realized he was hanging on the edge, and it was not a good place to be.

That was why he kept watch on the white car back there. That was why he wondered who was driving it, and why it kept such a constant speed. He thought about giving the troopers a call on his cell, identifying himself and asking for a little help in checking out a plate number.

"Who're you calling?" Terry asked when True took the cell out of his leather bag.

"Hang on a minute." But in only a few seconds True realized he wasn't calling anyone. No bars, no service out in this expanse of desert. He said, "Just checking something," and then he put the cellphone away.

"We ought to be almost there," Terry told him. "The sign'll say *Blue Chalk*."

"Okay," True answered, and he tried to concentrate on his driving.

Terry knew very well what he'd heard and kept when he was a child, and knew he had it still, hidden away in a place of safety. It was something from his grandparents' house. His mother's parents lived in a brick house a few blocks from his grammar school.

They were still there, Granddad Gerald in his mid-seventies and Grandmother Mimi just turned seventy. Some days after school, Terry had gone there to get a cold drink and sit on the screened-in porch as his grandfather listened to the early autumn baseball games on the radio and smoked a pipe with a face carved on the bowl that GeeGee said was a musketeer. His grandfather played board games with him, too. Any excuse to pull from the closet the old Milton Bradley *Dogfight* or the Mattel *Lie Detector* or the really cool Transogram 52-variety game chest with all the different colored boards. And then as the afternoon wore on, and Terry didn't want to leave because this house was small and warm and not like his own at all, Grandmother Mimi brought from the closet a small plastic keyboard that she plugged in and placed in her lap as she sat in the front room. He would never forget the sound of that keyboard coming to life when she flipped a switch. It was like hearing an orchestra warm up, the violins, the oboes, the flutes and trumpets just softly starting to awaken. An orchestra contained in a small plastic box. And then she played it with her supple fingers, and he was sure that her fingers were supple because she *did* play it, and maybe it called to her to play it, day after day, because they needed each other to stay young.

What stories that keyboard told! When Terry closed his eyes and listened, he could see the image in his mind of a boy on a raft with a beautiful girl clinging to him, and in the river the rapids ran fast over dangerous rocks and the boy would have to be quick and smart to get them through that treacherous stretch. Or he saw a hundred Cossacks on their horses, driving forward through the snow under a moon as bright as a new quarter. Or he saw himself, older but still young, playing that very same keyboard before a vast audience, in a great concert hall, and then the Cossack chief rode in right down the aisle and awarded him an official sword and the beautiful girl stood up from the front row and said she would be his forever.

And then, of course, GeeGee cleared his throat across the game table, and when Terry opened his eyes GeeGee puffed smoke from the musketeer's feathered hat and slapped down the dogfight's '5 Bursts' card, which meant Terry's Spad was going down in flames.

He began to think they were teaming up on him.

"Terry," said Grandmother Mimi, "do you want me to show you some chords?"

Chords? You mean...like...*ropes*?

"Sort of," she'd answered. "Only these ropes never wear out, and they always keep you connected to something wonderful."

Years later, the small portable organ just didn't wake up on one day. It was a Hohner Organetta, not the kind of instrument found in every neighborhood music store. It sat silent in the closet, gathering dust. Was it for that reason Grandmother Mimi's fingers began to swell and twist with the onset of arthritis?

"Let me try to fix it," said Terry Spitzenham, the high school freshman.

There was no owner's manual. No electronics diagram. Maybe somewhere in Germany there lived a Hohner Organetta expert, but he wasn't in Oklahoma City. Terry opened the keyboard up, and looked at the old wiring and the reeds. He replaced the electric cord, but no go. It had to be a voltage problem, according to his electronics books. Not enough voltage was being generated to produce sound. He tried this and that, and that and this, but the keyboard remained mute. Finally he decided to take it all apart, every last bit of it, and rebuild it.

It regained its voice too late for Grandmother Mimi, whose fingers would no longer let her play. But, she said, she would love to *listen*, because she said that when she closed her eyes and he was playing—just that small keyboard with its twelve black keys and seventeen white—she felt like she was right there with him.

His first vintage keyboard buy had been a Hohner Symphonic 320, a real nasal-sounding and nasty-ass bastard found in the back of a garage. If those old brutes weren't the heart and soul of rock, he didn't know what *rock* was.

And now, he was minutes away from seeing—touching, *playing* if he could—the legend of legends, Lady Frankenstein.

"There's the sign," he said, and he heard in himself the excited voice of a little boy.

Blue Chalk, it read. True noted that it was defaced by a pair of close-set bullet holes. He took the exit off Route 66 and started north along a cracked and uneven asphalt road. Ahead stood a mesa, purple above the burnt brown of the desert floor. True drove sixty feet and slowed the Scumbucket to a halt. He peered into the sideview mirror.

"What's the problem?" Nomad asked. True was acting shady this afternoon; something was up, and it wasn't just because of the second security team leaving, as True had told the band at lunch.

True was holding his breath. In his lap was the leather bag that held his pistol. He watched the exit curve very carefully.

"True, what is it?" Ariel had awakened when the van stopped, and now Berke opened her eyes and removed the earbuds.

"Where are we?" Berke asked.

True could see cars speeding by on the highway. He watched the curve for a white car that might suddenly take the same turn to Blue Chalk.

Nobody said anything else, because they realized True was not only working, he was a two-hundred pound tuning fork that had just been struck into vibration.

He saw the white car pass.

Then he let his breath go.

He gave the Scumbucket some gas and it rumbled onward.

"What was *that* about?" Nomad looked back, but of course could see nothing beyond the trailer's bulk.

"I wanted to make sure we weren't being followed."

"Why?" Berke's voice was tight. "Did you see something?"

"We're good," he told her, and drove on toward the distant mesa.

The road began to undulate, to rise up on small scrub-covered hillocks and then to fall into rock-walled gullies. Here and there were trailers with external generators because the power poles that marched this way no longer held electrical lines. They passed several houses that had collapsed under the weight of time. Maybe this had been a community when Route 66 was a leisurely scenic road, the theater of Buz and Tod in their red Corvette convertible, but now it was a footnote to progress.

The road curved in and out. If there was any blue chalk in these red walls of rock, it was hiding under camouflage paint. This place was so far off the track it was refreshingly clean, not a beer can or broken bottle or spray of graffiti to be found. An undiscovered country, True thought. Well, it had been discovered *once*, but in the end nature always won.

They rounded a curve and there stood the brown stone building Eric Gherosimini had told Terry to watch for in his letter. It was a hollow shell, really. An abandoned gas station. Long abandoned, from the looks of the two rusted-out antique pumps in front. A few tires that might have been perfect for a 1959 Ranchero lay in a dust-whitened stack.

"Damn!" Berke said, looking out her window. "Was gas ever twenty-five cents a gallon?"

A barely-legible metal sign leaning against a broken wall said it was.

"And who's Ethel?" she asked, but True didn't tell her.

Across the road were a half-dozen remnants of houses, not much left but the roofs and frames, and around them stood the boulders and shale that had over the years—decades?—drifted down from the rugged hill behind. Between two of the ruins was a rusted swingset, a slide and a seesaw. Once upon a time, a children's playground.

The Scumbucket negotiated another sharp turn, another descent into a washed-out gully, and there the asphalt ended. Ahead the road turned to dirt.

"Your boy wanted to get away from it all, didn't he?" True asked, easing on the brake. "You sure about this?"

"He said he lives a half-mile past the pumps," Terry said. "We're almost there."

"I think if I'd wanted to be a hermit I would've chosen an island in the Caribbean," True replied, but he pressed the pedal and the wheels of the van went round and round, raising whorls of dust behind them. "Maybe I'm crazy, but that's just me."

They continued on. True had been glancing every so often in the sideview mirror. It disturbed him that he couldn't see anything through the dust. They rounded one more snakespine of a curve and Terry said, "That's it."

On the right was a small, regular-looking adobe-style house, nothing special about it at all. It might have been plucked from any Southwestern city suburb, with a minimalist and rock-loving landscaper in charge. But then again, most adobe-style houses in city suburbs were connected to power lines and didn't have a pair of big metal boxes that could only be heavy-duty generators cabled up alongside. As they got nearer, they could hear a rumble like an old aircraft engine turning its propellor. An honest-to-God outhouse stood out back, along with a raised wooden platform that held a showerhead and some kind of waterbucket device operated by a pullchain. A sagging pickup truck the dun color of mole's skin was parked on the shale in front of the house. Berke thought that it had probably used its share of twenty-five-cents-a-gallon gas.

True was getting the picture of where they were. He could see two trailers standing maybe a hundred yards further on, where the dirt road ended at a rock wall that angled toward the sky. He figured the Zen masters of hermitry lived in those trailers. Either that, or they were cooking meth *and* hiding from the IRS.

"You guys ever watch Western movies?" he asked. They gave him blank expressions. "Know what a box canyon is?" When there was no reply, he wondered what young people were learning in schools these days. "Well," said True, "we're in one."

He stopped the Scumbucket in front of the house. A reddish-brown dog came rocketing off the shady porch, planted its paws in the stones and gave them a reception that could be heard even over the rumble of aircraft props.

Terry saw a man emerge from the house. The man stood on the porch, watching them climb out of the van. He looked as if he were trying to decide if he knew them or not. True clutched his leather bag close to his side.

Over the dog's barking and the generator noise, Terry called out, "Mr. Gherosimini? I'm Terry Spitzenham! You remember? From The Five? You wrote me a letter saying I could come—"

"My *brother*!" the man shouted, and lifted his hands in the air. He had a gray beard that hung over the chest of his overalls and was decorated with what appeared to be small metallic beads. His deeply-seamed face grinned. "*Finally* come home!" He came striding off the porch with the gait of an energetic younger man. The barking dog put itself between him and the visitors in a posture of defense.

Eric Gherosimini was making music as he walked, though they couldn't hear it. Tied in his beard with white and gold-colored cords were little bells. He was barefoot. Nomad thought the soles of those horny-toed feet must have been an inch thick to survive all the wicked edges. Gherosimini was thin and stoop-shouldered and bald on the top of his scalp except for a few remaining wild sprigs of gray, while the hair on the sides and back flowed down over his shoulders like opaque curtains. He wore wire-rimmed glasses that were not very different from Terry's.

My brother. Finally come home.

Oh my God, Nomad thought. This dude's going to ask Terry to change places with him so he can go out and paint the world red, and Terry will have to be the guardian of the secret fucking keyboards until the next sucker comes along.

But Eric Gherosimini raised his index finger to the dog and said sternly, "Stereo!" The mongrel stopped barking. Then the frail genius of the 13th Floors looked Terry full in the face, blinked his electric-blue eyes and touched Terry's shirt, which today was black-and-purple paisleys on a background of dove gray.

"*Boss* shirt," he said with admiration. "Vintage, '66? H.I.S.?"

"You got it." Terry remembered who he was talking to. "Sir."

Gherosimini put an arm around Terry's shoulder. "Come on inside. All of you. Come see the madman's dreams."

They followed him, with Stereo sniffing at their shadows.

TWENTY-EIGHT.

"I didn't know if you'd be here or not," Terry said, when he didn't know what else to say.

"Usually here, man. Don't get out much, but...how do you guys say it?..*it's all good*."

"Can I ask something?" True waited for Eric Gherosimini's eyes to focus on him. It looked to True as if the man had some difficulty in that department. "Why do you live so far from town? There's just nothing around here."

Gherosimini's gaze floated down along the creases of True's slacks to take aim at the black wingtips. An impish smile worked at the corners of his mouth. "Man, I know I've been out of action a *lonnngggg* time, but they sure don't make road managers like they used to."

They were sitting in what passed as the man's living room. It contained inflatable chairs in Day-Glo colors and a plaid sofa that must have come all the way from Scotland's Salvation Army. On the woodplank floor was a blue rug with the image of the moon and sun woven into it. Some type of scrawny leafless tree in a rusted metal pot stood in a corner, its limbs bearing a strange fruit of several different kinds of multi-colored glass windchimes. A fan powered by the generator continually stirred the chimes into musical tinklings. A blue cone of incense burned in a metal cup on a table made out of what True thought might be compressed telephone books. The faintly sweet smell of the incense reminded Ariel of the way the air smelled at Singing Beach, in Manchester, after a summer rain. Several unlit candle lanterns in an ornate Moroccan style stood about, indicating that the generators were not always running. Stereo sprawled on the floor at his master's bare feet, chewing on a green dental hygiene bone.

And it was not every living room that had walls covered, every inch except the front window, with white sound-dampening acoustic tiles. Bamboo blinds hung over the window. Tacked up in several places on the wall tiles were posters of San Francisco's Golden Gate Bridge, the rugged majesty of the Big Sur coast and the skyline of Seattle showing the Space Needle.

Gherosimini had brought them small ceramic cups of reddish-hued water that he'd said was sent to him by a fellow shapeshifter from the Lion's Head Fountain at a place called Chalice Well, in England. He offered a part-toast, part-prayer that the world should be healed by the power of mystic waters, and that it should begin right here in this room.

Nomad thought the water tasted like it had been soaking rusty nails. He took a couple of sips and decided, mystic waters or not, he wasn't going to run the risk of getting lockjaw.

"So far from town," Gherosimini said, repeating a portion of True's question. He was lounging in a bright orange inflatable chair. The windchimes tinkled softly as the fan's breeze touched them, and Stereo gnawed on his chewie. "Nothing around here. Why do you think that, Mr. Manager Man?"

"Because I have two working eyes."

"You *sure* they're working?"

"Pretty much." True took another sip of the water stained with iron oxide. It wasn't so bad, but what he would pay right now for a glass of iced tea!

"How about you?" Gherosimini's attention turned to Ariel. "You're very quiet. Do *you* think there's nothing around here?"

She shrugged, not sure how he wanted her to respond. "I guess I—"

"No," he interrupted. "Say what you really think."

"I think..." She saw he was forming an appraisal of her, and she decided to tell him what she really thought. "I think there's the wind at night, and when you walk in it you can hear music, or voices, or both. I think there's a silence that asks you who you are. I think there's a sky of stars that would knock a person's eyes out. I think the colors of the sunset and sunrise are never exactly the same. I think you could swim in the moonlight if you wanted to. I think you could stand in the blue cool of the evening and smell the ocean waves that used to roll here." She could smell those right now, from the smoky cone of incense. "I think the rocks might move when you're not looking, but if you keep looking one day you'll see it happen. I think you could see a hundred thousand pictures in the clouds and never the same one twice. I think maybe you could see angels out here, if you tried hard enough."

"And devils?" Gherosimini's thick gray eyebrows shot up. "Could I see those too, if I tried hard enough?"

She nodded. "Yes. But I wouldn't want to try that hard."

He looked at his other guests with a smile that told them the quiet ones always ran the deepest. "What do you think about that, Mr. Manager Man?"

"I think I must be nearsighted," he said, which really was the truth.

That made the genius of the 13th Floors laugh. The sound must've been unusual, because Stereo looked up from his chewie and made a weird questioning noise between a whine and a growl. Call it a whrowl. Then he went right back to chewing.

"My turn for a question," Nomad announced. He realized Terry was looking at him with fear on his face, not knowing what John was going to throw at his hero. Nomad had heard of the 13th Floors before, sure, and Gherosimini had earned his respect for blazing a trail, but this bell-bearded sixty-something-year-old bag of hippie dust was just plain ol' Jack to him. "You called Terry your brother and said he'd finally come home. What was that supposed to mean?"

"I don't have a computer here," Gherosimini answered, and then he sat there so silently and for so long that Nomad thought the tons of acid he'd swallowed back in the dark ages had come back to drop a psychedelic bomb on his brain. But then the man finished his cup of weird water. "After I got Terry's letter, I went to the Internet room at the library in town. I went to your website. Nice site, man. Very cool, easy to navigate. I watched your videos. I wrote Terry that I bought one of your CDs. They're hard to find. But...you know...I knew you before you were born."

"Really?" Uh huh, he thought. Acid bomb, bigtime.

"Really. You were the lead singer of the Mojo Ghandis. And you were the lead singer of Freight Train South. You were up on stage fronting The Souljers, and man did you work your ass off for Proud Pete and the Prophets. Oh yeah, I knew you. Watched you burn up a stage, work up a crowd, many nights. Many, many gigs." The wispy-haired head nodded, the blue eyes fixed on Nomad and unyielding. "I knew Ariel, too. She was the girl you went to when you needed to come down to earth. When it got real floaty and spooky up there in the high dark, and you needed a safe place to land. She was the one who told you what you didn't want to hear, because she was one of the few people—the *very* few—who gave a shit whether you lived or died. And Terry...oh, yeah. He was there. In how many bands and behind how many keyboards, who can count? But he was always where he needed to be, when he needed to be there."

Gherosimini looked at Berke. "I'm not sure," he said, "if I ever knew *you*. Not in my era. The female drummer was a freak. Shit, you may be a freak too. But I do know one thing: you can bust it up with anybody who ever sat behind *me*. So take that compliment from a gator who drove drummers so fucking crazy they'd do anything to get out of the band, including jumping out of windows. And that guy you've probably heard about, who jumped into a pool at a Holiday Inn and broke a woman's back?" Gherosimini grinned. "That spaz thought we were on the parking lot side."

A frown suddenly surfaced. "Your bass player. Where is he?"

It hit them all, at that moment, that Eric Gherosimini had no idea what The Five had been through in the past twenty-four days. Without a computer, without the Internet, possibly without a television or a radio, maybe adverse to reading newspapers and magazines...he truly had decided to put many miles between himself and modern civilization. Maybe, Nomad thought, he just didn't like the music anymore.

"Mike's not with us," Berke said. "But we'll catch up with him later on."

"Outta sight," was Gherosimini's comment, with an upraised thumb. "Oh, yeah...your question." He focused on Nomad. "Terry's my brother 'cause he feels the love. Of what we do. What we feel when we're playing. And I say he's finally come home, because he's wanted to come here for a long time. Not necessarily this place, man, but to wherever *I* am. I know what I've done. I know who I am. Terry's like family. He's finally come home, and I know the why of that, too. He wants to meet the lady. Isn't that right, Terry?"

The question made Terry's heart race. The moment was near. "Yes," he said.

Gherosimini stood up, and so did Stereo. "Let me introduce you."

They followed him into the small kitchen and then through a sliding metal door into a larger room at the back of the house. He flipped a light switch. When the fluorescents came on, Terry thought this must be the first step on the stairway to Heaven.

It was another room whose walls were covered with the white acoustic tiles. The floor was of gray concrete. Within the room were several sets of speakers of different sizes, a twenty-four-track mixing board on a desk, a chair for the board rider, and cables connected to an item True certainly recognized, a multitrack reel-to-reel tape recorder. Next to the console was a wooden rack holding what the others knew to be echo and effects boxes, compressors, limiters, and other studio necessities. None of the equipment looked very new, and most of it was definitely vintage, from the late '60s or early '70s. If any of this stuff still worked, Nomad thought, gear collectors would piss their pants with excitement in here. Various vintage microphones were on their stands waiting for use. A plastic crate held a rat's nest of cables, wallwarts and power cords.

On the left side of the studio stood a second desk, smaller than the one holding the mixer, on which sat a typewriter. A piece of paper was held in the rollers, with typing on it. Near at hand was a sheaf of paper, a tin cup holding some pens and pencils, and an ashtray with half of a plump brown cigarette in it that True decided he wouldn't stroll over and examine. On the right side of the studio was a workbench with various pieces of circuitry and wiring lying atop it.

Terry was focused straight ahead. Nothing in Eric Gherosimini's studio pulled at him but the array of mind-blowing vintage organs and electric pianos on their stands that dominated the space.

He felt for a few seconds that he couldn't breathe. He couldn't draw a breath. Something in his brain was so hit with the electric pleasure prod, and so deeply, that his automatic life-functions had gone on the fritz. But then he figured he really should concentrate on drawing in a long lungful of air, to clear his head and keep himself from passing out, because there never ever in his life would be another moment like this.

He went through a quick assessment of what he was looking at: a Vox Continental UK Version 1 with the cool black keys from about 1962; a fire-engine red Vox Jaguar 304, built to start a blaze on a dance floor; a silver-top Rhodes electric piano from 1968; a 1975 Rhodes Mark 1, a battered warrior; an ARP synthesizer...no, *two* ARPs, one opened up to show its internals and probably being cannibalized; a beautiful Roland Jupiter 8; a Minimoog Voyager and a Moog Sonic 6; a Prophet 600 with some missing keys on the high end; a Rhodes Chroma; an unknown thing labelled 'Sonick' in a suitcase with a blue keyboard and a control board with different colored knobs and what looked like a pegboard to chart the ocillators; a gorgeous wood-grained, double-keyboard early Mellotron; a glossy black Panther Duo 2200, the stage instrument of 'The Partridge Family' but capable of doing the nasty in any biker bar; an elegant, slightly arrogant gray Doric; two of the weird slabs of Kustom Kombos, the Naugahyde-padded "Zodiac" combined keyboard-and-stage-speakers, one in blue and the other yellow.

He saw sleek Farfisas and Cordovoxes with the 'AstroSound' effect. He saw a hundred-and-thirty-two pounds of double-keyboard vintage Yamaha, circa 1972. He saw the Gems: a Caravan, a Sprinter and a Joker 61. And then he came to the instruments he did not know, the ones that held no names or trademarks. The ones that were born from the acid-stretched mind of Eric Gherosimini.

He saw a sleek silver keyboard with wings, like a fighter jet awaiting takeoff. On the wings that curved back on either side of the player were dozens of rocker switches. Next to it stood a hulking black synthesizer five feet tall and about four feet wide. Above the blood-red keyboard were many banks of toggles, multi-colored cables plugged from one connection to another, knobs by the dozens and—ominously—a single broken wine glass sitting on a metal foil tray atop the brutish instrument's ledge.

He saw an instrument shaped like a hand, with rows of gray circular buttons designed to be pressed or played or whatever by each finger. A one-handed symphony. He saw a thing that looked like a harp crossed with a washboard. He saw a five-note keyboard, three whites and two blacks, with a control console that resembled a peacock's fan. Next to it was a red-painted upright acoustic piano with garishly-colored keys and desert plants and cacti bursting out of the open top. Was Gherosimini experimenting with organic sound-dampeners? Trying to create a naturalist sound using elements from nature?

"What's this one?" Terry asked.

Gherosimini craned his neck to see. "Oh, that's my planter," he said.

And there...right there...only fifteen feet away, on the other side of the planter, she was standing white and pure on four shining aluminum legs.

Gherosimini crossed to the wall, opened a metal box and pulled a lever. They couldn't hear the second generator kick into action, but they could feel its vibration in the floor. Green lights came on in a central command box. Lights of many colors, some steady and others pulsing like heartbeats, began to appear on the instruments. And there was a glorious hum of life.

"My brother," Gherosimini said to Terry, "you can play anything you like. This is your home."

Terry lowered his head.

Silently he wept tears of joy.

"Mr. Gherosimini?" Ariel was speaking from across the studio, where she'd wandered over to the typewriter to see, curious and writer-to-writer, what he was doing. "You have a new project?" She remembered the letter Terry had read. *I'm working on something real*, Gherosimini had told him.

"I do." He walked to her side through the maze. He knew every taped-down cable on the floor, and every plug pushed into every multi-plug floor unit; he could walk through here in pitch dark and not be tripped up. "It's something I've been writing for a while."

Ariel didn't want to look at what was typed on the paper, or what she'd glimpsed was typed and struck-out and retyped in the agony of creation on some of the other papers. She didn't want to be influenced by anyone else's lyrics, not with their song still unfinished. Mike had given his part, George had given his, Terry and Berke theirs. But not John. Not yet. And though she'd already added a line she felt it was going to fall to her to complete the song, to put it together from the different elements. To find a meaning in it, if a meaning was to be found. So far, in her nightly study of the words, nothing had come to her. Terry had tried to write a few more lines, but he'd ended up scratching them out. It seemed his part was done. Or was it? Berke was having nothing more to do with it, though she'd wished Ariel good luck.

Ariel thought John was afraid of the song. He didn't want to talk about it. He didn't want to even look at it. He had told her this morning that today, the 10th of August, was the seventeenth-year anniversary of the death of his father in Louisville, Kentucky. He'd said that he missed his father, and that Dean Charles had been a very good musician. Dean Charles had known how to play to a crowd. How to give them their money's worth. Dean Charles had known his role as a musician, he'd told her. But, John had said, his father had never quite figured out how to be a very good person, at least not to the people who'd cared about him the most.

I am not my father, John had said to Ariel.

I know you're not, she'd replied.

He'd said that someday he would tell her the whole story, and she'd said she would wait until he was ready to tell it.

But that song...John, who feared nothing, feared that song.

Yet he didn't say throw it away. He didn't say crumple the paper and burn it, or tear it into strips and leave it in a motel's trashcan when they drove away.

No. Ariel understood he was giving it to her to finish.

But she had fear too, and her fear was that she might make a mistake, that she might mess it up in some way, that the meaning and purpose of it might be ruined because of a slip of the human hand, or an imperfection of the human mind. Nothing created by a human was perfect and nothing could be perfect. But what did the girl at the well want this song to *say*? What did she want it to *be*?

"It's called *Ground Zero*."

"What?" Ariel asked.

"That's the title of my new project. My rock opera." Gherosimini was standing beside her, and a few feet away Nomad stopped in his inspection of all this old junk to listen, and True walked over to hear, and Berke had been scowling at the presence of a drum machine in the effects rack but she too cocked an ear in the old hippie's direction, and across the studio Terry had been about to touch the cool white beauty of Lady Frankenstein when he heard the words *my rock opera*. He turned away from her, and walked nearer her creator so he might hear.

"It's a work-in-progress," Gherosimini said. "I've got some bits and pieces done. You want to hear them?"

"No," Ariel said, and Terry almost hit the floor. But he understood when she added, "We're working on something very important. I don't think we should have anyone else's lyrics and music in our heads right now. Thank you anyway."

"Okay." Gherosimini looked disappointed, but he shrugged. "I understand. You don't want to muddy up the well."

"Yes, that's right," she answered.

"*Ground Zero*," said True. "It's about Nine-Eleven?"

"Oh yeah, man. It's about Nine-Eleven, and Nine-Ten, and Nine-Twelve, and Nine-Nine, and every day."

"Every day?"

"Right. It's about the war that goes on every day, Mr. Manager Man. Every hour, every minute. It's about the quiet war. The one that doesn't make headlines until something terrible happens, and people are left trying to make sense of *why* it happened. They're left wondering how they thought they could've known the nice guy who lives down the street. The same guy who woke up one morning and took a gun over to the shopping mall. The student who barricades other kids in a classroom and opens up with an assault rifle. The decent woman who can't stand the pressure anymore, and she hears voices in her head telling her to drown her children to give them a better life. That's Ground Zero."

"*What's* Ground Zero?" Nomad asked.

"Human suffering," said Gherosimini. "Ground Zero of the soul."

Nomad glanced quickly at Ariel but her gaze was fixed on their host, who said to Terry, "Go ahead. Don't be shy. You're not the first one to find her, but you're probably the youngest. She'll appreciate a young touch."

Terry didn't move. He was still registering what Gherosimini had said about his rock opera.

True spoke up. "What war are you talking about?"

"*The* war." Gherosimini stared at True for a few seconds. He wore a faint sad smile. "The spiritual war," he said. "The war between the spirits, man. For the souls of people. For their minds and hearts. For their *hands*, because that's what they really want. One to build, and one to destroy. Without human hands, they're nothing. Don't you get it?"

"You mean good versus evil, right?" Berke asked. "The cosmic wrestling match?"

"This one isn't fixed. It isn't predetermined. And okay, call it good versus evil. The light against the dark. The creation versus the destruction. I don't know what it is...but I believe it *is*."

Ordinarily Nomad would've thought the acid bomb was about to drop again, but now... after what they'd been through...especially that Connor Addison freak...

The angels are very disturbed with her, that trailer park nut had said.

It seemed to Nomad that the trailer park nut thought he was listening to a higher frequency than what was actually running through his comm line. He was picking up the low-down from Radio Stone Church, or from wherever the dark things on the other side of the glass sent out their bulletins to the branded.

As much as he hated hospitals, he thought he needed to check into one when they got back to Austin. He was going to have his head checked for brain tumors and even if they didn't find anything he wanted to lie on one of those beds that move up and down and get plenty of sleeping pills and feel-good drugs and watch simple-minded television until all this was the hazy memory of a particularly bad dream.

"At Ground Zero," Gherosimini said, speaking now to Ariel, "is where the war really happens. Everybody in the world suffers. Everybody knows some kind of pain, of disappointment or frustration. Because that's the world. Things don't go like you want them to. The richest man in the world and the most beautiful movie star...they know it. Nobody gets out without knowing it. And see, one side tries to winnow in, and drive a wedge to widen the crack that pain makes. Get in there, in the soul and the mind, and tell you you're a failure, and everybody else is taking your share, and people are laughing at you behind your back because you're a fucked-up old has-been with a heart full of regrets. Whatever they need to say, however they need to say it. And ohhhh yeah...they are real pros at what they do. But the other side wants to heal the crack. Not going to tell you there's never going to be any more pain or disappointments, or *unfairness*, because that would be a lie. It's a world of humans, so you've got to expect human failings. And that's just how it is."

"*But*," Gherosimini continued, in a quieter voice, "the side that wants to heal the crack won't do it for you. Maybe it'll nudge you a little bit, or show you the first step on a path, but it's not going to hold your hand and take you all the way. That's your decision, and you've got to do that yourself. *Why*?" He turned his bright lights upon True and let the question hang.

"You tell me," said True when Gherosimini's silence went on.

"Because," the genius of the 13th Floors said, "one side wants you to be weak and spread weakness around like a plague, and one side wants you to be strong and help other people find their own strength. But first you have to find it in yourself. That's *my* opinion, Kemosabe."

"Why should they even *care*?" Berke asked. Her voice sounded ragged. There was wildness in her eyes. "If these things are really out there, why should they even fucking care about us?"

"You'd have to ask *them* that question, sister. I doubt you'd get an answer. I never have. Maybe it's a game, but that would only be our word for it. Maybe it's a struggle of honor. Maybe it really does mean something, in the scheme of things. But I'll tell you, I don't think it's for nothing. If I did…I wouldn't be writing a rock opera about it, would I?"

Nomad looked at Ariel again, and this time she met his gaze.

"I need to ask you two," said Gherosimini. "Have you been fighting? Like with the fists? And the eye and the nose got in the way? Yeah, one thing about being in a band never changes: the more passion, the more smashin'. But, you know, you need to feel the love." He turned away and walked over the cables and between the keyboards to Terry. "Go on, man. What're you waiting for? She needs some attention." He pulled the swivel chair from his workbench and parked it in front of Lady Frankenstein, and Terry sat down.

The small red lights on the console burned steady, except for one at its center that slowly beat…beat…beat.

Terry began to play, just a testing of chords the way his grandmother had taught him.

Lady Frankenstein spoke. At first her voice was like one fresh from slumber, a little slurry, a little slow. She was, after all, up in her years. Her action was not the quickest. She had been in her prime long before the disco era, and now hers was the voice of a woman who had lived fully and freely with her long hair wild in the hot sparkle of the lights, her eyes glittering with expectations and opportunities, yet now she was graying and a little somber, and she wore a scarf of black velvet around her neck because she didn't really like the way her neck was evolving, darling, and she thought she would sit over there away from the lights and tonight—one night only—just be content to watch the dancers pass.

As Terry played first a variety of chords to get the feeling of the keys and then went into his self-written song 'Under My Window', about a young man who watches a beautiful girl go past everyday but can't find the courage to speak to her, he noted the red light at the center of Lady Frankenstein's console had begun to beat faster. And faster still.

What Eric Gherosimini had said was the truth. She did appreciate a young touch.

Her voice—feminine, warm and knowing—flowed from two external speakers, one on each side of her. It was like someone singing, a cool clear tone, but then he could hear a voice beneath a voice. Suddenly there were multiple voices, and he realized it was how much pressure he put on the keys. Soft, a single voice; harder, harmonic doublings and triplings. Lady Frankenstein was not just one woman; she was a female universe.

And then the most amazing thing. Eric Gherosimini came forward and stood at Terry's side and began to play right-handed along with him, and the voice was different—darker, maybe a little more rude—under his fingers, and Terry thought there might be heat-sensors in the keys themselves, something that transferred personal energy into the circuits and created the mood ring effect he'd heard about, that Lady Frankenstein's voice—many voices—changed according to the emotional state of her player.

He wanted to stop playing and ask Gherosimini how this could be. He wanted to know if within Lady Frankenstein's rapidly-beating heart there was a thermoacoustic element that translated human heat into sound. He wanted to know how her circuits were laid out, and he wanted to see for himself the intricate bundles of wiring that veined her together.

But no.

No, really, he did not.

Because she was what he knew to be the reason something had been awakened in them all, as children. Something they had heard and kept that other children had not. Something they still had, hidden away in a place of safety.

She was magic.

Listening to the music, hearing the voices of an angelic choir with a few bad girls among the bunch, True grunted and said, "Just when you think there's nothing new in this old world."

Ariel turned her head, as if to catch those words in her ears before they evaporated for all eternity. "What'd you say?"

"I said just when you think there's nothing new."

"No," she told him. "That's not all of it."

He had no idea what she was talking about. He was rewinding his memory when Stereo dropped the chewie and started barking furiously toward the front of the house. The dog jumped over cables and multi-plug boxes like a champ and ran through the open door, still barking his lungs out.

Terry and Gherosimini kept playing, and Lady Frankenstein kept singing in a dozen swirling harmonies.

"What's wrong with your dog?" True asked. "Doesn't like music?"

"He loves music." Gherosimini's eyes were heavy-lidded, drugged by the voices. "Got great ears. But he doesn't like cars."

"Oh," said True, and then it hit him.

"Neighbor drove by," Gherosimini said. "Maybe Wally on his 'cycle. Stereo hates it."

But he was speaking to empty space, because True had already moved and was on his way out of the studio. True looked to neither left nor right. He was unzipping his leather bag and putting his hand on the .38's grip as he reached the front door, where Stereo was raising canine hell in an effort to get out. That had likely been how Gherosimini had heard their arrival. True went to the window, pulled aside the bamboo blinds and saw nothing but brown waves of dust floating in the air.

He eased the safety off his pistol and cracked the door open. Stereo wasn't in a mood for caution; he pushed out like a barking battering-ram. Then True walked onto the shaded porch and looked for the car that wasn't there.

Only dust, and Stereo in the middle of the road, legs splayed, barker aimed toward the south.

The only way out.

The two generators created a continuous thunder. It echoed off the rocks. True looked to his right at the pair of trailers. The dust didn't go that far. He might be a little nearsighted, but he could see a VW van parked in front of one trailer. Alongside the other was an ugly old hulk that looked like an AMC Gremlin, up on four blocks. A friend of his had owned one of those in college. A death-trap, True had called it when parts fell out of the engine one day as it was being driven. Parked beyond the Gremlin was a motorcycle.

He turned his face toward the south. Stereo had stopped barking and was sniffing at something that scuttled from one rock to another.

Stereo was used to the muffled noise of the generators inside the house, True thought. But only a dog with great ears could detect the sound frequencies of a car or motorcycle through the acoustic tiles.

The only way out.

A car had pulled up in front of the house and then backed away. Probably had turned around on the other side of the snakespine curve. Its driver had surely noted the end of the road where the trailers sat.

True rechecked his cell. No bars, no service in this box canyon.

"What's the problem?" Nomad peered out through the door. He had to talk loud.

"Do me a favor. See if you can get a signal on your phone."

Nomad tried it. "Nope," he reported. He saw a shadow pass over True's eyes. His heart gave a kick. "What is it?"

"Listen," True said. "We probably need to leave here. Right now."

"You're starting to freak me out, man."

"My job is to keep you alive. If I need to freak you out to do that, I will."

"I thought your job *numero uno* was to catch Jeremy Pett alive and put him in a psych ward."

True watched the curve. Dust was still floating up from the road. Wasn't there a song called 'Dead Man's Curve'? He wished he hadn't remembered that. He made a move for the door, Nomad retreated to let him pass, and as True walked back to the studio where a chorus of ladies still sang he zipped his bag up.

"Guys," he said, "we'd better hit the road."

"Oh, man!" Terry cried out. He stopped playing and Gherosimini stopped and Lady Frankenstein stood silent but her red heart was still pumping hard. "We can't go *now*!"

"What's wrong?" Ariel asked, getting the distinct feeling from both True and John that all was not right in Blue Chalk.

"We need to hit the road," True repeated. "Yes. Now."

"Man, come on!" Gherosimini approached him. "You need to stay for dinner. I make a mean pot of chili and I've got some *fabuloso* magic mushrooms to share."

"We can't stay for dinner, thank you. Terry, let's go."

"*Please*, True!" Terry had swivelled his chair around, unwilling to leave it. "One hour! *Please*!"

Berke said tersely, "Shit's hit the fan. Am I right?"

True looked at the faces that watched him. They were waiting for an answer. He worked his hand on the leather bag, feeling the reassuring shape of the gun. Not much use against a rifle at long range, though. But they couldn't stay here. Not forever. Maybe it had been somebody lost, just driving. *Yeah, right*! But it might have been. Everybody believed Jeremy Pett was in Mexico. So why did he think that Jeremy Pett was sitting in his car on the other side of that snakespine curve? *His* car? The white car that had gone past the turn-off? Then what had happened to Pett's dark blue pickup truck?

"Cool it, Mr. Manager Man," Gherosimini urged. "Give Terry his hour. Anyway, if you don't like mushies I want you to try some kickin' ganja I got last time I was in Jamaica."

"*Jamaica*?" Nomad asked incredulously. "*You*?"

"Yeah, *me*." An expression of understanding spread across the old acid-head's face. He gave a wide grin. "Oh, *man*! Did you think I was...like...*destitute* or something? Far *out*! Listen, back in the '80s I sold a few of my ideas to Roland and they built some keyboards around them. My accountant says I'm worth more than the Six Million Dollar Man. I've never let any of my bandmates know. They're good guys, but some of 'em are slackers and they'd be on me for money. I take Stereo to Jamaica every year for a couple of months. Love the ocean. Deep-sea fishing, rum, good smokes, all that. Next year I'm having a contractor come out and remodel the place while we're gone. Converting to solar power. Terry, you play any Roland gear?"

"I've got a JV80."

"I'm in that," said Gherosimini. "Like I told you, it's all good."

True looked down at the floor, at his black wingtips.

He didn't know what to tell his band. He hoped his mouth would figure it out when he started speaking, because his brain was only doing a half-ass job.

"Berke," he said, "we're good here for a while. You know me. I just get a little anxious when we're not moving." He directed a quick glance at Ariel, who also knew him. Then he looked at Terry.

"How about thirty minutes?"

Terry thought about it. He cast an eye over the beautiful keyboards that most people in the world never knew existed. So many to play, and so little time.

"I can live with that," he decided.

"Good. That's very good." True nodded, and again he touched the shape of the .38 in his leather bag. It wasn't much use against a rifle at long range, but it was all he had. A thought came to him. "Ever do any hunting?" he asked Gherosimini. If he was a fisherman, he might be a—

"*Hate* guns," Gherosimini answered. "Worse than Stereo hates cars."

"Okay. Just curious." True smiled at Ariel. "I'm going to go for a walk. Not far. You know I get a little anxious."

Then he turned away from his band, and he walked toward the front door and the road that led south.

TWENTY-NINE.

He had dust on his wingtips. It was puffing up with every stride. Small stones grated underfoot. Then he caught sight of a second shadow on the ground, coming up behind him, rapidly closing the distance.

When the shadow got in step with True's, Nomad said, "Are you fucking *crazy*?"

True's gun was out, held in the right hand down at his side. He kept walking briskly toward the snakespine curve, the sun hot on the right side of his face, his back and his shoulder. Nomad kept up.

"You probably need to go back," True said.

"You think he's out there? You think he followed us and he's sitting out there waiting? If that's so, what good is it going to do to let him *see* you? You think you're going to walk right up to him, ask him to surrender to the FBI, and then it's hero time? Oh, *yeah*! Make me laugh, man. He'll blow your fucking head off before you can—"

True abruptly stopped and turned on him. "I've told you to stop that cursing," he said, his eyes intense. "You don't need that to communicate. It's *low*, and you are *not* low. Get yourself out of the *gutter*, how about it?"

They stared at each other for a few seconds, *mano-a-mano*.

Then True started walking south again, and Nomad lost a step but caught up.

"How's it going to help us if you get shot?" was the next question. "If you get *killed*, what are we supposed to do?"

“I’m just going to take a look. Very cautiously. I’m going to turkey-peek around that curve.”

“Okay, fine, but if he sees you before you see him—and from what you say about him, that’s what’s going to happen—he’ll put you down, reload and come after us. He might not know your face, but he’ll know you’re with the band. Gun in your hand...he’ll figure it out. Maybe he followed us from the club last night and he parked close enough to watch the motel. Maybe he saw the Yukon leave, and he’s figured that out too. Or maybe—*maybe*—he’s not sitting out there at all. But I wouldn’t want to walk around that curve and find out, because those fu...those bullets can run a lot faster than me.”

True kept going. Nomad said urgently, “How about asking Gherosimini to drive his truck out and scout for us? If he sees anybody waiting, he can get to a phone. Call for help.”

“If Pett’s there, he’s going to figure he has us in a prime position. I don’t think he’ll let anyone through. Would you like to be responsible for that man’s death?”

“The way this is heading, we won’t live much longer to be responsible for anything. Any*fucking*thing,” Nomad said, with gritty emphasis.

“This was a big mistake,” said True. “Coming here. A big, big mistake.”

“You want to tell that to Terry? Hold it.” Nomad caught at True’s white polo shirt and stopped his progress. The sun was fierce. Sweat sparkled on True’s forehead and Nomad felt it on his neck and the back of his Army-green T-shirt. “Don’t go any further. I’m asking you. *Please* will you not go any further?”

“John, I have to do my job.”

“Your *job*, Mr. Manager Man, is to get us *through*.” Nomad got his face right up into True’s. “Whatever it is. Keeping the van going, finding a place to sleep, a place for us to wash our clothes. Making sure nobody gets food poisoning, or if they have to see a doctor on the road you work that out too. Doing the best you can with a fucked-up sound system, or club owners who just don’t give a shit. You tell us we did really well when we all know we sucked, but we’ll do it better the next time. You get us *through*, man. The day-to-day grind. That’s your job. Because you signed on here as much a manager as you did an FBI gun.”

True wore a pained expression. He kept his eyes down. "John—"

"I'm not finished," Nomad asserted. "Maybe your gung-ho hero boy is around that curve. Maybe he's not. I hope to God he's not. You want to save him because he's sacrificed himself for a cause, because he's seen the hard battles that took so much out of him. Something you say we've never done. Are you *sure* we haven't? Are you sure we've never fought for a cause worth dying for?"

"And what would that be? To make music?"

Nomad shook his head. "To be *heard*," he said.

They stood together without speaking, their shadows on the earth, the snakespine curve on one side and on the other rocks that echoed the thunder of a storm about to break.

"Get us through," Nomad told him.

True looked toward the curve. Maybe Pett wasn't there. If he was...

"I'll try," True said. "But if he's set up with his rifle and he's ready, he can kill somebody today. Maybe more than one. Even with the tinted glass. We can't get a lot of speed out of that van, not with the trailer on it. Not much more speed even with it unhooked. He might go for the driver first, or for the tires. Do you hear what I'm saying?"

"I hear."

"Will you tell the others that, or do you want me to?"

"I'll tell them."

"We don't want Gherosimini involved. He'll think he has to do something to help, and he'll either get himself killed or slow us down. I'm planning on driving as fast as I can out of here. Everybody else needs to get small, as much as they can. That's not much of a plan, but it's all I've got."

"Okay."

"Okay," True said. He retreated from the curve, regarding it with a watchful eye, and Nomad did the same. Then at a distance they turned around and walked back to the house, the black wingtips and the black Chucks stirring up dust in equal measures.

When they got to the studio, Terry was playing Procul Harum's 'A Whiter Shade Of Pale' on the Vox Continental, and Nomad thought that beautiful song had never sounded so amazing. It brought tears to his eyes, watching Terry put his soul into it. Gherosimini was standing a few paces away, eyes closed, feeling the love.

< >

True beckoned Berke and Ariel over to him, and he began talking to them in a very quiet and serious voice.

After it was done, Nomad saw Ariel nod. She lifted her chin up like a fighter, daring fate. Berke walked away a few feet and put one hand against the wall; she stayed like that for a minute, her face downcast, and then Ariel put an arm around her shoulders and Berke nodded too.

< >

Terry kept playing. Nomad saw True check his wristwatch. Thirty minutes had gone past. True bent down, because one of his shoes must've come untied. Then the other's laces needed some attention too.

Terry finished the song, one of the greatest ever written for the keyboard. He blinked, as if emerging from shadow into sun. He looked around at True and asked if it was time to go, and True said it was, but first he needed to speak to him in the front room. They left the studio, and Gherosimini turned off the central switch, and all the voices went back to sleep.

Outside, as Stereo eyed the Scumbucket and readied himself for the hated sound of the engine, they wished Gherosimini well. Ariel told him she hoped he finished Ground Zero, and he said again that it was a work-in-progress. He asked them if they wanted any smokes for the road, and True had never been so tempted in his life but he said no thanks. They got into the van: True behind the wheel, Terry in the passenger seat, Ariel behind him and Nomad on the other side, with Berke in the back. Nobody spoke about the arrangement; it just happened. They would go out the same way they came in.

The engine fired, Stereo barked, Gherosimini waved, and True drove ahead to a place where he could back the trailer up and turn them around. Stereo kept barking and Gherosimini waved again—no, a salute this time—as they passed by. The dust welled up. Gherosimini and his dog were lost from view. True put his gun in his lap. He said, "All this may be for nothing. He may not be there, okay? But when I come out of that curve, I'm going to have my foot to the floor." He was already gaining speed. The trailer groaned. "I want everybody *small.* Down on the floorboard. Tuck your elbows in and get your knees up. Hell, get your heads up your butts if you can."

"Kinky," said Berke, but her voice trembled.

"Thank you," Terry said, as they entered the curve.

"For what?" True asked. The engine was roaring, as much as it could. The Scumbucket vibrated and the trailer slewed.

"For giving me time," came the answer.

True was fighting the wheel. The trailer pulled at the van and wanted to go sideslipping off into the rocks, but he held it on the edge.

< >

They came out of the curve.

Jeremy Pett was not there.

Ariel started to lift her head. True said sharply, "Everybody stay down!" The Scumbucket's speedometer needle gave up the ghost and started flipping back and forth across the numbers like a runaway metronome. Banners of dust flew back beneath the wheels. They went into another curve and then up a rise from the bottom of a gully. Loose rocks clattered against the Scumbucket's sides. True kept the speed up, as something in the engine began to emit a high-pitched whine.

They crossed the rough divide between dirt road and cracked asphalt, a jolt that made the van shudder and the trailer wag like Stereo's tail. Then they were coming around a sharp bend, and True didn't know if he could hold the van on it at this speed, so he tapped the brake just a fraction, just enough to keep them from flying off into the rocks, and as they whipped around the bend there was the abandoned gas station with its antique pumps and parked at an angle blocking the road in front of it a white car.

A Honda, True thought as he clenched his teeth, determined in the next onrushing second to jerk the wheel to the left and get by that car even if he scraped both vehicles down to the smoking metal.

Bastard stole himself an Accord.

A bullet came through the windshield.

It made a hollow *pop* as it pierced the glass, and a second *pop* as it continued through Nomad's window. With that, True realized Pett was on the right, maybe among the remains of the houses. He heard the front right tire blow, and then the Scumbucket pitched down on that side like a lamed horse and True lost control of the wheel.

They ran up over shale and rubble and crashed into the gas pumps, which sheared away in red whirlwinds of rust. Something metal caught up under the van's belly and seized it, and the engine screamed like a voice in agony. Another bullet shattered Terry's window and sent fragments of glass flying over him at True. The Scumbucket dragged itself to a halt, throwing sparks from beneath.

"Stay down! Stay down!" True shouted. He thrust his arm over Terry's glass-cut scalp and fired two shots at the ruins and the rocks, just to let the sergeant know he was packing. But exactly where the sergeant was, he couldn't tell, and he thought that by the time his eyes found Jeremy Pett he would be dead.

Berke, the tough girl, was gasping for breath. Nomad called out, "Berke? You okay?" but she didn't answer. A bullet came through Ariel's window, making a neat round hole.

True feared Pett was going to pick them to pieces. He felt blood trickling from a glass cut over his right eye. They had to get out of here. Get inside the building. Most of the front of it was wide open to the world. The interior was shadowy, but he could make out a tangle of stone rubble and collapsed roof beams. Make Pett come to him, so he could use the .38 at close range.

Some plan, he thought. And the idea of taking Pett alive, and getting him help…

Some effing plan.

"Listen up!" he shouted. "We're going to—"

He paused as a streak of heat zipped past his mouth and put a hole through his window that spread out a spider's web of silver cracks. He heard the whine of the ricochet off the building's stones. He slid down in his seat.

"We're going to get inside there!" he continued. They had a distance of about fourteen feet from the van to the building. "I'll get out first and cover you! Everybody's going to have to slide through my door! Fast as you can!" The other option was for them to go out the door on the right side, which would put them directly in Pett's sights. "Wait for me to tell you to move! Got it?" He burned a few seconds getting his nerves in order, and then his next-best plan went up in smoke because he couldn't get the driver's door open. The handle had no tension; the cable was broken. A knifeblade of panic twisted in him. This was the moment every man responsible for human life dreaded. He had to do something, and do it fast.

"John! Watch your eyes!" True put two more bullet holes through the large window on Nomad's side, and then Nomad got the idea and used both feet to kick the rest of the tinted glass out. True slid down again, opened his bag for more ammo and reloaded four chambers. He had another box of bullets, so he was okay there. "Terry, you stay where you are! I'm shooting over your head! Everybody else out! *Go*!"

As they scrambled out as best they could, True got off five shots. Pett would know what kind of pistol he had, from the sound. It wasn't going to put the fear in him, but it might keep his head down. *Might*.

True reloaded. He heard Pett's rifle fire, but where the slug went he didn't know. Shooting into the building, maybe. Shooting at the Band That Will Not Die. This time, they might.

"Terry! You okay, buddy?"

"Yeah. I think." His voice was shaking. "I'm cut up a little bit."

"Me too. I want you to crawl between the seats and get out. I'll cover you. Ready?"

"Yeah."

"Go!"

Terry crawled back and pushed himself through the window. True began firing through the passenger side, three shots at a ghost. Terry tumbled to the ground like a laundry bag. As he stood up to run for shelter, he was hit in the upper back on the right side and he gave a cry, almost of nothing more urgent than surprise, as he went down.

< >

He is where he needs to be. He is where he has been coming to. He has arrived, and today will belong to him. Gunny is with him in the rocks, close by his shoulder. His rifle is warm and it smells good. He is very glad that their van didn't hit his car, because he needs it to get to Mexico. His journey will begin after this is ended. Like they say... today is the first day of the rest of your life.

It has been a challenging hunt. Tracking them from city to city, driving past the clubs, marking where they stay, and being very careful not to let those men in the Yukons get a good look at him. He has not been trained for nothing. He knows his business, and he is a prince of his profession. A hero. The Bronze Star says so, and so does Mr. Salazar.

Gunny thinks very highly of him too.

Jeremy wears his Triple-T Truck Stop ball cap. He has taken his sunglasses off, the better to acquire his targets through the scope. The sunglasses had belonged to Grandmother America. They didn't look like an old lady's sunglasses, they were pretty cool. In the Accord's locked glovebox he'd found a hundred and sixty dollars in a bank withdrawal envelope. Why did they call it a 'glovebox'? Just wondering; it had been on his mind during the long drive from Tucson to San Diego. Gunny had occupied the backseat on part of that drive, but he had no opinion.

Now, Jeremy sees that they've gotten out of the van into that building. He feels a pressure here, because even though this place is a perfect shooting gallery—except for that van being in the way—somebody may come along at any minute and that would not be pretty. So he does feel a pressure. He felt that same pressure when he saw the van and the trailer go off the highway and he figured he'd better drive on a distance since the van was just sitting there, he didn't want to spook them, but then the next chance to turn around had been fifteen fucking miles west because a trooper got behind him and to cross the sandy median would have made him visible.

So here they are. He has just shifted his position a dozen yards, and it paid off because the different angle gave him a clear shot at the guy with the skinned head. He thinks that was a good shot, right through a lung. He's waiting for the man with the .38 pistol to get out. Okay… okay…here he comes, out the window the others shimmied through. And now he's leaning over trying to help the guy on the ground. The pistol in his right hand. Little piece of shit.

Jeremy sights and fires, just to let that man know what he thinks of the pistol, and he sees the man's right elbow explode and the pistol drop from the shot-stunned fingers.

Bite that, motherfucker, Jeremy thinks.

Oh, here comes the long-hair. The lead singer. Running out of the building. Jeremy wants to know if that dude, that fucking Nomad, thinks he's walking on a street under a burning sun. If he thinks that his blood is red, white, and blue.

"Hope they bury you where the grass is green," Jeremy says to the image in his scope. His finger is on the trigger.

Nomad has emerged from the building to help the man with the shattered elbow, whose arm is out of the action, Jackson. Now they both try to help the skinhead. Terry, that's his name. Spitzenfucken or something. Terry is up on his knees. They are trying to get him on his feet. Now, look at this: here comes the hippie chick to help, and the drummer girl stands at the edge of sun and shadow for a few seconds and then she comes out too, and Jeremy can hear their voices drifting toward him, telling each other to hurry.

He has a shot right on Nomad's head. Right between the eyes.

Gunny tells him to hit the hippie first. Gunny has gotten very troubled about that girl, though he won't say exactly why. He says hit her *now*, stupid!

Jeremy has a shot, but he hesitates.

Say what you will, those people are not Blue Falcons.

They've almost gotten Terry standing.

Jeremy shifts his aim and sends another bullet into Terry's back, and as Terry falls on his belly again and the others are frozen in shock Jeremy resights on the hippie chick's head but the drummer girl has her by the arm and is dragging her toward the building, and—shit, that bitch must be strong, because she's picking the hippie up and running with her the last few feet.

Then Nomad gets his head under the man's broken arm and drags his ass into the building too, and Jeremy fires twice more into the shadows that have covered them.

It is time to reload.

Gunny asks what he thinks he's doing. Gunny sometimes doesn't seem to understand who is in charge here. Gunny doesn't appreciate patience or understand that you can respect the bad guys, no matter how bad they are. Jeremy knows he would have been an outstanding gunnery sergeant, if they'd given him the chance. He would have been an example for the men. Of how you fight back from adversity. How you never say die.

Only they didn't want him, did they?

No, Gunny is quick to remind him. They did not. He tells Jeremy to get his mind back on his business, and that he is going to have to go down there and finish the job with the .45 that is tucked in his jeans.

And he is going to have to go down like right *now*, because this is what you call a Mexican standoff, except for the fact that Jeremy has two guns and the man who had one gun now has a broken arm and is bleeding torrents, so *move* before somebody comes along that road.

Jeremy wants to know what's so special about that hippie chick. She's a fucking *girl*, and maybe she's a liar and dark-spirited, but why is she so *special*?

Gunny tells him that it's over his head, that he's on a mission he needs to finish before he can start his new life in Mexico. That he just needs to go down there and kill *her*, and then he can leave the rest of them to rot, as far as he cares.

But *why*? Jeremy wants to know. What's the big deal about her?

Gunny seems a little agitated. A little pissed, really. He looks like he wants to spit blood and fire.

It's about the war, he says.

Yeah, Jeremy knows that already. It's about that lying video. About the lies that say we went over there and killed children. Just shot them right out of their shoes. Shot them *knowing* it was murder. And then came back over here and didn't tell a single solitary soul, because we were good guys, loyal and patriotic, and that's not something you can talk about, not even to your buddy who does nothing but offer you an empty smile from his wheelchair at the Veteran's Hospital in Temple.

Nice day for a white wedding.

Yes it is, he thinks.

Jeremy stands up like a soldier. He begins walking through the rocks toward the road, and the building beyond. He is hot and thirsty and ready to finish his mission. With two more strides he goes *crash* into the first moment of the rest of his life and he walked to the white car. He held the rifle at the ready, and his other hand went under his shirt to touch the automatic pistol. He could feel Gunny, walking at his side. He passed the skinhead, lying on his belly alongside the crumpled van. Where was the pistol? It had fallen somewhere around here.

One of the others must've picked it up. He drew his .45 and, holding it ready before him, he eased toward the building, step after step. Gunny was beside him, and Gunny began to chatter about killing the girl like an excited kid on his way to a carnival.

< >

Terry heard music. It was himself, playing 'A Whiter Shade Of Pale' on the Vox Continental. He was hurting. He was fading in and out, like a broken speaker. His wires were severely damaged. But oh, that music he could hear. He knew he was dying, but if he could hear music to the very last...then what was death, but an all-access pass to a bigger stage?

But this thing underneath him, whatever it was, hurt like fucking hell.

It was underneath his left side, pressing into his ribs.

He slowly shifted his body. His breathing gurgled like the pipes in a motel he remembered. He felt under himself to move that hard pain so he could listen to the music in peace, and his hand fell upon something metal. His fingers made out what it was: True's pistol.

He was aware of someone moving past him. Walking toward the building where his friends had gone. It was a man wearing a ball cap. It took Terry a few seconds to focus because his Lennon specs were gone and everything was blurry and turning red, but he could make out that the man was carrying a rifle and a handgun.

Terry thought he didn't have a whole lot of time or a whole lot of strength left. But maybe he was where he needed to be, when he needed to be there. He put his hand on the grip and found the trigger.

He sucked in his breath and rolled over to bring the gun up, and as the man caught the movement and started to turn Terry squeezed the trigger just as he used to do on the firing range in Oklahoma City. The bullet went in low on the left side, a few inches away from the spine, and when he felt the jagged ripping pain Jeremy knew he was in deep shit, because it had been a killing shot. He staggered, and he heard Gunny give a sigh of exasperation, as if this was the stupidest thing that could ever have happened in the world, but Jeremy thought Gunny had been too busy crowing about killing that girl to be watching his back.

Terry tried to pull the trigger again, but his finger and hand would not obey. His arm gave it up too. The pistol fell to the ground. Jeremy walked to him, more angry at Gunny than anything else. He thrust the .45 out at Terry's face, about to blow the head apart, and then he saw Terry faintly smile and Terry's eyes glaze over as he died.

Fucker looked like he was hearing something that could not be heard.

Gunny told him to get in there and finish it, because now he knew where the gun was. *Kill the girl*, Gunny said. *Okay, kill them all, but kill the girl* first.

Jeremy nodded. He could feel the blood running out of him. His shirt was wet back there. Maybe a nicked artery. Sonofabitch. Fucking *amateur* had gotten off a pro shot. He wanted to laugh, but he feared he might start crying, and that was not how he wanted to go out. Besides, he did have the mission to finish. But he wasn't getting to Mexico in this lifetime. Neither in this lifetime would he be working for the *federales*, or have a house on the beach, or find a new career as a hit man, or be much of anything in a very short while.

He did cry, just a few tears. He was crying when he walked to the edge of sun and shadow, and he saw them in there because they had nowhere else to go. Most of the roof had fallen in and the timbers and rubble blocked the way to the windows at the rear. The man with the shattered elbow was lying with his back against the stones, his face bleached by pain, a glass cut bleeding over his right eye, one arm supporting the shattered elbow. His polo shirt used to be white. The drummer girl was beside him, her eyes fixed upon Jeremy with terror. In her hand was a rock, like she was about to throw it. He said, "Don't do that." His voice sounded distant.

Nomad shifted his position. He was standing where he'd been desperately trying to dig through the debris to one of the windows, but it was hopeless. His right ankle had twisted as he'd tried to support Terry, and had twisted more severely when he'd helped True. Beside him was Ariel, her hands scraped and dirty from working at the same mound of rubble.

Jeremy sighed. He decided he would not finish them with the pistol after all. They were not Blue Falcons, and so he would take them out with respect. The pistol was so ugly, but the rifle was a work of art. He pushed the .45 into his jeans, and touched the wound at his back. His hand came back looking like a crimson glove. He chambered a round and saw with disgust that he was getting blood all over his weapon.

On the ground, True said hoarsely, "Jeremy. Sergeant Pett. *No*."

< >

Kill the *girl* first, Gunny instructed, as if Jeremy had forgotten already.

Ariel had realized two things: Jeremy Pett was probably bleeding to death from the wound Terry had delivered, and he was going to kill them all.

Those were the facts. Another fact was: she knew what had brought him here.

Though her knees trembled and she peed a little bit in her panties, Ariel stepped forward.

"You want me," she said.

Because it was the truth, and it was the only way.

"Ariel!" Nomad reached for her and limped after her but she didn't even look at him. When he grasped her shoulder and tried to turn her to face him, she pushed him back.

"Yes, you do," she told Jeremy. Her voice was calmer, now that she'd decided. She could look him right in the eyes and accept it. "I am what you want to kill. You and whatever's with you."

"Shit," he said, amazed. "That's Gunny. Can you *see* him?"

Ariel said. "I'll go with you, out of here. If you kill me, would you let my friends live?"

A trick, Gunny said with a wary sneer. *Kill her where she stands*.

But Jeremy, who felt his time streaming from him, frowned and said, "Maybe."

"No way! No way!" Berke's face was streaked with tears. She stood up, still gripping her rock.

It had occurred to Ariel that if she could get him far enough away from the others, even if he killed her—*when* he killed her—he might not be able to get back.

"I'm ready," Ariel told Jeremy. Her voice threatened to crack; she wouldn't allow it. "The thing that's with you wants me dead. So if you need to do that, I'm ready. I'm just asking you… *please*, to let my friends live."

A trick, Gunny repeated.

< >

Nomad picked up a board with nails sticking out of it. His face was gray and bits of glass were caught in his hair. He tensed, about to lunge forward as fast as he could—*if* he could—and start swinging.

Ariel saw Jeremy's bleary eyes fix on him, and she said quietly, "John, *don't*."

She came closer to Jeremy Pett. She came right up next to him. She looked into his face without fear, and she said the three hardest words she'd ever spoken in her life.

"Walk with me."

She reached out to take his bloody hand, and to guide him away from her family.

Jeremy stepped back.

Something is wrong here, he thought.

Something was all mixed up. The good and the bad and the weak and the strong, all mixed up. It seemed to him that she should be sobbing and begging for her life. He had the rifle. She had nothing. He didn't understand this; it went against all his training, that a weak unarmed enemy could look at a rifle and see their death in it, and not fall terrified before it. And she *was* weak. She was a weak, dark-spirited...

...liar?

He felt like he was about to pass out. It was close on him, this oncoming darkness. He could feel himself not only bleeding, but filling up with blood on the inside. He was a bladder, and something was about to burst.

I did kill a child, he thought. I did. I committed murder. I did.

It had eaten at him for so long. It had chewed and chewed at him, down in the belly of the beast. It had misshapen him, and warped time into a long midnight that never moved. It had driven itself into his bones, and made a nest in his heart.

It was pecking at him, even now. It never stopped.

Peck.

Peck.

Peck.

God had punished him for that murder. He was certain of it. Call it fate, if you wanted to, but it was God who made him pay. But Jeremy thought, as the world began to slowly turn around him and the taste of blood was thick in his mouth, that if only... if only he'd been able to tell *someone* about it. To tell Karen, and ask her to pray for him, but the accident took her away before he could. To tell his father, and get a kind hand on the shoulder, but it would only be another fist. To tell any of the officers, or the men, or any of the doctors at the hospital where he hoped one Wednesday somebody would ask him how he was doing. To have someone...*anyone*...listen, and say what he needed to hear most in this world. But, as the Christian In Action had said, *our meeting never happened.*

And now, in a place where it was the least expected, the person he'd least expected to help him with this burden was listening. Of all people, it was the hippie chick. She was standing before him, unafraid of his rifle, and he could tell she'd made up her mind to die for the others, and what more could you say about a person?

< >

"I murdered a child." Jeremy said to Ariel. "In Iraq." The words came out with thorns on them. They were tough to dislodge. "I'm not a good guy. But the others...the soldiers...they weren't all like *me*. You were wrong to say those things. We didn't go over there to kill children. We went to do our *job*. They weren't all like me." His voice shattered, and fresh tears began to course down his face. "Do you hear?"

She felt what he wanted. His eyes were frightened, and he was starting to waver on his feet. She focused on this moment, this moment alone, and with an effort that redefined the limits of her willpower she put aside her grief at the things this man had done.

She knew. And she knew that whatever was with him in this place, whatever had brought him on his long journey, whatever it had promised him, whatever it had proclaimed, it could not give him what she was about to offer. It was so simple, yet so important that the lack of it could crush a soul.

"I hear you," she said.

Oh my God, Jeremy thought. Oh Jesus...I have killed innocent people. "I'm sorry," he whispered. "I'm so sorry."

Maybe this band had been harsh in their interview with Felix Gogo. Maybe they'd been wrong in their judgement of his fellow soldiers...but how did the video itself lie? How was it not an accurate depiction of the choices that a soldier had to make, and no matter how tough you were trained you only had seconds to decide matters of life and death? How was it not the truth, showing the darkness that can swirl down in an instant and peck you to pieces?

I am the liar, he thought. Me.

And Gunny.

Gunny's a liar, too.

There is no need to kill anyone else today, he thought. This battle is over.

< >

Jeremy felt his face begin to come apart. A knot rose, writhing, on his forehead. He reached up and pushed it down. His right eye began to sag from its socket. He took his fingers and put it back in its place. His mouth opened, wider and wider, and his jaw began to unhinge, but he pushed his jaw up with one firm hand and his mouth closed and the little ripplings and tremors that moved across the plains of flesh and bone ceased to be.

< >

He shivered. He lowered his rifle, and when he did a small figure stepped out from behind Ariel Collier, and held onto the edge of her dirty blouse with one hand, and from the shadowed face the voice of a little boy said, *Daddy? You can come home now.*

Gunny screamed in Jeremy's ear that this thing *lied.*

Screamed that it was not what he thought. Screamed that it was a trick, that he should not—could not—let his eyes fuck up his brain. Screamed *You have a mission, you dumb fuckstick.*

But for a brief moment, as Gunny shrieked and babbled in first one ear and then the other, Jeremy Pett was allowed to see beyond the glass.

They were not alone in this ruined place.

There were other figures, at the edge of sun and shadow. They stood amid the rubble, behind Ariel Collier, John Charles, Berke Bonnevey and Truitt Allen. They stood silently, only watching. But Jeremy heard Gunny give a cry that began with bitterness and ended with ache. Jeremy looked from the hippie chick to the long hair to the drummer girl and then to the man on the ground. He looked at the small figure, whose eyes held centers of light that made Jeremy think of candles.

"Please forgive me," he said to all of them, to every listening ear. He backed away. He dropped his rifle.

He walked a distance, to get his bearings, and then he began to slowly and painfully climb a small rise of shale and stones that stood behind the building. Halfway up he took the .45 from his jeans and dropped that too, and then at the top of the rise he faced a huge expanse of open desert, brown-dusted and white-streaked under the hot blue sky.

He went on.

He was sure the Elysian Fields lay in the direction he was travelling. He wouldn't get there today, though. It would be a long, hard journey to—

He fell. He felt no weight on him, but he had the impression of hearing wings and the dry rattle of claws, and the sensation of something gripping his back and chewing at his neck. He tried to get up and could not. Tried again, but failed. He felt scrabblings at his flesh, and the noise of huge wings thrashing the air just behind his head.

Maybe on one side ten thousand times ten thousand screamed and capered, and on the other side ten thousand times ten thousand shouted and cheered for the man in the arena, the bloodied man, the man forsaken and cast aside, betrayed, yet the warrior spirit never broken.

It all came down to sharp edges, the wings of a crow, black origami.

That, against a Marine who was determined to stand.

Jeremy cast it off like an old skin. He walked on, staggering. The horizon was lost in the red descending mist. He knew he wouldn't get to the Elysian Fields today. He had too much to account for. Too much innocent blood on his hands, to be allowed entrance today to the Elysian Fields. But wherever he was going, it would be a step *toward* the Elysian Fields. He told himself that whatever he had to do to get there, even if it was the impossible, he would find a way. He would never give up the fight to reach his wife and son—whatever they had become—on the other side of this.

The thing descended upon him again, but this time did not drive him down. As he staggered forward it beat at him, and clawed his back, and tore at his head with a beak like a piston.

His back bowed but unbroken, Jeremy remembered something Gunny had said to him, in the truck on the highway outside Sweetwater. That had been a lie, too. Its opposite was the truth.

"Without me," Jeremy whispered to the enraged air, "*you're* nothing."

He shrugged the thing off. It whirled around him in a dark blur.

Gradually, whirl by whirl, the dark blur subsided. It did not vanish so much as it melted, oozing itself away in tendrils and chunks that also melted away into smaller and smaller pieces.

Jeremy fell to his knees.

He drew a breath, and he had a good look at the land that lay before him. Black clouds were rushing toward him, shot through with terrifying pulses of electricity. He smelled the ozone of war, the burnt scent of calamity and chaos. He figured he was in for a long hitch.

And in the last few seconds until his next mission began, he braced himself for the storm.

SIX

THE LAST SONG

THIRTY.

"Guys, we want to thank you for being here tonight," said Nomad into his microphone.

They had come to the end of their show at the Vista Futura, in Austin on Saturday night, the 16th of August. It was a packed house in this club, another black box on the knife and gun circuit. People had been turned away when the doors closed. It had been advertised as a free concert for those who came wearing a The Five T-shirt, which meant they'd been to another of their gigs or had bought the shirt off the website. All ages were welcome. It was approaching midnight, and it was nearly done.

Nomad stood cradling his Strat in a cone of clear white light. At his side, a few feet away, was Ariel with her acoustic Ovation. Behind them was Berke, at the center of her Ludwigs. Amazingly, only her snare and a floor tom had been damaged in the trailer. She was a firm believer now in styrofoam cubes and color-key labels.

Tonight there was no bass player, and there were no keyboards on the stage. It was just the three of them, and they'd had to improvise and fill in and do what they'd needed to do, but they were professionals and the show must go on.

But not, as Nomad had realized, on and on and on.

He looked out at the small lights of cellphone cameras. Some people had brought video rigs and set them up, but the space was tight. It was okay with the band that the whole concert was filmed. Put up on YouTube. Used to show the grandkids what grandmom and granddad did back in that long-ago summer of 2008, before musicians played everything in the air on virtual instruments.

It had been a quiet show. Nomad had done a couple of hot movers but his heart really wasn't in them, and they didn't sound so hot without Terry's keys swirling in and out. Tonight belonged to Ariel's voice. It belonged to her acoustic guitar, which she played with the precise passion of someone who wants not only to be clearly heard, but to clearly speak.

"I guess everybody knows, this is our last show." He held up a hand, palm outward, when the predictable moaning and groaning came from the audience, but they knew it already and they were just doing what they thought the band expected. It was like a heart thump that went into a peace sign.

"The Band That Will Not Die!" someone shouted, over on the right.

"Yeah!" another voice hollered, and then the crowd erupted into whoops and whistles and whatever they needed to do to express themselves, and Nomad waited until they were done until he smiled out at all the faces revealed by the reflection of stage lights and said, "Thank you."

He cleared his throat. "We lost three of our friends last time out," he said. It was the first he'd spoken of this tonight. There'd been a brief introduction from the MC, and then The Five had started right into 'When The Storm Breaks'. The songs had gone past with just a brief intro from either Nomad or Ariel between them. He didn't make any jokes about limping around like an old man, because his sprained right ankle was still bothering him though it was taped up under his jeans. Ariel said nothing about her slightly purpled nose. Neither did Berke offer any explanation about the bass guitar pin she wore on one lapel of her black jacket, and the keyboard pin on the other. The news stories had told everything, to everyone who wanted to know. Nancy Grace had done her interview and so had Greta van Susteren. Berke had done a telephone interview with Rachel Maddow on her radio show and was going to be featured in *The Advocate* next month. She would go again to the obvious tag the press wanted: Deranged Iraq war veteran stalks rock band, is killed in the New Mexico desert, hi ho.

That was the line they had pushed, with True's help.

The magazines and newspapers and networks and bloggers had emerged by their multiple thousands. Even Wally was a celebrity who found reporters hammering on his trailer door. Wally on his motorcycle, coming upon what appeared to be a wreck in front of the old Pure station that had once served the community of Blue Chalk, and then the people staggering out to the road, and all that blood.

Eric Gherosimini had been discovered by one of those tenacious door-knocking reporters. *Re*discovered. The genius of the 13th Floors, one of the most influential acid-rock bands of the '60s. Justin Timberlake said he'd been looking for him for years, to get permission to re-do a song in modern style. Lily Allen said she had all his old shit in a box in her closet. Eric Gherosimini announced through a spokesman that he was moving to Jamaica.

But not before he left a boocoodle of money to the University of Oklahoma to offer music scholarships at the American Organ Institute in the name of Terry Spitzenham.

They specialized in maintaining the tradition of the magnificent pipe organs that were played in churches, cathedrals and in the grand movie theaters, the kinds of keyboards most people never knew still existed.

George called them from the hospital when they were being interviewed by remote on MSNBC. He was doing some therapy now, he said. He was out of the woods. He was home free. He sounded strong. Nomad took the opportunity to ask him, on the air, why he wore pennies in his loafers, and George said that was easy to answer: for good luck.

"This is our last show," Nomad repeated to the audience. "We have one more song to do." He had to pause for just a few seconds, and Ariel wanted to touch his shoulder but she stayed her hand. He was a big boy now. "This will be the last song," he said. "We're not going to do an encore. It's late, and from the looks of some in this crowd it's past your bedtime. *Kidding*," he said to the exaggerated boos, but he really wasn't. "This song is one we wrote together on the road, all of us adding some lyrics. Ariel's going to sing it, and it's called 'New Old World'. Thanks again, guys." He stepped back, so Ariel could be front and center, and the audience applauded and waited as Berke started a steady beat, smack on 126 beats per minute, relying on the dark voice of the bass and the bright snap of a hi-hat.

Ariel strummed the intro on her Ovation. She was dressed tonight more funky than lacy, because she wanted to try something different.

She had on a pink blouse, black jeans and a sleeveless blue vest with large red and pink polkadots. She wore a blue porkpie hat, tilted jauntily to one side on her strawberry-blonde ringlets. She had made the decision that it was time for her to start having *fun* at this, her calling. She thought there'd been enough pain, and now it was time to let some pleasure in. Starting with her closet full of hippie duds. She would always go vintage, but she needed more and brighter colors. Like the song said, some things do change, and they change with you.

She began on the A chord. The song had a triumphant sound. It suggested just a hint of strut. It bore in its bones the strength of English ballads and smoldered with the earthy heat of Tejano. At its heart there was a touch of Soul, but at its heart of hearts classic rock 'n roll.

She sang in her warm, full voice.

"*Welcome to the world, and everything that's in it.*
Write a song about it, just keep it under four minutes.
Got to figure what to keep, what to leave behind, and like life it's never easy.
I wish you safe travel, and courage when you need it,
I wish you safe travel, and courage when you need it.
You'll need it. Oh, you'll need it.
Won't you move my hand, please tell me what to write.
I'm sitting here like a candle on the darkest night.
I've got my hot flame, got my flicker on, but where am I when my light is gone?
I wish you safe travel, courage, you're gonna need it.
I wish you safe travel, courage, you're gonna need it.
Gonna need it. Oh, gonna need it."

There had been a meeting in Roger Chester's office.

It had been yesterday afternoon, up on the fourth floor in the gray building on Brazos Street. The Five had cancelled their Friday night gig in Dallas. They'd stayed with True in the hospital in Albuquerque until his wife could get there. The Albuquerque FBI had been very helpful. They'd arranged for the contents of the wrecked U-Haul trailer to be truck-shipped to Austin, they'd taken care of Terry's body and brought Jeremy Pett in from the desert where he'd died, and The Five had flown from Albuquerque to Austin courtesy of Roger Chester's checkbook.

"I want you to look me in the face," said Roger Chester, sitting behind his desk in his office with a picture window onto The Live Music Capital Of The World at his back, and Ash sitting elegant, composed and expressionless in a brown leather chair to his left. "I want you to look me right *here,*" he said, pointing with one hand, two fingers, into his own dark brown eyes slightly magnified by the tortoise-shell glasses. "And tell me *why* Ash says you won't do a reality show."

Nomad, Berke and Ariel were all sitting together on one brown leather sofa. Before them was a glass-topped coffee table with magazines on it like *Money*, *Texas Monthly*, *Billboard* and of course the *People* with them in a small box at the upper right. Nomad wished Berke would put her black high-heeled boots up on it and sweep the magazines aside, but she didn't. His gaze kept being drawn to the huge horns on the bighorn sheep head mounted on the panelled wall between the picture window and the ceiling. If something like that fell, it could knock a man's brains out.

"Don't everybody talk at once," Roger Chester said. He glanced at Ash. "How come they'll spread it out thick to you, but to me it's as thin as a spick's wallet?"

Nomad almost said Mr. Chester ought to ask his pal Felix Gogo if his wallet was so thin, but he kept his mouth shut.

"Okay, I know you've been through some heavy..." Chester hesitated, seeking the right word for a man of his standing. He settled on, "Shit. Everybody knows it was rough. And I absolutely think you ought to take some time off. I guess you're shell-shocked. Well, who the hell wouldn't be? Right?"

"Exactly," Ash agreed.

"But we have to talk about your *future*. We have to get serious about it. We have to strike while the iron is hot."

Berke shifted her position. Nomad thought for an instant that she really *was* going to put up her boots and knock the magazines off, but the moment passed. He couldn't help it. He had to say, "That's a term used in branding cattle, isn't it?"

Roger Chester peered at him over the rims of his glasses. "Oh, mercy!" he said. "Mercy me and Johnny Jehosophat! What's your problem?" His voice not only took over the room, it nearly broke the picture window.

No problem, Nomad almost answered, but it would be a lie and that phrase could still send him into a rage thinking about a crazed waitress in Tucson. "We're breaking up," Nomad said. "Tomorrow night's the last gig."

"Yeah, I heard that from Ash." Roger Chester drank from a coffee mug with a UT logo. "Didn't listen to it, though. Didn't listen, because it didn't make any goddamned *sense*. You're telling me you're calling it quits, after all you've been through, all the shit, all the work, and now you've got network TV people interested in following you around with cameras and broadcasting your *life* to the world, and publishers wanting to do quickie books that ghost writers will write for you, and promoters crying out for you all over this country and in three foreign lands, and record deals hanging from money trees ready to be plucked, and you're calling it quits. *Quits*," he said to Ash, as if the suave fellow from New Delhi had forgotten his clipped English.

Ash just shrugged and smiled, showing some front teeth that Nomad thought would look so pretty on the floor.

"We need time," Ariel spoke up, "to decide what we want to do." She started to say *Sir*, but her lips would not let it through.

"And we definitely no way want to be in any fucking reality show," said Berke.

"Oh, is that *beneath* you? That's what this is about? You think it's *crass*?"

"I think it's unnecessary," Nomad said. "We all do."

"Do you think making money is unnecessary? Hm? Because that's what it would be. A whole big truckload of money. Plus super exposure, an opportunity to promote new songs and CDs, maybe a tie-in to a televised concert special, and—" He slapped the edge of his desk. "Jesus Christ, I don't believe I'm having to spell all this out! Look, you're on top right now! You're somebodies, instead of the nobodies you used to be. Your powder's hot and you're about to make one hell of a flash."

"Yeah," Nomad said. "Flash. That's kind of what I was thinking, too."

"Is there some cryptic meaning to that, or will you enlighten me?"

"I'll ask you a question." Nomad stared across the desk into the man's eyes. "Can you name one song we've ever done?"

"'*When The Storm Breaks*'," said Ash.

"Not you. I'd like Mr. Chester to answer that. Any song titles come to mind?"

Roger Chester stared back. He took a drink from his coffee mug.

"Any lines from any of our songs?" No response. "How about CD titles?" Nomad asked. He raised his eyebrows. "Anything?"

In the Vista Futura, on the Saturday night stage in a shaft of yellow light, Ariel sang.

"*You might be in a place where the old skin won't fit.*
You might feel as worthless as a cup full of spit.
Well some things don't change, you know they never do,
but some things do change, they change with you.
In this old world.
In this tough old world.
In this hard old world.
In this old world."

And now Berke's drums strengthened in volume, the cymbals spoke with their shimmering voices, and Nomad stepped forward to lay down a solo with his Strat. The solo was loose and easy, almost with a bluesy vibe. It sounded like something that might have spilled onto the rainslick street from a club where the sign said *One Night Only. Dean And The Roadmen.*

He was nervous, not because of the solo—he had that knocked—but because the verse he'd written was coming up next, and because deep down he feared this song.

"One CD title," Nomad had said to Roger Chester, in the fourth-floor office. "I'll give you the first two words of our newest CD. *Catch As*—"

"I don't need to know," the man across the desk replied. "That's Ash's job."

Nomad nodded. The way Roger Chester had said that spoke volumes.

"Do you even *like* music?" Nomad asked.

There was no longer any need for pretense. "Not your kind, no. Not particularly."

"Do you like any kind?"

"Listen, don't get *smart*. My grandfather started this business, friend. Started it from a travelling caravan of country singers who played places you people wouldn't *piss* in. And my grandfather was the barker, standing in the back of a pickup truck hollering through a megaphone. Bringing in the customers from the fields and the barns, and charging them a little money for a lot of entertainment." His voice was making the glass rattle. Nomad thought it was just a matter of time before the bighorn sheep had its revenge.

"Ohhhhh, *now* I get it," Roger Chester said, his eyes gleaming. But not in a good way. "Ash, take at look at these three. You know what you're looking at?"

Ash must've thought it was a trick question, because he refrained to commit.

"Ar*teests*," said the big voice. "I run into them occasionally. They go out to change the world and make grand statements, and they wind up living in their cars and playing on the street corner for lunch money. Well, can I tell you something?" He waited, but not very long. "Nobody gives one good fuck about art. About *messages*. It was true in my grandfather's day, and it is for *hell* sure today. People want to be entertained." He stressed that word with three distinct syllables, as if his guests had never heard it before. "They don't care what music says. They don't even listen. They want to go out to a bar on the weekend, have fun, drink some beer, maybe meet a girl or guy, and you know what you are to that? Background noise."

Berke put one boot up on the table.

Roger Chester glanced at it, but he was a mouth in motion now, a speeding fireball of truth, and he'd decided he was going to give these people what they'd asked for.

"This business is about *money*," he said. "Not art. Fuck art. Unless I can make a lot of money from it, and then I say 'Bring me more art!' But the profit on selling messages to people is mighty paltry. If it can't be branded, and packaged, and promoted, and sold to a demographic, as far as I'm concerned, friend...it doesn't exist."

It was the second 'friend' that almost sent Nomad over the edge. But he held himself back. He held himself. He put his hands on his knees and gripped hard, and he tried for a tight smile but it emerged as a grimace. He had nothing against entertainment. Entertainment was fine. The Five's material was mostly party band stuff, feelgood rockers or ballads, but still...to be told they had a boundary, a line they were not supposed to cross, a box they were supposed to be happy and glad and pleased not to ever climb out of. That seemed like a kind of death, in itself. The death of experimenting, the death of the noble failure from reaching too high. The death of caring whether what you did was good or bad. You just wanted to get paid, and to go home to your big TV, because nothing was more important than the cash.

"Mr. Chester," Nomad said, "you don't know anything about our music, do you? But it's the same as it's always been. A month ago... you're right, hardly anybody knew us. We were working, and we had fans, but—"

"You weren't going anywhere. I've seen your numbers."

"Right," Nomad said carefully. "So...what's changed? We're suddenly famous and all these people want a part of us—and you want to push us into everybody's living room and iPod—because two of our members are *dead*? And one was put in the hospital? What about the *music*? That's the same. We work, and we work, and we try our best, and we can't get anywhere unless we trade on the deaths of our *friends*?" His voice broke. He thought the rest of himself would fly to pieces at any second. "You didn't do these things for us before. That's not right. We agree on this, sir. The Five is done, because if we're ever successful again we want it to be for our music, not because of tragedy."

"John." Roger Chester let the name sit out there like an egg being fried. He smiled; it went away; he smiled again. "Nice speech, but pointless. Let's say you three walk out of here today, mad as hornets, and you decide that's it with this agency. You decide to *fire* me, for trying to make you lots of money and be very successful. Well...the thing is...I run this show. Not just me. Others like me, everywhere. See, we kind of guard the gate. We look for musical talent, sure. Got to have that. But there are *lots* of folks with musical talent. Then we look for the pretty people, or the people with something quirky about 'em. The people with attitude and personality. Something the mass audience would buy. We look for the rebels, or we create 'em. We line up the critics and the mentions in the magazines. We water grass, not weeds. So if we've let you in and you don't click, if you don't have the amount of sales we're looking for, if it's just not *right*, then...we kind of push you toward that gate again. And we'll hang with you for a while, but if it looks to us like our time can be used more productively...then we have to push you out the gate, and we hope you do real well in the future. So you can walk out of here, but where will you go? Oh, I forgot the Internet! Like you can ever make any real money, or a real career, off half-assed bloggers and low-rent CD pressers."

Roger Chester took a long sip of his coffee.

Then another long sip.

"Where will you go?" he asked.

Nomad's solo was finished. It was echoing off along the black walls. Ariel stepped to her microphone again, and sang.

"So welcome to the world, and everything that's in it,
It'd be a poor old world, described in just four minutes.
You got to get out there, see what's in it, don't let life make you crazy.
I wish you safe travel, courage, you can find it.
I wish you safe travel, courage, you can find it.
Was the old world,
Today the new old world.
Was the old world,
Today the new old world."

And then the drums quietened again, to the beat of the bass and the snap of the hi-hat, and Ariel sang softly, as if reciting a children's rhyme.

"*Try and try, grow and thrive,*
Because no one here gets out alive.
Try and try, grow and thrive,
Because no one here gets out alive."

Sitting on the brown leather sofa with Berke and Ariel, Nomad thought of the plight of Ezra's Jawbone, and the men in the suits saying that the awesome rock opera *Dustin Daye*, which followed no model nor copied any current sound, was no good because it lacked a single the kids would buy. And they made the members of Ezra's Jawbone think they had failed, when it was the suits who couldn't hear the music.

Nomad knew. It was partly why the man's speaking volume was so loud and uncontrolled. "You have a tin ear," he told Roger Chester. "Your hearing's fucked up. So you wait for someone else to say music is worthwhile, it has value, and then you rush around and gladhand people and say you knew it all along. Maybe you're afraid, because you have investors who are looking for quick money, and you can't—won't—support anything but the sure thing. But you make more money with the sure thing, right? The comfortable thing? So if you don't like music anyway, if you don't see the value in it beyond money, then how can you lose? And there *we* are…one day nobodies, the next day as sure a thing as you can get. Because tragedy struck, and we got some attention."

"Sounds like a golden opportunity to me," said Roger Chester.

"How you got yourself in control of people who really care about music, I have no idea. And *you*," Nomad said to Ash. "You've got your ears up your butthole."

Roger Chester took his glasses off and wiped the lenses with a white hankerchief. He still wore a slim smile. "All I can say to that is, we're talking about the age-old war between business and art. Correct? Friend, business won that war a long time ago. And if you don't already know that to be the truth, then…" He put his glasses back on, the better to see the face of the vanquished. "Welcome to the world," he said.

Nomad told Berke and Ariel that he thought it was time to go. They all stood up, and then Roger Chester went a buttkick too far.

"I guess this means your friends died for nothing."

Nomad stared at him across the desk. One month ago he would have thrown himself at the man, no matter who the fuck he was or how old he was, and he would've made that mouth regret its lips. He would've folded this man up at the joints and made him smile where the sun did not shine.

But not today.

He said, "You know where to send the checks."

"I certainly do, Mr. Charles. Minus our fifteen percent commission, and minus expenses for travel, various promotional considerations and extra expenditures as specified in the agreement. I certainly do."

They started out of the office. Before the door closed, Roger Chester said, "You'll be back."

On stage, Nomad couldn't help but wonder what this song would've sounded like with Mike's bass thumping at the bottom, and Terry's keyboards floating in and out like golden smoke. They were almost done, it was almost finished, and Nomad still feared this song because he didn't understand it, not the why of it, and he didn't know what was going to happen when the last note was played.

Ariel, her mouth up close to the silver microphone, repeated the rhyme once more.

"*Try and try, grow and thrive,*
Because no one here gets out alive."

Then the drums came in full-voiced again, Berke put her muscle into it, Nomad launched some soaring lines into the multi-colored air, and Ariel finished it out with an impassioned cry.

"*Oh yeah, from this old world,*
Could be a new world.
Could be a new old world.
Could be a new world,
Could be a new old world.
Might be a new world.
Just not the same old world.
It was the old world,
Today the new old world.
Might be a new world."

And she let the last line stretch out until her opera-trained voice roughened and rasped and held on to its control by the thickness of a thinned-out vocal cord.

"*Just not the same old world.*"

They approached the end, a few seconds away. The music began to quiet, and with one last sweep of electric guitar like a sword through the air Nomad was done, and Ariel went out with the same progression that had opened the song, and Berke hit the bass and snapped a hi-hat, and it was over.

As far as Nomad could tell, nothing changed in this old world.

The audience cheered and clapped, the cameras flashed and the videos were captured, the cries instantly went up for more, Berke threw her drumsticks into the crowd, Nomad said, "Goodnight, and thank you," and he unplugged his Strat and walked off with it. Ariel followed him, and then Berke. The house lights came up, saying the concert was done. Recorded music spilled from the speakers, the voices of some other band. The audience, nearly all of them wearing The Five T-shirts, began to file out in small groups. They were happy; it had been a good show.

Thor Bronson came backstage. He wore a white suit and his Five T-shirt. His tan glowed and his hair was lemon-yellow. Hanging on his arm was a blonde fox who could've been his teenaged daughter, and she was dressed like a Catholic schoolgirl and kept a BlowPop in her mouth. Nomad figured that Thor was now tapping the porn dolls. "You're one cheap sonofabitch," Nomad told him, referring to the fact that Thor had saved himself ten dollars by wearing the shirt, and Thor said that now the little prissy motherfucker had time on his hands he ought to come out to Cali and kick it with him. Nomad said he'd think about it, and Thor said don't think, *do*. He said he was staying at the Driskill, going to meet some studio people and party for the next few days, catch some Texas sun, hear some new bands, and he said that if Nomad didn't come visit him he would roast a pair of balls over a campfire and though he was not gay he would eat them on a slab of Texas toast with habanero sauce.

"Okay," Nomad said.

True and his wife passed Thor and his pony in the doorway to the Green Room, and Nomad thought that if the old world didn't crack itself wide open on that one, we were solid for the next few thousand years.

True and his wife sat in the Green Room with Nomad, Ariel, Berke, the Vista Futura's owner, a couple of guys who ran Internet fan sites, a sound tech, and the old bearded dude who wore a beret and owned

Play It Again, Man, which was a vintage vinyl and CD store out on West Anderson Lane. He'd wheeled in a handcart bearing two big boxes full of The Five CDs he was wanting to get signed, in silver marker, by the remaining members. A few other people came in and out, to meet-and-greet and take pictures. Someone, a kind soul, brought cold beers to the band. Two silver markers ran dry. The old dude supplied more from his massive backpack that smelled slightly suspicious to True. Sewn into the stained fabric was the depiction of a big marijuana leaf. True's wife, a small-boned, attractive woman named Kate, kept glancing uneasily at the bearded dude, who had the habit of staring at people, herself included, and not blinking his bulbous eyes for what seemed to her minutes at a time. He also had the habit of getting up, pacing around the room a few times, and then sitting down again in his chair with his legs crossed under himself Indian-style. She whispered to her husband that she didn't think that man was from earth. But True didn't say anything. He had a bandage over his right eye. His elbow was aching under the cast, and it was time they were getting back to the Radisson because they had an early morning flight home.

"Better head in," True announced. Ariel hugged him, and Berke came up stone-faced and sullen, and he didn't know what she was going to do. She balled up her fist and hung it in the air and he gave her one of those fist-bump things and then she grinned at him like the dumbass he was and she hugged him too.

"Glad it's not me having to sign all those," True said to Nomad, motioning with his good hand toward the boxes.

"Yeah," Nomad said. "Managers get off easy."

True nodded. He looked at Kate and saw her staring at the bearded man and the bearded man staring back at her, a battle of the X-ray eyeballs. "Do you have a card?" True asked Nomad.

"A *car*? I've got a car."

"A card," True corrected. He had one of those in his left pocket, ready to give Nomad, and he took it out. "A business card, with your phone number on it."

"Oh. No, I don't have one of those." Nomad accepted the card, which had True's office number and extension on the front, and on the back, in scribbly left-hand-written ink, his H.P. number.

"You should. People need to know how to get in touch with you." True knew that if he ever did want to get in touch with Nomad, he had the whole network of the FBI behind him as his White Pages. "Why'd you think I said 'car'? Are your ears ringing?"

"No, it's because nobody ever asked me if I had a card before."

"You might think about some kind of ear protection. All of you need that. You know, your hearing is very important."

"Yeah, I've heard that."

True stared at him. "You're a little asshole," he said, but he couldn't do it straight-faced, he couldn't keep the smile from creeping in.

"Yeah," Nomad said. "I've heard that too."

"You owe me some money, by the way. For certain dental expenses and mess cleanup on damage done at a Greek restaurant in Tucson, and the less you know about that the better. But I'm going to collect it from you someday. By then you'll be rich enough to pay me back."

"Maybe." Nomad shrugged. "We'll see."

"Well," True said, "better head in."

Nomad's heart ached. He put his arms around Truitt Allen and pulled him close, and True said, "Watch the elbow," but his voice cracked when he said it. Kate stepped away a few feet, and the old bearded dude blinked and aimed his eyes at the silver-signed CD in his lap, a picture of The Five standing against a statue of one of the descending snakes on the pyramid of El Castillo at Chichen Itza, a washed-out purple-tinged glow of light all around them, and the title in dark purple lettering *Catch As Kukulkan*. The old dude had no way of knowing it was all computer-generated and photo-shopped—no way could they afford the trip to the Yucatan—and had come from a dream Ariel had after eating a Mexican TV-dinner that evidently did not agree with her. She's been left with a compelling and somewhat frightening image of travelling through space and time on the back of a feathered flying serpent, Kukulkan the link between the gods and human nobility, the overseer of human sacrifice. The *Catch As* part came from the term 'Catch As Catch Can', which meant getting through a situation however you could, using whatever happened to be lying around that could help. It was just something she'd come up with.

"Keep it real," True said to Nomad, a statement he'd been planning on saying at this moment because it sounded like something a rocker would appreciate.

"Real, cranked to eleven," Nomad answered.

Which True couldn't make heads or tails of, but that was okay. This was where two worlds, having converged for a brief time in a circumstance of necessity, now by necessity moved again into their separate orbits.

"Thanks for getting us through," Nomad said, and that made sense enough, though True would have many nights to wonder if there had been any other way to get them through, and if somehow Terry Spitzenham didn't have to be dead. But he would never forget Terry playing in that studio, the voice of Lady Frankenstein rising from the speakers, and Terry saying *thank you for giving me time*.

He knew, though, that Ariel was the one who'd really gotten them through, and he'd told her so. Standing up to Jeremy Pett and his rifle as she had was probably the bravest—or most foolhardy—act he'd ever witnessed in his life. There ought to be civilian medals for something like that, but as Kate would be the only person on earth to hear the whole story, or what Ariel had impressed upon him to be the truth as she understood it, an FBI Certificate Of Appreciation was the best he could get for her. It was the best he could get for the others in helping put an end, however tragic, to a dangerous individual who had been a brother Marine. But behind the scenes he could have John Charles's money obligations taken care of and his record expunged. In his own case, he was to be awarded the FBI Star and the Medal of Valor at a ceremony next week.

True felt honored to have known them all. He felt like one of them. After all, Ariel had told him she'd realized what the song was about from that off-handed statement he'd made. *Just when you think there's nothing new in this old world*. She'd told him that after hearing those words, it was all clear to her. So part of him was in the song, too. He was a *songwriter*.

Sort of.

His wife took his left hand, because he was not moving and in his heart he wanted to stay until all the CDs were signed, every one, and the lights went out.

She led him from the Green Room, and when he looked back it was with the idea to tell them he planned to take up the guitar again when his arm was healed. But he let it go, because they needed to finish up their night and get home to bed, and so indeed did he.

THIRTY-ONE.

They were nearly done signing the CDs when a tall young man, maybe all of twenty, walked into the Green Room. He wore a The Five T-shirt under his red-striped jacket. He had long sandy-brown hair and gray eyes. He was handsome, but he was thin and angular and he had a darkly troubled expression. When Berke looked at him her first thought was that Gina Fayne, the new Janis Joplin and outspoken voice of the Nation, had died of too much life.

The young man's name was Ben Rivington. He was the bass player for the Mudstaynes. He came right up to Berke, and he said, "Can I talk to you?"

"Shoot," she told him, as she continued to sign the last two dozen.

He looked around at Nomad and Ariel, who knew who he was but didn't exactly know him personally. Berke had never spoken to the guy in her life.

"I'd rather talk in private," Rivington said.

"Okay," Berke decided. "Let me finish these first."

"It was a great show," he told Nomad and Ariel. "I'm a big fan, have been since your first CD. I wanted to speak to you at the Curtain Club, but...you know...sometimes you get hung up. People get in your face. You know."

"Do I ever," said Nomad, signing away.

"I bought the shirt online."

"Looks good on you," Ariel said. She was wondering, as Nomad was, why this gator wasn't playing somewhere tonight. Gina Fayne and the Mudstaynes were hot and hugely talented, they were young—the oldest being the twenty-two-year-old drummer XB4Y—and they had energy to burn. "I didn't know you guys were in town. Did you have an early gig?"

"No," he said. "I drove down from Dallas when I found out about this. Um…Gina's not feeling too well."

"What's wrong?"

"She's not well," he repeated, his eyes haunted, and Ariel knew not to go any further. He watched Ariel sign her name on a CD and then reach for another. "You really came through the fire," he said. "I don't know how you survived it."

"We were lucky."

"I heard you were more than lucky. I heard you were…" He looked down, and Ariel waited for him to find what he searched for. "Blessed," he said. "You'd have to be blessed to get through that. Does that sound fucking stupid?"

"No, not really," Nomad told him. "I mean…I can handle that."

"I liked that last song," Rivington said. "The 'New Old World'. It spoke to me."

Ariel lifted her eyes to his. She could tell he needed something, a desperate need, and he would not have come here if he didn't hope he could find it.

"After the gig, I was going to come back and speak but you had people on you, and I know how that goes. So I took off. Went to another club and had a beer. Heard another band finishing up. But that last song spoke to me. It told me to come back here. That part about, you know, changing things. That you've got to, like, step up to the plate if you want to get anything done. Take responsibility." He grinned suddenly, like a shy kid, and he actually blushed. "Man, does that sound fucking dorky. Me *saying* it that way, not the song," he corrected. "All props to the song, dudes."

"Thanks," Nomad said. He was still signing, but he was also listening very carefully.

"I believe a song can speak to a person. Like just jab a finger right in their throat, man, and say, like, 'Yo, wake up!' You know?"

"Got that right," Nomad agreed.

"Yeah," Rivington said with a kind of relief, as if an important bridge had been crossed.

They finished signing the last of the CDs. The bearded dude with the beret and the bulbous eyes gave them a million thanks and kissed Ariel's hand and started to kiss Berke's hand until he thought better of it. He pulled his handcart away to be unloaded. Everybody else was gone but the Vista Futura's owner and the manager, who were clearing things up in the office and writing down orders for more beer. Berke's drums had been loaded into the bed of her little black pickup truck, parked in the lot across the street. Nomad's three guitars and variety of stompboxes were in his 2001 red Ford Focus, also waiting in the same lot. Ariel's Ovation and her Tempest were packed in her silver-blue Corolla.

"Hey," Berke said to Ben Rivington as they walked with Nomad and Ariel through the club toward the door, "whatever you want to say, you can say it in front of my friends."

Rivington stopped. He was illuminated by the harsh light of the floods up at the corners of the room, the light of real life after the show is over and the fans have gone.

"Okay," he said. "Gina's sick. She's on smack."

No one spoke. Nomad remembered hearing that Gina Fayne was catching up to Janis in the department of drinking and drugs, and he'd hoped somebody wasn't stupid enough to let her try heroin to complete the picture.

"She needs help." He was speaking to Berke. "You know, she's fucking crazy. She's got all that voice, and the talent and the looks, and she fucking loves music more than anything, but it's eating at her. It's going to kill her, if she doesn't get help."

"Then get her help," Berke said.

"That's what the song said for me to do," Rivington answered. "To come back here, and ask for you to help save Gina's life."

"*Me*? Why me?"

"We've got a tour to do starting in two weeks. Going to England. First overseas gig, it's going to be a fucking grind. Gina's being Gina. Taking her shit, climbing into a hole and pulling the hole in with her. And let me tell you, when she wants to go deep, she can go to a place nobody else can get to. But a few days ago Lawrence walked out."

"Lawrence? Who's that?"

"XB4Y," Rivington said. "Lawrence Jolly. That's his real name. He says he's done with her shit, he's already hooked up with the fucking Beastie Crew. That's more his style, anyway. So our guy at PPK Management's looking for a drummer, but...it has to be somebody with *maturity*. And road experience too, you know what I mean?"

Berke thought she did. She wasn't certain she liked it either. "I'm only twenty-six."

"Well...that's like...older than everybody else. But I'm saying, we need...Gina needs... somebody she can count on. Somebody who, like, knows where she is."

"And you think that would be me?"

Rivington shifted his weight from foot to foot. For a few seconds he didn't dare meet the thundercloud where her face should be, and then he did.

"I was hoping," he said.

Berke turned her head and gazed across at where Nomad and Ariel stood, within earshot but far enough away to show that, if she wanted to be, she was free.

"The really weird thing," Rivington went on, "is that Gina's from a conservative family, and she rebelled and all that, she threw her talent and...you know...herself in their faces, but she loves them. I think she needs her family. She just doesn't know how to go home again."

Berke stared at the floor for a long time.

"Can I buy you a beer somewhere? Sit down and talk about it?"

When Berke looked up, Nomad and Ariel saw a muscle clench in her jaw.

"If you or anybody else ever calls me 'ma'am'," she said, "I will knock some fucking heads together. Got that?"

"Yeah." He nodded, very vigorously. "Sure."

Berke turned her attention once more to her friends. She gave them a wicked smile that Ben Rivington could not see. "And I *mean* it." she added.

"Understood," said Rivington.

"You can buy me a beer," Berke told him.

She cast one more look back at the darkened stage.

In the parking lot, she gave Nomad a high-five. She kissed Ariel's cheek. "Call you guys later," she said, maybe too brightly, as Rivington got into his Honda Pilot and started the engine. Then the brickhouse walked to her pickup, swung herself up under the wheel with easy grace, and she shot them a peace sign as she followed Rivington into her future.

Nomad and Ariel stood together, and alone.

"Cup of coffee?" he asked.

"I know a place I can get some silver needle."

"Lead the way."

< >

Kate Allen woke up when she realized her husband was not in the bed. It was dark in the Radisson room. She reached over to the table to find the lamp, but her husband said, "No need for that."

He was sitting in a chair at the window, in his crisp blue pajamas. The curtains were open. The lights of the city still glowed and winked, and up in the night sky a plane was passing.

"What time is it?" she asked.

"Late. Or early. Be dawn soon."

"Is it your arm? Hurting you?"

"Oh, it hurts all right." He had the cast propped up. She could see his profile against the glass. "But I'm okay. Just thinking, really. You go back to sleep."

She knew he had a lot to think about. He'd told her of going to visit Jeremy Pett's family in Reno. It was something he said he had to do. It had been a one day flight, there in the morning and back in the evening. He'd told her of going to the small house in a sad part of town, a place that he said had a sour smell in the air, a bitter burnt smell. He'd told her how Jeremy Pett's father, a decorated Marine, had never once looked in his eyes as they spoke, even as Truitt had expressed his deepest sympathy and his deepest respect for a young man who had lost his way.

Jeremy Pett's father had kept his right hand continually closed in a fist so tight the knuckles were whitened. Three fingers were missing from the left hand. Jeremy Pett's father had been a Marine sergeant who'd served in Operation Desert Storm, in 1991. Jeremy Pett's mother, Truitt had told his wife, wore a blank mask for a face, and when she'd very slowly moved around the room she seemed to be clinging to the walls, and once or twice she had appeared in a chair where she wasn't sitting a few seconds before, or she was no longer standing in a doorway where his last glance in a previous instant had placed her.

She had perfected the art of becoming invisible.

"Thanks for comin' by," Jeremy Pett's father had said at the door, his sunken eyes fixed on a patch of earth where no grass grew.

Kate lay with her head on the pillow, watching her husband in the dark. "I guess we could get to the airport early."

He nodded, but it was a small movement. He asked, "Would you listen to something?"

She said of course she would.

"Stone Church," he said. "It's on my mind. Has been for a couple of days." He'd told her all about that. The story Ariel had spun. It was disturbing enough to Kate, so he didn't know how he was going to tell her the rest of it, about Connor Addison and all, but he felt as her husband and her best friend, he needed to in time. She was his best friend too.

"Stone Church," he repeated. "Wouldn't it be amazing? Just incredible? If someday, who knows when, thirty or forty people came walking down the road from Stone Church?"

And, he said, wouldn't it be amazing if they were bruised and cut from climbing over chains and barbed-wire, and they wore old outfits that weren't costumes, and they blinked in a sun that they'd forgotten they had ever seen before, because all their lives had seemed to be a bad dream? They walked down that road, on this far future day, and among them were an old doctor, and a big bear of a sheriff with a thin Chinese girl holding him up, and four Civil War hellraisers who had come to fight a skirmish and found another war, and a couple of prostitutes with French perfume still fresh on their throats, and rough men and their rough wives and children. And right in among them, right at the center, walked two young boys, a woman who had endured much, and a dazed reverend carrying the body of a little girl wrapped carefully in his coat.

"A bad dream, they thought," said True from the dark. "A nightmare visit to a nightmare world. Like going to sleep in an instant, and waking up groggy, fogged, unable to figure out where you are. And that didn't pass, it went on and on. And maybe they stayed together, trying to find a way out of their nightmare, and maybe the reverend had the most reason to keep going, to urge others to keep going too. He had the most reason, because even in his fog and despair he wanted to give his child a Christian burial."

Wouldn't it have been amazing, True said, if as those people struggled onward through a land that had no horizon and no compass, no sunlight and no moon, from the deeper dark a figure came forward, misshapen and diseased, and whispered through cracked lips, *Follow me*.

What kind of journey would that have been? From where to where? Across what unknown plains, across what desolate mountains and valleys writhing with shadows? And time had no meaning, there was no time. Some might have fallen away, or drifted off, or been lured to follow other paths, and they were lost. The figure had to keep the rest moving. Because the figure had found a way out. Not for himself. His life was done. For *them*, because they had not yet lived their full lives, and that was the crack in the glass.

How would they get out? In the same nightmare haze that had brought them there? Like a clap of thunder, jolting them awake in the middle of the night? Was there, far ahead, a thousand miles ahead, a small hole of light against the darkness, and they followed that like the eye of a candle?

Would they find themselves and their clothes dusted with red rock, as if they'd been reformed, squeezed through the walls of the mountain and remade on the other side? Would they find little glimmers of silver in their hair? And what might the reverend say to the misshapen figure on the last day, at the last instant before escape? *What is your name*?

And he might answer, in a voice from the depths of suffering: *My name is—*

"Stop it," Kate said. "Really."

True breathed softly. His elbow was hurting, but it would be better soon.

"Something like that," he said, "would shake the foundations of the world."

"Well, you've got a big imagination. I've always known that. When you retire, you ought to write the story."

"No. I'll just wait for it to happen." True stared out the window, at the lights of humanity. Blue dawn was beginning to assert itself against the night. Interesting, he thought, to consider retirement. His injury would probably hasten it. And it might be good to go out as a big dog, with a big Medal Of Valor as his chewtoy.

"I'm thinking of a career in management," he said.

Kate dared not ask what that meant. But she thought she'd go ahead and get up and take him to the IHOP out by the airport for one of his favorite meals: the syrupy pancakes, crumbled-up bacon and yellow-drippy eggs all mixed together.

She decided she was going to stop worrying so much about his heart.

At least, for one day.

< >

Nomad and Ariel were on the road. She had left her car at their last stop, a place to watch freshly-baked doughnuts ride along a conveyor belt, becoming sprinkled with sugar or cinammon or sparkling with fresh glaze at the end of the line. They had climbed into his Focus, which was a blood brother to the Scumbucket with its crumpled front fender, its scrapes along the passenger's side, its dents and dings and bangs and bumps. He'd bought it cheap from another musician, with some of these imperfections already there, but he'd added a lot himself too. He realized now, as they followed the crooked headlights along a Texas road with the windows down and the pre-dawn air sweetened by night, that he probably could afford a new set of wheels.

It had been a full night, for sure. A mug of black coffee, not so bitter, and a cup of silver needle tea at a little downtown place called Selma's, which had about a dozen tables and served great chocolate brownies, though Ariel declined to order one. They'd started talking there, about the song. Then Nomad had decided he was really hungry, so they'd met again at the Magnolia Café, and this time Ariel had ordered a veggie Reuben when Nomad asked for a hamburger, and please make sure there's no cheese on it, and could the waitress make it, like, medium rare so it's a little pink in the middle?

And the waitress had said, "You got it."

They had continued talking about the song.

"So," Nomad had said, as the late-night crowd ate and drank and the waitresses buzzed around, "what happened, then?"

"I don't know that anything happened." They'd been over this ground at Selma's, but Ariel knew it was important for him to backtrack and go over it again, looking for what he might have missed.

"Something *had* to have happened. Really." He put his elbows on the table and looked her square in her mystic eyes. His ankle was sore from standing and sore from driving, but if the day ever came that he couldn't take a little pain, he would be ready to kick out of this strange old world. Which was definitely not new. Or was it? He didn't know. According to Ariel's belief, they'd been given the task of writing a song by a girl who was something other than human. They hadn't asked for it, but there it was. Then, according to Ariel's belief, Jeremy Pett had been given the task of stopping the song from being finished, by something he called 'Gunny'. Or was Pett just totally insane? What about Connor Addison, and the nutbag in the trailer park?

Nomad wondered about that trailer, parked in the flat hot desert on the 'angel line' radiating from the north side of Stone Church, or Apache Leap as it used to be called. That dumb fuck, the so-called Navy electronics expert, couldn't tell his angels from his demons. Nomad wondered if someone who—and this sounded like Ariel thinking—was able to pick up vibes and shit could stand in that trailer, in the room the nutbag had used as his comm central, and listen, or feel, or *sense*, or whatever, a quiet in the wires. Maybe a few scattered mutterings passed, like distant voices heard from a pirate radio station through a wallplug, just faintly there, or maybe a squeal of static that was not static at all but an ungodly voice raised in anger, and then drifting away in a whimper like a whipped dog. And maybe chatterings passed, like teeth being ground down to nubs, or a sudden "*You*!" jumping out, all fucked-up sounding and muddy, as if in recrimination for a battleplan defeated.

But, most of all, a quiet in the wires.

Maybe an ominous quiet. One that said there were other battleplans to be made, because it was a forever war.

It had been a bitch writing that song. Ariel had been adamant that he needed to write a verse. He wanted nothing to do with it. He feared that when it was done, and played as their last song, the whole of Vista Futura would be sucked down a cosmic drain—*gurgle, gurgle, gurgle*—to Hell, to Heaven, or to some dimension in between, and they'd have to be fighting off crows in the eternal blackberry brambles when they weren't filling baskets for Jesus. He just had no idea what was about to happen.

You need to write a verse, Ariel had told him with fire in her voice. It came from you *first*, do you understand that? Mike started it, but it came from you first. You have to write a verse.

In the Albuquerque hospital where they were waiting for True's wife to arrive, he'd looked at what she'd written, at the title she'd given it, and he'd asked, "What's this about?"

"Don't you know yet?"

He did, really.

It was about acceptance, he realized. Accepting who you are, within the limitations of a hard old world. It was realizing that sometimes things in the tough old world squeezed you, and crushed you, and drove you down into the dirt. But to survive, to keep going, you had to lighten yourself. To cast off things that no longer mattered, things that wore you down or weighed heavy on you. You needed courage to keep going, and sometimes you found it in yourself and sometimes in others. And it might seem hopeless, it might seem a fool's path, and it was never safe travel even though an angel might wish it were so for you, and some things never changed, they never would, but nothing ever changed unless you believed they could.

And it was still the same old world as it had been yesterday. It was still a hard old world, a tough old world. It would always remain so. But it was a world that could not be described in just four minutes, with all its universe of good and evil, strong and weak, light and dark. It was the world, as it would ever be.

People lived and people died, and the lives of people were precious; their time to create and exist, live and love, was also precious. The song said, keep trying, keep *living* in the fullness of life, keep growing and creating, because no one here gets out alive. It was not a cry of fear; it was a declaration. You are here today, said the song. One tomorrow you will not be.

The song asked: Between those days, what will you do? Who will you become?

Could it be a new world, in this old one?

It could be.

Might it be a new world, in this old one?

That was for each person to decide. Travelling there was an inward journey, across an often fearsome land. The world within each person, the private world held deeply within. That was where the change happened, where a world could be made new in the midst of the old.

And that journey took all the courage you had.

< >

But for certain, Nomad thought as he sat with Ariel's notebook in his lap, for himself it was not and would never again be the same old world.

That's what it was about.

In the end, he'd repeated Mike's opening with a variation, and added what he thought suited the song. He didn't think his part was very good. He had listened to Ariel's ideas about the music, the intro, the chord structure and the chorus. He'd given suggestions that he thought worked, but Berke didn't like his idea about speeding up the beat, and Ariel thought he was wrong about some of the chord changes. He was deadset on throwing a B-sharp in there at a particular point, but she didn't like that at all.

"Are we writing a fucking church song?" he'd asked in frustration. "We're a rock band, guys!"

"It'll come out well," Ariel had told him. "When it's finished. It will."

"Okay, *you* finish it, then! Shit! I'm going out to get a smoke!"

But the deal was, he feared the song.

"What was supposed to happen?" he asked Ariel again, at their table in the Magnolia Café.

She shook her head.

"Do you have any *opinion*? I mean, what was it for? Yeah, I know what it's about. Or at least I think I know what it's about, but we don't really know, do we? We're not sure, are we?"

"No," Ariel said, "we're not sure. How could we *be* sure?"

"Maybe it was for Gina Fayne. Maybe it was for that guy to hear, and for him to ask Berke to help keep Gina Fayne from overdosing on smack. Does that make sense?"

She could tell he didn't believe what he'd just said, but she answered, "Maybe it was."

"Uh huh. Tell me, then: You think the angels are that bent out of shape about Gina Fayne's heroin habit? You think they set up this whole thing to save Gina Fayne's life, so she could go on and be the next Janis Joplin? And you think whatever wanted to stop us—to fucking *kill* us—wanted to make sure Gina Fayne never became the next Janis Joplin?" Nomad almost pounded his fist on the table. He held himself back. "No way!" He was getting worked up, he had to eat his hamburger and ease down again. "I don't see the point," he said. "I wish somebody would tell me what it is. Or *was*. How come that girl, that...whatever she was...just didn't tell us what she wanted? What we were supposed to do. She could speak English. I mean, Jesus, I guess she could speak every language in the world, if she was what you think she was! So how come she didn't just *tell* us?"

"Because," Ariel said, "we would never have believed her. And how would you like to write a song knowing something we can't understand—something *awesome*, John—is asking for a command performance? She *did* want us to write a song. We wrote the song she wanted."

"You're sure of that?"

"Yes. And we wrote the song *we* wanted. It was as much for us, as it was for—" She stopped, because she couldn't finish the sentence.

"Gina Fayne?" Nomad asked.

Ariel ate some of her sandwich and drank from her bottled water.

Nomad watched her. There were so many things he wanted to ask her about all this. One question was: *Why us?* Another was: *Are those things in this café right now, only we can't see them?* And: *Are they everywhere all the time, and when I'm sitting on the toilet I ought to be a little more modest?* And, maybe the questions he wanted to ask the most: *Do they know everything? What don't they know? Do they sleep, do they eat, do they screw? Is everything around us a fucking illusion, the dream within the dream?*

And, oh yeah, one more: *Where do they come from?*

But she was eating her Reuben, really getting into it, and Nomad thought she could answer those questions no better than he could, no better than they'd been answered since the beginnings of time by scholars, priests, philosophers and thousands of others.

They were not allowed to know.

Nomad figured it was like the cosmos. You could only go so far, thinking about how many stars there were, and space going on into eternity. Where were the walls of the box?

"I just want to make music," he said, and Ariel looked at him over her sandwich and gave him a crooked half-smile, and before he could monitor his mouth the question jumped out of him: "Do you still need me?"

"*What?*"

"Do you still need me?" he repeated, and he answered it. "You really don't. You're ready to go out on your own. Maybe I was hard on you in Tucson, but I was telling you the truth. You could put your own band together. The *Ariel Collier Band*."

She wrinkled her nose. "Oh, that sucks."

"The Ariels. The ACBs. The Blue Porkpies. That's a good one. I like that look, it's cool. Okay, back to naming your new band. The—"

"Two," she said, and she gave him the mystic blast.

"I'm out of this for a while," he told her, averting his gaze. "I need some time. Just to think."

"I need the same thing."

The moment had come. It felt so natural now, so right to do this. The new old world, at this table in the Magnolia.

"You're better than I am," he said. "You're a better guitarist, a better singer, and I know for *sure* a better songwriter. And you're only going to get better still. I'm a party band type of guy."

"'*When The Storm Breaks*' isn't a party band song. You've written plenty of songs that aren't."

"You wrote all the parts that really said something. You wrote the parts that touched people. Their emotions, and all. I just hung on. You know what was driving me? Anger. At a lot of things, and I'll explain if you want to hear it. Anger's a tame word for it. More like fucking white-hot volcanic rage, which I guess you guys saw a lot of." He took a drink of his Pibb. "You can only go so far on that. I figured out, when we started getting the big crowds and the media attention…I started losing my anger. I started feeling like…you know…we were a *success*, which is what the lack of was making me even more angry. Without that in me, what do I have? I'm not nearly as good as I need to be. I know that. So what do I have?"

"You *are* good," she said. "Ask the fans if you are or not."

"I'm not good *enough*," Nomad said.

She sighed heavily and threw him a look of exasperation. "No one's good enough! Everybody has to push, and push, and try to break through some kind of wall. I *know* I'm not good enough. But I hope—I plan—on being better tomorrow, or the next time out. You start from where you are. You've broken through a lot of walls. *Yes*," she said when he made a scoffing noise, "you have. But maybe the next wall you have to break through will be with your *talent*, not your fists."

He thought about that, and he progressed a step further into his own new world. "Will you help me?"

"What? Like, give you *lessons*? I can see that happening!"

"No," he said. "Will you help me push *myself*?"

She looked at him across the table, across the half-eaten Reuben and the remains of a burger. It occurred to her that you might call this a 'date'.

"Yes," she said.

They sat for a while longer, until two young couples came up asking if they were who they thought they were, and Nomad wanted to ask *Who do we think we are?* but he was nice about it, he and Ariel had their pictures taken and the couples explained they wanted to get into the show at the Vista Futura but the doors closed, the fire code or something, and so they wound up over at Antone's hearing The Crop Circles. Nomad picked up the check and paid it—*My God, it really is a date*, Ariel thought—and then they were out of the café and Nomad said he wanted to take her one more place and it wasn't very far.

They watched the doughnuts file one after the other along the line. He ate a glazed and she ate a cruller. Then he asked her if he could tell her his story, about his father, and that he would like to drive as he told it, just drive, and keep driving toward morning.

They left the highway several miles out of Austin and followed the Texas roads. They passed towns waking up before the dawn. They passed dark fields and the lights of distant houses that seemed to be sitting on the edge of the world.

Nomad told his story, with the windows down and the pre-dawn air sweetened by night, and when he'd finished, when everything that needed to be said was said, Ariel leaned over and kissed him lightly, at the corner of his mouth, and she told him that yes, she did need him.

She needed the fighter, she said. She needed the rager against the machine. She needed the teller of truths, as he understood them to be. And if indeed some of his anger had dissipated, what had left him was self-anger, a crippling anger, directed at his own soul. She needed the man he was going to become, who dug deeply within himself, and pushed himself to create and to speak, to hear and to be heard, the man who said being just good was never enough. She thought she could love that man, if she didn't already. And she told him never, ever, to forget that.

< >

Besides, she said, he was just such a sexy bastard.

They had to get some gas. At an intersection of four roads there stood a small station, lights on, a Mom-and-Pop kind of place. Looked like a miniature bunkhouse. Still a little swoony from what he'd just heard, Nomad pulled up to the pumps. Ariel got out to stretch her legs. The air was still and silent; it was turning blue, and the last of the stars sparkled overhead. Nomad was about to unhook the nozzle from the nearest pump when a man's voice said, "No credit. Cash only. And here you pay up front."

Nomad and Ariel found the source of that voice. An overhead bug light shone on a man sitting in a chair next to the front door. Beyond him, in the interior, were shelves of stuff: paper towels, bags of chips, motor oil, detergent and the like. A mini-grocery, too. The man wore a cowboy hat, a faded workshirt, jeans and boots. He held an acoustic guitar, had obviously been playing it when they'd pulled in.

"Pay up front," he said again, his voice as harsh as dry wind. He strummed the guitar.

"I'll want to get twenty bucks worth." Nomad limped toward the man, taking out his wallet for the cash. He slowed down as he neared the cowboy, because though he couldn't fully see the face beneath the wide shadow of the brim, he had the impression of looking at someone who was older than the hills beneath the hills. Someone fence-post lean and shaved-leather raw, someone who looked meaner than a broken bottle of five-dollar whiskey.

The cowboy continued strumming his guitar—it had a nice full tone—and then took the money in one sinewy hand.

"Get your gas," he said. He began playing once more, a Tejano-flavored tune that Nomad did not recognize.

Nomad worked the nozzle. The gas flowed. Ariel walked a distance away. She lifted her face toward the fading stars, her hands on her hips. He thought she looked really hot in that outfit. He thought he might take her somewhere for breakfast. But he wasn't quite sure where they were, and he didn't see any signs.

"Sir?" he asked the man. "Where does that road go?" He motioned toward the intersection and the road that stretched east.

The guitar strumming stopped. Then it started up again, a slow, leisurely playing, all the time in the world.

"The road goes on," the cowboy said.

Nomad felt a slight tremor pass through him, like something waking up deep inside.

"What say?" he asked.

The cowboy continued playing, some trills up and down the neck. Just showing off.

"Got some cotton swabs in there if you want to clean your ears out," he said.

"John?" Ariel asked, coming nearer. "What is it?"

Nomad didn't reply. He couldn't speak.

It was the answer to a seventeen-year-old mystery. Maybe, too, it was a gift.

Johnny, there's no roadmap...but...

...the road goes on.

If it was not an answer, it was as near as John Charles knew he would ever find.

< >

He smiled at Ariel. He felt himself smile widely. He felt a weight leave him.

It was a very good feeling.

"You okay?" she asked.

He nodded, and he replaced the nozzle when he was done. He closed the gas tank's port. He stepped back and regarded his busted-up car as if seeing it in a new light.

"Sir?" he asked the cowboy, who kept his face lowered. "Do you have any spraypaint?"

"Cans of red, white, and blue. All out of red and white. Take your pick."

Nomad chose the blue. He paid for it, said for the cowboy to keep the change, and then as the guitar strummed at his back he shook the can of paint, popped the top off, and sprayed four letters first on one side, under the driver's window, and then on the other. Ariel stood beside him, incredulous, as the bright blue paint streamed down from the ends of the letters.

"You're crazy!" she said, with a grin.

"I'm a musician," he answered. That explained it all. His ankle was hurting him, not so badly but enough to want to rest it. He decided he needed some help. "Will you drive?"

"Sure," she said, and she took the offered keys.

John Charles climbed into the passenger seat. Ariel Collier got behind the wheel. He suggested they drive east, toward morning. As they pulled out, the cowboy was still playing his guitar, and he never looked up from the strings.

John thought every ship needed two captains. One to take the wheel when the other got tired, or heartsick, or ever doubted their destination. Maybe the two captains of this ship would never know what the song was about, or who it was for. But maybe it was enough to know that it was out there, on fan web sites and on YouTube, and in the memories of the audience. The Five would be out there, too, on those videos and CDs. You just had to look to find them.

Still gigging, still alive, after all these years.

The *Argo,* blood brother to the Scumbucket, headed east toward morning.

The indigo light of dawn cast a transformation upon the earth. It created waves from sand hills and whitecaps from pale stones.

And somewhere ahead, it washed clean against a distant shore.

THIRTY-TWO.

She awakened to the sound of a guitar, drifting through the wall between them.

Her heart beat harder. What time was it? Quarter 'til four, by the alarm clock. She would have to be getting up in a few minutes anyway.

A guitar. Imagine that.

She switched on the bedside lamp. She stood up, wrapped her cotton robe around herself, and left her room to go to Jenn's, which was two steps away.

The door was closed. She knocked.

The guitar playing immediately stopped.

"Open up!" she said.

There was a hesitation. She could feel Jenn inside the room, maybe sitting on her bed, staring at the door.

"I heard you playin', hon. It sounded nice."

Footsteps. Quiet ones. Jenn was light on her feet.

The door opened, and her daughter peered out.

"I didn't mean to wake you up," Jenn said.

"Aw, baby! You don't worry about *that*! I was glad to hear it." And that, she thought, was the biggest fish that ever passed as a minnow. She saw that Jenn must not have gone to sleep last night. She was still wearing her jeans and the T-shirt she'd worn to the concert. Jenn looked tired, her brown eyes were a little hazy. "Were you up all night?"

"I'm okay," Jenn said.

"Hm." She glanced into the room, at the posters on the walls. It was a typical room for a sixteen-year-old girl. Jenn's guitar, the old Washburn Joel had bought for her at the downtown pawn shop three years ago, was sitting on its stand next to the bed. "Well, then." Did she dare to ask the next question? She did. "You want a little breakfast? An egg? Slice of bacon?"

Jenn was thinking about it. She had a way of compressing her lips tightly together when she was thinking. "Can I have two slices?" she asked.

"Comin' up," said the woman, and when she turned away from her daughter to go to the kitchen in the small house on Lancelot Lane her mouth trembled and tears had jumped into her eyes.

Jenn retreated into her room, but she left the door cracked open.

She picked up her guitar. She sat on her bed and played a little bit. Nothing special, just strumming some chords. Hearing the ring of the notes. They looked copper-colored, like her mother's hair. She tried some hammer-ons and pull-offs, gradually picking up the speed. Those were okay, but her fingers were so stiff. She tried some tapping, again increasing the speed.

Ouch. That sounded like Pop Rocks dropped into a big bowl of mess.

Try it one more time.

No, she had a ways to go yet.

She returned to strumming, slowly, letting the copper orbs fly around the room and bounce off the walls. At least, in her mind they did. Some of them bounced off the posters. They evaporated in the air, after they were done singing.

She turned her head. She gazed past her ugly reflection in the mirror over the dresser to the cork bulletin board with pictures of herself and her dad on it. In those pictures, they were both playing guitars. She was fourteen, and he was still alive. In a corner of the board was a blue ribbon that said First Place Winner, Talent Show, Cedar Park High School, 2006.

Her eyes returned to the face of her father. He had been so handsome. A big man, and rugged. He had been an auto mechanic at the Felix Gogo Toyota dealership in Temple. He'd said there wasn't an engine made he couldn't fix. He'd driven fifty-seven miles there in the morning, and fifty-seven miles back at night. Every weekday for as long as she could remember. He had called her Birdy.

"Birdy," he said, "the crows *will* fly."

And that was exactly as he said it, the *will* pushed down like a thumb on a sore spot.

It was what he said to explain that bad things are going to happen, no matter how much you pray for them not to. No matter how much you ask God to save your father. No matter how much you cry in your room, and lie there on the bed thinking about how handsome he was, and how big and how rugged, before the cancer starting eating at him and shrinking him down. Those crows, they're gonna fly.

"You know what, Birdy?" he said in the hospital room, with the afternoon light streaming through the window and those tubes up his nose. "Have to take me down in size some. So I can get through the Pearly Gates. Aw, honey, it ain't nothin'. Come on, wipe your eyes. Laurie, get her a tissue. Listen, *listen*." He gave her the stern look, the one that always worked. "Get yourself together. Mom tells me you're not eatin'. Is that right?"

"Not hungry," Jenn had answered.

"You better *get* hungry, girl. One thing for a big ol' hoss like me to shrink down, and it's another for a twig like you."

"*Dad*," Jenn had said, and her eyes had almost flooded out of her head.

And he was such a good guitar player, too. His hands were big, sure, but they moved so lightly on the strings. Together they sat on the porch, and they played songs like America's 'A Horse With No Name', and Waylon Jennings's 'Luckenbach, Texas', and his 'Mama, Don't Let Your Babies Grow Up To Be Cowboys'. And so many, many others.

She was named after Waylon Jennings, who had taken the time to shake her father's hand and talk to him like a regular person at a concert in Austin long before she was born. Her name wasn't 'Jennifer', it was just 'Jenn'. Jenn Stewart, that was her.

"Birdy," he'd said one day in July on the porch, and this was just before he'd gotten sick, "you are a natural-born guitar player. And I swear, you've got lightning in those fingers. I can't even do licks like those! Lord girl, you put me to shame!"

But that was his way of saying he was proud.

Her nickname, Birdy, came from him too. He said she could sing the birds out of the trees. Said she must be half-bird herself, to sing like that. That voice going up and up, right to the clouds. Up and up, right to God's ear. You must be half-bird, Birdy. The other half's an ol' stinkbug! Ain't that right, Laurie?

And her mother Laurie would grin and say, "Just like her daddy!"

Jenn had her father's eyes, but she mostly resembled her mother. She was thin—much thinner now—and wiry, with the same copper-colored hair. She was a pretty girl—used to be—with high cheekbones and an elegant nose, again like her mother's. That was a good thing, because many of the Stewarts and the Ingrahams had honkers. She could be funny, she had a quick wit and she liked to dance, but there was a side of her that had some of the hard earth of Texas in it. That side was serious and sometimes moody. That side didn't go in for a lot of foolishness. An old soul, her mother called her when that side showed itself. Old beyond her years. That was the side that told her not to smoke pot or cigarettes, though her mother had admitted smoking pot herself back in the days when she was—and she said this with some pride in her voice—"kind of a hippie". Jenn had tried beer at a party after the Crosstown Showdown, but she went back to her sweet tea.

Sometimes she wore her hair like her mother did, in braids. Today, though, it lay loose about her shoulders. It didn't shine, though. It was dull.

She strummed the guitar some more, just trying it out again. Her fingers were not what they used to be. How long had it been since she'd brought this guitar out of its case in the closet? Three, four months? Half a year? Maybe so.

It had been a good concert last night at the Vista Futura. Her mom had told her about meeting The Five at the Denny's, where she was a waitress.

You know what one of them said when I asked him what that thing with the fist and the peace sign meant? He said 'Bullshit!' His exact word. I almost pooted, tryin' to hold back a laugh. But the girl was nice. She seemed kind. She's the one who gave me the shirt.

Won't you eat just a little dinner, honey?

< >

Jenn had seen them on television. She'd followed their progress, and in a way shared their tribulations. First off, the sniper shooting the bass player in Sweetwater. Her grandmother lived in Sweetwater, so it had riveted her attention. Then what had happened to their road manager in Tucson. And that Stone Church thing, and finally two deaths in the New Mexico desert.

It was a tragic story. She'd gone to their website, heard their songs and watched their videos. She thought they were very strong, very talented, especially Ariel Collier, and she thought Nomad's voice was as good as Waylon's. So when her mom had brought in a newspaper ad saying The Five was doing a last show at the Vista Futura, and all ages were welcome and you could get in free if you wore the T-shirt, well...

No, Mom, I can't go. I just don't feel like it.

Jenn stood up, returned the guitar to its stand, and looked at herself in the mirror.

That hateful mirror. That ugly, ugly mirror. It showed her that the crows *will* fly, even if you stay in your own room and stop going outside. They will fly if you stop eating. They will fly if you shun food, because at first the sight of it makes you think of your father throwing up his dinners and shrinking down to a sick, dying sack of bones, and you don't want to eat, either, if he can't. And then, later...you think... really...I want to be with him, and play guitars, and be a family like we used to be, and I love my mom with all my heart but I need my dad, and maybe if I get right to the edge...right to the very edge of slipping into a sweet sleep, he will come as a spirit, whole and well again, to tell me *you better eat, girl*, and I can let him know how much I miss him, and how since he's been gone all the music is gone too.

But he never came. He never could get through.

They call it *anorexia*. The doctor said: *anorexia nervosa*.

Jenn looked at herself. She really was a twig, now. Half of a twig. A sprig. Her bones could be counted.

No, Mom, I can't go.

Her mother had said she might enjoy it, if she let herself. Nobody was going to know her there, if that's what she was worried about. I'll pick you up when it's over. Jenn, *go*.

That band had gone through so much. Had seen so much death and tragedy. Yet still they kept going. They were unstoppable. So maybe...*okay, Mom, I'll go.*

She almost didn't make it in. She'd been outside the club waiting with about eighteen thousand people, it seemed like, and had started talking to another girl her age whose mother had let her off. The girl, whose name was Diane, wore very thick glasses and had a kind smile. She was wearing a The Five T-shirt and she said she was their Number One Fan. She said her mother had brought her from Waco. Then the doors had opened up and the crowd had started rushing in, and everybody was moving forward in a mob and there stood a man counting people on a little metal clicker, and when Jenn got up to the door with Diane behind her some people had pushed Diane back to get in front of her, and Jenn heard the man call out to someone inside, "We're about at the limit!"

So Jenn had reached a scrawny arm back through the surging crowd and caught Diane's hand and at first pulled her through and then pushed her forward so she could enter the door first, because Waco was a lot further away than Cedar Park, and Jenn had a cellphone she could call her mother with and Diane had just been kind of let out on the street.

But they'd both gotten in. The doors had closed about six people after Jenn.

"Breakfast's almost ready!" her mother called from the kitchen. "Orange juice? Milk?" It was a hopeful question.

Jenn stared at herself in the mirror.

She heard that song again.

The last song.

She heard the words *I'm sitting here like a candle on the darkest night.*

"Jenn, listen to me, now. Listen real close." It was her father's voice, speaking to her in the hospital room on one of the final days. "I don't want you to get sick. Do you hear me? You have *life* ahead of you. Hear me? I want you to be somebody's candle, Jenn. I want you to show somebody your light. I think, with your talent and your heart, that's what you're gonna do. But you can't get sick. You can't follow me. Do you understand that?"

She did understand, but it was something she couldn't control now. The crows were flying, and they destroyed little birdies.

But that last song...

And the part *Try and try, grow and thrive, because no one here gets out alive.*

Her father's voice once more, on maybe the very last day?

"Jenn," he whispered. "My beautiful Birdy. Don't cry, baby. Laurie, you don't cry either. It's all right. Do you think people get out of life *alive*? No, they don't. That's why you have to make every day...every minute...*count*. I love my girls. God bless you both."

And hearing that line in the song, in the Vista Futura, had made tears bloom in Jenn's eyes. Had made them trickle down her cheeks, until Diane had looked at her and said maybe Jenn ought to be the Number One Fan, if that song moved her so much.

Jenn had thought—had *known*—that at last, her father had found a way to get through.

It had been a good song. A really, really good song. It had deeply touched her. It had spoken to her in a way she thought it could speak to no other person in the audience.

But she thought she could do better.

She looked at her posters on the walls.

There was Gwen Stefani, who Jenn thought was one of the most beautiful and talented women in the world. Gwen Stefani had a sweet heart. Jenn could tell that about a person.

There was a woman named Joni Mitchell, standing on a stage before a huge crowd with her arms upraised. A vintage poster, bought off eBay. These two women, on the CDs she owned, were separate and distinct talents. Both had fire and passion in their voices. Joni Mitchell wanted to get things done. She wanted to give a voice to people who had none. She wanted to speak clearly, and to clearly be heard. And to do that, you also had to clearly *hear*.

Gwen Stefani used her talent as an entertainer. To enthrall and delight, to dance to a beat, to have fun, to laugh and help people shrug off the worries of the world for a little while. To help them find strength when the crows came flying.

Jenn enjoyed them equally, as she enjoyed listening to all the many different musicians in her collection. But these two...these two separate and distinct talents, were the ones she went back to again and again.

She thought…if someone could merge them together, could meld them into one talent, one voice, a single personality. The seeker of truth and the joyful entertainer.

And both of them, the combination, writing songs from the heart.

What music that would be.

Jenn thought she maybe should eat some breakfast today. At least try it.

You couldn't sing on an empty stomach.

You sure couldn't dance on one, either.

"Milk," she answered her mother.

"Alright, angel," her mother said, and her voice was husky.

That last song, Jenn thought. It had spoken to her, in about as clear a voice as anybody could wish to hear.

Some things don't change, they never do.
Some things do change, they change with you.

She looked again at the pictures of herself and her father, thinking about how much courage he'd shown when he was getting ready for his journey.

She thought she needed some too, for her own.

"Orange juice, too," she said toward the kitchen. And added, "Please, ma'am."

At breakfast, Jenn ate sparingly, like a bird, but at least Laurie thought it was a start. Just so long as she didn't go into the bathroom and throw it up. Laurie asked her what she planned to do today, it would be another clear hot day, and Jenn said she thought she was going to mess around on the guitar, and she might call Noreen Velasco and Anna Cope and ask them if they wanted to bring their guitars over. It had been a while since they'd done that.

"Will you try to eat some lunch?" Laurie asked.

Jenn crunched on a piece of bacon. "Do we have any peanut butter?"

Laurie got dressed for work, in her Denny's uniform. She would put on the tag that said *Hi I'm Laurie* when she got there. She put her hair in braids. She brushed her teeth. Thank the Lord Jenn don't have my big ol' choppers, she thought. The sun was about to come up.

She could hear her daughter playing her guitar again. Music was a beautiful gift.

She went in to say goodbye, and Jenn said, "Mom, I was thinking. Could I maybe start my lessons back?"

"I think you absolutely could. Absolutely." Jenn had quit her lessons months ago. Jenn was good, very good, but she was the kind of person—or used to be, before she got so sad and sick—who always wanted to be better.

"Can we afford 'em? I could probably find a job at the mall."

"Yes, we can afford 'em. And we'll talk about that later. You just enjoy your day." And don't *worry* so much, Laurie almost said, but today she didn't think she had to. She started to close the door.

Jenn said, "You can leave it open, Mom."

"Okay." Laurie listened to her daughter playing. Watched her hands moving on the strings. Sending music into the air. Who could say where it would go? "Love you," she said.

"Love you, too," said Jenn. "Thanks for breakfast."

"You can leave a tip on the table," Laurie told her, and she met her daughter's quick smile with one of her own, and then she left the house with music in her ears.

On the way to the car, she thought that money was tight, it always was, but she would figure out how to get those guitar lessons for Jenn. It seemed very important to her, and it seemed very right.

Because for someone you loved, sacrifice was no problem.

For someone you loved, it was no problem at all.

THANKS AND DEDICATIONS

I'd like to thank, first and foremost, Cass Scripps of the Metro Talent Agency in Atlanta for taking me through the life of musicians on the—his very excellent term—"knife and gun circuit".

I'd like to thank The Verve. I was having lunch in a California Pizza Kitchen restaurant when I heard a song over the speakers. It immediately spoke to me, and I had to ask the hostess to find out for me what the name of the song was and who the artists were. That situation gave me the seed of this book—the power of a song to speak to an individual. The song was 'Bittersweet Symphony'.

I'd like to dedicate this book to the following bands and artists. These are people I have listened to when I needed the balm or blast of music. All of them are in here somewhere. I have a long list to go through, and to be fair I put all the names in a blue porkpie hat and drew them out. They are not in any order of fame, or genre, or time-frame. They are in the order the blue porkpie hat decided.

So, thank you,

To Duane Eddy, The Haunted, The Red Walls, Nova's Nine, XTC, The Cuff Links, Pink, The Pretenders, Cat Stevens, Norman Greenbaum, Blood Sweat and Tears, Sex Pistols, Empire Of The Sun, Orchestral Maneuvers In The Dark, Panic At The Disco, The Grass Roots, Wang Chung, Prince, AC/DC, Crimson Metal Dragon, Adam and The Ants, Annie Lennox, Brian Wilson, Pearl Jam, Booker T &

The MGs, My Chemical Romance, The Hot Melts, Green Day, Allman Brothers Band, Cream, The Kingston Trio, The The, The Killers, The Trashmen, Elton John, the Beau Brummels, Dirtblonde, No River City, Carly Simon, The Clash, Chevelle 6, Delicate Balance, 10cc, Robert Fripp, Heart, The Fray, Moon Taxi, 13th Floor Elevators, Nirvana, Led Zeppelin, The Wheels, Spencer Davis Group, Cyndi Lauper, Gang of Four.

To Sonic Youth, Curtis Mayfield, 311, Soul Society, Metallica, Steppenwolf, The Specials, Procul Harum, Junior Brown, The Doors, Billy Joel, The White Stripes, Buffalo Tom, Spirit, Pink Floyd, Three Dog Night, the B52s, Amboy Dukes, Simon and Garfunkel, Uriah Heep, the Black Crowes, The Rolling Stones, Dion, the Human League, HIM, Pat Benatar, Herman's Hermits, The Yeah Yous, The Farm, Gonn, Edwin Starr, Simple Minds, Jethro Tull, Flock Of Seagulls, Robert Palmer, Grains Of Sand, Brian Eno, The Screaming Blue Messiahs, Famen, Tears For Fears, Leo Kottke, Bruce Cockburn, Red Hot Chili Peppers, Blue Oyster Cult, Janis Joplin, Things To Come, Filter, America, Beastie Boys, The Police, the Flaming Lips.

To Traffic, the Goo Goo Dolls, Johnny Cash, the Black Eyed Peas, Fear, Lovin' Spoonful, Alison Moyet, the Buckinghams, Elvis Costello and the Attractions, Johnny Rivers, The Moody Blues, Buckethead, Gary Numan, Toad the Wet Sprocket, Rare Earth, Billy Idol, Jan and Dean, Evanescence, the Ides of March, Blondie, Sheryl Crow, Royal Trux, the Yardbirds, the Motels, Kronos Quartet, The Kinks, Red Sky July, Rage Against The Machine, David Bowie, The Swingin' Medallions, Morning Bell, Mountain, Smashing Pumpkins, Slipknot, Black Sabbath, the Byrds, Mouse & The Traps, Talking Heads, Elvis Presley, INXS, Lily Allen, Alice In Chains, Joan Jett, Jefferson Airplane, the Pretty Things, James Brown, The Bold, Etta James, Supertramp, Chicago, Weezer, Donovan, Delphi Rising, 13th Omen, Ram Jam.

To Badly Drawn Boy, The Isley Brothers, The Cars, Crowded House, Squeeze, Insane Clown Posse, Guns N' Roses, Jimmy McGriff, the Dandy Warhols, Joni Mitchell, the Beach Boys, Concrete Blonde, the Kingsmen, Fading Tribesmen, the Geto Boys, Jimmy Smith, the Third Bardo, the Cult, Roy Orbison, Aerosmith, War, Nine Inch Nails, Dick Dale, Rob Zombie, KC & The Sunshine Band, the Chocolate Watch Band, Counting Crows, Vince Gill, Gwen Stefani and No

Doubt, the Seeds, Hole, Moby Grape, the Turtles, MC5, Joe Cocker, Sam The Sham and the Pharaohs, Count Five, the Beatles, Mary Chapin Carpenter, Oasis, Cheap Trick, James Taylor, U2, Band Of Horses, Wendy and Lisa, the Checkerlads, Jerry Lee Lewis, Journey, Dead Kennedys, Nameless, the Zombies, Strawberry Alarm Clock, Kings Of Leon.

To Warren Zevon, the Rockin' Rebellions, Les Paul, Bruce Springsteen, Beck, Crosby Stills Nash and Young, the Waitresses, the Breeders, the Righteous Brothers, the Grateful Dead, Run-DMC, Duran Duran, Wire Train, The Band, Adrian Legg, Peter Paul and Mary, the Osbourne Brothers, Fabulous DJs, Van Halen, Natalie Merchant, Fall Out Boy, Toronados, Yes, Iggy Pop, Jesus Jones, Electric Flag, Alice Cooper, Poco, Joan Baez, Brewer and Shipley, Grand Funk Railroad, Jimi Hendrix, Tony DeFrancesco, James Gang, The Eagles, The Call, The Who, Tina Turner, Pet Shop Boys, Sugarloaf, Def Leppard, Dead Tight Five, Candy Store Prophets, Billy Joe Royal, Sound We Sleep, Mitch Ryder and the Detroit Wheels.

To Van Morrison, the Troggs, King Crimson, Jackson Browne, Taylor Hicks, Sir Douglas Quintet, Melanie, ZZ Top, Bob Dylan, Marvin Gaye, the Electric Prunes, Molly Hatchet, Big Mama Thornton, the Velvet Underground, Bad Company, Black Oak Arkansas, Dire Straits, Judy Collins, T.Rex, Bob Seger, the Butthole Surfers, the O'Jays, Question Mark and the Mysterians, Iron Maiden, Free, Jane's Addiction, London Suede, The Fixx, Rickie Lee Jones, the Guess Who, Midnight Oil, Sheila E., Prefab Sprout, The Kytes, Kelly Clarkson, Judy Collins, the J. Geils Band, They Might Be Giants, The Acid Gallery, Boy George, Yer Cronies, Lucy Michelle and the Velvet Lapelles, Oingo Boingo, Karen Lawrence & The Pinz, The Fugitives, Fever Tree, Lord & The Flies, Emerson Lake & Palmer, Teenage Fanclub, The Turnstyle.

To the Castaways, the Bloodhound Gang, Orange Machine, Turfits, 'Til Tuesday, Emmylou Harris, the Psychedelic Furs, the Shadows of Knight, Foreigner, Steely Dan, Lynyrd Skynyrd, The Animals, Spring Heel Jack, the Standells, the Main Ingredient, Jr. Walker & The All-Stars, Doobie Brothers, Carole King, Otis Redding, Lemon Pipers, Marilyn Manson, Them, Todd Rundgren, the Dakotas, the Misunderstood, Bruce Hornsby, Soundgarden, Paul Revere & The Raiders, The Sinners, Zakary Thaks, Helmet, The Dream Academy,

Cypress Hill, Leon Russell, The Ting Tings, Sky Cries Mary, Dave Clark Five, Inspiral Carpets, Devo, The Clique, The Go-Betweens, Wimple Winch, The Poets, Toadies, The Lost Brothers, The Jaggerz, Sly & The Family Stone, Remember Tomorrow, Polly Mackey & The Pleasure Principle, Ten Wheel Drive, The Glass Menagerie, The Status Quo, Beyond Solace, Soul Inc., and the Field Hippies.

To all these bands and individuals, I want to say you have given so much, you don't even have any idea what you've given, and you can never be repaid for your talents and your gifts.

< >

I know I'm leaving out thousands of great bands. I'm leaving out bands who shot like fiery comets across the stages of small town clubs and burned out long before I was born. I'm leaving out bands who are being born as I write this. I'm leaving out the band who dyed their hair silver, and the band who tore it up on stage in togas. I'm leaving out the band who no one could understand, and the one who dared to smile for their picture.

I'd like to end here with three words, delivered with a jump and shout: Support live music!

Robert McCammon